KT-153-512

The Regency

LORDS & LADIES
COLLECTION

*Two Glittering Regency
Love Affairs*

Mistress or Marriage?
by Elizabeth Rolls
&
A Roguish Gentleman
by Mary Brendan

The Regency

LORDS & LADIES

COLLECTION

Volume 1 – July 2005
The Larkswood Legacy *by Nicola Cornick*
The Neglectful Guardian *by Anne Ashley*

Volume 2 – August 2005
My Lady's Prisoner *by Ann Elizabeth Cree*
Miss Harcourt's Dilemma *by Anne Ashley*

Volume 3 – September 2005
Lady Clairval's Marriage *by Paula Marshall*
The Passionate Friends *by Meg Alexander*

Volume 4 – October 2005
A Scandalous Lady *by Francesca Shaw*
The Gentleman's Demand *by Meg Alexander*

Volume 5 – November 2005
A Poor Relation *by Joanna Maitland*
The Silver Squire *by Mary Brendan*

Volume 6 – December 2005
Mistress or Marriage? *by Elizabeth Rolls*
A Roguish Gentleman *by Mary Brendan*

The Regency

LORDS & LADIES
COLLECTION

Elizabeth Rolls &
Mary Brendan

MILLS & BOON®

DID YOU PURCHASE THIS BOOK WITHOUT A COVER?
If you did, you should be aware it is **stolen property** as it was
reported *unsold and destroyed* by a retailer. Neither the author nor the
publisher has received any payment for this book.

*All the characters in this book have no existence outside the imagination
of the author, and have no relation whatsoever to anyone bearing the
same name or names. They are not even distantly inspired by any
individual known or unknown to the author, and all the incidents are
pure invention.*

*All Rights Reserved including the right of reproduction in whole or in part in
any form. This edition is published by arrangement with Harlequin
Enterprises II B.V. The text of this publication or any part thereof may not
be reproduced or transmitted in any form or by any means, electronic or
mechanical, including photocopying, recording, storage in an information
retrieval system, or otherwise, without the written permission of the publisher.*

*This book is sold subject to the condition that it shall not, by way of trade
or otherwise, be lent, resold, hired out or otherwise circulated without the
prior consent of the publisher in any form of binding or cover other than
that in which it is published and without a similar condition including
this condition being imposed on the subsequent purchaser.*

*MILLS & BOON and MILLS & BOON with the Rose Device
are registered trademarks of the publisher.*

*First published in Great Britain 2005 by
Harlequin Mills & Boon Limited,
Eton House, 18-24 Paradise Road,Richmond, Surrey TW9 1SR*

THE REGENCY LORDS & LADIES COLLECTION
© Harlequin Books S.A. 2005

The publisher acknowledges the copyright holders of the
individual works as follows:

Mistress or Marriage? © Elizabeth Rolls 2001
A Roguish Gentleman © Mary Brendan 2001

ISBN 0 263 84575 3

138-1205

*Printed and bound in Spain
by Litografia Rosés S.A., Barcelona*

Mistress or Marriage?

by
Elizabeth Rolls

Elizabeth Rolls was born in Kent but moved to Melbourne, Australia, at the age of fifteen months. She spent several years in Papua New Guinea as a child, where her father was in charge of the Defence Forces. After teaching music for several years she moved to Sydney to do a Masters in Musicology at the University of New South Wales. Upon completing her thesis, Elizabeth realised that writing was so much fun she wanted to do more. She currently lives in a chaotic household with her husband, two small sons, two dogs and two cats. You can contact the author at the following e-mail address:
elizabethrolls@alphalink.com.au

Chapter One

Lady Maria Kentham viewed her only surviving great-nephew in what appeared to be unmitigated exasperation. Lord knew the boy had always been stubborn, but this was beyond all belief! Not that there was much left of the youth she remembered, apart from the obstinacy, of course. Twelve years had wrought a greater change in him than they had in her.

He'd filled out rather nicely, she thought critically, as he stood glaring back at her, green eyes snapping. His breadth of shoulder and powerful chest were admirably displayed by the close-fitting black coat. His pantaloons were all they should be as well. Lady Maria did not always approve of modern fashions in clothing—indecent, some of them were. But when a pair of pantaloons was moulded to legs like those…well, she had to admit, if only to herself, that there might be a point in them.

His snowy cravat was a monument to discreet elegance—a single diamond, snuggling into the intricate folds, flashed its chaste fire without detracting from the artistry of the arrangement. All in all, his attire was everything a gentleman's should be, and more.

And he was just as handsome as ever, she thought approvingly, with the Melville green eyes and jet black hair. His mother's delicate bone structure had combined with the heavier features, which had characterised his father and elder brother James, to produce a chiselled strength, aristocratic in the extreme.

David Melville, the present Viscount Helford, eyed his Great Aunt Maria with mingled exasperation and affection. The last thing he'd expected when his butler announced Great Aunt Maria was that she'd stalk into his library and open fire without even a declaration of war. He thought ruefully that he had obviously been away too long, if he had forgotten Great Aunt Maria's tendency to speak her mind with frequently shattering candour. Nevertheless, he was damned if he'd dance to this tune!

'Don't you think, Aunt, that it might be a little early for this discussion? After all, I only arrived back yesterday. Perhaps I might be permitted time to look up my old friends before I exhaust myself in the hunt for an eligible bride. Or rather before they come hunting me. And would you kindly stop looking me over as if I were a prize stallion?'

A dangerous flash in her black eyes, Lady Maria corrected him on two points. 'This ain't a discussion, Helford! I'm telling you! The succession is in some danger and it is your duty to marry *at once*! James died over a year ago and the people are starting to wonder where you are. You have a ten-year-old niece who requires attention as well as a three-hundred-year-old title and estate in need of the same!'

She fixed him with a steely glare. 'As for looking up your friends, you have my full permission to look 'em up. On the dance floors!' A very unladylike snort escaped her. 'Who knows, if you run across Peter Darleston in town, then he might even help you! From all I can see, he's embraced the married state again with what I can only describe as vulgar enthusiasm! Which should be a lesson to you. Just because you had some stupid boy-and-girl attachment to

Felicity doesn't mean you can't form an eligible connection with another female.'

Her voice and eyes softened slightly as Helford stiffened at this blunt reference to his early infatuation for his elder brother's wife. 'Lord, boy, did you think I didn't know? It was obvious enough you was head over heels in love with her! The only person who didn't know was James!' She pursed her lips. 'Mind you, he never saw anything, not even Felicity's *affaires*. And God knows there were enough of them!'

Obviously startled, Helford was betrayed into revealing speech. 'James didn't know? That I—' The firm lips closed abruptly.

Lady Maria Kentham stared at him in disbelief. 'So that's it,' she said slowly. 'You thought James offered for Felicity, knowing how you felt about her. That's why you joined the army and stayed away all these years. Because you thought James had purposely stolen your bride. For heaven's sake, boy! Your mother suggested the match to James. If he'd known how you felt, he'd never have offered for her!'

Her nephew just gaped at her in stunned silence. She didn't really expect an answer. He'd never been one to confide, even as a boy, and she didn't think he'd changed all that much. Lord, so he'd been blaming his brother all these years for supposedly stealing a hussy who'd have broken his heart! Well, he knew the truth now and nothing more she could say on that head would be of the slightest use.

So she returned to the main thrust of her argument. 'You do intend to marry, I assume, Helford?' Using his title, she reasoned, would remind him of his duty. He was not merely the Honourable David Melville, younger son, any more. He had responsibilities…to his name, to his people. He must not be allowed to shirk them on any count, certainly not for the memory of his brother's wife, a woman who had been dead for more than a twelvemonth. A woman who, if the

boy were to be totally honest with himself, had not actually
cared for him in the least.

His jaw set hard, Helford answered. 'As you say, Aunt
Maria, I have no choice in the matter.'

She relaxed. Good. He was going to be sensible.

'Very well, then. There are bound to be any number of
personable young ladies out this Season. I will—'

'No!'

A frosty glare greeted this summary interruption of her
detailed and all-embracing plans.

It was met by one as chilly. 'I am entirely capable of
choosing a bride by myself, thank you very much!' grated
the Viscount. 'It may surprise you to know that I can just
about remember how to make myself agreeable to the
ladies.'

Lady Maria permitted herself an amused smile. 'Can you
indeed, Helford? From all I've heard, you're a little out of
practice with the ladies…'

'The hell I am!' exploded Helford.

'With the ladies, I said, dear boy,' purred Lady Maria
sweetly, not in the least put out by her nephew's choice of
language. 'I've not the least doubt of your expertise with
the brass-faced hussies of the Viennese Opera.' She rose to
her feet before her outraged nephew could think of a suitable riposte and continued, 'And if the way you've received
me is any indication, then I should think you can do with
all the advice you can get. No offer of tea, Madeira, cakes!
It passes all bounds.'

This backfired slightly. The blazing green eyes suddenly
crinkled with laughter, adding disastrously to their owner's
already nigh-on lethal charm.

'Oh, no, you don't, Aunt Maria! That cock won't fight!
I distinctly heard you inform Haversham that you never
maudled your insides with tea at this hour and considered
it far too early for anything stronger! You also told him to

concentrate on making himself useful rather than forcing you to eat food you neither wanted nor required.'

'Humph. You could still have offered!' she snapped, not in the least mollified. 'Still, it's all of a piece with your generation. Not the slightest notion of respect for your elders.'

She rose to her feet with the aid of a walking stick that Helford was morally certain was his grandfather's old sword stick. He supposed he ought to be grateful that she hadn't pressed her point with that.

'I'll take my leave of you, Helford. I'm putting up at Grillon's.'

He flushed. 'Whatever for? You're perfectly welcome to stay here for as long as you like. You know quite well that I have a considerable affection for you, quite apart from any respect you may feel I owe you!'

'Humph, I dare say!' Seeing that he looked quite sincerely upset, she relented. 'I've no taste for racketing about town these days. I'll stay another day or so at Grillon's, then go back to Helford Place. Shouldn't leave Fanny much longer. That child needs taking in hand.'

He frowned. 'Aunt Maria, did you come all the way down from Warwickshire merely to put me in the way of my duty?' The mildness of his voice belied the frown.

'Certainly not!' she lied unconvincingly. 'I've every intention of going to the opera!'

After seeing his great-aunt to her carriage, Lord Helford returned to his library, but somehow the peace and quiet he had been enjoying was shattered. The shabby old leather chairs seemed to repel him so that he paced up and down, and the leather-bound books lining the walls all nagged at him, reminding him of his forebears who had amassed them. The wisdom of generations was held in those covers, he thought whimsically. And all it could do was urge him to a step he had shunned for years.

Marriage. Something he had set his face against for over twelve years.

His memory lurched back to the day Felicity's father had calmly told him that he had received a better offer for her hand, that he was not to approach her again. An order which he had not the slightest intention of obeying. He had not found out who the lucky suitor was until he had reached home that night after riding all day in a thundering rage, fuming as he laid his plans for rescuing his love from an unwanted marriage.

He'd found out when he got home, muddied and exhausted, and discovered James celebrating with their mother. *She* had known. Had tried to explain to him later that James, with his title, had a better claim to Felicity's hand and fortune. She had smiled gently, cynically, when he'd cried out that he loved Felicity. Had told him that he would find another attractive fortune one day. He'd never spoken to her again.

The next day he'd managed to intercept Felicity on her morning ride with her groom. She'd seemed very embarrassed to see him and when he'd insisted on riding ahead with her, had agreed very reluctantly.

He could remember her light voice now. 'But, David, dear! You cannot expect me to marry you in the face of Papa's displeasure. Why, he has positively ordered me to marry James.' There was a brief, pregnant pause, during which he'd assimilated the variance of her claim that her father demanded the match, with her unruffled tone and demeanour.

She continued. 'We must be sensible about this, David. After all, once I have fulfilled my duty and provided James with an heir, there is nothing to stop us… I mean, if we were discreet.' Innocent-seeming blue eyes had smiled up at him beguilingly. The soft pink lips he'd longed to crush under his curved in the most tempting of smiles and the pale spring sunshine had glinted on golden curls.

He felt nothing but disgust. And fury. Fury with himself that he could still want her. That even knowing what she was, he could still desire her, long to have her as his wife.

Somehow he'd managed to speak. 'A gratifying offer, Felicity, but I think I'd rather stick to *honest* whores.' The words, and the biting tone in which he'd uttered them, had struck home. A flush had suffused the petal-soft cheeks, an angry glitter had sparked in the blue eyes and the delicate bow of her mouth hardened.

'Really, David!' she expostulated. 'You are being most unreasonable. You know as well as I that marriage in our class is a contract made for the better preservation of property and the provision of heirs. My father demands that I marry James. What more is there to say?'

'Absolutely nothing, my dear,' drawled David, wondering how on earth he had missed seeing her mercenary streak before this and realising that love could indeed be blind. 'It remains for me to congratulate you on your catch and beg your pardon for having distracted you from your duty to your ambition. Good morning.'

He'd spurred his horse into a canter, then a swift gallop, and left her. Not once had he looked back, either then or in the years of wandering that had followed.

The next morning he'd left, only pausing to ask James if he'd purchase him a pair of colours, and from that day to this he hadn't stepped across any threshold belonging to his family. James had looked puzzled at his request, but had agreed immediately with the easy generosity that had always characterised his dealings with his younger brother.

And he hadn't known. Helford swore bitterly. No wonder James had been so puzzled, particularly by his refusal to come home after that. His refusal to come to the wedding.

Even knowing the truth about her motivation, he had still found that the thought of seeing Felicity married to his own brother was unbearable.

By the time he'd come to his senses and realised that he'd made a fool of himself, he had been too proud to come home. And he could not have borne to see Felicity, to be reminded of the callow youth who had loved her only to discover that his idol had feet of clay. All during his years in the Peninsula and then in Vienna at the Embassy odd scraps of gossip had filtered through to him. Scraps which told him he was far better off out of marriage with her. Or with anyone.

Never again had he made the mistake of caring for a woman. They were toys, playthings. He avoided marriageable females like the plague, seeing in them only reminders of his own foolishness. And now he'd have to marry after all. Very well. So be it. But it would be on *his* terms. The terms Felicity had taught him so effectively.

His bride would be a woman of birth, beauty and fortune. And irreproachable conduct. He was damned if he would provide cover for a high-class little whore as James had obviously ended up doing for Felicity. He thought about it carefully. Titled. She needed to be titled and from one of the oldest houses preferably. That way she would have been brought up to know her duty. She would see her rank as an accepted responsibility rather than as a prize to be won at all costs. The bargain between them would be an equal one. And he would make damned sure he picked a bride with little disposition to flirt or encourage the attentions of other men. He'd learned his lesson the hard way and he was going to make quite certain that he profited by it!

And now that he had decided all that, he would go for a stroll along Bond Street and let the world know that he had returned.

* * *

He had quite forgotten what Bond Street could be like at this hour. The clop of hooves allied with rumbling wheels was deafening and overlaying it all was a buzz of chatter. It seemed that most of the fashionable world was here at three o'clock on a bright spring afternoon. For a moment time rolled back as though the intervening years had never happened. But for one inescapable fact, David thought, he might never have been away.

Twelve years ago he would have been recognised by any number of the elegantly gowned ladies whose fluttering muslins gave the street the appearance of a flower bed. The strolling gentlemen would have known him as well. He would have been most unlikely to have been walking alone. He would have been part of the milieu rather than this faintly cynical observer.

Just at the moment his anonymity suited him perfectly. There was an odd satisfaction in being able to view his world almost as though he were invisible to prying eyes and immune to gossiping tongues. He felt as though he were free to observe, not yet part and parcel of the glittering London world which all too soon would know of his return. No doubt by the time he had been back a week the news would be out and any number of people would be claiming long acquaintance. In fact, he rather thought he could count on Lady Maria to spread the glad tidings.

He strolled past Stephens' Hotel, wondering idly if any of his friends were inside but not sufficiently interested to find out. This feeling of being invisible was very pleasant. No one had seen him at all!

His feeling of invisibility was pure illusion, of course. Whatever the gentlemen might do, it was not likely that any lady could possibly pass by an unknown gentleman of his quality without observing him very closely, albeit surreptitiously. Naturally one would not like to stare and be thought a vulgar hussy, but one could and did cast a fleeting sideways glance at the tall, powerful figure, moving with such leonine grace and dressed with such unobtrusive elegance.

The illusion of invisibility continued as far as Jackson's Boxing Saloon. It might have continued even further had it not been for Helford's observation of an entirely new phenomenon. Never before in that distant time that had known him as a frequent and welcome visitor at Jackson's had he seen such a large dog sitting patiently outside the door. The creature was more than large, it was the size of a small pony, he thought. And what was even more amazing, no one, not even the ladies, seemed in the least bit concerned about it.

You would have thought, he reflected, that many of the ladies would have given such an animal a wide berth. But no, most of them went by without taking the slightest notice. The only ones to acknowledge the dog's presence were the ones who actually stopped to pat it. These attentions were received with a slight thump of the tail on the pavement, no more. Clearly a dog of discrimination, thought Helford in amusement.

He wondered who owned the shaggy grey beast. It had to be someone very highly regarded. Unless London society had altered out of all recognition, he could think of few men who would dare to plant an animal like that outside Jackson's and expect to get away with it.

Coming closer, he slowed to observe better. Sensing his regard, the dog turned its great head and gazed at him out of tawny brown eyes. The tail remained motionless and one was left in no doubt that only a fool took liberties with this animal if he didn't know you. There was nothing in the least threatening about his behaviour, just a sort of massive dignity.

He was conscious of an odd urge to incline his head to the dog before continuing, but all at once the dog's attention was not on him. He had turned to the shut door of Jackson's and was standing up, wagging his tail furiously.

Now we shall see who owns him, thought Helford. The door opened and a gentleman as tall as himself stepped out on to the pavement. An athletic fellow with curly black hair and dark brown eyes. He greeted the dog with a pat and then caught sight of Helford, who was staring at him as though seeing a ghost.

The brown-eyed gentleman's jaw dropped, just for a moment, then a smile of unshadowed delight lit a face which more than one romantically inclined damsel had in the past held to be positively Byronic in its brooding good looks. He held out his hand and it was taken at once in a strong grip. Blazing green eyes laughed into brown as they had not done for nearly eight years.

'David Melville! Good God! We all thought you were fixed in Vienna, distracting the ladies of the opera there! What the devil brings you to town? Apart from the opera, of course!'

Helford merely grinned at this reference to his generous, if scandalous, patronage of the arts and riposted, 'You can't talk, Darleston! I seem to have heard that you developed a bit of a reputation with the ladies too!'

The brown eyes laughed at him, 'All in the past, Melville, all in the past! Now come, what brings you...oh, of course! Melville, indeed! Helford, I should say! I forgot all about it. It's over a year since your brother died, isn't it?'

Helford nodded. 'Just over. I should have come earlier, I suppose, especially since I am guardian to James's daughter. But quite frankly I've little turn for children and Aunt Maria seems to have the matter well in hand. So...er...Vienna was more appealing!' There was a raffish twinkle in his eye.

The Earl of Darleston chuckled understandingly, 'Was she, indeed? How very pleasant for you! Where are you off to now? Are you busy or can you give me your company?'

Helford laughed and said, 'If you will promise not to

break my incognito to anyone, you may have my company for as long as you please.'

'Incognito?' Darleston grinned. 'Do you mean to say a whole, live, single Viscount managed to get this far along Bond Street without being mobbed? I had not thought it possible!'

He began to walk, the dog closely to heel. 'Eight years, isn't it? The last time I saw you was the morning we left Waterloo village.' His voice was studiedly light.

Helford nodded slowly, remembering that roaring, smoking hell. 'It probably was. Although I saw you much later in the day, I would doubt your having been in a condition to remember. Carstares was just heaving you on to your horse to have you led to the rear. Neither of us thought you'd survive.'

Darleston smiled. 'I still have Nero. My wife rides him now.'

His voice took on an oddly gentle cast and Helford looked at him sharply. His wife! Shouldn't have thought he'd let a female near a horse that had stood over his fallen body in the heat of battle, let alone ride it. Although hadn't Aunt Maria said something about Peter remarrying? Not to mention that letter he'd had from Carrington. Suddenly he remembered the letter.

Peter has remarried, you will be interested to hear. Married for convenience and an heir and it turned into the greatest love match of all time. Carstares and I are still laughing about it...

Something like that. 'That's right. I had a letter from Michael. Is it too late for congratulations?'

His friend shook his head. 'Not at all. And even if *you* think nearly three years is too long for congratulations, you can always congratulate me on the arrival of my children.'

Helford did some quick calculations and said, 'Children,

plural? In that time? Even for you…' He left the sentence hanging.

Darleston had the grace to look faintly embarrassed, 'Penelope is a twin, you see, and—'

'Twins? You are the father of twins?' Helford put back his head and roared with laughter. 'Well, well, well! And what are you blessed with?'

'Boy and a girl, just turned two,' said Darleston without the slightest attempt to disguise his pride.

'Congratulations!' said Helford in wholehearted delight. 'Now I have just one burning question. Where in God's name did you get this?' He indicated the great dog pacing beside them.

'Gelert? Oh, he belongs to my wife,' answered Darleston. 'Part of the marriage contract, you might say. Where she goes, he goes generally. Even into Sally Jersey's drawing room, would you believe!'

Helford mentally conjured up the image of this huge dog cluttering up the drawing room of London's uncrowned queen, one of the patronesses of Almack's, a woman who could destroy the chances of any aspiring debutante or hostess with a single word. It just wasn't possible! Lady Jersey would never tolerate such a thing, not even for the Countess of Darleston.

Grinning at the patent disbelief, writ large all over Helford's countenance, Darleston said, 'If you aren't otherwise engaged, come and have dinner with us this evening. George Carstares is staying with us and Penelope's youngest sister Sarah. Come and join us. An extra place at the table won't be a problem, I assure you.'

'If you are sure that Lady Darleston won't mind, then I should like that very much,' said Helford.

'Penelope never minds anything,' said Darleston with a sublime confidence that his friend was far from sharing. In

his experience, when a man married, his wife tended to regard his old friends as so many intruders.

They continued along the street slowly, filling in the past
eight years and laughing over old gossip and the fates of
various acquaintances.

'Now, are you settled in town? You say no one knows
you are back,' continued Darleston, as they strolled along
past Hookham's Library.

'For the Season,' answered Helford. 'I'll probably be or-
ganising a house party at Helford Place at some point during
the summer.' There was a faintly questioning note in his
voice.

'Oh, yes, we'll be home by then,' responded Darleston.
'The children are a great deal happier in the country and
Penny and I prefer it. We're really only up for Lady
Edenhope's ball in a couple of days. You come too. She'll
be so thrilled to be the first to entertain you formally, she
won't mind in the least if you turn up uninvited.'

'Seems as good a place to start as any,' was the enigmatic
reply.

'Start what? A mill?' asked Darleston with a wicked glint
in his eye.

Helford chuckled, 'I only did that once and the bounder
deserved it! Besides, I was foxed!'

'Once was enough, in all conscience!' said Darleston in-
dignantly. 'I still have nightmares about trying to persuade
Lady Edenhope not to call your father from the card room!
Now, enough! What are you up to?'

'Getting married, according to Aunt Maria.'

'Congratulations,' said Darleston and raised his brows in
mute surmise.

'You're a little premature,' said Helford. 'I haven't
popped the question yet.'

'Oh. I see.'

For a mere three words he managed to get a wealth of

unasked questions into them, thought Helford. But, after all, Darleston was almost as well acquainted with the formidable Lady Maria as he was.

With a sigh he said, 'You know how it is. I suppose you remarried for exactly the same reasons. Convenience and an heir.'

'I did, of course,' agreed Darleston. 'And very soon discovered my mistake.' His voice held more than a shade of amusement.

'Mistake?' Helford was surprised. 'Aunt Maria seemed to think your enthusiasm for the married state was positively vulgar.'

'Oh, it is!' smiled Darleston. 'I meant that I was mistaken in marrying for convenience. It didn't work at all! But enough of me. Tell me who you have in your eye.'

Helford shrugged. 'Does it really matter? Frankly, I've just got back. Aunt Maria descended upon me this morning and proceeded to enumerate to me my duties to the name of Melville. So...' He grimaced. 'Hence I'm in the market for a bride with the following qualifications: breeding—she must be titled—and good looks, of course. And a reasonable dowry. She must be well behaved and accomplished... sensible...capable of running a large household. You know the sort of thing.'

Darleston nodded slowly. 'Did Lady Maria stipulate all this? You surprise me.'

'Hardly,' said Helford with a reluctant half-smile, thinking that he must have sounded remarkably cold-blooded. 'That's my own recipe for a bearable marriage.'

'Oh,' said Darleston. Again he managed to invest the monosyllable with a world of meaning.

They strolled along in a silence broken at last by Helford in a tight, bitter sort of voice. 'I know what you are thinking, Peter, but I learnt my lesson early and I've no intention of mixing business with pleasure.'

'More than one lesson to be learned in life, old chap,' said Darleston thoughtfully. 'Mind you, I'm not saying it wasn't a good thing Felicity taught you to be wary, but one can take one's suspicions too far.'

Helford snorted sceptically. 'If you'll pardon my frankness, Peter, I should have thought that you of all men would have been doubly wary.'

Darleston did not seem at all offended. 'Oh, I was, I assure you!' He hesitated and then said, 'That's precisely what I meant. I didn't even recognise love at first! And probably just as well, since I should have run a mile if I'd realised. It just sort of sneaked up on me. I certainly didn't go looking for it. In fact, I caused Penny quite a deal of hurt while I was floundering about wondering why she bothered me so much!'

Helford was unconvinced. 'Well, it won't do for me. I'd prefer to know exactly where I am in my marriage so I'll settle for convenience. Come on, enumerate to me all the impeccably bred, attractive fillies currently parading in the auction ring.'

With a resigned smile, Darleston considered carefully. 'Well, there is the Clovelly chit, quite attractive and well behaved. Not titled, of course, but the Clovellys are looking high, I believe. And besides, she *would* be titled if her great-great-great grandmother hadn't told Charles the Second to keep his hands to himself! Or, if you insist on the title, there's Lady Lucinda Anstey—Stanford's chit, you know. She's held to be a very regal-looking girl. No doubt there are a score of others, but those two come to mind as… er…embodying the qualifications you mentioned.'

'Point 'em out to me,' said Helford. 'I thought to spend the Season looking about and courting here in town and then invite the girl and her mother to that house party I mentioned. You know, see her at closer quarters before making a final decision.'

'I see,' said Darleston, and his voice suggested that he did see. Perfectly. 'Very well. Penelope and I will engage to point out all the most impeccably behaved and bred damsels we can think of.'

Helford grinned. 'Aunt Maria, at least, will be eternally in your debt. I knew I could count on you, Peter. If you are quite sure Lady Darleston won't mind my turning up…'

'At eight, then,' said Darleston. 'We are keeping town hours. I must be off to the park now, David. Do you care to come and be presented to Penny?'

'No, no,' said Helford, hastily. 'I will look forward to that this evening!'

They parted and Helford turned back along Bond Street. Darleston's amused reaction to his matrimonial plans had thrown him slightly. Peter would never criticize, of course, but it was plain what he thought of Helford's marriage campaign. He shrugged. Peter *might* have been supremely lucky in his second marriage, but he'd reserve judgement until he'd met the second Lady Darleston. And he certainly wasn't going to run that sort of risk himself!

Helford presented himself in Grosvenor Square at the fashionable hour of eight and was admitted to Darleston House by the elderly butler.

'Good evening, Meadows. Are you keeping well?' asked the Viscount, handing the startled man his hat and cloak. He remembered the old boy from his school days when he had frequently ridden over to join Peter Frobisher and his other cronies at Darleston Court a bare ten miles from his own seat.

'Master David! That is…my lord! Well! His lordship did say he had a surprise guest for this evening, but he wouldn't tell anyone who.' The kindly old face beamed as wrinkles chased themselves delightedly all over it. 'You are looking well, if I may say so. Come this way, the family are all in the drawing room.'

'Thank you, Meadows.' He followed the old chap up to the first floor and said with a twinkle, 'I do trust you are going to announce me in style, Meadows.'

Suppressing a chuckle wholly at variance with his usual dignified manner, Meadows opened the door of the drawing room and said into a sudden silence, 'Lord Helford!'

The group before the fire stared in amazement, except, of course, for Darleston, who was obviously taking a mischievous pleasure in the shock he had given Carstares and the ladies.

Carstares had changed very little, thought Helford as his friend surged forward with outstretched hands.

'Helford! Good God! Where did you spring from?'

Helford seized the outstretched hand and wrung it. No, Carstares hadn't changed, still the same cheery blue eyes and tousled fair hair. The same merry open countenance.

He clapped George on the shoulder. 'Got off the packet yesterday morning and went on the strut down Bond Street. Just to see if anyone recognised me. Didn't see a soul I knew until I met Peter outside Jackson's.' He shook his head. 'Lord, it's good to see you two again!'

Darleston strolled forward, 'Come and be presented to my wife and sister-in-law.' The odd note of pride in his voice made Helford glance at him sharply. If George had not changed, Darleston most assuredly had. When last he had known this man, he had been in the depths of a bitter depression over the infidelities of his first wife. Now he was again the warm, easygoing man Helford remembered from his youth.

The reason was not far to seek. Penelope, Countess of Darleston, was a very lovely woman; a riot of auburn curls and smoky grey eyes were not the least of her charms. Her expression held a great deal of sweetness and a hint of mischief. And there was something in her eyes when they rested on her husband that made Lord Helford's heart contract sharply. Briefly he wondered what it would be like to have a woman look at you like that. Abruptly he dismissed the thought. He was not looking for love in his marriage. That was far too dangerous.

Lady Darleston came forward to greet him, 'I am so pleased to meet you at last, Lord Helford. Every time we drive past your gates in the country Peter is moved to reminisce about his long-lost youth and all the dreadful things you used to do!'

Helford bowed low over her hand and said, 'The pleasure is mine, Lady Darleston. Peter told me that it was not too late to offer congratulations on his marriage. And I understand that he is now a father. You cannot imagine how ancient I feel!'

The Countess laughed, 'I think it makes him feel old at times too. May I present my sister, Miss Sarah Ffolliot?'

She drew forward a slender girl with more brown than red in her curls but the same smoky eyes and friendly smile. But if Lady Darleston might be said to have a hint of mischief in her eyes, this chit had a great deal more than a hint. She seemed to be bursting with energy and, after being introduced, said to Helford, 'It must have been terribly exciting being abroad and in Vienna of all places. I should so much like to go there one day!'

He chatted to her for a few minutes, responding to her artless questions about life in the Austrian capital, until George came to lead her in to dinner. He was startled to see the look that passed between them. A look compounded of deep affection and, at least on George's part, of desire. Good God! Carstares thinking of marriage? How were the mighty fallen!

Helford enjoyed his first social engagement enormously. It was good to pick up his friendship with Darleston and

George Carstares. Their long separation had not loosened the bonds between them. Even Darleston's marriage did not seem to have affected his friendship with Carstares. It was plain to see that Lady Darleston held George in great affection, treating him with an easy camaraderie, and by the end of dinner Viscount Helford was in a fair way to envying his oldest friend.

That Darleston's marriage was ecstatically happy could not be held in doubt. His lovely auburn-haired countess was utterly delightful. Darleston was a damned lucky fellow, thought Helford, as his hostess had them all in stitches with her description of her first Channel crossing when she had been appallingly seasick.

'Poor Peter tried to be noble and hold the basin for me,' she said giggling. 'Which would have been fine had I not completely missed the basin and sullied his sacred Hessians! I don't know who was more upset with me, Peter, or Fordham, who had to clean them!'

Peter grinned and said, 'Not to mention the rest of my attire. Fordham was vastly put out.'

He changed the subject, 'Shall we escort Helford to Aunt Louisa's little do, Penny? He wishes to make his bow after such a long absence. Shall we lend him our...er... patronage?'

She smiled at Helford, seated on her right. 'Do you care to come with us? I am sure Lady Edenhope will not mind in the slightest. Will she, George?'

This last to George Carstares who said cheerfully, 'Devil a bit! Be glad to be one up on all the other tabbies, shouldn't wonder!'

Darleston eyed him in fascination, 'Are you referring to our esteemed friend, Lady Edenhope, as a *tabby*, George?' He shook his head. 'How very brave, isn't he, Sarah?'

'Or foolish,' suggested Miss Sarah Ffolliot with her usual candour. Helford was amused. Miss Sarah had a disconcerting habit of saying exactly what she thought and positively fizzed with naughtiness. He liked her, and hoped she was not going to hurt George. From a couple of remarks Darleston had made about minding her estate interests, it was plain she was an heiress. In his bitter experience, heiresses did not throw themselves away on younger sons, no matter how charming.

'Do come,' she said to Helford. 'It will be capital sport to see all their faces when you are announced!'

'Like the beasts at the Royal Exchange being fed?' asked Helford, amused.

'Something like that. I love going there with George. But would you consider yourself as a beefsteak?' laughed Sarah.

A groan of mock despair came from Darleston, 'We'll never marry her off, Penny! How can we when she refers to eligible *partis* as "beefsteaks"? Those that she doesn't beat all hollow at chess. There's nothing for it but to put her in a convent!'

Not in the least abashed, Sarah put her tongue out at him and continued to eat her syllabub. 'Oh, pooh,' she said between mouthfuls. 'If Helford is a friend of yours and George's, he must be perfectly accustomed to outrageous behaviour. Besides, George can beat me at chess now!'

'Well, thank God for that!' broke in Penelope. 'I've been tutoring him for months!'

Helford left Darleston House well after midnight to walk home. It occurred to him briefly as he strolled along that perhaps he ought to consider waiting a while before he married, see if he could find a girl to love, but he dismissed the thought immediately with something very like panic. Admittedly Darleston had been lucky and it looked as though George would be just as happy. But he shuddered at the thought of the risk he'd be taking. He'd made a crashing fool of himself once and he didn't fancy doing it again.

And it would take time and time was one thing that he didn't have. His brother's premature death had put the succession in some danger. It hadn't really needed Aunt Maria's intervention for him to realise the importance of his marriage. He was the last of the Melvilles now, except for his niece, and it behoved him to marry as carefully as possible to carry on the name creditably. No, he would marry for the title and family name. His own pleasures would be carried on as they had always been, outside the marriage bed.

Besides, he shuddered as he contemplated the sort of hurt that Darleston was wide open to. He did not for a moment think that Penelope would ever betray her husband. That was out of the question. Even his cynical mind could accept that. But how would Peter survive if anything ever happened to Penelope? It was better to guard against that sort of pain. He remembered the agony of grief after Waterloo as one by one he realised how many of his friends had died. No, it was safer to settle for convenience in marriage and attend to his pleasures elsewhere. Love, whatever it might be, was for others.

Three nights later he trod up the steps of Lady Edenhope's mansion under the gaily striped awning erected for the occasion in company with the Darlestons, Miss Sarah Ffolliot and George Carstares. Numerous glances were cast in their direction and Helford was tolerably certain that his incognito had been blown by the time Louisa Edenhope's very starchy butler announced their party.

'The Earl and Countess of Darleston, Viscount Helford...' Despite the stentorian tones of Lady Edenhope's butler, an upsurge of exclamations and chatter drowned the announcement of Miss Sarah Ffolliot and Mr Carstares. Neither of whom cared in the least. They were too entertained by the spectacle of such a crowd of fashionables jockeying to be among the first to greet the new beefsteak, as Sarah had christened him, without appearing odiously pushing.

As the hostess, Lady Edenhope was the first to greet him. 'David Melville! How dare you turn up like this without so much as warning me! I nearly fainted when I saw who Peter had in tow. So, you are back to plague us, are you? Well, I shall give up my box at the opera and I warn you, if you start a vulgar brawl this time then I will have Darleston and George cast you out! Not to mention having Sally Jersey and the others bar you from Almack's. Although I don't suppose that would bother you in the slightest.'

'Dear Lady Edenhope,' said Helford, bowing low over her hand and kissing it. 'I have lived for this moment!' He twinkled at her outrageously.

'I dare say,' she said. 'Stop trying to turn me up sweet and go and find some other female to play off your cajolery on. I'll have you know I'm far too old for your tricks!'

'Never, dear lady,' protested Helford dramatically. 'The day you are too old for me will be the day after I cock up my toes!' His lofty tones and resonant voice made the vulgar expression sound positively romantic.

His hostess snorted. 'You're cutting a wheedle, Helford! You can give me twenty years...more I dare say!'

'For you, I'd give them,' he assured her with a smile which she privately thought was enough to make any unwary female tumble head over ears in love with him. And as for those eyes! Well, they were enough to give any female, wary or otherwise, palpitations.

'Take him away, for heaven's sake, Peter!' urged Lady Edenhope.

'With pleasure, Aunt Louisa!' said Peter with alacrity. He looked at Helford in amusement. 'Are you practising for the benefit of the impeccables? Rest assured, you're in fine fighting trim.'

The evening passed in a blur of music and champagne

judiciously mixed with the stream of faces, familiar and new, which whirled past his lordship. True to his word, Darleston had persuaded Penelope to present him to as many of the young ladies as possible. Most of them he dismissed from his mind at once, including the charming Miss Clovelly. He found her giggle rather irritating and not all the legendary virtue of her great-great-great-grandmama was enough to reconcile him to a life spent throttling the urge to throttle his wife.

Lady Lucinda Anstey was quite another matter. Penelope had not at first presented him to her, but the dignified carriage and glossy black ringlets caught his eye.

'Who is that, Lady Darleston?' he asked very softly.

She followed the direction of his gaze.

'With the black hair,' he prompted, seeing her hesitate.

Damn! thought Penelope Darleston. Damn and double damn! She knew nothing against Lady Lucinda, but she just couldn't warm to her. The regal carriage people raved over always struck her as top lofty. The cool air of confidence said more to Penelope about Lady Lucinda's conviction of social superiority than anything else. She *was* lovely, though. Those glossy curls and rose-petal complexion were a lethal combination and, when added to deep blue eyes and a tall elegant figure, the sum total was quite out of the common way.

'That is Lady Lucinda Anstey,' she said reluctantly. If he married her, then any social intercourse with Helford Place would be of the most stuffy and formal variety, she reflected. Lady Stanford's entertainments were renowned for the positively stifling degree of pomp and ceremony which characterised them. Lady Lucinda, however, appeared to revel in it.

'Is it, indeed?' responded Helford. He looked the lady over with the eyes of a connoisseur. Tall, very elegant, a definite air of distinction. He supposed that she was beautiful—truth to tell, his preference was for smaller women of a more rounded aspect. Not plump, just a trifle more curvaceous than Lady Lucinda. The sort referred to as a *cosy little armful*, in fact. He reminded himself irritably that he was selecting a Countess, a consort, a woman to be respected, not tumbled in the heat of passion! He could set up a mistress later.

'Will you present me to her?'

He didn't sound terribly interested, but Penelope accepted the inevitable. Peter had warned her that Helford was not looking for a love match. 'The three Bs, my love: Breeding, Behaviour and Beauty,' he had said with a slight twinkle. Well, she certainly had all that, and if Helford didn't require a warm heart in his bride then it was none of her business.

With this in mind she led Helford up to the lady. 'Good evening, Lady Stanford, Lady Lucinda. May I present Lord Helford, who has recently returned from Vienna? He wishes very much to be made known to you.'

Helford bowed over Lady Stanford's hand and then Lady Lucinda's. Neither lady appeared to be in the least awed or flustered by his evident desire to make their acquaintance. He didn't mind that in the least. It suggested the sort of dignity and breeding he wished for in a wife.

They all exchanged polite pleasantries on the weather, the overcrowded room and the prospect of it becoming more so as the evening progressed. Helford was agreeably impressed by Lady Lucinda. Well bred, a serious turn of mind and definitely a young lady of striking appearance. Superbly gowned in cornflower blue silk which emphasised the sapphire blue of her eyes, she was clearly an eminently suitable candidate for the position he had in mind.

Of Lady Stanford he was not quite so approving. She had, he felt, a grating sense of her own superiority, not to mention a sublime ignorance of anything outside London.

'I am delighted to make your acquaintance, Lord

Helford,' said Lady Stanford. 'You must be glad to be back in England after so long abroad. You must have desired the sound of your own language very often. And I understand that the tone in Vienna is not always what one would like.'

He wondered sardonically just what language Lady Stanford thought they spoke at the Embassy. He had been in no danger of forgetting the sound of his native tongue and besides, when a girl whispered German sweet nothings in your ear as temptingly as that little charmer Lottie, then the only desire of which he was conscious had nothing to do with the English language. Certainly he had no complaints about the tone she had used. The thought was instantly dismissed.

'Quite so, ma'am,' he agreed politely. 'And I am the more aware of what I have missed when I see such a gathering as this.' Lord, what a stupid thing to say, he thought. I'd forgotten how polite and stuffy it can be!

He realised that the orchestra had struck up a waltz and smiled at Lady Lucinda, 'Might I have the honour of this dance? If you are not otherwise engaged…' He thought that it would be unusual for a girl of this quality not to be engaged for every dance, but to his surprise Lady Lucinda shook her head and said,

'As a matter of fact, I am not engaged and I should be honoured to dance with you, but—'

Her mama cut in. 'Of course she will be delighted to be your partner, my lord.' He missed the warning look Lady Stanford directed at her daughter and the disapproving look that Lady Lucinda returned. Smiling, he offered his arm and led her out onto the floor.

Completely stunned, Penelope Darleston watched Helford lead out a girl who had never danced the waltz in public on the grounds of her mother's disapproval of innocent damsels spinning around in a male embrace. She was only saved from a social indiscretion by the fact that her husband came up and said firmly, 'Our dance, my lady.'

He swept her on to the floor, saying, 'David has taken up quite enough of your time for one evening. He now knows enough impeccably bred fillies to found a stud should he wish to do so.'

She shook with laughter at this outrageous comment and felt his grip tighten.

'What on earth will we do if he marries that one, though?' she enquired, slightly breathless at the hard strength of his arms as they encircled her.

'Resign ourselves to some excessively tedious dinner parties at Helford Place, my sweet. And if Lady Stanford agreed to this dance, then I should say our fate is sealed as far as she is concerned.' He drew her closer so that her silk-clad thighs brushed against his and whirled her through a turn, effectively dismissing all thought of Helford's matrimonial concerns from her mind. If Helford wanted convenience, it was entirely his own business.

He held Penelope's gaze and whispered something that brought a flush to her face and a soft glow to the expressive eyes.

Watching them, Helford felt his heart lurch at the way Lady Darleston's mouth quivered into an adoring smile, the way she seemed to melt even more appealingly into her husband's embrace as they danced. The beauty in his own arms was quite unyielding. Much safer, he told himself firmly. Dull, perhaps, but safe.

Chapter Two

Lady Lucinda's first waltz took the *ton* completely by surprise and before it was over bets were being quietly laid that the Stanford stronghold was in a way to being stormed. It was well known that Lady Stanford deeply disapproved of the waltz for unmarried girls. At least, so the whispers ran, until a *parti* so eligible as to make a hopeful mama clutch her vinaigrette in excitement had solicited the Ice Maiden to stand up with him for the disgraceful dance!

Perfectly aware of the ripples of conjecture eddying out from them, Helford had continued to guide his rather unyielding partner around the dance floor, conversing with her on the most unexceptionable topics he could think of. While the sobriquet Ice Maiden did not occur to him, he did compare Lady Lucinda somewhat unfavourably with little Lottie, who had danced the waltz not at all as if she were laid out cold for her own burial. Sharply, he reminded himself of what he required in bride. Lottie's skills and charms were not part of it.

Lady Lucinda was also only too aware of the furore that this dance was causing. She was pleased to note, however, that finding herself in such an intimate embrace was not at all likely to make her lose her head. Indeed, she might as well have been dancing with one of her brothers, for all the thrill it gave her to be held in Lord Helford's arms. She had to admit, though, he talked like a sensible man and did not appear to be the amorous type.

Passing them on the dance floor in George Carstare's arms, Sarah Ffolliot said *sotto voce*, 'Do you think she's noticed that it's a waltz yet? Should we tell her?' Her grey eyes brimmed over with mischief.

In extremely un-loverlike tones George said, 'For heaven's sake, Sarah! Shut up, she'll hear you!'

'Well, but if she doesn't know it's a waltz…' Sarah encountered one of her lover's rare frowns and promptly shut up. If George looked like that, then he was serious.

By the time the *ton* left Lady Edenhope's ball the main topic of gossip was the Helford assault on the icy Stanford ramparts. Whatever might be Helford's intentions, Lady Stanford had clearly signalled hers. This was Lady Lucinda's second Season and there were two more daughters in the wings. Although the regal beauty had never lacked for suitors, none had ever come up to scratch. Obviously her ladyship was not going to put any rub in the way of my Lord Helford.

At the end of a fortnight society was still buzzing with gossip about Lord Helford's attentions to Lady Lucinda. He had ridden beside her carriage in Hyde Park during the fashionable promenade. He had called twice at Stanford House and had been admitted on both occasions. He had even danced the waltz with her at several balls. Lady Stanford had explained, most unconvincingly, that in her second Season a girl might be said to have proved herself.

By the middle of April most people regarded the match as a foregone conclusion. Helford had admittedly paid some attention to one or two other damsels, notably Miss Sarah Ffolliot, but no one was in any doubt about his intentions. Lady Lucinda was to be the lucky girl. The only bet you could get odds on in the clubs was whether Helford would pop the question before his friend George Carstares could get up his courage to offer for Darleston's sister-in-law.

Returning home one evening in early May from escorting Lady Stanford and Lady Lucinda to the opera, Viscount Helford found himself in a mood of introspection. He couldn't for the life of him think why. His courtship was going to plan. Quite obviously he only had to pop the question and he would be sending notices to the papers.

His intended choice was everything he had stipulated. She had breeding, conduct and beauty, even a respectable fortune. What more could he want? He entered his recently refurbished town house using his latch key. An argand lamp burnt on a marble-topped console table supported by improbable sphinxes. He took up the lamp and laid his opera glasses down in its place. What more, indeed? He had been startled to realise midway through the performance of *La Cenerentola* that he was paying more attention to the charms of one of the chorus than to Lady Lucinda.

Thoughtfully he mounted the stairs. Well, what of it? He had little doubt that Lady Lucinda would turn a blind eye to his amorous dealings if he were discreet and did not make her a laughing stock. Obviously she expected him to make her an offer, but it was ridiculous to suppose that there was any more sentiment on her side than his. Their marriage would be a business arrangement for the begetting of children, preferably sons, and the orderly devolution of property.

He reached his bedchamber and began to undress. Somehow he was dissatisfied. Now, when he had managed everything according to plan, suddenly the plan seemed flawed. Rubbish, he told himself sternly, as he divested himself of his black coat. You want a marriage of convenience and that's precisely what you are getting. He threw his shirt over a chair, resolutely thrusting away the vision of Peter and his lovely wife, who had also been at the opera. They had visited his box at the interval, the affection between them apparent for anyone to see. His breeches followed the shirt with unwonted violence.

A nightshirt was laid out for him. He donned it thoughtfully. His house party was nearly arranged. The Stanfords were off to Brighton for several weeks, but he had little doubt that if an invitation to Helford Place were extended, Lady Stanford would have no scruples in leaving her own spouse to the joys of Brighton while she secured a husband for her daughter. He had formed the intention of paying a morning call at Stanford House the following day to invite them. He had invited several friends, but Lady Lucinda was the only unattached female. It looked a little particular, but that suited his purpose admirably.

He sat on the edge of his enormous bed with its extravagantly carved headboard and blew out the lamp. It occurred to him as he lay waiting for sleep that perhaps he should have discreetly set up a mistress. That might have eased the odd feeling of dissatisfaction that haunted him. Too late now, he was leaving town in a couple of days to make sure all was in order for his house party. Besides which, it was probably time he introduced himself to his ten-year-old niece and ward, Miss Fanny Melville. He thrust away a feeling of guilt. After all, surely no one expected him to act as nursemaid to the child.

At ten o'clock the following morning Helford left his house in Cavendish Square to stroll around to Stanford House in Grosvenor Street. He met George Carstares in Grosvenor Square and hailed him with pleasure.

'Hullo, old chap. Haven't seen much of you recently. How are you?'

George grinned, 'Never better, thank you.' He appeared to be bubbling over with high spirits, unusual in one of his preferred matutinal habits. 'Offered for Sarah last night and she accepted!'

Helford stared, speechless for a moment, all his cynical, sceptical convictions flung into disarray. An heiress, and one much sought after, had accepted the hand of a second son with no chance of inheriting. Despite having expected this for weeks, the solid fact shook his cynical soul to the core.

'Congratulations, George,' he said, squashing the unwelcome tinge of envy that arose in his breast. He did not envy George *Sarah* specifically, just that look of transparent joy and completion that he and Darleston radiated. 'Please wish Miss Sarah happy for me. I will be leaving town tomorrow. Time I went down to Helford and sorted things out there. And I have a small house party arranged for next month— as a matter of fact, I'm just on my way to invite Lady Stanford and Lady Lucinda to grace it.'

George hid his horror very creditably. 'Oh! Then…?' He almost held his breath awaiting the reply.

'No. Not yet,' answered Helford, correctly interpreting his friend's unvoiced question. 'Only fair to let the girl see where she is going to live beforehand. Besides, it will be as well for us to spend some time together first. Make sure we don't annoy each other too much. I shall speak to Stanford this morning and make sure he has no objection.'

None of this gave George any comfort. There was no way Helford could get out of making the girl an offer if he spoke to Stanford. And he had little doubt that the offer would be accepted, if not with enthusiasm—for George could not imagine Lady Lucinda being so vulgar as to betray such a human emotion—then with dignified good breeding.

With no hint of his true feelings George said, 'I'll wish

you luck then, old chap.' No harm in that, he thought. Besides, if Lady Luck *did* happen to glance in the direction of Helford Place, she might just decide to meddle!

An hour later Helford left Stanford House, determinedly aware that he had set things in train for exactly the sort of marriage he had envisaged. Lord Stanford had given his permission for him to address Lady Lucinda with a complete lack of surprise. Lady Stanford and Lady Lucinda had accepted his invitation to Helford Place with a marked degree of gratification. Everything was as he had planned.

So why the hell did he feel as though a trap were closing about him? He had engineered everything himself. He had certainly not been caught by a scheming mama. On the contrary, he had been totally in control of the whole situation and would remain so.

He reminded himself of this frequently on his journey down to Helford Place, until his unacknowledged excitement at coming home at last finally rose up and drowned all other thoughts in a flood of expectation.

Indeed, he found the last part of his drive down to Helford Place to be a very odd experience. In the past twelve years, on the few occasions he had been in England, he had only visited London. Now, driving the last few miles, he found that everything was much the same as he remembered it. Yet he felt very differently about it.

The road was as rutted as ever, the hedges towering overhead crowded with pale pink dog roses and honeysuckle. Their heady scent drifted on the light breeze, seeming to float suspended in the golden aftermath of a brief shower. Glittering droplets bejewelled each blossom so that it sparkled. Twelve years ago he would not have noticed such things. Then, if he had been on this road heading for home, it could only have meant that he was in dun territory yet again, depending on his brother to give him a tow. Or to pursue his infatuation with Felicity. He'd certainly never had any inclination to notice the beauties of nature.

He thought cynically that, at least after he'd quitted Helford Place for the last time, he had learnt how to live on his pay as a soldier and his patrimony. Even added to it by careful investments, so that he'd been a relatively wealthy man in his own right before he inherited the title. So determined had he been to have nothing more to do with his family that he had learnt the value and handling of money.

He had made good time on the journey. He had sent his horses forward and this final pair of chestnuts he had picked up at Tattersall's had been an undoubted bargain, prime bits of blood and bone. Not quite sixteen-mile-an-hour tits, but nearly so. Their action was admirable, forward stepping and very easy. And their mouths were something to dream about. Better than the bays he had had twelve years ago, he reflected. Or perhaps it was just that he was a better whip now, capable of coaxing the best from his cattle.

His mind still in the past, he swept around the last corner before the village of Little Helford at a pace which he later admitted to himself to have been far too fast. He was within two miles of home and eager to reach it.

The road was not particularly wide and the church stood just outside the village with the parsonage beside it and it was from the lane beside the church that disaster so nearly struck. He could see a female on his left walking towards him alongside the churchyard. She looked up at the rumble of the curricle as it approached and he clearly saw her face turn to horror as she ran forward shouting and waving. Then, so fast that he could never afterwards be sure exactly what happened, a small boy on a makeshift trolley came tearing out of the lane. The trolley hit a rut in the road and flipped over, depositing its shrieking driver directly in the path of the oncoming vehicle.

Helford swore and hauled desperately on the reins with scant regard for his horses' delicate mouths. The pace was too swift. Seeing in a flash that he had not the slightest chance of stopping in time, he attempted to yank them around, but they were thoroughly upset and did not respond fast enough. Horrified, he realised that the child was going to be killed.

Then somehow the girl was on the child and had caught him under the armpits, swinging him out of the way before trying to leap clear herself. She was not quite quick enough to avoid a glancing blow from the shoulder of the off-side horse which sent her spinning into the ditch. There was an appalling cracking, splintering sound as hooves and wheels crashed over the trolley.

Petrified at what he might find, Helford pulled up his pair ten yards further on. White and shaking, he set the brake and flung the ribbons to his equally shocked tiger with a terse, 'Hold 'em!'

He vaulted down into the road and ran back, inexpressibly relieved to see the girl struggling to her feet and the small boy trying valiantly to control his sobs.

'Are you hurt, girl?' he snapped, fear making his voice sharper than it might otherwise have been.

The girl looked up at him, rubbing her left shoulder vigorously, and he was staring into the most appealing little face he had ever seen. She had a warm, creamy complexion, which just now was streaked with mud and becomingly flushed; the nose had the merest suspicion of a tilt and more than a suspicion of freckles scattered over it. Soft brown curls had escaped a knot on top of her head, adding to the disarray of her person. And a small, slender yet daintily rounded person it was too, he noted, despite the dowdy and rather shapeless grey dress she wore. Definitely what he would describe as a cosy armful!

He felt sick in his guts as a nightmare vision of what

might have happened rose before him. The slight figure lying broken and battered in the mud. He closed his eyes and shook his head to dispel the thought.

But perhaps her eyes were her most startling feature. He supposed one might describe them as hazel, but they were in reality the strangest mixture of green and brown, fringed with the longest, thickest black lashes. Delicate black brows arched over them in direct contrast to the softness of the rest of her colouring. Never had he seen lovelier eyes.

And never had he seen eyes quite so angry!

'No! I am not hurt! But it's small thanks to you if I am not! How dare you drive at such a *wicked* pace around a corner into a quiet village!' She positively quivered with fury. 'You could have killed Jemmy here!' She turned on the boy. 'Not but what you have been warned often and often not to ride that trolley on to the road! You ought to be ashamed of yourself. Why, you might have hurt the horses badly!'

'My thoughts precisely,' drawled Helford, relieved beyond all measure that the little vixen was at least unharmed enough to rake them both down. He reached into a pocket and drew out a shilling. 'Take this, Jemmy, and don't do it again or I'll warm the seat of your pants for you!'

Stunned at such largesse and barely able to mutter his thanks and apology, the boy accepted the coin and took to his heels before a crowd could gather. By some miracle no one was about and he could entertain reasonable hopes that his escapade would not reach the ears of his mam who would not wait for his next infraction to warm his seat for him. Especially if she ever found out how close Miss Sophie had come to being runned over!

Amused, Helford turned back to the girl and said, 'Are you quite sure you are—?' He stopped mid-sentence and swore. Her nose was bleeding copiously.

'Damn! Here, let me!' He found a large silk handkerchief

in his coat pocket and applied it firmly to her nose, cupping the other hand behind her head to hold her steady. Startled eyes stared at him in outrage over his handkerchief, but she remained still in his grip. His fingers, threaded through the soft curls, trembled slightly. There was a curious familiarity in the intimacy of silken locks tumbling over his hand in such disorder. It was far from the first time he had tangled his long fingers in such soft tresses. But under the circumstances he was shocked to feel a twinge of desire in his loins. Ruthlessly he shackled the unwelcome thoughts and concentrated on her bleeding nose.

After a few moments he released her carefully. 'That should do it,' he said with misplaced confidence.

For a moment the girl stood stock still and then he noticed that she was trembling and breathing rather oddly. His eyes widened in horror as he realised what was about to happen but there was no time to dodge. In sheer self-defence he grabbed her and clamped the handkerchief to her nose again.

'Aaaachhhoo!' The sneeze and its effects were thoroughly extinguished by the handkerchief, but he realized, while trying unsuccessfully not to laugh, that this time the girl had obviously had enough. Firmly she took the handkerchief and removed herself from his grip.

Her voice came slightly muffled from behind it. 'It's nothing! Please just go away unless you wish to see me reduced to a sneezing ruin!'

'But—'

She cut in coldly, 'I am perfectly all right and I can sneeze without your assistance! Please go away! I am not hurt in the slightest, despite your best efforts, and will be glad to see the last of you!'

'Damn you! The accident was not my fault!' he said, stung by her contempt. 'If you had stayed off the road—'

'Jem would be dead!' she flashed at him. 'I do not say he ought to have been there, but had you not been coming

at such a *wicked* pace you would have had time to pull up!
Did you not hear me? I called out to you to stop!'

He shook his head, 'No, of course I could not hear what
you were saying, you fool of a wench! The horses and
wheels were making far too much noise. In fact, I should
have thought that hell-born brat would have been able to
hear me coming and alter course! Now, if you are really
uninjured and require no further assistance, might I suggest
that you go on your way and permit me to go on mine!'

'Why you…you…arrogant, conceited coxcomb!' she exploded, while still trying to staunch her nose. 'How dare
you speak to me like that! No doubt in my position you
would have let Jem be killed!'

She was shaking with rage and Helford suddenly realised
that she was close to tears. Shock, he thought. Reaction. For
God's sake, man, control yourself! She's little more than a
child herself and you damned nearly killed her!

'No, I wouldn't have,' he admitted ruefully. 'But please
put yourself in my position. I dare say I was driving too
fast, but I was horrified when I saw the child and realised
that I couldn't avoid him. Can you imagine how I felt when
I saw you go flying into the ditch?' She stared at him in
shock and he continued, 'Come, you are undoubtedly upset!
Go home and try to believe that I would have been devastated if I had killed or injured either of you. I will even go
so far as to thank you for sparing me such an ordeal.'

'I…I beg your pardon,' she said stiffly. 'I should not have
lost my temper like that.' This grudging apology was uttered
into the blood-boltered handkerchief, but she cautiously
lowered it and sniffed carefully. Nothing happened, so she
folded the handkerchief up and held it out to him. 'Er, do
you want it back?'

He glanced at the gruesome relic and shook his head. 'Not
really! You keep it, in case your nose bleeds again.' She
nodded and bestowed it in the pocket of her gown.

He asked gently, 'Have you far to go? Might I take you up?'

'Thank you, but no. I have an errand to discharge on my way home and it will take some time. Good day, sir.'

'Good day,' he responded and stood watching as she walked away. She did not look back and he wondered who the devil she was. Her speech suggested that she was gently born, yet she had no maid to attend her, despite her youth. He did not think she could be more than twenty-three or so. Obviously she had no pretensions to wealth and fashion in that gown, but there was a certain dignity in her bearing which even her tumbled curls and muddied face could not destroy.

Puzzled, he went back to the curricle where his tiger was walking the mettlesome pair up and down.

'No harm done?' he asked.

'None, me lord,' responded his henchman. 'Leastways, not to these fellows. I'll warrant that mort'll pull up stiff tomorrow though! Lor', she did take a tumble! Thought she'd be kilt fer sure when I saw what she'd be at!'

His noble employer grunted. It had felt as though his stomach had fallen into his boots when he had seen the girl leap into the road for the boy. He had fully expected the pair of them to be trampled to death. And it would have been his fault. He had been going far too fast!

'Why the hell didn't you tell me to slow down, Jasper?' he asked crossly.

'Acos you mostly in general damns me eyes fer it,' was the very disrespectful answer. Jasper had been in Helford's employ since before he went out to the Peninsula in 1811. He had been in numerous scrapes with his master and had actually dragged him off the battlefield on two occasions. His was a privileged position and he spoke his mind very frequently.

'I dare say! Next time I do something this stupid, hit me on the head!' growled Helford.

There was a chuckle from behind him, 'I dessay the thought of that little bit of a lass tearin' strips off you like what she did will do the trick. Little spitfire she were!' The appreciation in Jasper's voice was marked.

Helford slewed around in his seat, 'You behave yourself, Jasper. She's a respectable lady!'

'You keep yer glims on the road, me lord. Don't have to tell me she's quality! Could see that fer meself! Real flesh-and-blood quality at that.' This last was muttered to himself. Jasper had his own opinion of Lord Helford's choice of helpmeet. For the life of him he couldn't think what the master was playing at. For his money, the little spitfire who'd raked him down in the roadway would be a better choice than that there statue back in London. Still, that was one subject where he'd do better to dub his mummer! The master wouldn't take no interference there! Not by a long shot he wouldn't!

Chapter Three

Miss Sophie Marsden wriggled her left shoulder irritably. It still ached from her tumble in the ditch two days ago. In fact, if she were to be strictly truthful, most of her still ached. She had woken up the following morning as stiff as a board. A careful examination had revealed her upper left arm and shoulder to be badly bruised along with her entire left side. Since this was where the horse had struck her and she had also managed to land on that side, the stiffness and bruising were only to be expected.

What really bothered Miss Marsden was that she could not get the gentleman's face and startling eyes out of her mind. He had been as white as a sheet as he came striding back to them. And his eyes! She had never imagined such blazing green eyes. And it was not just his eyes. The lean, powerful frame had simply radiated arrogant masculine strength. But it was the memory of his hand in her hair that was really occupying her thoughts. Those long fingers had tangled in her curls in a way that made her tremble when she recalled it.

Crossly she forced her attention back to the household accounts. Just because she had never seen such a handsome man before was no excuse to be making so many mistakes over these accounts. He was undoubtedly some traveller passing through whom she would never lay eyes on again and the quicker she stopped thinking about him the better. Even if she did see him again, the chances were that he would not even recall her face and, if he did, it would probably be in connection with her shocking loss of temper.

For a few moments the accounts reigned triumphant but then her pen slowed and her mind drifted. For some reason his face bothered her. She was nearly sure that it was oddly familiar, but she was quite certain that she had never met its owner before. Her reflections were interrupted by the door opening.

She turned around to see her elderly companion, Miss Andrews, and their maid Anna. The former looked distinctly apologetic. Anna, on the other hand, simply looked annoyed.

'Oh, dear! What has he done this time?' asked Miss Marsden resignedly.

'Can't find him nowhere, Miss Sophie,' asserted Anna. 'We've looked everywhere an' he's gorn.'

'Everywhere?'

''Fraid so, Miss Sophie. He's gorn.'

Miss Andrews said, 'I am truly sorry, my love. But I left him for no more than a moment, just to fetch the Latin primer. And I put him on his honour not to leave his books.'

'And he still left?' Sophie was shocked.

'Well, yes,' said Miss Andrews. 'But he took his books with him.' She seemed to feel that this in some way mitigated the crime.

'Little pest!' said Sophie indignantly. She sighed, 'Very well. I shall have to go and look for him. Again.' This was the third time in a week that her orphaned ten-year-old nephew had taken French leave from his studies. She shut the account book and stood up carefully, suppressing a curse at the soreness. She had not mentioned her escapade to any of her household, having a constitutional dislike of being fussed over. The muddied gown had been explained away as the result of a passing carriage.

Several applications of arnica had gone a long way towards relieving the soreness, but she was by no means her usual lively self and the thought of a long tramp after her truant nephew Kit did not appeal to her in the slightest.

She smiled cheerfully, realising that Anna was watching her closely. 'Never mind. I dare say a walk will blow the cobwebs away. I simply couldn't make my accounts add up.'

'I shall go over them for you, then,' said Miss Andrews, very pleased to think there was something she could do to atone for her foolishness in letting Kit slip his leash. She was vexed to think that she had not remembered to put him on his honour not to leave the room.

'Don't you dare, Thea!' Sophie was outraged. 'I am to have a pleasant walk over to the river, where Kit is no doubt tickling trout. Why should you not have a morning off? The accounts will wait. In fact, I have a very good notion about them. We will make Kit tot them up as his punishment. He can do it after dinner instead of his usual playtime.'

Miss Andrews was impressed. Like most small boys Kit loathed arithmetic. But he would certainly appreciate the justice in this arrangement!

Old Anna nodded sourly. 'Happen he'll think twice afore he does it again.'

Ruefully Sophie said, 'We can hope so, but I suspect there is something more to this than mere small-boy naughtiness. He doesn't even appear to *enjoy* his escapes. When I came up with him the last time he looked plain miserable, even before he saw me.'

Five minutes later, clad in a light cloak, bonnet and list boots, she was crossing the meadow behind the house, her skirts brushing through the purple clover. Several cows glanced up at her, their jaws moving rhythmically. She thought they must be getting used to the sight of her by now. Kit was making a habit of this.

It was odd, she thought. As she had said to Anna, he didn't seem to be enjoying his excursions. So why was he doing it so often? The only explanation she could come up with was the death of her sister six months ago. At the time Kit had been grief-stricken, of course, but he had appeared to recover, if not his usual spirits, at least some semblance of the merry boy he had been. Now he was playing truant all the time and even seemed to resent his aunt's authority. Oh, he still obeyed her, but she had the distinct impression that he didn't want to.

What exactly was behind it all, she didn't know. He wouldn't talk to her about it, just clammed up when she tried to discuss his behaviour. Give him time, she thought. It's hard for a child to lose his mother. She missed Emma bitterly enough herself. Even when she had been following the drum with her soldier husband, Emma had written regularly to her little sister, telling her all about their adventures, keeping in touch. Now she was gone completely and it would have been her birthday next week...

Sophie froze. Good God! How stupid of me, she thought. We always made such a fuss of Emma's birthday, picking flowers, making her a present. He's thinking about all that, of course. No wonder he's such a picture of misery. Oh, dear! What on earth can I do?

She continued on alongside the hedge until she came to the corner. There was a gap. Small enough to keep the cows in, but large enough for her to brush through the tangled honeysuckle, which spilled its scent and petals down over her shoulders. Large enough for Kit too, she thought, noting a scrap of wool caught on a twig. He's torn his stockings again! Well, at least I know what's bothering him now. Perhaps we can do something about it.

Insensibly cheered, she went on towards the river with an easy swinging stride. Her mind now largely freed of its concern, she was able to enjoy the walk. It was a favourite that she and her sister had often taken with Kit. Despite this being private land, the previous Viscount Helford, from whom she had rented her house, had always made her free of it.

'You can't do much harm,' he'd said in his bluff way, when he came by to apologise after one of his keepers had warned the three of them off. 'Just don't let the lad fall in the river.' He had waved aside their thanks. A kindly man with his green eyes and black hair. She and Emma had truly mourned his death…they'd hardly ever seen his fashionable Viscountess… Green eyes? Black hair? Good God! Now she knew why that face had been so familiar! He looked just like his brother. Well, not just like—Lord Helford had not had that air of rakishness about him and he had not been so appallingly handsome. But the resemblance had been enough to niggle at her memory.

Merciful heavens! She had actually had the effrontery to abuse her own landlord on a public road in the presence of a small boy and one of his own servants. If he ever found out who she was, she'd be lucky if he didn't evict her. No! The denial came sharply from an odd, secluded corner of her mind. It was inconceivable that he would be so churlish.

Little details of their encounter assured her of that. The look of sick terror on his face as he strode back, the gentle way he had held her while trying to stop her nose bleeding. The memory of his long fingers tangled in her curls brought a most peculiar sensation to the pit of her stomach. Firmly she dismissed it. He had been angry enough, she thought. But not because I nearly splattered him with blood! She giggled as she saw again the dawning horror as he realised what was about to happen. No, he hadn't cared at all! Just tried again to help her. He'd even laughed.

She felt a trifle guilty as she recalled how she had ripped up at him. No wonder he'd lost his temper with her. He wasn't to know that cologne sometimes made her sneeze. But he had curbed his anger almost immediately. Had he seen how upset she was? The whole affair had suddenly got home to her, making her quite sick with delayed fear. When she had seen Jem's danger there had been no time for fear. She had acted without even thinking. Only later, when she had been safe, had she begun to shake and feel cold. It was always the same, she thought ruefully. She went tail over top into action and then thought about the consequences later.

Even now...crossly she thrust the memory away. What a ninnyhammer, to be trembling like a leaf over an avoided accident two days old! Depend upon it his lordship—she entertained no doubts that it *had* been the new Viscount—had forgotten it already. If her memory served her correctly, then this Viscount Helford had a reputation as a considerable rake. Vienna! That was it! He had been at the Embassy, his brother had said. A badly dressed country nobody with no pretensions to beauty was hardly going to lodge in his memory.

Riding out that morning on one of his late brother's horses, his lordship was very far from having forgotten the encounter. He was strangely haunted by the business. He had seen death often enough in the army, horrible lingering deaths of mangled bodies and maimed limbs. Deaths which had been a mercy when they came. But none had ever affected him as did the thought of that girl battered by his horses and dragged under the wheels of his curricle. He had woken the previous night in a sweat having dreamed of it. The details were horribly clear and he had shuddered in relief to realise that it was merely a dream.

Now in the bright sunshine as he cantered across his

flower-starred fields he had leisure to wonder who the girl was. A lady, unquestionably. But who? He had casually enquired of his Great Aunt Maria about the various gently born families currently in residence, but none of the persons she had enumerated tallied with his little termagant. And why the hell was he bothering anyway? She could be nothing to him. He had applied for permission to court Lady Lucinda and that should suit him admirably.

Of course she can be nothing to you, soothed the odd voice in his mind. But it would only be polite to call on her and assure yourself that she really did take no hurt. And to suggest that her parents or guardians should take better care of her. A chit of her quality should not be wandering the countryside unattended. It was outrageous. The more he thought about it, the more he was convinced that he should find out who she was.

A movement on the far side of the hedge he was riding beside caught his attention. He stood up in his stirrups for a better view and there, on the other side of the meadow, was a familiar form. He could not possibly be mistaken even at this distance. There was something very distinctive about the way she moved. A suggestion of lithe grace about the lissom body. He was surprised that the unknown girl should have so wormed her way into his thoughts.

He watched for a moment and wondered where her companions were. He could see no one else, just one unattended girl heading, if his memory served him, for the river flowing beyond that belt of oaks. Riding further along the hedge, he came to a gap. Turning his mare, he rode back a little and then pushed her into a canter. Her ears pricked daintily as she saw what he would be at. A snort of enthusiasm told David that she was not at all averse to jumping. Gathering her quarters under her, she sailed over effortlessly, picking her feet up daintily.

The figure by the far hedge had obviously heard them.

She had stopped and turned to see who was coming. Now, thought David, I can find out who she is. And what the hell she is doing trespassing on my land!

The thud of hooves had alerted Sophie to the fact that she was not alone even before the familiar chestnut mare came over the hedge. She recognised her at once. Lord Helford's favourite mare, Perdita. And ridden by the gentleman in the curricle. His seat on a horse was magnificent, she saw at once, and he handled the lively mare with the ease of a born horseman. He was obviously coming to find out who the trespasser was so she waited, wondering if he would even recognise her.

His first words settled that. 'Do you never take a maid with you, or a companion? I cannot think it right for a girl your age to go about unattended.' He had not meant to be quite so direct but somehow the words were out before he knew it. It must be the eyes which unsettled him. They were even lovelier than he remembered.

Sophie stiffened. He would be quite within his rights to castigate her for trespassing, but how dare he call her to account for her behaviour! Insufferable man! With an effort she recalled that he was her landlord and a Viscount to boot, and that common courtesy required her to suppress her natural inclination to tell him to mind his own business.

'Good morning, Lord Helford,' she said sweetly. And observed with pleasure the jolt she had given him. He had certainly not expected her to know who he was.

'I confess, ma'am, you have the advantage of me.' He acknowledged her hit with a charming smile and dismounted, drawing the bridle over his mare's head. Perdita, recognising a well-wisher who on numerous occasions had bestowed an apple or even sugar upon her, promptly gave him a shove and insinuated herself between them, rubbing her face against Sophie's shoulder.

'I see she knows you,' said David drily. Damn, even his mare knew the chit!

'Yes, she was your brother's favourite. We often used to see him riding her,' said Sophie, petting the mare. 'I was sorry to hear of his death. He was a kind man and a good landlord.'

David nodded. Yes, that was James. Despite his hurt over Felicity, he had never denied James's sterling qualities; he had been kind and undoubtedly he had been a good landlord.

'May I know your name, ma'am?' he asked politely.

'Miss Sophie Marsden. And—' seeing that the name conveyed nothing to his lordship '—I live at Willowbank House.'

'Then your parents are my tenants!'

'No,' she corrected him gently, '*I* am your tenant.'

'And may I enquire what Miss Marsden is doing on my preserves completely unattended?' At last he had managed to return to his original question.

'I'm not poaching rabbits, if that's what is worrying you!' she snapped, unaccountably annoyed by his continual harping on her solitary state. 'I'm not a green girl, you know. I am five and twenty and my own mistress. If you must have it, I am trying to retrieve a truant and—' this with a mischievous smile '—I have to admit it, he *is* probably tickling your trout.'

'Tickling my trout? How old is this poacher?'

'Ten,' replied Sophie.

'And you are responsible for him?' An incredible suspicion was forming in David's mind. He could not believe it at first. She seemed so sweet and innocent. But a boy of ten and she was only twenty-five! He stole a glance at her left hand. No, it was bare of rings, he had not misheard her. He was conscious of a sickening jolt of disappointment, swiftly followed by anger. And she had known his brother! Damn

Mistress or Marriage?

James! And damn women, they were all the same! First Felicity and now this one!

His voice, when he spoke again, was cold. 'I think, Miss Marsden, that you had better remain off my preserves in future. In fact, I suggest you remove yourself now and remember that any *game* I find on my land, I am apt to consider mine. Since I am riding towards the river anyway I will send your…er…*ward* home.'

Completely taken aback by the sudden change in his tone, Sophie stared at him in amazement. He had swung himself back into the saddle and was looking down at her with a faint air of hauteur. And his eyes were different somehow. They seemed to rove over her body in a manner which suggested that he…that he was stripping her with them. She felt a blush rising to her cheeks. No one had ever looked at her like that!

'Just so, Miss Marsden. I shall consider you warned. If I find you here again…'

He smiled at her in a considering way and she suddenly realised what he was thinking. Disbelief robbed her of speech for a moment and she stood positively gaping at him. Before she could recover enough to tell him exactly what she thought of his high-handed, insulting, overbearing character, he had pressed the mare into a trot and was riding away. Calling out to him that he was mistaken was unthinkable. Let him believe her a *bit of game*! She hoped he would sink through the floor in embarrassment when he found out his mistake!

David rode away conscious of mingled fury and disappointment, trying to forget the look of startled surprise on Miss Marsden's countenance, which had been replaced by embarrassment. The whole thing was obvious enough. James, doubtless discovering Felicity's infidelities, had set up his own mistress in Willowbank House. It was not a large house, but quite commodious enough for a woman and child. Curse it! No doubt James had signed the house to the wench for a long lease on easy terms, just so everything would look above board. Well, he would have to do something about that. He was damned if he wanted her living there!

The thought occurred to him that he could always continue with whatever arrangement James had made. Not a doubt but what she was a dainty piece…and it would be deucedly convenient… No! He didn't want James's leavings! He hadn't wanted the scraps Felicity had been prepared to bestow upon him and he didn't want this one! At least he didn't think he did. She would be enjoyable though, he thought to himself. Those soft, voluptuous curves would nestle against him very comfortably…and that temper hinted at a passionate nature…

Still considering the matter, he reached the oaks and rode into the flickering shade at a walk. A narrow path led through the trees. He knew it well and tried to remember just how many times he had come this way as a boy in the evening or very early morning to catch a rise on the deep pool at the bend in the river. The mare's hooves made little sound on last year's leaves, damp from heavy rain overnight.

The trees eventually opened out on to the riverbank. On the far side the ground was marshy and bright with yellow flag irises. This side the bank shelved steeply, carved out as the river turned. Here in the deep, quiet backwater the trout lay up during the day. A demoiselle dragonfly skimmed across the water and he watched breathlessly, but there was no rise and the insect was gone again in a shard of blue. He looked further along and there in the long grass was a small boy lying on his stomach, peering over into the pool.

He dismounted and, dropping the mare's reins, walked quietly to where the boy was lying. His nankeens indicated that he had been sitting in wet grass and the soft brown curls were very familiar. A pile of books lay beside him. He had obviously not heard anyone approach.

David looked down at the child for a moment. There was something odd about the set of the child's shoulders which made him hesitate, but he cleared his throat warningly. The boy rolled over immediately and David saw in a flash that he had been crying and also from the surprise on his face that he had expected someone else.

Well, of course he did, you idiot, David castigated himself. Heavens! He had the same black-fringed hazel eyes, the same curls. It was uncanny. Nothing of James there.

The boy had rolled back on to his stomach, 'Oh. I thought you were someone else.' His voice was sullen.

'Your mother, for instance?' suggested David sardonically. And immediately regretted it. Those hazel eyes were fronting him again with a sort of suppressed anguish.

The small shoulders shook and a broken voice said in a whisper, 'Yes, but it's always Aunt Sophie!'

The riverbank heaved under David's feet. Aunt Sophie? *Aunt* Sophie? *Oh, my God! And she saw what I was thinking! Oh, hell and the Devil! What did Peter say about carrying one's suspicions too far?*

'Sophie Marsden is your aunt?' he asked gently as he squatted down beside the small figure.

'Yes.'

'I see,' said David. 'The resemblance between you is so startling I assumed she must be your mother.'

The tear-stained face looked up, puzzled. 'But how could she be? Aunt Sophie isn't married.'

How indeed, thought David ruefully. And to think *I* was that innocent once. I've certainly made a hash of this all right and tight! I must have been mad. James would never have taken a fifteen-year-old as his mistress!

His new acquaintance continued, 'I know we look alike.

Aunt Sophie and Mama looked a lot alike. I s'pose I took after Mama. I'm Kit Carlisle.'

David nodded, feeling his way. There was something here that he didn't quite understand. 'Miss Marsden was a trifle concerned about you. I met her coming this way and told her I'd send you home if I saw you.'

A sigh greeted this. 'Is she very angry?'

Well, yes, she probably was. But not with this youngster, thought David. 'Not very, I shouldn't think,' he said encouragingly. 'Did you have reason to think she would be?'

'It's the third time this week that I've given Auntie Thea the bag,' confessed Kit shamefacedly. 'She's my governess, you know. She left the room for a minute and put me on my honour not to leave my books...' He indicated the pile of books. 'So I...er...brought them with me.'

'Enterprising,' said David mildly.

'You're not cross?'

'Should I be?' asked David, surprised at the question.

'You don't think it was a bit mean?' asked Kit hesitantly.

'Well, since you mention it, I have to say it was not quite the thing to do,' acknowledged David. 'But I dare say I would have done it myself so there's hope for you yet.' He added feelingly, 'And if you never do anything worse to offend a lady then you'll be doing well!'

'I suppose I'd better go,' said Kit. 'If Aunt Sophie is looking for me...' His voice trailed off and he heaved himself to his feet.

'Why don't you wash your face first? It's a little dirty,' said David tactfully. He pulled out a handkerchief, reflecting that Miss Marsden was going to have quite a collection if this kept up. Reaching over to dip it in the pool, he asked casually, 'Any trout?'

Kit nodded as he scrubbed his face with the proffered handkerchief, 'Mmm. Three. But I put them back.'

'You tickled three trout out of there?' David was impressed. That rascally old poacher Twickenham had tried to show him as a lad how the trick was done without the least success. 'Who taught you that?'

Kit looked rather conscious. 'I s'pose I shouldn't say. They're your trout, aren't they?'

'What makes you say that?' Good God, the boy was as quick as his aunt!

'Well, I know Perdita and you look like Lord Helford a bit. Besides, I met your bailiff, Hurley, on the way and he said you were out riding, so it wasn't very hard,' explained Kit.

'I see,' said David, amused. 'Well, yes, I am Lord Helford and I suppose they are my trout, strictly speaking, and if you refuse to denounce the old scoundrel who taught you to tickle my trout I can only respect your discretion.'

Kit looked at him carefully. 'Does that mean you don't mind?'

'Mind? Of course I mind!' said David. 'I tried to tickle these trout for years and never caught one. Poor old Twickenham was ashamed of so clumsy a pupil!'

'Twickenham! But—' Kit stopped himself at once.

'You needn't tell me,' said David. 'If Twickenham's still alive I have no doubt that he was your master. You tell the old scoundrel I still can't tickle a trout when next you see him!'

A chuckle greeted this. 'You can't be as bad as Aunt Sophie. She fell in when I tried to show her.'

'Did she, indeed?' David tried to ignore the vision of Aunt Sophie in a wet and clinging gown, which promptly presented itself to his imagination for minute inspection.

'If you must be going, would you care for a ride home?' he asked. 'Since you and Perdita are acquainted I will presume on her good nature.'

'Is it out of your way?' asked Kit, obviously trying not to look too eager.

'Not in the slightest. You have reminded me that I have an errand to your aunts,' explained David, thinking that he certainly owed one of the lad's aunts an unconditional and grovelling apology.

'Auntie Thea isn't really my aunt, you know. I just call her that,' said Kit.

They walked over to the mare and David swung himself into the saddle and held a hand down to Kit. 'Put your foot on mine and up with you.'

Kit scrambled up easily enough and they set off back through the oak wood and across the meadows. Kit did not seem to be in the least in awe of a viscount and chattered away to David about the wildlife to be found around and about. To David's surprise he enjoyed the experience enormously. Children had not hitherto come much in his way. Naturally one had to have them to carry on the family name and title, but it had never occurred to him that they might be rewarding in themselves. Certainly the stiffly polite Miss Fanny Melville had not given him any such inkling.

Perdita's steady trot covered the distance very easily and as they pushed through the gap into the cow field behind Willowbank House a slim figure could be seen mounting the stile which led into the garden.

'There she is,' said Kit. He called out, 'Aunt Sophie, here I am!'

The figure turned at once and even at that distance David could see her stiffen in shock. 'Hold tight,' he said and pushed the mare into a canter.

By the time they reached her Sophie was standing on the lowest step of the stile, her face set and watchful. Nothing could have equalled her surprise at seeing Kit with his lordship. Her first assumption, that my lord must be taking the quickest way to remove an unwanted trespasser from his land, was quickly dispelled by a look at Kit's face. He was obviously quite happy with his company. A further look at

Lord Helford's face told her that he was perfectly aware that he had made an appalling gaffe and was thoroughly ashamed and vexed with himself. Well, far be it from me to make it easy for him, thought Sophie savagely. Arrogant beast!

She was the first to speak. 'Thank you for the return of my *ward*, sir. As you see, I am off your preserves.' The icy politeness of her voice spoke volumes for all the things she would have liked to say, but was prevented from uttering by the circumstances.

Not for a moment did David delude himself that either her good manners or his own high degree were in any way cramping her style. The only defence between himself and another sample of Miss Marsden's temper was perched on his saddle bow.

'I'm...I'm awfully sorry, Aunt Sophie,' said Kit. And Lord Helford had thought she wasn't very angry! Kit had never seen his merry aunt in such a pelter.

Her face softened slightly as she looked at him, 'Very well. You had better go inside and repeat your apology to Thea. And after dinner you can help me with my accounts since I had to leave them to come after you.'

Kit slid to the ground with a grimace. Trust Aunt Sophie to come up with that. 'Yes, ma'am.' He grinned up at David. 'Thank you, sir. Goodbye.' He swarmed over the stile and ran off to the house. If Aunt Sophie wasn't cross with him, who was she cross with? It couldn't be Lord Helford. She'd only just met him. Besides, he was a great gun!

Miss Sophie Marsden was left confronting the man she couldn't possibly be cross with and said, 'Naturally I will remove myself from your side of the stile. Good day, my lord.' Those dark eyes were showing more green than brown and they were narrowed to blazing slits.

David swallowed and began his apology with all the air of a man leading a forlorn hope. 'Miss Marsden, I...er...I made a frightful mistake. And I beg you to accept my profound apologies for the—'

He was cut off sharply. 'Your apology is of not the slightest interest to me, sir!' snapped the lady. 'I have nothing but contempt for anyone with such a horridly commonplace mind as to assume…to assume…what you assumed. And furthermore, even if I were a bit of game, as you so obligingly implied, you are the last man alive to whom I would consider granting my favours!'

'How dare you say such a thing to me!' exploded David in outrage.

'No?' asked Sophie, a dangerous gleam in her eyes. 'Would you prefer me to tell you that I am very disappointed and should be charmed to entertain your dishonourable proposals? Have you never had a female refuse you before?'

David glared at her. 'Of course not!' He stopped, aware of her incredulous gaze. Bloody hell! What was he saying?

'How very gratifying for you, my lord!' she said, patently disgusted. 'I am delighted to think that I have enlarged your experience so easily!'

'Damn your eyes!' He was really furious now at having made such a cod's-head of himself. 'What I meant was that a young lady of birth and virtue, which I assume you to be, should not say such things! Not even know of such things! I have apologised for misjudging you!'

'And of course you would know a vast deal about proper young ladies, my lord,' retorted Sophie sarcastically. She snorted in a very unladylike way and continued, 'I've no doubt that you judged me on exactly the same basis as you judge your mistresses! And if you had any thought that I might be persuaded to join their ranks you can think again!'

This was of course exactly what he had done, but to hear it said openly, and by a delicately bred girl who should have known nothing of such things, was a salutary experience for his lordship. The outrageous little termagant! He told himself that he was shocked, or ought to be. But he was conscious of a ripple of amusement and, damn it all, admiration for the little spitfire ripping up at him.

'All I have to say,' continued Sophie, who had already said more than enough, 'is that your *mistake* says a great deal more about *you* than it does about *me*!'

'You little vixen!' said David, even more outraged. 'What does a chit like you know of my way of life? Well, I can see when I am outgunned! Miss Marsden, I will leave you to recover your temper and will call upon you in a few days' time. I trust by then you will be in a way to forgiving me and will deign to receive me.'

Sophie glared at him from the stile, a slender form fairly bristling with indignation, even down to the eyelashes. 'Since you are my landlord I can hardly refuse!'

He was turning the mare, but he stopped at that and held her furious eyes with his. 'On the contrary, Miss Marsden.' His deep voice was very grave. 'If you feel that you prefer not to receive me after the insinuations I made and the very improper way I spoke to you, then I will respect your privacy. You need have no fear that it will in any way affect your residence at Willowbank House.'

He rode away without giving her time to reply, but stopped and looked back. 'Oh. Accept my compliments on your nephew. And tell him he needn't bother putting the trout back next time. He's a fine lad and you are both welcome on my preserves at any time. Without prejudice, of course.'

She stared after him in considerable confusion. Never had she been so puzzled by a man in all her life. From all she had ever heard of him he was the most dangerous of rakes but until he had considered her a...a *lightskirt*, to use a phrase culled from her military brother-in-law, she had felt perfectly safe with him. Unless, of course, you counted the fact that he had nearly run her over. Only when he had thought her a wanton had his manner changed and the way he looked at her. *As though I were a filly up for auction!*

She suddenly realised that she was still watching his lordship ride off through the cow pasture. Furious with herself, she jumped off the top of the stile into the garden and stalked towards the house. She wondered what he had thought when Kit had revealed their true relationship. Her ready sense of humour could not be denied and a choke of laughter had to be instantly suppressed. He must have been mortified! Served him right. Odious, arrogant...ooh! There were no words bad enough to describe him to her satisfaction!

And as for his insufferable charity in assuring her that she had nothing to fear in refusing to receive him! Had he threatened her with eviction she would have denied herself on principle. Now she would have to admit him!

Miss Marsden entered the house via the kitchen, where she found Anna industriously kneading bread dough. Anna took one look at her mistress's stormy face and decided not to comment. It was plain enough that Miss Sophie had had words with the gentleman. Anna had a good view of the stile through the kitchen windows and she had seen Miss Sophie on one of its steps and the tall gentleman on horseback who'd delivered Master Kit. Must be his lordship, surmised Anna. Looked like the old one, anyways.

'Miss Thea has took Master Kit into the bookroom to continue his lessons, Miss Sophie,' said Anna cautiously.

'Good,' said Sophie shortly and left the kitchen without another word.

The old woman smiled resignedly to herself. Not often Miss Sophie got into a tweak, but when she did all the storm warnings went up. Come to think of it, Anna couldn't remember when a mere man had managed to put her all on end. Miss Sophie took little enough notice of men one way or another. Which was a pity in Anna's opinion because if ever a better-natured, sweeter, prettier lass deserved a good husband, Anna had yet to meet her.

Her gnarled old hands automatically formed the bread into loaves and she put them by the fire to rise. Ah, well. There was time yet for Miss Sophie to meet a real gentleman. One who wouldn't mind her having Master Kit to provide for.

Chapter Four

My Lord Helford rode home in a state of considerable vexation. Not only, it must be said, with Miss Marsden, but with himself. He could not think what had come over him to leap to such an unwarranted and insulting conclusion. The little vixen was right. It did say something about him. About his way of life and attitudes.

He wondered if she would receive him when he called. He wouldn't put it past her to have a servant deny her. And he wouldn't blame her either. Lord, when he thought of how he had allowed his eyes to run over her body, making it quite clear that he was assessing all her charms and possibilities! Little wonder she was so angry with him.

Still, it was the outside of enough that she should suspect him of wishing to make her his mistress now that he knew his mistake, even if that thought had briefly presented itself to him. Firmly he repressed the delectable fantasy this thought conjured up. For heaven's sake! He had caused enough trouble without indulging in erotic fancies which were not only insulting to the lady, but were also guaranteed to cut up his peace. He had to come up with some way to make his promised visit to her perfectly unexceptionable and demonstrate that he did not view her as a prospective

mistress. It was a moot point as to who was in most need
of the demonstration, Miss Marsden or himself.

Still annoyed with himself, he handed the mare over to
Jasper when he reached the stables with barely a grunt of
thanks. His henchman said nothing aloud, rightly assessing
his master's mood as dangerous. But as he put the mare
back in her stall he muttered to himself, 'On the fidget 'e
is! Move over, lass. There'll be trouble over this 'ouse party,
me girl. Mark my words. Can't see 'im settlin' down to a
cold poultice for a wife. Not no how!'

With this very unflattering description of Lady Lucinda
Anstey, he removed the saddle from the mare's steaming
back and glared at the stable lad who had dared to peep
over the half-door.

'And what might you be wantin', Master Nosey?'

'N...nothin', sir!' disclaimed the boy hastily. 'Thought
you was callin' fer summat, that's all.'

It took Lord Helford time to hatch out a plan to make it
quite clear to Miss Marsden that he was not planning to
seduce her. When the solution finally occurred to him, he
wondered where his wits had gone begging, it was so obvious. A dry voice in the back of his mind suggested that
he might have thought of it all the sooner, had he been able
to concentrate all his mind on the problem, rather than
dwelling on the lady's fine eyes and pleasing form.

Accordingly, three days later, my Lord Helford rode out
of the main entrance to Helford Place with his niece, Miss
Fanny Melville, trotting beside him. In his brief acquaintance with her, Lord Helford had come to the conclusion
that his ward was far from being the meek little girl he had
originally thought. That was merely a façade for an abundance of mischief and energy. In David's opinion, she
needed taking in hand by someone who would stand no
nonsense. He had no turn for children, but he supposed that

as the child's guardian he should take some responsibility for her—which was another good reason to marry a woman of birth and breeding as quickly as possible. Then *she* could superintend Fanny's upbringing!

He wondered how Miss Marsden would receive him. In the time since their last encounter he had managed to find out a little about her. His Great Aunt Maria had known all about Miss Marsden, of course. Even seemed to approve of her, which did not surprise him in the slightest. Lady Maria was one of the most outrageous women he had ever known.

'Sophie Marsden?' she had barked in answer to his very casual query over the dinner table. 'Of course I know her. Good gal. None of your simpering niminy-piminy modern misses, that one! She and her sister took Willowbank House about two years back. Sister died last year. Sophie's got the boy in ward.'

'I see,' said David, understanding a great deal. No wonder young Kit had looked so devastated when he had suggested that his mother was looking for him.

'Got a bit of money,' continued the old lady. 'She don't lack for admirers, but I doubt she'll accept any of them. The way the money's tied up, her husband will assume control if she marries and she's determined to provide for the boy. That Garfield's dangling after her, but she'd be a fool to have him, boy or no boy. You may pour me another glass of wine.'

'Garfield?' asked David, obeying this last behest. 'Sir Philip Garfield? Fellow who called here yesterday? Good God, he must be forty-five if he's a day!' Somehow the thought of the gross Sir Philip making up to Miss Marsden revolted him. Nevertheless, he found it hard to believe that Miss Marsden would not eventually succumb to such an offer. What female in her position would not?

His distaste showed in his voice and expression. His great-aunt gave a cynical bark of laughter, 'What the devil has his age got to do with it? He's still a man, ain't he? And why should you worry? Besides, Sophie's not that stupid. She'll never take him!'

The conversation drifted on to the coming house party, Lady Maria only snorting disagreeably once or twice when she heard the projected guest list. It did not surprise her. She had her own sources of information. She at once realised the significance of the inclusion of Lady Lucinda and her mama, but forbore to comment. After all, she had set him on this path, even if he had taken her remarks about duty a little too much to heart.

And afterwards, when she retired for the night, she muttered to herself, So he's met Sophie Marsden. Well, she'd be a damned sight better than that pretentious chit of Stanford's! Not that Lady Maria had ever met Lady Lucinda, but the description she had dragged from her recent morning visitor, Penelope Darleston, had confirmed all her worst fears. Lord, what maggot had the boy taken into his head now? All these years he had avoided marriage and now he was setting himself up for the sort of union that would bore him senseless. And would do nothing to remove that expression of scornful cynicism that masked the daredevil, laughing boy she remembered.

Lady Darleston had tried very hard not to say anything derogatory, but her stilted replies and polite evasions to Lady Maria's searching questions had told their own story. The redoubtable old lady had ended by saying, 'Well, if she's anything like Aurelia Stanford I shall remove to the Dower House. And my fool of a nephew has invited them here for a house party, you say? Lord! The end of it will be that he's been so particular in his attentions that he'll have to offer for the chit. What the devil possessed you to present him to her?'

Penelope had disclaimed all responsibility. 'I can assure you it wasn't my idea. He requested the introduction.'

'Damned fool that he is!' said Lady Maria roundly. 'Well, at least the Dower House is vacant. There's little enough I can do.'

She recalled this conversation as her maid readied her for bed. Sophie Marsden, eh? David might think to pull the wool over her eyes, but she'd seen the recoil of horror when she mentioned Garfield's interest in the girl. Hah! Like a dog with a bone! She settled herself into her enormous feather bed and blew out the candle, chuckling wheezily to herself as she thought of the dance Miss Marsden would lead her nephew. And wondered what she could do to further it. On reflection she concluded that she could do very little, except sit back and watch. And pray.

David took his niece around by the road through Little Helford to Willowbank House. He found it difficult to know what to say to her. She seemed outwardly quiet and self-contained, but David had already discovered that when she didn't get her own way the screams were earsplitting. From all he could discover her nurse usually gave in to her, a tactic David heartily deplored.

She rode well enough and David commented on this. 'You sit very well, Fanny. If you would care for it, I will take you to watch a meet next hunting season.'

'Can I follow the hounds?' she asked at once.

David groaned inwardly. Why the hell hadn't he seen that one coming? He said cautiously, 'You'll have to ask the Master. It's for him to say who may follow. Even I have to obey him on the hunting field.' He wondered if his niece would actually ask Sir Philip Garfield who was the local M.F.H.

'Why?' asked Miss Fanny. 'You're a Viscount. Sir Philip is only a Baronet. If you tell him I'm to follow, then he has to let me.' This was said with an air of calm certainty which took David's breath away. More than ever he was convinced that the child had to be taken in hand. There was something grating in her cool assumption of superiority. He hoped to God that his own children would not develop it.

He changed the subject neatly. 'Would you care to canter, Fanny? We will have to practise that if you are to follow hounds one day.'

Miss Fanny being pleased to fall in with this suggestion, the final half-mile to Little Helford was accomplished without further conversational quagmires. Mindful of the last time he had gone through the village, David slowed his unwilling charge down to a walk as they approached the first houses.

'Why must we slow down, Uncle David? Blossom isn't tired. We can canter for much longer than that.' Fanny was seriously considering kicking her pony into a canter to establish her independence when she encountered her uncle's level gaze.

'Fanny?'

'Yes, sir?'

'Don't even think about it.'

They walked their mounts through the village, responding to polite greetings and tugged forelocks. The villagers all knew Miss Fanny and quite a number remembered David from his youth.

In particular one gabby old fellow seated outside the inn hailed him with great pleasure, 'Well! If it ain't little Master David. An' they tell me ye still can't guddle a fish!'

'Twickenham! You old rogue, and you're still catching 'em too young by all accounts.' David leapt down from his saddle and held out his hand to the rascally old poacher.

''Tis a sight better nor not catchin' 'em at all, me lord!' Twickenham took the hand held out to him in a gnarled grip. Ah, it took him back, so it did, seeing this lad again! 'Makes me feel an old man seein' you all growed up.'

'Gammon!' said David. 'I must have been at least two and twenty when last I saw you.'

'Were ye now?' Twickenham grinned. 'I'll tell 'ee summat, lad. When ye're my age, two and twenty don't seem all that growed up!'

'Nor five and thirty, I dare say,' said David with a grin.

'Not so's ye'd notice,' chuckled the old man. 'Now you be off. Ye're keepin' the little lass waitin' an' that'll never do.'

David glanced at Fanny who had remained mounted. She had a remarkably wooden expression on her face. 'Fanny, have you met Twickenham before?'

'No.' She sounded startled.

'Well, he is a very old friend of mine and I should like you to know him,' said David firmly.

'How do you do?' said Miss Fanny, meeting a notorious criminal for the first time.

'Very well, missy,' answered the old man, lifting his cap to her solemnly. 'I kin tell fine *ye*'re a Melville.'

'How?' she asked in surprise.

'Same green eyes, same pretty hair, o' course. But ye sit a pony like ye growed there.' David watched in amazement as his stiff little ward actually blushed scarlet with pleasure at the old scoundrel's compliment. And Twickenham was right, the child was all Melville. He realised that he didn't find himself constantly reminded of Felicity by her daughter. And felt ashamed that this very fear had kept him from doing his duty to James's daughter for over a year.

'Thank you,' she said shyly.

'Come along, Fanny,' said David as he remounted, still reeling under the revelation of the old man's comment. 'We have still to call on Miss Marsden.'

Twickenham pricked up his ears, 'Callin' on Miss Sophie, are ye? Well, ye'll find her and the lad in the churchyard. Layin' flowers they are on poor Mistress Carlisle's grave. Saw 'em go in twenty minutes back.'

Armed with this information, David led Fanny along to

the lych-gate which opened into the churchyard. Sure enough, there were Miss Marsden and Kit standing beside a small tombstone not far from the gate. A small posy of yellow flag irises and wild guelder rose lay on the grave.

He could hear Miss Marsden's voice reading softly from the book she held. *'Who shall ascend into the hill of the Lord and who shall stand in His holy place? He that hath clean hands and a pure heart. Who hath not lifted up his soul unto vanity nor sworn deceitfully…'*

David listened, entranced. The music of the words and the loving warmth in the girl's gentle voice washed over him in waves of peace. He thought guiltily that he had not yet even been to see his mother's tomb, let alone laid flowers on it. In fact, he had barely known his fashionable mother. He had gone to school at the age of eight and she and his father had frequently been away in his holidays. When he had received the tidings of her death six years ago he had been sorry, but not grief-stricken. He had long forgiven her for suggesting Felicity as a suitable bride for James.

A sudden pain shot through him at the thought that he had never cared for his mother as this boy so obviously had for his. Had never been given the chance. Ah, but then you can't be hurt, he told himself coldly. Or have the memory, another gentler voice said.

Miss Marsden had finished the psalm and was speaking to Kit. 'I think that one describes her, don't you?' David's heart twisted as he heard the love in her voice. 'And she will love the flowers—you gave them to her every birthday.'

David wondered what his mother's favourite flowers had been. Had he ever known? Had he ever gone out on her birthday and brought some in for her? Would she have appreciated a posy of flowers culled with love from the hedgerow? He found himself hoping that his children would love their mother with this depth. The vision of Lady Lucinda seemed to jar with this.

He watched dumbly as Kit nodded and slipped his hand briefly into Miss Marsden's. Suddenly he thought that this was an intensely private moment and that he should not intrude, but it was too late. The lad straightened his shoulders and turned to look directly at David and Fanny. Surprise, then pleasure, replaced the sadness in his eyes.

He came forward at once, saying, 'Good afternoon, my lord. Hullo, Fanny.'

Sophie spun around and nearly fell over. What was *he* doing here? She followed Kit through the gate, her thoughts in a whirl.

'Good afternoon, Miss Marsden,' said David with a smile which warmed his eyes. 'Er...may I present my niece, Fanny, to you? Fanny, this is Miss Marsden and her nephew Kit.'

'We've met before,' said Sophie with a faint smile. 'How do you do, Fanny?' She had previously thought his lordship's brilliant eyes rather cold. Now she perceived her mistake. They were positively glowing in a way which gave his chilly, handsome face even more charm.

David was surprised at the evident pleasure with which his niece greeted Miss Marsden and her nephew. Clearly she liked them.

He dismounted and handed his reins to Kit, saying, 'Perhaps you would oblige me by leading Perdita. I am going to escort you and your aunt home. Fanny, if you will promise me on your honour to stay beside Kit, then you may ride ahead of me. But you must solemnly promise to remain in a walk. Otherwise you won't ride for a week.'

Fanny had opened her mouth to protest but David said, 'Save your breath, child. Whatever may work with your nurse, it won't fadge with me. And if you start one of your vulgar displays here, I'll put you over my knee and spank you.'

Horrified at the thought of being publicly humiliated, Fanny gave her promise and rode off beside Kit.

Heaving a sigh of relief, David looked down at Miss Marsden, still with that glow in his eyes, and said, 'I was coming to call on you. I didn't intend to intrude like this, but once Kit saw us, well, I wouldn't like either of you to think I was cutting your acquaintance.' She did not reply and he continued, 'You may, of course, still prefer to cut mine, but I wish you won't.' He waited for her reply, amazed to find that it mattered enormously to him. For some reason he could not fathom, he very much wanted this outspoken chit to revise her first unfavourable impression of him.

The dark eyes glanced up at him briefly. Sophie was hard put to it to understand her reaction to this man. His deep soft voice was like a caress. She felt for all the world like a cat having its fur stroked at the sound. His eyes, which the other day had stripped her naked, now smiled at her understandingly, but she still felt wary. Something deep within her screamed that this man was dangerous to her. There appeared to be something seriously amiss with her lungs, which seemed incapable of performing their function with any degree of certainty. Anger at her own missishness steadied her. She would *not* behave like a silly fluttering debutante just because Helford chose to converse with her.

'I can't think why you should wish for my acquaintance, my lord,' she said bluntly. 'At least, I can, but since—'

He cut her short. 'Of course, I always present my niece to girls I plan to set up as my mistress.' There was an unmistakably teasing note in his deep tones.

Sophie glared up at him but reined in her temper. 'That was my "but", sir!' she said sweetly. 'Despite your reputation, which I am afraid I know all about, I never heard anyone describe you as quite that outrageous. So I feel moderately safe in your company.'

'Do you, indeed?' said David astringently. 'I suppose I ought to be flattered.'

'Not in the least,' said Sophie. 'I am merely doing you the courtesy of assuming that you can on occasion conduct yourself in a mode befitting a gentleman.'

'Why, you little hornet!' said David, amusement warring with outrage. 'I'll have you know that I always conduct myself as befits a gentleman!'

'Then my first impressions were quite off and I am perfectly safe,' said Sophie blandly. 'And since Kit seems to think you are, as he put it, *a...a right one*, I have not the heart to disabuse his mind of such an error of judgement.'

'I see,' said David wryly. He decided to change the subject. 'Do you often lay flowers on your sister's grave?' He saw the solitary tear slip down one cheek to be hastily wiped and felt his guts wrench at the pain in her face. This, then, was what it was to care too deeply!

'Today was my sister's birthday,' said Sophie simply. 'Kit has been playing truant rather frequently and I thought that if we could do something to get him to talk about Emma it might help him to tell me what is bothering him.'

'I should have thought that was pretty plain to see,' returned David.

'Yes, I know he misses her,' said Sophie. 'But why has he suddenly begun to resent me?' She rubbed her nose thoughtfully. 'At least, not resent precisely. I can't quite describe it and I can't think why I am saying any of this to you at all!' She finished in a rush and walked on in silence, embarrassed to have burdened him with her concerns.

David said nothing. He was conscious of an odd desire to help Miss Marsden, who was far removed from the outraged girl he had insulted the other day. And he could not remember ever having wanted to help a woman before in his entire life! At least, not with a problem of this nature! Pecuniary problems were another matter. The only emotional problem his mistresses ever laid claim to was being in love with him. And that was definitely their problem to solve. Not his.

Strangely, he could understand her speaking what was on her mind. Obviously her softened mood was engendered by the circumstances and the feelings were too close to the surface to be hidden. But why the hell did he want to do something about it? It was none of his bread and butter. Stay out of it, he told himself firmly. You should have as little to do with this girl as possible!

Despite this excellent advice, something suddenly occurred to him. What had Kit said by the river the other day? Something about expecting his mother and…oh, come on…what did he say…expecting his mother and…and it was always Aunt Sophie!

'You look like your sister, don't you?' he asked at length.

She nodded. 'Yes. Anyone could tell we were sisters. Kit looks like both of us. Why?'

'I think it bothers the boy,' said David slowly. He told her what Kit had said.

There was silence while she thought it out. He noticed with an odd clarity that she again rubbed her nose in that appealing way.

'Then if he is pretending that Emma is still alive…' she said hesitantly, still working it through. 'And…and coming to find him…then there is that awful moment when he realises that she is dead after all…'

'And you look like her,' finished David.

'Which makes it worse,' said Sophie with catch in her voice. 'Poor little chap. Well, at least now I know. Thank you, Lord Helford. I don't think I would have thought of that.' His understanding, the mere fact that he had remembered what Kit had said, amazed her. Well, he might be a dangerous rake but he had a kind heart.

David himself was startled at the ease with which he had seen the problem. He was even more startled at the fact that for a moment he had felt her anguish as a knife twisting inside him.

They walked on in a companionable silence for a while. It was rather pleasant, thought David, to be with a female who didn't strain every nerve to entertain him with vivacious chit-chat. If Miss Marsden had something to say then she said it, bluntly. Otherwise she seemed content to hold her peace.

Peace was the last thing that Sophie was conscious of. She found Helford's quiet presence by her side extremely disturbing. She had no illusions about what he had been thinking the other day. She supposed that, since he had acknowledged his mistake and apologized, she would have to forgive him. What she found far harder to forgive was the fact that his speculative glance had awakened all sorts of immodest and dangerous imaginings. What would it be like to…? No! She must not think of it! It was wrong! Quite improper! And it terrified her.

The sound of the children's voices floated back to them, rather stilted at first but becoming more and more vociferous as they found a subject in common. Horses. David grinned as he heard Fanny telling Kit how high she could jump now.

'She's exaggerating just a little,' he informed Sophie in a teasing undertone. 'My headgroom won't let her attempt anything over two foot six yet, so three feet is a distinct bouncer.'

'Kit is romancing a little too,' admitted Sophie, with a chuckle. 'That seventeen hand colt he's just mentioned is Farmer Gillies's new cart horse. I'm afraid he hasn't got his own pony. And Megs, the mare I have for the gig, is far too lively for a beginner. He's tried to ride her a couple of times and she puts him straight over her head. She's hardly ever ridden anyway and I only have a lady's saddle so he has to ride bareback.'

David thought that Miss Marsden's finances must be rather straitened, but said nothing. Sympathy would smack of patronage and condescension which she would resent mightily. He had the distinct impression that she was still not quite easy in his company. For some reason he could not fathom, he wanted her to feel comfortable with him.

'Would you like him to ride?' he asked cautiously, the seeds of an idea sprouting in his head.

'Naturally yes,' said Sophie wistfully. 'But I cannot afford the upkeep of another horse. At least I could, but I try to put money aside for when he must go to school and to add to our principal, you see. So, no pony, unless I sell Megs and buy another, but we are rather fond of her.' She clipped her lips together firmly. I'm doing it again! It's none of his business and he can't possibly be interested. All she could think of was that going to Emma's grave had released a need to talk, a need to share some of her burden. A need she had not hitherto recognised.

David nodded thoughtfully. 'Then that makes it easier for me to ask for your help.'

Sophie stopped and stared at him. 'My help? What do you think I could do for you?'

Quite a lot, thought David as he looked down at her up-turned face. He tried not to imagine what it would be like to cup that face in his hands and kiss her, feel that soft mouth open under his and hold her in his arms as he deepened the kiss. He wondered what she would taste like and had to give himself a mental shake. *You have presented your niece to her! She is off limits!*

'My lord? Is something wrong?' Her concerned voice recalled him to reality. The black-fringed eyes were puzzled and a slight frown knotted her smooth brow.

Good God! What was he thinking of, that he wanted to smooth the frown away with a caressing finger? 'Fanny needs company of her own age and a woman of her own class to give her some much-needed guidance,' he explained. 'I wondered if you would consent to have her at Willowbank House for, shall we say, an afternoon a week?' He rushed on before she could answer. 'I realise that it is an appalling imposition, so what you say about Kit makes it easier. In return, I will bring Fanny this way for a ride once a week with her second pony and take Kit out with us.'

He waited for her reply, wondering why the devil he had made such a suggestion. Why on earth did he want to do something for Kit? Was it just to show this impossible chit that he could behave like a gentleman? Show her that she was wrong about him? That must be it. He ignored an ironic voice in his mind which assured him that Miss Marsden's pithy and unflattering reading of his character was not, after all, so very wide of the mark.

Sophie was stunned. What did he imagine she could teach Miss Fanny Melville? Why not a governess? What about Lady Maria? Why not find a little girl for the child to play with? All these questions and more whirled in her brain. In some confusion she tried to explain all this to him.

He cut her short. 'I know. But I want someone who isn't beholden to me in any way. Someone who will have no qualms in handing out a bit of discipline when necessary. Her governess, Miss Harris, is a meek creature and doesn't stand a chance, but I haven't the heart to dismiss her. She is old and would be unlikely to find another position. I could pension her off, but she tells me she would prefer to be working. Aunt Maria says herself that Fanny needs the attention of someone younger. As for finding a girl for her to play with, nothing could be easier, but I would like her to be with a child who won't take any of her tantrums. Kit won't.'

'I shall have to ask Kit,' said Sophie. 'After all, he is the one who will have to do most of the entertaining! Er…you do realize, my lord, that Kit's afternoons are spent mostly in such pursuits as fishing, climbing trees and playing cricket when he can persuade me to bowl. I have no intention of sitting him down to learn sewing or domestic economy.'

'Excellent.' said David. 'Do her the world of good. Ask Kit by all means.'

By the time they reached Willowbank House the details had been thrashed out. On Mondays Fanny would come over in the afternoon for two or three hours, and on Thursdays David would collect Kit after lunch and take the two children riding. He suggested that Miss Marsden might like to join them, but she declined firmly and refused to budge.

'It would start a great deal of gossip if I were to do that, my lord,' she said bluntly. 'You may be immune or indifferent to gossip, but as a single woman I am not!' He took her point. The last thing he wanted to do at the moment was stir up gossip. It would be fatal to his matrimonial plans.

By this time they were at the front gate. 'Would you care for some refreshment, my lord?' asked Sophie politely. 'A glass of cowslip wine? A cup of tea? And I have little doubt we can run to a slice of plum cake.'

'Cowslip wine?' David blanched. 'Good heavens! Who makes it?'

'I do!' said Sophie stiffly. 'And it is perfectly palatable, if a trifle alcoholic.'

David laughed, 'Very well, the cowslip wine it shall be. Let's hope I don't end up in my cups!'

Sophie opened the front gate, saying, 'I shall give you

half a glass just in case. Although,' she quizzed him, 'I should have thought you were well able to carry your wine!'

'Baggage!' he said in amusement, noting in some surprise that when she smiled, an utterly fascinating dimple peeped at the corner of her mouth, simply begging to be kissed. Why the hell hadn't he noticed the dimple earlier? He must be going blind.

Quite unaware of the temptation she was presenting, Miss Marsden merely laughed. 'Kit, why don't you take Fanny around to look at the new ducklings on the stream?'

'Are we stopping, Uncle David? What about the horses?'

'Yes we are stopping and the horses may be tied to the fence,' said David firmly. 'No one is going to steal them, so go and look at the ducklings. And, Fanny, behave yourself. If Kit feels he can stand it, you are going to come here to visit on Monday afternoons. On Thursday afternoons we will come past with a spare pony and Kit can come riding with us.'

Sophie was not really surprised to see that Kit's face broke into smiles at this. What did surprise her was the undoubted pleasure on Fanny's face. She knew that Kit would be glad of a companion, even a girl, but the little she knew of Fanny had led her to think the child would consider Kit beneath her touch.

'Come on, Fanny,' said Kit. 'I'll show you the ducklings. We're going to eat one for Christmas!'

'Bloodthirsty little beast!' said Sophie feelingly as the children disappeared around the side of the house. 'I used to cry my eyes out when one of my ducklings got killed.'

David laughed as he followed her into the house. 'Never mind. Now come, where is the dreaded cowslip wine?'

'Oh, Thea,' said Sophie as Miss Andrews came out of the parlour into the hall, 'this is Lord Helford. Lord Helford, may I present Miss Andrews, who is good enough to lend me respectability and to act as Kit's governess?'

His lordship smiled and held out his hand to Miss Andrews. 'Ah, the lady who was given the bag by Master Kit. You will be relieved to know, ma'am, that he harboured grave doubts as to the duplicity of his action in taking the books. How do you do?'

Thea Andrews thought that she had never seen a more handsome man as she placed her hand in his. Her reply was somewhat flustered. 'Oh, my lord, I should have known better. After all the years I have been a governess! Especially for dear Sophie and Emma.'

'Did they give you a great deal of trouble, ma'am? I can well believe it and you have all my sympathy.'

'Come and have a glass of wine with us, Thea,' said Sophie, trying unsuccessfully not to giggle. 'Lord Helford is convinced I am trying to poison him, I believe.'

The dimple quivered again, giving his lordship the most peculiar sensations in the pit of his stomach. He had met dimples before, but never one that tantalised as this one did!

'Well, perhaps just one, dear,' said Miss Andrews. 'Your cowslip wine always makes me a trifle sleepy.'

Within a very few moments they were seated in the parlour with the sun pouring in at the window. David sipped his wine suspiciously. He had never tasted anything like it in his life, but was obliged to admit that it wasn't as bad as he had expected. Which was not, as Sophie pointed out, saying very much at all.

'Well, I wouldn't quite say that, Miss Marsden!' protested his lordship. 'I will grant you that it is perfectly potable.'

'Would you care for a second glass, my lord?' asked Miss Marsden in deceptively demure accents. Her eyes twinkled engagingly.

David rose to the challenge admirably. 'If only to drink to your eyes, Miss Marsden!'

'How...how very *heroic* of you, my lord!' achieved Miss

Marsden with a delightful choke of laughter. 'I am rebuked indeed.'

'Rebuked?' Helford was amused. 'I meant to flatter you!'

Again that appealing gurgle. 'Then you must be losing your touch, my lord!'

'Sophie!' Miss Andrews was shocked. Or would have been if she were not used to her young charge making such outrageous remarks from time to time.

Helford blinked. The little baggage was actually daring to laugh at him! And at his reputation! Most women would have been cast into a flutter by a sally of that nature. This impossible female just giggled, setting not the least store by his gallantry. He was damned if he didn't like it! And why hadn't he noticed that dimple earlier? Ruefully he admitted to himself that their previous meetings had given Miss Marsden little cause to favour him with her delightful smile.

Through the window they could hear the faint sound of the children's voices.

Miss Andrews, seizing the opportunity to change the subject, commented on the fact that she could hear another child. Sophie was just explaining the arrangement she had come to with Helford when a splash followed by a loud shriek came to their ears.

Even before the yell of, 'Aunt Sophie! Hurry!' was heard, Sophie was on her feet and racing down the hall with her skirts hitched up. Taken completely by surprise, Helford was well behind her as she ran out a side door, across the garden and through a gate into the orchard. In fact, he was amazed that any woman could run so fast.

In the stream Kit was up to his shoulders trying to help Fanny who appeared to be in a state of complete panic. A small jetty jutted out into the water which Fanny had obviously fallen off. Before Helford could stop her Sophie had plunged in and was hauling the struggling child to her feet.

'Stop wriggling!' Sophie commanded sharply. Fanny continued to struggle and two sharp slaps rang out. Stunned, Fanny stopped, gasping and spluttering.

'Now, why don't you stand up?' suggested Sophie in matter-of-fact tones.

To her utter amazement Fanny found that she could do so and, still holding her hand, Sophie led her out on to the bank, closely followed by Kit, to stand dripping and shivering in the fresh breeze. All three of them were liberally festooned with mud and water weeds. Fanny's black curls were plastered around her face and Kit was probably the worst of the three, being covered in mud from head to toe, having slipped in it on his way out.

After one shocked glance at Miss Marsden, Helford set his jaw tightly and turned to survey his filthy and bedraggled niece. She was not meeting his gaze, a sure sign that she had been responsible for the disaster.

'Kit! What on earth were you thinking of to let her fall in?' asked Sophie in dangerously quiet tones.

Her nephew opened his mouth and then shut it again. 'Just looking at the ducklings, Aunt Sophie,' he said at last.

Sophie was about to favour him with a pithy description of his idiocy, but Helford forestalled her.

'Fanny. Would you care to tell us how you came to fall in?' His voice was deceptively bland, but there was an indefinable hint of authority in its depths.

Fanny hesitated for a moment, then said, 'I leaned over too far. Kit told me to get back but I...I didn't. So I sort of slipped. And Kit fell in trying to grab me, I think.'

Sophie stole a glance at Lord Helford. He was not looking at her and his face was icy. Oh, dear! He won't think this such a good place to leave Fanny now, she thought. She was rather surprised to discover how much she had been looking forward to Monday and Thursday afternoons. It would have been so good for Kit to have the companionship of a man, she told herself. Not to mention someone of his own age to play with and get into mischief with. The thought that it would be rather pleasant to see his lordship was ruthlessly suppressed.

She looked at the unrepentant Fanny. The child would take a chill, standing there in that soaking habit! She was getting a little cold herself.

'Perhaps we should get Fanny into some dry clothes,' she suggested tentatively.

'Good idea,' said his lordship curtly. He glanced at her briefly and averted his gaze at once.

Sophie flushed. He was obviously furious about the accident. Well, at least the child knew she could stand up in the blasted stream now! Even if she did fall in again she wouldn't drown! And he was the one who had suggested that Kit would be a suitable playmate. It wasn't my idea, thought Sophie rebelliously.

Miss Andrews, who had rushed out after them, said gently, 'I think, dear Sophie, that you had better change as well. And Kit, of course!'

'Yes,' said Sophie. 'Ask Anna to try and find some clothes for Miss Fanny. There are some of Kit's old ones in the chest on the landing and she can be bundled up in a cloak of mine so that no one sees her. And if his lordship takes her home across the fields they will be less likely to meet anyone. Kit, you may change in the scullery! Ask Anna to bring you some clean clothes.'

Having said this, she stalked off into the house and up to her chamber, leaving a trail of water and aquatic flora behind her from her sopping gown. Just before she began to strip her gown off she caught sight of herself in the looking glass and saw exactly what Lord Helford had seen.

No wonder he had refused to look at her! She might as well have been naked for all the good her light muslin gown was. It clung to her body in the most appallingly revealing way. And it was not only her form that was revealed! The material was rendered practically see through and the rosy tips of her breasts were quite apparent. Sophie blushed, a deep, hot crimson. He had no need to use his imagination to strip her now. There was not really a great deal left to imagine. How on earth was she to face him downstairs? What if he thought she had done it on purpose to gain his attention? How very mortifying!

When she did eventually leave her chamber it was still with heightened colour and in a very high-necked, long-sleeved grey gown which was a trifle too large for her and did not suit her in the slightest. There was no need to give his lordship anything more to think about, she thought as she went downstairs. Not that he could possibly be in the least interested, she admonished herself. With his reputation he must have seen hundreds—well, dozens anyway—of much prettier women without any clothes at all. Seeing Miss Sophie Marsden in damp...no, soaking muslin was hardly going to set his pulses racing.

David waited in the parlour while Miss Marden and her nephew changed their attire and while Miss Andrews and the maid rushed about finding clothes for Fanny. Not only were his pulses racing, but there was solid evidence that his lordship's carnal experience was not sufficiently broad to have rendered him immune from Miss Marsden's charms as displayed by a wetly clinging muslin gown. And the reality was every bit as delightful as the vision he had conjured up by the river the day he had met Kit.

He groaned audibly as he tried not to think about it. Unfortunately, that only made it worse. Her body was beautiful, so dainty and rounded. A slim little waist and those flaring hips! He could imagine his hands on them, holding her against him as his arousal throbbed between them. And, oh God, her breasts! He thought he would die at the memory of how the cold water had teased them into life. They would respond to his caress in the same way, springing up under the ministrations of his hands and tongue. His mouth felt dry at the very thought of cupping those breasts in his hands, of touching his tongue to those dainty pink morsels which had peeped through the soaking muslin.

And she would be his, all his! Never had he touched a virgin in his life. He had thought his preference was for experience. For a woman who knew how to entertain a man. A woman who would cry out in pleasure when he took her, rather than an untouched girl who would doubtless feel pain. The thought of teaching an innocent had always rather bored him.

Now he was burning with desire for a girl who would not have the slightest notion of how to satisfy his needs. And he didn't care in the least. He wanted to please *her*! He wanted to be the only one who had ever possessed her, heard her cries of passion. And they *would* be cries of passion when he was finished with her!

The only thing which acted as a lifeline in the sea of confused emotion and desire which threatened to engulf him was the knowledge that she would most certainly be hurt if he seduced her and not just physically! He couldn't do it! If it leaked out, she would be ruined and besides, she was not a woman of the world who could play the game for a time and then go on to the next lover. If she gave herself, it would only be because she cared for him. She was not the sort of woman he wanted to be his mistress. He did not wish to hurt her in any way. It would be best to see as little of her as possible. Thank God she had refused to ride with them! He could drop Fanny off and collect the boy with as little intercourse as possible.

He swore savagely as he paced back and forth, wishing to God that he too could go out and take a dip in the stream. For the life of him, he could not see how he was otherwise going to be able to ride home in any sort of comfort.

Fortunately for his lordship's peace of mind Kit, whose

ideas on drying off and dressing neatly were rather rudimentary, was the first to make an appearance.

He came into the room, looking very embarrassed. 'I say, I'm awfully sorry Fanny fell in, sir. I should have dragged her off the jetty.'

'Never mind,' David replied. 'She's probably learned her lesson. Just keep her out of the river when she comes here.'

'You'll still let her come?' Kit asked in surprise.

David nodded. 'Oh, yes. If your aunt doesn't consider her too much of a liability after this.'

'What's a liar...liar...liarbilly?' asked Kit, very puzzled. 'That's what Aunt Sophie says about the open range in the kitchen because it uses so much fuel.'

By the time David had explained what he meant by a liability and decided to undertake a few improvements at Willowbank House, namely a modern closed stove, he was in a fair way to regaining control of himself. Miss Marsden's reappearance, camouflaged in an extremely unbecoming and voluminous gown, told him two things immediately. Firstly, that she was perfectly aware of how she had looked and, secondly, that she was very embarrassed by it. He acknowledged her very stiffly. He wanted to reassure her that she had nothing to fear, that he had not been in the least affected but, even if he could have lied convincingly, the presence of Kit and, a moment later, of Fanny, made any such thing impossible.

Fanny looked excessively improper in Kit's old clothes. David was highly amused despite his personal confusion, not least at the apologetic look on Miss Andrews's face as she shepherded the child into the room.

'So indelicate, my lord. I do beg your pardon but there is nothing else. All Miss Sophie's old clothes were given away years ago!' She held out the cloak over her arm, 'But I am sure you can contrive to bundle this around her and no one need know. None of us will breathe a word, you may be sure.'

David took the cloak with a charming smile. 'Miss Andrews, you are so calm about the whole thing that I can only assume that Miss Marsden and her sister must have given you almost as much trouble. Tell me—do you quail at the thought of being afflicted with my niece every Monday?'

'Certainly not,' asserted Miss Andrews. 'It would be very odd if I were to mind any arrangement Miss Sophie has made. Does that mean Fanny is still to come?'

'Most definitely,' said David without meeting Miss Marsden's eyes. She had looked thoroughly discomfited at his abrupt greeting and he did not dare to look at her lest his hard-won control deserted him. After making final arrangements to collect Kit two days later, he took his leave, firm in his conviction that the less he saw of Miss Marsden the safer she would be.

Sophie was heartily glad to see the back of him. Odious wretch! How dare he look down on her because she pulled his niece out of the stream! It wasn't as if she were used to having a man around to do things for her. Besides, he would not have cared to plunge into a muddy stream in his immaculate riding boots and leathers!

She wished she could refuse to have anything more to do with him, but it would be too infamous to deny Kit the opportunity to learn to ride, still more infamous to deny him the opportunity to be in a man's company. Even if he was a man whose morals and way of life she thoroughly despised, Sophie did his lordship enough justice to realise that he would not allow anything unfitting to come to Kit's ears. And besides, he had shown himself to be very understanding of Kit. Remembering what the boy had said and recognising its relevance to what she had said, suggested that he might be the very person to give Kit's thoughts a happier turn.

* * *

It was with this in mind that she went to bid Kit good-night that evening. He put his book down at once when she came in and said, 'Shall you mind having Fanny here?'

'Not in the least,' she assured him. 'Will you mind having to ride with her?' She sat down on the edge of his bed.

'Gudgeon!' he said affectionately. He was silent for a moment. 'Aunt Sophie?'

'Yes, love?'

'I'm sorry about all the running off and I've been rude to you…and…'

'Don't worry about it,' she said gently.

'But it's so silly,' he said. 'It's cos you look like her and I kept thinking you were her and then being sort of disappointed an' *angry* cos God took her an' not you. Remember how the Vicar said God wanted her an' loved her more than we could? Well, I just wanted to hit God for being such a skirter! I…I thought he could have taken you an' never known the difference.' He stopped, very embarrassed. 'An' then I'd feel awful cos you're so good to me.'

So Helford was right.

Sophie stroked the soft curls. 'Don't feel awful, Kit. I thought exactly the same thing when the Vicar said that! Believe me, I would have died happily to save you this! And I don't think God could possibly love your Mama *more* than you do. Differently, yes. But not more.'

They sat enveloped in a comforting silence as the house martins chattered under the eaves.

Eventually Sophie spoke again. 'What made you say all this?'

'Lord Helford,' said Kit slowly. 'It was when he found me by the river and I thought it would be you behind me and I wanted…Mama…and he said she was looking for me. Before that I didn't really understand what was wrong, but I said it to him. I…I don't know why. Do you think he minded?'

'No,' said Sophie, reasonably certain that after some of the things she had said to his lordship, nothing Kit could say would startle him in the least.

Another long healing silence.

'Aunt Sophie, those flowers we took to Mama will die, won't they?'

'Yes.'

'Well, should we take some more? I mean, if they die, they won't look as nice.'

Sophie groped for an answer. She didn't want him to mope over Emma's grave. At last she said, 'I think, you know, that it is all right for the flowers to die. You see *their* souls will go to Heaven as well, so your Mama will have them there just the same. So perhaps we should just put them there on the days when you would have given her flowers anyway. You know—her birthday, Mothering Sunday, your birthday and also the day she died.'

Kit thought about it and said, 'I never thought of that. Of course the flowers have to die. Thank you.'

Sophie bent to kiss him and was half-suffocated by the enveloping hug. 'I like Lord Helford,' he said. 'I'm glad he likes you.'

'Likes me?' Sophie allowed her surprise to show.

'Well, he must!' said Kit logically. 'Why else would he take me riding?'

Faced with this undeniable logic Sophie went back downstairs to curl up in a chair by the fireplace with a book. After a few moments her rather battered volume of poetry was allowed to fall unheeded to her lap. Staring into the empty grate, she gave up the singularly useless attempt to banish Lord Helford from her thoughts. Why should he go out of his way to help her? And why did she feel so threatened by him? Because she did! His big powerful frame positively radiated danger of the most potent masculine variety.

And his reputation suggested that appearances were not

deceptive. He was an acknowledged rake. Used to having his way with women at all times. Sophie had no doubts at all that he would be quite unused to being refused. She could understand why. His lazy smile held a world of temptation reflected in the wicked green eyes. And the thought of being surrounded and overwhelmed by that powerful, male body sent shivers of excitement wriggling up and down her spine… She caught herself up crossly. This would never do! He was just being kind to make up for his embarrassing gaffe.

He was a gentleman and would not pursue an unwilling female of birth and virtue. She could have no fears that he would allow his inclinations to obscure that fact. Reluctantly she faced the dawning knowledge that it was her own inclinations that she most feared. His lordship might be a gentleman, but he was no saint. The slightest hint that she might welcome his attentions would place her in the gravest danger!

Chapter Five

Two days later Lord Helford called to take Kit riding and return the clothes. Nothing could have exceeded the polite propriety with which he greeted Miss Marsden on this occasion unless it was the cool dignity with which he was received. He informed her that he wished to speak with her upon their return and promptly realised that his manner of doing so had well and truly set up her bristles.

'Do you indeed, my lord?' she asked in dulcet tones. 'Then naturally I will hold myself at your disposal. I shall give Anna instructions that I am at home to you.'

He glared at her. Curse the chit! He always seemed to say the wrong thing to her. What was it about her that made him such a clodpole? His mind sheered away from the obvious answer which was that never in his life had he wanted a woman this much. Especially one that he couldn't have. He told himself bracingly that if he had her in bed, it would break the spell. He could slake his lust for her and be done with it. He had never known a woman whose charms and skills did not bore him in the end.

Angry at the trend of his thoughts, he checked the girth on the pony he had brought for Kit and showed the boy how to mount. He swung himself into the saddle, raised his hat to Miss Marsden and rode off fuming with his youthful charges.

Sophie went back into the house to do a fair bit of fuming on her own account. After half an hour of savagely kneading bread, all the while pretending that she was wringing his lordship's arrogant neck, she calmed down enough to laugh at herself. Whatever would Emma think to see her little sister, who never took the slightest bit of notice of a man, so utterly furious over the opinion and overbearing ways of a comparative stranger?

By the time his lordship returned with the children, she had assumed a dignified and calm attitude towards him. This was dispelled by his first words to her after dismissing the children to the garden with a rider to stay out of the stream.

'I cannot see that your situation, Miss Marsden, is in the least eligible for either you or the grandson of an Earl. Why have you not enlisted the aid of Kit's paternal relations in your rearing of him?'

'What?' she gasped. 'How *dare* you imply that I am not capable of bringing him up as a gentleman!'

'Rubbish!' he said angrily. 'I meant only that Lord Strathallen should provide some assistance. Yet, from what Kit tells me, I should doubt of his even knowing that he has a grandson!'

'You can't possibly have got that from Kit!' said Sophie furiously. 'How dare you poke your nose into my affairs!'

'I have done no such thing! I was slightly acquainted with Jock Carlisle, though,' David informed her coldly. 'When Kit mentioned that his father died at Waterloo, I asked him what regiment. You may imagine my surprise when he told me the Scots Greys! Why the devil have you not been in touch with the Carlisles? Kit knows nothing of his birthright!'

The fury in her countenance made him take a step back.

He thought he had seen the worst of her temper, but this was something quite different. Her eyes practically spat with rage and when she spoke it was in tones of the most bitter contempt.

'If Lord Strathallen had not refused to receive my sister when Jock was so ill advised as to marry her in the teeth of his father's threat of disinheritance, not to mention our own father's implacable opposition, then perhaps I might have done so!' blazed Sophie. 'As it is, since he did not even reply to my sister's letter informing him of Jock's death and, I might add, the birth of Kit, I feel I am absolved of any charge of denying Kit his birthright!'

'He disowned Jock? Why?' David could not believe his ears.

'Oh! Did you not know that?' Sophie was even angrier. 'Then might I suggest that you find out all the facts of a case before you pass judgement! Lord Strathallen is, as you may be aware, a Catholic. I understand many Scots hold to that still. He was affronted that his son chose to marry a Protestant and a Englishwoman at that. His family having fought at Culloden, he considered Jock doubly a traitor to have married south of the Tweed!' She paused for breath and to dash her hand across her eyes. 'As for my father, as a minister of the Church of England he took the gravest exception to Emma's marriage to a Catholic. She was also disinherited! The result is that I inherited ten thousand pounds, which I cannot touch except for the income until I am thirty-five. If I marry before that date, the money passes into the hands of my husband. My father did his best to ensure that I was powerless to help Emma and Jock.'

David was horrified. 'He did *that*? The bastard!' He caught himself up sharply. 'I beg your pardon. I had no idea and did not intend to offend you.'

'No! You just thought you would tell me what to do! Like Sir Philip, who would have me marry him and trust

him to *settle a suitable sum on the lad*!' Her voice dripped
with scorn. 'Well, he can take his offer and you can take
your advice and—' She managed to stop herself right on
the brink of saying something that would not have reflected
at all well on her vicarage upbringing.

'Go to hell.' David finished the sentence for her. 'I don't
blame you. No. I knew nothing of this. My acquaintance
with Jock was of the slightest. I knew he was married, but
I never met your sister. Miss Marsden, I apologise unreservedly, but I do feel that Strathallen ought not to be allowed to ignore his responsibilities. If you would like, I
could—'

'No!' Sophie cut in. 'You are going to offer to write or
see him and shame him into doing something for Kit. I
would rather die than beg for his charity after the way he
treated Emma. From all I saw, Jock's marriage was the making of him. He was the wildest, most spendthrift good-for-
nothing! But he actually settled down with Emma and reformed all his appalling ways.' A tear ran down her cheek,
unnoticed except by David who was conscious of an overwhelming desire to kiss it away. What had he done, un-
leashing all the hurt she obviously kept bottled up lest it
should overwhelm her?

Sophie continued, in a hard little voice to hold back the
tears which threatened to spill over. 'She…she used to write
to me you know, through Thea. We were very close despite
the seven years between us. So many things she told me.
They were so happy and then Kit was born just before the
peace in 1814. Papa was dead and it was all settled that they
would come and live with me. But then Napoleon escaped
and Jock died in that awful charge.'

'I'm sorry,' said David very gently. 'I will do nothing
without your permission. But I will say that I do believe it
is a matter not of charity but responsibility.'

Sophie looked at him unseeingly. In fact, he wondered if

she had even heard him. She seemed to be miles away. In truth she was years away in the past, seeing the heartbroken agony of a widow who cared nothing for the fact that her husband had died a hero. A woman who held a fatherless child and wept over him in a despair that her young sister could feel but not fully understand.

At last she spoke in a husky voice. 'I'm sorry, my lord. I should not have spoken as I did. It is just that…I…I loved Emma and…and it was her birthday and…and…' Two more tears rolled down her cheeks unheeded.

'Damn!' David took two quick strides across the room and had her in his arms, her face pressed against his chest. There was nothing even remotely amorous in his embrace. He held her as he might have held Fanny or Kit to give comfort. Sophie accepted it as such, leaning against him trustingly, conscious of the sense of peace that seemed to radiate from his powerful body and the firm circle of his arms. One hand stroked her curls lightly.

Never had he known such a feeling of tender admiration. Her proud independence and determination to stand alone he found incredible. He knew that many women would have had no hesitation in forcing the boy's paternal relations to take charge while they used their inheritance to secure a good marriage. And with ten thousand pounds she could have done it easily. She was attractive enough to tempt any man.

Instead she had chosen to live in quiet obscurity, husbanding her money against the day when Kit should need it and refusing a more-than-eligible offer to ensure his future. Without conscious volition his arms tightened around her protectively.

They stayed that way for a moment before David released her. Even if his intentions were good, his unruly body was not capable of surviving that sort of abuse for long. He became agonisingly aware of the softness of her body against his, the silken feel of her curls under his caressing fingers. He knew it could not be long before he slid that hand under her chin and brought her mouth up to receive his kisses. And they would most certainly not be mistakable for mere comfort.

Feeling him pull back, Sophie stepped away at once, telling herself that it was the novelty of being held so intimately that made her heart pound, her knees feel wobbly and created that sensation of scorching heat that was melting her entire body. *He offered comfort, you little ninny! Comfort! Nothing more!*

She looked up and caught his green glance which seared through her, causing a tremor to ripple up and down her spine. She had wanted to know what it would feel like to be held in his embrace. Well, now she knew. It felt simply wonderful! His embrace had engulfed her in its tender warmth. Never had she felt so safe or content.

'I beg your pardon, my lord,' she said carefully, not quite certain that her voice was to be trusted. Her breasts tingled at the remembered sensation of being pressed so firmly against a powerfully masculine body. 'You may be right about Lord Strathallen's duties but I would prefer not to be obliged to him in any way.'

He looked at her searchingly. Was she aware of how deeply he had been affected by their brief embrace? She seemed oblivious. At least she was calmer now.

Sighing, he said, 'I think I should leave you now.' *Because if I don't I will be embracing you again. And not for comfort this time.* 'Don't trouble yourself to see me out. I will find Fanny and go. Goodbye, Miss Marsden, and please don't fret yourself in any way.' He turned back at the door. 'I nearly forgot what I had to say to you. I have been considering improvements to the estate and have decided to install a closed stove in the kitchen here. I will arrange for the newest and most up-to-date model. It should arrive within a week or so.' With that he was gone.

She was only too relieved to see him go. Her own feelings were skittering here and there and it was difficult to think straight when the mere sight of him made her recall the sensuous motion of his long fingers tangled in her hair, the strength of his arms and the warmth of his powerfully muscled chest under her cheek. She sank into a chair as the door shut behind him. What was she thinking of? She couldn't be falling in love! Or could she? And why was he concerning himself with her old-fashioned, fuel-greedy stove? If he had ever so much as stepped into a kitchen in all his life it was as much as he had done! She was surprised to hear that he even knew what a closed stove *was*!

My Lord Helford's next few visits were remarkable for their brevity. He dropped Fanny off and collected her with dispatch, greeting Miss Marsden with punctilious civility. And when next they came to take Kit riding, he didn't even come into the house. Kit was waiting eagerly at the gate and Miss Marsden nowhere to be seen. Kit informed him that Aunt Sophie was out visiting in the gig.

It was a pleasant ride. The children, he was fast discovering, were amusing and delightful companions. They argued and teased each other, occasionally appealing to him to settle some point. As far as David could tell, there was very little they agreed on but this did not seem to disturb their friendship.

One thing they did agree on was their united affection for Kit's aunt, whom Fanny had taken to calling Aunt Sophie. As they rode Kit often let fall odd scraps of information about his aunt that told David just how hard she tried to make up to the boy for his orphaned state. He found himself thinking this afternoon that it was a pity Miss Marsden had set her face against marriage, since she would make such a wonderful mother. But the thought of Miss Marsden marrying was strangely disturbing, making him grit his teeth in anger. The idea that someone else should possess her was thoroughly unsettling.

They had just turned for home when Kit said, 'Oh. Look, there's Megs. Aunt Sophie must be visiting Mrs Simpkins and her baby.' He pointed to a little dappled cob harnessed to a gig tied up outside a farm labourer's cottage.

'A baby?' Fanny sounded interested. 'How old is it?'

Kit shrugged with typical male uninterest. 'Lord, how should I know? A week or so. I say, Lord Helford, could we stop and see if Aunt Sophie wants us to ride back with her?'

'Oh, yes!' Fanny was enthusiastic. 'And then I could see the baby!'

Standing at the open door of the cottage a few moments later, David could hear Miss Marsden's soft voice speaking in accents that made his heart turn over.

'Are you getting hungry, little pet? You won't find anything there for you!' Low and soothing, all of a woman's tender, protective love for a child resonated in her tones. 'Never mind, Mama will be out in a moment. She'll have something for you.'

Inwardly shaking, David stood stock still on the threshold. Miss Marsden was seated on a wooden settle with a tiny woollen bundle nestled in her arms. She did not even notice him, caught up as she was bending over the baby, who was nuzzling hopefully at her breast. The expression of yearning regret on her face tore at David's very soul. Clearly this was something she would have desired above all else but thought never to have.

Swallowing hard, he thrust away the longing to see her nursing a child of her own and tapped belatedly on the door.

She looked up slowly from her happy dream, hazel eyes soft and vulnerable. For a moment she could not think as that green look seared into her with unmistakable tenderness. She could not tear her eyes away from that regard, but stared back transfixed, conscious of her pounding heart and uncertain breath.

With difficulty she found her voice. 'My lord? Have you come to call on Mrs Simpkins? She is in the bedroom.' What on earth was he doing here? And why was he looking at her like that? As if he could see exactly what was in her heart and understood her pain! She was imagining things! How could he, of all people, possibly understand how she longed to have her own children? Not to replace Kit, of course, but the longing to hold and nurse a child of her own.

'Er, Kit saw your mare and thought you might like our escort,' explained David. He cleared his throat of an uncharacteristic lump and went on. 'And Fanny would like to see the baby, if Mrs Simpkins would have no objection.'

At this moment Mrs Simpkins came into the room and gasped at the exalted visitor. With practised ease David set her mind at rest, saying that his little niece would love to see her baby.

Polly Simpkins was only too delighted to oblige. Accordingly Fanny and Kit came in, and in a flash Fanny was on the settle beside Sophie, being shown how to hold the baby. David watched the two women instruct his niece with a strange feeling of growing emptiness. Never before had he been so conscious of a longing to have children of his own. Not heirs—children. The raw longing in Sophie's face had shown him something within himself, the existence of which he had never suspected.

Entranced, he watched them with the baby, the gentle, tender hands and protective arms. He knew, had any danger threatened, that they would have turned like tigresses to defend the child, whatever the cost to themselves. He had seen something of it in Sophie's reaction to his suggestion that she should contact Strathallen.

*   *   *

On the way back to Willowbank House Fanny and Kit cantered ahead while David held his mare beside the gig. Sophie seemed rather quiet and disinclined to conversation. David fell in with her mood, content to study her surreptitiously.

Her brown hair curled softly, drawn back into a simple knot resting on her nape, a few stray tendrils brushing her cheek, which made his fingers itch to tuck them back and caress the soft cheek himself. The greeny-brown eyes were faintly abstracted, an odd frown puckering her brow. The impertinent little nose still had that sprinkling of freckles over it. Freckles, he knew, were considered a blemish. These were enchanting.

The frown worried him, combined as it was with a pensive droop to the mouth. He knew beyond doubt what was bothering her. The baby. She had purposely gone to see another woman's baby, had cuddled it and loved it when she knew perfectly well it would set off all her own yearning for a child. Why did she court that sort of pain? Why not just avoid babies?

At last he could bear it no longer and asked gently, 'Why did you go, Miss Marsden?'

She negotiated a bend in the road before answering, giving herself time to think of an appropriate answer. How much had he seen? Just that she wanted a child of her own? Or had he seen that she had been pretending the baby was her own? That he might be pitying her was unbearable. He must be deflected at all costs.

Settling for face value, she responded with spurious brightness, 'Why, to see the baby, of course! Women like to do that, my lord.'

He was not to be deflected. 'Even when holding a baby is a reminder of all you cannot have? Surely you would be wiser to avoid such thoughts.'

Her hands trembled on the ribbons. What business was it

of his how she chose to live? And how could he possibly understand how she felt? She knew it was foolish to pretend, but the joy of holding a baby was too precious to be denied, even if it hurt a little.

But she found herself struggling to explain. 'You see, I love babies and children. Even if it makes me a little sad, why should I lose the pleasure of holding a baby or looking after one? Why refuse little joys because the greater one is denied? That's not living. How can you even know what joy is unless there is some pain or risk of pain to temper it?'

'You see life like that?' he asked curiously. It was oddly at variance with his own decision to marry for convenience and avoid any risk of hurt. Sophie's way was so dangerous, especially for a woman. She could be hurt so badly. He didn't like the thought of that and tried stumblingly to warn her.

She interrupted at once. 'You were in the army! How can you possibly be so scared of life when you faced death and maiming almost daily?'

'A physical risk.' He shrugged. 'Perhaps because I faced them and grew to some degree inured. But I prefer not to lay myself wide open to the sort of pain you obviously felt back there. And all for an illusory joy.'

She flushed to think that her thoughts had been so apparent. Making a gallant recover, she said, 'We will have to agree to differ. My joy in Polly's baby was no illusion and I could not live if I had to avoid all the things that might hurt me or frighten me. It may not be wise, but it is how I am made.' She paused for a moment and then said, 'Emma felt the same. She told me once after Jock had been killed that their love had been, was still to her, the reality. That it was death that was the illusion. She said it was better to have known that joy than not. That even had she known the grief in store for her, she would still have grasped the joy. Lived every minute of it as though it might be the last.'

Her acceptance shook him to the core. In some odd way it made sense. She had enough courage to take what joy she could and accept the accompanying pain. Just as she had had the courage to leap into the path of his curricle to save a child's life. She was a risk taker, then. She would take the risk and reckon up the cost later. He shuddered to think of the sort of hurt she was courting.

The rest of the drive was accomplished in silence. David was trying hard to convince himself that the way Sophie chose to conduct her life was none of his business. He tried even harder to convince himself that his way was better. Far more sensible, far more practical and certainly safer. He tried to ignore the irritating voice that suggested his safe, comfortable existence might be a little dull.

He did not dismount to bid her farewell, merely saying, 'Goodbye, Miss Marsden, Kit. Please convey my regards to Miss Andrews. Come, Fanny.'

Sophie drove the mare around to the stables in a daze. Despite her avowal that she could not avoid everything that might hurt her, there were some things she would prefer to avoid. Having Helford read her heart and soul like a book was one of them. It was far too dangerous and there would be no joy to counter the hurt. She was literally playing with fire and it was her heart that was likely to be burnt. She would have to see as little of Lord Helford as possible.

Accordingly, the next time he brought Fanny, she greeted him briefly at the door, saying, 'You will not wish to keep your horses standing, I dare say.' Then she had swept Fanny into the house, the door closing firmly behind her. David was conscious of a feeling of momentary pique and then berated himself for an arrogant fool. She was not to be blamed for keeping a safe distance between them. She gave

Fanny back into his care later in the afternoon with the same quiet dismissal.

It was the same when next he came for Kit. She was baking, she informed him calmly. Just as well, David told himself sternly as he rode away with the children. It would be most unwise to see any more of her than was absolutely necessary. Somehow she got under all his defences. Unfortunately he would have to speak with her when he brought Kit home. His house guests would be arriving from the following day and he would be unable to continue with the arrangement personally for the duration of the visit. It was, however, only polite to assure himself that Sophie had no objection to Jasper taking Kit out with Fanny.

He tried to ignore the fact that he wanted to see her. His efforts were not successful and he was irritated to realise that he resented the chit having to spend her time on such domestic drudgery as baking. She was just a child, he told himself, and ought to be having fun.

Unaware that his lordship intended to speak to her later, Sophie flung herself into the baking with a vengeance, just as she had flung herself into all manner of domestic activities in the past few days. If she kept busy there was little enough time to think—and thinking was a dangerous pastime at the moment. Whenever her thoughts were permitted to drift a tanned, aristocratic face invaded her mind and emerald green eyes seemed to peer into her soul, seeking out her innermost secrets. Night time was even worse. Then she found herself imagining his arms around her again and his hand caressing her hair. And not only her hair.

Bread was kneaded and set to rise. A cake compounded, the joint for tomorrow's dinner dressed, several pounds of plums were turned into jam. In this way did Sophie try to ward off the disturbing daydreams that plagued her. Dreams of tender kisses and powerful arms enfolding her to rest against a hard, masculine body. At this point her dreams broke down. She could not imagine what might come next. Or at least she could, but was far too shocked at the thought to allow it houseroom.

Curse it! You're doing it again! Sophie dragged her mind back to the pastry she was making for a raised pie and blinked at the soggy mass. Too much water, damn! The door bell pealed loudly as she was adding more flour and she frowned. Too early for Helford to have the children back. Besides, he wouldn't use the bell if he wanted to see her, he'd come straight in with or without the children.

The bell pealed again. 'You answer it, please, Anna. And I am not at home.'

'Aye, Miss Sophie.' Anna wiped her hands on a cloth and left the kitchen. She returned a few moments later. 'It's that Sir Philip Garfield, Miss Sophie.' She sounded annoyed.

'Well, did you deny me?'

'Aye, but he weren't takin' no for an answer,' replied Anna. 'Settled in the parlour like as how he owns it.'

Sophie used an expression which she had certainly not culled from her vicarage upbringing and stripped off her apron. 'Curse and blast the man!' she muttered. 'He never does take *no* for an answer! Well, I've tried being polite. This time I am going to leave him no room for doubt or hope or whatever he bloody well calls it!'

Anna was scandalised. 'Miss Sophie! You watch your tongue!'

Sophie stuck her tongue out and squinted down her tip-tilted nose at it. 'Hmm. Looks perfectly fine to me. Let's hope this time it can convince Sir Philip that I won't accept his offer and that he would be better off if I don't!' She was gone, leaving Anna unsure whether or not she ought to scold her highty-tighty young mistress or cheer her on.

One thing was for certain, Anna would be just as glad to see the back of Sir Philip. *Fetch your mistress at once, my good woman. You forget your place. Miss Sophie will not deny herself to such a trusted friend as myself!* Trusted friend! Bah! Miss Sophie would never take him! Good woman, indeed! She'd give him *good woman*, so she would!

Sir Philip, a large, florid man in his mid-forties, rose to his feet as Miss Marsden entered the parlour and said, 'My dear Miss Sophie, you must allow yourself to be guided by one who is older and wiser. That servant of yours actually tried to tell me you were not at home. You should turn her off at once if she does not know her place better than that.'

'Anna was merely following out my instructions,' said Sophie, very much on her dignity as she went to stand by the chimney-piece. 'And I have no intention of dismissing a servant so much devoted to my interests.'

Sir Philip frowned at the unwonted sharpness in her voice. 'You must not resent the advice of another who is devoted to your interests, my dear. You need a servant who can distinguish when an unexpected caller is a close enough friend to be admitted.'

Miss Marsden smiled sweetly. 'Oh. Well, I assure you that Anna always does that, Sir Philip.' She waited with bright-eyed interest for her suitor to absorb the implications of this set-down.

'Now, now, Miss Sophie! You must not be naughty with me!' chuckled Sir Philip. He lowered his frame into a chair only to encounter a pair of raised black eyebrows from his hostess, who remained standing. Hastily he stood up again. What the devil had gotten into the chit? Always before she had received him with a deference which had encouraged him to think that her refusal of his suit lay in her natural modesty and the disparity between their estates. In his self-importance, it never occurred to him that Miss Marsden might find his advances repugnant.

Having decided at last to marry and beget an heir, Sir Philip was not the man to be put off by a little feminine coquetry. Sophie Marsden was as dainty a morsel as ever he'd seen and she'd warm his bed quite nicely, thank you very much! Her resistance to his suit merely added spice to the pursuit. The thought of overpowering her refusal was exciting. Doubtless he would have to overpower her in bed as well. All the better, for his money! He'd enjoy a struggle. Nothing worse than a wench who lay there like a corpse. Naturally one would not expect or wish one's wife to actually enjoy the business! That was for lightskirts and farm wenches one could tumble in the straw!

All this ran through his head as he stared at his unwilling hostess. No doubt she had forgotten to sit down. She'd do so at once now that she realised *he* wished to do so. To his amazement she did not. Instead, she remained by the chimney-piece, her dark eyes holding a faintly questioning look, as one who says, *Are you staying for long? Is there something I can do for you?*

Indeed, she was saying something very like that.

'I am very busy this afternoon Sir Philip. If there is something which you particularly wish to say to me I wish you will say it.' *And then get out of my house!*

Sir Philip smiled complacently. Aha! So she was going to listen sensibly at last!

'Well, well. I don't mind saying I think it is time that nephew of yours was taken in hand by a man's authority,' he said. 'Should be sent off to school by now! Won't do him any good to be tied to your apron strings, you know.'

'Might I remind you that my nephew is only recently orphaned?' snapped Miss Marsden. 'I consider sending a child to school at his age to be barbarous anyway and doubly so in these circumstances!'

'Oh, tush! Make a man of him!' said Sir Philip bracingly. 'Don't you worry. I'll take the lad in hand for you. He needs a man's authority.'

Miss Marsden was seized by a spirit of devilry. 'I am so

much in agreement with you there, Sir Philip, that I have arranged for him to ride out once a week with Lord Helford, who has very kindly offered to mount him.'

Garfield stiffened like a wolf scenting the hunter. *Helford?* Mount young Kit? He'd warrant that wasn't the only thing his lordship was planning to mount! His colour rose in anger.

'I cannot think that to be an eligible arrangement,' he opined forcefully. 'Had I known you wished it, I would have taken Kit out myself!'

'I do not choose to be under any obligation to you, Sir Philip!' said Miss Marsden in chilly tones.

'Obligation? I wonder you will choose to be under one to Helford! A young lady like yourself can know nothing of his reputation, but I assure you it will not do, Miss Sophie. I will not permit it in the woman I intend to marry!'

Miss Marsden had had quite enough at this point. 'Sir Philip, this has gone far enough!' she said in tones of unmistakable anger. 'You have no authority over me and I do not intend that to change! You have several times in the past offered me marriage. I have refused unequivocally on each occasion, but I have tried to avoid giving you pain by too blunt a reply. This time I will tell you plainly that the thought of marriage to you is repugnant to me and I would not consider it under any circumstances. You will please take my reply as final and cease to importune me with your suit!' That, thought Sophie, surely ought to be the end of it.

With any other man it probably would have been, coupled as it was with a look of frozen disdain from eyes which glared like chips of ice from under haughty black brows. Unfortunately Sir Philip was so far enthralled in his own conceit that he took Miss Marsden's declaration of repugnance as a challenge to his virility and acted accordingly.

Before she could so much as grab the poker, Miss

Marsden found herself in a suffocating grip. One hand was at her throat trying to force her chin up and his wet mouth was fumbling clumsy kisses all over her averted face in an attempt to reach her lips.

'Stop it! What are you do—?' Her protest was smothered by his lips which at last reached their goal and forced greedy, rapacious kisses on her soft mouth.

Revolted, Sophie fought desperately, only to realise that in some horrible way her struggles were pleasurable to the brute beast assaulting her. Her very fear and anger seemed to spur him on. She tore her mouth free and was about to scream for Thea and Anna when a familiar voice ripped through the room in accents of blazing fury.

'That will be quite enough, Garfield! Release Miss Marsden immediately, unless you wish to sample my riding whip!'

A vice-like grip took Sir Philip, dragging him away from his victim and spinning him around. Something drove itself into his midriff with crashing force and its identical twin smashed into his jaw as he staggered backwards. Winded and stunned, he collapsed moaning on the floor. Sophie staggered slightly, dazed and confused. A gentle hand under her arm supported her to a chair and pressed her shoulder as she stared up gratefully at her rescuer.

My Lord Helford, who had been sitting outside on the garden seat under the open window waiting for Miss Marsden to get rid of her unwanted visitor, then turned to Sir Philip Garfield. He was still writhing ignominiously on the floor, a circumstance that David viewed with immense satisfaction as he said in a voice laced with biting scorn and a fine unconcern for the fact that Garfield was ten years his senior, 'In my day, Garfield, no *gentleman* would have dreamt of pressing his suit on a lady who had declared herself unwilling to entertain it. And he certainly would not have forced his attentions on her! I suggest that you get out of here before I am tempted to use my whip on you.'

Sir Philip regained his feet. He was brick red and said with some degree of physical difficulty, 'I...I am making Miss Marsden an...an...honourable proposal of marriage which—'

He was cut off coldly. 'Which she has refused. Now get out!'

For a moment Sir Philip looked ugly, but Helford's reputation with his fists was no less awe-inspiring than his reputation with the ladies of the Viennese Opera. And calling him out would be decidedly worse. He was reputed to be just as deadly with swords or pistols. Sir Philip decided that discretion was the better part of valour. He was a fair shot and a reasonable swordsman, but he knew that to challenge Helford on a matter like this was to sign his own death warrant. With a curt nod to Miss Marsden he left, one hand pressed to his solar plexus, the other cradling his fast-swelling jaw.

Sophie said nothing at first, but sat shaking in the chair Helford had placed her in. After taking a thoughtful glance at her David went to the side table which held that bottle of cowslip wine and poured her a glass. He could see that she was seriously upset and said, 'I think you need not worry, Miss Marsden. He is most unlikely to risk a challenge from me, you know. Here, take this.' His words and tone gave no clue to the turmoil of emotions raging within.

She looked up in white-faced horror. 'No! You mustn't!' A feeling of sheer panic shot through her at the thought of him courting such danger. A hideous vision of him dead or badly wounded rose in nightmarish detail before her.

He stared at her. Surely she wasn't going to feel sorry for the lecherous brute! Could he have mistaken her sentiments? Did she in fact plan to accept Garfield? The thought sickened him. That she might surrender herself to Garfield! To anyone!

Her next words as she took the glass showed him his error. 'I...I couldn't *bear* it if you were to be hurt for my stupidity!' She sipped the wine gratefully.

She's worried about me? David found the notion immensely interesting, not to say novel. On the only other occasion when he had challenged a man over a woman, she had been quite excited by the prospect of two men going out, each with the expressed desire of putting a period to the other's existence. After that, Helford had declined to offer challenges over women. They just weren't worth it— until he had heard Sophie Marsden struggling with that lecherous bastard! That had enraged him as nothing else had ever done. He had scarcely been aware of moving as he had leapt from the seat and hoisted himself through the window. He would have fought a dozen duels for her sake!

He tried to speak lightly to cover up his feelings, 'Very sweet of you, my dear, but you need not worry. I can assure you that if Garfield is fool enough to challenge me, it will be his corpse the surgeon has to deal with, not mine.'

Sophie managed a faint smile and said, 'I just wanted to make it clear to him that I wouldn't marry him! I thought that perhaps I had been too *gentle* on the other occasions when I refused his offer. So I told him that...' She hesitated. No matter what his crimes, it was scarcely the done thing to boast of Sir Philip's offer and then tell Helford how rudely she had refused it.

Understanding her sudden silence, David smiled, relief lightening his mood. 'You don't need to tell me what you said. I was right outside the window and overheard. I can only say that Sir Philip is a more conceited man than I, if he could possibly suppose, after a refusal like that, that he could change your mind by, er...*force majeure*.'

Sophie shuddered in disgust. 'No! I...I had no idea it was

so *horrible!*' She continued without thinking, not realising how surely she was betraying her complete innocence, 'Why on earth do women get married? Ugh! How can they put up with it?'

David felt a surge of tender amusement at the inexperience evident in this. 'I am obliged to point out to you, Miss Marsden, that if the lady is willing it does not have to be a horrible experience for her. And not all men are as singularly inept and brutish as your erstwhile suitor. I trust I am not myself. And I certainly do not force my attentions on unwilling females!' A trace of indignation crept into his deep voice.

She looked up at him over the rim of her wine glass. How dreadful. She had offended him! 'I…I'm sorry. I shouldn't have said that. It was very rude. I am sure that you…I mean, that you wouldn't—' She stopped, very embarrassed. Better not to inform Helford that she was persuaded his attentions would have been far more acceptable to her!

'Never mind,' he said consolingly. 'It's far from being the rudest thing you've ever said to me. Now, to business.' *Probably better not to know exactly what she was about to say. And it would definitely be better not to think about correcting her misapprehension by a demonstration!*

He explained gently why he had wanted to see her. Sophie was silent. She told herself that she ought to be relieved that she would see nothing of him for a period. It would give her time to regain some measure of control over her thoughts. Especially after this afternoon. It would be all too easy to view Lord Helford as a gallant Perseus rescuing Andromeda and dream of living happily ever after. All he had done was to act as any man of honour would have done in his position. Yes, it would be as well if she were not to see him and the little stab of pain in her heart was undeniable confirmation of that.

'Very well,' she said at last. 'If you are happy to entrust

Fanny to your tiger, then I can have no qualms about sending Kit with him. Thank you, my lord and…and thank you
for your intervention just now. I am very grateful.'

She rose to her feet and held out her hand. It was taken
in a warm firm clasp, but to her surprise Helford did not
release it at once. Rather he held her eyes in his gaze and
raised her suddenly trembling hand to his lips. He pressed
a gentle kiss to her fingertips. He knew he should release
her at once but then, unconsciously, her fingers returned the
clasp and the dearest and shyest of smiles quivered on her
lips. The dimple hovered uncertainly at the corner of her
mouth, as if unsure of its welcome.

He wondered despairingly if she had the slightest idea of
how devastating that wide-eyed look was, of what it did to
him? It burnt its way into his very soul. And her fingers
were still trembling in his suddenly tightened grip. Slowly,
deliberately, he turned her hand over to caress the palm with
his thumb. She stared up at him, her lips slightly parted in
amazement at the shudders of pleasure that rippled through
her at the implied intimacy of his action.

David was lost, all his virtuous resolutions forgotten as
he drew her gently into his arms and lowered his mouth to
hers. All the reasons why he should not kiss her were overwhelmed by the temptation of those softly yielding lips and
the desire to show her what a kiss could be like. Her complete innocence was both spur and curb to his passion. He
was very gentle, moving his mouth over hers in a tender
caress as he marvelled at her sweetness, reining in his rapidly mounting desire.

Sophie, whose first kiss had left her shuddering in revulsion, was stunned at the difference. It seemed my lord was
right when he said it made a difference if the lady were
willing. She was of the opinion, though, that the skill of the
man made a great deal of difference as well.

The seductive pressure of Helford's mouth was a far cry

from the lustful slobbering of Sir Philip. Helford's lips were persuasive, exerting a subtle command to which she responded instinctively, her arms clinging to him for support as his tongue ran over her lips, seeking entrance.

With a little sob that shook David to the core, her lips flowered under his. Dizzy with passion, he plunged his tongue into her soft, vulnerable mouth, tasting and exploring in slow, sensuous strokes. *Oh, God! She's so sweet, so soft!* He was racked with desire as he felt her body melting against him. One hand rose unbidden to fondle her breasts through her bodice. Even so he felt her nipples harden in response to his action, felt her sigh of pleasure, which his mouth absorbed.

The sensations coursing through Sophie's body robbed her of all power of thought. She had thought his kiss seductive enough before he deepened it, but when his tongue invaded her mouth she realised her mistake. Boldly sweeping and plundering, it hinted at all sorts of other intimacies.

She felt one compelling hand slide sensuously down to her hip, pulling her against his body in a way which should have shocked her. Beyond caring, she allowed herself to kiss him back, pressing herself against his powerful body, revelling in the hard muscles and glorying in the contrast between that and the gentleness of his touch.

Her breasts ached at the knowing caress of his large hand which was yet so gentle and she felt a strange tension building in her, which seemed to centre itself between her thighs. His kiss became more demanding, more intimately probing as her body's response set her trembling. And his loins moved back and forth against her in slow, erotic suggestion, telling her exactly what he wanted of her. No longer gentle, but fiercely possessive, his mouth and hands arousing her senses almost to the point of pain. And she acceded to his demands, surrendering totally to his mastery.

David was fast losing control of himself and it terrified

him. His own arousal was pure agony. The sheer innocence of her response had set him ablaze with a desire stronger than anything he had ever experienced. A desire to have her nestled naked in his arms in bed, while he explored her body with ever-increasing intimacy. A desire to kiss and suckle her soft breasts and finally to take and possess her fully. A desire to make love to her until she cried out in the ecstasy of fulfilment. His loins were throbbing, positively screaming at him to do something—*anything!*—to relieve their torment.

With a groan of frustration he released her gently and, realising that her legs were unlikely to support her, put her back in the chair. What the hell was he doing? He looked down at her flushed face and swollen, trembling lips, bruised with his passion. Her eyes were dazed as she met his searching look and he felt a stab of appalling guilt. *I'm worse than Garfield! At least he was offering marriage! And who the devil is going to protect her from me?*

'I...I beg your pardon, Miss Marsden,' he said with difficulty. 'I did not intend...did not mean to take advantage...I...I hope you will not misconstrue...no insult was intended...I...I mean...' *Lord! What a meandering morass of rubbish! What the devil do I mean?*

Drawing a deep breath, Sophie Marsden reached for her tattered composure, draping it inadequately over her raw and naked emotions. It was better than nothing, even if it couldn't keep out the chilly reality which was seeping into her and quenching the fire which had raged through her body. *His kisses mean nothing, save that he wanted to kiss you.* All very well, but what was she to say?

Keep it light! Don't let him see how you feel! It was not that she feared he would take advantage, but she feared his pity if he saw how much he had affected her.

There was only a faint tremor in her voice as she said, 'It...it was most educational...my...my lord. You are indeed an improvement on Sir Philip.' *Oh, dear! Did I really say that?*

He stared at her in disbelief. *Educational? Educational, did she say? Good God!* He'd heard it called some funny things before, but that card took the trick! Then he saw the slight quiver of her lower lip, swiftly bitten down on, and realised how hard she was trying to control herself. *Help her, you arrogant fool!*

'If you can consider it as such, then I am obliged to you,' he responded, not feeling obliged in the least. He did not wish Sophie Marsden to consider him in the light of a passing stage in her worldly education. He was damned if he knew what he *did* want her to think of him, but it certainly wasn't that!

He went on smoothly, 'Naturally I am gratified that you found me an improvement.' *And I had best get the hell out of here before I improve on my own record!* He saw her mouth tremble again. *Damn! I can't leave it like this. It's too cruel!*

The door burst open and Fanny and Kit came tearing in.

'Aunt Sophie! I jumped a hedge! Truly I did!' Catching the quizzical eye of his mentor upon him, he grinned and said, 'Well, a gap in a hedge. And Lord Helford says I'll be a bruising rider!' He was absolutely ecstatic and went on charitably, 'Fanny jumped it quite well too, for a girl, of course.' Master Carlisle didn't dodge quite fast enough to avoid the thump Miss Melville landed on his shoulder.

'Uncle David didn't say it was good for a *girl*!' she said fiercely. 'And he said you'd be a bruising rider when you stopped riding fast at timber. Otherwise you'd be a bruised rider!' And she stuck her tongue out in a manner calculated to bring despair to the gentle soul of her governess.

Helford just laughed and said, 'Out, you revolting child! It is time we took our leave, and don't strike Kit again. It is not at all the thing when you know he is not permitted to hit you back.' *Damn the brats! Why did they have to come in just then? Not that I have the faintest idea what to say to her anyway.*

Sophie rose to her feet. 'I will bid you good day then, my lord, Fanny. I hope you will enjoy your house party.'

She held out her hand to his lordship and he took it reluctantly. It was as though a knife twisted in his guts as he heard her dismiss him so coolly, but he had no choice but to accede. With a brief pressure of the fingers he was gone, pulling Kit's ear and telling him to be good to his aunt. Fanny paused only to bestow a hug on Sophie, of whom she was becoming very fond, and rushed out after him.

Kit went off about his own pursuits and Sophie was left alone. Why had he kissed her like that? Her fingers touched her lips in wonder. Never had she imagined a kiss could possibly make you feel like that. As though you were on fire and melting all at the same time! *Did he feel the same? Could he possibly kiss me like that without feeling anything beyond desire? Are men really that different?*

Suddenly exhausted, she sat down. Her muddled thoughts were interrupted by Anna.

'Miss Sophie. That Sir Philip, what happened? I saw 'im go. Did he try to make up to you?'

Sophie nodded. 'Yes. It…it was very unpleasant. Fortunately Lord Helford came in and…and…'

'Gave 'im a settler, I'll be bound! You be careful, Miss Sophie. You didn't ought to be receiving gentlemen alone. Mind you, his lordship's safe enough.'

Sophie did not feel it advisable to correct this false impression and Anna went on, 'Courtin' he is or so they say in the village.'

If Anna had dumped a bucket of cold water on her young mistress, Sophie could not have been more shocked. 'Courting? He is courting? Who?'

Anna shrugged, 'One of the young ladies comin' to stay

up at the Place, I did hear. Good as betrothed to some Lady Lucinda.' She looked closely at Miss Sophie. Proper wore out she looked. 'You go an' have a rest, Miss Sophie. I'll look after things. Go on, now.' She shepherded Sophie out of the room like a large sheepdog with a very small lamb.

In the privacy of her bedchamber Sophie sat on the bed, staring blindly into space. He was courting. So what could he possibly want with her? At best he was amusing himself with a little flirtation, and at worst…at worst he would offer her a *carte blanche*, ask her to be his mistress. She shuddered to think that, after her disgraceful response, he could hardly be blamed for thinking that she would be a willing conquest. Well, he would learn his mistake!

At least she hoped he would. It was as she had known deep down at the start—if he wanted her and so much as suspected her willingness then she was lost. She would surrender herself even though she knew it would destroy her.

Chapter Six

All the next day Helford Place resounded to the rumble of arriving carriages and clattering hooves on the gravelled sweep of drive before the main portico with its lofty Grecian columns. Servants scurried hither and yon, conveying mountains of baggage to the various apartments assigned to the guests. The house echoed to the influx of new voices, footsteps and the whisper of silken skirts hushing over the floors.

Lady Maria viewed all this rather sardonically. Her eagle gaze had been quick to descry the tension in her nephew when he returned home the previous day. He had almost winced whenever Fanny spoke of Sophie Marsden, which she did very frequently, referring to her as *Aunt Sophie*. Well, not winced precisely. Frozen was more like it, as though he were trying to control or counteract some powerful emotion. And in Lady Maria's long and varied experience, there was only one emotion likely to bring out that sort of reaction over a woman.

So she waited with intense interest to see how he would greet the guests of honour. Snatches of conversation came to her ears when people thought she wasn't attending. 'Has

he offered already?...forgone conclusion...probably announce it towards the end of the visit...'

Sometimes, thought Lady Maria, it paid to let people
think you were a little deaf and more than a little senile.
The irritation of being spoken to like a halfwit was more
than amply compensated by the information you picked up.
For example, Ned Asterfield would never have referred to
Lady Lucinda as *a cold poultice* had he thought his hostess
could hear him.

She sat in the Green Drawing Room, which was considered hers by long tradition, receiving the guests as Helford
presented them to her, watching their approach across the
empty expanse of carpet and knowing perfectly well that
they found the experience singularly unnerving.

The old-fashioned, formal arrangement of the room assisted in the impression of approaching a throne. Gave you
a chance to have a good look at the person. Humph! None
of this new-fangled rubbish about cluttering up a room with
furniture higgledy piggledy all over it. While she had breath
in her body her apartments would be arranged in the old
way with the furniture in its place against the wall. The way
it was when a gown was a gown, thank you very much, and
had a decent hoop to it! Not one of these scandalous modern
muslin draperies calling itself decent attire for a modest female!

At length Lady Stanford and Lady Lucinda Anstey were
announced and Lady Maria eyed her nephew's quarry as
she made her way regally down the long room to be presented to her hostess. Tall and elegant, Lady Lucinda glided
across the carpet to greet the old lady. *A beauty? Oh, yes,
she's that, all right. The right girl for David? We shall see.*

She was demurely respectful, but Lady Maria was quick
to detect a hint of patronage. And by the sudden frown in
his eyes Helford had caught it as well.

Lady Maria responded to the young lady's greeting with

a blunt, 'How d'you do?' Then she turned her fire on Lady
Stanford. 'Good evening, Aurelia! How is Stanford these
days? Still an eye to the fillies?' This enigmatic question
left most of the assembled party in doubt as to whether the
old girl referred to the absent Earl's sporting interests or
other less respectable proclivities.

Everyone except Lady Stanford and Lord Helford, that is.
The latter managed to disguise an unseemly crack of laughter as a fit of coughing, but Lady Stanford went purple with
fury and barely returned a civil reply. Lady Lucinda was
somewhat taken aback. Never had she seen her mama so
put out by an innocent question. Lady Lucinda was one of
those young ladies of birth, so recently extolled by Lord
Helford, who knew nothing of a gentleman's reputation. Not
even when the gentleman was her own father and carried
on his amours with much the same regard for discretion as
a stag in rut.

Oddly enough, his lordship was not delighted at her obvious ignorance. *Lord! What a pea-goose she must be! Stanford's peccadilloes are common knowledge!* Helford had,
manlike, completely forgotten his dictum, so forcibly expressed to Miss Marsden, that young ladies should not know
of such things. He found himself thinking that Sophie would
have made some outrageous comment to put the old devil
in her place. And Great Aunt Maria would have loved it!

Belatedly remembering his role as host, he strolled forward to rescue the seething Lady Stanford.

Fixing his outrageous relative with a look which would
have wilted almost any other female and most men, he said,
'Perhaps you and Lady Lucinda would like to rest after your
journey before you must change for dinner. It is after four
now and we will dine at six. Country hours, you know.'

'Thank you, my lord,' responded Lady Stanford. *At least
he knows what is due to me. Disagreeable old hag! When*

Lucinda marries, Lady Maria can retire to the Dower House or Bath. I'll see to that!

She permitted Lord Helford to lead her from the room and show the pair of them to the suite of rooms they were to occupy. The grandeur and appointments of these rooms went a long way towards mollifying her. These were the state apartments, their wainscoting lavishly gilded and the furniture luxuriously upholstered in gold silk damask. A large salon separated the two bedchambers, which boasted elegant and enormous beds surmounted by canopied drapes in gold and ivory silk.

It would be too much to say that Lady Lucinda was impressed by this display of ostentation, but she certainly appreciated it as her due.

'Lord Helford uses us with great respect, Mama,' she observed when she joined Lady Stanford in their private salon.

'Quite so, my love,' agreed Lady Stanford. 'And I am sure that he will not make a fuss about any little changes you may like to make.'

'Changes, Mama?' Lady Lucinda was surprised. As far as she could see the house was fitted up in the first style of elegance. Lofty rooms, a certain formal dignity. Some of the furnishings were a trifle old fashioned, but no doubt they could be relegated to less public rooms bit by bit. What could Mama be talking about?

'Yes, my dear. For example, I believe that Lord Helford's niece is living here at the moment. Understandably he has not had time to look about him and dispose of the child suitably. That will be a task for you, my dear. The child will be very much better off in a good school or with other relations. She must not be encouraged to think of this as her home now, you know. Orphans,' she spoke with a delicate shudder, 'can be sadly encroaching.'

Lady Lucinda nodded thoughtfully. Indeed, she did not wish to be troubled with someone else's child.

Lady Stanford continued, 'And, of course, Lady Maria is becoming quite peculiar. And she has been so used to ordering everything here just as she pleases. It will be very much better if she retires to the Dower House or even perhaps to Bath. Yes, Bath would be best. Her health, you know. I am sure the waters would be most beneficial.'

This point of view struck Lady Lucinda forcibly. Most certainly she did not want Lord Helford's Great Aunt interfering with her management of the house. She went down to dinner in a thoughtful frame of mind, determined to ask her mother's advice on how best to achieve these evictions.

By the end of dinner Lady Maria was determined on one thing. Her nephew was not going to marry that insufferably superior wench if she could stop it! And if he *was* fool enough to take her, then she would betake herself to the Dower House before the bridal trip was over. Never had she been more irritated by a female in her life, which was saying a great deal since most women irritated Lady Maria.

She made two exceptions. One was for Penelope Darleston, who was an impudent baggage, but at least kept that handsome rake she had married in *her* bed where he belonged. The second was for Miss Marsden, who was, she opined, a good gal and one who would give as good as she got. Not one of these mealy-mouthed modern misses who swooned if someone mentioned *breeches*. Lady Maria had had a soft spot in her heart for Miss Marsden ever since the day she had called upon her to find her chasing a piglet out of her parlour and using language which Lady Maria had not heard since one of the grooms had been kicked by one of her carriage horses.

By the end of the evening Lady Maria had added to her resolve about removing to the Dower House. She would take Fanny with her. The child had been brought down to the drawing room before dinner and Lady Lucinda had treated her with a mixture of condescension and patronage which grated on Lady Maria intolerably. *Damn it! This is the child's home, ain't it?* Not a doubt but that Lady Lucinda would be packing the child off to school faster than the cat could lick her ear. *Not if I have anything to say to it!*

By the time she retired and had heard Lady Lucinda assuring David that she would be delighted to see over the house on the morrow and give him the benefit of her advice in his plans for refurbishing the west wing, Lady Maria had heard more than enough. Lady Lucinda Anstey would marry David Melville over her dead body!

To this end she emerged from her bedchamber the next morning well before her usual hour. She wished to catch Helford before he began the day's entertainments which were to include a ride around the estate and a visit to Darleston Court. She found her nephew in the library just before breakfast.

He looked up in some surprise. 'Good God, ma'am! Has someone invaded the nation? What the devil are you doing up so early?'

'Don't you swear at *me* as if I was one of your troopers!' she snapped, secretly delighted at the easy, down-to-earth way he spoke with her. Hah! She'd like to see Madam Anstey's reaction if Helford addressed her like that!

Now, to be devious. 'Had an idea,' she said. 'Are you going to see anything of the Darlestons while you've got the house full of all these people?'

'Well, of course,' said David. 'In fact, I had arranged to call on them this afternoon while we are out riding. I sent a note over yesterday and Lady Darleston sent one back saying to bring as many as I liked.'

Lady Maria smiled in an odd way which made David feel

very nervous. He remembered that look from his childhood and it always meant trouble for someone, generally the recipient.

'Why don't you suggest to Penelope that she calls on Miss Marsden?' suggested Lady Maria. 'Those two should deal extremely well together. Not a hair's-breadth between them when it comes to speaking their minds and, as far as I'm aware, they've never met.'

David perceived that his memory must be at fault. He could detect no danger at all in this brainwave. Penelope Darleston would be just the right friend for Sophie. He was shaken to find that he thought of her as *Sophie* now, rather than *Miss Marsden*. There was something about kissing a girl which seemed to do away with such formalities. Especially when the memory of the girl's response haunted your sleep and left you feeling as though your bed were stuffed with nails. Damned chilly nails at that.

'Very well, Aunt Maria. I'll suggest to Lady Darleston that she calls on So…Miss Marsden. Good God! Look at the time. I'd best get to breakfast. If you can be out of your room this early, I can make it to breakfast on time.'

Lady Maria permitted him to escort her from the room, not betraying by so much as a quiver of her lips that she had caught his telltale slip. *Sophie, indeed! Once that impudent creature Penelope gets wind of this, I can trust her to do something about it without my having to say a word.*

True to his word Helford showed Lady Lucinda around the house after breakfast.

Lady Lucinda had reminded him that she was all eagerness to give him the benefit of her advice. 'Indeed, it will be a pleasure, my lord. You must know that Mama recently had several rooms done up at Camberley in the Chinese style. I fancy that the result is not just in the common way and I should be happy to assist you.'

David was conscious of an unexpected twinge of pure fright, since it was evident from her arch comments that Lady Stanford had no intention of accompanying them on this expedition. He was at a loss to understand his dismay since, logically speaking, it should be just what he wanted. A chance to become acquainted with his prospective bride. *It looks so particular! You'll have the entire party gossiping by noon if you take only her. Think now, some camouflage is called for.*

'Perhaps Mrs Asterfield might care to come along as well,' he said, smiling in the direction of a young matron who showed every sign of having a *tendre* for him.

'Why, I should be delighted, my lord,' responded Kate Asterfield, a faint smile curving her lips. She was no fool and understood exactly what his lordship was at. Perfectly happy with her husband, an old friend of Helford's, she was nevertheless quite happy to spend a morning in the company of a man who was the most handsome thing God ever put in breeches. Especially if it would annoy that insufferable Anstey chit. Not that Lady Lucinda would ever do anything so human as to show annoyance, but she must surely be conscious of a little chagrin that she was not the sole recipient of this signal honour.

The tour was a mixed success. The two ladies had enjoyed themselves enormously. Mrs Asterfield was not a woman who had to be the centre of attention to be happy. On the contrary, she was quite content to stand back and observe the foolishness of others. She derived no small satisfaction from listening to Lady Lucinda instruct his lordship in the principles of modern taste, consigning several obviously valuable heirlooms to the attics in the process. She was relatively sure Helford had been quite shocked at some of the suggestions put forth, but he was the soul of tact, merely saying quietly that he had a liking for this piece or that and would prefer it left in its place.

Blissfully unaware that she was not showing to advantage, Lady Lucinda gave full rein to her ideas and was tolerably certain that Lord Helford was much struck by her understanding and taste. With her mama's advice in mind she even ventured to enquire when 'dear little Fanny', as she described the child, would be off to school.

'Surely a wise move, my lord. It must be painful for the child to be constantly reminded of all that she has lost,' said Lady Lucinda with an air of sincerity which made Mrs Asterfield long to smack her.

David merely replied, 'Indeed, I am of the opinion that she has lost so much that I prefer not to remove her from her home while she is so young. I must say I can see little need for her to be sent away to school at all. Her governess appears to me to be doing an admirable job.' It was said quietly and in the friendliest of tones, but Mrs Asterfield was convinced she had seen a flash of anger in those green eyes.

Oblivious to her blunder, Lady Lucinda said, 'Oh, but she would benefit from companionship.'

David inclined his head, 'Just so, ma'am. I have arranged for her to visit a friend of my aunt's once a week so that she may play with Miss Marsden's nephew. And I even take the pair of them riding so that Miss Marsden does not feel imposed upon.'

He was startled at the pang of longing which shot through him in just mentioning Sophie. He thought of the way in which she had taken on the responsibility for her orphaned nephew and wondered at Lucinda's lack of understanding. It suddenly occurred to him to wonder how Lucinda would deal with Fanny. He was coming to have a fondness for the child and felt a stab of uneasiness at the thought that his bride might not wish the child to remain with them.

Mrs Asterfield was speaking. 'Besides, dear Lucinda, Helford will be setting up his nursery one day and will no doubt provide lots of companionship for Fanny.' It would be too much to say there was a glint of mischief in the lady's eyes. She had, his lordship judged, a perfectly straight face. Which was more than could be said for Lady Lucinda, who actually glared at her.

With a strange tightening of his throat David found that all he could think of was Sophie with that tiny infant cuddled to her breast, her tender voice as she dreamed over it. And with a jolt he realised that it was that that had started him thinking of her as *Sophie*, not merely kissing her.

'And, of course, so many little girls become positively maternal where babies are concerned,' continued Mrs Asterfield with, David considered, malice aforethought. The look of extreme distaste on Lady Lucinda's face had obviously not been lost on her. 'Why, I did myself after my eldest sister was brought to bed with her children and I was not so much older than Fanny is now, being the youngest of twelve. I believe it all kept my parents shockingly busy.'

They were standing in the Round Parlour in the South Tower at the time and Mrs Asterfield caught sight of a Gainsborough over the chimney-piece depicting the wife and very numerous progeny of the fourth Viscount.

'I am sure another picture of that nature would gladden his lordship's heart,' she said sweetly, indicating the painting with an airy wave. The children surrounded their mother, the youngest nestling on her lap, her arms curved around him protectively.

'Quite so, ma'am,' responded Helford drily, as visions of Sophie surrounded by children assailed him. He wondered whether Ned Asterfield would accept a plea of extreme provocation when his wife was found strangled.

Lady Lucinda was looking absolutely outraged at the impropriety of this conversation. Lord Helford could not help thinking that Sophie would in all likelihood have succumbed to giggles by now and probably would have said something just as outrageous. It clearly behoved him to bring the tour to an end as quickly as possible, which he did by suggesting that the ladies might like to repose themselves before partaking of a luncheon prior to their ride over to Darleston Court.

Entirely satisfied with the morning's activities, Mrs Asterfield took this gentle hint. She retired in good order, reflecting as she did so that poor Helford deserved *some* time alone with the chit if he really was desirous of making her an offer.

David found himself left alone with Lady Lucinda, giving him the chance to say, 'You may not know that I spoke to your father before leaving town. Naturally I feel it to be of the first importance that we are both quite sure of our own minds before coming to any final agreement but...' He smiled at her meaningly.

'Of course, my lord,' said Lady Lucinda without the slightest trace of coyness or embarrassment. 'There is no need to be hasty over such an important matter.'

Telling himself that he ought to be pleased that she so obviously viewed the match with the same cool propriety that he did, Helford escorted Lady Lucinda back her bedchamber. As they went he tried to imagine her with children, a baby snuggled in her arms, and failed dismally. The image just didn't fit. He took his leave of her very formally and departed to think over his morning in the solitude of the library.

The visit to Darleston Court was very pleasant. The Earl and his Countess received the party with great hospitality, and if Lady Lucinda thought that the presence of Lady Darleston's extremely large dog was inappropriate she left her opinion unvoiced.

Helford noticed, however, that she avoided Gelert assiduously and wondered how she would react to dogs in the house. He had every intention of selecting a couple of puppies from his keeper's current litter of springer spaniels. Dogs always made a house seem…well…more like a home. He had not kept a dog since leaving England and was looking forward to it very much.

He took the first opportunity of suggesting to the Countess that she might care to make Miss Marsden's acquaintance.

'Great Aunt Maria thought you would be pleased with her,' he said in explanation of his request as he absentmindedly fondled Gelert's ears.

'Did she, indeed?' asked Penelope. 'Then, of course, I will do so. Willowbank House? Oh, yes, I know it. Very well. I shall call in the next day or so. I often ride out that way.' *What now is Lady Maria up to?* Penelope was far too well acquainted with his lordship's aunt not to detect a distinct whiff of rodent in the seemingly innocent suggestion.

Thinking Kate Asterfield and Lucinda might well be tired, Helford took the party back by the shortest route which led them straight past Willowbank House. For the preceding mile the temptation to stop briefly and visit Sophie warred with the knowledge that to see her would be extremely unwise. Positively dangerous, in fact. He could place no reliance on his ability to keep the line with her now.

As the house came into view he decided firmly that he would ride straight past and resist temptation. Therefore he was understandably stunned to hear his own voice say, 'Please ride on ahead. I must stop and speak to my tenant here about some improvements I have in hand for the house. I will catch you up in a very few minutes.' *Where the devil did that come from?*

He dismounted, rather dazed at the lack of control he seemed to have over his behaviour, and tied the mare's bridle to the gatepost. All the way up the path he issued mental instructions to himself to keep his hands and mouth off Sophie, that she was his tenant, a lady of breeding and undoubted virtue, and as such should be treated with respect. And also that he had as good as offered for Lucinda Anstey, who had every qualification he had demanded of his bride. She was beautiful, titled, well behaved and well dowered— a veritable paragon.

To his mingled relief and chagrin Sophie received him with Thea Andrews in attendance. If she was surprised to see him again so soon, it did not show in her demeanour.

'Good afternoon, Lord Helford. It is very pleasant to see you again.' Her voice was quiet and dignified, giving no hint of the turmoil raging within. *Why is he here again so soon? What does he want? Surely he is not going to…to offer a…carte blanche. Stop it! Stop it at once! He can't do so with Thea in the room. And if he is, it doesn't matter! Unless you are fool enough to accept!* But it did matter. She knew she would be immeasurably ashamed if he thought that her disgraceful response to his kisses meant that she would consider such a connection. And she would have no one but herself to blame. She should not have talked in that indelicate fashion about marital duties. Of course a man of his reputation would be unable to resist such a challenge.

She indicated a chair to his lordship, 'Please be seated, my lord.'

'I…I should not stay, Miss Marsden. I…I wished merely to say that I have been calling at Darleston Court this afternoon and I mentioned you to the Countess. She…er…intends to call upon you in the next day or so. I…I hope you do not mind?' *Good God! Stop stammering like a lovesick schoolboy!*

Miss Andrews was all a-twitter. 'Why, how very kind of you, my lord. I am sure that Miss Sophie could not possibly mind. Indeed, why should she? Sophie, dear, you say nothing?'

Sophie was staring at Helford in complete confusion. Her eyes met his with a look of puzzlement. At last she spoke. 'It is certainly very kind in you, my lord. But I can think of no reason why you should do such a thing. What can I have in common with a Countess?'

She undervalues herself so dreadfully. Aloud he said, 'Well, my Aunt Maria approves of both of you. In fact, it was her suggestion that I should mention you to Lady Darleston. I am quite sure that you will like her, you know.' He continued reassuringly, 'She is not in the least top lofty or condescending and I don't think she cares in the slightest about rank or degree or any of that nonsense. So don't tease yourself on that head. Now, I must be going. I am supposed to be escorting my house guests home. They are riding on ahead.'

Sophie rose gracefully to her feet. 'Then I will escort you to your horse, my lord, and thank you for your kind offices. I shall look forward to meeting Lady Darleston.'

Helford bid Miss Andrews a polite farewell and held the door open for Sophie to precede him from the room. The soft fragrance that hung around her hair drifted past him teasingly. He shut the door behind them, wondering just what the scent was.

'Miss Marsden. I hope you will forgive my behaviour the other day…it was infamous of me—'

'You need not consider it, my lord.' Her voice was cold. 'I am well aware that I ought not to have received Sir Philip alone. I would not have done so had I not intended to refuse his offer in such blunt terms. And you have certainly demonstrated the folly of receiving you alone. The responsibility is mine.'

She was blaming herself for his behaviour? Damn! *She* shouldn't feel guilty because he had behaved like a cad! He knew that many people would assume that she had asked for it in some way or another, but such attitudes stuck in his gullet. A man should not hide behind such cowardly untruths. He had kissed her because he had not been able to help himself, but the fault was not hers. Unless she was to be blamed for being too lovely, too appealing.

'The fault was not yours, Miss Marsden,' he said gently. 'It was mine. You are not to be blaming yourself or thinking that I will read anything into your...er...into what happened.'

Into my response? Into the inescapable fact that I kissed you back? That I did not merely permit but encouraged the liberties you took? That I enjoyed it? Sophie did not answer as she went down the path to the front gate. She did not know what to say.

'Goodbye, my lord. I will expect Fanny on Monday.'

He nodded, accepting his dismissal. 'Farewell, then.' He held out his hand. She looked at it for a moment and then placed hers in it hesitantly. The long fingers closed around it in a light grip and before she could withdraw he raised it swiftly to his lips to drop a kiss on the inside of her wrist.

Her eyes widened in shock at the ripple of delight that ran through her. 'No,' she whispered. 'This must stop. I am not for you, my lord. Look elsewhere for your amusements and leave me in peace!' She wrenched her wrist from his grasp, her cheeks stained scarlet.

'My amusements?' David was shocked. Was that what she thought? *What else could she think?*

'What else can this be?' asked Sophie fiercely, echoing his thought. 'I do not know whether you are simply indulging in a little flirtation or something more serious, but I tell you this, Lord Helford: I want none of it! Goodbye!'

She nearly ran back into the house, leaving David wondering what the devil had possessed him to do such an addlebrained thing. He'd only just apologised for the previous day's familiarities and there he was doing it again. Always with other women he had been in full control of himself. Oh, he had desired them right enough, but he had always been in command of his actions. Never had he felt so completely powerless to restrain himself.

It's because I can't have her. If I could have her in bed, then she would cease to have this power. Ah! But you can have her. She responded yesterday. How much effort would it take to—?

No! Horrified at the turn his thoughts were taking, Helford spurred his mare into a brisk canter. He couldn't, he simply couldn't take advantage of her in that way. Had he only defended her from Garfield's mauling to destroy her himself? It was unthinkable. Or it ought to be. She deserved better than that. Why the hell was he interested in her, anyway? She had no extraordinary degree of beauty, her connections were no more than passable and she had a tongue on her like a wasp when she was annoyed.

And her mouth had opened under his in the sweetest, most trusting way, her body melting into his embrace as no woman's ever had. Her very inexperience and shyness set his senses blazing. But through it all was this inexplicable urge to protect her, even, or rather especially, from himself.

Stay away from her. It's the best thing you can do. Unless you are prepared to offer marriage. And the last thing you want is marriage to a woman you care for…a woman who can hurt you.

The thought seared itself into his mind just as the tail end of his guests came into view around a bend in the high hedges and he cantered up to them, a terrible suspicion forming in his mind that he might have made an appalling mistake. That he might have all unwittingly fallen into the very trap he had sought to avoid. While he made polite conversation to Kate Asterfield and Lady Lucinda, a remark

Peter Darleston had made on the subject of love pounded mercilessly in his brain.

I didn't even recognise it.

He gritted his teeth. If he had fallen in love with Sophie Marsden, then there was only one thing to be done about it. Avoid her. Like the plague.

Sophie ordered herself to forget about Lord Helford. She knew now why she had instinctively recognised him as dangerous. He wielded a power over her that no man ever had. A few more interludes like that, she thought, and I won't be able to refuse him. No matter what he asks. His mouth and hands robbed her of all ability to think rationally. She lay in her bed that night for hours, waiting for sleep, trying to convince herself that this madness would pass.

It's just a physical attraction. You can't be in love. You hardly know him. What do you like about him apart from the fact that he kissed you out of your senses?

But there were many things she liked about him. His kindness to Kit and his understanding of the boy's problem. The way he had actually taken some time to acquaint himself with his niece. Kit was full of things that Helford had said to him in the most casual way which told Sophie that she could not have found a better man to influence him. And he had seen unerringly to the heart of her make-believe with Polly Simpkins's baby.

She cursed and thumped her pillow. *Damn! Try and think of things to his discredit, you little fool. His reputation for a start. And what about the way he nearly ran you over? Thought you a bit of game? Accused you of keeping Kit from his family? Arrogant, interfering oaf!*

Her natural sense of justice was no help at all.

But he apologised for all of those things, unreservedly owning himself at fault.

It only made her love him the more. For it was love, she

could not lie to herself, even if she did manage to preserve a cold front with Helford. And she would have to preserve a very cold front. She knew he would never press her if he believed her unwilling. She must take care never to be alone with him again. It was the only way to be safe from her own weakness which would surrender to him at the first opportunity.

Elusive sleep came at last but brought her no peace, haunted as it was by his voice and tender caresses. She woke several times, her body trembling as it had in his arms, her heart pounding and that strange tension building in her belly. The dreams were so real that each time she sank back into sleep, confused to have found herself alone.

Chapter Seven

After dinner the next day Sophie dismissed Kit to his afternoon pursuits and Thea went to her usual afternoon rest. She knew that the best thing she could do was to keep busy, so she fetched the beeswax from the scullery and set about polishing the furniture in the parlour. Most of the pieces were very old with no pretensions to fashion. They had belonged for the most part to her father's family and showed signs of wear and aging. Nevertheless they glowed with care and lent the small room an air of home for her. She had lived with this furniture all her life. To her they spelled safety and security.

She flung open the casements, allowing the fresh air to flow into the room. The garden was full of flowers and their scent drifted through with the light breeze. Humming a soft air to herself, she went about her work.

Piece by piece she moved around the room, applying the wax sparingly, knowing that a small amount of wax to a large amount of elbow grease was the best combination. As she went the hum became a song and her rich, warm voice floated out to mingle with a whistling blackbird. After she had waxed several pieces she judged that the first one, a small drop-sided dining table, would be dry enough to buff and returned to it, still singing.

> *I will give my love an apple without ere a core,*
> *I will give my love a house without ere a door.*
> *I will give my love a palace wherein he may be*
> *And he may unlock it without any key.*

The visitor coming up the path with her dog stood as though petrified as she heard the plangent air and the poignant intensity of the voice. She waited for a moment, and then walked up to the door. She had been very nervous about calling on a complete stranger, but she just had to know what that song was.

Just as Sophie picked up the clean cloth the door bell jangled loudly. She frowned. Who on earth—surely, surely not Helford again? Anna's footsteps were heard in the flagged hall and the sound of the door opening. A charming, feminine voice was heard inquiring if Miss Marsden were at home.

Before Sophie could so much as stuff the jar of wax and the cloths in a drawer, Anna was opening the door and announcing, ''Tis Lady Darleston, Miss Sophie.'

Sir Philip might have had a point, thought Sophie in horror. A Countess comes to call on me and Anna has to show her in before I even have time to tidy myself. Horribly conscious of untidy hair, a streak of wax on her cheek from pushing a curl out of her eyes and a shabby old gown, Sophie came forward to greet her exalted guest.

Her first impression was one of extraordinary beauty. A tall, slender figure in an elegant dark blue habit, the skirt looped up gracefully over one arm. Glowing auburn curls nestled under a charming hat with one curling feather and set off a delicately fair countenance.

Sophie drew herself up proudly. *I have nothing to be*

ashamed of! A second glance revealed the caller's laughing grey eyes and merry smile. Suddenly Sophie was reassured.

This was confirmed by the first thing Lady Darleston said. 'Oh dear, I am interrupting you. Should I come another time? I...I...don't mean to intrude, but when Helford said Lady Maria wanted me to meet you...we are to dine with them, you know, and she is bound to ask me how I liked you.'

Despite herself Sophie started to laugh and her extraordinary guest joined in. 'Oh, good! You looked so dreadfully stern for a moment that I was quite scared. It didn't fit in at all'

'Fit in with what?' asked Sophie.

'That lovely song you were singing. You're going to sing it for me again so I can learn it,' explained the impossible Countess.

'Won't you sit down, Lady Darleston?' asked Sophie, still smiling. 'Anna, bring some cakes and sandwiches, please, and tea.'

'Yes, Miss Sophie, and what should I do about the dog?'

'Dog? What dog?' Sophie was puzzled.

'Her ladyship's dog what's taking up the entire hall.'

'Can he come in, Miss Marsden?' asked Lady Darleston. 'He's enormous, but very well behaved. Or I could leave him outside with my groom.'

'Bring him in,' said Sophie. 'And, Anna, tell Lady Darleston's groom to take the horses around to the stable. He may put them in the spare boxes.'

Lady Darleston gave a soft whistle and Sophie stared as the largest dog she had ever seen came in and sat beside his mistress.

'Good God! Do you *need* a groom with him to escort you?' The question was out before she could stop it. Oh dear, that probably wasn't the right way to address a Countess. But this particular Countess did not seem to have

the slightest notion of fitting into any of Sophie's precon-
ceived ideas.

'Of course not. Gelert would simply savage anyone who
accosted me. But you know what men are!' she said with
an infectious chuckle. 'Darleston insists if I am off our own
land. On our estate I never bother with a groom.'

Sophie laughed and said, 'It must be nice to have someone fuss about you that much. Please sit down. I am glad
you called. Lord Helford warned me that you might, but I
didn't think it would be so soon.'

Lady Darleston grinned as she sat down with the dog at
her feet, 'How well do you know Lady Maria?'

'Not terribly well,' admitted Sophie. 'She used to call
here once in a while, but she doesn't get out much now, I
believe.'

'And you don't call on her?'

'N...no. I...er...I didn't think...' Sophie didn't quite
know how to tell Lady Darleston that she would not dream
of presuming that she was welcome to call at Helford Place.
Although the previous Viscount had been kind enough, his
wife had certainly never indicated that she wished for any
sort of intimacy.

'You didn't want to be thought encroaching?' Lady
Darleston smiled understandingly. 'Next time I'm calling on
her I shall come in the carriage and take you up if you would
care to come. She likes visitors, even if she does always
give one a tremendous scold for not coming next or nigh
her for months. You should have heard what she said to me
after I didn't visit for a month when my twins were born.'

Sophie was fascinated. She found it hard to believe that
this slender creature could be the mother of twins. 'I had
heard you had twins,' said Sophie shyly. 'How lovely for
you.' She felt a pang of envy for this girl who had everything she would never have. A husband, who by all accounts
worshipped the ground she trod on, and children of her own.

At least I have Kit. She pushed away the thought of Lord Helford. Whatever he might offer, she did not think love would come into it. At least not love as she understood it.

Lady Darleston was speaking again, 'What were you singing when I was walking up the path? I had never heard it before. It's very old, isn't it? It sounded lovely.' She hummed part of the melody.

'One of our maids taught it to me when I was a child,' said Sophie. 'It's just a country song, but I like it.'

'Will you play it for me?' asked Lady Darleston, indicating the harpsichord in the corner.

Sophie shook her head. 'I play very badly.'

Lady Darleston stood up and went to the old instrument. She lifted the lid and sat down, twinkling at her hostess. 'Very well. Sing. I have to learn this song. Darleston would love it.'

Slightly self-conscious, Sophie sang the old air and was amazed when her guest joined in with a light accompaniment on the second verse. Her touch on the keys was sure and light and she played with a delicate sensitivity. 'Again,' she commanded at the end. This time she played the whole way through, adding an improvised interlude between the verses.

Penelope Darleston had never heard a girl sing like this one could. The voice was so warm and vibrant and there was that peculiar aching quality. It made Penelope's heart contract to hear it, as though the singer's soul was bared. Enough to break your heart, she thought as she struck the final chords.

Their eyes met and held, the song's spell still holding them in thrall. In that moment friendship was born as each recognised in the other the power of music to stir them and express all the things that could never be spoken.

At last Penelope spoke. 'I hope you will come to dinner one evening and sing that for Darleston.'

'Oh, I couldn't, Lady Darleston!' said Sophie in horror.

Penelope laughed. 'Oh, yes, you could. He'd love it. And I think since we are going to be friends that you had better stop calling me Lady Darleston. Everyone I like calls me Penny.'

'You want me to call you Penny?' Never had Sophie imagined that a Countess could be so unaffected and charming. No, not charming. Warm, friendly and yet there was a dignity about her that would preclude anyone taking liberties with her.

Penelope nodded. She definitely liked this girl with her soft brown curls and greeny-brown eyes. She had an oddly taking face with its impertinent freckled nose. Far more welcoming than Lucinda Anstey's aristocratic countenan— Good God! Is that what Lady Maria is up to? Does she think that Sophie Marsden can cut that insufferable girl out with Helford? Well, if he ever hears her sing! But from all I hear he's as good as offered for Lucinda. How the devil can he get out of it now?

'Please do,' she went on aloud. 'Now we have met I would like to be friends. And if Lady Maria likes you that's something we have in common. She's terribly choosy.'

'Well, I can't imagine why she does like me,' confessed Sophie. 'The first time she called here to see how we were settling in I nearly knocked her flat, chasing a piglet out of this room and the language I was using was not precisely…polite.'

Penelope burst out laughing. 'I can imagine. The little beasts can run so fast and they are so *slippery*! Nothing at all to get hold of. That wouldn't bother Lady Maria. She can't bear people to be what she calls mealy mouthed!'

'I certainly wasn't that,' said Sophie with a grin. 'Quite the opposite.'

'Good for you. Tell me, do you know Helford well?' She

watched carefully and saw the slight stiffening of Sophie's
expressive face.

'Not very well,' said Sophie lightly. 'He brings Fanny
over once a week to play with my nephew and he takes
them out riding another day so I...sometimes see him when
he calls. He has been very good to Kit.'

'I see,' said Penelope thoughtfully. Why on earth should
Helford do that unless he was interested in Sophie? And if
he was interested, why was he still pursuing Lucinda
Anstey? He couldn't possibly be intending to offer Sophie
a *carte blanche*. Surely not if he brought his niece here and
had suggested that she should befriend the girl. Besides, she
was not the sort of girl whom a gentleman *would* set up as
his mistress. She was plainly of good family and Helford
would have to be an utter scoundrel to ruin her. Penelope
couldn't believe that of any friend of Peter's.

She chattered on about Helford and came to the conclusion that Sophie was very uncomfortable. Her voice, thought
Penelope, was a complete giveaway. Too expressive to hide
her feelings.

Tactfully she changed the subject to children, asking
Sophie about Kit. 'Is he dreadfully naughty? Or do they
really grow out of it? My two-year-olds are frightful at
times!'

By the time Penelope left she was convinced that Sophie
Marsden was not at all indifferent to Lord Helford. Whether
it was love or not Penelope had no idea, but she was sure
of one thing: Sophie Marsden would be a far more popular
choice than Lucinda Anstey with Helford's friends and his
aunt. With the child too, thought Penelope suddenly. She
could not for the life of her see Lady Lucinda Anstey per-
mitting the residence of another woman's child under her
roof.

'Goodbye, Sophie,' said Penelope. 'Now we have met at
last I shall call again and, if you are coming past, please

call and see me. I shall send a note over to Lady Maria telling her how much obliged to her I am.'

Her groom put her up into the saddle as though she were made of porcelain and said, 'Best be quick, me lady. Master don't like it if ye're too late.' He swung himself into his saddle and raised his cap to Sophie.

'Oh, pooh!' said Penelope. 'His lordship worries if I'm five minutes late. Come along, Gelert!'

They trotted off and Sophie went back into the house, feeling as though a ray of light had broken through heavy clouds. In her straitened circumstances she had held aloof from most of the local gentry, not wishing to be thought encroaching.

Except for Lady Maria, none of the women had bothered to call on them more than once and there had been no suggestion that they would welcome any further acquaintance. Several of them had sons of an impressionable age and they had made it quite plain that Sophie would not be acceptable. Until, that is, they had found out after Emma's death that she did have some money. Then one or two had called with their younger sons in tow. One lad had gone so far as to offer for her and had been told gently that she would require him to settle half her fortune on Kit.

He had hummed and hawed. Like Sir Philip, he had thought it quite unnecessary. The lad did not need the half of such a sum, surely. He did not know what his mama would think of such an arrangement!

Sophie had suggested sweetly that perhaps he should discuss it with her and renew his offer if the lady approved. He hailed this idea with obvious relief and had not called since. Nor had anyone else, except, of course, Sir Philip, who had tried on several occasions to turn her polite refusal into an acceptance.

She reflected on all this rather sadly as she went back to her polishing. Even as the furniture glowed under her vigorous rubbing so too did the dull ache in her heart deepen. Why had fate put Helford in her path, if only to torment her? *Ah, but he sent you a friend. No doubt he is trying to be a good neighbour.*

For the next week it rained without ceasing. The countryside lay dripping under a grey, sodden sky, an apt reflection of Sophie's depression. She longed to get out of the house and go for a long walk to burn off some of her fidgets, but Thea would not hear of anything of the sort.

'Dear Sophie, you would catch an inflammation of the lungs, I am persuaded, or a putrid sore throat!' she protested. 'It cannot rain forever after all, and then you may go out again.'

Sophie forbore to comment on the likelihood of its raining until at least Christmas and submitted with a docility which made Thea wonder if she were sickening for something. She had fully expected her erstwhile pupil to don a heavy cloak and boots and be off into the meadows.

Fanny came to play with Kit and they nearly turned the house upside down with their chasing and romping, which served to cheer Sophie up insensibly. Helford's tiger, Jasper, ensconced himself in the kitchen and held Anna spellbound with his tales of the army and Vienna.

He viewed with equanimity little Miss Sophie's presence in the kitchen. She was as good as ever twanged, she was and asked as many questions about his foreign travels and army days as what Mistress Anna did. He noted sapiently that she never asked about the master, but if he happened to enlarge on the more respectable exploits of his noble employer she listened with great attention. A shame and a pity it was that his lordship seemed not to have noticed what a good 'un Miss Sophie was, but had settled with that Lady Lucinda.

The new closed stove was installed with the maximum of

confusion and upheaval, but afterwards Anna was like a child with a new toy, hardly daring to cook on it lest its gleaming newness should be sullied.

'Never seen nothin' like it, Miss Sophie, Miss Thea, not in all me days. Why, the fuel it saves on! An' when you think it was his lordship's wood we was buying—well, I can't see where 'is profit's comin' from!'

It occurred to Sophie briefly that perhaps his lordship was trying to ingratiate himself, but it didn't match her knowledge of him. He was not the sort to entice a woman with anything except himself. *He wouldn't have to.*

The rain finally stopped the day before Kit was due to go riding with Fanny and Jasper. He was in tearing spirits all morning, barely able to concentrate on his lessons until Thea had the bright idea of practising French conversation and picked the subject of horses and riding.

'I was surprised at how much he knew, dear,' she confided to Sophie later. 'It just goes to show! He really did very well.'

'Aunt Sophie,' said Kit suddenly over his apple dumpling, 'Why don't you come with us this afternoon? You could ride Megs. She needs exercise. Jasper says she is as fat as butter!'

'Ride Megs?' Sophie laughed. 'She hasn't been ridden for ages. She'd have me off in no time.' Megs was notorious for her dislike of being ridden.

'Oh, do come,' he urged. 'If she is too awful, you could swap with Jasper. He wouldn't mind. He said last week he didn't know why you didn't come.'

Sophie was sorely tempted. She had given up riding the little cob because it seemed so unfair to ride her when Kit could not. In fact, before Helford's offer she had been seriously considering selling her and buying something Kit could handle despite her fondness for the lively little mare.

But buying a horse was such a risky business. Unless you really knew what you were doing it was so easy to be cheated. She had turned her back very firmly on the insidious suggestion that she might ask Lord Helford for advice.

There seemed no reason not to go. Helford would not be coming. She could go out with the children and enjoy herself. But not on Jasper's mount. Nothing would induce her to ride one of Helford's horses. If Megs got rid of her, that would be her bad luck.

Kit watched her breathlessly. She was thinking about it! He could tell by the way she rubbed her nose. Aunt Sophie always did that when she was undecided. 'Please?' he said in tones that would have moved a sterner guardian than Sophie.

'Very well, Kit,' she said, smiling, unable to resist his obvious desire for her to share the treat. 'I'll come, but I'll expect you to rub arnica into my bruises later on.'

'Hurray!' yelled Kit. He bolted the remains of his dumpling and leapt up from the table. 'I'll ask Grigson to get her ready!'

The sound of his flying feet dwindled into the distance.

Thea looked at Sophie. 'Do you really think you should, dear? I mean, if Megs is too lively for you...'

With a wry smile Sophie said, 'I have no doubt at all that I will return with a muddied habit, but the ground is so wet after all this rain that I am more likely to drown than break anything.'

She was not quite so sure when Jasper and Fanny arrived and the little dappled mare was brought around from the stables. Megs had not been out at all for several days and had not been ridden for months. The unaccustomed saddle was obviously annoying her and she was in what might have been charitably described as a fidget, with her nervously flickering ears and rolling eyes.

'Goin' ter join us, are ye, Miss Sophie?' asked Jasper with

obvious pleasure. He ran an expert eye over the restless cob. Too much for a lady. 'Better swap saddles, Miss Sophie. I'll ride the mare an' you have old Ben. He's a nice ride.'

'Certainly not, Jasper,' said Sophie firmly. 'If Megs is too resty it's my fault for not keeping her exercised.' She was damned if she'd let Helford have the mounting of her. In any way!

He shook his head, 'Master won't half kill me if'n you gets hurt...'

'Are you going to put me up or not?' asked Sophie crossly. 'Megs will settle once we get moving.' How dare he suggest that Lord Helford had anything to say to which horse she rode!

Jasper bowed to the inevitable and put her up. He had to own that she handled the cob well. Kept a short rein on her and never gave her the least chance to get her head down and buck. And them short-backed cobs could really put you down if they got half a chance. He'd like to see that Lady Lucinda manage as well. Looked good on a well-bred, mannered horse but he'd lay she'd be in trouble on this 'un. Lor', she'd be off so fast it 'ud make yer head spin. That is, if she had the gumption to get on at all!

They set off across the fields towards the river and had a wonderful ride. Megs, after her initial carry on, was so pleased to be out of her stable that she seemed to overlook the shameful circumstance of having a rider and behaved herself so well, only fidgeting with the bit and plunging very occasionally, that Sophie was moved to comment.

'Megs must be getting old. I thought she'd have me off in the mud by now.'

Jasper snorted his disapproval. 'I'd say she's a proper varmint, Miss Sophie! An' if the master could see us he'd have me hide! Still, you handles her proper, I'll say that fer ye.'

They had just turned for home when a series of hunting

cries from the other side of a tall hedge told them that they were about to have company. Jasper pulled up at once. He knew one of those voices at least.

One after the other, half a dozen horses came sailing over the hedge. Most of the riders would have galloped on but one, on a familiar chestnut mare, seeing the little group, pulled up.

Helford was delighted to see his niece and Kit. He had half suggested that they might join his riding party, but Lady Lucinda had been quite taken aback at the idea. She had seemed to think that it would be far too much for the children. They could all ride back together now, that would be quite unexceptionable. Their horses were tired after a long ride. Jasper could escort Kit home and…and *Sophie*!

He had spent the last week trying not to think about Sophie Marsden. Trying to ignore the voice in his brain which whispered her name incessantly. Trying to convince himself that what he felt for her was just a passing fancy and would die as swiftly as it had been born. For a moment he was tempted merely to greet them and then ride on, but his party had followed him over and Kate Asterfield was speaking.

'Hullo, Fanny. Are you going to ride back with us? Do introduce your friends.'

And Fanny was doing the honours, 'Aunt Sophie, this is Mrs Asterfield and Mr Asterfield and Lord Mark Reynolds and Captain Hampton and this is Lady Lucinda Anstey.' She paused for breath. 'And this is Miss Marsden and her nephew Kit Carlisle and Uncle David's tiger, Jasper.'

She looked at Helford a little nervously. 'Did I get that right, Uncle David?'

'Perfectly right, sweetheart. But you didn't need to introduce Jasper. They already know him.' Helford's friends had all managed to keep straight faces at being introduced to his tiger as their social equal. In all conscience he could do no less, even if Lady Lucinda was looking daggers at the child, whether in fury at being introduced to Jasper or being left until last he wasn't sure.

Ned Asterfield was saying, 'Well, we do, of course, but I can't recall that you ever introduced him so politely. Delighted to make your acquaintance at last, Jasper. And yours, Miss Marsden.' He eyed her with an unmistakable approval, which made David's hackles rise. 'I call it most unkind that you four didn't join us this afternoon, don't you, Tom?'

'Very shabby indeed,' said Captain Hampton, smiling at Sophie and Kit. Sophie warmed to him at once. He had a kind face, not precisely handsome, but pleasant and distinguished by smiling grey eyes. He looked more closely at Sophie with a little frown. 'Have we ever met, Miss Marsden? Your face is familiar, but I don't recall your name... Wait! Did not Fanny say this was Kit Carlisle?'

'Yes, sir,' said Sophie quietly. 'If you find my face familiar, then I think that you must have been acquainted with my brother-in-law, Major Carlisle, and met Kit's mother, my sister Emma. We were very alike.' Megs began to sidle and toss her head restlessly, impatient at the delay in returning to her comfortable stall. Sophie soothed her with a gentle hand and murmur.

'Of course! Jock's wife.' Captain Hampton slapped his thigh. 'And this is their son! How amazing to meet you like this.' He rode up to Kit and leant down from his saddle. 'Kit, I am delighted to meet you. Your father was a very close friend of mine and I am proud to meet his son. And how is your mama?'

Kit held his head up proudly and said very steadily, 'I am sorry, Captain, but my...my mother died last year. Aunt Sophie looks after me now.'

Hampton grimaced. 'I'm sorry to hear that. She was a lovely person. Please accept my condolences.' He turned to

Sophie. 'So you have him in ward. Surely Strathallen has made some provision, though, in the circumstances.'

David held his breath, but it seemed that Sophie saved her temper for his benefit. To do her justice, Hampton had touched upon the subject far more tactfully than he had.

'Lord Strathallen,' she said calmly, 'has never shown the least interest in Kit's existence. I believe my sister wrote to him and informed him of her husband's death and that they had a child, but he never replied. He did not approve of the marriage.'

'I see,' said Captain Hampton slowly. He looked as though he would have said more, but then exclaimed, 'Well, this is indeed a coincidence. I shall look forward to meeting you again, Miss Marsden. Perhaps you would permit me to ride over one day to call upon you?'

Sophie smiled and said, 'I would be happy to welcome any friend of Jock and Emma's. Lord Helford can direct you to Willowbank House.' Again she steadied Megs, who was beginning to pull at the bit in an attempt to get her head down. Firmly Sophie brought it up again, wondering if she could politely go before the mare really got annoyed. Stopping for any length of time with Megs under saddle was always risky. Besides, she was beginning to feel decidedly nervous about Helford, whose glittering green gaze was boring into her in a very uncomfortable way.

'I'll do better than that,' said David, by no means sure he liked the way Sophie had smiled up at Hampton and aware that he was being ridiculous. All the more so since he had decided to ignore his own inclinations. 'We'll escort you and Kit home now and Fanny and Jasper can ride back with us. It is only a couple of miles further. If that is agreeable to everyone?' He glanced around questioningly, not really expecting anyone to mind.

That was quite enough for Lady Lucinda. How dare Helford suggest that they should go out of their way to escort a shabby, little provincial nobody mounted on a badly mannered farmer's cob? It was beyond anything. And the effrontery of announcing that Helford could direct anyone to her house! Besides which, she did not at all like the way Helford looked at the creature. There was something most unbecoming in such warmth.

'I must confess I am really rather weary and would much prefer to ride straight back, Helford,' said Lady Lucinda in the fragile tone of one who holds herself in the saddle by will power alone.

David looked his amazement. Only moments before she had been challenging them all to jump the last hedge. Good manners forbade him to say anything and he was about to agree to escort her home when Kate Asterfield spoke up.

'I'm a little weary too, Helford. If Miss Marsden will assure me that she does not believe me to be cutting her acquaintance, then I will accompany Lucinda and the rest of you may extend your ride as much as you like.' This was said with a convincing sweetness and gave no hint of the annoyance she felt. *Little cat! Of all the snobbish, ill-bred things to do! If Helford marries Lucinda I wash my hands of him. Ned can visit by himself!*

'Oh, but we should never find our way!' protested Lucinda. Kate Asterfield, she thought, was in need of a good set-down. The only problem was that giving Kate a set-down had a nasty tendency to backfire. As when her mama had commented on the flightiness of so many of the younger matrons and Kate had smiled in that *insincere* way, agreeing that her grandmama had said just the same only the other day.

'If I might make so bold, me lord,' said Jasper. 'If'n you and the other gentlemen is to escort Miss Sophie an' Miss Fanny, there baint no need fer me to come along of ye. I dessay I kin guide the ladies back safe.'

Before Lady Lucinda could open her mouth, Kate had

said, 'Heavens! What an honour for us. Helford's tiger to escort two lowly females, neither of whom is a Melville. Come, Lucinda, not even my grandmama could accuse us of impropriety with that escort.'

Helford had the oddest feeling that something he didn't understand was going on here. Kate was looking as though butter wouldn't melt in her mouth, almost as big a danger signal as that peculiar smile Great Aunt Maria had been wearing recently. Lucinda, on the other hand, was glaring at her, the blue eyes hard as ice and a decidedly pinched look about her mouth.

Very embarrassed, Sophie said rather more sharply than she intended, 'There is not the least need for anyone to escort us. If Fanny is to ride back with you, Helford, I am sure that Kit and I will find our way home.'

It was plain to her that Lady Lucinda considered a little dab of a country nobody far beneath her exalted touch. As for Sophie, she wished Helford joy of his courting. She felt an ache inside at the sight of Helford's chosen bride. Lady Lucinda was the most beautiful girl she had ever seen and only a ninnyhammer would continue to indulge dreams which left her weeping on her pillow each night.

Little fool! Why would he look twice at you when he has her?

Something of her irritation must have communicated itself to Megs, who suddenly flung her head up and down in annoyance. Sophie was quick to get her head up again and shorten the rein before the mare could give more than a token buck.

'Jasper!' said David sharply. 'What the devil do you mean by letting Miss Sophie out on this little varmint? Why did you not swap mounts?'

His tiger did not get a chance to reply. Sophie said rather breathlessly as Megs swished her tail and lashed out, 'Jasper offered and I refused. I am perfectly capable of managing

Megs, thank you, Helford! And now it is time Kit and I were getting along. Good day! It was so nice to meet you all. Captain Hampton, Kit and I will be glad to welcome you if you care to visit us.'

'You are not riding back alone on that mare,' said David firmly. 'I at least will come with you.' He felt suddenly nervous at the thought of Sophie riding the flighty mare with only Kit for escort. Anything might happen! He told himself glibly that his concern arose not for personal reasons, but from motives of the most disinterested chivalry. *And since when has disinterested chivalry had anything to say to your dealings with any woman?*

Lady Lucinda bridled angrily, but was careful not to show it. What was Miss Marsden to Helford that he should be so concerned about her safety and offer to mount her? If she could not handle her own cob, then she was certainly not fit to ride one of Helford's well-bred horses. And how dare she give such an intemperate reply to a lord of the realm! Especially after such a forward invitation to Captain Hampton! Brazen little hussy! Obviously her mama's dictum that she must turn a blind eye to his lordship's vagaries held force before as well as after marriage.

Observing her, Kate Asterfield was moved to murmur to Lord Mark that a little temper did wonders for dear Lucinda's looks, did it not? Beautiful, of course—but ever so slightly…inanimate? Lord Mark's imperfectly concealed choke of laughter earned him a chilly blue stare. He straightened his face at once and informed Kate in a pithy undertone that she was born to be strangled, and the sooner Ned attended to it the better.

'Oh, well, then,' said Lady Lucinda, 'let us all go. I am sure I would not care to go home early if you are all set on a longer ride.' She brought her horse up beside Megs and addressed Sophie directly for the first time. 'I vow you are a famous horsewoman. Myself, I prefer a *well-bred* horse to give me a comfortable ride. My papa, Lord Stanford, you know, is always so careful to choose for me.'

Sophie met the faintly patronising blue eyes and replied, 'How very fortunate you are. As a parson and the son of a bishop, mine was always more concerned with selecting an appropriate psalm for me to memorise.'

Lady Lucinda's blue eyes widened. Outrageous! The little hussy had actually dared to imply that the Earl of Stanford was not as good a father as some provincial clergyman! And daring to claim a connection with her betters! A bishop, indeed!

Captain Hampton, riding on the other side of Sophie, chuckled. 'Did he? So, too, did mine, although he wasn't a parson. Tell me, Miss Marsden, when did your sister die? I meant to keep in touch after Jock's death, but with one thing and another I lost track of her and the boy.'

Captain Hampton was being sadly taken in by her airs, thought Lady Lucinda scornfully. She looked Sophie over coolly, noting the well-worn habit and unfashionable hat. No pretensions to beauty either. The nose was decidedly unpatrician. And such dull brown hair! It was curly enough, no doubt owing more to art than nature, but brown! And as for her eyes! Well, if you could decide what colour *they* were, you would be doing better than most. No doubt those preposterous lashes and brows were darkened. Altogether Lady Lucinda could not understand why Helford or any other gentleman should take the slightest interest in this bumptious little provincial.

She dropped back slightly to ride with Helford and was annoyed to see him move up beside Miss Marsden. But before she could push forward to ride on his other side Lord Mark, deserted by Kate, brought his mare up and said, 'Do you care for another gallop, Lady Lucinda? Asterfield and I are going to have one. Do join us.'

'Why, certainly, Lord Mark,' agreed Lady Lucinda and

then, as an idea occurred to her, 'Do go on. I shall have to adjust my stirrup.' She bent down and reached under her flowing velvet skirts to fiddle with the leather. 'I will catch you up directly.'

'Can I assist you?' asked Lord Mark politely.

'No, no. *I* am well able to manage for myself,' said the lady, continuing to fiddle. Lord Mark nodded and cantered off to join Asterfield.

Lady Lucinda cast a quick glance around. Kate Asterfield, who obviously had a taste for low company, was actually riding slightly ahead with the groom. How *could* she, thought Lady Lucinda with a slight shudder.

No one was watching. Still bent over, she put a hand to her hat and drew out a hat pin. Captain Hampton had ridden forward to catch some comment thrown him by Kate. Lady Lucinda saw her chance and spurred her mount as she straightened up. Drawing level with the little cob's hind-quarters, she reached over to jab her hard in the rump and quickly swung her own mount out of the way, dropping the pin as she did so.

Chapter Eight

Megs went absolutely mad. With an outraged squeal she leapt forward, got the bit between her teeth, flung her head down and began to buck. Taken completely by surprise, Sophie tried in vain to get the mare's head back up.

'Sophie! Look out!' cried David in horror as he watched helplessly. Swearing, he forced his mare up beside the cob in an attempt to grab her bridle. He was not in time. Sophie had sat the first few bucks firmly, but Megs had taken quite enough for one afternoon. On the sixth buck she gave a peculiarly malicious twist which unseated her rider.

Sophie went straight over her head, landing on her bottom with an audible thump and then lying motionless on the wet grass. Having achieved her goal, Megs took off across the meadow, still bucking and plunging.

David's cry of alarm was almost drowned by the scream of childish terror from Kit who had been trailing behind with Fanny. White with fear, he flung himself from his pony and ran to Sophie. David was already beside her, feeling for a pulse in her wrist. He looked up at the boy and his heart lurched at what he could see in the blanched face and those great hazel eyes. This, then, was what it meant to love someone!

'Aunt Sophie! No!' Kit's voice was shaking and small trembling hands groped for the wrist Helford wasn't holding. Not Aunt Sophie! She couldn't be! God couldn't be so cruel! It was because he had wanted God to take her instead of Mama. God was telling him how wicked he had been to think such a thing.

Under David's suddenly nerveless fingers a pulse beat strongly. 'Thank God!' he whispered huskily. Kit's eyes flew to his face, hope flaring. I have never cared like that about anyone, thought David, as he saw the tears on the boy's cheeks. The thought hit him like a body blow that he did now. He cared about Sophie Marsden in a way he had never even imagined and it was the most frightening thing he had ever known.

He reached over and ruffled the boy's curls, wishing he dared caress those other curls which were now very muddy.

'Just stunned, I think, Kit. All the wind knocked out of her too, I shouldn't wonder.' His voice cracked slightly and Kit stared at him. He nodded. 'Oh, yes. I thought the same as you. My heart nearly stopped!'

He began to pat Sophie's cheeks gently, trying not to think about how soft her skin was. A movement at his elbow made him look up.

Tom Hampton was holding out a silver flask. 'Never move without it, dear boy. Not since the night I got caught out in the rain with a lame horse ten miles from anywhere. Take it and welcome.' David took the flask in a shaking hand and tried to avoid Tom's puzzled eyes.

He could almost hear Tom thinking, wondering what had got into him to be so upset over a fall. She was all right, just stunned, her eyes would open in a moment…so why was he still feeling as though his stomach had parted company with him? As though the whole world had tilted under him, leaving him dizzy and…frightened.

Conscious of Tom's steady gaze, he looked up and said, 'Thank you…I…think she's just winded…I…I…'

His voice trailed off under the dawning comprehension in Hampton's clear grey eyes. The startled disbelief. He reached for control. He didn't want this!

The rest of the party had come up. 'Tom, what happened?' asked Kate.

'Don't know,' said Hampton slowly. 'That little cob went absolutely berserk. Miss Marsden did well to stay on as long as she did. I think she's just stunned.'

Kate went on in a low voice, 'From the look on David's and the boy's faces, I should say they expected the worst.'

'Surely there is no need for dramatics over a paltry tumble,' said Lady Lucinda in rather bored accents. 'Although I do quite see now why Helford felt she should be escorted home. Why, that bad-mannered animal nearly kicked my poor Rufus!'

Kate did not waste subtlety on her this time. 'Lucinda,' she said quietly. 'Hold your tongue.'

At this point Sophie opened her eyes to find Helford and Kit bent over her, the latter with tears on his cheeks.

She smiled up at him. 'Gudgeon! I told you Megs would have me in the mud!'

'It's my fault!' said Kit pitifully. 'Because I was so angry with God!'

Sophie cut him off. 'Fustian! I should have kept a shorter rein on her.'

'Can you sit up, Sophie?' asked David gently, without realising that he had used her Christian name, so used was he to thinking of her that way. 'The ground is very wet. You shouldn't lie here too long. Come. Drink some of Tom's brandy and we'll take you home.'

She blinked at the tender note in his voice and the merest suspicion of unsteadiness in the deep tones. Why should Helford be so upset? Surely, surely he didn't care for her?

And he had called her Sophie, something he had never done before.

While she was still puzzling over his behaviour, Helford slid an arm under her shoulders to support her as she tried to get up but she cried out as pain shot through her. 'My back!'

Suddenly terrified again, David lowered her to the ground, unable to meet Kit's eyes.

'Wiggle your feet!' he commanded harshly. She did so. 'Thank God!'

Ned Asterfield said diffidently, 'Not an expert, of course, Helford, but did you happen to see where she landed?'

David looked at him in withering scorn. 'Right here, of course, you cod's-head!'

'Not what I meant at all, old chap. Which bit of herself did she land on?' explained Ned patiently.

'Oh.' David thought hard. He was so shaken he couldn't think straight.

Fanny answered for him. 'On her bottom, Uncle David. I saw everything!' She cast a fuming glance at Lady Lucinda as she said this. She was sure she had seen her hit Megs as she passed. Not quite sure enough to accuse, but sure none the less. She couldn't understand. Surely grown-ups didn't do mean spiteful things like that?

'Did she, now?' Asterfield nodded. 'Then I should say she's jarred up all the muscles in her back.' He got down and removed his coat. 'Excuse me, young man.' Kit made way reluctantly. 'Lift her up again, David.' He did so and Asterfield put the coat under her. 'Right. Turn her over. Going to feel your back, Miss Marsden. You tell me if it hurts anywhere I touch.'

David watched in mounting possessiveness as Ned's hands moved firmly over Sophie's body. *Don't be a fool! He's only doing what a doctor would do!* He gritted his teeth and clenched his fists in the effort not to strangle his well-meaning friend who was taking such unpardonable liberties with a woman he considered *his* and his alone!

What a fuss about nothing, thought Lady Lucinda scornfully. She might have known the girl would make a to-do over it. Hurt back, indeed! And Ned Asterfield as foolish as Helford!

'Hurt there?' Ned was speaking.

'No.'

'Here?'

'No.'

'Here?'

'No.'

'You can start breathing again, David. Like I said, jarred all the muscles. Did it myself once. Miss Marsden, you'll be stiff and sore for a while. Stay lying down rather than sitting and move around as much as you can without tiring your back muscles. If you must sit, put a cushion behind your back to support it. Er…no riding that cob for a few weeks. You see that she don't, young Kit!' He cuffed the boy's head lightly.

'Not at all!' David struck in. He lifted her carefully to a sitting position.

'Me lord?'

'Yes, Jasper?'

'I've caught the mare—which horse should I put her saddle on? Should be gettin' Miss Sophie home now an' the mare's mighty upset.'

David nodded but said, 'She's not riding. At least not alone. I'll take her up before me on…Ben…isn't it? He's quiet enough.'

Completely ignoring Sophie's protests, he forced her to drink some of the brandy before carrying her to the horse. She was lifted up by Asterfield and Captain Hampton and found herself nestled in Helford's arms, leaning in a position of appalling intimacy against his chest. She tried to sit up straight, but the throbbing ache in her back defeated her; anyway, the brandy that Helford had poured into her so liberally was creating a delicious feeling of warmth and lassitude.

Helford said gently, 'Lean on me, my dear. We'll have you home directly.'

Tears stung her eyes at the unconscious endearment uttered so softly in her ear. How lovely it would be if he truly cared for her and were not just being kind because she had so foolishly allowed Megs to get away from her. She could feel the hardness of his powerful chest under her cheek, the easy strength of his arms as they held her there. His big frame was a strangely tender cradle for her aching body. She had never felt so safe or cosseted in all her life.

The little group set off at a walk, chatting soberly.

To take her mind off the agreeable sensation of being held in such a tender embrace Sophie smiled down at Kit, who was riding as close to them as he could.

''I'll be all right, Kit. Why don't you and Fanny ride on ahead and ask Anna to draw a bath for me? That will help the stiffness.'

Kit nodded, his voice still too wobbly to use, and looked around. Where was Fanny?

She was off her pony looking at something on the ground.

He trotted back to her and jumped off. 'What are you doing? Hurry up, we have to get Aunt Sophie home!' he said impatiently.

Fanny looked up at him and asked, 'This is where Aunt Sophie fell off, isn't it?'

'Pretty much. Come *on!*' Kit could hardly bear to see the torn-up ground where Megs had bucked.

'Well, look at this!' Fanny held up a long shiny hat pin. 'That Lady Lucinda went past Aunt Sophie just before Megs started bucking. I thought she might have hit her, but maybe…maybe it was this!'

Kit stared in disbelief. 'Why should she do that? Aunt Sophie might have been killed! Are you sure? Why didn't you *say* something?'

'Because I *wasn't* sure!' Fanny flashed at him. 'And Lady Lucinda doesn't like me. If Uncle David marries her it's going to be simply horrid! I'm sure she means to pack me off to school!' She pushed the hat pin into her own hat and said, 'Help me mount, please, Kit.'

Kit was astounded. 'Lord Helford's going to marry her? Why would he want to do a bacon-brained thing like that?' He jumped down and made a stirrup for her with his hands.

'For an heir,' explained Fanny as she vaulted into the saddle. 'I heard the servants talking about it. None of them like her either!'

Kit remounted. 'Then why on earth would Helford bother marrying her? If no one likes her, it's silly!' Kit could not imagine why any sensible chap would want to marry anyone. Except Aunt Sophie, perhaps, or Thea if she wasn't so old. They didn't nag at a fellow. If you stepped out of line they told you and made sure you stepped back in and there was an end of it. And they didn't make spiteful, cattish remarks at other people. Like that Lady Lucinda did to Aunt Sophie.

'Come on,' he said. 'We'd better hurry. Aunt Sophie asked us to ride on and have Anna get a bath ready.'

They pushed their ponies to a canter, quickly catching and passing the other riders. Kit was thinking furiously. He'd sneak out later to look at Megs's quarters, and if Fanny was right then he'd pay Lady Lucinda out if it was the last thing he ever did. He ground his teeth in rage. How could anyone do such a beastly thing?

Helford watched them go. Kit's face was bleak as the pair raced by them. A nasty shock for the lad, thought Helford, unconsciously tightening his hold on Sophie. He knew exactly how Kit had felt. Never had he felt so helpless in his life, always excepting the afternoon he had met the wretched chit and nearly run her down. His heart was still pounding at the memory. At least he hoped that was the cause.

Gradually, however, he could no longer ignore the fact that his heart was not just pounding because of Sophie's fall. His body was becoming increasingly aware of the glorious sensation of holding Sophie nestled trustingly in his arms. The temptation to rest his cheek, even briefly, against the soft, disordered curls was almost irresistible. His arm about her slender waist longed to hold her in a more intimate embrace, feeling the texture of her skin, not just her shape. Somehow he knew she would be silky smooth, pliant… Oh, God! Yielding! *Stop thinking about it!*

Riding was nigh on unbearable, the pain of his arousal like nothing he had ever experienced. *Think about something else!* He spared a glance for Jasper leading Megs who, if her flattened ears and switching tail were anything to go by, was still upset. What the devil could have set her off like that? He forced himself to consider it. Despite his own reservations about Sophie riding a horse that tricky, he had to admit that she had been handling the mare with great skill. He had been taken by surprise just as much as Sophie when the mare started bucking.

Hampton came up alongside. He cast a knowledgeable glance at Helford, noting that he appeared to be in almost as much pain as his fair burden. Most interesting! He would have a little chat with Kate Asterfield in the near future.

'How are you, Miss Marsden?' He smiled at her kindly. White as a sheet, poor child, he thought.

'A bit sore,' she admitted, understating the matter very substantially. *But terrifyingly comfortable apart from that. Stop it! It's just the brandy! Now you know why Papa disapproved of spirits!*

'Never mind,' he said comfortingly. 'Funny how the mare went off like that. Has she ever done it before?'

'Not like that,' said Sophie, who had been puzzling over it as she lay in Helford's arms. 'I mean, she does buck from time to time. She doesn't really like being ridden. We keep her to draw the gig. But I've never known her to go off like that without a bit of warning. I hope she isn't going to make a habit of it.'

'You don't mean to say you'll ride her again?' This from Kate Asterfield, who had ridden up.

'Like hell she will!' growled David and felt Sophie stiffen in his arms. The thought of Sophie riding the mare again sent extremely unpleasant sensations shooting through his entrails.

'Since she is the only horse I possess, naturally I will ride her again,' she said defensively. 'Something must have alarmed her. Maybe a bee stung her or…or something. Anyway, it is quite my own affair.'

'The devil it is!' exploded David, before he could stop himself. His arms tightened visibly around her, protective, possessive.

Oh, bloody hell! He saw Kate's eyes flicker to Lady Lucinda, riding a few yards away with Lord Mark. Outwardly she appeared to be engrossed in conversation, but she would have to be deaf not to have heard his outburst. Would everyone know what a fool he was making of himself by the time he got Sophie home? First Tom, and now Kate Asterfield and his intended bride?

He went on quietly. 'Sophie, I mean, Miss Marsden, if you could have seen Kit's face! He thought you had been killed for a moment.' *As I did!* 'Think of what the boy will suffer every time you mount that mare.'

Sophie was silent. He was right, of course, but she couldn't bring herself to condemn Megs out of hand. After all, she had never behaved quite that badly before.

Hampton added his mite. 'You must consider that you know, Miss Marsden. Helford does not mean to sound dictatorial. It is just a bad habit that he has picked up some-where!'

Sophie had to stifle a giggle, despite the pain in her back.

Helford was speaking again. 'Will you at least agree to a swap? Send her over to Helford Place for a while and let Jasper exercise her. See if she does anything like it again. I will lend you a pony to draw the gig. There will be no obligation.' He knew what she was thinking, that people would talk, draw conclusions. 'If you were to call on Great Aunt Maria every so often I think that might silence any wagging tongues. And she would enjoy it.' *As I would.*

'I should accept, my dear,' said Kate quietly. 'There can be no objection to you swapping horses with Helford for such a reason and, if Megs turns out to be too unreliable, then I dare say Helford can put you in the way of replacing her without being cheated.'

David shot her a look of heartfelt gratitude and she smiled slightly before turning to Lady Lucinda. 'What do you think, Lucinda? I should merely think that Helford was being a good neighbour, but of course there is no telling what the minds of the vulgar will invent.'

Lady Lucinda froze. Was Kate Asterfield actually daring to insinuate that *she*, an *Anstey*, could be classed as vulgar? Somehow she managed to bite back the very unladylike response which rose to her tongue and said merely, 'Oh, it is his own business after all. Myself, I should have the horrid brute shot out of hand. I dare say it will come to that in the end.' *After all, the animal must be a dreadful commoner to behave like that over a little prick.*

'No, it won't!' said Sophie fiercely, firing up in defence of Megs. 'If Helford considers her unsafe to ride, then I shall take his advice and not ride her. She is always perfectly well behaved in harness so there is no need to have her destroyed.'

'Then I am satisfied,' said David equably, determinedly

ignoring Lady Lucinda's uncharitable remarks. It struck him for the first time that Lucinda's high degree did not necessarily render her an agreeable companion. 'She would not be the first horse to be perfectly reliable in harness and useless as a saddle horse. Would she, Hampton?'

'Hardly!' answered Hampton with an unholy grin. 'When, I should like to know, was the last time anyone put a leg across your chestnuts?'

'Silence, Rattle!' Kate admonished him in mock severity. 'You blaspheme. A leg across Helford's chestnuts, indeed! Why, the mere thought is sacrilege, is it not, Helford?'

'Something very like it.' Helford's deep chuckle rumbled in his chest, sending some very peculiar sensations rippling through Sophie's belly.

'What's that?' asked Ned Asterfield, who had not really been paying attention for several minutes. 'Ride Helford's chestnuts? I wouldn't do that, Kate! Probably react like the cob!' He went on cheerfully, 'Tell you what, Miss Marsden! You swap horses with Helford for a few weeks. Let one of his lads ride your mare. See how she goes. Helford's got more horses than he knows what to do with anyway. He can very well spare one until your mare is sorted out.'

'What an excellent idea, Ned.' Helford's voice was very dry. 'Where would we be without you?'

'Where, indeed?' asked Ned's undutiful wife. 'You great oaf! We decided that ages ago!'

Sophie gave a choke of laughter. It seemed she had little choice. Everyone was taking it for granted that Helford should lend her a horse and undertake to vet Megs for her. The notion of someone taking care of her for a change was immensely appealing. You'd better enjoy it while you can, she thought sadly. Lady Lucinda was simply beautiful with those gleaming curls and sapphire blue eyes. So tall and elegant, too. Why should Helford, who could doubtless have his choice of brides, look twice at a poor little dab of a girl with dull brown hair and eyes which even their owner stigmatised as muddy? *Stop dreaming and get on with your life. You are intended for a spinster aunt, not a wife and mother.*

Helford glanced down at the brown curls resting against his chest. The little spurt of suppressed laughter gave him a dizzying sense of intimacy. He had a vision, instantly throttled, of those curls resting against his naked shoulder and spreading over his arm, of running his fingers through them and…his overactive imagination had no trouble filling in the rest of the scene.

Looking around for someone to speak to and distract his thoughts, his eyes met Lucinda Anstey's hard blue gaze. A faintly supercilious smile curved her rather thin lips.

'Poor Helford,' she said sweetly. 'Your chivalrous nature must be such a burden to you.'

Kate Asterfield squashed her at once without compunction. 'Dear Lucinda, has no one told you yet that men like to feel chivalrous! It panders to all their baser instincts! And since earlier heroes have accounted for all the dragons, Helford will have to content himself with reforming Miss Marsden's mare for her. A far less dangerous proceeding, especially since Jasper will undertake it.'

'Quite so, Lady Lucinda,' said Helford with another grateful look at Kate. 'At the moment I am feeling a veritable Sir Galahad.' He reflected ruefully that if the legendary Sir Galahad had ever felt like this, then he had been sadly misinformed.

By the time they reached Willowbank House and Sophie had been carried upstairs to her bedchamber by Helford, he was in such a state of frustrated desire that he could barely speak without gritting his teeth. The worst of it was that he was quite certain Tom Hampton had a very fair idea of what he was going through. Not that he would say anything. But that quizzing look was the outside of enough.

Having deposited Sophie on her bed in the fussing care

of Thea Andrews and Anna, David gave an inward groan of relief. Never again, he thought. There was a limit to what he could be expected to endure and he had definitely reached it. In future he would avoid Sophie Marsden. For both their sakes.

All he said was, 'I'll leave you in safe hands, Miss Marsden.' *Safer than mine at all events.* 'I'll send another horse over with Jasper and Fanny on Monday. Goodbye. We won't stay now. It is time I got the others home.'

Sophie looked up him gratefully. 'Thank you, my lord. I…I hope this has not caused you any…well…trouble. I think some of your party were a little put out. I…I should not like to be the cause of any unhappiness.' Even if she did dislike Lady Lucinda exceedingly, the girl was apparently as good as betrothed to Helford and could not be expected to like him paying attention to another woman.

Perfectly aware of what she meant, David said firmly, 'You need not concern yourself in the slightest. The only thing of any consequence is that you rest quietly as Ned recommended. Goodbye.'

He left very quickly, consumed by the knowledge that he had indeed fallen in love with Sophie Marsden. Had done the very thing he had sworn he would never do. He could almost be glad he was practically honour bound to offer for Lucinda Anstey. If he didn't have to offer for her, he would be in serious danger of committing the crowning folly of offering for Soph—Damn it! Miss Marsden!

He groaned inwardly as he went back downstairs to find his guests awaiting him in the parlour. They were chatting quietly amongst themselves, except for Lucinda, who was wandering about the room, casting a disparaging eye over everything.

'So quaint,' she was saying to Lord Mark as she glanced at the harpsichord. 'I had not thought anyone still possessed such a thing!'

David clenched his teeth. Despite his growing distaste for the idea, he had better offer for Lucinda as fast as possible. In that way he could escape the worst consequences of his idiocy. Being shackled to a woman who could, if she ever so wished, deal him an even crueller lesson than the one Felicity had so generously taught him.

'Is everyone ready?' he asked abruptly. 'Miss Marsden is in safe hands now. We should be going.' Before he was tempted to rush back upstairs and beg her to resign herself to his hands. Before he offered his own heart again for a woman to break.

Chapter Nine

By the following Monday Sophie was feeling a great deal better. Her back still ached like the devil if she tried to do too much and, as Ned Asterfield had predicted, she was more comfortable standing or lying down than sitting, but it had improved. Kit had been rather subdued for a couple of days, but he seemed to have recovered his spirits and had even protested at the idea of selling Megs.

'Sell Megs? But, Aunt Sophie, she's never done that before! At least not like that.' His face was flushed and earnest. 'I'm sure she won't do it again. Please don't sell her!'

Sophie was startled. 'Lord Helford has offered to have Jasper ride her for a few weeks and lend us another horse. If Jasper thinks she is safe, then I shall keep her.'

'She *is* safe!' said Kit.

The discussion was dropped and when Fanny arrived on the Monday she was immediately dragged out to the stables after barely being permitted to greet Sophie and thrust a note into her hand, telling her it was from Lady Maria.

Captain Hampton, who had brought her over in Helford's curricle, laughed as the two children disappeared. 'Some mischief they are brewing! Fanny is up to something, if you ask me. She barely spoke two words on the way over and

I thought myself quite a friend of hers. God alone knows what it is and I can only be grateful that I have not been admitted to His confidence. The thought of being implicated in any plot of Fanny's hatching fills me with dread.'

He sat down by the sofa where Sophie was resting. 'How is your back, Miss Marsden? And I should mention that I brought a pony over behind the curricle. Helford insisted. We are to take Megs back with us.'

'Oh, dear. Very well,' she said, putting Lady Maria's letter down unread on the little sewing table beside her. 'It is very kind of you all. I cannot think why you and the Asterfields should have been so concerned. Or…or Helford for that matter,' she went on, flushing slightly.

'No, well, it was only sensible,' said Hampton dismissively. Not for worlds would he have informed Miss Marsden that he and the Asterfields were desperately hoping that Helford could be brought to his senses in time to realise that just because he'd suffered one disappointment in youth, did not mean he had to condemn himself to a loveless match if something better offered.

'Is it?' she asked with a smile. 'I think it is very kind indeed and especially kind of you to come all this way to ask after my back, which is much improved.'

'Not at all,' he said. 'As a matter of fact, there was something I wished to say to you. About Kit.'

'About Kit?' she echoed. 'What do you mean?'

He was silent for a moment. 'How much did you know about Jock's family?'

'Very little,' said Sophie. 'I was only ten when Emma eloped with him. All I knew was that he was a younger son of the Earl of Strathallen and very wild. At least that was what Papa said. And I only heard that because he had forgotten that I was in the corner learning Psalm 51 as a punishment.'

The captain nodded. 'He *was* wild. Strathallen was a fool

to disown Jock over his marriage. It was the making of him. Your sister was very good for Jock. He cared for her so deeply that he actually settled down.' He paused and then asked, 'Are you quite sure Strathallen knows about Kit? You may say that Kit is none of his business, but I do have a reason for asking!'

'I believe Emma wrote when Jock was killed,' said Sophie slowly. 'Well, I know she wrote to let him know something about Jock's death. Quite a number of his friends wrote to her, you see, to tell her how it had happened. She...she thought that his father ought to know how they had thought of him...read for himself that Jock had died a hero.' Sophie's eyes filled with tears. 'She actually copied extracts from those letters for that hateful old man and it...it took her *ages* because she wept over them! And he never even acknowledged the letter!'

Angrily she blew her nose hard. 'I am sure she mentioned Kit in the letter. Thea might remember better, you know.'

'I hope you won't think I am interfering,' said Captain Hampton thoughtfully, 'but I believe you should contact Strathallen and remind him of Kit's existence. You see, his eldest son Alastair died two months ago and, as far as I can recall, Jock was next in line, which would mean, of course, that Kit is his heir.'

Had he struck her in the face Sophie could not have been more devastated. 'But that...that means they would take him away! No! Emma would not have wished for that!'

Hampton looked at her white face compassionately. 'Would she have wished him to be denied his birthright?'

'I'm sorry,' said Sophie after a moment in which she regained control of herself. 'That was a foolish thing to say. And selfish.'

'Not at all,' said Hampton gently. 'After all, you have stood as a mother to the boy. Known him from infancy and cared for him. It is hardly surprising that you should view any thought of losing him with abhorrence.'

'What should I do?' asked Sophie. 'How should I go about it? Can you advise me?'

Hampton said diffidently, 'If you wish it, I will discuss the matter with Helford and we will write to Strathallen on your behalf. I did indicate to him today that I intended to mention Kit's grandfather to you. He...er...seemed to think I would be in some danger by doing so.'

He grinned understandingly as he took in Sophie's blush. 'He is a trifle dictatorial, but I assure you there is no one who can be kinder. No doubt he expressed himself badly.'

'If you and Lord Helford would not mind doing so, I would be most grateful,' said Sophie, not feeling in the least grateful. The thought that his paternal relations might assume responsibility for Kit when they had totally ignored his existence for ten years hurt abominably. But it was as Captain Hampton had said, she could not stand between Kit and his birthright even if it were possible.

In the meantime, the subject of their discussion was seated on a pile of hay in the hayloft with his little playmate, doing enormous discredit to his upbringing.

Fanny was staring with undisguised horror at the wooden box he was proudly displaying to her. 'A *rat*! Ugh! Is it alive?' A loud scrabbling from the box informed her that the inmate was very much alive.

'Of course it is! What use would a dead rat be to us?' asked Kit impatiently.

Fanny gave him to understand in no uncertain terms that, whatever his own requirements, a rat was of not the slightest use to her, dead *or* alive.

'Don't be such a nodcock, Fanny! It's not for you!' said Kit, seeing that she was about to decamp down the ladder. 'It's for Lady Lucinda.'

She stared at him, her mouth open. 'For…for Lady L…Lucinda?' She sat down again. 'Why? Do you mean that—'

She got no further. 'Because I looked at Megs the other night after she calmed down and you were right!' said Kit savagely. 'I could see where she had been jabbed with that hat pin! So I caught the rat to put in her bedchamber!'

'H…how?' Fanny was awed.

'Used a sticky trap. Glue, sugar syrup. Made an awful mess of one of Anna's old pots. I had to catch it alive, you see,' explained Kit.

'Er…that wasn't quite what I meant,' said Fanny nervously. 'How are you going to put it in her room?' She had a sinking feeling that she really didn't want to hear the answer to this question.

'Well, you are, of course!' said Kit in surprise, confirming her worst fears. 'You aren't actually scared of a rat, are you?' He conveniently forgot the unaccountable squirming sensation which had assailed him in the region of his belly when he saw the large and ferocious rodent struggling in his sticky trap.

'No, but I'm scared of Uncle David!' lied Fanny.

'Why should he think it was you?' asked Kit.

'Well, who else would do it?' she asked impatiently. 'One of the servants? My great aunt?'

'I wouldn't put it past Lady Maria,' said Kit with a grin. 'She's a great gun! No, really, Fanny. Everyone knows that old houses like Helford Place are always teeming with rats. Why should anyone suspect you?'

'We are *not* teeming with rats!' said Fanny indignantly, justifiably incensed at this slur on her home.

'You must have a few!' argued Kit. 'I'll tell you what. Suggest to a few of the maids that you've heard some scuttlings and squeakings. Ten to one half a dozen of them will have seen a big rat within a couple of days. Then, when no one will be at all surprised, you sneak into her room one night while she's at dinner or something and put it on her bed with a half-eaten apple. With a bit of luck it'll still be there when she comes to bed!'

Fanny thought about it. It was true. Mention a possible rat to even one maid and they would all be seeing things within a few hours. And she did want to pay Lady Lucinda out for hurting Aunt Sophie. The thought of her face when she was confronted with a large, revolting rat in her bed-chamber was simply irresistible.

Seeing her wavering, Kit said cunningly, 'Just think, Fanny, if you're scared of it, she'll be even more scared!'

'She will?' Fanny found the idea that anyone could possibly be more scared than herself hard to swallow.

'Well, of course!' said Kit. 'To start with, she's a coward. Only a coward would have played that trick on Aunt Sophie. And she won't be expecting it!'

Nothing, thought Fanny, could be more certain than that! But she rather liked the implied compliment that Kit didn't think her a coward.

'Besides,' said Kit on a note of inspiration, 'If she thinks the place is teeming with rats, she won't want to marry Helford!'

Even if Fanny hadn't already made up her mind that would have taken the trick. 'Can you catch a few more?' she asked hopefully.

Kit grinned. 'I knew you'd do it! Have you still got the hat pin?'

'Yes, I thought I'd better keep it as evidence,' said Fanny.

'Good. Give it back to her.'

'Whatever for?' Fanny was very surprised.

'To let her know you're on to her,' explained Kit. 'Then even if she does suspect you, she won't dare say anything to Helford. Give it to her in front of as many people as possible and say she dropped it the other day. No need to say when. Just say you saw her and kept forgetting to return it.'

'You think of everything!' said Fanny, simply lost in admiration.

Kit had the grace to blush. Never before had a female gazed at him in quite such approbation and it was really rather nice, he was rapidly discovering.

'Well, I don't want you getting into trouble,' he said roughly. 'Now mind, if they do bubble it, you tell Helford at once that it was my idea and that I gave you the rat!'

'We Melvilles,' said Miss Melville in lofty tones, 'don't rat on our allies. I mean, we don't give them away!'

'And we Carlisles,' said Master Carlisle in even loftier tones, 'don't leave our allies in the lurch!' He looked at her seriously. 'If Helford does work it out, don't you dare try to stand buff! I won't have it! That's *my* rat and I won't have you pinching all the credit! Promise!'

Immensely moved by this touchingly expressed concern for her safety, Miss Melville gave her word, reflecting as she did so that Great Aunt Maria could be counted on to stand her friend in an emergency. Especially if it involved a rat in Lady Lucinda's bedchamber. Fanny was tolerably certain that Great Aunt Maria liked neither Lucinda nor Lady Stanford.

The sound of hooves on the cobbled yard made the pair of them scramble to the edge of the loft and peer over. A strange groom was leading in an old black hunter.

'Hullo,' said Kit.

The groom looked up and grinned at the two faces. 'Afternoon, young master and mistress.'

'Whose horse is that?' asked Kit.

'Lady Darleston's horse.'

'Oh,' said Fanny. 'She's nice. Even Great Aunt Maria likes her.'

Quite unaware of the high approval bestowed on her, Penelope Darleston was greeting Sophie. 'I only heard this morning. Are you all right?' She looked at Sophie questioningly. 'It must have been a rattling fall. You're still terribly white.'

Sophie hesitated for a moment and then said, 'It's not just that.' She turned to Captain Hampton. 'I would like to tell Lady Darleston if you have no objection.'

'None at all,' he said.

The news made Penelope's jaw drop in surprise. 'Goodness! How amazing! And that wretched old man has ignored Kit's existence? But that's impossible. If the estate's trustees find out, he would be liable for an action at law. He can't be that vindictive, surely! You'd better find out quickly, Captain Hampton.' She smiled at Sophie, 'Well, that's good news, then. Why the long face?'

'What if Strathallen decides to remove Kit from my care?' asked Sophie miserably. 'I...I know it's selfish but...but...I just can't—'

Penelope interrupted, 'Of course you can't! Did your sister leave a will?'

'Yes,' said Sophie. 'She left everything to Kit.'

'Did she name a guardian?' asked Penelope intently.

'Well, me, of course,' said Sophie. 'There was no one else. I...I have a deed of guardianship.'

'That's that, then,' said Penelope triumphantly. 'I doubt there's anything Strathallen can do to remove Kit from your charge. If he tries Helford would support your claim, I'm sure, and I think I can safely guarantee that Peter would also back you up.'

Sophie heaved a sigh of relief. 'I never thought of Emma's will. And now I think of it, Jock's will named her as Kit's sole guardian. He specifically cut his family out at the time.' Her lovely smile transformed her face. 'Thank you, Penny. I...I never thought to find such good friends.'

'Now,' said Penelope, 'I heard about your accident be-

cause Lady Maria sent a note over this morning inviting us
to dinner next week. Apparently Helford is inviting quite a
number of locals.' She grinned at Sophie. 'Quite apart from
saying you had taken a tumble, she also wrote that she is
inviting you to dinner the same night.'

'*What?*' Sophie felt as though she had been invited to her
own execution rather than a dinner party. 'No! I couldn't
possibly go!'

Penelope nodded, 'I see.' With an inward smile she recalled Lady Maria's note,

*No doubt the silly chit will refuse to attend. I'm relying
on you to nip any such intention in the bud...*

There was no need, of course, to tell Sophie that so she
just asked, 'Could you tell me why not? I mean, Lady Maria
will be terribly disappointed.'

Captain Hampton said thoughtfully, 'That must be the
invitation there.' He indicated the forgotten note Fanny had
thrust at Sophie before being hustled out by Kit. 'Lady Maria gave that to Fanny just after breakfast and told her to be
sure not to forget it. Maybe you should read it.'

Sophie picked up the letter, broke the seal and read.

My dear Miss Marsden,
*Take pity on a poor old woman beset with a lot of
boring house guests and accept an invitation to dinner
on Tuesday next. We are inviting a number of residents,
including that rake Darleston and his baggage of a
wife Penelope so you will not lack for agreeable company. We will expect you at 5:30. I am sorry to hear
that you parted company with your mare. Fanny was
very put about by it, as was Helford.*
                    Your affectionate friend, Maria Kentham

Despite herself Sophie was tempted by the invitation. But
it was not to be thought of. The less she saw of Helford the

better and if, as was likely at a dinner party for the locals, he announced his betrothal to Lady Lucinda that night she did not wish to be in the room. It would be unbearable.

Resolutely she looked at Penelope and said quietly, 'No, I would very much prefer not to attend. I...I have nothing suitable to wear and, besides, I refuse to drive myself up to Helford Place for dinner in a gig. Old Grigson who looks after Megs for me is not up to driving at night.'

Unfortunately Penelope demolished these very cogent reasons in no time. 'Oh, pooh! We shall go up to your chamber presently and look something out and as for driving up in a gig; it would be most ineligible! Darleston and I shall be delighted to take you up.' She turned to the Captain. 'Please tell Lady Maria that Miss Marsden is delighted to accept her kind invitation and is looking forward to it very much.'

Left with no room to retreat or manoeuvre, Sophie capitulated. She could not bring herself to tell Penelope, even privately, her real reasons for not wishing to attend, so she permitted herself to be whisked upstairs. She even became mildly enthused as Penelope opened her armoire and chest to find an old gown of Emma's in amber silk, which she held up against Sophie with a cry of triumph.

'This is it! It will look lovely. Just the right colour for your eyes and hair.'

Sophie flushed scarlet. 'If anyone could tell what colour my eyes are, I might agree with you,' she said drily.

Penelope grinned wickedly. 'It never hurts a man to be kept wondering. Even if it's only over the colour of your eyes.' She giggled, a naughty, chuckling ripple. 'Besides, if he can't decide what colour they are, he'll gaze into them all the longer!'

Before she could stop herself Sophie said, 'Lady Maria refers to you as a *baggage* in her letter. I begin to see why!'

'Does she?' Penelope giggled again. 'You should hear what she calls Peter!'

'That rake Darleston..?' quoted Sophie with a twinkle. Penelope nodded and they collapsed on to the counterpane in fits of laughter.

The gales of laughter which echoed through the chamber were faintly audible downstairs. Anna, chopping vegetables in the kitchen, smiled grimly to herself. That Lady Darleston certainly had a way with her. And thank God one of the local ladies had decided to give Miss Sophie a bit of a hand. Bout time it was.

Tom Hampton, idly flipping through a book in the parlour, smiled as well. Do the poor girl good to have a bit of fun. He wondered what Helford would say when he heard that Miss Marsden was invited for dinner. Tom had a sneaking idea that Helford was more than a little confused. He had decided he wanted one thing and gone all out to get it. Now he was presented with something else and he wanted that too. Well, he'd have to make a choice because he certainly couldn't have both. At least he could, but Tom Hampton didn't think David Melville the man to take a girl like Sophie Marsden if he wasn't offering marriage. Too shabby by half that would be!

Lady Lucinda would be very put out, thought the Captain. He grinned to himself. He found that he could bear the prospect of Lady Lucinda's discomfiture with great fortitude. It occurred to him that, if he and Kate Asterfield handled things carefully, they might be able to ensure Helford had no opportunity to offer for Lucinda Anstey or in any way commit himself before that dinner party.

Seeing the two women together in company and realising that all his friends, not to mention his aunt, liked Sophie, might just tip the balance, he mused. He was fairly sure that in issuing an invitation to Miss Marsden, Lady Maria was

sending a clear signal of approval to her unexpectedly ob-
tuse nephew.

At this point in his cogitations Sophie and Penelope returned. They chatted away merrily until it was time for Captain Hampton to take Fanny home. She and Kit were extracted from the stables where they were found admiring
Penelope's horse Nero, a hero of Waterloo, the groom had
told them.

'Home, young lady,' said Hampton sternly. 'Before your
uncle has a search party out after us and accuses me of
kidnapping you. Miss Marsden, I will see to that business
for you as soon as possible. Lady Darleston, your most obe-
dient servant. Kit, I shall look forward to making your better
acquaintance on another occasion.'

He swung Fanny up into the curricle and drove out of the
stable yard in fine style with Megs trotting behind, and if
he had had reason to complain of his companion's lack of
conversation during the drive over, there was no cause for
complaint on the way home. If asked, he would have said
ruefully that he had never realised Fanny could be such a
little bagpipe. To do him credit, though, he studiously
avoided inquiring about the large and highly suspicious bundle upon which she was resting her feet. It was none of his
business after all.

When their visitors had left, Sophie and Kit walked back
to the house together after duly admiring the little Welsh
grey Helford had sent over to take Megs's place.

'He's complete to a shade,' said Kit reluctantly. 'But I'd
rather have Megs. Even if she does misbehave. It…
it…wasn't her fault, Aunt Sophie!' He stopped, unwilling
to say more. It would never do if she found out about the
rat.

Sophie looked at him closely. 'You sound very certain,
Kit. Is there something you aren't telling me?'

'Yes,' he admitted.

'And you are convinced that it wasn't Megs's fault.' There was no question in the way she spoke.

He nodded.

'Then I'll keep her no matter what Helford says,' declared Sophie.

Kit stared at her. 'Just because I said so. Without even telling you why?'

Her eyes quizzed him gently. 'But of course. Your word is good enough for me, Kit. Just as your father's or mother's would have been.'

His heart swelled with pride to think that his word was believed in this way. Trust Aunt Sophie to know how a fellow liked to be treated. She was as good a gentleman as Helford, who had never pressed to find out who had taught him about tickling trout. He told her so in gruff tones which imperfectly concealed the depth of his affection.

Even the best of aunts, however, is prey to the complaint that killed the cat. Sophie Marsden was no exception. She spent quite a long time that night wondering just what Kit, and, by implication, Fanny, knew. That they were plotting something she was sure. It had not needed Captain Hampton's remarks to tell her that.

What could they have seen? Carefully her mind went back over her fall. Where had everyone been? At last she had it. The only person right behind her had been Lucinda Anstey. If Kit swore that Megs had not been at fault then…the idea was ludicrous…why should she do such a thing? *To make you look no how!*

The answer presented itself with startling clarity. Lady Lucinda, if she had somehow caused Megs's explosion, must have meant for her to look a complete fool. Which confirmed that she resented the attention Helford had paid to her. She must have been as cross as crabs when it backfired, thought Sophie with a reluctant grin. She couldn't possibly have anticipated that Helford would end up carrying her victim home.

Drat the man! Why couldn't he have just left her alone and stayed out of her life? Dismally she thought that the sooner Helford took himself back to London where he belonged, the better. It occurred to her that he might decide to live at Helford Place for much of the year. That she might have to live with him as a neighbour. She couldn't do it. Perhaps if the Carlisles wanted Kit, she could go too. That would be better than seeing Helford and his wife constantly. There would certainly be no joy to alleviate that pain.

Later that evening Helford sat in his library, listening to what Captain Hampton had to say with increasing concern.

'You think Kit is the heir?' He was incredulous. 'Are you sure?'

Hampton shrugged. 'Of course I'm sure. You don't think I would have told Miss Marsden if I weren't, do you?' He poured himself a brandy. 'Look, David, Jock Carlisle was a very close friend of mine. I stayed with his family once or twice and I'm as sure as I sit here that Kit is Strathallen's heir.'

'Good God!' said David blankly. 'What did Sophie... Miss Marsden say?'

'She was horrified,' admitted Hampton. 'Seemed to think Strathallen might try to remove the boy. Which is very possible. He disinherited Jock for marrying Emma Marsden, after all.'

'He might try, but he won't get away with it!' said David fiercely.

Hampton grinned. 'That's much what Penelope Darleston thought,' he said. 'She felt that you could be counted on to support Miss Marsden and even pledged Peter's backing.'

David nodded. He couldn't stomach the thought of

Sophie losing Kit to a vindictive old man who had refused to acknowledge the lad's existence all these years.

He sipped his brandy. 'You told her we would write to Strathallen? Good. I'll do it now and you can add your signature to mine in the morning. Have you got the old man's direction?'

Hampton was rather taken aback. 'Er…aren't you joining the ladies in the drawing room?' He had pulled Helford aside as they left the dining room after the port.

'No,' said David in a tired voice. 'Make my apologies, Tom. Say something urgent came up and that I must get this letter off first thing. It's true enough. Besides…well…I need to do a bit of serious thinking.'

Hampton looked at him sharply, but said nothing beyond, 'Just as you like but, you know, Lady Lucinda won't like it!'

'No, I don't suppose she will,' agreed David, still in that weary tone.

Hampton left him, but turned back at the door to say, casually, 'I like your Miss Marsden, David. She's as gallant a lass as you'd meet, isn't she?'

David just nodded with a rueful smile. The door clicked shut. *Trust Tom to spot it!* He wondered how many others had realised his attraction to Sophie Marsden. Kate Asterfield, no doubt. Ned? Lord Mark? Most unlikely. That pair rarely noticed anything beyond their dinners and horses. Well, that was a little unfair. Ned certainly noticed his wife. But that was probably because she made quite sure he remembered her existence.

Lucinda? Certainly. That would account for the way she had behaved, although he was surprised to find that she could feel jealousy. Justifiably expecting an offer from him, she had no doubt been miffed at his behaviour. He couldn't blame her.

At last he faced the fact that he had been trying to avoid

for over a week. He had to offer for Lucinda quickly before his passion for Sophie led him into the snare he feared. Before he lost control of himself and rode over to Willowbank House and begged her to marry him. And what he felt for Sophie was a far cry from the youthful infatuation he had succumbed to with Felicity. This was the most terrifying emotion you could possibly imagine. That appalling fear when he had thought her dead. The fury that consumed him when Sir Philip's importunities recalled themselves to his memory. More than ever it confirmed his notion that to care too deeply was dangerous. That he would be better off, safer, if he never saw her again. If he allowed his passion to die a natural death.

A marriage of convenience, wasn't that what he had wanted? A well-bred wife who would cause no scandal. A wife who would make no demands on him, who would turn a blind eye when he sought his amusements outside her bed.

And, after all, Lucinda was a very attractive woman, he told himself. One who conducted herself with the right degree of maidenly modesty. With breeding. She had been brought up to know his world and her place in it. There would be no surprises there. She'd certainly never rip up at him about his morals as Sophie had!

But she's so…so cold. He could not dismiss the thought, and groaned. Surely once they were wed she would thaw out somewhat. Surely with all his skill and expertise he could…seduce her?

Perhaps. If you wanted to… Frankly, the idea left *him* cold. Somehow the words *seduce* and *Lucinda* did not seem to belong in the same world, let alone the same thought.

For the first time he wondered just how Lady Lucinda would take to her marital duties. Unfortunately, his imagination was not even remotely interested in speculating on the possibilities. With difficulty he conjured up an image of her elegant figure, white skin and silky black curls. He was rewarded with not the slightest twinge of desire. Determinedly he thought about kissing her, but again his imagination refused to cooperate.

That might have been due to the fact that it was unceremoniously thrust aside by his memory, which interposed the remembrance of Sophie melting in his arms and that little moan as her mouth opened under his… For a moment Helford allowed himself the pleasure of this recollection and felt more than a twinge of desire and guilt. He was tolerably certain that Sophie was not in the least indifferent to him. She was not a wanton, could not possibly have responded to him like that had she not cared.

Worse than his own misery was the knowledge that he had hurt her. That she would continue to think he had amused himself with her innocence. That she had been nothing to him.

Grimly he faced the fact that for him his memories could hold no joy, only a bitter cynicism. He had recognised love far too late. He told himself that, had he been able to gaze into the future after their first meeting, he would have ensured that he never saw her again. Because now he would have to banish Sophie Marsden from his thoughts completely.

Perhaps, he thought in resignation, I should try kissing Lucinda. Maybe that would banish these…these fantasies. *Tomorrow, then. Surely she won't be too shocked. After all, she must be expecting an offer.*

It occurred to him that she might reasonably expect the offer first and the kisses later.

Or not at all.

Resolutely he thrust his cogitations aside and concentrated on writing a letter to an elderly Scottish peer which combined tactfulness with clarity of expression and in no way hinted at the writer's opinion that Strathallen was a curmudgeonly old fool.

Chapter Ten

Having made his bitter decision, David found that over the following week he had no opportunity to be alone with Lady Lucinda Anstey. Tom Hampton and both the Asterfields seemed to be afflicted with an incredible lack of tact. Kate in particular appeared to have a hitherto well-concealed predilection for Lady Lucinda's company and sublimely ignored all hints to make herself scarce. Nearly all hints, anyway. On the few occasions when David managed to get rid of Kate, Aunt Maria turned up and was impossible to shake.

Tom Hampton and Ned were also extremely demanding of his time. Both of them had developed a bloodthirsty urge to rid his estate of rabbits and were constantly dragging him out to shoot at the hapless creatures with the result that rabbit was appearing on the menu rather frequently.

By the time he was dressing for dinner on Tuesday night he had not had even the smallest opportunity to kiss Lady Lucinda. Nor had he offered for her, which he had told himself he ought to do.

To the immense disapproval of his valet, David dressed for dinner with unseemly haste. It was not that the result was anything less than perfection, thought Meredith grudgingly. It was just that these things ought to be done properly and haste could lead to slovenliness, a tendency to be heartily deplored. He firmly suppressed his horror as his master even hurried over his cravat, taking twenty minutes where usually half an hour was considered quick.

The reason for this callous assault on Meredith's sensibilities and professional pride was simply that David had asked Lady Lucinda to meet him alone before dinner. He was starting to suspect that he was being outmanoeuvred. When the thought first flashed into his mind he had dismissed it, but then all the little things started to add up. Tom and Kate had been as thick as thieves for days past and they had been extremely attentive to Aunt Maria. Ned, he decided, was simply along for the ride. Such strategy was beyond the scope of his kindly, but limited, thought processes. He would, however, be only too happy to fall in with whatever devilry his wife might be plotting. He was terribly proud of Kate's quick brain and hardly ever called her to order.

David reflected on this grimly. Yes, he began to see now. Kate and Tom were orchestrating the whole thing, but why? The answer was not long in coming to him. They didn't want him to offer for Lady Lucinda. Now he thought about it, that was fairly obvious. Damn it all! Did they think he didn't know his own mind?

So, as he escorted Lucinda upstairs to change for dinner, he had said, 'Would it be too shocking of me, Lady Lucinda, to ask you to come down, shall we say…fifteen minutes early? I should very much like some private talk with you.'

She had inclined her head graciously. 'I think I may safely agree to that, my lord, in our situation.' She accorded him a gracious smile. 'I am sure Mama will see no harm in it.'

David started. Damn! He didn't want Lady Stanford to know. Irritably, he realised that this was precisely what he had wanted in his bride. A well-bred and virtuous damsel above all gossip. He went away to his own chamber to violate unthinkingly all his valet's cherished notions of the way in which a gentleman should dress for dinner.

Entering her chamber, Lady Lucinda found her maid there waiting. She glanced at the clock and realised that she would have to hurry. Her bath was unwontedly swift, and the maid was shocked at the haste with which her ladyship arrayed herself in the gown of jonquil silk laid out for her. Neither did Lady Lucinda change her mind half a dozen times over which pieces of jewellery to wear. Her pearl necklace and matching earrings were chosen without the least hesitation. Kid slippers and a silk reticule completed the ensemble.

'I will ring for you when I come up to bed, girl,' said Lady Lucinda coldly. She had the greatest dislike of her maid waiting for her in the evenings. Why, once she had found an impertinent servant actually asleep on her daybed. Without even waiting for Betsy's respectful curtsy, she sailed through to her mama's bedchamber.

Lady Stanford was still in her petticoat and chemise.

'Not that dress, girl! Lilac, I said! Cannot you see that one is mauve? Stupid wench!'

In very different tones, 'Lucinda! You are very early!'

Her daughter looked significantly at the hapless maid who was clutching two dresses of identical colour with a countenance devoid of all expression. Lady Stanford took the hint at once.

'Take yourself off, girl. I wish to speak to Lady Lucinda. Wait in the sitting room!'

The maid bobbed and removed herself, wondering if she could get another position. She'd gladly take a drop in status and wages to find a more pleasant mistress.

'Helford has asked me to come down early, Mama,' explained Lucinda. 'You do not object?'

Lady Stanford gave it some thought. No doubt Helford wished to offer for Lucinda privately. That was not how it had been done in her young days, but one must move with the times. It was not surprising that he should wish to see her alone. She could depend upon Lucinda to keep the line.

'No, my dear. You may do so. But I would be failing in my duty as your mother if I did not drop a word of warning in your ear. He may well attempt to kiss you! You must not repulse him. Nothing could be more fatal! I say this only to warn you not to allow your instincts as a lady to rule you. Nothing could be more natural than that you should find it excessively distasteful, I do myself, but you must not flinch. Such a thing would be very bad! A lady does not shrink from her duty and you would not wish to give Helford any cause to think you would be less than dutiful.'

'No, indeed, Mama,' agreed Lady Lucinda and after some more of her mama's advice, all of which made it perfectly plain why Lord Stanford had, since the moment of his marriage, sought the consolation of a string of mistresses, Lady Lucinda Anstey descended the stairs to the Green Drawing Room.

David was before her and he looked up with raised eyebrows as she entered the room. It would not have surprised him in the least if Lady Stanford had been with her daughter, but to his relief Lady Lucinda was alone. As she came across the room he told himself that she really was very lovely—those blue eyes were quite extraordinary and her figure was excellent.

'At last, Lucinda,' he said with a forced smile, dropping her title for the first time.

Her eyes widened, but she reminded herself that it was quite the thing for a gentleman to assume a more informal manner with his intended, at least in private. The way Darleston always used his wife's Christian name among friends was, she considered, most unseemly.

'Good evening, Helford,' she responded to his greeting.

He held out his hand to her with a slight lift of his black

brows. With all the dignity of an aristo going to the guillotine, she placed her hand in his and allowed him to draw her into his arms. It was not too distasteful, she thought. He had put one finger under her chin and was pushing it up slightly. His mouth covered hers and moved in a very peculiar way while his free hand moved over her back and urged her to stand closer. Obediently she did so and was rather surprised when he moved one of her arms to encircle him. Surely he did not expect her to embrace him! She did not move the arm, but certainly its fellow did not join it.

David was finding Lucinda's lack of response most disconcerting. It was not merely a lack of response, he thought, as he moved his lips over hers as seductively as he could. It was a complete lack of interest. Even disgust would be better than this ice-cold submission. At least that would be something with which to work. To make matters worse his body, which had ignited just holding Miss Sophie Marsden, categorically refused to work up the slightest spark of enthusiasm for the far lovelier siren he was providing for its pleasure. He thought whimsically that if his body could have yawned, it would have!

Determined to try a little harder, he allowed the hand caressing her back to move around to the front, or rather, since it had showed no interest in doing so, he put it there and cautiously essayed to sample one breast. That did get a reaction. Lady Lucinda opened her mouth, to which David responded by reluctantly pushing his tongue inside and sweeping it across the roof of her mouth.

Unfortunately Lady Lucinda had only opened her mouth to request Helford to keep his hands to himself and his disgraceful invasion revolted her to the core. Her blue eyes opened wide in shock and she could not repress a shudder of revulsion. It was only with great self-control that she did not break away from his hold. He was releasing her anyway

and seemed about to say something when the door opened
to admit Lady Maria.

Lady Maria cursed mentally as she saw the two alone by
the fireplace. *Damn! Hope I'm not too late. Might have
known he'd try to get down early. Thank God Kate told me
Lucinda was down.* By the look of things she'd interrupted
something. That chit was looking as close to discomposed
as she'd ever seen her.

'Good evening, Aunt Maria,' said David awkwardly. He
was not sure whether he was furious or relieved at her appearance. Having kissed the girl, he had intended to offer
for her, but his aunt's arrival had put paid to that.

'Helford, Lucinda.' She stalked across to her accustomed
chair and her nephew at once handed her into it. Sitting
down, she said, 'I beg your pardon for not being down before you, Lucinda. I trust Helford has kept you tolerably
well entertained.' Her eagle gaze did not miss the way Lady
Lucinda stiffened as she responded.

'Yes, I thank you. But I was early. You must not blame
yourself, Lady Maria.'

'And where's your mama?' she continued. 'Not at all the
thing for a chit to come down alone with a rake like Helford.
Lord, girl, don't you know his reputation?'

The look of utter distaste frozen on Lucinda's lovely
mask was balm to Lady Maria. She'd lay anyone handsome
odds that Helford had been kissing the girl and she hadn't
liked it above half. Good! That would put Helford off if
nothing else did. He was the sort of man to like 'em willing.
He wouldn't like the idea of sharing his bed with a wench
who only entered it on sufferance.

'Thank you, Aunt Maria,' said David coldly. This was
going too far! 'Perhaps we could leave my reputation out
of it.' What the devil was the old lady up to? Anyone would
think she was trying to put Lucinda off. Which seemed, he
thought, to be a work of supererogation. Not that Lucinda

had repulsed his advances exactly, but he had received the distinct impression she would have liked to do so.

Perfectly satisfied with Lucinda's reaction to her comment, Lady Maria went on as though no one had spoken. 'Well now, who's coming this evening? Let me think. The Darlestons, of course, and Sir Philip Garfield. Someone else...oh, yes, the Vicar and his wife...now, who else...ah, here is Mrs Asterfield. Good God! Does she call that thing a gown?'

Lady Maria raised her quizzing glass the better to survey Kate Asterfield's nearly transparent pink silk gown. It was plain that whatever she was wearing beneath it did not constitute any protection at all against the chill of the room.

'Humph! Well, it may not warm her,' observed Lady Maria acidly, 'but I can guarantee it'll warm Asterfield! Wouldn't you say, Helford?'

Lord Helford, completely forgetting his company, was moved to reply in tones of great appreciation, 'Not a doubt of it, Aunt Maria!' There was a slight movement beside him. Lady Lucinda had taken a very definite step away. He looked at her and surprised a look of utter scorn on her face.

He frowned slightly. Kate's gown was outrageous, he supposed, but damn it! She and Ned were his friends and it was as plain as a pikestaff that Lucinda disliked her intensely. And that was another thing that concerned him, apart from the fact that Lucinda had relished his attentions not at all. It would be deucedly uncomfortable if she disapproved of all his friends. *Oh my God! It's a bit late to think of all this now!*

Kate's greeting interrupted his thoughts. 'Really, Helford! Why can't you keep your rooms properly heated?'

He grinned at her and said most improperly, 'We do. Would you like me to find you some clothes? I'd give you my coat, but then Aunt Maria would accuse *me* of being indecently garbed.'

Lady Maria gave a crack of laughter, but Kate just twinkled up at him.

'Never mind, Helford, I can assure you that I won't remain cold for long!'

Disgusting, thought Lady Lucinda. The woman was shameless! No doubt she was trying to ensnare Helford! Well, if it kept him from taking those foul liberties with her more often than was necessary for the begetting of an heir, then she would gladly look the other way when he strayed!

Lady Maria was speaking again. 'My memory's not what it was, Mrs Asterfield. I can't remember who's joining us tonight.'

'Oh, the Darlestons, didn't you say?' responded Kate helpfully. 'And the local Squire, Sir Philip Whatsit? Did you say something, Helford?' A disgusted snort had erupted from her host. 'Now let me think. Oh yes, that charming girl who fell off her mare last week.' She smiled brightly at David. 'Miss Marsden, is it not?'

David stared from her to his aunt and said in a constricted voice, 'Sophie Marsden is coming tonight, Aunt Maria?' He was aware of Lucinda Anstey's gasp of shock from behind him, but Lady Maria's reply was lost as the gentlemen of the house party came in together with Lady Stanford.

Ned Asterfield lived up to everyone's expectations by exclaiming when he saw his wife, 'I say! That's a devilish pretty gown, m'dear. I like that!'

Lord Mark and Tom Hampton merely looked their appreciation at Kate, who ignored them as she bestowed a glowing smile upon her husband.

'Dear Ned, you always say the right thing! Helford practically told me to go and put my clothes on.'

Ned Asterfield just grinned and said, 'You leave me to worry about my wife, old boy. Time enough for you to tell a wife what to do when you've got your own.' Clearly unconscious of having said anything in the least untoward, he looked around and said, 'No one else here yet?'

At this moment the door opened and the butler announced, 'Sir Philip Garfield. The Reverend Mr Henshaw and Mrs Henshaw.'

David eyed Garfield with disfavour and pointedly greeted the Vicar and his lady first. He had not been able to veto Sir Philip's inclusion in the dinner party without telling his aunt just why he had taken such a dislike to the man. Any other man, he thought disgustedly, would have politely declined the invitation.

Not Sir Philip, who entered the room with a slight swagger, sure of his welcome. He had come to the conclusion that Helford had been under the mistaken impression that Miss Sophie would accept a *carte blanche*. By now he would have discovered his mistake. Miss Marsden's unwillingness to receive his own suit he put down to her expectation of a more respectable offer from Helford. She was far too unworldly to realise that a man of Helford's rank did not offer marriage to a little country nobody. Even if he wasn't betrothed to the daughter of an earl. By gad, the wench was lucky *he* was prepared to offer marriage.

So he greeted his icy host with all the bonhomie of a man who had not recently been laid low by the host's punishing left. 'Ah, Helford. We meet in more gracious surroundings. I fancy our little misunderstanding is all cleared up?'

David permitted himself a frosty smile. 'I am afraid any misunderstanding of the situation was on your side, Sir Philip.'

Before anything more could be said the door opened again to admit the final guests.

'The Earl and Countess of Darleston, Miss Marsden.'

David moved forward to greet them, scarcely able to take his eyes off Sophie. Shimmering amber silk clung to her lissom body, the perfect foil for her creamy complexion and complementing golden highlights in the simply arranged curls. It was years out of fashion with its crossover bodice and raised waist and, compared to the jewellery worn by the other women, her ivory beads were mere trumpery, but she carried herself proudly as if she were dressed like a princess.

His greeting to Peter Darleston and his wife was disjointed to say the least, which brought a twinkle of amusement to the Earl's eye. Resignedly David wondered just *who* had told Peter *what*. It didn't bear thinking about. Gritting his teeth for control, he turned to greet the woman he both wished miles away and, at one and the same time, locked irrevocably in his arms.

Sophie felt absolutely terrified. Never in her life had she been in a room like this. Its grandeur and formal elegance overwhelmed her. She wished desperately that she had not come. There was Lady Lucinda looking as scornful as ever and an older lady who must be her mother.

She dragged her attention back to Helford. He was greeting her.

'What a pleasant surprise, Miss Marsden.' His voice cracked slightly. Seeing her like this just as he was about to offer for Lucinda was shattering. His heart was like lead in his breast, all his resolution destroyed.

'A…a surprise?' A puzzled frown creased her brow. 'Did…you…did you not invite me?' For a horrible moment she wondered if she had misread the note from Lady Maria.

'Aunt Maria did not mention your name to me until just now,' he said in some constraint. And could have kicked himself when he saw her reaction.

Her dark eyes widened as her cheeks flushed crimson 'I…I beg your pardon, my lord. I assumed you were aware…' She floundered to a halt.

Oh, God! She thinks you don't want her here! There was nothing he could say to reassure her even if they didn't have an audience. Because in some ways it was true. Had he known in time he would have confided in his aunt and begged her not to invite Sophie. He could only repeat inadequately, 'A pleasant surprise. Come and talk to my aunt and be presented to Lady Stanford.'

Sophie greeted Lady Maria with real pleasure. The old lady tapped her on the cheek with her fan. 'Pretty colour. That gown suits you and at least there's enough of it to keep *you* warm. I fancy you know most of the others here. Ah! Aurelia, this is Miss Sophie Marsden. Sophie, this is Lady Stanford.'

Lady Stanford was very cool. She had heard an edited version from Lady Lucinda of the riding accident and considered it very likely that the scheming chit had engineered her own fall. She had said as much to Lucinda. Now, as she looked Miss Marsden over, she could see precisely why her daughter had considered the girl ill bred. That nose! Freckled! And the gown! It was positively archaic! No one with the least pretension to fashion would wear such an outmoded creation. And the way she held herself as though she were quite as good as her betters. Daring to come in with the Darlestons as though she were a member of their party!

Determined to show this little nobody the gulf that lay between the aristocracy and an encroaching little mushroom, she extended two languid fingers, uttered a brief, 'How do you do?' and turned away without waiting for an answer.

Lady Maria chuckled silently to herself. This was better than a play! David was quite obviously upset. Just far enough off balance to forget his manners and do something foolish for a change!

Lady Lucinda came up to Sophie and said with spurious interest, 'And how is your back, Miss Marsden? I do trust that Helford's services won't be required tonight.' She smiled sweetly at the look of embarrassment on Sophie's face. 'No doubt you find Helford's horse far better mannered than your, er…cob.' She could almost be said to have smirked.

This was too much! Sophie pulled herself together and replied with the utmost charm, 'He is very well mannered. And since you mention the incident, I do hope you had sufficient time…er…*left* to pull your own mount out of the way.' Her eyes rose challengingly to Lady Lucinda's.

Lady Lucinda stared at her in sudden doubt, but at that moment Miss Fanny Melville was escorted into the room by her governess. Sophie could see at once that she was up to something. The green eyes were just too modestly down-cast and she was looking just too innocent. She greeted her uncle and great aunt with pleasure before glancing around the guests.

Her eyes widened and a huge smile of delight transformed her face. 'Aunt Sophie! I didn't know you were coming. How is your back?'

'Much better, thank you,' said Sophie with a twinkle. 'Kit sent his greetings, by the way.' Now, what was there in that to make the child look so smug?

Fanny had turned to Lady Lucinda and was saying in her clear, bell-like tones, 'Oh, Lady Lucinda, I believe this is yours!' She was holding out a hat pin. 'I saw you drop it the other day and kept forgetting to return it.'

'Good God, child!' exclaimed Lady Lucinda impatiently. 'Give it to one of the maids!' Then, as Fanny continued to hold out the hat pin, she said uncertainly, 'You cannot be certain it is mine.'

'Oh, yes,' Fanny assured her, smiling seraphically as her victim whitened. 'I saw you drop it.'

Sophie stared at the smiling child in sudden understanding. So Kit was right! Heavens! No wonder Megs had bucked, having that thing stuck into her. What a pair of monkeys, though, to declare war on Lady Lucinda in this way! In front of everyone! For Sophie had not the slightest doubt that it was a declaration of war. Nothing could be clearer. Fanny Melville had flung down the gauntlet at Lucinda Anstey's satin-slippered feet with a resounding clang.

Lucinda took the hat pin and put it in her reticule with a forced little laugh. 'I suppose I must thank you, Fanny.'

'Oh, no,' said Fanny. 'Thanks are not necessary. Good evening.' She cast an affectionate smile at Sophie and said, 'Please tell Kit that he was quite right about the maids and that it will be done just as he wished.'

Sophie agreed to pass on the message with a perfectly straight face.

Lucinda was looking most uncomfortable and Sophie said, as Fanny went to greet Captain Hampton, 'Really, I don't know when I have met a child as bright as Fanny. She is charming, don't you think?'

Still flustered from the realisation that at least two people knew of what she had done and possibly three if, as seemed likely, Miss Marsden's horrid nephew had found out, Lucinda was betrayed into an unwise rejoinder.

'She would be all the better for the discipline of a good school rather than tearing about the countryside in unsuitable company!'

A deep voice behind them said, 'I would hardly consider Kit unsuitable. You do Miss Marsden a considerable injustice in saying so, Lucinda.'

Lucinda turned in consternation. Helford was looking down at her with a dangerous glitter in his brilliant eyes. 'Oh, I meant merely that a girl should be with a member of her own sex. Nothing more.'

'I see. Ah, here is Bainbridge to announce dinner. Miss Marsden, Tom Hampton will take you in. Mine is the pleasure of escorting Lady Darleston. I understand they brought you over. I need hardly say that had Aunt Maria had the sense to tell me she had invited you I would have sent the carriage. As it is, I am glad you did not drive yourself over.' He kept his tone light and cheerful, ignoring the leaden misery in his heart.

The light in his eyes warmed Sophie insensibly and she smiled up at him in relief. 'Naturally when I told Lady Darleston that it was impossible for me to attend if I *did* have to drive in the gig, she agreed that it would not do at all.'

He looked down at her, conscious of the usual desire to take her in his arms. Abruptly he said, 'Here comes Hampton. I shall talk to you later about Kit's affairs.' He turned away to seek his dinner partner, thinking that, despite the undoubted charm of Peter's wife, this was like to be the worst evening of his entire life!

Chapter Eleven

While Sophie was delighted to have Captain Hampton as her dinner companion, finding Sir Philip on her other side was a considerable penance, since he took the first opportunity to lean over and assure her that he would not mind their little misunderstanding.

'No doubt you were misled by the circumstance of Helford's attentions,' he said in an undertone, unaware that he was distressing her deeply. 'But you were not to know how a fellow of his rank views things. Stanford's chit, eh? A very fine young woman and will make him an excellent wife.'

Sophie swallowed a spoonful of the delicious turtle soup which suddenly tasted as though it had been seasoned exclusively with hyssop and wormwood. Would he never give up? She thought despairingly that it would take more than her word to convince him that she would never marry him! Or anyone else for that matter. It would be impossible now to surrender herself to any other man. Helford had seen to that.

She attempted to turn the conversation into more acceptable channels, aware that Lady Maria was not so much taken

up by the outrageous flattery of Lord Darleston that she
could not hear every word Sir Philip was saying.

Lord Darleston, thought Sophie, was simply delightful.
He was every inch a gentleman, but she could see precisely
why Lady Maria called him a rake. He would be irresistible
to most women if he were not so obviously devoted to Penelope. She had met him for the first time that evening and
his easy kindness and good manners had charmed her completely. Penelope was the luckiest of women, she thought.

With Lady Maria he was at his best, teasing the old lady
by dredging up some long-forgotten scandal about her family and assuring her that the secret was safe with him.

The old lady snorted. 'Humph! All I can say is it's a good
thing that baggage Penelope keeps you in line. You and
your flummery!' She turned her attention to Sir Philip. 'And
how are you keeping, Garfield?' Better draw his fire from
Sophie. Chit was starting to look as though she were about
to give him a set-down.

Relieved, Sophie returned her attention to her dinner, accepting a helping of duckling and green peas. She found
Tom Hampton's kindly smile a positive Godsend and returned it with interest.

The unshadowed sweetness of her smile at Tom seared
through Helford at the end of the table. His heart contracted
as though a fist had tightened around it. No. Surely not. It
would be appalling to see her married to Tom. *Better than
Garfield!* He was surprised to find that the thought of Tom
Hampton pursuing Sophie was almost as offensive as
Garfield. Savagely he reminded himself that it could be none
of his business if Sophie chose after all to marry. And Tom
would at least be a kind and affectionate husband.

Not entirely oblivious to the fact that his host was toying
with the idea of calling him out, Tom Hampton set himself
to entertain and please Miss Marsden. Their conversation on
the topic of boring punishments inflicted upon them in their

youth was laced with laughter. Sophie's account of how she had made Kit add up her accounts after his last truancy impressed Hampton enormously.

'What a capital idea, Miss Marsden! I'll warrant he took the hint!'

'Well, yes,' acknowledged Sophie, chuckling. 'But I am bound to own that he did it a great deal better than I do. Even Thea, his governess, said so.'

'Should have taken a riding crop to the lad,' growled Sir Philip. Namby-pamby idea! Adding up accounts, indeed! 'Boy needs a man to show him what's what. I'll soon take care of that!' This remark was dropped resoundingly into one of those dreadful pools of silence which seem to attract embarrassing speeches.

Sophie flushed scarlet, every eye at the table was upon her and there was nothing she could say to rebut the impression made by Sir Philip without being appallingly rude to him.

David was not so nice in his notions. He could see the Vicar pricking up his ears, about to enquire if his services were to be needed. He had to head the man off at all costs before Sir Philip put Sophie into the position of having to refuse him at the dinner table. Despite the convention which dictated that conversation should be confined to the persons seated immediately to left and right, he fixed Sir Philip with an icy green stare.

'I thought it had been agreed, Sir Philip, that you were not to be granted that, or any other authority?' His voice held only mild inquiry, but it made Lady Maria shoot a startled glance at him over the forkful of game pie she was raising to her mouth. She almost laughed aloud. Lord! If ever she'd seen the boy so angry! Just as she'd thought— he'd completely forgotten his manners!

David returned to his conversation with Lady Darleston, supremely conscious of having made bad infinitely worse.

He didn't dare look at Sophie. If he did he was entirely likely to find himself making a declaration over the dinner table. Damn Aunt Maria's scheming! She'd probably planned the whole thing!

It was a moot point as to whether Sophie was more horrified by Sir Philip's crass assumption of authority or the chilly way in which Helford had depressed his pretensions. It might not be convenable to converse across the table, but that wasn't stopping both Lady Lucinda and her mama from looking down their long noses at her.

While Sir Philip assumed an unwonted interest in his dinner, Captain Hampton was speaking to her very softly. 'Now that really was bacon-brained!' She looked up at him and found an expression of understanding sympathy on his kindly face. 'David,' he went on, 'has not the slightest notion of tact. It will be a wonder if any woman of rank can be prevailed upon to accept him.' This last was uttered so quietly that she could not doubt it reached her ears only.

Swallowing hard, she said with difficulty, 'I cannot understand why you should say such a thing to me, sir, but—'

His eyes twinkled as he interrupted her. 'Because I am as tactless as David, my dear. Do not allow this little contretemps to upset you, Miss Marsden. The only persons likely to be at all upset do not matter in the least. You may take my word for that.'

Both those unimportant persons had stiffened in wrath at Helford's very proprietorial expression of interest in Miss Marsden. Lady Stanford was furious. How dare he have the effrontery to include his mistress at a dinner party where her daughter, his intended bride, was present! Let alone making the situation clear to everyone! No doubt that little hussy Kate Asterfield was laughing up her non-existent sleeve and planning to let everyone in town know just as soon as she could!

Lady Lucinda was no less disgusted than her mother, but

her fury was somewhat tempered by the reflection that if Helford was planning to set Miss Marsden up as his mistress, or had already done so, it would keep him from sharing *her* bed more than was seemly. She looked up to find Helford's eyes on her and could not repress a shudder as she recalled the liberties he had taken with her person.

This reaction was not lost on David, who was of the opinion that he had completely lost his senses. How on earth was he to share a bed with this girl if he married her? With a shock he realised that he was casting serious doubt on their union for the first time, and that the thought of marriage to Sophie was suddenly far less terrifying.

Once admitted openly, the idea that he might not marry Lucinda Anstey refused to be banished. It developed itself into a fully fledged conviction as he continued with his game pie. But he was practically honour bound to offer for her now! How the hell could he get out of it? There had to be a way. A marriage of convenience was one thing, but he was damned if he'd spend the rest of his life tied to a female who made it clear she would welcome a crawling slug to her bed only slightly less enthusiastically!

And as for his reaction to Garfield's idiocy! What on earth had he been about to call attention to the situation in that way? He had meant only to erase the distressed look on Sophie's face and block the Vicar, but he had made matters immeasurably worse. For the rest of the meal he confined himself strictly to addressing his remarks to Lady Darleston and Lady Stanford, all the while trying to persuade himself that he was grateful for Tom Hampton's protective presence beside Sophie.

In truth, the fact that Sophie was so obviously comfortable with Tom galled him unbearably. He watched her surreptitiously as the first course was removed and the second course set out. She appeared to have recovered from her discomfiture and was talking happily to Tom while Lady Maria held Garfield's attention.

Gallant as ever, he thought. Far too proud to let any hint of her embarrassment show.

He smiled automatically at Lady Stanford as she informed him that his chef's way with a saddle of venison was quite something out of the way. She was far too canny to let Helford see her outrage. The last thing she wanted was for him to assume that an offer would not be acceptable. It was of the first importance now to marry Lucinda to Helford. If she returned to town unbetrothed, Lady Stanford would be the laughing stock of all her acquaintance.

So she continued to compliment Helford on his chef. 'I vow, I cannot imagine how you persuaded such a treasure to come into the country!' she said archly.

David said with a polite smile, 'I pay him very generously, Lady Stanford. There are few services that enough money cannot secure. Even a French-trained chef.'

'Quite so! A lowering reflection, is it not?' agreed Lady Stanford. Unguardedly she allowed her eyes to rest on Miss Marsden and a scornful smile curved her lips as she conjectured what price the little slut had put on *her* services.

Following her gaze, David's black brows snapped together as he realised what she was thinking. Sheer fury that anyone could think he would take advantage of an unprotected girl like Sophie rendered him utterly speechless. And the insult to Sophie was beyond anything! An insult he had laid her open to!

At this unfortunate moment Sophie happened to glance towards the end of the table to find Lady Stanford's sneering eyes on her and Helford glaring at her as though she had somehow offended him mortally. Her fork rattled uncontrollably as she set it down. Unable to help herself, she stared back at him, confusion and hurt evident in her dark eyes which could not tear themselves from his scowling face. *What have I done?* Trembling slightly, she dropped her eyes and schooled herself to an expression of cheerful interest as she turned back to Tom Hampton.

David saw the pain on her face, saw her turn back to Tom and flinched as he realised that he had unwittingly hurt her and that she had unhesitatingly sought comfort of his best friend. Dear God, would he never stop wounding her? It struck him with all the force of an exploding shell that she was just as vulnerable to being hurt as he was.

How the hell was he supposed to survive this? Never before had he been conscious of a desire to soothe away all hurt, protect a woman from the slightest breeze, ease all her burdens and make sure that she never looked at another man again. And he could do nothing but hurt her, forcing her to turn to one of his oldest friends for reassurance.

Love seemed to confuse everything. He couldn't think straight, he wanted her so badly. And even that had a different quality to it. In the past it had always been *his* desire, *his* pleasure that had been the main focus of his affairs. That was why he had always ensured that he bedded with women of experience, skilled in entertaining a man. To please them in return was simply part of the payment. Nothing more.

Sophie would have been different, he thought despairingly. It would have been…like…like…*making love for the first time*. For the first time he wanted to *give*, not just take his own pleasure in a woman's body. More, he wanted to give *himself*, not merely pleasure.

'Lord Helford?'

Penelope Darleston's warm voice drew him back.

He looked at her in confusion. 'I beg your pardon! My wits were wandering. What were you saying?'

'Merely that your aunt is signalling to me that it is time for the ladies to retire to the drawing room,' she said drily.

He looked down to Lady Maria, who had a particularly wicked smirk on her lined old countenance.

Turning back to Penelope, he said very softly, 'Tell Miss Marsden that I need to speak to her privately and will have her escorted home. Will you do that for me?' He could not allow her to think he had held her so cheap. He had to apologise to her. And he could not do it in front of an entire roomful of people!

Penelope looked at him with suddenly narrowed eyes and said slowly, 'Since you ask it of *me*, my lord, I can only assume that you will take all due care for her reputation.'

David blinked. Never had he heard such an implacable challenge in a woman's voice. Before he could answer Penelope had responded to Lady Maria's signal and was standing up to leave the room for the servants to remove the covers and set out the port and brandy decanters. The gentlemen rose to their feet and waited politely until the door shut behind the ladies.

As they sat down again David resolved that they were not going to sit over their wine for very long. For a start the Vicar's presence made the usual round of ribald stories quite ineligible and even were this not the case he himself had no stomach for them.

He could not have borne to hear tales of loose living and even looser women bandied around while his mind was reeling under the appalling knowledge that he had left Sophie vulnerable to the worst of insults. The only benefit his love had brought Sophie Marsden was that it had prevented him from seducing her. It was not her quality or her unprotected situation that had stopped him. It was quite simply because he had fallen shatteringly in love with her, even if he had been such a fool as not to recognise the fact consciously soon enough—and to distrust it even when he did. Some deeper, surer instinct had held him back from an act which would destroy her. He would explain that to her and then he would let her go.

In the drawing room Sophie was conducting herself gallantly under fire. Lady Lucinda and her mama were probing with condescending insolence into the meaning of Sir Philip's insinuation.

'Are we to offer you our congratulations, Miss Marsden?' purred Lady Lucinda insultingly.

'Sir Philip has often been concerned enough to offer his advice on my handling of Kit,' Sophie replied with outward calm. 'I can hardly see that as a matter for congratulation.' Inwardly she seethed at the implied insult in offering her congratulations. It suggested that a woman had schemed successfully to snare a man. One wished a woman happy and congratulated a man!

'Oh, how disappointing! I quite thought he meant something else!' said Lady Stanford with vast insincerity. 'But I do think Sir Philip would be the very man for you. No doubt he would be able to mount you most satisfactorily. Far more so than Helford.' She smirked triumphantly.

Sophie went absolutely white with fury and opened her mouth to deliver a blistering reply, but Lady Lucinda chipped in first.

'Yes, indeed! I dare say *marriage* had never crossed your mind.'

'No, it hasn't,' said Sophie with deadly emphasis. 'I'm afraid the examples I have seen of women on the catch for a husband, the stratagems they use and the offensive insolence of their behaviour, have quite decided me to leave thoughts of marriage to others.'

'Well spoken, Miss Marsden,' came a light voice at her elbow. 'You remind us all of the pitfalls of vulgarity that await those who seek the married state too eagerly.'

Sophie turned in consternation to find Kate Asterfield twinkling at her in amusement. 'I did not mean—' she began but was cut off.

'Of course you did not,' Kate reassured her. 'Your meaning was plain to the meanest intelligence. Now come and explain to myself and Penny Darleston just exactly how to bring up boys. She is in despair over Darleston's heir, who has painted his sister's face bright blue! And I am expecting an interesting event in the winter and will take all the sensible advice I can get.'

So saying, she drew Sophie's hand through her arm and bore her off, leaving Lady Stanford and Lucinda seething at her effrontery.

'Well!' said the latter in tones of revulsion.

'Quite so, my love!' agreed Lady Stanford. 'How disgusting. To make such an announcement! And in that gown! But it is all of a piece. She was always a trifle fast and a dreadful flirt. One wonders that the Asterfields countenanced the match.'

Perfectly content that her character was being ripped to shreds behind her back, Kate said cheerfully, 'Now you are in the best of company, my dear! Helford's tactlessness will be in a fair way to being forgot with that for them to gossip over.'

'Are…are you really…?' Sophie was too shy to go on.

'I am indeed!' said Kate with a grin. 'But I haven't told Ned yet. I'll do that tonight. Penny has been warning me what a fuss Peter fell into when she was increasing. No doubt Ned will do the same!' She and Penelope kept Sophie beside them as they quizzed her on methods of dealing with naughty toddlers and even naughtier schoolboys until the gentlemen joined them.

Helford's eyes sought Sophie as soon as he crossed the threshold. Ah! There she was! He was relieved to see her with Kate and Penelope, apparently quite at her ease with them. He longed to go to her immediately, but he could see that the Vicar's wife was in urgent need of assistance.

Lady Stanford and Lucinda were discoursing to the long-suffering Mrs Henshaw on the best way to deal with a country parish and keep its members on the path of virtue. Mrs

Henshaw had never before realised just what an atrocious piece of work she and Lucius were making of their job. She smiled with delight at his lordship as he joined their group, making it quite plain, as he bowed over her hand, that she was the object of his interest.

'Tell me, ma'am,' —and his voice radiated an unlikely innocence— 'that sermon your husband preached last Sunday on the power of faith—do you ever have the feeling that your prayers have unequivocally been answered?'

Emerald eyes quizzed her wickedly and she suppressed an undignified chuckle with difficulty. 'Sometimes, my lord. And I always find that my deliverance comes in the most unexpected guise.'

Lady Stanford rushed into speech. 'I was just explaining to Mrs Henshaw the importance of making sure the members of the choir are beyond reproach. One cannot be too careful and one must not condone sin.'

'No, indeed,' agreed Mrs Henshaw. She took the opportunity to change the subject. 'And speaking of music, I am sure Lady Lucinda is a most talented performer. Perhaps if it would not be too much…' It was uncommonly like toad-eating, she thought ruefully, but…if it would shut Lady Stanford up…

Lady Maria, who had been having a quiet word to Penelope, heard this and said, 'Excellent notion. Go on, girl. A little music will be just the thing.'

Lucinda was not at all averse to displaying her talent. She had studied under the finest masters and knew her performance on the pianoforte to be superior. And it would remind Helford of her eligibility. No doubt Miss Marsden was but an indifferent musician. After all, the instrument in her parlour was a mere harpsichord, old fashioned and dowdy in the extreme.

With a fine show of demure reluctance she went to the Broadwood instrument and sat down. Having placed some of her own music there much earlier in the day, she found a piece quickly and began to play.

Her performance, thought David, was indeed superior. Touch and execution were faultless, but increasingly he felt that there was something lacking, some vital spark that would bring the music and the instrument to life. At the end he joined the clapping and nodded in polite agreement when Lady Stanford murmured to him that she considered Lucinda's taste to be irreproachable.

Lady Lucinda stood up and smiled graciously, accepting the applause as her due. She would have been quite happy to favour the assembled party further but Lady Maria had other ideas.

'Very well indeed. I think we'll have some more.' And then, just as Lucinda was about to sit down again, 'Lady Darleston, you play quite prettily.'

Sophie noticed with delight that Penelope did not bother to demur or protest archly that she was sure no one wanted to hear her poor fumblings. Instead she smiled at Lady Maria and went straight to the piano. Her fingers drifted over the instrument for a moment in rippling arpeggios as she explored its tone and feel.

Then she stopped, turned to her audience and said simply, 'Beethoven. *The Appassionata.*' Without any further ado and without music she plunged unhesitatingly into the first movement of the sonata.

Sophie had never heard music played like this. The instrument sang and wept under those slender fingers which held such an unexpected power to move the passions and senses. She found that she was actually trembling as Penelope unleashed the full strength of the music's fire and vigour.

As for David, he had realised the moment Penelope began to play what had been missing from Lucinda's performance. Passion of any sort. Certainly there had been no passion for music. To Lucinda the music was merely a means to display her cleverness and skill. To Penelope it was a means of entering another world where passion and emotion were paramount and she transported her audience with her.

At the end there was a moment's stunned silence, during which David sneaked a look at his old friend Peter Darleston. That gentleman was regarding his wife, still seated at the piano and seemingly oblivious to the wild clapping, with a burning intensity. He was seated on the edge of his chair and David somehow doubted that Penelope Darleston would get very much sleep that night. My Lord the Earl of Darleston was positively ablaze.

David swallowed hard. He knew exactly how Peter felt. Sophie was seated a few yards from him, her creamy complexion warm and flushed with her emotion, a sheen of tears in her expressive eyes as she stared at Penelope Darleston who had shown them all what music was for.

Lady Maria was looking at Penelope with an odd tilt of her head, David noticed suddenly.

Penelope returned that look as she said, 'I think a song is called for now.' She gazed straight at Sophie and said, 'Come, Miss Marsden. Kate, you must know, has a croak like a raven's. You sing for us.'

For one dreadful moment Sophie thought she would die as all eyes in the room rested on her, but Penelope's gaze held her. Those smoky grey eyes were full of encouragement and laughter as Sophie rose to her feet and went to stand by the instrument without the faintest notion of what she was to sing.

Wordlessly Penelope told her. Softly, without bothering to glance down at the keyboard, she slipped into the old tune Sophie had been singing the day they met. The haunting melody drifted through the room as she improvised an introduction.

Sophie stiffened. She couldn't sing that! Not with Helford

in the room. It was impossible. Then her eyes met Tom Hampton's, full of confidence and with that kindly smile on his face. Imperceptibly he nodded at her. In a flash she realised that in this way she could say what was in her heart without shame. She had not chosen the song. If Helford understood, then he could make what use of the knowledge he chose. If he did not understand, then no harm was done.

On the final questioning chord Sophie drew a deep breath and began to sing. Penelope at the keyboard thought she had never before heard any voice echo with such poignant sorrow. There was a simplicity about the song and the performance which tore mercilessly at the heartstrings.

David listened transfixed, his heart pounding. She would give her love an apple without a core, a house without a door and a palace which he might open without any key. The riddle she had set hung between them in the quivering air as a simple interlude led into the second verse.

Her head was the apple without any core, her mind the house without any door and her heart…oh, God! Her voice soared in the final pleading phrases…her heart was the palace where he might dwell and for which he did not require a key because it was his. His mouth suddenly dry, he realised what she was offering. Herself, body, mind and soul. And something in the plangent voice told him that she had not the slightest expectation that her gift would be accepted. True to her nature, she had taken the risk of telling him what she felt in the certainty that her sentiments were not returned. Leaving herself wide open to the full hurt of his rejection. She'd done the very thing he had most feared to do.

As the song closed he stared at her in disbelief. Such a slender, vulnerable figure in her amber silk, the wide dark eyes unfocused as she waited for Penelope to strike the final chord. In that moment he knew only one thing. Sophie Marsden was his! He couldn't possibly offer for Lucinda!

If it caused a scandal, that was just too bad! He might have been able to sacrifice himself on the altar of duty, but he was damned if he'd immolate Sophie!

Sophie was conscious of a burning regard as she curtsied to the applause. Shyly she looked up at Helford and turned a fiery crimson as she met his searing gaze. He seemed to devour her with his eyes, daring anyone to gainsay him. He alone was not clapping, but what she saw in his face made her swallow hard. She had openly declared her love for him and he was telling her that he had understood. What he would choose to do with the knowledge she did not know. She had offered herself unconditionally whatever the cost.

The Vicar, sitting next to Lady Maria, thought he must have misheard the old lady. Surely she couldn't really have said, 'About bloody time!' No, it must be his hearing. Unless, of course, her ladyship was becoming a trifle peculiar.

The tea tray was brought in half an hour later. The talk in the meantime had all been of music.

Kate was positively bubbling over Sophie's singing. 'It was wonderful! Where *did* you learn that song?'

She was delighted at Sophie's explanation. 'How lovely. I must ask my maids at home if they know any like that.' She twinkled at Penelope. 'I may have a voice like a raven. Indeed, I do not deny it. But I still know a good song when I hear one.'

Lady Lucinda turned to her mama and said audibly, 'A maidservant's song! I suppose the tune is well enough in its way, but the words! I dare say its origins account for the very vulgar sentiments expressed.'

'Quite so, my dear!' agreed Lady Stanford fervently. 'And I believe it to be a sad mistake to shower too much praise for what may be achieved by any person of moderate taste and talent. And I am not quite sure that I approve of

Beethoven. After all, he was a supporter of that monster, Bonaparte.'

'Vulgar?' asked a lazy, husky voice just behind them. 'Do you reckon love as a vulgar emotion, Lady Lucinda?'

Lady Lucinda turned to meet the faintly sardonic brown eyes of Lord Darleston. She drew herself up proudly. 'I think persons of our rank should be above being moved by the sway of strong emotions, yes. There is something most unseemly in such things, be it temper, excessive grief or…love.'

Darleston nodded. 'I see. Well, well, well. I never knew I was such a vulgar fellow. Poor Penny, she won't want to know me now. Unless—' in tones of discovery '—unless, of course, she feels vulgar too. Perhaps, since she chose Beethoven, there is yet some hope for her poor, vulgar husband.' With a friendly smile he strolled away from the two speechless and furious ladies.

Lord Mark Reynolds, upon hearing this masterly set-down, nearly choked on the cup of tea just handed to him by Lady Maria. 'Good God, Darleston, what on earth are you about?' he spluttered. 'Are you aware that Helford is about to offer for that chit?'

The black brows rose slightly. 'Do you care to have a little wager on that, Mark?'

'A wager?' Lord Mark was astounded that Darleston should suggest such a thing. 'You ought to know I don't bet on certainties like that! Be robbing you, dear boy.'

'I'll lay you a monkey Helford doesn't marry Lucinda Anstey,' said Darleston calmly.

Lord Mark goggled at him.

'You see, Mark,' he continued, 'Helford is not quite that much of a fool.' He smiled at Lord Mark's stunned countenance and went over to sit down beside Lady Maria.

She handed him a cup of tea which he accepted with

thanks. 'I trust you are satisfied with the evening's results.' His countenance was gently mocking.

Shooting an irritated glance at him, Lady Maria asked bluntly, 'How much did Penelope tell you?'

Darleston grinned. 'Not much beyond the fact that you had set her on to stop the match. She certainly didn't give any clue as to what she intended, apart from asking if David liked music. Put it down to my knowledge of David and my powers of observation.'

She chuckled wheezily. 'You always were as sharp as you could stare. Lord! How could David be such a zany as to contemplate...' She paused. 'Well, I suppose that was my fault. I handled him badly. Should never have mentioned the word *duty*. But I think we've done the trick, with a certain amount of help from the lady herself, I might add. It now remains to be seen whether he has enough brains to offer for the right girl.'

Darleston's roar of laughter attracted the attention of his wife who was speaking quietly to Sophie. 'Heavens! Lady Maria must have said something utterly outrageous.' She turned back to Sophie and said, 'He asked me to tell you he would have you escorted home in one of his carriages.'

At this point they were interrupted by Sir Philip, who came up and said, 'I have ordered my carriage, Miss Sophie. We will be leaving very shortly.'

Sophie looked at him innocently. 'Oh, did you bring the Vicar and Mrs Henshaw? I hadn't realised. Goodnight, Sir Philip.'

A look of annoyance crossed his face. 'I will escort you home, Miss Sophie. I wish to...to discuss certain matters with you.'

Penelope watched with fascination as a hint of steel entered into Sophie Marsden's face.

It was echoed in her voice as she replied, 'I find your manner of discussing the matter repugnant, Sir Philip, and have no wish to endure it again. My opinion on this topic remains the same as ever. I have no need of your advice, no need for your carriage and no need or desire for your discussions. Goodnight, sir.' And, as he looked as though he would have argued further, 'Sir, I have spoken elliptically out of respect for your feelings, despite the fact that you have shown none for mine! Unless you wish me to speak more plainly, leave this subject!'

Red with bottled fury, he turned on his heel and stalked away to bid farewell to his host and hostess.

'Goodness!' said Penelope, visibly impressed. 'Do you always refuse offers so categorically?'

A little conscious, Sophie said, 'Oh, dear. I suppose it was rather obvious.'

'Moderately,' agreed Penelope. 'Never mind. He did ask for it.' She had every expectation that Miss Marsden would not respond to Lord Helford's inevitable offer in the same way.

Chapter Twelve

The house party had made its way up to bed without realising that their host had disappeared. He had handed them their candles on the landing and bidden them all goodnight with every appearance of having all night at his disposal. Lady Lucinda had lingered slightly, thinking that he might like to take the opportunity to make her an offer since Lady Maria had interrupted them so tactlessly before dinner. She thought that even if he wished to kiss her again, she was prepared now, and could endure it without too much difficulty.

Her affront when Helford smiled at her charmingly and thanked her for her pretty playing as he handed her the candle was considerable. He did not move as she went off down the corridor to her chamber, but as soon as he heard the door close behind her he was off the opposite way along the corridor at a run. Down some narrow back stairs, usually frequented by servants, three at time. Down another corridor to a side entrance and out into the night.

Sophie was waiting in the Great Hall for Helford. All the others had gone and he had disappeared muttering something about bidding his house party a goodnight. She waited with increasing nervousness, wondering if Penelope had made a dreadful mistake, until a familiar face appeared at the door.

'Evenin', Miss Sophie. Got yer carriage outside.' Jasper smiled at her in a friendly fashion.

'Oh.' Sophie looked around wildly. There was only a sleepy-looking footman who appeared to be waiting for her departure to lock up.

'Should I…should I not bid his lordship farewell?' She was conscious of a feeling of sickening disappointment. Helford had not returned. If he had wished to speak to her, he must have changed his mind. He was probably avoiding her. She could not tell his servants that she wished to see him. It would look as though she were throwing herself at his head.

Jasper was shaking his head. 'His lordship asked me to tell ye to go straight home, miss.'

She blushed in mortification. Damn Helford! If he couldn't keep to what he himself had arranged, then he could go to the devil! Throwing her cloak around her, she said, 'Very well, then. Thank you, Jasper. I am ready.'

Proudly she went down the broad flight of steps to the waiting carriage. Jasper handed her in. After the brightly lit hall and the flood of light pouring from the open door, her eyes took a moment to adjust to the darkness inside the carriage. She heard Jasper spring to the box and call, 'Let 'em go!'

The pair of horses moved off and she suddenly realised that there was someone else in the carriage, sitting in the darkest corner. For a moment she thought she must be mistaken, but the figure moved and she found herself caught in a hold as tender as it was unbreakable. A seductive mouth was on hers, warm and caressing. A gentle hand was under her chin, stroking her throat, her cheek, adding its mite to the persuasive lips which held her in thrall.

* * *

At about this moment Lady Lucinda, having rung for her maid, was removing her pearls at the dressing table when a movement in the glass caught her eye. She spun around, but could see no one. Just the flickering candles in the sconces, she thought. Shrugging her shoulders, she removed her bracelets and began to unpin her hair. She could not remember ever having been so disgusted by an evening's entertainment in her life. How dare that insufferable man Darleston give them such an insolent set-down! And Helford! Making it plain for anyone to see that that little trollop was his current inamorata! While as for the girl herself! It was obvious enough what Helford saw in her!

Again that movement caught her attention. She turned again, but could see nothing. As soon as her maid came she would have her light a lamp, this candlelight was quite inadequate. The girl should have come up earlier and lit the lamps. And where was her maid? How long must she wait for the lazy wench?

And then she saw it. Sitting up on the middle of her bed with a piece of apple between its paws was a rat. And not just any rat. A big rat. In fact, a *very* big rat. It did not seem to be particularly concerned about Lady Lucinda's presence. But then, given its size, it really had no need for concern. It just sat there, nibbling on its apple, bright eyes gleaming in the candlelight, looking totally incongruous on the silken counterpane.

That was before Lady Lucinda screamed. At the very first scream the rat whisked around and disappeared into the shadows of the bed hangings. Lady Lucinda kept on screaming, becoming more hysterical by the second.

Within half a minute Lady Stanford came racing in, brandishing the poker from her bedchamber, clearly convinced her daughter was being raped. She found her standing on an elegant bergère chair as far away from the bed as she could get, clutching a smaller gilt chair in an attitude of defence. A second later her maid burst into the room from the corridor, closely followed by the entire house party, Lady Maria, the butler and two footmen who appeared to have left behind their usual expressions of bovine stolidity.

A babble of noise broke out as everyone tried to ascertain from the shaking lady exactly what had induced her to seek the dubious sanctuary of a French chair. Eventually Tom Hampton's calm voice got through to her, after he had silenced everyone else by the simple expedient of telling them plainly to shut up.

'Come now, Lucinda, tell us what has alarmed you.'

She raised one shaking hand and pointed at the bed. 'A…a rat! On…on my bed!'

'A *rat*?' exclaimed Lady Maria in disbelief. 'We do *not* have rats at Helford Place!'

'Ugh!' Kate Asterfield was for once entirely in sympathy with Lady Lucinda. 'How utterly revolting!'

'A rat, eh?' said Asterfield, not at all convinced by Lady Maria's belief in the ratless state of the house.

The butler, Bainbridge, however, drew himself up and said in tones of deep disapproval, 'Her ladyship must have seen a large mouse. I do not deny that there may have been a mouse in the room, but it cannot have been a—'

This categorical denial was rudely interrupted by a startled exclamation from one of the footmen. 'Gor…bloody 'ell! It's enormous!'

Never in all his life had Bainbridge been so shamed by one of his underlings. Turning to annihilate the offender, he found James staring and pointing at the canopied top of the bed hangings. The forceful rebuke died on Bainbridge's lips as he beheld the largest rat he had ever seen perched on the apex of the canopy.

'Gawd!' gasped the other footman. 'What a whopper! That ain't no mouse, beggin' your pardon, I'm sure, Mr Bainbridge, an' yours, milady. That's a *rat*, that is!'

Screams of horror erupted from all the women, who scrambled as far away from the bed as possible. Except, of course, for the redoubtable Lady Maria, who stalked over to the bed and peered up at the rat with an outraged expression on her countenance.

Satisfied that it was not, after all, a mouse, she pronounced, 'There seems little doubt. It is a rat. Remove it *at once!*' She swung around to glare at the hapless footmen and Bainbridge.

'Remove it?' James seemed to have totally forgotten his place. 'Remove it? Just like that? Not bloody likely…milady.' This last did not in the least suggest that his respect for Lady Maria would lead him to tackle a rat of these proportions. His colleague and boon companion Samuel nodded vehemently in support of this revolutionary attitude. Even Bainbridge looked flabbergasted at the suggestion.

'I say!' said Lord Mark, 'I've got a capital idea! Helford's head groom Highbury has a champion terrier. He was tellin' me the other day. It kills rats on sight. What say I nip down to the stables and fetch him up with the dog? Be capital sport!' He rubbed his hands together in glee. And, as all the ladies stared at him in outrage, he added lamely, 'Get rid of the rat, you know. Capital terrier it is…just the… er…job.'

Trying not to laugh at a scene which was rapidly deteriorating into a farce, Hampton looked at his hostess for guidance. 'Ah…Lady Maria…what do you say?' It seemed like a good idea to him, although he would not have cared to wager any sum on the motives behind Lord Mark's enthusiasm. He could not, however, adopt the idea over Lady Maria's head. And where the devil was Helford? he wondered. Damn it all! It was his job to deal with things like this. His chamber wasn't so far away that he wouldn't have heard all the racket Lucinda had kicked up, let alone the rest of them.

Lady Maria snorted and said shortly, 'If that seems best to you, Hampton. I have no experience of rats, I am happy to say! Lucinda! Another room will be made ready for you while the gentlemen amuse themselves!' She shot an ironic glance at Lord Mark, who blushed deeply. 'You will not wish to sleep in this chamber again. Come, Mrs Asterfield.' Accompanied by Kate, she stalked out, her rigid back proclaiming her complete disapproval.

'I'll fetch the terrier, shall I?' suggested Lord Mark with unconvincing diffidence. At Hampton's nod he went out quietly, but a moment later he could be heard fairly running down the corridor. A faint cry of, 'Yoicks! Tally ho! Gone awaaaaay!' drifted back to them. Only the knowledge that Lady Stanford, apoplectic with fury, was observing him enabled Tom Hampton to keep a straight face.

'Oh, I say!' said Asterfield in tones of deprecation. 'That's a little off! Mean to say, he don't need to be that pleased!'

Lord Mark returned fifteen minutes later with Highbury and an excited terrier whose tattered ears bore mute testament to his many battles with the foe. Lucinda and her mama were, with the assistance of their maids, removing all her belongings to Lady Stanford's room for the night where the sofa bed was to be made up.

'Evenin', milady,' said Highbury, not at all averse to being called upon to perform duties outside his province. 'Now, where's this 'ere rat 'is lordship's tellin' me about?'

James pointed silently to the bed hangings and there was the rat, scuttling back and forth. The terrier did not need to ask, his nose alerted him to the presence of his greatest enemy and he pranced forward, barking loudly.

Highbury swore softly. 'Righto. Clear the room. We'll soon 'ave 'im down and then Nelson can do 'is stuff.'

Asterfield spoke up. 'Hope we didn't drag you out of bed, Highbury. Jolly sporting of you to bring the dog along.'

'Oh, I weren't in bed, Mr Asterfield, sir,' Highbury assured him cheerfully. 'I never goes to bed without all the 'orses is in safe. An' Jasper an' Bob ain't brought 'is lordship in yet.' Patently unaware of having uttered anything at all out of the way, he turned his attention back to the rat.

Oh, my God, thought Hampton. It only needed that!

Lady Stanford and Lucinda had frozen on their way out. Lady Stanford turned back and enquired icily, 'And where, may I ask, is his lordship?' Her tones suggested that no excuse for his absence would be sufficient to redeem him in her view.

'Hmm?' Highbury's thoughts snapped back to his betters. 'Where's 'is lordship? Gone in the carriage to see Miss Marsden 'ome safe. Now...Captain Hampton, sir, if you'd just fetch me that chair, I can stand on the bed an' give 'im a bit of a poke, like...'

A stunned silence greeted this revelation. Lady Stanford's jaw hung open in disbelief. Not all her spouse's infidelities over the years had prepared her for anything this outrageous. Shameless! Utterly shameless!

A stifled snort of laughter from Ned Asterfield settled the issue. Her head held high, Lady Lucinda said, 'Come, Mama. It is clearly not at all the sort of establishment with which we wish to be connected. In any way whatsoever!' She stalked from the chamber in what could only be described as suppressed fury. Lady Stanford followed in full agreement. Had Lucinda shown the least disposition to accept his lordship's suit after this comprehensive insult, she would have disowned her!

Twenty minutes later Hampton strode back to his bed-chamber, having persuaded Asterfield and Lord Mark that to finish up an evening's sport by returning to the library to try and drink each other under the table would be in the worst of bad taste. They only agreed when it was pointed out that they didn't even have the rat's mangled corpse to gloat over as it had hurtled around the room to evade the terrier and had found an open window. The rat had disappeared along the ornate stonework which afforded ample holds for a rat, if not for a terrier, who had had to be forcibly restrained from attempting to follow his craven enemy.

As he settled into bed, he resolved that in the morning he was going to give David Melville the finest trimming of his unregenerate life for putting Sophie Marsden in such an appalling position. He ground his teeth in rage. If Helford hadn't already offered for her he, Captain Thomas Hampton, was personally going to stand over him while he did it!

On reflection, though, he had to admit David had certainly solved his problem about having to offer for Lucinda. Someone with David's best interests at heart was plainly looking out for him, he thought with a chuckle. Where on earth had the rat come from? On the heels of this question came another: just what had Fanny had in that box she'd brought home from Willowbank House the other day?

'*Helford!*' Sophie gasped, stunned, unable to think. His kisses were possessive, demanding. Her mouth was released briefly as he whispered against her hair. 'Call me David, please, Sophie...oh, God! Sophie! My little sweetheart...' She could feel his ragged breath on her ear, creating the most dizzying sensations, and then he took her mouth again. She felt his tongue flicker against her lips, seeking entrance.

She opened her mouth with a moan of pleasure, feeling his tongue plunge in and take complete possession, boldly plundering and exploring as his hands gripped her waist, pulling her closer to his hard muscular body. She yielded totally, pressing herself against him, returning his kisses, her arms clinging to him desperately as he removed her cloak.

David felt as though he were on fire. He could think of nothing but the innocent response of the girl in his arms, the sweetness of her trembling body and mouth. Desire raged in him fuelled by her passionate embrace. One hand slid up her bare arm to her sleeve and slid it off her shoulder, easing her bodice and chemise down until the breast was exposed. He touched it lightly, wondering at the texture of velvety flesh. He felt, rather than heard, her instinctive murmur of protest. He smothered it with his lips and tongue, ravishing the vulnerable, moist mouth in a way which brooked no argument.

Her senses entirely overwhelmed by his sensual onslaught, Sophie offered no further resistance, but gave herself up to the utterly wonderful way he was making love to her. His teasing fingers were fondling and stroking her breast in a manner which made her gasp in pleasure.

Circling and tantalising at first, he at last brushed his thumb very lightly over the nipple. He groaned deep in his throat as he felt it hard and erect. He could feel the tremors running through her body and lifted his mouth from hers. Then with another groan he lowered it to her breast and ran his tongue over it lightly before sucking and biting with gentle savagery at the rosy peak.

Sophie was conscious of a feeling of intense heat burning through her whole body; it seemed to be concentrated in her breasts and in an increasing tension in her belly and even lower. David was now beside her, encouraging her to lie back along the seat. She knew she ought to resist, but lacked the willpower to do so. It felt so wonderful, so right to be lying in this intimate embrace with him practically on top of her and his mouth literally devouring her breast.

She felt one hand slide down the silk of her skirt, caressing the line of her thigh through the fabric, then he was lifting her skirt, pulling it up to expose her bare leg to his hand. It glided up past her knee and on to her thigh. Shock blazed through her, partially recalling her to sanity. The last remaining corner of her brain screamed feebly that she had to stop him. Right now! At once! Before things went too far. But that mesmerising hand crept further to tease and caress her soft thighs, which fell apart in obedience to his seductive probing.

His mind reeling, David's mouth lifted from her breast. Never in his life had he felt so totally out of control, so totally possessed by his own desire. The carriage lamp outside cast a faint glow and he could see her face very dimly. Tenderly his free hand stroked a wayward curl back from her brow, then drifted over her cheek to linger by the corner of her mouth. Oh, God! Her mouth, so soft, so yielding, like her body! With a shuddering groan he took her mouth again, his tongue echoing the rhythm and action of his searching fingers.

Dazed, melting in surrender, yet that small, sane part of Sophie's mind still shrieked its warning. This must stop! Her fainting reason panicked. Soon it would be too late! If, indeed, it were not so already. Desperately she tried to summon the willpower to tear herself free. But she wanted him, longed to give herself. She sobbed in passion, words of love germinating in her heart, where they had lain dormant, ready to flower on her lips in response to his loving.

Releasing her mouth momentarily, David whispered in a deep voice, cracking with emotion, 'Sophie, dearest Sophie. I want you so much!' His lips drifted over her temples, her cheek, to the wildly beating pulse at the base of her throat.

She froze. He wanted her...was that all? Suddenly Sophie's mind cleared and she realised where this was going to end. That she had to stop him. Before...before he could not be stopped...before she begged him to take her.

His mouth was on hers again, seducing her to his will,

his fingers teasing and probing until he found the tangle of soft curls at the base of her belly. Tenderly he cupped the mound and one long, expert finger slid down to caress the quivering dampness between her thighs. Shock lanced through her at the sensation. Aching, empty, her body throbbed to the gentle rhythm, to the overwhelming temptation to yield. But a vision of Kit flashed before her dazed mind. What was the use of remaining single to protect his inheritance if she ruined herself in this way? Desperately she pushed against the solid wall of his chest, crying out in protest as she wrenched her lips away.

'My lord, no! Please!'

She felt him pull away from her, heard his groan of frustration as he released her. Frantically she pulled and pushed her skirts down over her trembling thighs, dragged the bodice of her gown back over her aching breasts. Her hands shook uncontrollably as she realised what she had so nearly permitted. What it could have meant to Kit.

Her whole body sang with the burning, raging need his caresses had unleashed. She prayed that he would not press his advantage, try to overcome her resistance. She knew if he did that her defences would crumble swiftly, that she would not be able to stop him, would not even want to stop him.

To her horror she felt him reach for her, his hands gentle but compelling, drawing her into the warmth and strength of his embrace. Terrified of her own melting response, she clung to reason as to a life line and flung herself to the other side of the carriage.

'No!' It was a cry of despair.

And finally the blind terror in her voice got through to David. It shook him to the core. *Oh, my God! What the hell have I done? She's terrified!* Shame surged through him that he could have lost control so totally as to actually scare her. *She trusted you!* Breathing hard, he forced himself to sit back against the squabs, forced his limbs to relax. Tried, with even less success, to force his mind to think about something other than the girl sitting shaking in the darkness not three feet from him. And conscious all the while of the frantic urge to wrap her in his arms again. To comfort her, to reassure her. He dared not.

The pain of his arousal was appalling, but it was as nothing to the pain of guilt in his heart. She had told him...No! Begged him to stop. And he hadn't wanted to. He knew even now that if he pressed her she would not have any real defence against his lovemaking, that she would surrender to his demands, give herself without reservation.

He couldn't do it. She deserved better than that.

They sat in shaken silence, letting the rumble of the carriage wheels soothe their ragged breathing, each as insanely aware of the other as if they were still in each other's arms.

Sophie was beyond speech and even if she hadn't been she had no idea of what she could possibly say. So she sat, grateful for the friendly veil of darkness that masked the tears slipping down her burning cheeks. So close had she been to declaring her love for him, that she could still feel the words bursting to escape, clamouring in her heart for release.

David, his mind still reeling from the sheer intensity of his physical and emotional response, drew a deep breath, and said as evenly as he could, 'Sophie...you must not misunderstand me. I did not mean to insult you...I never intended...' His apology trailed off. What hadn't he intended? To make love to her? Nearly seduce her?

To his horror he heard her response. Light and bitter.

'You need not fear, my lord. I have not misinterpreted your actions.' The briefest of pauses. 'I am well aware of your intentions...' He thought her voice shook slightly, but an instant later it was as cool as ever. 'I confess I had no idea you meant to go beyond flirtation. Forgive me if I decline to join your game.'

At this extremely inopportune moment the carriage began to slow down.

David cursed fluently. And then realised he was wasting time.

'Sophie, listen,' he said urgently. 'You must know I love you. I...I know I shouldn't have even touched you tonight. God knows I find it hard enough to keep my hands off you at the best of times, but you can't think I merely want a quick tumble with you!'

At this inopportune moment, the carriage drew to a halt. And before the horses' hooves had fully stilled, Sophie had the door open and had leapt out into the road.

She did not dare wait to find out just how long a tumble his lordship envisaged. The likelihood of her acquiescing in his ideas was too great to be risked. 'G...good night,' she whispered, staring up at him with wide, dark eyes.

'Sophie! Wait!' His voice was frantic. 'My house party is going tomorrow. I will come the next day to see you, to...to arrange everything...'

She bit her lip and turned away before she could respond to the urgency of his tone. She fled to the open gate and up the path without a backward look. Fumbling with the latch, she opened the door and slipped inside. The house was quiet and she could hear the rumble of hooves as the carriage was turned. Holding her breath she listened...there it was, the sound of the carriage leaving. With unsteady hands she shot the bolts home and went up to her chamber quickly.

Still shaking, she sank on to the bed, her thoughts in turmoil. *Arrange what?* He had not said what he was offering. She did not dare hope that he offered marriage. He was as good as betrothed to Lady Lucinda. At the most he wanted her to be his mistress. At the worst he wanted a brief affair. She dismissed that. *He said he wanted you.*

Surely if all he wanted was to have you, he had every opportunity. He must have known how little effort it would have taken to persuade you.

She flushed in shame, knowing that, had he chosen to press her, one touch, one word of love, would have done it, would have had her in his arms, begging him to take her. Bitterly she realised that he had only spoken of love when it was plain that she would resist him.

She shuddered. He knew she loved him after that song. Would he realise how easy it would be to breach her defences even now? What would her answer be when he returned? She knew what it *should* be, but she could not bear him to think her a tease. Or, worse, that she was trying to lure him into marriage by refusing him. And she did not want to refuse him. Had it just been herself she would have surrendered and taken the risk. Taken what he offered.

She could not afford to think of just herself. She had to protect Kit. And now that meant shielding him from her own disgraceful impulses. Fiercely she forced herself to envisage how his life would be ruined if she accepted a *carte blanche* from Helford and gave Strathallen a weapon with which to challenge her guardianship in court.

Slowly she undressed and readied herself for bed, laying aside the crumpled silk gown. As she washed herself at the jug she found that her thighs were sticky, that cleansing between them was enough to set her trembling at the sensations which coursed through her. She pulled on her nightgown and slipped into bed as she faced the undeniable fact that if Helford came to take her and claimed to love her the temptation to surrender would be overwhelming.

Furiously she gritted her teeth and fought for control over her unruly heart and body. She was *not* going to add her name and heart to the list of Helford's innumerable conquests.

* * *

David watched her go and collapsed on the seat with a groan of frustration. He sat with his head in his hands, trying to regain some measure of control over his body. Never in his life had he felt so utterly insane with desire. The pain in his loins was beyond bearing. He tried hard not to think of Sophie's warm, yielding body, and wondered if she would ever forgive him for what he had done. The only saving grace, he told himself grimly, was that he wanted to marry her.

It was at this point that he realised he'd been so damn flustered that he had not made his intentions absolutely plain even at the last when he'd told her he loved her. He had not actually asked her to marry him. Swearing, he sat back against the seat as he realised that she had every reason to think he wanted an affair!

Chapter Thirteen

The following morning David was somewhat startled to hear from his valet that a rat of large and ferocious aspect had been discovered in Lady Lucinda's bedchamber.

'A rat?' he asked in amazement as he flung back the bedclothes. 'We don't *have* rats here! Not in the house. I suppose there are bound to be a few around the stables. It must have been a big mouse.' He drew on a resplendent grey silk dressing gown.

Meredith shook his head mournfully. 'No, my lord. It was a rat. Mr Bainbridge will bear out James and Samuel. They all say it was the biggest rat they'd ever seen. Even Lady Maria agreed it was a rat.' He handed Helford his shaving water.

David nearly dropped the jug. 'Lady Maria saw it? Why on earth did she see it?'

'Every one in earshot saw it, my lord, as far as I can make out,' he explained. 'Very upset the young lady was, which I'm sure she's not to be blamed. She wouldn't stay in the room, I'm told, but had a bed made up on the day bed in Lady Stanford's chamber.'

'What happened to the rat?' asked David in failing tones. If everyone had appeared in Lucinda's bedchamber to discover what the disturbance was, then his own absence must have been glaringly apparent.

With a singularly abysmal effort to maintain a straight face Meredith said, 'I am…er…given to understand that Lord Mark, who is, as your lordship knows, much addicted to sports, he…er…suggested that Highbury and his terrier might be fetched up from the stables.'

'What?' David stared at Meredith in patent disbelief in the shaving mirror as he lathered his face.

'Yes, my lord,' affirmed Meredith. 'Mr Bainbridge and James and Samuel refused to budge when Lady Maria told them to remove the rat. Very outspoken on the subject James was, I am informed.' The corner of his normally well-trained mouth twitched convulsively.

'It must have been a bloody big rat to make them disobey my aunt!' said David with a shout of laughter. 'Come on, Meredith, what happened? Did Highbury bring Nelson up? Lord, what a kickup!'

'As to that, I was not an eyewitness, my lord,' said Meredith, in tones of infinite regret. 'But Captain Hampton is in the library, I believe. He asked me to tell you that he would appreciate a word with you before breakfast.'

David snorted. 'Did he, now? And tell me, was Captain Hampton present at this bloodbath?' He carefully negotiated his chin.

'I believe so, my lord.'

'God help me, then,' said his lordship in restricted tones as he shaved around his mouth. Tom, of all those present, was bound to have a very fair idea of where his host had been. He comforted himself with the thought that Tom was far too discreet, not to mention too good a friend, to have given him away.

Half an hour later his lordship, immaculate in breeches, top boots and a coat of dark green superfine, strolled into his library to find Tom Hampton sitting at his own *bureau plat*, by the open French window, writing a letter.

He slewed around when his host walked in and said grimly, 'Good morning, David. I hope you are up to a few shocks.'

David cocked his head and said, 'Well, I know about the rat. Something, however, tells me the mere fact that a rat invaded Lucinda's bedchamber would not be sufficient to make you look like bull beef. Out with it. What am I supposed to have done?'

Hampton's mouth did not so much as quiver at this. 'I will rather ask you, David, what are your intentions towards Sophie Marsden?'

'And if I give the wrong answer?' asked David, the lightness of his voice at odds with the watchful gleam in his green eyes and the alertness of his stance.

Hampton stood up slowly. He was not quite as tall as Helford, but just as strongly built. And he looked positively dangerous. 'I tell you, David, if you mean to take that child and make her your mistress, I'll call you out.' Despite the softness of his voice, no one in possession of his senses could have doubted that he was in deadly earnest.

David relaxed. 'Well, I certainly mean to take her,' he began and flung up his hand hurriedly as Hampton started towards him. 'Oh, take a damper, Tom! I want her as my wife, not my mistress.'

'Thank God for that!' said Hampton, sitting down again. 'I couldn't believe that you were really going to seduce her, but when it came out that you had taken her home…'

David stiffened. 'Who the hell let that out? I didn't realise anyone knew!'

'Highbury,' said Hampton. 'I dare say he was distracted by the rat! Mind you, we were all wondering where you were. You missed a scene of high drama, let me tell you. And you may yet be thankful for Highbury's lack of discretion! Sit down, David! You're making me nervous, looming over me like that.'

'I thought you were going to call me out,' protested David, sitting down on the edge of the *bureau*.

'Only if you were planning to seduce Miss Marsden,' Hampton replied.

David thought it might be as well not to tell Tom how close he had come to doing just that the previous night. 'For God's sake, tell me about this blasted rat, Tom! I can't believe it, we don't *have* rats!'

Hampton complied, explaining in laughing detail what had happened. He looked a bit more serious at the end. 'When Highbury said you'd taken Miss Marsden home, well! You should have seen the look on Lucinda's face! Not to mention Lady Stanford's. You're in trouble there, my boy. Made it quite plain that you would not be accepted. Er…just how deeply were you entangled with Lucinda?'

'Deep enough,' acknowledged David with a grimace. 'It's going to cause a lot of talk, but I'm damned if I'll marry her just to avoid unpleasantness. And if she's indicated so publicly that an offer won't be welcome, it doesn't matter. I approached Stanford before leaving town to ask his permission to pay my addresses, but I hadn't actually asked her to marry me. You and Kate put paid to that in the last week, didn't you?'

'Mmm,' said Hampton with a twinkle. 'Don't leave Lady Maria out of the reckoning. She was quite as determined to prevent the match. May one ask why on earth you even considered Lucinda? I don't say anything against the girl, but I wouldn't have thought she was quite your style.'

'She's not,' said David promptly. 'Put it down to sheer stubbornness. I intended a marriage of convenience because I thought myself incapable of falling in love after Felicity. Thought it didn't really matter who I chose as long as she was a girl of breeding, beauty and virtue. You must own

Lucinda is all that.' He shrugged. 'It never felt quite right. I knew I wasn't in love, but that didn't worry me at first. Nor that Lucinda doesn't know the meaning of the word. But I kept seeing Peter and Penelope. I suppose it gradually dawned on me that a marriage doesn't have to be convenient to be happy. And that just because a man makes one mistake he doesn't have to keep on making it. And then I met Sophie!'

'I see,' said Hampton. 'And that was it. She bowled you out!'

David looked at him. 'You could say that. One day I'll tell you how I met her. But now, if you will excuse me, I need to write a note to reassure her that I really do intend marriage. Unless, of course, you feel that you could make a better fist of it. I suppose I should be thanking you and the others on bended knee for your kind offices.'

'No, no!' said Hampton with a grin as he stood up. 'I'll leave you to it in the sure and certain knowledge that Lady Maria approves your choice this time.'

'Oh, go to the devil,' recommended David, sitting down at the *bureau*. He watched Captain Hampton depart with a light step and wondered just how quickly his friend would be able to tell his co-conspiritors of the success that had attended upon their efforts. With a shudder he contemplated just what might have occurred without their intervention. He would have offered for Lucinda and been accepted.

He groaned as he realised just how close he'd come to an appalling scandal. He had no doubt that he would not have married Lucinda. Would probably have jilted her for Sophie, which would have made the position for both women intolerable. Thanks to his aunt and his friends and…yes, and that impossible rat, he'd been spared all that!

The chiming of the clock on the marble chimney-piece warned him that he was running out of time and that if he wished to write to Sophie before breakfast, he'd better stop dithering.

His lordship found paper, mended his pen and wrote hastily for a moment. It would have to be a brief letter if he were not to be hopelessly late for breakfast. To his exasperation his seal was missing.

'Hell and damnation!' he muttered. 'Where is the confounded thing?' He thought hard and remembered that he had put it in his pocket the day before to take down to the estate room. 'What I need,' he said to the standish, 'is a seal ring. I shall suggest it to Aunt Maria as a wedding present.' He folded the letter over and wrote *Miss Sophie Marsden* on the outside. Then he left the room to find his seal.

As soon as the door clicked shut a tall slim figure gowned in pale blue muslin stalked into the room through the open window. Fury and chagrin blazed from cerulean eyes; even Lady Lucinda's black ringlets seemed to radiate anger. How *dare* he! It was bad enough to think that he had been pursuing the Marsden wench right under her nose with a view to making the slut his mistress. But to find that he actually wished to marry the little trollop in preference to herself was insupportable!

Never mind that she would not now accept him if he got down on his knees and begged. Lady Lucinda Anstey had never been so insulted and humiliated in her entire life. She'd make the pair of them pay for this if it took her the rest of her life!

She clenched her fist in rage and brought it down on the vacated *bureau*, making the quill pen and standish jump slightly. The unsealed letter to Sophie caught her eye. Her hand went out to it and drew back. There was no point in destroying it. He would only write another.

But her hand went back to the letter as if drawn irresistibly. She hesitated, never in her life had she read someone else's letter but the temptation to see what sickly, vulgar rubbish Helford had penned to the presumptuous whore was too great. Quickly she unfolded the letter and conned it.

> *My dearest Love,*
> *I thought that I had better write and reassure you as to my intentions after my behaviour last night. We arrived at Willowbank House far too soon. Believe me, Sophie, I mean to have you with all honour. I am rather rushed now but please accept this in earnest of my intentions.*
>
> > *All my love, David.*

She snorted in disgust. How pathetic! Had she not actually heard Helford tell Hampton point blank that he intended marriage she would doubt it from that letter. She was about to refold the letter again when a sudden idea presented itself for her inspection.

Carefully she re-read the letter. It was as she thought, he did not actually mention marriage. Not that she doubted his intention. But would Madam Marsden see it like that? If, as the letter implied, he had taken liberties with the wench, then she might well be expecting a very different sort of offer.

Lucinda thought fast. Helford could be back at any moment. He must not find her here! Swiftly she opened her reticule and drew forth two ten-pound notes. Swiftly she folded the letter around them, and placed it back on the desk. At the worst, if Helford found the money, he could prove nothing, might even think he had got the notes muddled with the letter. At best, it might even ruin the marriage if Miss Marsden thought he had considered making her his mistress.

With a coldly triumphant smile Lady Lucinda left the room, giving all her consideration to how she could ensure that Miss Marsden should be as sullied as possible by the fact that Lord Helford had taken her home and not kept the line with her!

Entering the room a bare two minutes later, Helford sat down his desk and pulled the letter towards him.

Just as he was about to open it the door opened and a small voice said, 'Uncle David?'

He looked up in some surprise. 'Hullo, Fanny. Something wrong?'

Inserting her self into the room, Fanny nodded. 'It's... well...it's about that rat.'

Smothering a smile, he said comfortingly, 'You don't have to worry, sweetheart. Highbury's Nelson saw it off. It won't come back.'

'It's not that,' muttered Fanny. 'All the maids are quite hysterical and Aunt Maria is talking about having the whole house gone over and...and...I thought I'd better tell you...'

'Tell me?' he prompted as she hesitated.

'That it was me.'

A feeling akin to awe stole through David as he eyed his shamefaced niece. 'You put the rat in Lucinda's room?' He couldn't quite believe it.

'Yes, sir.'

Choking back a wild desire to laugh, he asked simply, 'Why?'

She hesitated and then said, 'Because I didn't want her to marry you. And I thought...'.

'That if she believed the place to be infested with rats she wouldn't,' he finished drily. 'You were quite right, but why tell me now?'

Fanny blushed even more deeply. 'Because I heard Captain Hampton just now telling Aunt Maria and Mrs Asterfield that you'd decided to marry Aunt Sophie instead...and...and...well, we...I wouldn't want *her* to say no because of the rat! And, he...he kept on looking at me and saying that Lady Lucinda wouldn't have you because of the rat…and…and I thought I'd better tell you before he did!'

'I see,' said David, wondering if he was allowed to laugh or should, in the name of discipline, preserve a disapproving front. But for the life of him, he couldn't find it in him even to pretend to be cross. 'Well, since you've saved me from a fate worse than death, to wit, an appalling scandal, I'll let you off this time.' He shook slightly. 'Just don't unburden your soul to Aunt Maria!' Seeing her look of puzzlement, he explained. 'Don't tell her what you've just told me. I think that it had better be our secret.'

He held out his hand to her and with a smile of relief she ran across to him. He hugged her and said lightly, 'Just don't import any more rats, pet. Where on earth did you catch one anyway?'

She looked very conscious and said, 'I think I'd better not say…really, Uncle David. I promise I haven't been anywhere I'm not allowed, but I can't say…'

Memories of his own misspent boyhood suggested only one reason that she would refuse to answer; an ally to incriminate—which meant—no, he wasn't going to ask! There were some things a wise guardian just didn't want to know. Officially, anyway.

'Very well,' he said. 'Now, you'd best be off. I have to get to breakfast and be extra polite to everyone! Out!' Then, as she reached the door, he asked casually, 'By the way, Fanny, how big was it?'

She turned and shuddered. 'Oh, it was enormous! I nearly screamed when it came out of the box on her bed and I saw it. I didn't think rats got that big!'

'Hmm,' managed David in the face of this innocent revelation. 'Greater love hath no niece…my thanks, Fanny. Off you go now, and remember—don't tell Aunt Maria!' That joy, he vowed, was going to be his, and his only.

Only after the door shut behind his niece did he give in to his laughter. Kit and Fanny! And he'd have the pair of them under his guardianship! What on earth was he letting himself in for?

Belatedly remembering his letter, he cast a horrified glance at the clock on the chimney-piece, sealed the missive hurriedly and rang the bell. When James appeared, he merely gave it to him and said, 'Have one of the grooms deliver that to Willowbank House immediately.'

'Very good, my lord.' James took the letter and prepared to depart.

'Oh, James, about last night…'

James turned with what could only be termed reluctance. 'Yes, my lord?'

'It must have been an extremely large rat.'

The corner of his lordship's mouth was twitching uncontrollably and a wide answering grin split James's normally stolid face. 'It was that right enough! Cor! I never seen the like! Even Mr Bainbridge was shocked!' He flushed. 'I hope her ladyship didn't take it too badly amiss, me speakin' out of turn like as how I did. Don't know what came over me.'

'Never mind, James,' said his lordship with an even broader grin as he wondered how Fanny had steeled herself to the task. 'Should her ladyship chance to mention the incident, I will undertake to convince her that had she given me that command, my response would have been even less respectful. I understand Highbury's terrier put the beast to flight?'

'Aye, he did that all right,' said James, with a chuckle. 'Shame it got away. Not but what it would of made a nasty mess which the maids wouldn't of liked. All for the best, like as not, my lord.'

'I dare say!' said his lordship in heartfelt agreement. He was sorry that Lord Mark and Ned Asterfield had been disappointed in the evening's sport, but a rat fight in the State

Apartments would have been in very poor taste. Besides, he owed the rat a debt of gratitude!

An hour later Sophie broke the seal of Helford's letter in the privacy of her bedchamber. Her fingers shook as she slid the knife under wax. As she opened the letter something inside fluttered to the ground. She frowned. It was a bank note, no, two bank notes. Her stomach lurched sickeningly as she bent to pick them up.

Shaking with horror she read the letter…*accept this in earnest of my intentions*… She dropped letter and money as though they had burned her. She could not blame him after the way she had behaved last night, but somehow she had allowed herself to hope that he had meant…she could scarcely think the word…marriage. It was plain he did not! *I mean to have you in all honour*… What did that mean? That he would engage to keep their liaison secret?

It was not, however, his intent to take her as his mistress that really hurt. Were it not for Kit, she would have gone to him regardless. It was the money. And she'd allowed herself to think he might mean marriage! Doubtless he'd decided that having her in bed would be far more comfortable than a draughty carriage!

What does he think I am? Her mind shied away from the obvious answer. He had sent the money as a down payment on her services. No more, no less.

He calls you his dearest love! He told you he loved you!

Not as you understand it, obviously. Grow up, Sophie Marsden, and stop dreaming. He regards you as a cheap little strumpet. Just imagine what he would have sent if he hadn't decided that it would be more comfortable for him in bed!

'I hate him!' she said furiously. 'I hate him!' But she didn't. That was the problem. She loved him and she had thought he at least cared for her. Even if he hadn't been able to marry her…she had thought…now she knew that she had been close to destroying herself for a man who thought of her as a…a…business transaction…a filly to be bought, and doubtless sold when she tired him or if her action did not please. All that had saved her was Kit.

She sat for a long time, staring at nothing, dry eyed although her throat ached with unshed tears. It would be impossible to stay here after this. She could not allow Kit to ride with him any more or have Fanny here even if Helford would have permitted it. She did not think he was unprincipled enough to use the children to disguise an affair. No, she would leave as soon as possible. She would be able to think of some reason to satisfy Thea and Kit.

At last, though, a solitary tear trickled soundlessly down her cheek. It was followed by another and another until her face was wet and her shoulders shook with the force of the sobs that racked her slender frame. Never, not even when Emma died, had she known such complete despair. Emma's death, she had known, would in time be accepted, and in truth she never felt that Emma was far away. She was always conscious of her as a silent but friendly presence.

This was not something that could be transmuted into a joyful memory as Emma had become. This bitterness would haunt her for the rest of her life. Never would she be able to seek or accept love again. She felt soiled. Helford might not have actually taken her maidenhead, but she knew that any man would consider the distinction to be academic. She felt it so herself. She was damaged goods now.

When she finally emerged from her chamber her face was white and her eyes red-rimmed. Her cold expression forbade anyone to ask what was troubling her and she went about her household tasks with unwonted efficiency and vigour. When Lord Helford came tomorrow, he would be sent about his business and requested not to call again.

* * *

Discovering the next morning that the milk had gone sour, Sophie took a can and walked down the lane to Gillies's farm. It was usually a pleasant walk and she was always sure of a welcome at the farmhouse. Mrs Gillies was never so busy that she didn't have time for a comfortable chat.

On this occasion, however, Sophie was met at the door to the dairy by one of the maids, who said cheekily, 'Missus don't hold wi' your sort! She says ye can go elsewhere fer yer milk after this. She'll fill it this onct but not anymore.' The girl grabbed the pail and departed before Sophie could utter a word. When she came back she said, 'There y'are. Now ye're t' go. Missus don' want none on us ter be dirtied wi' your sort.'

Her cheeks flaming, Sophie took the can and left, crossing the farmyard with her head held high. Two farm hands on seeing her, made it clear that they considered her fair game, standing in her path, calling out obscene remarks as she approached.

She ignored them and walked on defiantly. Something in her eyes made them give ground, but one of them grabbed her bottom as she went past, squeezing it hard and saying, 'Sure an' 'is lordship was on to summat sweet an' juicy 'ere!' As she kept going he yelled, 'I can give yer what 'is lordship give yer! Stuck-up slut!'

By the time she reached home she was raging. The driver of a passing farm wagon had offered her a lift in return for a kiss. It was obvious that the entire countryside had been informed of Helford's intentions. So much for his promise to have her in all honour! She opened the front door and heard Thea's voice in the parlour. 'No doubt this is Sophie now, my lord.'

Damn him! He must have sent his horse around to the stable. Just as if he owned the place! Which he did, of course. No doubt he thought he owned her too. He was about to discover his mistake.

As Thea came out of the parlour Sophie said, 'A moment, Thea. There is something I must return to his lordship. I will be down directly.' She ran upstairs to her bedchamber and took the letter from a drawer. It was refolded with the note inside and resealed. Holding it, she went back downstairs with her head held high.

Upon her entering the parlour Helford stood up and smiled at her tenderly. Then the smile faded. His little love was looking anything but loving. Thea Andrews was excusing herself and he politely bade her farewell. Then he turned to Sophie warily.

She was holding out his letter, her eyes cold and her pale face like a mask. 'I would prefer you to take this back. I am afraid that I cannot entertain your obliging proposals, my lord, and I would infinitely prefer it if you ceased your visits to this house.' Her voice was laden with contempt.

'What!' He couldn't believe his ears. She was actually refusing him! 'You…you can't be refusing…Sophie, why?'

'I do not return your sentiments, my lord!' She had expected that question. Her answer was true enough, she considered. She didn't return his sentiments. She was in love with him and he thought of her as a convenient bit of game, just as he had once implied.

Helford's temper began to rise. What the hell did the chit mean? She'd returned a fair bit in that blasted carriage all right and tight! Fair enough if she had thought him to be suggesting a less respectable union before she received his letter, but now! What more did she want?

'Damn it all! You certainly gave a good imitation of it the night before last! I wasn't the only one making the running!'

She had no answer to that but blushed a deep crimson. 'Please leave, my lord. There is nothing more to be said.'

'Isn't there?' Helford's voice was savage. 'I'll say one thing more, Miss Marsden! You have behaved like the veriest *trollop*! If I *had* taken you in that carriage, it would have been no more than you deserve! Obviously I should have availed myself of the opportunity! Good afternoon!'

He snatched the letter from her and stormed out, leaving a white-faced girl behind him. She stood rigidly until she heard the thunder of his horse's hooves on the road, then she sank into a chair and sobbed her heart out. Thea Andrews, returning to the room, stood dumbfounded on the threshold and then ran to kneel beside her, slipping an arm around her shoulders, murmuring softly and stroking the brown curls. Gentle, soothing words flowed from her but Sophie continued to weep until Thea thought she must break apart.

Thank goodness Kit was out of the way, she thought. Finally she managed to urge Sophie to her feet and up to bed. After tucking her in and drawing the curtains she went back down to the kitchen to consult with Anna on this puzzling departure from the norm.

Anna had been to the village and had got a fair idea of what was being said.

She passed it on to Thea at once, saying, 'If'n we don't do summat fast, Miss Sophie's ruined. His lordship oughter be ashamed of hisself! But what to do is beyond me, Miss Thea.'

'It can't be true!' said Thea, shocked. 'I mean, I have suspected that she is not so indifferent to him as she would like us to think, but she wouldn't—'

'Lor', miss! You don't need to tell me that. I've knowed Miss Sophie since she was a baby. It's what others'll believe that's the problem. An' there's no gettin' around it, if 'is lordship did bring 'er 'ome then 'e oughtn't 'ave done!'

Thea racked her brains. 'Lady Darleston!' she said at last.

'I'll write to her at once and have Grigson take the note over. She'll know what to do!'

Anna nodded her approval. 'Aye, that might help. Not a blind bit of notice would they take of us what've known Miss Sophie fer years, but they'll take the word of a Countess what's known 'er five minnits!'

Chapter Fourteen

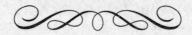

After pushing through a hedge into the fields and urging his horse into a gallop for some four miles, Lord Helford was no closer either to regaining control of his temper or understanding why Miss Marsden had refused his offer. Surely she didn't think he would object to her settling her money on Kit! Not that the boy was likely to need it if Strathallen could be brought up to scratch.

At last he turned for home, his mood bleak. His temper had finally ebbed, giving way to a numb despair. As much as he tried to convince himself that Sophie Marsden was a teasing little trollop, his heart stubbornly refused to take the slightest notice. If anything had been needed to assure him that what he felt for her was love, it was the fact that he could not shrug her off. Bitterly he remembered the morning he had gone to beg Felicity to marry him. He had felt only rage and hurt pride, he now realised. Not this aching, leaden despair.

Briefly he considered offering for Lucinda Anstey after all, only to dismiss the notion with a shudder. Even if she accepted him, which he seriously doubted after the cool way she had spoken to him in farewell the previous afternoon, the knowledge that all his friends were dead set against the match was enough to give him pause. Had he loved her, that would not have signified, but it would hardly be a convenient marriage if his friends and aunt actually disliked his bride. Besides, he could not bear the idea of making love, or rather consummating a union, with Lucinda. Not after the innocent abandon of Sophie's passionate response.

Which brought him back to Sophie. Why the devil had she refused him? He found it hard to believe that she did not return his love. He hoped he was not the arrogant coxcomb she had once called him, but he had been sure that she loved him. There was something odd about this and he didn't know how to deal with it. All he knew was that if Sophie didn't marry him, the name of Melville would die with him. He could not imagine ever wishing to marry someone else.

Upon reaching the stables he dismounted and threw his reins to Jasper without even a grunt of greeting and stalked up to the house, prey to the blackest despair he had ever known. Far worse even than when Felicity had chosen to marry James and the title rather than himself. He'd thought he'd hit rockbottom then, but somewhere deep down he had known that it was inevitable. That had Felicity truly cared for him, she would not have hesitated for a moment.

Somehow it hurt far more that Sophie had rejected him. She was not choosing something else. Merely rejecting him. He thought he could have borne it better had he thought that she was in love with someone else. *Dear God! Was she? But who? Not Garfield. That was unthinkable. But Tom?*

He groaned. That was not at all unthinkable! Tom would make her, indeed any woman, a splendid husband. Comfortably circumstanced, kind…and he'd made it quite plain that he liked and admired Sophie. Even if he had not encouraged her, he had supported her through that ghastly dinner party. David realised that the thought of Sophie being in love with anyone save himself did not help in the least.

It merely made him want to plant Tom a facer and drag Sophie to the altar by the hair!

Jasper had watched his master's bleak-faced departure with interest. He had a great deal to say to his master when opportunity presented itself, but he judged that now was not the moment. The master would be settling down for a long session this evening. Jasper decided to slip up to the kitchen later on to visit his good friend, Jeffreys the chef. Time enough to ask his lordship what the hell he was playing at with little Miss Sophie once he'd had time to down a decanter or so of brandy.

By the time Lord Helford was halfway down the decanter, his leaden misery had settled firmly and showed no sign of responding to the time-honoured remedy known as drowning one's sorrows. The noble vintage he was quaffing so recklessly might as well have been drained off from the kennels for all the satisfaction it afforded his numbed heart. His determination never to darken Miss Marsden's doorstep again had been replaced by an equally irrational desire to leap back into the saddle and ride straight back to Willowbank House, sweep her into his arms and force her to consent to marriage. It would not do, of course, she'd tell him to go to the devil in as many words.

By the time Bainbridge came to the library to announce dinner he was extremely well to live and merely favoured the butler with a morose grunt.

'Should I, er...take the brandy decanter into the dining salon or would your lordship prefer to dine here?' enquired Bainbridge tactfully. 'Lady Maria is dining off a tray in her room, being rather tired.'

'Neither,' was the reply. 'I am not hungry. Apologise to Jeffreys for the trouble he has been put to.' It would be too much to say that his lordship's deep voice was slurred precisely, but it was evident that he was expending a great deal of effort to avoid that indignity.

Bainbridge tottered away, quailing inwardly at the likely reaction of Jeffreys at this cavalier rejection of his labours. What, apart from the jug, of course, had bitten the master? He bore all the signs of a man badly crossed in love, but that was impossible! It was common knowledge that his lordship had been on the point of offering for Lady Lucinda Anstey, and it would be news to Bainbridge if love had entered into his master's dealings with her.

Steeling himself for the inevitable explosion, Bainbridge entered the kitchen and relayed the fell tidings in as placatory tones as he could muster. On the whole Jeffreys took it quite well. Apart from jumping up and down forcibly expressing the desire that, if England had a revolution, his ungrateful master should be the first to mount the block, he only threw the rolling pin he happened to be holding and one silver chafing dish which had the misfortune to be close at hand. His underlings all ducked for cover and the scullery maid, who had put her nose in from the scullery to see what was amiss, retreated at once to her pots and pans.

Of all the occupants of the kitchen, the only one unmoved by Jeffrey's wrath was Jasper, who was seated at the table devouring bread and cheese.

He pricked up his ears and said, 'In a tweak, is 'e?'

Bainbridge eyed him with marked disfavour. His lordship's tiger had no business whatsoever in the kitchen, but if Jeffreys chose to allow it, he had nothing to say in the matter.

'His lordship,' he intoned frigidly, 'is not at all himself.'

'Jugbitten, eh?' Jasper correctly interpreted this genteel euphemism. He grinned cheekily at Bainbridge. 'I'll deal with 'im. Where might 'e be?'

Not for all his disapproval of his lordship's vulgar, make-bait tiger, could Bainbridge deliver a fellow man up to such a fate as he reckoned would be in store for anyone disturbing the master.

'Don't you do it, Jasper!' he said earnestly. 'Be more than your job's worth. If I didn't know better I'd say he'd been crossed in love!'

'Would you, now?' said Jasper slowly. 'Then thankin' yer fer the warnin' all the same, but I'd best see 'im afore 'e shoots the cat, as the saying is! Jeffreys, you keep things warm a bit. There's no sayin' but what 'e mightn't fancy a bite after I'm done with 'im. Now, where is 'e, Mr Bainbridge?'

'In…in the Library,' said Bainbridge, thinking that no doubt his lordship, having an affection for Jasper, would reemploy him in the morning if he turned him off tonight.

Upon entering the Library, one look was enough to inform Jasper that his master was in as bleak a mood as ever he'd known. He hadn't even noticed the door opening but was gazing into the empty fireplace with an expression of bitterness, twirling his empty brandy glass. The usually immaculate cravat had been loosened and his black hair tousled.

Jasper shut the door quietly, watching as his master reached for the brandy decanter on the floor beside his wing chair.

'Beggin' your pardon, sir, but I'd say ye'd had enough.'

David turned sharply, focusing his gaze with difficulty on the figure by the door. 'Jasper? What the hell are you doing here?'

'Need a word with yer lordship afore you gets any further,' said Jasper bluntly. He walked over to the fireplace and looked down at his master with friendly concern.

'Damn you, Jasper!' exploded David. 'You go too far!'

'Aye,' said Jasper equably. 'An' I'll go a bit farther. 'Tis about Miss Sophie—'

David erupted from his chair. 'Jasper, if you mention that name again, you'll be seeking a new master!'

Seemingly unperturbed, Jasper nodded. 'That's as may be, my lord, but was you wishful to have all the folks around Little Helford talkin' about how Miss Sophie was your bit o' muslin?'

'What?' David was dumbfounded. 'But she's not! I mean…I didn't…why the hell am I explaining myself to you?'

'I didn't think ye knew,' said Jasper. 'But that's what they're all asayin'. That she's no better than what she oughter be an' that she's a disgrace to the…'

'My God!' He felt sick. 'Does she know what's being said?' Could this be why Sophie had refused him? Had she been misled by scurrilous gossip? Had she thought he intended to recant his offer of marriage? Take her as his mistress? That he would callously ruin her?

'As to that my lord, I did hear as 'ow she got a pretty nasty greetin' at Farmer Gillies's farm this mornin'. Full of it the village was when I was down at the smithy afore.' Jasper watched his master sympathetically. Not a doubt but what it was a facer for him.

Ashen, David swallowed hard. It was all his fault! If only he hadn't decided to take Sophie home! Somehow the story must have got around. Damn Highbury! He shuddered to think what she must have thought. That he was laughing at her naïvety. That he had let it be known she was his mistress. No wonder she had refused him if she thought he was offering her a *carte blanche*! But what about his letter? He had offered her marriage, hadn't he? Surely, even if people were talking, she must have been reassured by that. But then why had she returned it to him as though it were the embodiment of an insult?

At this juncture the door opened and Bainbridge announced, 'Captain Hampton, my lord,' in tones which suggested he envisaged an immediate entry to the workhouse.

The groan which broke from his lordship betokened that the unexpected sight of one of his closest friends was in no way welcome.

Captain Hampton, taking in the scene with an experienced eye, said, 'Bainbridge, have dinner served at once in the small salon before we have to put his lordship to bed in a bucket, there's a good chap.'

The door closed behind the outraged butler.

'What the hell are you doing here?' asked David. 'You were going home.'

'Broken wheel about thirty miles from here. Thought I might as well come back. So I hired a horse. But do enlighten me. What now have you been about that Jasper feels called upon to give you one of his jobations?' enquired Hampton as he lowered himself into the vacated wing chair.

'Ruining Sophie Marsden!' said David in accents of utter despair. 'Tell him the worst, Jasper, and then you may as well leave me to my fate.'

'You did *what*?' Hampton stared at him. 'You said you were going to offer for her!'

'I thought I had, too!' said David. 'Tell him, Jasper!'

Jasper obeyed, noting that the Captain, usually so cheery, looked as though he was like to give the master a fair bit more than a jobation.

'But didn't you write to her, David?' Hampton was puzzled. 'Maybe the letter was not delivered.'

'Of course I wrote to her!' said David. 'And, yes, the damned letter was delivered. She almost threw it at me when I saw her!' He paced the floor in frustration. 'She must have thought that I...that I...had... Oh, God! Tom, what she must have thought? She told me she did not return my sentiments! And well she might if she thought I meant... to...to...take her as my mistress!'

'It all hinges on that letter,' said Hampton thoughtfully. 'I don't suppose you can recall precisely what you wrote?'

David shook his head. 'No. I was in such a damned hurry. I had to go and find my seal and just as I got back Fanny came in and told me she'd put the rat in Lucinda's room…'

'It was her, was it?' Hampton choked on a laugh. 'How very enterprising of her. Where the devil did she get it? And why?'

David grinned. 'Yes. She thought you'd smoked her. I'm prepared to wager she got it from Kit. As for why—she told me that she wanted to make Lucinda think the place was infested with rats to stop her marrying me. Anyway, what with trying not to laugh in front of the child, and thinking I'd better get to breakfast on time and smooth Lucinda down a trifle, I was a little rushed. Turned out she was breakfasting upstairs, though.'

'What?' Hampton was surprised. 'But I passed her in the hall on my way to the library that morning.'

Helford shrugged. 'Must have changed her mind. I dare say she was furious with me. If Highbury let out that I had taken Sophie home…and with the rat thrown in…'

Jasper piped up. 'Not me place, o' course, to say, but…' He hesitated.

David looked at him in resignation. 'Since when has that consideration ever stopped you, Jasper? Out with it.'

'Well, I was agoin' ter say that mebbe 'twas her ladyship what started all the talk 'bout Miss Sophie,' said his henchman reluctantly. ''Twas her maid talkin' the loudest in the servants' hall. Could be she was takin' out a bit o' spite.'

'You're sure you can't recall that letter, David?' asked Hampton.

'Quite…no, hold on! I think I've got it with me!' exclaimed David. 'I shoved it in my pocket and stormed out. It's probably upstairs.'

'Well, for God's sake go and get it!' recommended

Hampton. 'And bring it to the small dining salon, I'm famished.'

With a broad grin, Jasper opined that it would be as well if so be they were wishful to keep Jeffreys in good skin.

Ten minutes later the two gentleman were seated at one end of the dining table, a vast expanse of mahogany even with all the leaves taken out. The letter lay unopened beside Helford while the first course was set out.

'We'll serve ourselves, Bainbridge,' said David impatiently.

Scarcely had the door shut before he picked up the letter and broke the wax. As he opened it the twenty pounds fluttered to the table top.

He stared at it as though he had never seen a pair of ten-pound notes in his life. 'What the hell is that doing there?'

Hampton blinked. 'You didn't…no…of course not.'

David was reading the letter with a gathering frown. When he had finished he put it down and said in constricted tones, 'I should have let you write it after all, Tom. I don't actually say anything about marriage…here, you read it.'

He passed it over. What a bloody fool he was! For want of a bit of care, he had ruined Sophie and made her life hell. He wouldn't blame her if she refused to have anything more to do with him, even after he explained.

Hampton read the hurried note and handed it back. 'Not exactly explicit, is it? You damned idiot! But what really has me gapped is the money. How did that get there?'

David shook his head. 'I couldn't hazard a guess. I certainly didn't put it there! She…she must have thought I was…buying her…services.' He buried his face in his hands with a ragged groan.

Hampton was thinking hard. 'You know, David, if Lucinda started the gossip, then I think we need look no further for the origin of this twenty pounds.' He nodded at Helford's dropped jaw and darkening brow. 'Think about it.

You didn't put it there. And I spoke to Lucinda just before going to the library. In fact, I told her that I was going to see you. The window on to the terrace was open and…you didn't re-read it, did you, when you came back? Didn't you say you left the room to find your seal? And then Fanny came in?'

'The little bitch!' David exploded. 'I'll…I'll…'

'Do nothing,' finished Hampton. 'You can't prove it and you've already done quite enough to stir up the tabbies. The only thing you can do is marry Sophie Marsden as fast as possible and get her up to London with Lady Maria and Penelope Darleston to silence the gossip. The pair of them can launch her in the Little Season.' He looked at David sympathetically. 'You know, old chap, I think when you explain yourself and apologise for being such a bloody fool, she might just forgive you. There's really no occasion for quite such despair. After all, the girl's tail over top in love with you, for some God-unknown reason!'

'How the hell would you know anything about it?' asked David irritably. 'Or did she tell you that when you were making up to her at dinner the other night?'

'Oh, take a damper!' recommended Hampton good-naturedly. 'I should imagine everyone in the room knew what was going on when Penelope Darleston got the girl to sing that song. Damn it all, if she'd been singing it for me, I'd have fallen in love with her myself!'

By the end of dinner David had talked himself into a more hopeful frame of mind. Tom was in the right of it. He'd see Sophie tomorrow and sort things out. Have the banns called immediately. And if Sophie tried to kick him out again, he knew perfectly well how to get her attention and stop her talking for long enough to convince her that his intentions were entirely honourable.

In the event Lord Helford did not arise from his slumbers at all early on the following morning, and when he did he came to the immediate conclusion that the sun was far too bright and the sky far too blue. That was before Meredith drew back the curtains of his bedchamber to reveal a cloudy, weeping day outside. At which point he winced audibly and visibly as he buried his aching head under his pillow.

'Should I return later, my lord?' asked Meredith solicitously.

'What time is it?' asked David carefully.

'Nearly noon, my lord.'

Nearly noon? Oh, God! He'd have to get up. He couldn't leave Sophie in this damned coil any longer.

'Coffee,' he said shortly as he eased himself out of bed. 'Black and strong.'

And blinked as it was handed to him in a delicate basalt-ware coffee cup.

'Captain Hampton's orders, my lord,' explained Meredith, laying all blame squarely where it belonged.

David throttled an overwhelming urge to laugh. It was bound to make his headache even worse than it was already. Instead he accepted the coffee and sipped at it gratefully. Gradually he began to feel less scratchy and was able to contemplate getting dressed in a more optimistic spirit. He still didn't feel quite so sanguine about facing Sophie.

He would have to explain that damned twenty pounds for one thing, and despite being morally certain Lucinda had been responsible, he had no proof and hesitated to make an accusation he could not substantiate. Besides which, he just had a sinking feeling that everything was not going to be quite as simple as Tom had suggested.

For God's sake, David! Just tell her you're head over heels in love with her, beg her to marry you, in as many words, and kiss her senseless! How difficult is that?

Which was all very well, thought David. The last time he'd tried to do that, he'd got the order confused and kissed her first. And just look at the bumblebroth that had landed him in!

Having made a brief stop at the Vicarage on his way through the village that was guaranteed to stir up even more gossip, he rode up to Willowbank House alone in the middle of the afternoon to discover a chaise and four standing in the road outside. Frowning, he wondered who could possibly be visiting Sophie in a chaise. The crest on the door was unfamiliar, but when he looked more closely he realised that what he had taken for a leopard was actually a Scottish wildcat.

Shock lanced through him as he realised who must own it.

'Is this Lord Strathallen's chaise?' His question was addressed to the lad holding the wheelers.

'Yessir.' The boy touched his cap politely. 'Come special all the way from Scotland he has, sir. Hold your mare, sir? Jim ain't doin' much.'

David nodded. 'Thank you.'

Another boy came forward and took the mare's bridle.

Steeling himself, David walked up the path, breathing the misty, heady scent of the lavender that lined it brushing against his sleeves. He always smelt it when he came here, he realised suddenly. And Sophie always smelled of it.

Smiling slightly, he went through the open door into the hall and wondered where she might be.

A harsh voice from the parlour, raised in anger, gave him the clue.

'D'ye think I've not heard all the gossip, ye little southron whore? Full of it the village was! Twasn't hard to pick up that his lordship's taken you as his latest lightskirt! Aye, and I only wish Jock had had as much sense with your sister! Why he had to marry her I'll never know! But since he did, I'm damned if I'll have my heir raised by you! Ye'll hand the lad over and there's an end of it! D'ye hear me, ye little doxy?'

David froze in horror. The countryside must indeed be humming if a chance traveller had heard the gossip. Despairing guilt racked him. No wonder Sophie had refused him if this were the sort of thing to which she was being subjected!

Sophie's answer came furiously. 'You have not the least right, my lord! You have known of Kit's existence for years! Emma named me his guardian and I have the deed to prove it! You are entirely welcome to visit him and I will be happy to bring him to visit you so that he may learn to know his family and become familiar with your people, but...'

A bark of scornful laughter interrupted her. 'Aye, so ye may have a deed! And how long do ye think that will stand in court if I bring a claim and can prove ye're not fit morally to have charge of the lad? Precious little good Helford will be then!'

This had gone far enough! Rage exploded through David that anyone might threaten his love in any way whatsoever, let alone with a weapon he had forged.

He stalked into the parlour without even bothering to knock.

Sophie, facing the door, was on her feet, her face white and stricken. 'You...you can't...it's not true...you *couldn't* be so cruel...*Helford*!'

She broke off as she saw him, shock and despair evident in her wide eyes and trembling mouth. Unbelievable pain pierced through David as he realised that in his arrival she saw the vindication of Strathallen's claim.

The old man had turned to face him. Nearly as tall as David, he was a striking figure in his kilt. Fierce blue eyes glared forth challengingly over a beak of a nose in a face lined with years. A thick head of white hair was the only other discernible evidence of his advanced age. He held himself as straight as a man half his age and exuded a vigour that many a younger man might have envied.

When he spoke his voice held nothing but scorn and triumph.

'Ye're mighty prompt, Helford! Come for a word with this little doxy, have ye? Or have ye been here all along?'

'You may thank God for your advanced years, Strathallen!' rapped out David, white-lipped with fury. 'Only they protect you now, and if you insult my betrothed wife any further, I can assure that they will not continue to protect you!' His voice was icy. 'I have no idea what gossip you have been listening to, but I made Miss Marsden an offer of marriage yesterday morning and I am here to inform her that the banns will be published next Sunday. I suggest that if you have any further requests to make of her, that they be made through me. I would point out to you that once Miss Marsden marries me, I will automatically assume all legal responsibility for Kit. And perhaps if you have any doubt of the nature of our relationship you might better apply to my aunt, Lady Maria Kentham, or to the Earl and Countess of Darleston, rather than the taproom of whatever hostelry you are dignifying with your custom!'

Thus my Lord Helford at his most arrogant and overbearing.

It was probably fortunate that Strathallen was too taken up with goggling at David to observe the shocked disbelief on Sophie's face. Her jaw had dropped open and she was clutching at a chair back for support as the room whirled around her in a very dizzying manner.

Marriage? Had he said marriage? That he was here to inform her that the banns would be called on Sunday? She had to be dreaming…it just wasn't possible!

Strathallen was speaking. 'Do I understand you, my lord? You are betrothed to…to this…'

'To Miss Marsden!' grated David. 'And you will speak

to her and of her with respect, Strathallen! Starting now! You owe Miss Marsden an apology, I believe.'

A harsh laugh broke from Strathallen. ''Tis no matter to me if ye're fool enough to marry the little slut just because the whole county is awash wi' the tale...'

'*Take that back!* Or...or I'll *kill* you!' Kit had stormed into the room. Small fists were clenched and hazel eyes were bright with childish rage. The black eye he was sporting suggested that he had already been defending his aunt's honour. 'Aunt Sophie isn't a...a...what you said. Take it back, I say!' He advanced threateningly on Strathallen, evidently intent on ramming his insults down his throat.

'That will do, Kit,' interposed David, laying a firm hand on his shoulder. 'Lord Strathallen is under a misapprehension. You may trust me to protect your aunt.'

'She's *my* aunt!' said Kit fiercely. 'And I won't let anyone insult her!' Suddenly he rounded on Helford. 'Not even you! Do you know what they are saying?' His distress was plain in the overbright eyes, the wobble in his voice. For a moment it looked as though he would fly bodily at Helford, but all of a sudden he seemed to regain control of himself.

Fixing David with a steely glare, he said, with commendable steadiness, 'My lord, I...I demand to know what your...your intentions are towards Aunt Sophie!'

Sophie froze. She saw David's jaw tighten.

'Kit, no!' she said frantically.

David held up one hand. Meeting Kit's fierce gaze, he said quietly, 'A moment, Sophie. He has every right to ask that question.'

Drawing a deep breath, he continued. 'Yes, Kit, I am aware of what has been said. It was all a misunderstanding which has made both me and your Aunt Sophie very unhappy. People did not realise that my intention is to marry your aunt. But I assure you that I intend, have always intended, to marry her.'

Tension ebbed visibly from the small body. 'You're going to marry Aunt Sophie? Well, that's all right and tight then!'

'If she'll have me,' said David diplomatically.

'Why ever wouldn't she?' asked Kit in surprise. 'Fanny thought you were going to marry Lady Lucinda.'

David strove to keep a straight face. 'Lady Lucinda is not at all fond of rats, Kit.' He raised one brow in mute query.

'Oh.' Kit grinned. 'Well, serves her right. I mean, after she stuck that beastly hat pin into Megs! Does this mean that we will live with you and Fanny at Helford Place? I mean, it's bigger than this house. And Lady Maria wouldn't like it if you came here, would she?'

David's jaw dropped slightly as he realised the full extent of his erstwhile intended's perfidy, but he managed to say, 'No. But she has already informed me that if I mean to fill the place with scrubby schoolboys she will remove to the Dower House. Now, might I suggest that you take yourself off about your business and leave us to ours?'

Kit seemed to remember Strathallen's presence. 'Oh, very well, but if *he* starts slanging Aunt Sophie again, will you tip him a leveller?'

David's face was grave as he said, 'Something of the sort. But it's not good form to hit a man twice your own age. Not at my age anyway.'

This was given frowning consideration. 'I suppose not.' He swung around to Strathallen again. 'Then if you insult Aunt Sophie again, you'll be the most rotten skirter, since Helford won't hit you. I don't care who you are!'

'Kit,' said Sophie. 'Out! I am sure Lord Strathallen has understood your position.'

'Just long as he does!' said Kit trenchantly. He left the room with a final fierce glare in his grandfather's direction.

A stunned expression on his face, Strathallen turned to Sophie. '*That* was my grandson? Jock's lad? That young varmint who juist aboot called me oot and challenged a mon he knows to be a peer?' His accent became decidedly more marked.

Sophie swallowed hard. 'My lord, recollect, Kit had no idea of your identity and he is well acquainted with Helford…please do not—'

She was rudely interrupted. 'Losh, girl, I'm not repining! If any mon had spoken to my mother as I spoke to you, I'd be after rammin' the words back down his gullet wi' me ridin' whip! The sperrit of the lad! An' he's been kept frae me all this time!'

'No doubt if you had acknowledged the letter Jock's widow sent you eight years ago you might have known the boy! And he would have known who you are!' snapped David. 'You must have known the boy was your heir long before Hampton and I wrote to you!'

'Aye. I knew,' admitted Strathallen. 'But no one else knew of his existence. Ye may be sure I did not boast of the whelp of a—' He caught David's eye and stopped. 'Weel, I was wrong. Any lad who could do what that lad juist did has no cause to complain of his dam or his raisin'! Lord, he looked as though he'd be at me throat!'

'As he would have been at mine,' said David drily. 'That is, if he didn't persuade my niece to put a rat in my bed-chamber.' He went on, 'Seriously, my lord, there has been no attempt to keep Kit from you. You were informed of his birth in the letter Emma Carlisle sent you when she wrote of Jock's death. A letter which I understand it cost her great pain to write.'

Sophie's eyes flew to his face. She remembered telling him of that, how he had comforted her grief. That had been the first time he'd held her, his powerful body a refuge from pain, his arms a barrier to ward off all trouble. And now…what was he trying to do now? Simply protect her with his name since, contrary to expectation, the story of his intent had got about? Did he actually think she would accept such an offer? Or was he merely intending to smooth things over with Strathallen before breaking the engagement?

Strathallen's voice, low and ashamed, broke in on her thoughts. 'I barely read the letter before I burned it. Sure, it hurt so much... And ever after I wished I'd not done so, or that I'd copied the extracts she included...' The old eyes were suddenly misted over, their fierce blue softened.

'The original letters are here,' Sophie told him gently. 'If...if you would like to read them...copy them...I am sure Kit will bring them when he comes to see you. He is so proud of Jock. I am sure he will wish to show them to you.'

The old man sighed. 'I've been a damned fool, then. Alastair tried to tell me for years and I refused to listen. I never intended to deny the lad his inheritance. 'Twas just so damn hard to climb down...an' when I heard what folks were sayin'...weel, I juist saw red. I'll be takin' meself back to the Helford Arms. Your servant, Miss Marsden, an' I beg your pardon for...for everything. Bring the lad to me when it suits you to do so. I'll not be raisin' a claim against ye.'

He left quietly, leaving Sophie and David facing each other.

She supposed that she would have to sort the mess out. Now would be best. There was Kit's future to arrange. As long as he didn't renew his offer. Over the past day she had forced her battered heart and pride to accept the hand dealt by fate.

Despite what Penelope Darleston had said when she visited yesterday evening, Sophie did not believe he had ever intended marriage. Why should he when she had made it quite obvious that with a little effort he could have her without? Had he chosen to press her the other night, she might well have given herself. No doubt with Penelope's support and that of her husband the scandal would blow over, but the fact remained that she had nearly ruined herself.

She would not destroy herself for the gratification of his desire no matter how much she wanted to do so. He could go to the devil and leave her in peace. If such a thing were possible for her now.

Bleakly she told herself, as she met his eyes, that it would come to that in the end anyway. He would tire of her and leave, his only legacy a load of bitter memories. She did not delude herself. The memories would not ease the pain of parting. Rather the nature of the relationship would sour the memories. And there was Kit to consider. She could not ruin his life for the transient joy of Helford's arms.

She was the first to break the silence. 'I have to thank you, my lord, for your intervention. It was most timely.' Her voice was cold and light, a brittle armour for a breaking heart. Gallantly she continued. 'You may be sure that I will not hold you to your foolish declaration. Lady Darleston has been kind enough to engage herself to scotch the unfortunate consequences of the other night.'

The strange glint in his eyes disconcerted her. 'Is that what you think, Sophie? That this is merely a ploy to mislead Strathallen?' He smiled oddly. 'I am desolated to contradict you, my dear, but I can assure you that nothing less than our marriage will satisfy him. You will marry me or see Kit whisked off to Scotland before the cat can lick her ear.'

She stared up at him in horror. 'You...you mean I have to marry you to keep Kit?' She had thought it was painful enough to be offered a *carte blanche* by the man to whom she had given her heart. That was as nothing in comparison to the pain of being forced to accept an offer of marriage from him, an offer he had made only under duress.

For a wild moment she considered hurling the offer back in his teeth. But the vision of Kit arose before her, as it had done the other night. She couldn't, simply couldn't, betray his trust now, just to salvage her own pride. If she didn't accept Helford's offer, then Strathallen would have no trouble at all in convincing a court that she was unfit to be Kit's guardian. For Kit's sake she had to accept. Furiously she suppressed the surging joy in her own heart, the joy which cried out in exultation that now she would belong to Helford, no matter on what terms.

From between clenched teeth she said, 'Then I have no choice but to accept your very obliging offer, my lord. You will forgive me if I am less than enthusiastic about accepting your very reluctant hand in marriage!'

'Sophie, you cannot possibly think that I am only offering for you out of obligation...' In absolute horror, David realised that his final, instinctive attempt to mask the terrifying reality of his own need had backfired very badly. Her next words confirmed it.

'What else should I think?' she blazed at him. With a massive effort she drew a deep breath and forced her voice to calmness. 'You had no thought of *marriage* the other night, my lord. You can hardly expect me to be flattered at an offer made out of necessity. And made, no doubt, at the prompting of your friends.'

The cool steadiness of her voice was gratifying, but she hoped keeping it that way was going to get easier rather than harder. A flutter in her breast and a rising lump in her throat were not helping in the slightest.

'David.' He corrected her with a challenging look. 'I asked you to call me that the other night if you recall.' A hot flame flickered in his eyes. 'Of course you might not. You were somewhat distracted at the time, I believe.'

'No!' What had been intended as a firm and categorical denial came out as a frightened squeak as his words brought the memory flooding back to her body as well as to her mind. Horrified, she felt her knees turn to jelly and that same melting sensation take control as her body remembered the power this man had wielded over it.

Desperately she forced her brain to keep functioning. She had to keep him at bay—had to remind herself that this marriage would be one of obligation—on both sides.

He came closer, green eyes glinting, reminding her irresistibly of a prowling cat, one of the larger ones.

'No!' This time there was a note of panic in her voice. Furious with herself, she forced a lighter note. 'And marriage is a high price to pay for your pleasure, is it not, my lord? Yesterday morning it was only worth a down payment of twenty pounds to you!'

She was unprepared for his reaction. Embarrassment she would have understood. Or outrage at her most improper suggestion. But not this sudden and genuine roar of laughter. His whole face was alive with it, green eyes sparkling as he continued to chuckle.

'Oh, Sophie! What next will you say?'

Her hold on her temper, which had been precarious to say the least, finally slipped completely. Scarcely knowing what she was doing, she grabbed for the nearest available missile and hurled it at him. Years of bowling for Kit had given her an enviable aim and she heard with immense satisfaction the thump as the heavy family bible struck him above the eye.

He staggered backwards, clutching his head. 'For God's sake, Sophie! Calm down, you little termagant, and give me a chance to explain myself! I didn't put that money in the letter!'

She stared at him in disbelief. If he hadn't put it there, then who had?

He sat down on the sofa and tenderly felt the spot where the bible had struck him. 'You've got a better aim than most females, I'll grant you that. I should have dodged!'

His voice held tender amusement and his eyes laughed up at her. She saw that he was going to have quite a bruise and felt a twinge of remorse. Ruthlessly she stamped on it.

But his smile was turning her bones to water as she clung desperately to her resolution, reminding herself that he didn't really love her. That he must never know how much she loved him.

He was speaking again. 'Tom and I think that Lucinda overheard when I told him I intended to marry you. That she slipped the money into the note when I left the library to find my seal. Tom thinks she was on the terrace.' He sighed. 'I'm sorry, Sophie. That letter was the most useless bit of correspondence I've ever penned. My only excuse is that I've never actually written a proposal of marriage before, or even a genuine love letter. And I was a bit pressed for time. Can you forgive me?'

It was becoming harder and harder to breathe, let alone speak. The lump in her throat combined with a burning prickle in her eyes to make speech nigh on impossible.

At last she spoke in a voice that seemed to break. 'My lord, surely there need be no pretence between us. You offer marriage because you have accidentally compromised me and in so doing have given Strathallen a weapon to use against me. I have accepted your offer because if I do not, I must lose Kit. What more remains to be said?'

She saw his fist clench.

'Just this, Sophie.' He dragged in a deep breath. Their misunderstanding had gone far enough. 'I'm offering marriage because I damned well have to!' This was said with considerable violence. And then, as the bitter agony of despair flooded her soft eyes, he added, 'But not for any of the reasons you might be forgiven for thinking.'

He stood up and crossed the remaining space between them and set his hands on her shoulders, looking straight into her overbright eyes. Her whole body stiffened at the touch of his hands, his nearness, his overwhelming masculine strength.

There was a hint of laughter in his voice as he said,

'Leaving aside the minor circumstance that there are four people in line to call me out if I don't marry you as fast as possible, namely the Earl and Countess of Darleston, Tom Hampton and my Aunt Maria, to which you might as well add Anna and Thea Andrews as well as Kit and Fanny—I have to marry you because if I don't, I'm going to be infernally unhappy!' A sudden responsive tremor ran through her and he went on. 'And I did think marriage was necessary the other day, you little idiot! I know that letter of mine was less than explicit and I grant the money must have been a facer, but didn't it occur to you that if I didn't want marriage I would have just taken my pleasure with you in the carriage? Do you think I don't know how easily you could have been persuaded the other night? For God's sake, Sophie, I'm in love with you! Take my word for it—that's the only reason you're still a virgin.'

There was a moment's silence while Sophie took in this impassioned declaration. She wanted to believe it, her heart begged for its release, but still she hesitated. The shadows of doubt still weighed in on her. That he desired her was obvious, and she knew that he was fond of her, but marriage? Was that really what he wanted? And if so, why on earth had he been courting Lucinda Anstey?

Lord Helford, however, did not hesitate. Seeing her mouth open and feeling that enough had been said and that further explanations or arguments could wait, he swept her into his arms and stopped her mouth in the only effective way he knew. His lips claimed hers irrevocably in a searing kiss and she was held in a grip which threatened to break several ribs. Despite her lingering doubts, she yielded completely, her mouth opening under his assault with all the sweetness he remembered.

With a wrenching groan he deepened the kiss, whirling her into the vortex of a dizzying passion. Irresistibly he backed her to the sofa until her calves hit it. And then with

a satisfied grunt he scooped her up to dump her unceremoniously upon it, where he joined her at once without ever
breaking the kiss.

His hands were everywhere, caressing and stroking. The
light muslin gown was no protection against his wicked expertise. He revelled in the softness, the sweetness of her
breasts, kneading and teasing until with a deeply plundering
kiss his long, experienced fingers found a taut nipple and
massaged it tenderly. Encouraged by her moan of pleasure,
he abandoned himself to the task of convincing her that their
marriage was inevitable, a glorious necessity.

Her mouth clung to his, a miracle of loving surrender.
Her whole body under his was warm and pliant. But when
he finally raised his head to gaze down at her, her eyes,
when they fluttered open, told him that he had only been
partially successful. She had yielded…she loved him…but
the shadowed eyes told him that still she doubted—could
not quite believe that he loved her.

'Sophie…' he whispered, despairingly.

She trembled in his arms. 'I…I have agreed, my lord.
Please, I do not require protestations of devotion… When
are we to be married?'

His heart contracted in pain as he sat up, releasing her.
So calm, so hurt. How the hell could he reassure her?
Passion was patently useless. It might bind her to him,
thereby increasing her sense of hurt, but would she ever
believe that it meant anything to him? Unthinkingly he said
bluntly, 'The banns will be called for the first time on
Sunday. It's all arranged.'

'Arranged!' Sophie stared at him in dismay. Had he been
so sure of her? So sure that she would be so desperate to
retrieve her reputation that she would leap at his proposal?
Did he care so little for her that he had actually arranged
the wedding without so much as asking her who should be
invited? Fury surged up again to mingle with the mind-

numbing pain. She was not going to be organised and...and managed like one of his mistresses!

Seething with hurt outrage, she scrambled to her feet.

'If I am going to marry you, my lord, we had better get something clear.' she said in shaking tones. 'Firstly, even if I do manage the word *obey* without choking on it, I haven't said it yet, and I do not appreciate being ridden over rough-shod! I have no intention of being treated as one of your *convenients*.' She blushed fierily as she said this, and added, 'Not even a convenient wife.'

He stared up at her. And then he groaned. 'Oh, hell! I'm sorry, Sophie. I didn't mean to be so damned officious! Tom's right, it's a shocking habit and I'm counting on you to cure me of it. For God's sake, don't think I take you for granted, or that I mean to be arrogant. It's just that I want you so much that I tend to get carried away! And when I found out what was being said...I saw the Vicar on the way over because I wanted to straighten everything out as quickly as possible...'

Sophie flinched. She was right, then. For a moment, when she had seen the hurt in his face, she had hoped... But he was, after all, marrying her only to protect her name. Every nerve in her body tightened.

'No!' His voice, harsh and shaking, dragged her eyes to his. He surged to his feet and grasped her hands, drawing her to him inexorably. The green depths held a fear and a pain that shocked her, the planes of his face set and tense. 'For goodness' sake, you have to listen to me, Sophie. I do want to protect you. I can't deny that. But it's because I love you. Not because I nearly ruined you. Sweetheart, it's not my honour, but my heart that's begging you to marry me. Please, Sophie.'

'You...you really want me?' She still couldn't quite believe it. Didn't dare to believe it.

Her heart trembled at the intensity in his voice as he said,

'Three weeks, Sophie. The banns will be called on Sunday. Give me that time to convince you, my love. I know I've been a fool, that I've hurt you and confused you. Will you trust me, just this one last time?'

Words would not form, and even if they had, would not have made it past the choking lump in her throat. She could only nod helplessly as he raised her hand to his lips.

Chapter Fifteen

The following morning Penelope Darleston descended upon Willowbank House like a whirlwind and removed Sophie to Darleston Court, effortlessly squashing David's plan to remove his bride to Helford Place. She said cheerfully that her chaperonage was the best way of stopping any malicious tongues dead in their tracks and forestalling any more difficulties. Just what she meant by difficulties was left unsaid.

And somehow her matter-of-fact attitude did wonders for Sophie's uncertain spirits. She seemed to take it for granted that Helford was tail over top in love and that his near betrothal to Lucinda had been a minor aberration.

'Peter did exactly the same, you know,' she confided in the carriage. 'The only difference was that he actually chose me, for all the wrong reasons, but then had the sense to fall in love. Helford has merely muddied the waters a bit more. The main thing is that he has come to his senses at last.'

David swiftly realised that, despite Lady Darleston's amused attitude towards his very obvious frustration, she had actually assisted him indirectly. As had Lady Maria by inviting Kit and Thea Andrews to move into Helford Place immediately. She had also invited Lord Strathallen to re-move from the Helford Arms, in order that he might become acquainted with his heir.

Not unnaturally, Kit was eager to see his aunt nearly every day and, since this involved Helford and Strathallen escorting both Kit and Fanny over on their ponies, David's visits to his betrothed were thoroughly and unexceptionably chaperoned. A situation which his supposed friend and ally, Peter Darleston, laughed at openly.

Nevertheless, despite the fact that he could barely steal a kiss without interruption, David had to admit that the three weeks' enforced propriety gave him the opportunity to fully convince Sophie of his love for her once and for all. He found that taking the children riding was the best way of at least being able to talk to Sophie without interruption.

With their innocently efficient chaperons cantering ahead with Strathallen on one of their earliest rides, he was able to explain all his confusion to Sophie without being dis-tracted by the passion simmering beneath the surface, flaring into life.

As they rode he was able to tell her what a fool he'd been.

'I never intended to offer you a *carte blanche*, sweet-heart,' he assured her. 'At first I didn't realise why I kept wanting to see you, why I worried about you.' He groaned. 'I should have realised when Garfield tried to persuade you to marry him, but I was so damn confused. I was practically betrothed to Lucinda and I'd convinced myself that she...or rather the sort of marriage she offered...was what I wanted.'

'A marriage of convenience?' she asked quietly. 'You never cared for her?'

'That was not part of the bargain,' he answered. 'Lucinda made it quite plain that ours was to be a...a union of dy-nasties, not individuals. And I was so damned cynical about

love and women that I thought I wanted it as well. Until I
met you and you turned all my stupid notions inside out!'

'Me?' Sophie was stunned. 'What did I do?'

He laughed harshly. 'What did you do? You risked your
life to save that wretched urchin. You refused to marry for
money or security, instead you protected Kit's interests just
as gallantly as you saved Jem. And the day I saw you with
the Simpkins baby, realised how much you longed for your
own children, and tried to warn you to protect yourself from
hurt, you forced me to see that I'd spent twelve years running scared, rather than living.'

He saw joy leap into her eyes and understood at once.
'It's not just desire I feel for you, my love,' he avowed very
softly. 'I won't deny it's there, but that didn't prompt me
to marriage. If I had simply desired you, I'd have been able
to control my longing to see you. I would never have asked
you to be my mistress under any circumstances.' He laughed
oddly. 'I also wanted to protect you, even from myself. A
fact which was brought home to me when Garfield tried to
force his attentions on you. I'd never felt like that in my
entire life. Oh, I dare say I'd have defended any woman in
that situation, but I wouldn't have felt so…so personally
involved…as though something belonging to me had been
violated.'

Trembling, her hand stretched out to him. He grasped it
at once and held it reassuringly. 'Trust me, Sophie. If I
hadn't loved you, my betrothal to Lucinda would have been
announced before we sat down to dinner that ghastly night.
At that point I was still dithering. I knew I loved you and
it scared the hell out of me. What your song did was force
me to realise that I couldn't run away from what was between us. That all my supposed conviction that I wanted a
marriage of convenience was no more than a smokescreen
for my own fear of being hurt again. I meant to offer for
you in the carriage, but like a fool I kissed you first and lost

control. I was so stunned by what I felt for you that I couldn't even express it.'

He felt her fingers cling. Her voice, soft and shaking. 'Then you have relieved my mind, my heart, of its only fear: that you were marrying me for a combination of obligation and desire. That you were fond enough of me to sacrifice what you really wanted.'

Tears hung on her lashes as he said harshly, 'No, Sophie. I've made the right choice. I've chosen love.' To his inexpressible joy he saw the shadows lift from her eyes and knew that she was his. That she had finally and irrevocably accepted the truth of his love. As he had.

With that concern off his mind, by the wedding morning the only consideration weighing on David was how soon he could decently remove his bride from the wedding feast and take her back to Willowbank House. To the enormous bed that he had arranged to have installed in Sophie's bedchamber.

As weddings go, it was small, with only close friends and family. To wit, Lady Maria, the children, the Darlestons, Tom Hampton, Strathallen, the Asterfields and, to David's startled delight, George Carstares and Miss Sarah Ffolliot. Kate had sent a letter announcing that they were coming. And would Helford please ensure that there were no more rats? George and Sarah simply appeared at Darleston Court, the day after the notice appeared in the *Morning Post*.

''Fraid we just assumed, old chap,' had said George, wringing the groom's hand in obvious delight. 'We're not getting married for another month so we left Sarah's mother with the preparations and came!'

So David Charles Melville, Viscount Helford, took to wife Miss Sophia Ann Marsden, a woman who embodied none of the virtues he had so coldly deemed necessary in a wife. And he spoke his vows in the full and certain knowledge that he had finally got it right. The blast of approval at his back from family and friends assured him that they knew it too.

By eight o'clock that evening he was settling his dazed and sweetly exhausted bride safely in his arms. Her naked, pliant body was intimately entangled with his, her head resting on his shoulder. He viewed with intense satisfaction the fact that Sophie was, at long last, his. Totally and irrevocably.

Completely ignoring Anna's offer of refreshment when they arrived back, he had picked his bride up and carried her upstairs to her bedchamber. He had not even dared to kiss her in the carriage on the way over. He was going to have her in bed, but he was not going to wait a moment longer!

Sophie lay stunned in his embrace. Not even his near seduction in the carriage after the dinner party had prepared her for the joy and ecstasy that had flooded her when he at last took possession of her trembling, arching body. He had been so tender with her, despite the blazing desire that was consuming him.

When he had set her on her feet after carrying her up to her bedchamber, he had taken her mouth in the most gentle of kisses, framing her face in his hands. It was only after several minutes that she realised that one of his hands had somehow found its way to her lacings and that her gown was in some mysterious way sliding down over her breasts, her waist and pooling in a silken whisper around her feet.

He had drawn her back into his arms as he released the bow of her chemise and cupped one breast in a large possessive hand, rubbing his thumb back and forth over the nipple, calling forth a whimper of pleasure as her senses spiralled in a dizzying vortex of passion. This time at last, there would be no drawing back, no more frustration. This time he would take what was his and she pressed herself to him urgently, eager to give him everything he wanted.

She had felt him feather burning, searing kisses along the neck line of her chemise, teasing her until she wriggled to be free of the wretched thing and with a deep, seductive chuckle he had obligingly removed it as well as her petticoat. Then he had swung her into his arms again, placing her gently on the bed, which she had dimly realised was rather larger than she recalled.

His eyes had never left her as he stripped. Blazing with incandescent desire they had roamed her quivering body as she had watched him divest himself of his clothes. Only when he unbuttoned his breeches had her virgin shyness asserted itself, her eyes fluttering shut almost unwillingly.

Then he was beside her on the bed, his arms enfolding her to lie in his embrace, a large, compelling hand on one satiny hip moulding her to him as he moved his throbbing loins against her in a slow, yet inexorable rhythm.

Despite his screaming need, David had held himself in check as he made love to her. Never rushing her, he lavished untold attention on every exquisite detail, bringing into play all his expertise. He savoured to the full her unhesitating and glorious surrender to his demands, to his caressing hands and his increasingly possessive mouth.

When at last his hands and mouth had brought her to the point of insanity she had heard a sobbing voice she could barely recognise as hers begging him to take her. It seemed that was all he had been waiting for. His weight had shifted immediately, pinning her to the bed, vulnerable in the aching emptiness that cried out within her. His hand had pressed her thighs apart in unspoken command, a groan of deep satisfaction tearing from him as he settled himself between them…for a moment he had continued to caress her, his arousal pressing against her…and then with a tender murmur…oh, God…he had taken her in one gentle, but

masterful movement of his loins…he had lain motionless
for a moment, soothing her involuntary cry of pain, waiting
for her to relax before he allowed himself to move…and
when he had! She had thought she would die of the agony
of delight his powerful body evoked as gradually he allowed
her to feel the full force of his passion.

His loving had brought her to the limits of ecstasy and
further, to a place where thought was suspended and only
passion and breathless, searing sensation existed…a world
of feeling where she had soared in unfettered joy. And now
as she lay nestled in his arms, her body relaxed in sweet
exhaustion, his tender, adoring whispers assured her beyond
all doubt that she was loved.

She was his. Completely and irrevocably. David held her
and gloried in the thought as she drifted towards sleep, her
silken limbs and body entwined with his. Never had he felt
like this in all his life. This sense of completion, of total
possession, of being possessed in return. That he had not
merely taken, but had actually given. He remembered that
he had once thought that in lying with Sophie he would be
truly making love for the first time. It was all that and more.

His arms tightened about her and she sighed peacefully.
'Dearest.' His voice was husky, the merest whisper, but she
turned slightly in his arms, her silky softness caressing him,
and pressed a kiss on his shoulder. Smiling, his lips gently
brushed her hair.

Finally, after all his years of wandering, he had come
home. And love was, after all, the most convenient choice
he could possibly have made.

*   *   *   *   *

A Roguish Gentleman
by
Mary Brendan

Mary Brendan was born in North London but now lives in rural Suffolk. She has always had a fascination with bygone days and enjoys the research involved in writing historical fiction. When not at her word processor she can be found trying to bring order to a large overgrown garden or browsing local fairs and junk shops for that elusive bargain.

To Amazing Grace
Also for Elaine, Doreen, Jane, Amanda, Marie and all
the other Friday-nighters at 2-HOD

Chapter One

'Elizabeth!'

Lady Elizabeth Rowe turned in the spacious hallway of her grandmother's elegant townhouse to see the elderly lady bearing down on her, nose pinched between thumb and forefinger and what was visible of her face, behind her podgy hand, set in a grimace of utter distaste.

Elizabeth understood. Sheepishly she glanced down at her hem. It *was* suspiciously clogged. She sighed and shrugged an apology. It was possible the stains were mud from the hedgerow she had skipped over moments ago on alighting from Reverend Clemence's gig. Unfortunately, she suspected, as did her grandmother, that it was rather more offensive detritus. Probably ordure from the gutters in Wapping where she'd been assisting the vicar in teaching at Barrow Road Sunday School.

'Look at you!' Edwina Sampson shrieked at her granddaughter, jewels flashing on her fat fingers as they flicked floorward in disgust. 'There's no mistaking when you are home. I simply follow m'nose!'

'Don't nag so, Grandmama,' Elizabeth said mildly. 'There are worse things in life than a little muck. I have just been amongst poor wretches who live with the stench daily in their nostrils as well as beneath their feet.'

Edwina Sampson bristled. 'Decency and hard work is

what's lacking! Shut that door!' she suddenly bawled at a tall, stately man who was standing by the draughty aperture, steely eyebrows slightly elevated as he phlegmatically assessed a trail of dung on formerly pristine marble. 'Quickly, man! Do I warm this house simply to let it out and encourage vagrants to congregate on m'step? Do you know the cost of a sack of coal? A cartload of logs?'

'Indeed, I do, madam,' Harry Pettifer calmly responded. 'I have just this week settled the fuel bill.'

'Is that insolence, Pettifer?'

'I am never insolent, madam,' her butler informed his mistress, inscrutable of face as he regally paced the hallway poker-backed. One bright blue eye disappeared as he passed Elizabeth and she stifled a smile at the unobtrusive wink.

Harry Pettifer had been in service to the Sampsons for almost thirty years. In the few years Elizabeth had lived with her grandmother in this quiet part of Marylebone, she'd witnessed far more entertaining exchanges between the short sexagenarian and her statuesque butler.

As Elizabeth carefully eased off her suspiciously slimy shoes, she noticed the commotion had drawn other servants to gawp at the spectacle. With supreme aplomb, Pettifer clicked his elegant fingers at mobcaps. 'Brush... mop...hallway...now,' was his brusque instruction to them to dispose of the mess.

Edwina Sampson frowned at his back. 'For what I pay him, I could take on two footmen, or pay m'butcher for a twelve-month.'

'I think not, Grandmama. I doubt poor Pettifer's salary would even cover your confectioner's bill.' She teased her grandmother's fondness for marchpane with a meaningful nod at her sizeable girth.

Pettifer allowed an appreciative smile to touch his lips, prompting his employer to snap, 'Less of your sauce, miss! I might have a sweet tooth,' she admitted while twitching Elizabeth's skirts this way and that, her smooth, plump face a study in revulsion. 'And why should I not? A woman who's worked her fingers to the bone is entitled to a little treat in her twilight years.'

Elizabeth padded to the stairs in her stockinged feet. 'You know very well that we need Pettifer…far more than he does us, I suspect. I hear that Mrs Penney is stalking him again. She's keen to lure him away to her Brighton townhouse,' Elizabeth warned.

'Is she? Who told you?' Her grandmother's lips compressed into a tight, indignant line, her pale blue eyes narrowing.

Elizabeth removed her bonnet, dropped back her ash-blonde head and laughed while the hat swayed on its strings. 'I shall just freshen myself, then join you in the parlour and share some gossip regarding Pettifer's popularity. Meanwhile, perhaps you ought go and curry a little favour with him, lest he really is tempted to go this time,' she taunted over her shoulder as, grimy skirts held high and shapely ankles displayed, she ran easily up the curve of stairs.

Moments later, in her lavender-fragrant chamber, Elizabeth grimaced down at her hem, then up at her maid. Josie distastefully wrinkled her small pert nose, shook her head and gingerly helped her mistress step out of the serviceable garment before bundling it away for the laundry.

Her grandmother was right, Elizabeth mused while bathing her face with petal-scented water. It *was* the stench that disturbed the most. Even when home and decked in fresh clothes, the reek of the slums would haunt her nostrils.

She'd been assisting at Barrow Road Sunday School every week for some thirteen months. In all that time, it seemed that the air never got sweeter or more foul. The fortitude of unwashed humanity, seething middens and the proximity of the docks contributing salt and tar spillage, remained stoically unchanged. Even the recent heat of summer seemed to make little difference to rank poverty. Only the flies came and went. As did the school's pupils.

At times a gap would appear on the rough pew on which the boys and girls sat, slates balanced on tattered laps.

'A'workin' t'day, m'm. Ailin' t'day, m'm,' would gruffly answer any enquiry as to where was the absentee. 'Dead, m'm,' on one occasion was the toneless reply to the condition of a sickly child.

The philanthropic owner of a spice warehouse had allowed a spare, bare corner to serve as a classroom to a score or more local urchins, aiding their escape from a little petty larceny along the wharves or watching young 'uns on the Sabbath to scratch out scripture instead. On arrival at the premises on Sundays, a mass of skeletal arms and legs would jostle and elbow for a place on a splintery bench as determinedly as they doubtless fought for a portion of what was available to eat or earn. The weakest would sink cross-legged to the cold, stone floor.

Seating herself on her velvet dressing-table chair, Elizabeth studied her well-nourished appearance. As Josie worked pins from her hair, pearl-blonde tresses sinuously spiralled to bounce either side of her oval face and slender column of neck. A healthy flush was still rimming her high cheekbones from the brisk walk earlier.

Each Sunday, she and Hugh Clemence hurried through a maze of narrow alleys to reach Barrow Road. Even a clergyman who was afforded a respectful nod or word from ragged parishioners never chose to tarry in such an area. Their route never differed. Winter and summer, lines of greyish washing crisscrossed overhead between grimy tenements. When the air froze in front of their mouths as they talked and walked, the rags hung stiff and unmoving; at other times a tepid oily breeze might flutter the tattered flags of a community surrendered to its fate. Dead-eyed women and rickety children crowded the dank doorways or squatted on the cobbles sifting through the rubbish for something useful.

Elizabeth closed her violet-blue eyes and relaxed into the chair as Josie gently but firmly drew a brush through her blonde tangles. She sighed as she thought of the children. Was it enough to simply suspend reality for them for a while on the Sabbath? What were they really thinking as they gazed, glassy-eyed, at her and rubbed at streaming noses or chapped skin? Their empty bellies? The chores they had just come from or were soon returning to? The nonsense of hearing tales of a Benevolent Father when in their short lives most had experienced nothing but hunger and harshness?

'If but one child escapes the ravages of the gin house or the bawdy house through our work today, I shall die a happy man,' Hugh Clemence had once expounded his philosophy on it all. Enduring the stench of poverty in her nostrils once a week was a paltry price to pay to help just one poor soul.

'We must make it two,' she had answered him, and he had taken her hand to hold. And she had allowed him to…for a few seconds, before extricating her fingers.

'Ah, that's better,' Edwina Sampson praised the sight of her granddaughter's pretty, petite figure. Elizabeth entered the cosy, flame-flickering parlour, dressed in rose-pink crepe with her shiny blonde hair piled elegantly atop her head, making her look taller than her five feet three inches. 'Now you look and smell more like my sweet Lizzie.'

'On the subject of odours, Grandmama…have you been smoking in here again?' Elizabeth quizzed, wrinkling her small nose. 'It reeks of a gentleman's gaming room,' she chided, fanning a space in front of her with a small hand.

'And how would you know of such places? Have you lately *been* in a gentleman's gaming room?' her grandmother shot back distractingly while the heel of a slippered foot sent a dark stub skidding under her chair.

'You know Papa and his cronies could set up quite a fug in the blue salon at Thorneycroft when playing at Faro. I am well used to identifying tobacco smoke.'

'Hmmph,' Edwina rumbled. 'I thought perhaps you'd been spending time with a real man instead of that whey-faced clergyman who limps after you.'

Lady Elizabeth Rowe sent her grandmother a prim look. 'Hugh is a very conscientious and kindly gentleman, and I cherish him as a good friend.'

The demure description was dismissed with one plump hand while the other dived into a silver dish and extracted a piece of marchpane. Chewing and eyeing her granddaughter speculatively, Edwina demanded, 'Has he yet proposed?'

Elizabeth sank daintily into a fireside chair opposite her grandmother's seat. Holding her hands to the glow in the grate, she allowed a small smile. 'No, he has not. Neither will he. Hugh is well aware I have no fondness for him in…that way.'

'Thank God for that!' her grandmother muttered. 'I live in dread of you arriving home with some paltry bauble on your betrothal finger to announce you're to move into some roof-leaking rectory in a godforsaken part of town.' With a finger-wag, she added, 'That's not to say I've given up on your nuptials, miss. It is far and away time you were wed. You are soon to be twenty-nine and can't live with your old grand-mama forever. I might soon get notice to quit and first I must know you're settled.'

'You're as robust as ever and as like to see a score more years. And you're well aware that I shall never marry. Now then,' she speedily changed subject, 'are you interested in learning how I know that Mrs Penney is again batting her lashes and her banknotes at Pettifer?'

'You shan't sidetrack me that easily, m'girl. I meant what I said. I'm sixty-five years old and often afflicted with a pain right here.' She thumped a spot beneath her ribs. 'It could be a serious malaise; it might see me off!'

'It's indigestion,' Elizabeth mildly reassured her. 'And as like to disappear if you cease eating for…let's see…one hour a day?' A cheeky smile made her look no more than nineteen, and immediately melted her grandmother's indignation.

'Elizabeth,' Edwina wheedled. 'You are a beautiful woman and need a husband. You can't let a tragedy that occurred a decade ago blight your entire life. It is forgotten. People have forgotten.'

'I haven't forgotten! Neither have I any wish for a hus-band…especially not a gentleman from the *ton*. Were I to marry, I would choose a kind, caring man such as Hugh, which would rile you greatly and have you ranting of a *mé-salliance*. After all, I *am* the daughter of a Marquess and poor Hugh comes from a long line of impoverished men of the cloth. So please, no more of it.'

A theatrically languid hand displayed despair as Edwina flopped back in her chair. Her fingers began straying comfortingly towards the silver dish. 'Tell me then why that cat Alice Penney is after Pettifer.' She resorted to sighing in a martyred tone.

Elizabeth smiled winsomely. 'I imagine it is because he is so handsome.'

'Pish! He is an old codger: a year older than me!' emerged through a mouthful of marchpane.

'He is still a very sprightly and handsome man, despite his age. According to Sophie, many a matron in Mrs Penney's set would like him to greet their guests and grace their hallway. They are to have a wager, so I hear, on who can steal him from under your nose. I believe a great deal of money is in the pot.'

'A *wager?*' Edwina spluttered. 'On who can steal my *butler*? He's been my man for nigh on three decades and my man he will stay. I'll…I'll never give him a character if he leaves me.'

'I rather think he might not need one,' Elizabeth chuckled. 'I'm sure Mrs Penney will snap him up without.'

Edwina shook her salt and pepper ringlets back from her plump cheeks, her eyes narrowing, her mouth twitching angrily. A gleam appeared in her light blue eyes. Wager? If there was one thing Edwina liked as much as a good gobble, it was a good gamble. She'd give those wanton alley cats a run for their money!

Harry Pettifer was a fine figure of a man and he had noble blood in him. Had it not been for his idiot father, Sir Roger Pettifer, taking the family into penury through his love of hazard, his youngest son might have had an inheritance to smooth his path through life. Instead, fate decreed he take up a position as butler to a friend.

Harry and her late husband had been chums, even though, at one time, Harry had been frowned upon for keeping company with a lowly 'cit'. For Daniel Sampson had made *his* tidy fortune through commerce, progressing through hard work from humble mercer to retail baron, dealing in all manner of luxury commodities. At that time, Harry had been an eligible bachelor who lived off a generous allowance. Then bankruptcy came; no more funds were forthcoming for the Pettifer sons and Harry would not hear of a loan from Daniel Sampson being written off. So his services were taken up, half in jest, half in earnest, for Harry had always been a proud man. What ensued was an employment lasting half a lifetime. On her husband's death some thirteen years ago, Harry had stayed on. She hadn't expected him to: her relationship with her husband's friend, confidant and man of all trades, had at times been quite prickly.

Edwina had never been generous or mean in her dealings with him. Since his financial obligation had been cleared, Harry had drawn a reasonable salary. Edwina had always paid him an acceptable rate: what was fair. And now, if he wanted to go, she had no right to detain him. In the past, when she had casually interrogated him for his opinion on their status quo, a slightly quizzical look would sharpen his blue eyes. Politely he would assure her he was content. Perhaps he no longer was content. Perhaps he missed not having a wife, children of his own. Perhaps he regretted only ever observing family life rather than engaging in it himself. Perhaps, Edwina mused with a leaden feeling in her stomach that she knew was nothing devoured, she regretted that she had never rewarded her loyal gentleman butler with gratitude and generosity instead of a remote fairness. Annoyed at the melancholy that the possibility of losing him evoked, Edwina suddenly barked irritably, 'What time are we to go to the Heathcotes'?

'At eight,' Elizabeth confirmed the hour of the quiet soirée planned at Sophie's parents that evening. At twenty-two, Sophie Heathcote was six years her junior. Her closest friend was an attractive brunette who possessed a sharp wit she refused to disguise. That rendered Sophie far less attractive in the eyes of the *beau monde*. Sophie was a blue-stocking, an odd creature who was happier pursuing knowledge than an eligible man. Which was as well, for no man would want a wife whose intelligence was superior to his own. The two young women were outcasts in a society which despised and isolated women who didn't conform to an accepted ideal. Since Elizabeth moved to town from the countryside when her father, the Marquess of Thorneycroft, died, some few years ago, she and Sophie, both lonely yet lively, had gravitated towards each other and become firm friends.

'Would you mind terribly if I cried off tonight, Lizzie? You know it is all a bit dull for my taste and I have an invitation to Maria Farrow's salon. Josie can accompany you there.'

'No, I don't mind. I shall not stay too late, in any case. There is a visit to Bridewell planned tomorrow—' Her grandmother's snort of disgust cut her short, making it clear she had no interest in learning any details of her visit to the correctional institution, with Hugh Clemence and some other charitable ladies. Elizabeth, undeterred, ploughed on, 'Actually, Grandmama, we are hoping for some kindly people to donate—' She got no further.

Sixty-five years old and portly, maybe, but Edwina was out of her chair in a flash and soon at the door. 'I have told you, young lady, I have no spare fortune to be squandered housing foundlings and fallen women!'

'I am not asking you for a fortune, Grandmama,' Elizabeth sighed. 'A few pounds would be very welcome. It would buy cloth for the women so they can make things to sell: pinafores, handkerchiefs…'

'Had they not stolen such articles in the first place, they wouldn't now be stitching scrappy rags to while away the time till their release!'

Elizabeth sprang to her feet and glared at her grandmother. 'One mistake in their miserable lives—perhaps to put bread in their children's mouths—and they should pay forever? I made a mistake once; have you forgotten that? I made a bad mistake. But I refuse to feel ashamed. I, too, was wrong for the right reasons. Some of those gentlemen you would like to see come a'courting are the worst immoral riffraff. If one or two of them still loiter about me, it is for far less honourable reasons than proposing marriage!' Her small oval face flushed with anger, her fingers clenched. After staring stonily at each other for a moment, Elizabeth sighed and gestured apology.

'I'm sorry Grandmama. I had not meant to shout. But…' She dredged up a weak smile, reseating herself. 'I have been meaning to ask you for some weeks now…' She paused, striving for coaxing words to unlock her parsimonious grandmother's purse. 'The portion you have put by for my marriage is money likely to stay untouched. I shall not marry. But if you really intended it to benefit me, I beg you allow me just a small sum from it so that I can—'

'You are right in one respect, miss,' her grandmother interrupted tightly. 'The money is for *your* benefit. If you think I will pass over some of my hard-earned cash—from the days when I worked dawn till dusk in your grandfather's mercery—so you can then transfer it to such drabs as used to rob us blind the moment our backs were turned, you are much mistaken! Never a week went by but a pair of gloves, silk stockings, handkerchiefs and ribbon went missing from our first shop. And now you want *me* to support those miscreants' descendants in their thievery?'

'No, Grandmama,' Elizabeth reasoned wearily. 'So it can assist such poor wretches to perhaps gain employment, a little self-respect; to help them start a new life. Just one hundred pounds…please? It is my money and it would make such a difference to so many; children as well as their mothers.'

'I'd as lief hand it straight to your husband to squander at dice.'

'And the men you would see me wed would do exactly that!' Elizabeth snapped bitterly. 'Perhaps I shall wed the

vicar after all, I'm sure I might persuade him to give it me
straight back!'

'Hah…you think I've not thought of that? No clergy. It
states in the terms. Marry a clergyman and the dowry is forfeit.'

Elizabeth threw up her hands in despair. 'I love you dearly,
Grandmama, but your misanthropy disgusts me.'

'And I love you dearly, granddaughter, but your misplaced
charity disgusts me,' was flung over a plump satin shoulder
as Edwina quit the room.

Lady Rebecca Ramsden raised her glorious turquoise gaze
from the paper and stared into space. It couldn't be true! Luke
surely would have said! She shook the page to straighten it,
dipped her golden head and read the paragraph again. It *was*
true! It was there in black and white! Springing from the chair,
the paper clutched tightly in a hand, she sped for the door.
Out in the hallway she gasped at their aged butler, 'Have you
seen my husband, Miles?'

'Er, no, Miss Becky,' Miles returned with a frown at his
mistress's agitation. Neither of them were in any way put out
by him addressing her so informally. Miss Becky she had
been prior to her marriage to Baron Ramsden and Miss Becky
she was now to all old and trusted servants at Ramsden
Manor, who had known her since childhood. Now approaching his seventy-seventh year, Miles would never think of her
as anything else but little Miss Becky. In all other respects,
Lady Ramsden was accorded every respect due to her station
as the much-loved chatelaine of this grand house.

'I expect he's about the stables, putting young Master Troy
through his paces on his pony,' Miles added helpfully.

Rebecca had already reasoned that and, with a laughing
wave of the crumpled *Gazette*, was off again. She ran in mellow late-afternoon sunlight towards the stables. 'Luke!' she
called breathlessly as she hurtled into the cool, musty building.

Only a few young stable-hands, toiling at one end of the

brick-and-timber building, were within. They looked curiously at her. 'I think his lordship be in the barn wi' young master. Right tired he were after his ride, m'lady. Practic'ly a'snoozin' on his feet,' the more gregarious of the grooms told her.

Rebecca nodded in appreciation of the information and was gone. She pushed open the barn door and located her husband at once. Against the yellow straw his dark breeches, white cambric shirt and jet hair were a striking contrast. He looked up as a shaft of warm, mote-ridden sunlight bathed him. Earth-dark eyes locked on to his wife's curvaceous figure, silhouetted by hazy golden light. He smiled slowly in that special intimate way that quickened her heart. A finger beckoned her in, moved to touch his lips, then indicated their small son, curled up on his side on soft straw close to his father.

Rebecca sank gracefully down onto her knees close to her husband. Even casually reclining on his side, dark head propped on a hand, one black knee raised, the powerful masculine lines of his body were immediately apparent. She shook the paper at him and hissed in an undertone, so as not to wake their sleeping son, 'Why did you not tell me? Isn't it wonderful news?'

Luke frowned at the paper, removed a stalk of sweet straw from between his even white teeth and said softly, 'Whichever marriage you've seen announced...I've no knowledge of it, Rebecca. I've not yet read the paper today. And don't be cross if I'm not about to be as enraptured as you at the prospect of some acquaintance's impending nuptials.'

'No...no, not a wedding!' Rebecca chided in an excited squeak. Then her turquoise eyes were sparking mischief. 'You've not seen it? Guess, then, what I have just read,' she teased, standing up and whipping the paper behind her back, out of reach. 'I promise it will interest you. It should delight you...'

'Enough...I'm curious,' her husband growled, snaking a powerful hair-roughened forearm about her slender blue silk figure to catch at the paper.

'No! Guess!'

A peaty-brown gaze swerved to his son, then raised to his wife's beautiful flushed complexion. His hands jerked her forward and his mouth approached a rounded hip close to his face. Slender fingers wound into long dark hair, holding his hot trailing mouth against her midriff as she insincerely discouraged, 'Oh, Luke, not here…not now; Troy might wake and…'

'Give me the paper, then,' her husband whispered in a throaty growl against warm silk. 'Or I'll have no option but to wrestle it from you…'

Heat flooded Rebecca; her fingers tightened in his hair, but, with her eyes on her sleeping son's profile, she again sank, with an expression of very ironic submission, to her knees.

Demurely she handed over the paper, pointing at a paragraph before resting back onto her heels and watching his face.

Luke Trelawney, Baron Ramsden, slowly pushed himself upright, a slow grin moving the lean dark planes of his handsome face. 'I didn't tell you, my love, because I didn't know,' he emphasised for Rebecca. 'Only Ross would keep quiet the fact that he's being gazetted as a peer of the realm.'

'Viscount Stratton! How noble it sounds,' Rebecca said on a musical laugh. 'You had no idea?' she quizzed her husband. 'He had said nothing?'

'Not a word. But then I've not seen him in six months. Neither, I imagine, has Mother or Katherine or Tristan.'

'Oh, but it's too bad of him, Luke! He really should have written to let his kin know of such an honour.'

'Ross? Write a letter? My little brother is more likely to turn up unexpectedly after half a year's absence than he is to pen a couple of lines.'

Rebecca flung her arms about her husband's neck. 'It's such wonderful news. Viscount Stratton of Stratton Hall in the County of Kent. Ross must be so proud.'

'Is Uncle Ross coming soon?' a small voice quavered from beside them.

Rebecca relinquished her husband to stroke her son's silky black hair. 'No, my love. But your uncle Ross is now a nobleman. The honour has been bestowed by the King. Uncle Ross is now a Viscount and will be Lord Stratton.'

Troy Trelawney looked singularly unimpressed by this news. He fully opened his sea-green eyes and looked at his mother from beneath black curly lashes. 'Will Uncle Ross still play pirates with me?' he asked with all the gravity of his six years. 'Now he is so important?'

Rebecca stifled a laugh and looked helplessly at her husband. Luke gave his son a lop-sided smile. 'I think that's still very likely,' he gently reassured Troy while a stray thought acknowledged that, at thirty-three, his recklessly intrepid brother still looked and acted like a dashing young buck. 'Besides, if he doesn't, then I shall.'

Again Troy Trelawney looked unimpressed. 'But you're not such a good Blackbeard, Papa, as Uncle Ross. He teaches me to fight with his sword. The one with the silver hilt, not a pretend wooden one...'

'Now I think it's time a certain sleepy man was snuggled up,' Rebecca hastily interjected, on noticing her husband's murderous look. Her brother-in-law might never live to enjoy his new rank.

'Excellent suggestion, darling,' Luke murmured. 'Tend to Troy first, though.' In a lithe movement he was on his feet and tousling his son's glossy raven hair with long fingers. 'Come back here when he's settled so we can enjoy the sunset?' he quietly requested.

Rebecca took her son's hand, picking stray straw stalks from his hair, before she met her husband's gleaming dark eyes. She smiled, then murmured on a virginal blush that never ceased to enchant Luke, 'Yes. I want to...'

Within fifteen minutes, Rebecca, Lady Ramsden, having seen her eldest son safely within the nursery and settled close to his sleeping infant brother, was again speeding over the vestibule flags, blue silk skirts scrunched in her palms, on her way to rejoin her husband.

'Dinner is served in ten minutes, my lady,' Judith called at her back as she rushed lightly past.

Rebecca came to a halt and spun about at her housekeeper's words. 'Oh…oh…' She looked towards the open great doors. An orange ball was visible, dipping low on the horizon. 'Lord Ramsden and I have…er…a few estate matters to discuss, Judith, while we…er…enjoy the sundown. Will dinner keep awhile?'

'Twenty minutes?' Judith offered on a smile.

Rebecca looked into middle distance and frowned, unsure.

'Thirty?' Judith amended neutrally. 'I know these estate matters take time.'

'Yes,' Rebecca said. 'Thirty. Thank you, Judith.' She spun away and was gone in a flash of blue silk.

Judith looked after her and grinned. Eight years married, two handsome sons tucked up in the nursery, and still they pulled together like magnets. It was the longest honeymoon of any couple she'd ever known.

'What's that you're fiddling with?' Edwina barked at her companion as they rocked together in her cosy old coach en route to a private card evening with Mrs Farrow.

Evangeline Filbert held up her knitting so the light from a passing gas lamp illuminated it. 'Stockings. I've finished ten pairs so far for Lizzie. She's taking them tomorrow to Bridewell for the inmates.'

Edwina Sampson snatched the needles and threw them onto the seat. 'Not you, too! Is everyone now with attics to let over these misbegotten felons?'

Evangeline looked mortified, her lips started to quiver.

'Oh, for God's sake, don't blub. Here.' Edwina plonked the knitting back on her lap. 'Finish a few more rows if you must. Just don't blub or I shan't again let you accompany me to m'friends. You shall sit at home alone.'

'Oh, I like to come,' Evangeline whispered. 'Your friends are all so…so…'

'Yes…?' Edwina snarled. 'So?'

'Exciting. And glamorous. And thrilling,' Evangeline expounded in wonder. She was a spinster of forty-three who had led a very quiet and careworn existence tending her ailing mother. When that lady—who had been a long-standing friend of Edwina Sampson's—finally accepted the notice to quit delivered some years earlier, Edwina had kindly taken Evangeline under her wing. The arrangement suited them both: a few times a week Evangeline escaped boredom and solitude, and Edwina gained an unpaid and unaware companion to accompany her to some of the unconscionable venues she favoured.

Tonight their hostess was an exceedingly glamorous widow, fêted for being the Duke of Vermont's current mistress. She was more notorious for cuckolding him quite openly with any lusty young buck who caught her eye. Still the ageing duke remained besotted. Mrs Farrow ran an exceedingly fine salon, Edwina judged, if a little *demi-monde*. Certainly more interesting than sitting with her granddaughter on the Heathcotes' sofa and listening to young Sophie spout about the position of ploughs and bears and how the planets might form a conjunction and alter one's fate.

Despite Maria Farrow being some twenty years her junior, the two women had a lot in common. They *were* common. But now Edwina had mighty connections: her late husband had hobnobbed with the gentry. Their beloved daughter had married an aristocrat. She had a beautiful granddaughter, sired by the late Marquess of Thorneycroft. Edwina frowned. What she really would have liked was a grandson. But her daughter had fallen foul of an icy winter before producing further children. It galled her greatly that, when the Marquess had remarried, desperate to produce an heir to prevent his detested cousin gaining the entailed estate on his demise, the sour-faced cat of a second wife had produced an heir within the first year of the nuptials.

A grandson-in-law was still an option, despite dear Lizzie's protestations that she had no wish to wed. A decade had passed since that fateful midsummer evening when she'd been compromised. When all was said and done, it had been no more than a silly little slip.

Chapter Two

'It's hot enough to roast an ox in here, Maria!' Edwina expostulated with her friend, feverishly fanning her sanguine complexion.

'Lawks, Edwina, but you'll have to make do with the veal pies,' Maria quipped. 'Spitting an ox, even for you, dearest, is totally too…mediaeval.'

Edwina gave her comrade a playfully indignant knock with her fan.

'The blaze in the hearth is for his Grace's benefit,' Maria confided, inclining her auburn coiffure in the direction of a sparse-pated, august gentleman engaged in a rubber of whist at a nearby table. 'Charlie, bless him, is keen to keep me warm since he discovered that young Carstairs had overnighted here last week. I pleaded it was so chilly in my chamber I was doomed to freeze to death a'bed lest a hot-blooded member of the regiment slide in and warm me. Next day, a forest of logs had sprouted in the gutter outside.'

Edwina chuckled, then gestured with her glass. 'What in heaven's name is this foul potion? Has he spent so much on your fires that the wine cellar's gone begging? It tastes like infant's cordial.'

'His Grace is keen for sober company tonight.' Maria sighed. 'Yesterday, I over-imbibed and he couldn't wake me.

Not that it mattered to me. I'd as lief the old goat got on with it while I'm unconscious.'

Edwina smothered a guffaw. Maria floated daintily away to greet some new arrivals, a vision of virginal loveliness with her alabaster skin and fiery tresses, and her willowy body draped in white muslin.

Edwina inclined her head at some acquaintances and smiled serenely, but she was vexed. Her enjoyment had been spoiled before it had begun, yet the company, the food and the music seemed as fine as ever. Even the stifling heat was just bearable. It was another matter which had dampened her humour.

On drawing up outside Maria's modish address, she had noticed Alice Penney's carriage stopping at a house along the street. Mrs Penney had made a point of loitering and simpering very deliberately in her direction on alighting from her barouche. Now Edwina could concentrate on little else but what that snide look signified. She'd concluded a wager was won: Harry Pettifer was to quit her service for pastures new. His resignation letter might, even now, be awaiting her, and she felt irritably inclined to rush home to discover if her gloomy prediction was correct.

With her lace fan whizzing before her ruddy countenance, Edwina was oblivious to Evangeline huddled in a corner seat, needles flying through the wool in her lap. Knitting her brows, she marched towards doors that led to a terrace, seeking refreshing night air. She stalked over stone flags to the iron balustrade that overlooked the lawns, gripping at it as though she'd reshape it with her bare hands.

'You look fit to do battle, Mrs Sampson,' drawled a voice from one side of her. 'Have you been sucking lemons to perfect that sour look?'

Edwina's brow smoothed, her eyes peeked sideways as she grinned in delight. But, despite that husky baritone sounding so familiar, it probably wasn't who she'd thought. Having clawed back some awesome fortune for the King's hungry coffers by confiscating a shipload of smuggled gold bullion destined for the continent, her favourite scoundrel, so she'd learned, was now much in favour with Georgy Porgy and very welcome at court.

The new Viscount Stratton was unlikely to be sitting alone in the dark on a mature courtesan's terrace, even if the lady did run a damn fine salon and her aristocratic lover was present tonight. Edwina didn't imagine the Duke of Vermont and Viscount Stratton were chums: there was a score or more years' difference in their ages and a vast discrepancy in their energy. Stratton was always up to carriage racing, pugilism and cavorting with enthusiastic strumpets; his Grace sometimes left unfinished a game of whist and a brief romp with an indifferent woman. Were it indeed the Viscount, even as plain Mr Trelawney, there would be an ambitious young female loitering somewhere hereabouts, keen to turn his head.

A cigar glowed in the night to one side of her. Edwina raised her lorgnette strung on the pearls that were lost in the folds of her neck. 'Is that you, Trelawney? Slumming this evening, are you? Taking a little break from the Carlton House Set? Must I curtsy?' Edwina ribbed. She chuckled delightedly as a tall, dark and exceedingly handsome man pushed to his feet from the stone bench he'd been resting on and strolled into the shaft of weak light filtering through the french doors.

'I accept your congratulations, Edwina,' he commented drily. 'And how have you been?'

'I have been better,' she snarled, suddenly recalling what had brought her out here. 'I'm in high dudgeon, Ross. But it's good to see you. It must be…' She looked reflective, trying to recall the last time she and this man had socialised.

'Two years or more, as I recall,' Viscount Stratton supplied. 'At Vauxhall two summers ago. I don't get to London as much as I used to.'

'And when you do it seems you skulk about in the dark. Are you grown shy all of a sudden?' she laughed.

'I'm always shy when a woman has commitment on her mind; especially when I figure in her delusion. That's not the real reason I'm out here,' he admitted, with a flash of a white smile. 'The whole house is hellish hot, is it not? I wasn't sure whether to drink that odd brew being doled out or throw it on the fire.'

'I sympathise on both counts,' Edwina said, peering distastefully at her glass, but her eyes were narrowing thoughtfully. 'So you're still unwed…I imagined some young minx must have cornered you by now.'

'They do, Edwina,' he agreed wryly. 'But not well enough that I might submit.'

'You're a heartless rogue,' Edwina chided, her mouth aslant and gimlet eyes sparkling with a crafty light. 'Of course, I understand why these flighty young misses straight out of the schoolroom don't appeal. Why…you must be thirty-three if you're a day. You're a sophisticate who would suit a more mature lady. Someone older and wiser in the ways of the world…'

'Are you proposing, Edwina?' Ross asked with studied gravity.

Edwina tutted, rapping her fan on his arm in mock outrage, but her pale eyes were veiled behind her lashes and her mind whirred.

'So what's set you so glum-faced this evening?' Ross asked idly. 'Apart from the lack of a good cognac to be had, of course.'

Edwina looked shrewdly at him. 'Well, I'd like very much to tell you actually, Stratton. I need a friend to confide in. It's all about some underhand thievery in the offing, so I'd value your expert advice on the subject,' she teased with a wicked smile. 'You must visit me tomorrow; we shall dine and catch up on all our news. You can impress me…and m'granddaughter…' she mumbled on a cough, 'with all your heroic exploits.'

Ross frowned, and ruefully moved a hand as he mentally sifted through prior engagements.

When he seemed unsuspecting, Edwina hurriedly encouraged, 'It's time you met m'granddaughter…' At his slow, speculative look, she hastened on, 'You'll find the tale amusing…very droll. And perhaps there might even be a little side bet in it for you. You know you and I always manage to make a good wager. There was that two thousand guineas we shared when the Duchess of Marlborough didn't survive the Duchess of Cleveland…remember? It was strange fortune indeed that day; you'd needed a doctor y'self and it happened he'd come straight from her sick-bed. How are those old wounds?' she asked, prodding maternally at his arm through his jacket as though testing his fitness.

He allowed her ministrations for a moment before extricating his arm. 'Those are forgotten, Edwina. I've added a few more scratches since that have also healed well.'

Edwina shook her head and started a lecture on the necessity of early stitching that had barely begun before it was rudely interrupted.

'I've been searching for you, Lord Stratton. I thought we were to go elsewhere in search of a real drink…'

Ross looked about rather than responding to Edwina's fussing.

'I hadn't realised you were with your grandmama.' The young woman placed apologetic gloved fingers over her rouged mouth. 'Oh, dear, *is* she your grandmama?' Cecily Booth was lounging against the door frame, the candle flame behind clearly outlining her voluptuous figure beneath diaphanous voile.

Edwina squinted through the gloom at her firm, youthful face, guessing her to be barely twenty. But she *was* polished and confident—probably already had several years as a kept woman beneath her tiny belt. Glancing enquiringly at Ross, she saw he was laughing silently. Her scowl prompted him to give an easy shrug.

Striding regally for the door, Edwina glared at the young woman until she moved aside. 'Yes,' she purred, with curled top lip, 'I might be his grandmama. But what, pray, might you be, I wonder?' Thin, sooty eyebrows winged disdainfully. Her lips twitched in triumphant satisfaction as Cecily's mouth knotted into a rouged rosebud. Peering down her nose, Edwina turned with a sniff and a raised shoulder. 'I'll expect you tomorrow at seven then, Stratton. Don't be tardy. Re-heating game makes it tough. A soufflé doesn't like to wait and neither do I.' With that she marched through the stuffy, crowded salon, barked at Evangeline to find her cloak, and within five minutes was hoisting herself with a footman's help back into her carriage.

Cecily peeked sulkily up at her lover. She angled her bru-nette head, and pouted at him. Ignored, she trailed a fingernail lightly back and forth on the lean dark hand resting idly on the iron balustrade. When he still gazed, starstruck, into the night, a possessive hand slipped through the crook of a mus-cular arm. 'Who was that fat lady, Ross?' she finally sighed.

'A good friend.' He drew on the stub of his cheroot, then sent it in an arc of glowing ash into the darkness.

'I told you yesterday evening that I was to be abroad today, Grandmama.'

'Yes…yes. Well, I forgot. It is important you are back to dine. We rarely have guests and today we do.'

'Do I know them?'

'Er…no. It is just the one guest. He is a…well-travelled gentleman. A friend of mine of some long standing who I've not seen in an age. We used to play cards and have a little flutter during the years you lived at Thorneycroft with your papa. You would not know him. As I say, he is…an adven-turous gentleman who has sailed the seas and has tales to tell. Presently he is in great favour at court.'

Lady Elizabeth Rowe pulled on her gloves and straightened her bonnet over her smoky-blonde hair. 'Well, I dare say he has a deal more enthusiasm for your company than mine and will never miss me. It is good you are to see one of your old friends again. If we are early back from Bridewell, then I shall be happy to meet him.' She smiled at her grandmama, pleased that their tiff yesterday seemed forgotten. 'He sounds great fun…' she added amiably on wandering off to the window and pulling back the curtain. 'Oh, Hugh's gig is just arrived. I must hurry.'

Edwina followed, hot on her granddaughter's heels, into the hallway. 'Seven o'clock. Tell the Reverend I expect you home by that hour to dine with Viscount Stratton…'

Elizabeth skipped lightly down the stone steps and allowed Hugh Clemence to help her alight. He politely raised a leather-gloved hand at Edwina. She scowled back a greeting.

Elizabeth settled herself on the seat, then slid forward again. She indicatively shook the carpet bag she had dropped to the floor. 'Twenty pairs of knitted stockings, a roll of twill donated by Mrs Heathcote, four of my own woollen shawls and three quite serviceable kerseymere gowns that my grandmother is grown too large for.' Elizabeth gave him a sparkling amethyst look. 'She doesn't know I have purloined them, but she will never miss them. She believes she is the same size, but the dresses are shrunk from the laundry.'

Hugh Clemence's eyes lingered on her sculpted, ivory profile. 'Did Mrs Sampson mention Viscount Stratton? Or was I mistaken in hearing that name?'

Elizabeth's smooth brow puckered in a frown. 'No. I believe that is the name she mentioned. She tells me he is an old friend of hers who is to visit and dine later. He sounds rather an intriguing character!' At the protracted, crackling silence, Elizabeth studied her companion's twitching jawline. 'Is something wrong, Hugh?'

He forced a tiny, prim smile. 'No. I realise your grandmother is a little…eccentric in her ways and the company she keeps is at times a little…bizarre. I have to own to surprise, though, that she and the Viscount are acquainted.'

'Why?' Elizabeth asked with idle curiosity.

'He…he is a bachelor of a…a certain reputation, Elizabeth. Perhaps you might know of him better as Ross Trelawney. He has recently received honours from the crown. Did you not see it gazetted?'

Elizabeth frowned and shook her head. Then her eyes widened and she gave an incredulous little laugh. 'Not the Trelawney...the pirate? The Trelawney from Cornwall...who is always in some fight or scandal? The robber bandit?'

'A clan of marauding smugglers rather than pirates or bandits, I believe.' Hugh sniffed. 'Now, of course, he is fêted as a smuggler catcher and has recovered over the years for the crown some fortune in currency and contraband. It is why he has been ennobled. Dark deeds indeed have shrouded that man over many years...' he added ominously.

Elizabeth stared into space. 'It cannot be,' she muttered in a tone that harboured horror and humour. 'Why, I'm sure I heard a ridiculous tale that Ross Trelawney cut out a foe's liver and fried it for breakfast.'

'I think that's a little *too*...fictionalised an account of his villainy. But villain he is, without a doubt. And young ladies who cherish their virtue would be well advised to give he and his friends a very wide berth!' He reddened at his evangelical zeal, fiddled with the reins, then sent them undulating like leather snakes over the horses' backs. 'Don't make an ironic comment, Elizabeth, as to your own reputation,' he gently charged her. 'You know I judge a person by deeds. In my estimation, never was there a more virtuous and charitable lady than sits beside me now.'

Elizabeth smiled on a frown and turned her head. 'Thank you, Hugh. Now, please don't forget that Sophie is to join us later when she has finished attending the lecture on Nostradamus at the Taverners' Hall. I have said that she can travel home with us, if you have no objection.' But her mind was not on Sophie; or the Reverend's compliments, as he assured her he was more than happy to escort her friend home to her door. It wasn't even at Tothill with Bridewell and its wretched inmates. Time and again she ruminated on the intriguing possibility that, if it wasn't all a case of mistaken identity, her grandmother was intending to dine later with an infamous rogue. And she had said that he sounded fun!

If gossip was to be believed, the new Viscount Stratton was as hardened a rake as her worst enemy, the repulsive Earl of Cadmore. But whereas the Earl was a youngish dandy about town, Ross Trelawney rarely set foot in the metropolis and was more likely to feature in tales of far-flung places. Perhaps a coast in Kent or a port in Bristol. Or even on foreign shores. She believed it was in France, during the war, that he was rumoured to have dined on liver. She stuffed a fist in her mouth to stifle an hysterical giggle, wondering whether he'd managed to uproot a Gallic onion to make it more palatable. As Hugh said, it was too outlandish to be true.

But why was her grandmother keen for her to return and dine with a disreputable old sea dog she'd known for years? She gave a delicate shudder. He probably talked with his mouth full of food and guffawed at inappropriate moments, showering the table with peas or wine. And if he was anything like the portly Mr Hollyrood…! The noises emitted by that ancient gentleman over the canard a l'orange had been accompanied by such a sulphuric smell that Elizabeth had been forced to quit the room, pleading a migraine, for fear of bursting into very unladylike laughter in front of him.

If only half she had heard gossiped about Trelawney was true, he was hardly fitting company for a spinster of gentle birth. Her grandmother would enjoy his salty tales, of course: Edwina liked a little raucous talk.

Elizabeth had been so relieved when it seemed that there were to be no long silences, no frosty-faced looks from her grandmother following their quarrel yesterday. Perhaps something had occurred to sweeten her so quickly. She'd been known to sulk for three days following an altercation. *I want you settled*, her grandmother had stressed yesterday and with more finality in her tone than usual. Why was she seeking to introduce her to this old friend? A moment ago Hugh had said he was a bachelor. The reprobate was now a peer of the realm. Perhaps he was keen to complete the transformation from villain to gentleman by acquiring a high-born wife. Did his unsavoury history render him unacceptable to respectable ladies of the *ton*? Despite his newly acquired title and lands, perhaps he was cold-shouldered by the *beau monde*. Perhaps her grandmother believed he might be persuaded to settle for a consort whose reputation was as sullied as his own.

Or perhaps she was just being ridiculous, she exhorted herself as she wriggled against the upholstery. The man was possibly as old as her grandmother. If he was a decade younger, he would still be in his fifties and unlikely to be desperate to saddle himself with a wife. Besides, he was a renowned rake who probably had offspring scattered around the countryside. He must like one well enough to nominate as his heir. With that safe, inspiriting thought, she gave Hugh such a sweet smile as made him almost swoon. Scrambling for his wits, he madly shook the reins at the horses while clicking and clucking with his tongue at the startled animals.

'Wager you can keep him, then bribe him to stay on,' Ross remarked, then sipped from his glass. 'That way you can recoup his bribe from your winnings if he agrees to go along with it.'

'Yes. I considered doing that,' Edwina said waving a fork full of pheasant at Ross. The meat soon disappeared and she chewed and looked thoughtful. 'I'm sure that Pettifer would not be averse to an early retirement gift. Problem is, Stratton, that I've little cash I can quickly lay hands on. If I'm to keep m'butler, and lay down some wagers that will wipe the floor with that slut Penney, I've to act without delay. By the time I've sold a little stock, that bitch will have made of me a laughing stock. I need a fairly substantial amount… Have some more red currant jelly,' she offered through a mouthful, sending the silver sauceboat skating along the polished table. 'It's m'own recipe, fortified with a little orange liqueur.'

Ross arrested the flying dish and carefully positioned it by the ornate candelabra. He glanced about the cosy, elegant dining room, wondering what odd fancy had prompted him to do this old termagant's bidding and dine with her tonight. True, the food could be relied upon to be excellent; true, Edwina was entertaining company. But so was Cecily, who had the added advantage of being far easier on the eye, and she could be relied upon to divert him over the dining table with an altogether more sensual banquet. Instead, he was spending a substantial part of the evening with a woman in her sixties and suggesting ways and means for her to outwit her cronies over some old cove they all fancied.

Perhaps he'd spent too long at court in George's company. The King was renowned for favouring ampled-bodied mature women, yet even he chose them a little less long in the tooth and broad of beam. His own preference was for lively young women who enjoyed a roistering good time as much as he did and never grew possessive or tearful when he disappeared to carouse elsewhere; which made his choice of current paramour rather an enigma. He smiled privately at his loaded plate. Cecily liked slavish attention and lavish payment. In return she was liberal with her body and her devotion. Although happy enough with the former, the latter was becoming tedious. He didn't want her to unexpectedly materialise at his side every evening. He enjoyed being unattached while with male friends and spare women and was growing irritated at being constantly stalked.

He glanced at Edwina, to see her ladling more vegetables onto her plate. He smiled. He'd come here this evening, he realised, because he thrived on diversity. And there was something exceedingly diverse about a woman lacking in vanity and at ease with her appetite, and him. There were no devious games, no arch looks while hinting at putting commitment into what he regarded as a casual liaison. No allusions to trinkets favoured. No requests for cash so non-existent family paupers could be saved from starving. Edwina wanted only his company, his advice and a little reminiscing. And they had aired some extremely amusing anecdotes over dinner. He picked up his knife and fork again, feeling content and amiable. 'This is a fine house, Edwina. You don't look to be short on blunt.'

Edwina shot him a hasty look. 'Oh, I'm not. Never better. But I like my money accruing. Investments should be where they can't easily be got. I'm charier than you, Stratton. I know you've always a little on hand for those necessities of life which thrifty mortals like me class as luxuries. That's why I'm a little…er…embarrassed for liquid funds, right now…'

Ross smiled at the fire roaring away at one side of him. Then he laughed ruefully in comprehension. He'd been uncharacteristically naïve in congratulating himself on having found a female companion who wanted nothing from him. 'Edwina…why don't you just ask?' he drawled wryly.

'Twelve thousand…and you'll have it back within two weeks, plus a nice rate of interest,' she immediately responded, wiping her mouth with a snowy napkin and eyeing him shrewdly over it.

'Twelve thousand?!' he repeated slowly, in disbelief. 'I thought you wanted to keep your butler, not set him up in a residence with a staff and carriages of his own. Are you sweet on him, Edwina?'

Edwina flapped a dismissing hand, but couldn't prevent a girlish giggle. 'It's not all for him, you fool! Harry Pettifer would be as pleased as punch with a tenth of that amount. The balance is to be used wagering against Alice Penney…once I've contrived to convince her she's every chance of snatching Pettifer. Bertram Penney left her ten thousand a year and a sizeable estate in Surrey to go with that mansion in Mayfair and the townhouse in Brighton. She can afford to lose a little face…and a little cash…and deserves to.'

Ross leaned back in his chair, raised his glass to his lips and looked at Edwina over the rim. She was aware of his perusal despite her eyes being fixed on her busy cutlery, and fidgeted beneath his calculating gaze.

Ross studied her thoughtfully. He had been expecting some stout, plain young woman to be blushing and giggling at table while they ate. Since his peerage had been gazetted, it seemed he couldn't venture out of the house without some matron trailing a younger version of herself, accosting him on street corners, reminding him of some short acquaintance they'd enjoyed years previously. In this instance it seemed his fears for his bachelorhood were unfounded. 'Where is your grand-daughter this evening?' he asked idly.

Edwina choked, thumped herself on the breastbone. Damn! She'd been confident he had forgot! It was only when ruminating on her strategies an hour before his arrival, that she realised she wished she'd never mentioned dear Lizzie to him at all. And she was also hoping her headstrong granddaughter wouldn't have an uncharacteristic fit of meekness and rush home to obediently join them at dinner. If she stayed out late this evening it would be a blessing. Things had been going so well... Now he looked...too cynical. And this wasn't a man you played for a fool...

'Oh, she's off doing good deeds,' Edwina gasped, still hammering at her ample chest, making the satin undulate. 'No interest in anything else, don't you know. Spends all her time with bores and vicars. You wouldn't like her,' she dismissed with screwed-up face and wrinkled nose. 'Now don't change the subject, Stratton. You owe me a favour. There was that time I paid your marker at Almack's when you were fifteen hundred down and due to be carted to the Fleet. Then there was that other time when I took your place for over an hour while you disappeared for a snooze. You'd sat at that gaming table all night and couldn't keep your eyes open, let alone your credit.'

'All right...I give in.' Ross laughed. 'What the hell? It's only money. But ten thousand tops and for just two weeks,' he said soberly. 'I can no longer afford to be as liberal as I might have been. I've a cash-eating country estate to restore and a few dependants. You aren't the only one with old retainers to keep happy, Edwina. Stratton Hall's also saddled with the quaint aspect of allowing one to stargaze from the comfort of one's bed. I'd guess the roof hasn't had a full set of slates for almost a decade.'

'Well, make a little side bet with me and you can buy your roof out of your winnings. Come, you know I'm good for the money,' Edwina purred persuasively. 'We've known each other some fifteen years. When you were first in London as a callow youth, I took to you at once…treated you as my own kin. I would have liked a grandson. Still would…' she rumbled to herself. 'Even at eighteen you could charm the birds from the trees,' Edwina chattered on.

'I remember you were good to me, Edwina,' Ross said on a smile. 'That's why I'll lend you the cash. Send your man to Jacey's in Lombard Street tomorrow and he can collect a contract for signature.'

'A contract?' Edwina barked. 'Don't you trust this old friend who once saved your miserable young hide from a rat-infested cell in the Fleet?'

'Of course I do, Edwina,' Ross smoothly said, dazzling her with his fabled charming smile. 'For I've a notion you've no liking for the Fleet any more than I, and would hate our friendship to founder at such an establishment should things turn awry. The contract is as much for your benefit: I might come to my senses and try to renege on such lunatic generosity.'

Elizabeth put down her teacup and glanced at the clock on the wall. It was approaching nine-thirty and she was tired and ready to leave this little gathering of members of the Society of Friends. Following their weekly visits to Tothill Fields, the members who'd attended the correctional institute for women and children usually congregated at Mrs Martin's residence for light refreshments and earnest debate. Usually the lively talk held her attention. Tonight she had barely contributed a word.

The whole afternoon and evening had been dominated by her fascination with Viscount Stratton. She'd seen pictures in books of dark-visaged men with tangled, dusky locks and wicked grins. Did he sport a gold earring or a gold tooth, from his smuggling days? Or keep a parrot and a monkey as pets? Part of her wanted to rush home now, and find out, and part of her wanted to linger here as long as possible, lest she returned too soon, and did.

Hugh intercepted her next glance at the clock as it chimed

the half-hour. He inclined towards her. 'Are you ready to leave, Elizabeth?'

She smiled and sent Sophie a meaningful look. Her friend understood the signal and nodded. Elizabeth had decided. She *did* want a glimpse of this intriguing scoundrel. Perhaps, if they were back in Marylebone before ten, he might still be at her grandmother's house. After all, from past experience, she knew that Edwina's guests could linger over some score or more dishes.

'What's your opinion on the usefulness of the treadmill as a deterrent for felons, Elizabeth?' Hugh Clemence conversationally enquired as they jogged along. They had five minutes ago dropped Sophie off at her home in Perman Street and were now making good time past the new gas lamps towards Connaught Street, where Elizabeth lived.

'It's a soul-destroying contraption,' she opined at once. 'When used to grind corn or draw water, I suppose it gives some purpose to the discipline; but to make the poor wretches step it simply to beat the air! What a stupid and inhuman exercise! It's more likely to produce bitter recidivists than reformed characters…' Her words tailed off. Hugh's gig had turned into Connaught Street and her stomach fluttered excitedly as she noticed that fine matched greys were approaching along the street at the head of an elegant carriage.

Hugh was agreeing with some of her comments and tendering his own but she was barely listening, for within that glossy coach might be… The horses drew level and, heart pumping exceedingly slowly, she slanted a wide-eyed violet glance from beneath her bonnet brim at the carriage window.

She had the impression of staring at the top of an ebony head. A flare of a match illuminated a cupped hand and a cigar pointing towards it. A hard lean profile was momentarily gilded by sulphurous light, and strands of hair slipped forward to soften a strong jaw and planed cheekbone. Abruptly the man's head snapped back with an inherent shake that took the obscuring locks away from his features. A slash of white teeth were visible, clenching on the newly lit cheroot, then his sensual mouth moulded around it. Aware of the gig, his idle glance strayed sideways, skimming casually as he extinguished the match with a hand flick. A second too late he was aware of glossy wide eyes and whitish curls peeping from a dark bonnet. His eyes ricocheted back, but the vehicles had passed.

Chapter Three

'What on earth is up, m'dear? You look positively peeky,' Edwina exclaimed, looking up from her novel. 'You really must stop visiting the prisons, Lizzie. I swear you look more forlorn each time you return. And I go in fear of the gaol fever creeping within these doors…or the lice.' A shudder undulated her purple satin bosom.

'Has Viscount Stratton just left?' burst from Elizabeth as she snatched her bonnet from her dishevelled fair hair and paced back and forth.

Edwina looked curiously at her. 'Yes, not more than a few minutes since. You have just missed him.' Relief lilted her tone at that realisation. 'The dinner was fine; Stratton enjoyed it…'

'What age is he?' Elizabeth interrogated. 'You said you had a long-standing acquaintance. I imagined him to be old…as old as you.'

'Why, thank you for making me sound a veritable decrepit dodderer,' Edwina huffed drily. Discarding her novel on the sidetable, she absently picked over pieces of marchpane in the silver filigree dish. 'I have known him some fifteen years, but he was probably only eighteen or nineteen when first we met. He ought to have been sent down, you know. He was hardly scholarly…always gallivanting…' She frowned at her restless granddaughter. 'Do stand still, Lizzie! You're turning me giddy, wheeling about like that. Why are you so concerned about any of it?' A knowing glint narrowed her eyes. 'You caught sight of him in the street, didn't you? Handsome devil, is he not? Is that what's vexing you? You're now wishing you'd forgone that whey-faced vicar's company and dined at home? Well, you're not the first young woman to be overset by his good looks. With my own eyes, I've seen shameless hussies in a pretended swoon at his feet just so he might pick them up.'

Elizabeth's violet eyes flashed at her grandmother, her colour heightening. 'I am overset, Grandmama, because you were half-right in your description of *his Lordship*! By all accounts, he is, indeed, a devil. Even I, out of circulation for so long, have heard gossip of Ross Trelawney. You conveniently omitted to mention that he and Viscount Stratton are one and the same. Hugh Clemence told me and was as shocked as I that you would know such an individual, let alone invite him to dine with us.'

Edwina flapped a dismissive hand. 'Don't be priggish, Lizzie. Do you think I give a fig for that milksop clergyman's opinion? Do you think Stratton would care?' A shrewd glance at her granddaughter preceded her declaring, 'You're showing a deal of interest in a man you've only ever heard tattled over and only ever glimpsed in passing. Did he see you?' she demanded.

'No…I don't know.' Elizabeth was flustered, still pacing about. 'It was dark and the vehicles had passed so quickly. He might have glanced my way, I think.'

'Good,' Edwina muttered to herself with some satisfaction.

Elizabeth slanted a frown at her grandmother. 'From what I could distinguish of him in the half-light, he resembles a Romany…a heathen. Which is what he is, by all accounts.'

'He has dark colouring, it's true. But he's not unattractively swarthy. And never fret over all those ludicrous tales of marauding on the high seas and eating Frenchies' offal and so on,' Edwina scoffed through a sweetmeat. 'Now he's so sought after by the *ton* I expect there'll be more wonderfully concocted fables of his warrior habits: maidens in distress either spoiled by his virile lust or saved on a romantic whim. He won't bother denying any of it. I think, beneath that cool, detached air he has, he deems it all faintly amusing.' Edwina grinned widely. 'Besides, now he's the King's favourite and so eligible, he could spitroast a street urchin for his dinner in Pall Mall and still be invited to Lady Conyngham's ball. If he bothers to attend, he must bring along his cane...to beat off the petticoat set.'

'I don't see anything amusing in it,' Elizabeth admonished tightly, fingers dragging through her thick, pearly hair. 'Wretched street urchins are not a case for banter. And there's always a grain of truth in gossip.'

'You of all people should know that's not necessarily so, miss!' Edwina brusquely reminded her granddaughter. Noting Elizabeth's wince and flush, she gestured apology with a plump hand. 'Stratton was good enough to ask after you,' she added, with every intention of alleviating the tension.

'*Me?* He doesn't know me!' Elizabeth squeaked in protest, renewed agitation sending her in another turn about the room. Inwardly she prayed, *Please don't let such a man know of me or my misfortune, especially if he's going to be a regular visitor to Connaught Street. I receive more than enough lecherous looks and whispered propositions from Cadmore as it is.*

'I told Ross I now live with m'granddaughter and he politely enquired after you. He is cultured and mannerly.'

'He is a rogue, Grandmama, and well you know it.'

'Rogue, maybe, but he's a gentleman too. He has excellent connections. His eldest brother is a baron and has a large estate in Brighton. His father amassed a vast acreage in Cornwall which another brother now administers. They have business interests embracing mining and shipping and banking which extend the globe. They are an exceedingly wealthy and influential family who are on good terms with other important aristocrats. Sir Richard Du Quesne and Lord Courtenay are but two of his close friends and business associates. Ross courts danger and excitement from choice, not financial necessity.'

'In that case, Grandmama,' Elizabeth stressed quietly, 'surely it behoves us to studiously avoid the company of such a madman.'

Their conversation ceased as Harry Pettifer entered and bowed. 'Excuse me, madam; may I lock and bolt now that Lady Elizabeth is home?'

'Ah…indeed,' Edwina said, a little flustered. 'And, Pettifer…'

Harry Pettifer pivoted politely, poker straight.

'I should like to speak with you before you retire—' Edwina broke off to bid her granddaughter good night as Elizabeth pecked her cheek and informed that she was ready for a warm bath and a soft bed. As the door closed behind Elizabeth, Edwina shifted her purple satin bulk in her chair and looked up at the tall, imposing man standing close by. He seemed relaxed, yet she had stiffened with tension while fiddling with small buttons on her cuffs, and it needled her. She forced her fingers still. 'Am I right in thinking I've treated you fairly over many, many years?' she burst out.

'Indeed, madam,' Harry Pettifer replied, inclining his pewter head.

Edwina stared at him, hoping he would contribute more. He didn't, merely watched her with a clear, untroubled gaze. But amusement lurked far back in his bright blue eyes, she was certain. She shifted again in her seat. The silence protracted. 'Are you perhaps keen to discover if the grass grows greener in Sussex?' she hinted, irritated by his composure and how stately he looked: all grey and black and rigid-backed. She bit her tongue to prevent herself simply snapping out that she knew he was planning to quit.

'Would you like me to tell you whether I intend to take up Mrs Penney's offer of employment at her Brighton townhouse? Or accept a similar offer from Mrs De Vere or Lady Salisbury?' he blandly offered.

'You know dam' well I would,' Edwina gritted through her teeth, abandoning any attempt at nonchalance. Flinging herself against the chairback, she grabbed a handful of sweetmeats and chewed ferociously.

Harry inspected his immaculate shoes. His mouth twitched. Then his eyes levelled on his fiery-faced employer.

'I have not yet responded to those ladies' offers, but I have little desire to…er…investigate the shade of turf outside London,' he said solemnly.

'Why not?' She eyed him suspiciously. 'I know, without you telling me, all those…*ladies*—' she spat on a sneer '—have offered you more than I pay you.'

'Money isn't the first consideration, at my time of life. I have adequate funds for my needs, and a little to spare. I have no wish to leave Lady Elizabeth…or you.'

Finished with the sweetmeats, Edwina chewed her full lower lip, eyeing him thoughtfully. 'You have a deal of fondness for Lizzie. I've noticed a rapport strengthening between you the few years she's lived with us. You would spoil her as a child when she visited with her papa: bring her titbits from the kitchens.'

Harry Pettifer bowed his head. 'As you say. I have a great fondness for Lady Elizabeth…and her family,' he added quietly. 'I have been employed by Sampsons for a long while now. I believed you deemed me loyal.'

Edwina fidgeted and grew hot at the gracious reproof. A finger commenced twirling absently in the silver dish. She suddenly lifted the bowl and proffered it, by way of reparation. 'Have a sweet,' she said, shaking the dish. 'Come… take one…' she cajoled with a coy smile.

Harry Pettifer approached and his long, patrician fingers selected a small piece of marchpane. Edwina watched as he carefully chewed.

'It seems to me, Pettifer, we both want the best for Lady Elizabeth. I imagine you, as much as I, would like to see her happily settled, before we are grown too crotchety to hug her children. She is in her twenty-ninth year, you know, and no nearer to swallowing her pride and socialising properly than she was immediately after the…um…delicate situation.'

'I understand the predicament, madam. Lady Elizabeth, I think, is proud. And not without reason. She is of noble birth and character. Of course I crave to see her happy.'

'You think she's not happy?' Edwina pounced.

'I think she is at times a little…wistful,' Harry said, choosing his words carefully.

Edwina nodded slowly, eyeing him thoughtfully. 'Yes…wistful…that's it. It is time she was wed…not wistful.'

'I heartily concur, madam. Lady Elizabeth would make some fortunate gentleman an excellent wife.'

'And children would never find a better mother,' Edwina added. 'She has a lot of affection going begging. Succouring waifs and strays is no substitute for having a husband and children to love. Mayhap she just needs a little nudge in the right direction…to realise it.'

'I think those are very wise words, madam. My sentiments exactly,' Harry said, emphasising his approval with a movement of his steely head.

Edwina's flushed visage cocked to one side; she watched her plump fingers pleating the satin of her skirt. 'It was nice to see Trelawney again after such a long absence, don't you think?'

'Indeed, I do, madam. In all the years I have welcomed that gentleman into your houses, he has never grown too coarse or too fine to speak to me and ask how I do. To my mind, Viscount Stratton is an altogether grand fellow, for I always judge as I find.'

'I think those are very wise words, Pettifer. My sentiments, exactly,' Edwina said, an affable look slanting from beneath her lashes at him. 'It seems we share a deal of common sense where m'granddaughter and the Viscount are concerned. I wonder if there's a way in which both might benefit from it?'

* * *

It was when her grandmother described him as cool and detached, yet given to a latent amusement, that something far, far back in her mind started to stir.

Relaxing back into warm, scented bathwater, Lady Elizabeth Rowe allowed corners of banished memories to pierce her consciousness. People…events…conversations…trickled in, pulled together to surface from a deep well of pain.

Agitated, she pushed jerkily upright, causing the towel turbanning her newly washed hair to unwrap and flop into the tub. Tutting impatience, she wrung it out, then dropped it onto the mat while her loose topknot of damp platinum hair uncoiled. Her creamy, narrow back and firm rose-tipped breasts were soon screened by sleek pale tresses falling to float on soapy water.

A decade ago, during a summer that had seemed unremittingly hot and humid from the months of May to September, she, her beloved papa and her grandmother Rowe had moved to London. Her maternal grandmother and paternal grandmother detested each other in equal part, so Edwina Sampson had immediately removed herself from the City to avoid breathing the same air as the Dowager Marchioness, and spent the summer in Harrogate with her sister.

On her eighteenth birthday, in May of that year, Elizabeth was presented at court and thus began the most memorable, the most thrilling, the most devastating period of her young life. But in May, when all was heady excitement, and all she and her dear papa rued was that her mother hadn't survived to see her looking so blissful and beautiful, it seemed that nothing could mar the utopia. She was blessed with everything any young lady could want: beauty, vivacity and an indulgent and doting parent.

A popular debutante, the daughter of a Marquess, a descendant of one of the noblest, if no longer the wealthiest dynasties in the land, gentlemen had vied for her favours, sighing that her silky silver hair and violet eyes were incomparable. She was that season's rage. Constantly besieged by gay, modish acquaintances gathering at her father's Mayfair townhouse, constantly plied with invitations to the most lavish balls, the smartest soirées, she had attracted the attention of many eligible partners: one duke, two earls and three baronets. In all, nine and a half offers of marriage were forthcoming in one month. The half, her sweet papa had gently joked, was from one blushing young admirer who, having stuttered and suffered through an earnest speech praising Elizabeth's loveliness, had then stumbled away, too embarrassed to deliver his proposal.

With youthful vanity and an arrogance borne of her spoiled and privileged upbringing, Lady Elizabeth Rowe had flirted a little with each devoted beau, broken at least a half-dozen hearts and deemed it all so trivial and amusing, for secretly she had made her choice within a month of arriving in London. Despite the Dowager Marchioness's eagle-eyed vigilance and chaperonage, Elizabeth had fallen madly in love. With all the naïve idealism of youth, she was adamant trusting to her heart must be the only right way.

The man she'd loved had not been *a catch*. He had impressed upon her that her relatives would tell her so, and that, ergo, they must proceed stealthily. Blinded by infatuation, buoyed by the self-assurance of her youth and inexperience, she'd entered into the spirit of the romantic adventure, oblivious to the havoc her behaviour might wreak. She chose badly, acted rashly, tasted a little of her own medicine. But what really hurt was that in the doing of it she'd shattered and shamed her papa, besmirched his illustrious name and broken his heart. That she had degraded herself beyond redemption, too, seemed of less consequence in the face of her beloved father's despair.

She tossed her head aside, clamping shut her eyes, not wanting the sorrow to knife her insides. She forced her concentration to another man instead. A tall gentleman with hard, dark features who had never figured amongst her languishing suitors, but he did figure in her memories. They had never spoken but she had espied him during that sultry summer.

Roistering on the fringes of the ton were young rakehells: Corinthians who mostly shunned conventional socialising in favour of their own riotous assemblies. They rarely bothered entering Almack's stately portals where a marriage mart took place under the guise of fusty regimented assemblies. Neither were they lured by lavish balls arranged by fond mamas with nubile daughters and an ulterior motive in mind. If they did deign to show at such insipid venues, within an hour or so of arriving, they were gone in search of more bacchanalian entertainment. Arrogant and affluent, their spendthrift ways were legendary. Gambling large amounts of money on a whim was rife. Bets of hundreds of pounds might be made on the most ridiculous eventualities: whether a drunk would fall before he reached the end of the street. If he did, whether he would topple forward or backward. Whether an acquaintance with pockets to let would pawn his silver ice pails, or sell on his Spanish mistress. Those were just a few of the outrageous wagers that she could recall.

Apart from the customary sporting activities of fencing and boxing at Gentleman Jackson's, more hazardous pursuits drew them: racing high-flyer phaetons had resulted in the death or maiming of more than a few daring young bucks. Duelling over the favours of immoral women—whom genteel young debutantes such as she would never have acknowledged existed—had taken several others…either to the grave or to a sojourn abroad until the scandal died away.

An especial amusement of younger sons with no stately pile or peerage to polish was the sorrowful sight of impecunious heirs found planted amongst the pillars in Almack's, loitering to barter a title for a fortune and perhaps buy back freedom and licentiousness with a dowered bride. Elizabeth recalled thinking that marriage to such a selfish debauchée must be hell. And when her thoughts ran that way, the enigmatic man with a rugged, gypsy visage and long chestnut hair had dominated her mind. Languour hooded his hazel eyes, yet his muscular physique was testament to a regime of regular, punishing exercise.

Indolent amusement had hovered on his hard, handsome features when he glanced at her and her friends. But then he did so rarely, for he was in demand elsewhere. On the few occasions fate had manoeuvred them close, he had seemed insolently unmoved by her blonde beauty and petite sensual figure hemmed by a throng of fawning admirers.

Once or twice as she'd sneaked a fascinated peek through seething humanity at that group of distinguished men and their exuberant female companions, her amethyst eyes had tangled with his. Captured, held fast, she recalled how his golden-glinting mockery had burned. Flustered, she would eventually drag her eyes away, feverishly indignant that he dared laugh at her. Yet, piqued, too, that he didn't notice her more often.

Since she had turned fifteen and her chubby body began dipping and curving in exactly the right places, she had come to realise that men liked to look at her. In her naïeveté, she had revelled in the power her femininity bestowed. At eighteen, her face shed its youthful plumpness, and wide-honed cheekbones sculpted her countenance to a symmetrical, classical loveliness. Her blue eyes deepened to violet, her lashes and eyebrows darkened, while her hair retained its light pearly sheen. It was as though time and nature had conspired to perfect her looks in readiness for her first outing in society.

Even strangers told her she was beautiful. She already knew it…and used it. She'd enjoyed knowing that male eyes followed her when she left a room, then observed her return. She'd been amused by the compliments, by the gifts, by the constant attention, and had fostered it. But it wasn't until it was too late that she had understood that male interest could be dangerous as well as gratifying, and her gentle birth and innocence was no guarantee of kindness or respect. Now when men sidled looks at her, her chin might tilt, but it was in undefeated pride, not vanity. Once she might coquettishly have sought eye contact with an admirer—now she studiously avoided it. What had unsettled her so this evening was the momentary glint of interest that had whipped Ross Trelawney's eyes back to hers as their carriages passed. Yet, if truthful, she couldn't deny she'd hoped to catch his eye…

Elizabeth sank lower in her bath, drank in the soothing scent of the lavender-scented water as she dwelt on the memory of a less-menacing man: Guy Markham had kept company with that wild set. His father, Sir Clive, had been her papa's friend. The baronet would often grumble to the Marquess that he feared his heir would turn out bad because of the company he kept. She wondered what Guy Markham might be doing now. She had quite liked him. On the few occasions she had met him through their fathers' friendship, he had seemed civil and amiable. Now that she was out of circulation she had no idea, nor did she care, what occurred in the *beau monde*. She imagined Guy to be much as he ever was, for she knew from her grandmother's casual chatter as to what went on that Sir Clive was still enjoying robust health and seemed unlikely to relinquish his baronetcy yet awhile.

Her thoughts veered, unbidden, back to Viscount Stratton. Never once had she made the association between him and the scandalous rogue, Ross Trelawney, whom the gossiping matrons used to whisper about. Perhaps if her come-out had not been curtailed, fate might eventually have remedied that…

'You should allow me to do that for you, my lord.'

Ross half-smiled. 'If there's one person I would allow to hold a blade to my throat, it would be you, Henderson,' he told his valet as, slowly, he drew a razor carefully up the column of tanned neck to his square, shady jaw. He dipped the soap-edged steel into warm water, then angled his head and proceeded to shave the other side, his eyes on the mirror. At a gruff laugh, Ross's eyes strayed to another man's reflection.

Guy Markham was standing by the window of the dressing room, shaking his head in amused disbelief as he observed an entertaining spectacle in the street below. Moments ago a pickpocket had caused havoc by fleeing straight across the path of an elderly gentleman. Having overset that man, who in turn accidentally brought a matron to her knees, the lad, now sure he was free and clear, had turned and was making an exceedingly lewd and triumphant gesture. Having given chase for two yards and decided the sport too arduous, the fallen woman's companion instead began shaking his cane at the taunting, dirty-faced urchin. The gentleman on the floor was rolling about clutching a leg, the tumbled matron was trying to preserve her modesty by rearranging her skirts, and the lady who had been robbed of her reticule, but managed to keep to her feet, was prancing on the spot and squealing, red-faced, for assistance from any who would listen. And it did seem that the majority of Grosvenor Square's residents were a captive audience: people were either craning from windows or emerging onto elegant front steps to investigate the hullabaloo.

Ross glanced at his friend's profile as Guy's head tipped back and he guffawed at the ceiling. 'Did he get clean away?'

Guy grimaced disappointment through his smile. 'I'm afraid so...'

Ross continued shaving with one hand, his other extended meaningfully.

Guy stepped away from the window and, having foraged in a pocket, dropped a note into his comrade's damp palm.

The bank note was deposited on the dressing table and Ross's attention returned to his toilet. 'I think I'll take a place in Cheapside,' he mentioned drily, swirling the razor in water again. 'I've paid a premium for a salubrious address and genteel neighbours and what do I get? Daylight robbery. Dockside manners.'

Guy returned to the window to watch the injured parties hobbling away, no doubt in search of a Bow Street runner.

'I bow to your superior knowledge of daylight robbery and dockside manners, Stratton,' Guy chuckled.

Henderson was still hovering behind his master, dipping this way and that in time with the blade's movement as he judged Ross's dexterity with the razor.

'A close shave is much appreciated by the fair sex,' Guy informed the limber valet with a suggestive wink and a nod at his friend. Henderson responded to this piece of information with a sniff and an extremely old-fashioned look. He straightened his back and shoulders, stalked to the four-poster bed and busied himself with extricating discarded shirts and breeches from amongst the blankets.

Guy took out his pocket watch. 'Well, it's after noon. Speaking of the fair sex: I imagine the delectable Miss Booth might be even now loitering outside. You've been out of her clutches some twelve hours,' he warned Ross of his young mistress's increasingly determined pursuit.

Ross examined his lean features in the mirror. His angular, clefted chin rested in the fork of a hand as long fingers and a stroking thumb tested the smoothness of his skin. He raised his eyes to his friend's laughing expression. 'Sit down,' he ordered, as he pushed himself to his feet and dried his face with a towel. 'Maybe it's time I gave you an equally close shave. It might help you do better than last night's lanky strumpet.'

Guy put out two defensive hands. 'No, thanks; I'll stick with last night's strumpet, and stubble.' A hand wiped across his bristly jaw as he moaned, 'God, I'm ravenous. My belly's complaining my throat's been cut and I've been nowhere near a razor.'

'Toast…crumpets…tea?' Henderson offered over a starchy black shoulder.

'Yes, thank you, Henderson,' Guy Markham enthused, rubbing his hands together and smiling as his stomach loudly endorsed its ability to do justice to the breakfast selection.

With his long, dark fingers busy at his neck folding a sepia silk cravat, Ross strolled to the window and looked out over

Grosvenor Square's resumed gentility. Smart vehicles thronged the street, people strolled and a few liveried servants could be seen weaving busily between the gentry. To a newcomer, the fracas a moment ago would seem unimaginable.

Ross inwardly sorted through his business affairs. There were several matters to finalise before he journeyed later to Kent; several messages to relay: Luke and Rebecca were bringing his mother to London to visit and wanted confirmation from him that it was convenient to arrive this week. A few good friends were also soon due in London, keen to personally congratulate him on his elevation to the peerage. It was incumbent on him to throw some sort of celebratory party for them all, he supposed. His younger sister Katherine had written to say she wouldn't be travelling to London because she was still confined after the birth of her son. But he was to be godfather. Yet possibly what occupied him most was that a fortnight had passed and no repayment had been forthcoming from Edwina Sampson.

Before he left for Stratton Hall it would be prudent to pay her a visit and remind her of her contractual obligations regarding his loan. Not that he wanted to harrass her; but commencing restoration of his very own stately pile was a pressing concern. Besides, he smiled inwardly, he was still intrigued to know the identity of the blonde who had been peeking at him as she passed in that rickety gig. He'd caught a brief glimpse of the man beside her: he'd looked like clergy. It would be his luck to lust after a vicar's wife…or daughter. He hadn't seen enough of the man to guess his age. Perhaps they were neighbours of Edwina's. It might be interesting finding out, especially as something in her shy stare had seemed to stir memories…

'White's or Watier's?' he asked Guy while shrugging into the tan tailcoat his valet had laid out. He was adjusting spotless cambric cuffs just as Henderson reappeared with a silver salver rather than the breakfast tray he had been expecting.

'Watier's…the food's better,' Guy decided, having given the matter a moment's thought.

'Are you attending Maria's rout later? She's promised the comely Clarke sisters are to be there. I imagine the King's favourite contraband-catcher might do rather well with one or t'other…or both. If you can escape Cecily's eagle eye, you're guaranteed a pleasurable evening. You could travel to Kent in the morning.'

Ross shook his head. 'No, I want to reach Stratton Hall this afternoon. There's an architect I've to see…' he muttered in explanation, taking the letter Henderson was proffering on the salver.

Guy frowned at him. 'You're becoming a building bore, Ross. You sound like my father. Renovate this wing…pave that terrace…sweep those chimneys… You'll be holding forth on cooking ranges or roof pitches next.'

'Well, when it's all yours, you'll know why,' Ross said with a grin.

As Ross turned his attention to the missive and broke the seal, his valet cocked his head as though he would read it too. Green-flecked hazel eyes levelled at the servant. 'Thank you, Henderson,' Ross said, mildly amused at the man's inquisitiveness. 'You may organise breakfast. A pot of coffee, too, if you please.'

Henderson pulled a supercilious long face on turning for the door.

Guy settled himself before the dressing mirror and, unwinding his canary-yellow cravat, picked up the razor.

Ross strolled back to the window to read his letter. Seeing the elegantly scripted address at the top of the parchment, he smiled. Trust Edwina to come good before he needed to chivvy her about the loan. She'd been a good friend and a good business partner on occasion. He had owed the old harridan a favour or two and had felt obliged to help her out. But he knew she could be trusted…

It was some moments later that the silence made Guy stop shaving and look curiously at his friend. Ross was staring at the letter, his face an inscrutable, granite mask. Slowly, he crushed the paper in a powerful hand. His lips strained back against his teeth, then formed an inaudible blasphemy.

'Bad news?' Guy asked quietly, the razor poised over lathered skin.

'Bad move...' Ross said softly with a smile that chilled his friend. 'Very bad move, Edwina,' Ross expanded on a humourless laugh and, leaving Guy staring after him, quit the room.

Chapter Four

'Calm yourself, Mrs Sampson…there is no need for panic.'

'Calm myself! No need for panic!' Edwina parroted in a hiss. 'M'granddaughter shouted at me not two hours since that she never again wants to see me…doesn't give a fig if I end in the Fleet catching rats for m'dinner! Loathed by m'own flesh and blood and after I've taken her in and boarded her these past few years when that sour-faced bitch turned her out. And now Trelawney is come and you say he has a face like thunder! It is all gone awry! How can I be calm?'

'You must expect Lady Elizabeth to be overset at first, she is…independent…strong-willed. Such news would naturally come as a shock. And I described the Viscount as thunderous, not thunder-faced; there is a subtle difference. Outwardly he appears unperturbed, but inwardly…ah…inwardly he is turbulent,' Harry opined with a nod, his customary reserve lost to admiration. 'I must say he conceals his anger exceedingly well. There was some coolness in his request to know how I do today.'

Edwina stared at her manservant, recognising again the wry humour lurking in his eyes. 'It is not a matter for jest!' she snapped testily. 'I am in a tizz over whether I am a fit grandmother. Dearest Lizzie has no other close kin, apart from the hag of a Dowager Marchioness and her little stepbrother who can do her no good turn as he is but seven years old. Perhaps

I should not have meddled, but let well alone. What if Lizzie never forgives me? I might get notice to quit before it all comes right! What if Stratton rejects her? Oh, what will I do then?' She whirled about, displaying some stamina as she marched away, then speedily stomped straight back. 'And do you realise what sort of man we are dealing with? This is not a fool to be trifled with. Oh, no! And now I have forgot what I must say to him.' She flapped a hand and, eyes closed, waddled around in a circle, rehearsing inaudible lines.

'Of course he is not a fool. He is a fine fellow: a lesser man might be making matchwood of your stair spindles, instead of demolishing his shoe leather in the hallway. Lord Stratton must have covered a mile over marble since arriving. Yet still he remains self-possessed. It should greatly reassure you that, if all goes to plan, Lady Elizabeth's future well-being is entrusted to worthy hands.'

'Do you imagine I would have risked her to anything less?' Edwina squealed, puce-faced.

'No, of course not, my dear. Calm yourself, please,' Harry Pettifer soothed. To obscure the casual endearment, he pressed on steadily, 'I simply congratulate your choice. But you must have expected that the Viscount would be…miffed, on receiving your note.'

'*Miffed?* You think Trelawney is *miffed* to discover he cannot have back his ten thousand pounds and a little extra? I think the Viscount, self-possessed or no, is a deal more than *miffed* with me,' Edwina emphasised, bulge-eyed. 'And so is m'granddaughter! My sweet, dear Lizzie is fair spitting mad. Are you sure her chamber door is secure?' she demanded, prowling the cosy drawing room searching surfaces for a dish of sweetmeats. Finding none, she resorted to chewing on a fingernail. 'If she should bolt to that vicar, she'll wed him just to spite me. But…I shouldn't have done it. Locking her in her room like a naughty schoolgirl will guarantee a fit of the sulks.'

Abruptly she ceased perambulating and summarised matter-of-factly, 'Lady Elizabeth has long needed to be properly settled. All this loitering in slums and prisons makes her vulnerable, as does her...unlucky past. Cadmore sent another letter only last week. I wish to heaven I had managed to intercept it. But she had received the post on her way out to meet Sophie. If I was younger I'd shoot the blackguard down dead! She needs a man to care for her. A man other fellows respect and will not dare cross. I can't imagine any man...unless he is moonstruck...attempting to cuckold Stratton, can you?'

Edwina received a smile and gesture of absolute agreement. 'Just for a moment I s'pose m'nerves had the better of me. It is all too late for second thoughts, anyhow. The deed is done; and done for Lady Elizabeth's own good. Should I turn up m'toes impecunious, she'll never need to beg a living from that miserly crone of a Dowager Marchioness, or her vinegar-faced daughter-in-law. Stepmother to Lizzie?' She snorted in disgust. 'She's never shown the dear girl a jot of affection. So, I must set to, rally m'courage and cut this crazy babbling...'

'I'm happy to hear that, Mrs Sampson,' drawled a voice from the doorway. 'I'll admit I was beginning to fear for your sanity, too, when I received your letter. My apologies for the intrusion, but I find myself a little pushed for time. I think we should...*set to*...right now,' was added in a deceptively mild tone that brooked no refusal.

Edwina smoothed her skirts, then strained her generous lips into a welcoming smile. 'Come in...come in, Stratton. Good of you to respond to m'note so quickly. Tea, Pettifer,' she ordered with a hand flick. 'And don't be tardy. You heard the Viscount: he is a busy man and must fly off before he is properly arrived.'

Harry Pettifer arrowed a glance at the tall, imposing man just inside the door. The Viscount's narrowed hazel eyes were most definitely upon him, too. An almost imperceptible movement of Ross's dark head acknowledged the butler's neat bow.

'Oh, and Pettifer...' Edwina said casually. 'Don't forget you were to attend to m'granddaughter...'

Harry Pettifer inclined his head, tacitly indicating that nothing had slipped his mind.

Elizabeth yanked at the door again. She rattled at the knob, peered into the keyhole, then banged angrily on the panels with two small fists. After a moment spent glaring at the wood she turned, marched back into the room, her blonde head flung back, and closed her eyes, trying to calm herself. It wasn't her grandmother's fault...was the mantra that echoed in her aching head. She must not blame Edwina. In her own idiotic way no doubt the woman truly believed she was securing her a nice future. Her grandmother must have been swayed by that...Elizabeth's soft lip curled into a sneer, her violet eyes glittered...*roguish gentleman,* as Edwina was wont to quixotically term him.

Walking on stiff legs and with rigid fists at her sides, Elizabeth moved to her bedroom window and looked out over the gardens. She forced her humour to lighten; made herself appreciate the dazzling late summer flowers in the borders, the laurel hedging glistening grass green in the noonday sun. A small smile unclamped her compressed lips. Such a ridiculously transparent plot, too, she dismissed on a faint laugh. Between them, they really ought to have managed something slightly more plausible. But then her grandmother had let slip that the Viscount had been keener on gallivanting than studying in his youth: he was no doubt a dullard who relied on his fabled charm or his fists to get by.

In the two weeks since Ross Trelawney had dined here, all Edwina had seemed to talk of was the Viscount: his future prospects, his past heroics, his good connections. Yet to Elizabeth's knowledge he had not paid a return visit. Had he again set foot over the threshold, she was sure the honour would have been brought to her notice...many times.

She was surprised by Edwina: her grandmother had a sharp, quite devious mind when it suited her. Now she appeared to be held in thrall by this villainous acquaintance of hers. Perhaps her grandmother's advancing years were unhappily telling on her now. Perhaps she was beginning to lose sense and logic and was allowing herself to be manipulated.

Elizabeth managed a sour smile at the azure sky. Her own reason, however, seemed never more acute. It transpired that her thoughts on the Viscount seeking a consort of good birth to cement his aggrandisement were sound, almost prescient. Two weeks ago, she had been prepared to dismiss the notion as fanciful. Now, according to her grandmother, she was to soon receive a marriage proposal from the upstart.

Obviously Edwina had let slip her granddaughter had a pedigree and a portion, then fallen in with his mercenary plot because she was keen to see her granddaughter wed. Well, they were both about to find out that *she* refused to be manipulated. She had no wish to marry but, if she must, it would be preferable to wed a comfortable friend rather than a disreputable stranger. And if that meant the dowry was forfeit, so be it. With a little encouragement, Hugh would propose and they would live, hand to mouth, in that dilapidated vicarage her grandmother had scorned. Better that, than endure the ignominy of having a husband bought for her…especially a coarse ruffian with pockets to let and no interest in her other than filling those pockets with her grandmother's money.

Ross placed his teacup down carefully and leaned back in the chair. 'I hope that's a joke, Edwina,' he said softly.

'A joke! You think I would joke about such a thing? I've no more liking for the way things have turned out than you. I can't keep the man here against his will longer than to work a month's notice. He's accepted another position and I've lost m'wagers. I even made some more to try and get you your cash back. I've never been so out of favour at the tables. Whatever I tried…Faro, Hazard, Picquet…all duds. Unlike me, too…you know that, Stratton. I bet you'd have wagered on me turning up trumps. I'm not a pauper, but neither have I adequate funds at present. I've some merchandise on a trader

returning from the Indies and due to dock in a few months'
time. Once that's sold you will be welcome to the profit. It
might prove a little short of ten thousand…' She flapped an
impatient hand, flounced her pudgy visage away from him.
'Oh, you simply must wait a while, that's all.'

'I *must* do nothing of the sort,' Ross corrected in a tone
that sent a shiver down Edwina's spine. 'I want my money.
Our contract states repayment was due yesterday. I've builders, bricks, timber and slates on their way to Kent and I've
no intention of cancelling any of it.' He watched her plump
hands clasping and unclasping in her lap. He knew she had
other funds. So did he…but he didn't see why he should damn
well use them. Unravelling a maze of joint business ventures
held with friends and family would take time. He also was
loath to present himself as some sort of gullible fool to those
gentlemen when they questioned his reasons for selling out,
when by right he should have adequate liquid funds pooling
in his business account.

Edwina was one of the richest widows in London, if chary
of advertising that status. She was certainly one of the can-
niest. Why she was lying was beyond him. Some instinct told
him that she wasn't intending to defraud…just delay; deceive
him for her own benefit. But he felt too preoccupied with
other matters to be bothered dissecting the workings of the
female mind for probable motives. What he did allow himself
to indulge in was utter irritation. Not only directed at her, but
himself.

Perhaps the whole sorry state of affairs had come about
because she was getting senile and he was getting soft. His
attitude to money had always been too cavalier…as had his
attitude to women. Now he was reaping the cost of that double
folly and at a time when he was least able to afford it. A few
weeks an aristocrat and he was already done with *noblesse
oblige*.

'We've been friends a good amount of years, Edwina. I'd
hate this to end badly between us.' A charming smile accom-

panied the remark but it failed to soften the glitter in his golden eyes or the hard line of his lips.

'There's only one tidy amount of Sampson money going begging,' Edwina quickly spluttered. Her mouth felt dry, her tongue clumsy, her complexion fiery beneath his astute observation. She and this man had never before crossed swords, other than in banter. She knew he had a savage, ruthless side, of course, but was certain it was directed only at deserving foe. She had never anticipated experiencing it personally.

Her needling fears subsided. Pettifer was absolutely correct. Stratton had every right to give vent to the frustrated anger she could sense seething below his suave exterior. Yet he was ever the perfectly mannered gentleman. He was, she realised with a burgeoning serenity, exactly right for provocative, proud Lizzie. As she slanted a sly look at his handsome, rugged features, for the first time it occurred to her just how wonderfully well they would complement each other: Elizabeth with her fragile, pale femininity and Ross with his dark, virile strength. But looks apart, their temperaments and characters would mesh too. She was growing impatient to get them in the same room. Sparks might fly…in fact, she would wager on it. But the blaze they ignited might just warm them through a lifetime.

'The cash is tied to terms and conditions, Stratton,' Edwina snapped, defensively brusque on realising she had been quietly brooding too long.

Ross elevated dark brows, wordlessly demanding to know what they were.

Edwina fiddled with her salt and pepper ringlets. 'There's a trust fund for m'granddaughter that was set up some years ago: fifteen thousand lump sum and ten thousand a year to be paid each January for her lifetime.'

'Why didn't you say so at once?' Ross sighed, peeved at the circuitous route they had taken to achieve a settlement. 'Surely you didn't think taking some chit's inheritance might trouble my conscience? I'm confident you'll replenish her fund…when your ship comes in,' he reminded her ironically.

Pushing up abruptly out of the chair, he straightened his cuffs. Sauntering to a large gilt mirror, he adjusted his cravat. 'I'll take the money, thank you, Edwina.' He was speaking and frowning at his own reflection rather than hers. 'Now, if you'll excuse me, I'm journeying to Kent this afternoon and want to arrive before dusk.' He was halfway to the door when he asked, 'How soon can I collect a banker's draft?'

'As soon as you produce the marriage lines,' Edwina shot back, on a wickedly triumphant grin.

Pettifer approached the chamber door, silently turned the key in the lock, then knocked.

Elizabeth threw down her knitting, rolled to the edge of the bed and scampered to the door. 'Grandmama?' she hissed angrily, not bothering to try the handle.

'It's Pettifer, Lady Elizabeth. Your grandmother would like to speak to you in the parlour.'

Elizabeth yanked at the door, stumbling backwards as it unexpectedly opened. She glared at Pettifer, who looked back kindly, she thought. Looked almost as though he might say something soothing. Should she upbraid him for leaving? Beg him to stay? No. It wasn't his fault her grandmother was a fool. Besides, the wagers were already done and won. What use in that? Restoking her anger at her grandmother, she gripped her skirts, streaked past Pettifer and rushed down the stairs.

She found Edwina sitting sipping Madeira by the fire. With a deep, steadying breath, Elizabeth carefully closed the parlour door. 'I am not going to argue any more, Grandmama,' she stated in a tone that was quietly adamant. 'But I should like to know why you locked me in my room in such an unnecessary and puerile fashion. Did you anticipate I might flee like a frightened rabbit after listening to that daft tale? Why…it is just a laughable fiction. Now I have had time to reflect on it, it is so transparently false that I am amazed you and the Viscount bothered concocting it at all.' She gave a scornful little laugh, paused and awaited her grandmother's comment.

Edwina simply frowned as though weighing up what she'd heard, before moving the glass to occupy her mouth.

'So,' Elizabeth blurted, a trifle disconcerted at the lengthening silence, 'I shall apologise for shouting at you earlier and take it that you have either been under the influence of too much alcohol or too much of that savage heathen's company.'

Uncharacteristically, Edwina, again, had nothing to contribute. Elizabeth eyed her grandmother anxiously as she sipped her Madeira. Tentatively she asked, 'Have you over-imbibed, Grandmama? Or has that scheming rogue intimidated you? You need not be frightened of him! I have every intention of writing this very afternoon and letting him know exactly what I think of his ridiculous attempt to embezzle us. As if you would ask him to loan you a penny! You have money enough to buy and sell half the *ton*! Has he forced you to sign some document? Coerced you? Be assured I shall write and...'

'There's no need for that, Lizzie,' Edwina interrupted, placing down her empty glass and savouring the sweet stickiness on her lips. 'You can reprimand the Viscount in person. He's in the drawing room.'

'I hope that's a joke!' Elizabeth whispered, her eyes huge violet pools in her alabaster face.

'He used exactly the same phrase, no more than twenty minutes ago,' Edwina said with some satisfaction. 'You think alike, Lizzie. That's a good sign. Perhaps on meeting him, you might no longer want to tell him off.'

Elizabeth glared at her. 'He is here? *Now?* And without you even allowing me notice of his arrival?'

'You would have refused to see him, Lizzie, you know that. Actually, he has kindly loaned me money and repayment is overdue.'

'This is the outside of *enough*! I'll listen to no more of your Banbury tales! I know you have no need of a loan from anyone. You have stock bonds and investment documents spilling from your bureau. You must be insane if you think I shall be taken in by woeful tales of some imaginary poverty we are soon to endure.' Elizabeth flung her hands in the air in hopeless despair. 'To broker a marriage with a gentleman would be bad enough. To bribe a rogue to take me....'

'Gentleman rogue,' Edwina interceded with a nod of her head. 'And handsome too...'

'Enough! I'll listen to no more!' Elizabeth gritted through teeth so firmly set she was in danger of taking the pearly edge off them.

'Come, Lizzie,' Edwina wheedled. 'The Viscount is here...in the drawing room...and he is prepared to defer his travel to give you a brief audience.'

Lady Elizabeth Rowe pivoted back very slowly to meet her grandmother's innocent expression. '*He* is prepared to give *me* an audience,' she faintly echoed, her face rigid, bloodless from furious indignation. Once more in her mind's eye she could see those mocking dark eyes catching her peeking at him ten years previously. She could sense his ennui, his laughter at her inexperience as confident, voluptuous women vied for his attention.

Edwina studied her granddaughter's proudly tilted little chin and began relaxing into the chair. Suddenly, she felt more content than she had all day. 'He is a busy man, Lizzie,' she sighed. 'He bade me impress upon you that he cannot tarry long. But he has agreed to spare you a few minutes of his time, before he is away to his Kent estates.'

Lady Elizabeth Rowe's full, soft mouth tightened into a hard little knot. 'Has he? How exceedingly good of him,' she murmured in a voice a-quiver with rage.

'Your gown is a little crumpled, your hair a bit wispy...' Struggling from her chair, Edwina bustled over, circled Elizabeth, tutting as she began winding silky soft blonde tendrils back into their pins with one hand while fussing at rose-pink crepe with the other. Two angry high spots of matching cerise now adorned Elizabeth's otherwise flawless ivory complexion.

'Ross is used to keeping company with beautiful, stylish women. He is not seeing you to best advantage. Most days, you could easily compete with any of them…even the youngest. But I suppose today you look…well enough. The years hardly show…'

Elizabeth snatched herself from her grandmother's touch with two crisp backwards steps. Her whole being felt as taut as a coiled spring. She wasn't sure when last she had been in the throes of such all consuming white-hot wrath. And she wasn't sure on whom to vent it: her idiotic, well-meaning grandmama or the pompous, egotistical villain in the next room. What she *was* sure of was that she didn't now want him to quit the house before she'd had the opportunity to impress on him a few things. She stalked to the door and pulled it open with such violence that, Edwina, just behind, had to catch at it to prevent it damaging her cream silk wall.

As Elizabeth marched the few yards to the drawing room, her quivering fingers found some pins in her hair and yanked them out. So, he was used to keeping company with beautiful, stylish young women, was he? She tossed the pins carelessly aside, then messed the trailing pearly locks into snarls. When satisfied with that disarray, she scrunched the expensive material of her skirts in her fists, just stopping short of ripping into it in her fury.

She halted before the drawing room door, oblivious to Edwina a few paces behind hissing at her, flapping her hands in wild gestures, then watching her, transfixed. Elizabeth closed her violet eyes, took a huge breath, then reached for the handle…

She made her entrance fast, before her courage deserted her, her eyes fixed forward to where she envisaged him to be: either lounging on a sofa or perhaps posing regally by the hearth. The momentum of her pace having taken her a way into the room, her first impression was that it was vacant. The unoccupied sofas, the uncluttered mantel made her thankfully certain that he had deemed himself too important to wait after all. Her head swayed back on her graceful, stalk-like neck, her eyelids drooped and she sighed relief. Dragging forward the few paces to the fire, she warmed her hands against the leaping flames, rubbed her glowing palms along her goose-pimply forearms. The sudden knowledge that she was timorously grateful for his absence, and the reprieve, had her flinging herself around in self-disgust. She had retraced barely a pace when she froze.

He had actually stationed himself on the right-hand side of the room, by a window adjacent to the double doors. Once the doors were opened, the narrow casement was obscured from view to anyone entering. He was still turned slightly towards the glass as though he had been observing the street scene. Now he was looking at her.

For what seemed a small eternity, yet was probably no more than seconds, she stared at him, her heart in her drying mouth while all manner of disjointed messages raced through her mind. It *was* him. Although all trace of youth was gone from his hard, rugged features, this was the same man who had held court amid a band of wild Corinthians a decade ago and occasionally bestowed on her an idle mocking glance on catching her spying on him. He *was* gypsy dark, his hair bronze-black and long with a slight curl where it rested on his collar. Sartorially, he was all stylish elegance. His powerful broad-shouldered frame was garbed in shades of brown: buff trousers, tan tail coat. An amber stone glowed in the intricate knot of his sepia silk cravat. With a skipped heartbeat she realised the tiger's eye resembled the hue she could discern between his close black lashes. He seemed taller than she remembered; if she stood against him she guessed the top of her head would barely reach his chin. The thought of being placed that close to him jerked her out of her trance and into awareness that she was openly staring. A fact that had not gone unnoticed by him: a corner of a finely chiselled mouth had tilted in acknowledgement.

Heat stung into her complexion. But despite her embarrassment, she became aware he was assessing her equally closely. A sardonic, hooded gaze was roving her tangled blonde hair, her crumpled rose-pink gown. Spontaneously, a hand jumped to attend to the self-inflicted damage. She forced it to clench before it could smooth one ruck, undo one snarl. It returned to her side, then slipped behind her to be joined by the other. Her fingers gripped together and her chin tilted, her beautiful flushed visage a study in hauteur.

'Have you had an accident?'

For no reason she could understand she flinched at the sound of his husky, baritone voice. At that moment, she hated him simply for the lazy humour in his voice, in his eyes, as he alluded to her disarray. She moistened her lips. 'Accident?' she echoed as though attempting a foreign tongue.

'You seem a little…dishevelled,' he mentioned taking a step towards her.

Elizabeth took a step back. 'Oh, that.' She launched a freezing smile at him while an unsteady finger worked its nonchalant way into a blonde tangle. 'I have been reclining in my chamber, but thought you would prefer me not to tarry and primp in your honour. My grandmother said you impressed upon her your eagerness to soon leave. So here I am, come directly to impress upon you how well that suits me.'

A slight movement of his dark head acknowledged the insult, as did his dry tone as he said, 'I'm greatly obliged.'

'Good.'

So here she was, indeed, Ross mused wryly to himself. The one place he hadn't expected to find the blonde beauty he had glimpsed in the street, was within Edwina's house…within her family. Her granddaughter had figured in his imagination as a dumpy, uninteresting young woman: an insipid version of Edwina. A sense of chivalry had made him stay and at least meet her. He couldn't have been more wrong about it all. And he couldn't have been more right, thinking he'd seen this woman somewhere before. Such exquisite loveliness was rare, unforgettable. It was also, oddly, unmarred by the fact that she looked as though she'd been dragged through a hedge backwards. If only he could bring to mind where and when they'd met. 'I'm afraid Edwina has left me a little at a loss. I don't know your name...Miss Sampson...?' he ventured.

'Lady Elizabeth Rowe,' Elizabeth stated, her voice wobbly but her tone strong with pride. Her worst fears were realised; she felt her stomach tumble at the immediate intelligence in his eyes. Oh, she knew what caused the strengthening smile, his lashes to droop to conceal the base interest...

His memory finally served him correctly and everything had suddenly become crystal clear. Not least, Ross realised, cynically, why Edwina had omitted revealing her granddaughter's identity and was so damned keen to buy her a husband. He had imagined the chit to be impeded in the marriage stakes by homely looks, not by her ruined reputation...or her age. Not that she looked approaching thirty, but he guessed she must be. If she'd been seventeen at her debut she'd now be in her twenty-eighth year.

Edwina Sampson, he laughed inwardly, really was the most unpredictable woman. He'd never known of her connection to the Thorneycrofts: a less likely mother-in-law to the late Marquess, he couldn't imagine. Now Edwina wanted her sullied granddaughter wed and thought she had found the perfect sap to take her...in him. In fact, despite the lady's haughty disdain, they were probably in cahoots. They wanted to manipulate him to get her off the shelf and respectable before she got too much older and started losing those beautiful looks. And she was desirable...barely five minutes in her company and his body was already impressing on him just how badly he wanted her.

Elizabeth could sense his contempt! But she knew his interest was growing. But then gentlemen were always more interested once they'd discovered her identity. She had come beneath lingering male appraisal too often to be ignorant of what excited it. Because her stupid temper had made her burst in like some unkempt virago, he would now brand her every manner of slut. She scoured her mind for some insolence to send him quickly on his way, for she was horribly afraid she might not manage to brazen it out today...with him. She could feel her throat closing, feel ice shivering her lower lip. She clamped teeth into it. She would not bolt from the room, hide away ashamed…

'I hear you do good works.'

'I hear you don't,' was flung back at once with a childlike defensiveness, even though he had spoken conversationally.

Ross smiled. 'Our sovereign might challenge you on that. He seems happy enough with my services.'

'How well a King so easily pleased befits this great nation,' she sneered.

Ross laughed and his head fell back a little. He frowned at the ceiling. So much for polite chit-chat. 'Look, I'm trying to make this easier for both of us,' he said affably. But his steady gaze, as it levelled on her again, was quite devoid of amity or humour. 'As you appear to disdain small talk…and most other things…let's get straight to business. I imagine you're aware that your grandmother owes me a sum of money?'

'I'm aware that you allege she owes you a sum of money.' Elizabeth slanted a contemptuous purple stare at him. Softly, fluidly, she announced, 'However, there are things, sir, you should be aware of: firstly, I do not believe any transaction has taken place between you and my grandmother. I think you have bamboozled her in some way to lay hands on my dowry. You may fool her, you will never fool me. Secondly, the whole matter of money loaned or borrowed is of no consequence whatsoever. I have no intention of marrying you, now or at any other time. You will need to look elsewhere for money to embezzle.' She turned her face from his. 'I think that is all. Oh, now you may go,' she added with an idle wave of a slender hand at the door. Although she had shown him her back, she knew he was yet there. The silence was deafening. Unable to bear the tension longer she gathered her creased skirts, tossed her shaggy head and, chin up, headed for the door.

She barely saw him move but somehow he had managed to station himself in the middle of her escape route. She made to sweep first one way, then the other around him. Whichever way she stepped, he seemed to block her path.

Backpacing from his proximity, she raised flashing eyes. 'Come, my lord. I thought you were in a tearing rush. Please go before me, if you'd rather impress me with your status and quit the room first. Conscious of your aggrandisement, I did offer you the opportunity…'

Ross took a moment before lowering his face to look at her. He then gave her a smile so laden with deceit, so obviously unmeant and threatening, it took her breath away. As did his eyes. They were cold as metal yet extraordinarily beautiful in hue: green-flecked gold and fringed with thick black lashes that were incongruously childlike in their length. Her face quickly lowered. I do just reach his chin, scuttled deliriously through her mind as she blinked at the cleft in it.

'Are you naturally this rude? Or have you been practising insults in my honour, instead of…primping…wasn't it?'

Despite herself, Elizabeth turned scarlet. 'Remove yourself from my way. I wish to leave this room…right now,' was all she could manage in response.

'And I wish to receive back my money…right now,' flowed back, honey-voiced.

'You're lying! My grandmother has no need of your money. She has more money of her own than she knows what to do with,' Elizabeth spat at him.

Ross smiled coldly. She was a damn good actress. And very aware, he was sure, of the effect she was having on him. His fingers itched to touch her, slide her gown from shoulders that looked as fragile as milky glass. They clenched at his sides. Barely two feet separated them. He was so damned aroused that if she locked the door and gave him a taste for an early wedding night on the sofa, he'd get a licence this afternoon.

'I don't doubt Edwina's lying about her ability to repay,' he gritted, angry and frustrated. 'Nevertheless, two weeks ago I was foolish enough to be taken in by some bleeding-heart story concerning the loss of her butler to a rival and her eagerness to try a little deviousness to outwit the woman and keep him. In short, she persuaded me to loan her ten thousand pounds to fund the chicanery.' He withdrew a parchment from his inside pocket. 'The contract states that repayment was due yesterday. Patient soul that I am, I have allowed her one day's grace already.' He moved the document, indicating Elizabeth should take it to check his story's veracity.

Elizabeth eyed the proffered paper as though it might bite. From sounding like lies, it now all sounded horribly plausible. How would he know of Alice Penney poaching Pettifer unless Edwina had related it all? Why would he bother mentioning their domestic arrangements at all unless he had a vested interest in them? Why would he let her read the contract? Her hands seemed welded together behind her back. Suddenly they sprang apart, snatched at the paper. Swishing about, she ran to the fire and fed it to the hungry flames. Her defiance was almost palpable as she put up her chin and shook back tangled locks from her sculpted white face.

'I'm lucky in my man of business,' she heard him say in a voice that dripped irony. 'He's thorough…sometimes tiresomely fussy. He sets a clerk to duplicating documents and nothing else. And Mrs Sampson was obliging enough to sign the set…even that spare lodged in my safe.'

'I don't care,' Elizabeth gasped through the mounting rage and fear tightening her chest. She was behaving with reckless abandon. More stupidly than she had in a long…long while. It seemed the more patient and polite he was, the more rude and abrasive she became. But she couldn't seem to stop. Everything was running out of control. 'I won't marry you. I will never marry you,' she stormed.

'Progress at last,' Ross drawled. 'We've come to something we agree on. You appear to be under the misapprehension that I have proposed. I don't recall doing so, or ever intending to do so. I am done, my lady, with enduring your puerile insolence and disdain in the hope we might amicably solve this problem. I want payment. To be honest, I would much prefer the cash, but I'll take retribution in its stead.'

Chapter Five

'What do you mean?' Elizabeth forced out through her sandpaper throat.

'Well, I'll tell you my dear. I think that the lady doth protest too much. I think you are an accomplice, possibly the instigator, in this feeble plot to trick me into marrying you. I think your pathetic insults are perversely intended to endear you to me in some way.' He walked away from her, braced a hand against the window sill. It looked heavy and dark against the narrow white-painted ledge. Idly he looked down, scanning the street, then up at the clear blue sky. 'You may tell Edwina it might have worked. It's true I like women who are novel and present a challenge. But not that much. If you were planning to ride back into the *ton* on my wedding coat tails, I'm afraid I'm about to disappoint you. Forgive me for being blunt, but I'd never take to wife a rude, supercilious little bitch ruined by scandal.' His sweeping gaze relinquished the heavens and he pivoted about to lean back against the wall. His hands were thrust into his pockets, an indolent look levelled at her. 'I also mean that it's in your best interest to persuade Edwina that you both now act sensibly. Concede defeat. Return my money and the whole trifling matter is at an end... finished.'

He couldn't be sure if her chalky pallor stemmed from shock or fury at his explicitness. More gently he added, 'I'm not a fool, neither am I a vindictive man. I don't want to give credibility to my infamy as a ruthless swine by finishing your grandmother in a debtor's cell…or finishing you in my bed. And I will bring you down…' Between them was catastrophic silence, absolute stillness for a moment. 'If I'm generous and allow you to work off the debt at two thousand a year, including interest due, that's six years service. You might be a trifle sullied now; after a lengthy stint as one of my paramours, you'll be a professional courtesan approaching her mid-thirties. It would be a kindness if I took the trouble to prepare you for meaner partners before ejecting you. Eventually you'll have nothing left but base standards and spoiled looks. You'll be grateful to scrape a living as a tavern whore in Whitechapel.'

Elizabeth moistened her lips, swallowed, tried to speak. No words formed. Dumbfounded, she couldn't find a voice. Never in all her life, even directly after that horrible shame he alluded to, had anyone spoken to her with such deliberate brutality.

But she couldn't fault his honesty. She had encountered similar wretched specimens of womankind as those he alluded to almost every week on visiting Newgate or Bridewell. Sometimes she saw them at a mean liberty, lolling hollow-eyed against a wall in Barrow Road or its environs. At first glance they seemed no different from the rough trade they now lived amongst. Then there might be a hint of once-graceful deportment, or a cultured inflection to an overheard word, and they were betrayed as once having known gentility. And she would try to glimpse, beneath grey, gin-cracked masks, the pride and vivacity that must once have sparkled beneath. And he wasn't being vindictive. His words were harshened by impatience, not malice. His desire to be elsewhere, his indifference, made it all so much worse.

She accepted it now. He was owed a fortune by her grandmother and he wanted it back. Dealing with her was just a vexing waste of his time. She wanted to shout at him that she wasn't involved, that she had known of her grandmother's plot less time than he. Instead she simply stared at him, un-blinking, her glossy violet eyes huge in a face that was cold, milky, immovable as marble.

'Persuade your grandmother that a banker's draft for ten thousand pounds would do well to find its way to Grosvenor Square by four this afternoon. I'll forgo the interest for now. Inform her that the cuisine at the Fleet leaves a lot to be desired and she's in danger of fading away. I'm told by dis-gruntled paramours that my selfishness leaves a lot to be de-sired. So you choose,' he offered dulcetly. 'But know this, my lady. I want what's due. Parting with the cash might be relatively painless. In your position, that's what I'd choose. That's all I mean,' he stressed in conclusion.

Elizabeth finally unstuck her tongue from the roof of her mouth. The shuddering, indrawn breath she took was barely perceptible. 'Thank you for that explanation, sir. I do now know exactly what you mean.' Her voice strengthened from thready whisper to gruff choke. 'Perhaps I might be permitted to trespass on your precious time a few moments more and let you know what I mean.' Her tousled blonde head came up and she stalked away from the fire towards him, suppress-ing the shock and bitter humiliation that had moments ago threatened to humble her, crumble her like a rag doll at his feet as his lazy contempt withered her bones.

She approached him, emboldened by a wrath that tightened her fists into quivering, knife-edged balls. She forced them close to her sides lest they lashed out at him, beat at his arrogant, heathen head. She half-circled him at a distance, looking his powerful physique up and down. 'Firstly,' she enunciated carefully, frowning in concentration, 'I must con-gratulate you on your excellent memory. Yes, I was compro-mised ten years ago; yes, I have been shunned by people who class themselves as better than me. People like you who shield their disgusting habits behind sham morals and manners. Sec-ondly, had I any wish to sneak back into the *beau monde*, I would choose nobler coat tails than yours to cling to. Perhaps in your conceit you believe I should be grateful…flattered, even, at having been propositioned by an upstart Viscount; a thug who has managed to brawl his way into favour. I'm afraid I must now disappoint you. I've had far better offers than yours. Over ten years, two dukes and two earls have pursued me, along with numerous less eminent but often wealthier gentlemen. A coal merchant once offered me the freehold of a house on Park Lane, together with all the servants, clothes and carriages I could use. Oh, and an allowance of two thousand a year.'

She stared, vivid-eyed, into middle distance. 'The Earl of Cadmore is less generous but more persistent. Just a few weeks ago he wrote again to let me know how greatly I would benefit from allowing his ardent attention.' She spun about to gaze at her tormentor as though he had crawled from the wainscotting. 'And you...a paltry Viscount...a paltry, parsimonious Viscount at that, think to stable me amongst your mongrel harlots? Are you really so stupid, so vain, that you imagine a Marquess's daughter, even a sullied Marquess's daughter, would ever contemplate a union with a Cornish brigand? If my silly grandmother hadn't made the circumstances so tiresome, I swear I might die laughing at your pathetic fantasies...'

She got no further. Two hard, brown hands gripped the tops of her slender, ivory arms, abbreviating her jeering tirade. The speed and ease at which he lifted her made her sure he would jerk her up against him so their faces were level. But he dropped her just before him, abruptly, as though she had become scalding. Her silky, silver head grazed his dark chin, then recoiled to rest inches away.

'Quiet! Or I might now share those pathetic fantasies...just for the hell of it. I promise you won't laugh,' he added with a hint of apology that chilled her.

Elizabeth back-paced, rubbing at her arms as though removing taint. 'Oh, I believe that. I was being ironic, of course. Anyone less diverting than you I cannot imagine,' she sneered, contempt sliding from beneath dusky lashes.

'Well, let me imagine for you,' he whipped back mellifluously. 'How diverting did you find Lieutenant Havering? Was it his pathetic fantasy or yours that you play mongrel harlot for some gentlemen of the road?'

Elizabeth stumbled to a halt. Her pale complexion lost what little colour stained her cheeks. She ran a dry tongue over arid lips. So there it was. He had to let her know that he recalled all her disgrace. Every sordid part. And at that moment it seemed as though the raucous guffaws that had echoed in her ears as she and her stiff-backed papa quit Caledon Square in their elegant carriage were rolling within this room. The walls seemed to undulate with the vicious male amusement that accompanied the start of their journey back to Hertfordshire and thence into exile. Ross Trelawney might not have bothered witnessing her banishment with those crowing dandies, but he was gloating now, determined she understand how equally he despised her. A shaking hand went behind to grip at the sofa-back, as her legs weakened. Slowly her chin came up. 'I have considered it. No, I still cannot imagine anyone less entertaining than you,' she whispered.

Threat of retribution savaged the mockery in his eyes making her sure he was about to come after her. It shocked her out of petrification and into a tottering retreat. 'I must again impose on your patience, sir,' she croaked distractingly. 'Please wait here. It is in your interest to stay for I hope to return in a moment with something that ensures neither of us need ever again endure the other's company.' Without awaiting his agreement, Elizabeth swished about and sped from the room.

Ross watched her go. He stared at the door for a moment before closing his eyes. He felt shattered. He'd limped away from battlefields with more energy and better spirits. A grunt of laughter scratched at his throat as he looked about the sedate, cosy room with its tasteful mix of blue and gold furnishings. But this was a war zone and no mistake. And he had the feeling, despite holding the high ground and an arsenal of weapons, he'd just lost and made an implacable enemy. And for some reason that wounded him to the core.

And then it came to him, sidled into his mind and wouldn't leave. She hadn't withdrawn to find a gun to level at his head, or even to collaborate with Edwina on better strategies. She wasn't involved in Edwina's scheme to get her wed at all. She was innocent of that and he was guilty of barbarism. She'd retreated to fetch something valuable to offer as loot rather than risk his revenge. He smiled ruefully, hoping she wasn't about to struggle back with a sackful of family silver. Idiotically, he didn't even want her to return with a banker's draft...not yet. So much for tactical, wounding words and manoeuvring to keep distance between them. He hadn't resisted the lure of her small, sensual body. He hadn't managed to keep his hands to himself. Now his palms seemed to tingle with the loss of satiny skin beneath them. The fragrance of flowers that had wafted up from her tangled pearly tresses teased his nostrils anew, the infinitesimal stroke of silky hair against his jaw made him irritably toss his head to prevent another phantom caress. The memory of her was narcotic. He wanted more. Now. He wanted her back so he could look at her again...touch her again.

He'd called her a bitch and, innocent or not of plotting with Edwina, his opinion hadn't much altered. Yet Lady Elizabeth Rowe aroused something in him Cecily never touched: few women stirred his mind as well as his body. She fascinated him. He wanted to know everything about her. Everything that had occurred, good and bad, since the first time their eyes met at Vauxhall Gardens. He placed a hot palm against cold glass, then curled it into a fist as his thoughts weaved back through the years to a sultry summer and a blonde debutante.

He'd wanted her then too. But she was too young, too popular...and so was he. He'd known if he approached her, joined that band of fools awaiting a kind glance, permission to call...to dance...to flirt, it might have finished him. For as she had just rightly proclaimed, daughters of marquesses, especially those of rare beauty, didn't forge unions with sons of Cornish freetraders. They married aristocrats; and she hadn't exaggerated the number of noblemen who had pursued her. She had constantly been surrounded by the bluest young bloods. So that summer he'd steered himself clear of her innocently provocative glances, too youthfully vain himself to face enduring the rebuff that was sure to come.

At that time he had wealth but no status...apart from a reputation as a marauder. But there were always women, some classed as ladies, who wanted him because of his rough lineage rather than despite it. Women who were excited by his piratical looks and cavalier manners, who liked him to relate tales of sea skirmishes and plundered cargoes while they traced the marks on his body with sharp fingernails and shivered naked in his arms. The only time they were disappointed was on realising he was happy to stimulate any number of them and no one in particular. It was pleasurable and easy that way and, at twenty-three, he saw no reason for strife or self-denial.

Yet, along with the rest of society, he'd been wrong in guessing Lady Elizabeth Rowe to be ambitious in the marriage stakes and stalking a title and wealth. Her lover had been the youngest son of a baronet and impecunious to boot.

Their reckless elopement had floundered into disaster. En route to Gretna Green, the callow youth was alleged to have panicked and fled, abandoning Elizabeth to a couple of highwaymen who'd stopped his carriage. Her father, so the tale went, eventually tracked her to a tavern in Cambridgeshire where she'd been found partially clothed and alone. A natural conclusion had been drawn to her fate once given over to the felons' tender mercies. And apparently she'd offered no defence to that. Neither had her father.

The scandal had rocked society. Ross first learned of the affair at White's, while playing Faro with Guy Markham and his brother Luke. The redolence of cigar smoke and stewing beef mingling, hanging thick in the air, filled his nostrils. He recalled losing heavily as the ribald jesting crescendoed around him. Inwardly he had felt the angry sorrow of desecration. Outwardly he had chipped in some cynical comment about the sanctity of virgins.

From that moment, for about a month, the gentlemen's clubs had resounded with ever more salacious conjecture on the circumstances of her abasement and how best to tempt the lady back to town for an encore after such a promising debut. And many a titled rake had put his money where his mouth was and offered her his protection. He assumed, from what she'd said, none had tempted her sufficiently.

But one had persevered. He could believe that: Linus Savage, Earl of Cadmore, was known as a man to hold grudges. He was also once known as the man believed to be leading the field in Lady Elizabeth Rowe's affections. A decade ago their betrothal had been expected. When it was discovered she had played a rich peer of the realm for a fool, using him to camouflage an affair with an indigent officer in the army, the Earl became a risible figure, too. Ross could imagine Cadmore to be unremitting in his need for vengeance, even though years had passed and he'd since wed an heiress.

As Lady Elizabeth was guessed to be in the marriage mart to lure a fortune to reline her papa's pockets, Cadmore had seemed a natural choice. When it foundered into farce, in every sense the Marquess was sure to have been disappointed. Thus, for a while, wild predictions on his jezebel daughter's fate were bandied about. He would incarcerate her in the nearest convent; he would despatch her to some remote relative; he would negotiate a discreet deal with a wealthy gentleman prepared to take her as concubine or, paradoxically, borrow the means to buy her a modest husband and respectability. But the Marquess did nothing of the sort. The last Ross heard, as gossip faded for want of any fuel to fire the rumours, was that the Marquess was still devoted to his lovely daughter and they were living a reclusive life at Thorneycroft.

A woman of gentle birth was to be congratulated for retaining her pride after such degradation. Ravished and ostracised, maybe, but she had spirit. She despised him and was quick to let him know it. And there had been no reason for him to know it, or to have met her again at all and now be brooding over ten-year-old tragedies and regrets like a sentimental fool. His teeth met. 'Damn you, Edwina,' he muttered irritably into the mellow afternoon.

Her fingers were shaking so much it took several attempts before the key slotted into the lock. Jerking open the secret drawer in her grandmother's escritoire, Elizabeth withdrew the burgundy velvet roll. Her first instinct was to open it out, feast her eyes one last, private time on the treasure within. She resisted, simply snatching it up, and within a moment was rushing headlong down the stairs. The thought that the beastly bastard might leave without a settlement being reached today; that she might toss and turn the night through, uncertain if the vile man was firmly banished to her past, made her burst through the double doors in a most unladylike fashion.

Although Elizabeth ignored him, and slowed to a graceful walk, she did utter with cool civility, 'Thank you for waiting.' It was honest gratitude and helped to steady the quivering of her fingers as they hovered, then reverentially laid bare her peace offering on the sofa table.

The diamond-and-amethyst collar glittered as sunlight dappled over it. As always when she looked upon it, its magnificence caught the breath at the back of her throat; as did memories it evoked of a certain person. She took a few steps back and tossed up her head, meeting green-gold watching eyes.

A nervous gesture indicated the heirloom. 'It was my mother's,' she brusquely explained. 'Now it is mine. It was Edwina's gift to my mother on her twenty-first birthday. Soon after that she married my papa, the Marquess of Thorneycroft.' She hesitated in reciting the gem's provenance as she became aware of him approaching. She moved away to the other side of the table, wordlessly inviting him to fully appreciate its opulence.

'You might be thinking it is not worth ten thousand pounds. I expect you are.' Elizabeth hastily removed his need to scorn her sacrifice. 'And…and that is quite true. This piece was last valued at two thousand guineas.' She glanced at him, at intervals, searching for signs of anger or impatience.

He raised his eyes from the superbly matched violet and white stones and gazed into something similar. Her eyes were equally cold, equally beautiful. 'Your mother looked like you…' he stated with a half-smile.

Elizabeth blinked, swallowed, half-turned away from him. 'How could you possibly know that?' she demanded, angrily, absently dragging fingers through her tangles. 'This is her necklace, not her portrait.'

'It was bought by someone who loved her…to reflect her beauty. You've the same eyes. I'm guessing you look like her in other ways, too.'

Elizabeth glared accusingly at the collar as though it had betrayed her. It lay glistening between them, shieldlike, protecting a flimsy treaty. Ignoring his astute personal observation as best she could, she recommended stiltedly, 'My papa was pleased with how well this suited my mother and wanted to add to it. He had a matching suite made by the same craftsman and presented it as my mother's wedding gift. It includes a bracelet, two styles of eardrops, a brooch and a small hair ornament. I believe the parure was last valued at approaching eight thousand pounds. It must be worth more now. A decade has since passed. All the pieces, save this one, are kept in a bank vault. But they are all mine. I own it in entirety so you need not fret they are the property of the Thorneycroft estate and will be reclaimed. My mama left them to me. Edwina likes to keep this one here. As she purchased it originally, I saw no reason to deny her the pleasure of looking at it from time to time.' She met his watching gaze, trying to glean from his expression whether he intended rejecting her proposal.

'Are you expecting me to feel too ashamed to take it?'

Elizabeth sensed her face flame but said icily, 'Not at all, my lord. In our brief acquaintance there's been nothing that would let me credit you with a conscience. Your reputation as a heartless villain is quite safe with me.'

His smile strengthened, the crinkles at the corners of his

eyes and mouth deepened. She realised he was, for the first
time, genuinely amused. 'That sounds like a challenge to
prove equal to such trust, my lady.'

'I should like a receipt…' Elizabeth burst out.

That made him laugh. 'Of course. And how shall I lay my
pillaging hands on the other pieces?'

Elizabeth moved to the small writing desk by the window
and selected quill and parchment. She dipped, began to write,
tutted as her unsteady fingers caused a blot of ink to mar the
paper. She hesitated, dithering over whether to crumple it and
restart. She finished quickly, in a few sentences, sealed, then
immediately proffered the note. 'That gives you the right to
remove and dispose of the set as you will. No doubt Sir
Joshua will first contact me for verification. It is an unusual
occurrence….'

Ross took the letter she was holding by its very edge and
slipped it in a pocket. He rolled the velvet into a cylinder
again, obliterating her inheritance with deft casualness. The
rich, red cloth looked lost in his large dark hand.

'Receipt…' Elizabeth whispered, realising that he could
walk away now with all her financial security…her most precious possession…and no one would ever be the wiser. She
held out the quill towards him. 'Please…' she forced through
a clog in her throat, while her mind chanted, *I'm sorry,
mama…I'm so sorry…so sorry…*

He wrote fast, fluently, then placed the pen back in its rest.
Her rigid fingers stabbed the paper, drew it towards her as
though frightened he might take it back. She looked blankly
at him. 'Thank you,' she murmured in the tone of voice that
let him know she'd sooner curse him as a devil.

A tiny movement of his head acknowledged her faux gratitude. Unable to take a polite leave of him, any sort of leave
of him, she stood, backed off two steps, then turned immediately for the door.

'You'll want it returned,' was addressed to her stiff back.
'Persuade Edwina to be sensible and repay me within a week

and I'll let you have it. After that time, I can't promise anything.'

Elizabeth swallowed. She should face him, thank him again, but the two simple words burned like acid in her throat. She felt her eyes fill with needling tears. Without another word or glance, but with dignity in every endless step that eventually brought her to the door, she left him.

'I thought you were long gone, Stratton!'

Ross tore his eyes from leaping flames and turned. He removed from the mantel the glass of whisky he'd helped himself to from the decanter on the sideboard. Sipping, he looked at Edwina over the rim.

'Thought you had to be in Kent before sundown.' Edwina consulted the clock on the wall. 'Doubt you'll make it now…' At his continuing silence she mentioned drily, with a flick of a fat finger at the tumbler now held low by a muscular thigh, 'I see you found the decanter.' She smiled. 'Or perhaps m'granddaughter remembered her manners and served you refreshment. She can be a charming hostess. Did she look after you?'

Ross's smile was intensely sardonic. 'I think you know damn well she didn't.' He assessed her from under low lids until she shifted uneasily. 'You know when I arrived here earlier, Edwina, I was worried you were losing your mind and didn't know what you were about.'

Edwina adopted a shocked look. 'No! What made you think that?' she asked, humour quivering her voice.

'Oh…just some odd notion that you might be foolish enough to intend defrauding me.'

'And what do you think now?'

'Now I think you're an extremely devious woman with an extremely…intriguing granddaughter. I imagine that's exactly what you want me to think.'

'So, how did you like my sweet Lizzie? Pretty girl, isn't she?'

Ross laughed at glowing logs. *'Pretty girl?'* he echoed sarcastically. 'You'd never have bothered putting a pretty girl in my way, Edwina.'

'That's true.' She paused before opining innocently, 'I believe you already like her.'

'No, I don't like her. But we both know that's immaterial, don't we?'

Edwina's eyes narrowed. 'I'll pay out on marriage only, Stratton. No wedding, no dowry. I don't want her settled in any other way. Her papa could have arranged that other way ten years ago. She could have arranged it for herself last week. She's still in demand, you know.'

'I'm sure,' he drawled drily.

'Well, don't keep me in suspense. What occurred? Have you proposed?'

'No. But we came to an acceptable arrangement.'

'Which is?'

'She's paid me.'

Edwina stalked forward. 'She's done *what*?'

Ross placed his glass down on the mantel and withdrew the velvet roll.

Edwina looked at it resting on his palm, then at him. Quickly she shielded her frustration with her sparse lashes. 'She must truly dislike you, Stratton. I believed never in this world would she part with that necklace.'

'She's parted with the rest of the collection, too.'

'Then she's frightened and that's not like my courageous Lizzie.'

'No doubt you'll do the decent thing then and buy them back for her.'

'Oh, no,' Edwina said airily. 'Why should I? I've not given up hope of you doing the decent thing. After all, you're still here, aren't you? And you so busy 'n all, and desperate to get to Kent. I would hazard a guess, Ross, that you've behaved boorishly and now you're feeling guilty. After all, you might not like her now, but tomorrow…'

A tight-lipped smile quirked his sensual mouth, his dark brows hiked with sceptical enquiry. But the way he then shot whisky down his throat, slammed the glass onto the mantel and brushed past, made Edwina indulge in a secret smile before she turned to follow at a careful distance. She watched as he strode out into the hallway, his steps cracking like gunshot as he neared Pettifer. He took his coat and cane from the butler without slowing pace.

'Tomorrow you will…' Edwina murmured slyly at the closing front door.

'Are you not going to talk to me, Lizzie?'

Lady Elizabeth Rowe placed down her breakfast coffee cup and gave her grandmother her attention. 'Are you going to repay that man his money?'

'I cannot. You know I cannot. I have explained about m'funds at present.'

Elizabeth snatched up her cup, raised it to her mouth. 'Then I am not going to talk to you. There is nothing more to say.'

'Lizzie, dear…' Edwina cooed in her most wheedling tone. 'Come, it is two days now since Stratton was here and still you punish me. You have had time to sulk and berate me as a foolish woman. And I have said m'sorrys. It is true I hoped that you and the Viscount might like one another. But if it is not to be…' She shrugged as though it mattered little. 'You cannot blame me for wanting to settle m'debts with money that's just mouldering in the bank. Neither can you blame a fond grandmama for wanting to introduce her granddaughter to such an eligible gentleman. Besides, why take against him so? Don't you find Ross handsome? Charming? Be truthful now. All the ladies sigh over him…'

Elizabeth scraped back in her chair and jumped to her feet. Forgetting her speech embargo, she snapped, 'Handsome? He looks like a romany who has thieved himself fine clothes. Charming? He called me a rude, supercilious little bitch!'

'Did he?' Edwina barked, more surprised than outraged. 'You never said so before. He is usually unfailingly civil to the fair sex; even to those creatures who hardly warrant it.' She sniffed, recalling Cecily Booth boldly soliciting his company at Maria's soirée. 'You must really have got under his skin, my dear, to upset that courteous nonchalance he maintains. Were you…?'

'Was I what?' Elizabeth demanded, peering through the parlour window.

'A rude little bitch. I know you can act haughty at times.'

Elizabeth flushed, leaned her hot forehead against cool glass as she gazed into the gardens. If honest, she knew she had behaved badly. No, worse than that: with anyone else she would have felt thoroughly ashamed of her conduct. Not with him. Never with him. He deserved all her rancour.

Yet there was an irritating niggling in the pit of her stomach. Had she been pleasant, perhaps he might have been so, too. But she had acted purely on aggressive instinct. She never used feminine wiles now. It was ten years since she had flirted and acted girlishly to get her own way. But now she was tormented by regrets…missed opportunities.

It would have been a shrewd move to flatter his pathetic conceit and angle for a little more time in which to nag Edwina to pay him. It would have been wise to batten down her stormy emotions. But it seemed the more cool sophistication he displayed, the more fraught she had become. She still couldn't quite believe that while in the throes of temper she had forfeited her mother's treasure…her treasure.

'Well, were you rude?' Edwina's query cut sharply into her pensiveness.

Elizabeth spun about at the window. 'I had every right to be as unmannerly as he was. For all his failings, Stratton's memory doesn't lack. He was at pains to let me know just how well he recalls my disgrace.'

'And were you at pains to enlighten him to the facts of the matter?'

'Why should I tell him anything so personal? He is of no consequence. I don't need his approval,' Elizabeth flared, sculpted chin arrogantly tilting.

'So he knew of your misfortune, yet was still reluctant to go,' Edwina muttered to herself. Noting her granddaughter's haughty expression, she added lightly, 'Well, if you peered down your nose at him like that, I can see how he might arrive at such a description.'

'In case you have forgotten,' Elizabeth snapped, 'your nasty friend now has my mama's jewellery in his grubby possession.' She covered her face with her hands. 'Oh, why did I do it!' Her head shook behind her palms before they curled into fists. 'I should have never agreed to meet him. I should never have allowed him to browbeat me into settling your debt. I should have let him dun you as he threatened. It is what cheats deserve. You have made a grave mistake in this, Grandmama, and you must put it right. Give him the piffling cash. Please! The Thorneycroft parure is irreplaceable!'

'Don't think badly of me, Elizabeth. I don't always get things right. Neither do I often get them wrong. I would never jeopardise your keepsakes, or my sweet Valerie's memory. The Viscount is an honourable gentleman. I'm as confident of that as I am of seeing you again wearing those amethysts. To tell the truth, they have lain idle in a metal box too long. In a way, I'm glad Stratton has them. At least they will see the light of day again.'

'Oh, yes,' Elizabeth choked. 'No doubt they will also reflect candlelight: strung about one of his naked doxies! How will you like *that*?' She flung furiously past her grandmother to quit the room just as Harry Pettifer was entering. The butler jumped aside then tilted backwards at the waist and turned his stately steely head to watch Lady Elizabeth fly along the corridor.

'Come, tell me, Pettifer, am I right to persevere in this? I swear I need a little proof this might succeed or I shall give it all up, right now,' Edwina sighed.

Pettifer raised the salver he had dropped close to his leg to prevent it catching the young mistress as she burst upon him. Stooping agilely, he swept up from the floor a letter and placed it back upon the silverware. 'Never fear, Mrs Sampson; I think a timely confirmation that you're on the right track has just arrived,' Harry said with a twinkle in his blue eyes and a chuckle rumbling in his throat.

Chapter Six

He would like the opportunity to speak to her again, would he! With a view to reaching a more congenial settlement this time—perhaps negotiating the return of her family's heirlooms. How noble of him! And what would he like in their stead? Elizabeth wondered acidly. Perhaps her head on a platter. Or more likely, her naked body on his bed. How odiously predictable these men were, she inwardly scoffed, flicking aside the letter with brave disdain. But the sudden, fierce pumping of her heart forced her up jerkily from the edge of her bed. Linus Savage always used similar phrases in his little notes: opportunity to negotiate…compatible terms…

Dropping onto her velvet dressing stool, she dragged a brush through her thick flaxen hair for a few moments before impatiently discarding it onto the polished wood of the dressing table. Its clatter masked her deep sigh.

She studied her face in the mirror, raised a finger to touch a small laugh line close to her pouty mouth and wondered why she'd not noticed it before. Wondered, too, how she'd come by it. She'd done precious little laughing recently. The finger moved to press against a frown line between her delicately arching brunette brows. That tiny furrow was probably less an imperfection than her moods and history warranted. Yet, on examining each feature by angling her head back and forth, up and down, she realised her appearance was barely touched by the years that had passed since her come-out. She'd been proud of her looks as a debutante…quite vain, she accepted, dropping her tilted chin and grimacing humility at fingers gripping the edge of the dresser.

Since then many men had attempted to make her life squalid and ugly. And now there was another to add to their number, and what terrified her was that of them all he might know how to succeed…

Her mouth pursed with indomitable spirit. She wanted her jewellery back. She wanted it so much, her stomach clenched into a hurting cramp. 'If I reclaim the Thorneycroft parure I swear I'll never again let it go…' she promised her dead parents in a vehement whisper. But she could dredge up no devious plan likely to outwit a mercenary and make him forfeit his booty. If he returned her jewellery, she rather imagined it would be on his terms…

Pushing it all determinedly to the back of her mind, she concentrated on the day ahead. It was Sunday and, after attending morning service with Edwina at St Mary's, there would be barely time for a quick change into serviceable clothes and a bite to eat before Hugh Clemence arrived and they made their way to Barrow Road Sunday School.

She picked up a pen. Replaced it on her writing desk. Picked it up again and tapped at paper with the nib. She firmly, neatly, put it back and pushed the parchment away. She would reply later, when she'd had time to construct a suitably scathing rebuffal to his impertinence.

'Reverend Timms seemed a little peaky, I thought.'

Elizabeth nodded. 'I thought so, too. I hope his wife has just a chill and talk of influenza is unfounded.'

Edwina leaned forward in her sumptuous barouche to raise a gloved hand at a neighbour just emerging from the churchyard. 'Look at that ridiculous turban,' she hissed at Elizabeth from a corner of her mouth. 'Have you ever seen such a concoction of feathers? I swear she has a whole farmyard roosting atop her head. Of course when one is as sparse-thatched as she, a little borrowed plumage is understandable.'

Elizabeth glanced at Mrs Vaughan, a woman of her grandmother's age, and her two gangly nieces accompanying her. Her soft lips quirked at one corner. 'You can be very unkind, Grandmama. Very duplicitous, too. I heard, with my own ears, you praise her rig-out when she settled on the pew behind us.'

Edwina chuckled, then slid her granddaughter a look. When Elizabeth refrained from rebuking her over more serious duplicity, and appeared content to inspect passing scenery, she mentioned casually, 'Pettifer tells me you received a letter today. He says it was delivered by a young footman in very smart livery. He believes it to be the new Viscount Stratton's colours. Black and gold…'

'How vulgar. Obviously it *was* his servant, then.'

'Have you received a letter from him, Elizabeth?'

Elizabeth turned a pansy-blue stare on her grandmother. 'I'm sure if I have, t'would be my own business.'

'Come, don't be missish! You're m'granddaughter,' Edwina huffed. 'I've a right to be interested in what goes on between you and m'friend.'

'A little late with your worries, I think. But, yes, indeed, a fond grandmama should be concerned,' Elizabeth said sweetly. 'And, yes, I did receive a letter from your good friend. In it, he insinuates he is willing to re-negotiate terms of payment. The lure to meet him is a hint at immediately returning my jewellery…'

'Well, that's mighty nice of him. You see; I told you he was a gentleman.'

'In exchange for being so nice, I imagine he will require my immediate agreement to another of his propositions.'

Edwina shot her granddaughter a sharp look.

'Oh, did I not say?' Her tone was all innocent apology. 'The Viscount was exceedingly obliging in offering various options should I be unable to persuade you to give him back his cash.' She unfurled slender, white fingers and ticked them off. 'There was the Fleet for you; and Gin Alley for me. For him, first of all, of course, came my services as paramour to pay him in kind. He calculated six years before he was done…and so was I.'

'I'll speak to him,' Edwina spluttered. 'Enough is enough. The matter is at an end.'

'Because you say so?' Elizabeth choked a despairing laugh. 'No. You told me he was a powerful and influential man and I didn't want to believe you. Unfortunately, now I do. I think money is not so terribly important to him now. He didn't mention the cash in his letter. He wants reprisal. It appears you have outwitted him and he will not be bested in this.' She jerked her head away, staring sightlessly into September sunshine. 'I believe you meant well and hoped to see me safely settled with him, but…' Elizabeth sighed a sigh that seemed to well from deep within. 'But I think your friend has his own ideas. I think he will make a bad enemy. What *have* you done, Grandmama?'

Elizabeth held her breath as she leaned over the child's scrawny shoulder. Valiantly ignoring a stirring in his wiry hair and the acrid smell of his unwashed clothes, she gently took the piece of chalk from his bony fingers. 'Samuel is spelled with the *u* before the *e*,' she told him, correcting his work by writing his name again beneath his own spidery effort. She returned his chalk, and with a smile moved on. Clara Parker was next in line. She was about ten years old and Elizabeth was aware the little girl hero-worshipped her. Glassy grey eyes were adoring her while a dirty finger twirled a stringy strand of mousy hair. 'Have you finished your writing, Clara?' Elizabeth asked on a smile.

'Yes, m'm,' Clara responded gruffly with an unobtrusive little stroke at the blue wool of Elizabeth's oldest, least fashionable pelisse. 'I'd like my hair in curls,' Clara added shyly, twirling faster at her rat-tail tress, while gazing admiringly at Elizabeth's pearlescent ringlets peeping from beneath an old felt bonnet.

Elizabeth's hand hovered over the child's head. Gingerly she took a section of limp hair and wound it round and round a slender finger. Carefully she withdrew her digit from the loose spiral. 'Now do some letters,' she whispered at the girl's glowing, grubby face. Clara immediately cradled the treasured curl on a palm. 'Come, attend to your lesson or the Reverend will be cross!' Elizabeth looked at Hugh as, hands clasped behind his back, he leaned forward to listen to a youngster falteringly reading the few lines of scripture he had chalked on his slate.

Conscious of Elizabeth's petite figure moving closer, Hugh arrowed her a smile and straightened. Taking out his watch he tapped it indicatively. It was time for school to end. His double clap brought heads up. Then the score or more pupils filed forward at the signal and handed their boards and chalk to the Reverend. The warehouse emptied slowly, the children becoming jocular as they emerged into welcome evening sunshine that warmed their chilled little bodies. Finally it was just Hugh and Elizabeth left in the cold, dingy interior of the warehouse.

'It's a shame this window doesn't face south and let in more light and warmth,' Elizabeth observed as she peered up at a small pane of glass and the uninspiring sight of a neighbouring warehouse's sooty wall.

Hugh grimaced agreement as he locked away the few precious articles into the cupboard. 'Without Mr Grantham's benevolence in allowing us this room, the school would have to shut. It's here or the vicarage, and I don't think Mother would relish the thought of twenty mucky urchins shedding lice on to our carpets.' He laughed a trifle uneasily at the uncharitable admission. 'If only there were funds to build a parish hall...' he sighed.

Closing and locking the warehouse door, he gallantly drew Elizabeth's arm through his to aid her progress as they started negotiating a path over uneven, slimy cobbles. In front of them lay a ten-minute walk through the back lanes of Wapping to the vicarage. Once there, Elizabeth would graciously accept a cup of tea and a slice of dry cake from Hugh's elderly, widowed mother, before being taken back to Connaught Street in Hugh's gig.

Hugh touched a gloved hand to his hat as a woman shouted a greeting from a doorway. She was lounging comfortably, basking in a shaft of dying sunlight that glossed a paint-peeling, bottle-green doorway and mellowed crumbling brickwork. As she exposed her face to the soothing warmth, the pipe gripped in her teeth angled skyward. A child, barely knee high, huddled into her skirts, two tiny thumbs lost in its mouth.

Before they had properly passed the tranquil scene, a man dressed in vest and patched breeches appeared. Grabbing the woman's arm, he shoved her inside with a string of slurred curses concerning the lateness of his dinner and her sluttish ways. She answered him in some colourful language of her own, but slunk away into the darkness with the child wailing in her wake.

Hugh shook his head and increased his pace.

'Lady Elizabeth…?'

The call was so buffered by neighbourhood cacophony that at first both Hugh and Elizabeth herself missed being hailed and continued discussing the likelihood of an influenza epidemic.

'Lady Elizabeth Rowe…?'

The questioning shout strengthened, bringing both Elizabeth and the vicar to an abrupt halt. Extracting her arm from Hugh's, Elizabeth falteringly approached the nearest tenement doorway. Several pairs of eyes swivelled to her. Even after all these months of hurrying back and forth through these alleys on a Sunday afternoon, she still drew curious stares from the locals. The women, especially, picked over with jealous eyes her blonde hair and fine features and her clean serviceable garb. Hugh was a more prosaic sight to his parishioners. Elizabeth knew that her safe passage through the slums was wholly attributable to the respect these people had for their local minister. But never before had anyone addressed her directly. Never would she have expected them to.

'Did someone call me?' Her pupils widened, blackening her eyes as she squinted into the dim interior of the building. The unwholesome stench of rancid food and unwashed humanity had her retreating a pace. In any case, all that was discernible was a broken stairway and a few huddled figures propped against the newel post. About to turn thankfully away, sure she had been mistaken in thinking she'd been summoned, a woman slid from behind the splintered doorframe and simply stared at her. Elizabeth stared back. She knew her. Beneath the sallowing bruise on her face that extended from brow to lip and the matted dark brown hair that tumbled wildly about her thin shoulders was a person she should recognise. But she couldn't fit a name to that poor, gaunt visage.

The woman laughed wryly at the confusion on Elizabeth's face, but the sound couldn't escape her bobbing throat. Her head fell forward into one quivering, cadaverous hand. 'You don't remember me, do you? That's not surprising: I like to think I don't look the same.' It was a cultured voice, just a hint of cockney dialect taking the edge off the vowels and running words together. She shook back her snarled hair, squinted sideways at Elizabeth, a poignant arrogance in the slant of her mouth, the tilt of her head. ''Ere, take a proper look. Know me now?' she challenged, adopting the local nasal twang for all its worth. 'Ain't a pretty sight no longer, wouldn't you say?'

'Jane? Jane Dawson?'

'As was. I married Colonel Selby, remember? Did well, didn't I?' she gutturally mocked herself. She stared at Elizabeth with eyes like wet black pebbles. 'I certainly thought I'd done better than you that year,' she commented slyly and chuckled as the colour rose beneath Elizabeth's pale complexion. 'Never can tell how things'll turn out...' she added with a toss of her tangles. She cocked her head to take a look at Hugh Clemence who was hovering a pace or two behind watching, listening to their exchange. 'You married now? To him?' Jane demanded, cuffing her nose and sniffing. 'You a parson's wife?'

'No! No, the Reverend and I teach Sunday School together. In Barrow Road,' Elizabeth explained with a hand flick back the way they'd just come. Aware that this unusual discourse between a lady of quality and one of their own had drawn inquisitive bystanders, Elizabeth placed a hand on Jane's thin arm and drew her outside to shelter behind the open door. 'What on earth has happened? Where is your husband? Is the Colonel dead?' Elizabeth asked with a perplexed frown.

'Damned if I know,' Jane said on a dull guffaw. 'It turned out he wasn't my husband after all; he wasn't a colonel either. It transpired, my lady,' she mocked in a soft, precise drawl, 'that the bounder already had a wife in Yorkshire and another in Portugal.' She blinked rapidly and bit her lip before choking, 'I think he married the foreigner while in the army during the war. He lied about being invalided out and his rank and regiment. He was a sergeant who had been cashiered from the infantry for cowardice and thievery. I never did any better than you, with that Lieutenant Havering. Army bastards!' She spat. She looked Elizabeth up and down, her glittering black eyes lingering covetously on her fair, classical features. 'But that's not right. You've done well enough by the looks of things, if not as well as you ought. Looks like scandal slid off you like water off a duck's back...'

Elizabeth managed a wan smile. 'Not quite. But I've been lucky in that my grandmother—my maternal grandmother, that is—has never shunned me. In fact, without her, after my papa died a few years ago, I don't know how I would have survived...'

'Same way as me, I expect.' Jane's light spite transformed into a conversational, 'I heard that the old Dowager Marchioness cold-shouldered you.' She leaned forward, giggled conspiratorially, 'She always was a toffee-nosed, miserable old biddy. Do you remember our first time at Vauxhall, when you and Sally Treacher and me got lost in the walkways?'

Elizabeth bit her lip and laughed. 'Yes, I do. The Dowager nearly had an apoplexy!'

'So did my mama. She accused me of losing more than my shawl in the bushes that evening! That silly cow, Mrs Treacher, told her that Trelawney and his band of lusty chums were spotted in the same grove. They both needed reviving with hartshorn after that. When I found out we'd missed them, I was bloody angry...' she exclaimed on a ribald laugh.

Aware that Hugh had moved closer on hearing mention of that particular gentleman, Elizabeth demanded in a low tone, 'But what on earth has happened to you? Why is it come to this, Jane? What of your parents? They surely don't know how you're living?'

Jane put a hand to her trembling mouth, spoke from behind it in gasping bursts. 'They wouldn't care if I was dead. No, that's not true. They'd prefer it if I was. And it's come to this...because I loved him. Because when my father told me...he had discovered sordid details...of Frank's past...I wouldn't believe it. My papa told me to choose...return home with him...or stay with my bigamist...in which case they no longer had a daughter. So I chose...because I was sure he loved me...but he's gone...abandoned me...and our son.'

'You have a *son*?' Elizabeth whispered, aghast. 'Living *here*?' She shot an anxious glance at Hugh who was frowning back, listening intently to all that passed between the two women.

Jane nodded. 'Upstairs.' She jerked her head to indicate the doorway. 'Dosed little Jack with laudanum this evening. Keeps him quiet and out of harm's way.'

Elizabeth closed a firm hand on her friend's wrist. 'That is too much! Fetch the little lad now and come home with me to Marylebone. I shall see what can be done.'

Jane wrenched from her grip and backed off, eyes wild with terror. 'I can't do that. You don't understand. I can't do that. He'll never let me...not till I pay him...'

'Who? Who do you mean?'

''S'pect she means me,' came drifting in an oily drawl on the river-pungent air.

Elizabeth spun about to see a stocky man, sallow of complexion, with greasy-looking dark curls corkscrewing on to his wide forehead. His eyes were an incongruous bright blue, the edges a sunburst of creases as he squinted foxily at them. He slid along the wall as though he might have been spewed from one of the many doorways agape in the rotten brick. Reaching Jane, he slung a possessive, brawny arm about her shoulders. His hand clenched into a thick fist, making the muscle in his forearm jump beneath a matting of wiry hairs. Jane seemed to shrink, become ever more brittle beneath the mean embrace.

'Aren't yer goin' t'intradoos me to yer friend?' he silkily enquired. ''Course me 'n the Reverend's 'kwainted.' When Jane remained quiet with head lowered, he gave her thin body a brusque shake. 'No manners, gel? 'Oos the luvlie lady wiv the vicar?' The cap pushed to the back of his head at a jaunty angle was doffed in a travesty of respect. It was swept low towards his dirty dark trousers, before resting against a dapper corduroy waistcoat.

Hugh laid a heavy hand on Elizabeth's arm and determinedly drew her away. At the same time, he said coldly, 'I see you're at your old tricks, Leach. No dock work to keep you? Have you tried earning your own living?'

''S'not me, Reverend,' the man whined craftily. 'S'these bad girls wot know the tricks and get's me inta trouble. You ask 'm if'n they don't. Badgers me ta look out for'm, they do. So that's wot I do, 'cos I'm a carin' sorta feller.' He shook Jane masterfully again. 'Tell the vicar jus' 'ow good Leachie looks out fer yer.'

Jane raised wide, jet-black eyes. 'He does,' she whispered. 'Go away. I'm sorry...I shouldn't have troubled you...I beg you not to come back...' Grabbing her grubby skirts in her fists, she pulled out of the man's restraint and was swallowed by darkness inside the dank portal.

'Come, Elizabeth!' Hugh's voice was aquiver with urgency and anger.

'No!' Elizabeth swivelled back to glare at the swarthy man who was leering unpleasantly at her. She watched his tongue tip protrude, then work its slow way about his fleshy lips.

Heavy lids weighted over eyes that crawled her primly dressed figure while rough, wiry fingers thoughtfully massaged an unshaven chin. 'Don't yer go takin' no 'eed o' Jane now,' he growled. 'She's poor wiv manners at times. I've 'ad ta speak sharp wiv 'er over that 'afore. 'Specially when *she's* sharp wiv the gents 'oo want ta treat 'er right. You come back an' see Leachie offen as yer like…'cos I've a notion there's plenty a gent might jus' luv ta treat you right. Might even be me.'

Elizabeth opened her mouth to flay him with her disgust but could only think that, if she did, Jane's plight would be that much worse. Her impotent rage put her teeth on edge, curled her shaking fingers.

Leachie recognised her angry frustration and smirked, then laughed raucously, bending over at the waist. Elizabeth turned away and blindly groped for Hugh Clemence's arm so he could lead her away.

'Be sensible, Elizabeth. Listen to what Reverend Clemence is telling you. These vermin are not to be trifled with. They are vicious miscreants who have their own codes; their own underworld hierarchies…'

Elizabeth continued shaking her head at her grandmother until Edwina flung her hands up in despair. She glared at Hugh Clemence, who was still standing close to the door as though uncertain whether he would be welcomed further into the parlour. 'Oh, you speak to her again, vicar. But know this: I hold you responsible for it all. You should never have begun this nonsense of encouraging a gentlewoman to slum visit. See what you have done! Oh, never mind.' She illustrated her impatience with his red-faced distress by flapping a fat hand. 'For now, just impress again on Lady Elizabeth the dangers of associating with this lowlife. And that she must never return.'

'I do not need to again be told,' Elizabeth enunciated angrily. 'I do not need you to blame Hugh for my behaviour. I am a woman of nearly twenty-nine and quite capable of making up my own mind about helping the needy. Today I have sincerely understood just how important it is that such work continues. I have seen with my own eyes just how squalid and mean life can be. I have had paraded before my own eyes living proof that there, but for the grace of God, go I. And if you think for one moment I am about to abandon an old friend, and her son, to that foul man...'

Hugh hastened forward. 'Listen, please, Elizabeth. It is not simply a case of rescuing a...er, fallen woman and her child. Men like Leach tie the wretched creatures to them with debts as well as fear.' An unsteady hand scraped through his brown hair. 'I doubt you have heard of Old Mother Leach. I pray you have not. She is a notorious fence and a bawdy-house keeper. Her name should bring trepidation to the hearts of all decent folk. Nathaniel Leach, whom you met today, is her son and in the same line of business. He knows nothing else. That isn't to excuse him, it's simply the truth. They deal in prostitutes and pickpockets. They are parasites of the worst kind.'

'*I don't care!*' Elizabeth raged, her beautiful eyes sparking blue flame.

'Please listen,' Hugh again begged. 'As hard as it must be for you to accept, the sad truth is that Mrs Selby is very much in his power and unlikely to leave. Leach will have gained her trust by posing as a concerned friend when she was vulnerable and isolated. He might have presented food or clothes, insinuating they are gifts, then introduced her to an usurer when it is time to pay. He will have told her how easy it is to borrow to settle her dues; how soon she and her son will be able to escape to a better life if she only does as he bids. He will have snared her with her own hope. None of it ever comes about. Only the debt collector comes about. So does Leach, to take what she earns from clients he finds her. He'll give her a little back, keep a tally and encourage her to borrow more. So the debt mounts and the trap closes. She will never have the means to break free; Leach will make very sure of that. And inhuman as it may seem to you, her parents will never now want to know how you found her…or where…'

'Give me some money, Grandmama,' Elizabeth demanded, turning her back on Hugh's pained expression. 'I am begging you as never before to allow me some of my inheritance to help someone far, far worse off than I have ever been.' Heartfelt appeal throbbed in her voice, blazed in her violet eyes.

Edwina stalked away. 'This is madness, Elizabeth. Have you heard *nothing* the Reverend has said? You cannot help in these instances. Do you think I will allow you to involve us with such scum? Do you imagine this Leach is likely to allow you to steal his meal ticket from under his nose without a fight? If he discovers we are two women living alone save for servants, he might send his evil accomplices to rob us blind. He might murder us in our beds!' Edwina pointed a finger at Hugh Clemence. 'Am I not right in m'fears, vicar?' she asked loudly, daring him to contradict.

'Possibly, Mrs Sampson,' Hugh admitted on a lingering sigh. 'And, forgive me, but there is no peace in agreeing with you.'

Edwina nodded vehemently, her salt and pepper ringlets dancing crazily. 'I'll listen to no more foolishness from you, m'girl. I forbid you to go back there. If you defy me, I swear you will be sorry!'

The door slammed after her grandmother's dumpy, bristling figure. Elizabeth looked at Hugh. He needed no more encouragement than that doe-eyed glance. Approaching her, he took both her small, cold hands into the warm comfort of his. 'I'm so sorry, Elizabeth. It's my fault. Your grandmother is right to reprimand me. Involving you in a project in such a stew was not wise. Had I not done so, this evening's chance meeting with Mrs Selby would never have come about.'

'I'm glad it did,' Elizabeth interrupted quietly, squeezing at his fingers. 'At last I feel there is an opportunity for me to truly make a difference. And please don't feel guilty. I volunteered to become involved in Barrow Road. And I want to continue helping. More so than ever now.'

'If you truly mean that, Elizabeth, you must allow me to protect you properly,' Hugh uttered hoarsely. 'You must let me shield you with every means in my power. I would be so very honoured if you would allow me to protect you with my name and my humble vocation...'

Elizabeth squeezed his hands more firmly to make him stop. 'Please don't say any more, Hugh. Just know that I am greatly obliged to count you amongst my true and loyal friends.' Disengaging her hands, she choked a wry little laugh. 'It has been rather an exhausting day, to say the least. I think retiring early is in order. First, I suppose I had best find my grandmama and make my peace. 'Twill in some small part help me sleep.'

Hugh managed a wavering smile and a fleeting touch of his lips to her fingertips before she gently withdrew.

'No, the long-sleeved one, Josie. There seems to be a chill in the air tonight,' Elizabeth told her maid. Obediently, Josie folded away the frothy sleeveless nightdress and replaced it in the clothes press. She removed another and began shaking out heavy brushed cotton that dragged on the floor.

Elizabeth wandered to the fire in her undergarments, holding the fragrant warmth of the washing cloth flat against her face. With a sigh, she moved her face up and down against flannel-covered palms, scouring away the day's grime. It dropped from her fingers to plop back into the shallow bowl, slopping splashes of steaming water onto her writing desk. Retrieving and wringing out the cloth, Elizabeth wiped her arms, dipping her head as she washed a shoulder, reached beneath her heavy hair to scrub her nape. Her lowered eyes encountered the note on her bureau. She immediately relinquished the cloth and picked up the letter, her heart missing a beat. With all the commotion and consternation surrounding her reunion with Jane Selby, she had forgotten about the Viscount and her own problems. But then, in comparison with what she had witnessed today, her feud with Stratton paled into insignificance. She had a doting grandmother, enough food to eat, clean clothes and bedding. She had no problems.

Water droplets had swirled with ink to form a small black pearl upon the paper. She touched a fingertip to it; withdrew it to read again the curt suggestion they once more meet. *Perhaps return your family's jewellery* was untouched by greyish smears. The words were clear and precise and seemed to leap significantly out from the paper. And what came to her next was so simple yet so shocking that she clutched at the bed edge and sat down.

If she could brave the pitfalls of Wapping on a Sunday afternoon, she could do this. What had she to lose? No good name and no keepsake. Both were already gone. And if she didn't act immediately, while the horrors of Jane's predicament still churned her stomach and the thought of a small boy drugged into oblivion on a filthy bed sent bile to her throat, she might never in her life act from true, selfless compassion at all. The seed was in her mind, needing just a sprinkling of stalwart courage to help it blossom.

The note drifted from her quivering fingers onto the bureau. Elizabeth stared out of the window into the gathering dusk. Treetops swayed close to the glass in a stirring breeze. It wasn't so late. Barely nine of the clock, she guessed. She knew Edwina had already retired. She had said her goodnights to her grandmother in her chamber, kissed away her grumpiness and smoothed her soft cheek with appeasing fingers.

She glanced at Josie; her maid turned the nightgown she was holding up before the fire to air it. Satisfied it was cosy enough, Josie approached, holding out the snug garment.

'Not that one, Josie,' her mistress said with a note of hysterical humour. 'My blue velvet gown and black satin cloak…the one with the hood. No, not in which to retire.' A shrill giggle escaped her as Josie gaped in astonishment. 'I must yet go out; and, I'm sorry, but you must accompany me, I'm afraid.'

Chapter Seven

If he deemed it unusual for a lady to arrive, unexpectedly, at nearly ten of the clock, then demand to see his master, the man kept the surprise to himself.

Elizabeth seated herself on the chair the butler indicated, a gracious dip of her head his only thanks. In turn she indicated that Josie take a seat, too. Josie obediently sank down, but with her goggle-eyed stare clinging to her mistress's face. Elizabeth was conscious she had stupefied her maid by acting in such a bizarre manner.

'I shall see if Viscount Stratton is available to see you,' the butler intoned, pessimism barely discernible. Elizabeth again inclined her blonde head in haughty acceptance of his cool courtesy. Perhaps the man's sang-froid indicated that it was fairly customary for women to turn up at late hours, soliciting an audience with his lordship.

The fact that the Viscount was at home was both alarming and reassuring. From Marylebone to Mayfair, she'd been alternately fretting or praying that her reckless sortie might be in vain. Once out and upon the road in a hired hackney, her daring had ebbed a little. Logic had flowed in its stead.

A hedonist such as Trelawney was unlikely to spend his evenings at home alone twiddling his thumbs. If he wasn't abroad, it was likely he might have a pack of cronies around him, which would only make things so much worse. Well, it was too late to demand to know if his master already had company. She peered after the smartly uniformed butler disappearing into the heart of the quiet house.

Elizabeth refused to be impressed by the splendour of this residence. She refused to look about at all to admire the soaring marble pillars, or the glorious paintings, or the chandeliers that blinded with diamond-fire as scores of candles flickered amid icy droplets.

She had been reared amongst such grandeur, she reminded herself. In her papa's heyday, they had leased just such wonderful residences as this. During her come out, they had rented a Nash townhouse in Caledon Square which was the envy of all who were invited within. Wellington had visited; so had numerous other dukes, earls and titled families. She was unmoved by evidence of a hefty chandler's bill, she decided, sweeping a jaundiced eye over stately mahogany furniture and a huge gilt-framed mirror. Her attention was arrested by the pretty unicorn central to its intricate carving.

So, she had been correct in thinking the Viscount wasn't on his uppers. Which meant her theory, voiced earlier to her grandmother, was sound. Stratton wanted retribution. The fruits of his ill-gotten gains were displayed all around. Porcelain artefacts resting on polished surfaces were probably priceless spoils from confiscated cargoes. Her meandering eye returned to a delicate jade figurine close by. Her suspicions as to its provenance were interrupted by the sound of footsteps. The butler had reappeared; behind him came two footmen and a maid. All were dressed in the same neat uniform of black with dull gold embroidered waistcoat and braid trim. Quite a sober livery, she had to admit, as she recalled denigrating it as vulgar earlier today. The servants appeared industrious, while giving her discreet glances.

Elizabeth had witnessed few housemaids dusting so late. Either the Viscount was a hard task master or his menials were curious for a glimpse of the bold hussy visiting a bachelor at his home, uninvited, at such a late hour. She frowned at Josie, gesturing at her to straighten in the chair and look less cowed by the whole affair.

'The Viscount will see you now.'

Elizabeth identified vague surprise lilting the butler's adenoidal tone as she got to her stylishly shod little feet. Her chin edged up; only the rim of colour accentuating her sharp cheekbones might have betrayed how jittery she actually felt. 'Good,' was the sum of her acknowledgement to the favour. Then, 'Please find my maid a little refreshment while she waits for me.' She ignored his raised eyebrows and Josie's quivering. She knew the poor girl simply wanted to be left alone to shrink against the wall.

I am not afraid, neither am I ashamed…beat through her head in time with her footsteps as she followed the butler over a plush carpet. As he came to a halt, pivoted precisely to open the door, then marshalled her within, she clung to the haunting image of Jane Selby and her little son. What was her own humbling compared to their pitiful predicament?

The Viscount was ready to receive her. He was standing, with one arm propped against a high mantel, one booted foot resting against an ornate brass fender. On a table close to a fireside chair was a brandy balloon containing a considerable amount. A book had been placed open, face-down, as though he had just reluctantly relinquished it to gain his feet. It was such an unexpectedly homely scene and one that she would never have associated with Ross Trelawney, bounty hunter, that for a moment she felt disorientated…tempted to apologise for disturbing him. The words were swallowed unuttered.

She realised, with a wrench, that the cosy tableau reminded her of Thorneycroft and her dear papa: a glass of cognac, a weighty tome laid open by the blazing logs. How many quiet evenings had they spent so, happy in each other's company, in their countryside retreat, before her stepmother's arrival? But for her papa's need to remarry and produce a male heir to prevent his detested cousin gaining the entailed estate, it might have continued so… Had she only been born a boy, things might have been so different…for both of them…

'Come in…please,' Ross invited, breaking into her wistful thoughts. He extended a hand to welcome her further into the oak-panelled small salon.

Elizabeth felt herself flushing at his unfazed manner and civility. To cover her confusion at what she knew was a shameful intrusion and breach of etiquette, she blurted out, 'I know I should not have come. I realise it is quite outrageous behaviour. But…but as you and I have no good reputations to keep, I thought…as there is nothing to lose, you would not mind.'

He smiled a lop-sided smile. 'I don't mind.'

Elizabeth nodded, moistened her lips. 'It is important, or I would not have come.' Small, white teeth sank into her lower lip. She was repeating herself unnecessarily. He had already gallantly accepted her explanations. *The lady doth protest too much, I think*…echoed in all its sarcasm, in her mind.

'Of course it's important,' he soothed.

She looked at him, really looked at him, but in glances that quickly strayed. Yet they lingered long enough on his broad shoulders clothed in fine white cambric, his dark, angular features and dusky hair, to come to a profoundly disturbing conclusion. At first sight, he would appear the perfect man. Any woman ignorant of his dubious reputation and lineage would simply see before her an imposing, handsome gentleman who enjoyed a quiet evening reading amid the trappings of his wealth. It would have been unremarkable if, in the other fireside chair, his refined lady wife worked at her tapestry.

She had supposed him an ill-educated oaf, yet she had no proof it was so. And this domesticity wasn't stage-managed for her benefit. He had no warning of her visit. Even if he had, why would he bother seeking the good opinion of a rude, supercilious little bitch? She had simply caught him unawares about his private business. She was seeing the man, not the myth.

'I take it you received my letter earlier?' he prompted, interrupting her startling insight.

'Yes. 'Tis why I'm here.'

He nodded. 'Thank you for responding so quickly.'

She shot him a sharp, violet look, searching his face for sarcasm.

'Would you like some tea?'

'No,' she snapped. 'No, thank you,' she amended, recalling her manners. 'I think it best to get directly to business.' She flushed again as she saw his smile at her bluntness. 'That is…I cannot tarry.'

'I understand.'

He was being too polite. Far too polite. It was as though the ruthless stranger who had menaced her with abuse and a harrowing future had never existed.

As though exactly reading her thoughts, he volunteered quietly, 'As you've found the courage to come here this evening, my lady, I must find the humility to apologise for my crude behaviour when last we met.'

'I'd rather you did not,' she rebuffed him immediately, increasingly unsettled by this change in him.

'Why not? Because my apology might demand yours?'

'I've no need to apologise!' she burst out hotly.

'Yes, you have,' he mildly corrected. 'I imagine you feel as ashamed of your conduct as I do of mine.'

'A rude, supercilious little bitch ruined by scandal never feels obliged to say sorry,' she whipped out icily, but her face was flaming beneath his unwanted perception, his unwanted chivalry.

'We'll leave proprieties till later then,' he said drily, but with an indulgent smile.

'Proprieties are not required between us at any time. This is not a social call,' she retorted, flustered by this bewildering need to keep him in the role of uncouth lout. 'I said a few days ago that I hoped never again to endure your presence. My feelings have not changed.'

'So, why are you here?' He pushed away from the mantel and took two steps towards her. As she back-paced in time with his advance, he halted and swung his head sideways to frown in defeat. 'If my company is that odious and you already regret coming, go. Go away now. I'll not stop you.'

If only she could do just that: whip about and storm out! But she was a Marquess's daughter and above being dismissed by a barbarian such as he! Elizabeth's insides somersaulted with frustration and humiliation. She wouldn't go…couldn't go. How could she leave without the necklace when it had taken every ounce of audacity she could summon to come and fetch it?

Ross watched colour ebbing and flowing beneath her translucent complexion. He could sense her turmoil as she strove to curb her temper and force herself to be pleasant. And as his eyes discreetly roved her alluringly garbed little figure, her pearly hair, he felt the crazy need to stalk her down, corner her…just so he could take her in his arms and comfort her. For the moment, though, he judged keeping his distance and tendering another olive branch might be the best move. 'If you want to stay, come and sit down. I can't talk business if you're going to hide in the shadows.'

'I'm not hiding…I'm not afraid…'

'Very well,' he conceded softly. 'You're not hiding and you're not afraid of me. That's good. Come and sit down.' He pivoted slowly, watching her evade him by keeping to the perimeter of the room on her way to a fireside chair. He returned to the wingchair opposite, mirroring her pose by perching on the edge. Lifting his glass indicatively, he asked, 'Would you like a drink? Wine? Ratafia?'

'I don't drink.'

'Ah, yes. Good works.' He smiled. 'Are you a member of some temperance society?' He took a long sip while awaiting her reply.

'No. But I've sympathy with the cause,' she said, primly eyeing his glass. 'I've witnessed the damage alcohol wreaks on poor wretches.'

'Where? Where have you seen that?' he asked interestedly, placing down his brandy and frowning at her.

'Bridewell, Newgate, the back alleys about Wapping where

I assist at Sunday School…' She broke off, grateful for that timely reminder of her reason for being here, alone with him, at this time of the night, flouting all decent codes of conduct.

Ross leaned forward to rest forearms on knees. 'You prison visit and slum visit?'

She was aware of the surprise, and the hint of disapproval in his tone. 'I haven't risked fresh opprobrium in coming here this evening, my lord, to discuss the charities I support. Might we please get to business? I am keen to return home before I am missed.'

'Edwina doesn't know you are here?'

Elizabeth gave a slight shake of her head. 'No,' she murmured. 'But I doubt she would raise much objection if she did know…' She dropped her eyes, unable to meet the humour lurking in the hazel depths of his at that unguarded observation.

The silence lengthened and she glanced at him from beneath a curtain of lashes, then again more openly. He held her gaze easily that time, moved his glass, gesturing that he was ready and willing to listen. Now the time had come her mind seemed to have frozen. She had lost all her clever phrases, all her rehearsed persuasiveness. All that battered monotonously at her fraught mind was the need to recover her precious necklace. So, unembellished, that's what tumbled out.

'I want back my necklace.'

'I know you do.'

'May I have it?'

'Yes.'

She stared at him suspiciously.

'Now you'd like to know what I want in return.'

She nodded, a jerky movement that swayed silverish tresses against the graceful column of her alabaster neck.

He watched her eyes clinging to his. They both knew what he wanted. She'd spurned his sweet talk, so now it was time to get down to brass tacks and proposition her properly. Yet he couldn't immediately do it. And he wasn't sure why. God knows he'd had enough practice taking on mistresses over the years. Perhaps it was that poignant look of resignation making him hesitate. Of course, she'd heard it all before, lots of times, from other men. He noticed her pearly teeth sinking deeper into her lower lip to keep it still…but that might be simply to prevent a tirade of disgust hurtling at him. She was conquering her pride, solemnly awaiting the further indignity he was about to deliver. That's how she would see it; just as she read his attempts at conciliation as calculated sophistry now he was on home territory. He took an abrupt swig of brandy, noting that his prevarication was unnerving rather than reassuring her. Her fingers were in knots in her lap. He sensed a gentle protectiveness washing through him, again making him want to comfort her. Intense irritation swiftly followed. She'd come to him, uninvited, risking, as she'd rightly said, all manner of censure. She was here to barter. She knew exactly what he wanted. So why couldn't he open negotiations? What the hell else did she expect he might say? Marry me?

'I've decided that Edwina's original offer to settle her dues wasn't such a poor suggestion…' He heard the words and supposed they must be his.

Elizabeth frowned, trying to bring to mind, in her numbed state, what that offer was. Then she remembered. Her violet eyes widened expressively on him. 'She won't release my dowry for your sake. I've asked her several times before to advance a small amount to me but she refuses. She really is a tight-fist,' she confided on a sweet, self-conscious smile.

And that did it. Gentleness was back with a vengeance. She was actually looking at him with something akin to shy camaraderie. For the first time she was letting him see the real woman behind the defensive shell of hauteur. And he knew it was what he'd been waiting for: just a glimpse of the lovable, vivacious creature he'd watched from afar a decade ago. For the first time, too, he felt more kindly disposed to Edwina for getting him embroiled in this mess. 'I'll agree to your grandmother's terms,' he said hoarsely. He cleared his throat, then added, 'It's what she planned all along.'

'She planned getting me wed all along,' Elizabeth contributed to the conversation with the same trace of amicable confiding in her voice and smile. And then, barely established, it was gone. She finally comprehended his meaning. She moistened her lips, waiting for him to scoff at Edwina's idiotic presumption he might take a scandal-wrecked woman to wife. Just as he had before, at her home. But he didn't laugh; he simply looked at her, his golden eyes merging mesmerically with hers. Her gaze fled to her lap; slowly she rose to her feet, one hand behind her steadying against the chair as though frightened her strength might collapse.

So he wanted money after all, not retribution. He wasn't quite the noble savage she had thought. And she wasn't sure whether she hated him more or less. He believed she had come here to brazenly broker a marriage. He had told her, had he not, that he judged her the instigator in this derisory plot to snare him as a husband. He probably thought he was doing her a huge favour by succumbing to the lure of her fortune. Thus, he would not laugh now, during the prelude to his proposal, but he was sure to later when he recounted to his chums how she had come begging him to make an honest woman of her. He would laugh harder on boasting how well he would upkeep his riotous life-style with her dowry and the plump annuity that came with it. She felt her heart thumping achingly slowly, her pride smarting equally painfully. If he imagined she was just some risible toy who would allow herself to be sold, then show gratitude for a soulless sham of a marriage, he was much mistaken.

'If you would allow me two weeks' grace, my lord,' was forced out of her stiltedly, 'I promise to persuade Edwina to be sensible. She is already wavering over the whole stupid affair. I know you have been patient, but if I might again beg your forebearance, I vow she will soon relent.'

Having looked at her, listened to her, Ross stared at the toes of his boots for a moment before pushing to his feet and immediately walking away. He was seething mad, yet simultaneously felt crushed, drained.

So much for being a sentimental fool and taking the honourable way. She'd refused to even acknowledge his tentative overture…his pathetic fantasy, as she no doubt still termed a union between a Cornish brigand and a Marquess's daughter. Having spent all his adult years studiously avoiding the marriage trap, he'd actually begun to propose, and before the words were properly out, it was made very clear they were unwelcome. A double-handed grip tightened on the mantel's cold marble. 'Very well. Two weeks only. If no firm decision is reached by then, I'll dispose of the suite. I'll get a servant to escort you home,' he clipped out curtly.

Violet eyes flew to his rigid, dark profile as he strode determinedly towards the door. He was going to make her leave, empty-handed. She could sense exasperation in him beneath that icy courtesy and guessed that it sprang from having been denied early access to her money. She had no time to further ponder its cause: he was reaching for the door handle. Instinctively she pursued him, raised a hand to detain him, fearful he might dismiss her right now. 'No, you don't understand. I want…that is…I hoped that you would let me have back my necklace.'

'So I shall, when settlement is reached,' he growled, his eyes riveted on the slender, white hand straddling the breadth of his forearm.

'No…tonight. I must have back my necklace tonight…'

'Why?'

Elizabeth's timid violet gaze floundered beneath the narrowed hawk's eyes just visible between those long black lashes. A gleam of curiosity was darkening into something else. Something that alarmed yet oddly reassured her. She swallowed and stared fixedly at his abrasive chin. He might want her out of his house…but he did still want her. Her hand slipped unobtrusively from his shirt-sleeve, as though she hoped he might never have noticed it spreadeagled there. 'I have come here specifically to collect my necklace…please don't make me leave without it. I swear to you I can persuade Edwina to give you back your money, if you will only be patient a while longer.' Her voice was light and breathy. Only the colour creeping beneath her skin betrayed her desperate uneasiness.

'That's not good enough. I want a firm contract before I'll let you have it. You can't expect me to give you back what little collateral I hold,' he reasoned in a voice of gravelly velvet. 'I only have your word that there is anything at all of value in a bank vault.'

'You've had time enough to find out. I would have imagined a grasping opportunist would already have done so,' she sniped, uncontrollable frustration making her insolent.

'I've been too busy grasping other opportunities,' he returned silkily.

The small space between them seemed to throb with tension yet she couldn't seem to withdraw. When she finally managed a step back, she knew before his hands moved that he would bring her close again. His touch felt warm, firm, yet not callous as he swung her about, stranding her between his body and the door.

Her heart seemed to have jumped to her throat; she could sense the wild pulse there. Her tongue tip wet her lower lip, then hid. She peeked up into his thick-lashed watching eyes, wishing he'd say something. He did, and she immediately wished he'd not.

'Tell me why you came here tonight.'

'I've already told you: to collect my necklace.'

'And you imagined this hard-hearted villain would simply hand it over? I don't think so. What did you plan offering me in exchange?'

'A sincere promise that I would extract your payment from Edwina,' she whispered, frowning at the onyx stone set in his snowy cravat.

'You could have written that in a note. Besides, it's not much of an incentive for a hardened rake. I'm afraid I still don't think so,' he purred. A tanned hand spanned her ivory chin, jerking it up. 'Shall I tell you my theory?' He shifted his fingers so their length caressed a cheek as she nodded.

'I think, my lady,' he said softly, 'that you came here, in person, with every intention of tempting me to take a few liberties with you. And you would allow me to take just a few, wouldn't you? Whet my appetite and my trust that you'd deliver what I wanted another night…so long as I delivered what you wanted tonight. You seem desperate to get back home with that necklace, which gives me quite a bargaining stake. So, promise me something else…something convincing, and we'll play it from there. Perhaps we might both end up satisfied.'

She jerked back, clattering her heels against the door. But her face burned where he'd touched it. Burned, too, because he'd put into words something she'd not allowed herself to acknowledge. From the first moment she'd scrambled into fine clothes, prettified her hair, misted her body with her favourite perfume, she'd been…primping in his honour…before quitting the house. 'You're despicable,' she whispered in a shaking voice.

'You've never believed me anything else. Have you?'

Ross observed raw emotion tightening her lovely features. He could tell she was torn between stamping and demanding he give her what she wanted, or ceding and giving him a taste of what he wanted. She was favouring trying just a little flirtatiousness, but didn't know if it would work. What made him smile so wryly was that he knew. And he'd settle for that, because it was a game at which he excelled. If he chose to, he could lead her from one kiss to heaven…or hell. He could make that soft, silky skin that had shivered beneath his palms burn with passion, turn her choked little insults into moans of pleasure. Maybe…he mocked himself, as his eyes wandered her fragile, stony face, her eyes alight with purple fire. Tonight, for his ego's sake, he would take just one kiss, then take his future wife home. Those were his terms, his only terms.

'One kiss,' Elizabeth bit out. 'One kiss only and then you give me the necklace.'

'One kiss?' Ross echoed scornfully. 'I thought I said be credible…'

'One kiss!' Elizabeth wailed, a sob of panic in her voice.

'Very well, if you insist.' There was barely a hint of triumph in his eyes as he drew her forward.

Her eyes were closed tight by the time she was against him. After a heart-stopping moment, when there was nothing other than the sensation of being held against a warm, male body, they fluttered open again.

'Put your arms around me,' he said as she met the hot golden glow in his eyes.

She hesitated for a moment, then her arms rose to rest woodenly against the sides of his broad torso.

'Not there. About my neck,' Ross instructed with all the ardour of a man tutoring a pupil in combat skills.

Elizabeth obediently moved her hands to slide up the front of his muscled chest and hover on his shoulders. But her mouth clamped in a hard, mutinous little line.

'About my neck…'

'You're too tall, I can't reach,' she snapped.

'I've had no complaints before…'

'Well, now you have mine…' she commented icily.

'Perhaps if we sat down…'

'No!' Elizabeth cried, flustered, fretting he might lead her to the sofa set back against the wall. It was long enough to take someone supine. She guessed it might be her. With that disturbing knowledge motivating them, her hands shot up past his powerful shoulders and linked behind his nape. She felt the stroke of his long thick hair against her quivering fingers.

'See how easy it can be, Elizabeth,' Ross murmured. 'Now you've learned to curb that temper, and take a little good advice, you'll make me an excellent, dutiful wife…'

Her violet eyes flew open, her jaw dropped in absolute astonishment. He smiled crookedly at the unwitting invitation of her soft, slack mouth. 'Just a joke…I'll take you the way you are,' he murmured before his lips swooped to cover hers.

This isn't right, was all that paraded back and forth through her head as her knees buckled. No one had kissed her like this before. She had been infatuated with Randolph Havering for two months, and he had never kissed her with such tenderness, such devotion that her bones began melting. Never before had she deliciously shivered beneath male fingers trailing her nape, her collarbone, her ears, every available exposed part of skin, while a careful onslaught of caressing lips and teasing tongue on her mouth made her sigh at its seductive sweetness. Never before had any gentleman during her short debut taken a liberty and made her feel as though her body was swirling in such honeyed pleasure she might die if it stopped. She was losing her mind. And that's why she drew a shuddering breath from his mouth and made it stop.

Working her lips back and forth, she endeavoured to break free from the dangerous magic, while her head chanted, *It's seduction…just sly seduction…* For a moment she was sure he would let her go. The long fingers lost in her hair withdrew to curve over her fragile shoulders. Their mouths unsealed, his tongue tip lightly trailing her lower lip as though in parting salutation…then it was plunging back. This time she wanted it to stop at once; fought to make it stop. His mouth was hot and hard and hurting. This was no subtle wooing. This was selfish lechery: savage and punishing, and the more she twisted her face to free it, the more cruel the assault became. Finally she stood rigid in his arms and within a moment he lifted his dark head.

Two small palms flattened against the rock-like wall of his chest, then pushed. He remained unmoving but, unanchored, the momentum sent her back against the door. A hand went to soothe her throbbing mouth. Her eyes glittered odium. But all she could lash him with, was, 'I said just one kiss.'

'It was one; one for you and one for me.'

His expression was hard, sardonic. He was unmoved by either kiss, she knew. He'd gained little satisfaction from pleasing her or himself. It was all just an exercise, a lesson for her benefit: be amenable and I will be too. Show your claws and that suits me equally.

'Fetch my necklace, at once,' she commanded.

He ignored her demands. Reaching past her, he opened the door. 'As liberties go, my lady, I've taken better,' was all he said.

Elizabeth flung her petite frame back against the door, slamming it shut. 'My necklace!' she squeaked, almost incoherent with fury at his louche, insulting attitude. A small foot stamped down on polished mahogany. 'Fetch it now! You lying…cheating…bastard! You said I might have it. I swear I won't leave without it!' Tears of frustration sparkled in her night-blue eyes, her graceful, slender body a-quiver with temper.

Ross leaned a hand against the door, moved the other to touch her cheek, pursuing her evasive headflicks with idle doggedness until she gave in and allowed the caress. 'I don't recall ever being held hostage in my own home before. It's something I've always fancied: being held captive by a beautiful, belligerent woman. There…we've shared one pathetic fantasy already.'

Elizabeth shook free of his fingers, glared at him through misty eyes.

'If you're determined to wreck my reputation and remain here the night, the least you can do is make an honest man of me.' His thumb caught a sprinkling of tears sliding towards her mouth. 'Come,' he soothed, 'be sensible. I want to return your jewellery. In truth, I'd rather not have the trouble of selling it. But I also want back what I'm owed,' he added reasonably. 'Your dowry is what Edwina wants me to have. I'm not too proud to take it.'

'But you know it won't come unconditionally,' Elizabeth jeered on a watery choke. 'I'm surprised at you, my lord. You'll stoop to take a sullied woman to wife just to lay hands on her money. For a short while this evening, when I saw how well you live, I deemed you a gentleman of some standing.' She paused to sniff. ''Tis all show, is it not? I doubt you can call one candle your own. Now you want to procure my portion to squander!'

'Will you marry me, Elizabeth?' Ross asked quietly.

He watched the conflict on her face. Watched her large, luminous eyes raise upwards, slide sideways away from him as she delved deep to find a way to outwit him. She was weighing up whether to feed him false promises again; tell him whatever he wanted to hear, then rescind it all tomorrow. Would he be gullible enough to let her leave with her necklace on those terms?

'I should be pleased to accept your marriage proposal,' she finally ground out, in a voice throbbing with bitterness.

There was such resentment in her tone that it seemed natural to conclude she had decided against chicanery in the morning. 'I'm greatly honoured,' he said softly. 'I shall call tomorrow and speak with Edwina about the financial implications. But now, it's high time I took you home.'

'I shall return as I came: in a hackney cab, accompanied by my maid. I wouldn't dream of imposing on you. Fetch my necklace now,' was all she deigned to answer him.

'No.'

'No?' she gasped. 'No?' Her small fists flew up. Immediately they were covered by two large hands. She tried to jerk them free, crying, 'If you think I will let you treat me like this…'

'How am I treating you? Far better than you deserve, I think, Elizabeth. Do you really imagine I'll allow my fiancée to travel at night in a hired rig with a valuable gem in her possession and a maid for protection? I'll bring the necklace with me tomorrow when I meet with your grandmother.' He watched her eyes, saw the confliction of reason and vexation. 'You'll just have to trust me to do it. Come, I'll take you home.'

She opened her mouth to fling his courteous offer to escort her back in his face. She managed to bite that back, but not the note of sourness in her voice. 'If you are to kindly escort us, then I trust such a renowned warrior is man enough to protect me and the jewellery?'

Something in the amused twist to his mouth told her he

was anticipating the barb. 'It's nearly eleven o'clock at night, Elizabeth. What are you planning to do with it at such an hour? Wear it to a ball? Stake it at the tables? Pawn it?'

Elizabeth spontaneously coloured, yanked at her hands within his. A dawning comprehension in his eyes had them hardening, as were his fingers on hers. Abruptly he flung her hands aside with a muttered oath.

Once more at liberty, Elizabeth was soon out in the corridor and hastening towards the brightly lit vestibule. Although he let her alone, she knew he was following behind on the thick carpet. He had won, was all that beat repetitively in her aching head. She had come here to get something valuable and leave nothing but empty promises in her wake.

He had turned the tables on her so completely! She had agreed to wed him! Now he had her dowry and her jewellery. He was also suspicious of why she wanted the necklace so desperately. She had nothing other than the word of a renowned rogue that tomorrow he would return it to her. She had utterly failed herself and, more importantly, Jane Selby and her little son. She was a fool! An incompetent fool!

Chapter Eight

'I'll see you safely within doors.'

'There's no need!' Snatching her hand from his, Elizabeth swept disdainfully past and up the steps of Number Seven Connaught Street.

Ross signalled to his driver to wait and followed her to the base of the steps, where he braced a foot idly against the lowest. 'Elizabeth,' he called in a voice that was at one and the same time discreetly quiet yet authoritative.

An indefinable inflection accented her name, making her hesitate. Turning majestically by the door, she bestowed a quizzical look. Inwardly she felt piqued that she couldn't continue to ignore him, as she had on the journey. She had felt childishly triumphant at not once having yielded to glancing his way, despite being very aware of his saturnine features facing her. She hadn't thanked him for his escort, or for the use of his luxurious carriage, or even for his gallant assistance in handing her and Josie both in and out of it. She was not, by nature, unmannerly. The fact that he caused her to act so out of character just added to her sense of squirming exasperation.

His expression was concealed by shadow: the flickering coach and porch lamps did little to augment the glow misting about the street lanterns.

'Come here.'

'I'm tired.'

'Come here.'

Grinding her teeth, and with her fingers flexing furiously on air, Elizabeth flounced down three steps, then stopped, so that her pearly complexion was level with his dark face.

'I expect a little more gracious goodnight from my betrothed than the one I've just received. I think it as well to start as we mean to go on.'

Elizabeth's eyes glittered pure disgust but, with a toss of her fair curls, she lilted, 'And I, sir, will witness a cold day in hell before taking lessons in gentility from an upstart Vis—'

'Scapegrace! Minx!'

The sudden sibilant screeching directly behind had Elizabeth jumping on the spot and only Ross, steadying her against his solid body, prevented her stumbling down the remaining steps.

'Where have you been? What have you been doing? Do you know I have sent Pettifer twice along to the vicar to see if you had gone there?' Ignoring Josie cowering by the door, Edwina flew out of the lighted hallway, night rail flapping about her stout legs, and peered down at her granddaughter's back. 'Where have you been? Don't lie now. I shall know if you lie. Have you been to see that drab of a friend in the stews?'

It was at that point that Edwina's myopic vision located a man's muscular figure behind that of her granddaughter. She noticed, also, that the two of them seemed to be locked in some sort of embrace. With a scandalised gurgle, she thumped herself on the breast bone, a pudgy hand searching for support from the wrought iron balustrade. 'Oh, my God! Now she really *is* ruined...'

'Lady Elizabeth has been with me.'

'Stratton?' Edwina barked, astonished, recovering remarkably quickly. 'What are you about? Have you seduced her? Oh, never mind. Come inside, all of you, before we give every nosey parker enough gossip to keep them up guessing all night.' Without another word Edwina shuffled about on her slippered feet. She huffed back up the few steps she'd descended and disappeared into the honeyed glow behind the half-open door.

Gently, Ross put Elizabeth's quaking form from him. With a hand lightly on her elbow, he urged her up the steps. Drained of further resistance by jangled nerves and dismay at the utter failure of the entire evening's enterprise, Elizabeth allowed his assistance.

'Thank Heavens it's you she's been with, Stratton! For a moment there I thought dearest Lizzie had taken leave of her senses and gone slumming at dead of night!' Edwina burst out when they were all inside the drawing room. She managed a relieved little snort of laughter as she wrapped her thick, cord night rail snugly about her embonpoint.

Elizabeth glared at her grandmother. Personally, she deemed it preferable for a spinster to be discovered doing good works at close to midnight than clinging to a disreputable rogue's neck on her own doorstep.

Oblivious to her granddaughter's theory on impropriety, Edwina continued to flap a hand and smile as she relaxed. 'I've been fair frantic since discovering you abroad when I imagined you safely tucked up in bed.'

'You may retire, Josie,' Elizabeth quietly directed her maid. The girl needed no second telling; speedily she slipped from the room, her nervous backwards look speaking volumes. Pettifer, however, impassively traversed back and forth, lighting candelabra and coaxing the dying embers of the fire into a cosy blaze, as though just such catastrophes were commonplace.

'You know, the silly thing is, Lizzie,' Edwina rattled on with the verbosity of stupendous relief, 'I came along an hour or more ago to your chamber, with m'good idea to help your wretched friend, and dam' me if you haven't had the exact same one. Although I didn't know it then, of course, and have been out of m'mind with worry…and twice resorted to m'salts. And I do think, dear, t'would have been wiser and a lot more seemly to wait till morning to seek the Viscount's good advice…'

'Please be quiet, Grandmama,' Elizabeth gritted over her grandmother's rambling.

'Pray, continue, Mrs Sampson,' Ross contradicted, arrowing a brooding look at his uneasy fiancée. 'I should, of course, still be pleased to help, once I know a little more of the problem.'

Edwina stood with her back to the fire, warming herself. 'Do you know I was foolish enough to think that Lizzie might have gone to that revolting rookery tonight? And taken with her something of value to buy her friend's freedom from her fancy man. I was convinced enough to check m'silverware in case she'd absconded with a candlestick or two.'

Ross's dark expression became ever more sardonic. 'I take it from these few odd clues, Edwina, that your granddaughter has a friend languishing in a slum somewhere in very unhappy circumstances. A friend she's desperate to help…at any cost?' Although the conversation seemed to be flowing between the Viscount and her grandmother, Elizabeth knew that every word he uttered was directed at her.

'Well, of course! Has she not told you anything? Have you not told the Viscount anything?' Edwina demanded with a perplexed frown at her granddaughter.

Elizabeth managed a tight little smile for her interfering grandmother before turning a particularly impudent look on Ross. 'Did I not tell you anything?' she echoed, all surprised apology. 'Well, let me make amends, sir, and tell you now. The reason I acted with such temerity tonight and bothered you at home was…not what your arrogance led you to believe at all. I hope that hasn't wounded your conceit too greatly. Goodnight.' With a cursory little bob she immediately turned for the door.

'It would take more than a puerile subterfuge…which, by the by, didn't succeed…to deflate my ego. And before you retire, my lady, I think we should let your grandmother in on our happy news.'

Elizabeth swished about, attempting to freeze his words and his person with a purple glower. But he kept on coming until his powerful physique was towering over her petite figure. 'You should have been more honest, my dear. I just might have been sympathetic.' The words were light, his expression leaden.

'Now, it's my turn not to think so,' she sourly muttered. 'There is no news to impart to my grandmother,' she added in a more audible underbreath. 'As I have just said, nothing tonight was what it seemed. Especially your understanding of my motive in visiting you. I apologise for taking up so much of your evening.'

'I'm glad you did. Now that we are to be married, it would be churlish, indeed, to deny you an hour or two of my time; or assistance with any problems you may have.'

Edwina hurried closer. Although Ross had spoken in an intimate tone, it was obvious from the woman's rapturous smile she had overheard. 'Married, did you say? You have agreed to the match, Elizabeth?' she demanded excitedly. Her glowing eyes spontaneously swerved to Pettifer, loading logs onto the hungry flames in the grate. He acknowledged her triumph with a quirk at one corner of his finely moulded mouth and kept on about his work.

Elizabeth fidgeted beneath a tawny stare. She knew he was challenging her. She could revoke her consent and risk his displeasure and his revenge, or she could honour their agreement. She could deny ever having agreed to wed him; but that would be an outright lie and she knew she was not capable of that. She wanted him to generously release her from their pact. She also wanted him to generously return her gems. She wanted too much, she knew. Nevertheless, she raised her jewel-bright eyes.

'No,' Ross murmured to her unspoken entreaty. He refused to look directly at her, smiling privately in wry acknowledgement of her persuasive powers.

Edwina demanded again, 'So, you have agreed to the match, m'dear?'

After a further silent moment, replete with inner wrangling, Elizabeth muttered, 'Yes.'

Edwina seemed oblivious to the bad grace which accompanied her answer and hugged Elizabeth, delighted. 'Oh, that is wonderful. Quite the best news I've heard in an age!'

Elizabeth kindly reciprocated the embrace, patting at her grandmother's rotund back. Her eyes looked huge in her wan face; dulled with weariness. They livened enough to dart violet arrows at the man who was watching the emotional scene with an amount of rueful amusement.

As Edwina bustled away to direct Pettifer to fetch champagne, Ross approached Elizabeth. Taking both her hands in his, he raised them, bringing first one then the other to briefly touch his lips. His fiancée couldn't summon the energy to snatch them back. She allowed his thumbs to brush soothingly back and forth over the backs of her small fingers.

His eyes held hers and for a moment she thought she glimpsed a look of tender praise in them. But all he said was, 'You must be keen to retire. I'll not keep you longer.'

Elizabeth could do no more than nod at their touching hands while, way back in her mind, she was fretting that perhaps she should have lied after all: he looked too content. He was congratulating himself on his victory. He now had her fortune. He had her, too: a minor encumbrance was doubtless how he saw that. Perhaps he was already planning to banish her to his Kent estate, while his life in London, funded by her money, carried on regardless. Oh, yes; he had what he wanted! He had won! And the crushing knowledge made her lower lip wobble while her lashes fluttered low over glistening eyes.

As though cognisant of the reason for her distress, his fingers tightened on hers and he jerked her gently forward. They were so close she felt his words stir her hair. 'Everything will be fine, Elizabeth. Trust me.' Abruptly she was released. 'We'll celebrate another time, Mrs Sampson, if you don't mind. It's been a hectic night for us all. I'm sure you must be more than ready to retire.'

At the door he executed a polite bow to the two ladies. 'If I may, I should like to return tomorrow and discuss a few details concerning the wedding and so on. You might like then to tell me more of this unlucky friend's plight. Oh, one other thing,' he added conversationally. 'I'm sure Elizabeth would be interested in seeing just what sort of Cornish stock I spring from. My mother and eldest brother are due to arrive in London tomorrow, as are a few close friends. I would be honoured if you would both dine with us one evening soon. If you are agreeable, I shall announce our engagement that night. Thereafter a notice will be put into *The Times*.'

'That sounds delightful!' Edwina gushed.

'Elizabeth?' Ross said quietly.

'Of course, I must come; I should very much like to inspect your pedigree,' she retorted with all the bitter sweetness of lamented defeat.

'I still cannot believe you were that rude!' Edwina rebuked next morning at breakfast. Her knife plunged angrily into the jam pot.

Elizabeth couldn't believe it either, and her face grew hot at the memory. It seemed that, lately, never a day passed without her feeling ashamed of some aspect of her behaviour. The reason for her cringing was always the same: Stratton! She was sick of the man! 'The Viscount and I are well used to exchanging insults,' was all she offered in mitigation. 'It is a bad match, Grandmama. You should never have interfered. I can only hope he will eventually come to his senses and release me from my consent.'

'He is not likely to do that, no matter how objectionable you contrive to be,' Edwina spluttered through a mouthful of toast and jam.

'No, indeed! Not with so much money riding on the wedding lines,' Elizabeth commented caustically. 'I'm sure he'll put up with any amount of my slights, so long as you pay him to take me.'

'I've a notion, m'dear, that Stratton would wed you whether I paid him or not.'

Oddly, that lightened Elizabeth's mood. She gave a little guffaw. 'And I've a notion, m'dear, that you must have been early at the Madeira, to say so,' she returned in a droll approximation of her grandmother's gravelly tone.

The affection and gratitude she felt towards her grandmother prevented her ever staying mad at her for long. If only she hadn't taken it into her silly head to get her wed! It was idiotic! It was infuriating! It was Stratton's fault! she unreasonably judged as she gave her grandmother a fond peck on a chomping cheek. 'I'm going to fetch my pelisse. Sophie wants to choose dress material. I said that Evangeline might accompany us. She likes a carriage ride and a scout through the warehouses.'

After a frantic swallow, Edwina choked, 'You're surely not going out today?' She snorted her disapproval. 'Ross will be here this afternoon. He sent word he is to attend us at three. You must ensure you are home.'

Elizabeth faced her grandmother again, ivory ringlets a-sway about her graceful neck. 'I must do nothing of the sort! I'd rather not be present to oversee my sale.'

'Ross will expect you to be here…'

'It's as well, then, that I shall be absent,' Elizabeth announced petulantly. 'Stratton has yet to learn that I have no intention of fulfilling his presumptuous expectations.' Her small mouth slanted contumaciously as she recalled him yesterday evening requiring her apology, requiring her answers, requiring her gracious goodnights. He would soon learn not to treat a Marquess's daughter so high-handed, she decided on sallying forth, chin-up, from the room.

Sophie widened chocolate-brown eyes on Elizabeth's face. 'You have received a proposal from Viscount Stratton?'

Elizabeth nodded, simultaneously grimacing understanding of her friend's shock. Evangeline continued knitting as though deaf to the riveting news. She was simply glad to be invited on an outing with two lively young ladies…or so the earnest pair seemed to her.

'But, Elizabeth, isn't he the one…the rather savage gentleman?'

'Yes,' Elizabeth admitted calmly. 'The very same. But I have to own the tale of breakfasting on an adversary's liver seems a trifle *de trop*. Grandmama has had him for dinner, so to speak. She maintains he's table-trained.'

'Well, I don't see how you can joke about it, Elizabeth!' Sophie scolded squeamishly. 'Is he terribly handsome?' she immediately demanded. 'I've heard Mama talking about him. She and her crony, Mrs Talbot, seem to think he has a raffish appeal…like a corsair…'

'Or a gypsy…' Elizabeth added with a curl to her lip. Offhand, she said, 'I suppose he might pass as good-looking. If one likes sallow men.' The injustice of that bitchy remark made her shift on the upholstered seat. He wasn't sallow-skinned. He had acquired a healthy tan from being outdoors in the elements. He was handsome…*very* handsome. He was impeccably well dressed, too. Yesterday she had deemed him the perfect man.

The memories of her clandestine visit, that blissful kiss, that hurting kiss, made her stare sightlessly out of the carriage window while heat bled into her complexion. With a stubborn set to her soft mouth, she determined to wriggle free of this stupid betrothal at the very first opportunity. Yesterday evening, when tired, she had allowed defeatism too much rein. Now refreshed, she rallied her pride and confidence. He might have won that battle, but he had not yet won the war!

'Have you accepted him?' broke into her pugnacious thoughts. It was the second time Sophie had posed the question, while leaning across the carriage, gazing into her friend's faraway amethyst eyes.

'I have…but not irrevocably. My grandmother has landed herself in a financial mess with Stratton and my dowry has been dangled as settlement. The engagement is still unofficial.

I'm hoping they will both discover what idiocy it is trying to manipulate me.'

Sophie frowned. 'I see,' she said, when she quite patently did not. The last she had heard from her own mama concerning Mrs Sampson's financial mess was that it involved wagers with that harridan, Alice Penney. Slumping back against the squabs, Sophie asked, 'What of Hugh? Have you told him?' She pulled a little face. 'I'm quite sure, Lizzie, he is harbouring hopes of his own, in that respect.'

'I've not seen him to explain,' Elizabeth said truthfully. But again her thoughts were troubled. She had written Hugh a brief note this morning, and despatched it with a servant. In it she had apologised for Harry Pettifer twice bothering him yesterday evening. She had lightly implied her grandmother's eccentricity was to blame, and left it at that. It was rather unjust; it was also unlikely to appease Hugh for long. When next they met, he would expect proper explanations. It was another reason why she was so keen to be abroad today. She would wager—if she were a betting person, of course—that at some time in the next few hours, Hugh would pay a visit to Connaught Street. The way her luck was running, it would probably coincide with the Viscount's visit. She banished all thought of it. She was determined to enjoy this shopping expedition with Sophie. She needed a little peaceful interlude with a good friend before anxiety again dominated her life.

Having alighted at Harding, Howell & Co.'s warehouse in Pall Mall, the two young ladies, with Evangeline in tow, entered an Aladdin's cave certain to enchant any modiste. A wealth of fabric bolts in every conceivable weight and hue were shelved to ceiling height behind polished wooden counters flanking two long walls of the shop. From mahogany poles, interspersed in the room, silks and satins, lace and damask flowed in a confusion of fabulous colours.

The friends slowly promenaded, turning their heads from left to right, up and down, to survey the shimmering array. From time to time their attention was arrested enough by a

sheen or shade to pinch a piece of material between thumb
and forefinger and test its quality.

'Have you anything particular in mind?' Elizabeth asked
her friend.

Sophie stopped by a roll of coffee-coloured velvet, cocked
her brunette head. She unrolled a little, smoothed her fingers
along its luxuriant pile, then with a negative sigh, walked on.
'I thought perhaps apricot satin, but I have seen nothing that
is quite right.'

Elizabeth caught at her friend's arm and urged her between
milling customers to the opposite counter where she had spied
a length of peach voile. The gauzy material was woven
through with gold and silver string ribbon. A length was
swirled off the roll, ready for cutting by the draper.

'This is beautiful,' Sophie enthused. 'The best I've seen, if
a little too transparent. But as it is to be a splendid ball,' she
chattered on about her parents' forthcoming anniversary cel-
ebration which was to mark their quarter century together, 'I
fancy something a little daring and eye-catching…'

'I must say, so do I,' stressed a drawling masculine voice.
'And, lucky dog that I am, I believe I've spotted the very
thing,' was whispered at the back of Elizabeth's neck, disturbing her flaxen curls and making her skin crawl. 'How are
you, my dear? Did you receive my billet-doux?'

Elizabeth marched sideways to escape the interfering fingers on her small rounded buttock. Even through the thickness
of her velvet pelisse she could feel the heat and determination
in that kneading hand. Furiously twisting about, she glared
absolute loathing at the Earl of Cadmore.

He simply grinned at her disgust. 'Still my proud beauty, I
see; that's good,' he taunted in a low, familiar tone. An idle
glance slid to Sophie, who had only just become aware of his
presence. He mocked her look of arrant distaste with an exaggerated dip of his head. 'Send your priggish little friend on
with the old woman so we can talk,' he muttered. He leaned
his snake-narrow hips back against the counter, seemingly
quite confident of Elizabeth complying with his orders. She

did; merely to prevent Sophie and Evangeline witnessing her acute embarrassment or suffering likewise on her account. A few quick, quiet words and an explicit look soon had Sophie leading away a blithely smiling Evangeline.

While Cadmore waited for them to distance themselves, his effeminately thin white fingers flicked open a japanned snuff box. He took a pinch, his lizard-lidded weak blue eyes lingering on Elizabeth's small bosom, heaving visibly beneath the straining buttons of her pelisse.

'Go...*away*! At once!' was all she managed to choke between huge calming breaths. Livid-faced, she spun back to clutch at the counter, her white-knuckled fingers rigid on the smooth wood. She was trembling with such fury at his outrageous assault that her shame was soon suppressed. He had cornered her before, slyly touched her before, but never in such a public place. Never with such blatant intent and disrespect. And then she learned why he was feeling so cocksure.

'I hear Mrs Sampson has been unlucky at the tables lately. I hear Alice Penney is holding her vowels for quite a ridiculous figure. In the circumstances, a dutiful granddaughter ought swell the family kitty. I could be of service there.'

'And in the circumstances, a dutiful husband ought swell his own family. Should you not go home and paw your wife in private rather than molest a stranger in public? For I certainly cannot be of service there,' she bit out through her teeth.

Incensed colour began mottling his face as she alluded to something freely tattled and smirked over: in five years of marriage, the Earl and Countess of Cadmore had failed to produce any progeny.

Cadmore advanced on her with such a ferociously snarling mouth that, for a moment, Elizabeth was sure he would strike her. Barely a foot away, he seemed to gather his wits and recall where he was. He halted, darted a circumspect look about to see if they had attracted attention. A pink tongue tip flicked out between his taut, bloodless lips, then recoiled. He nodded a greeting at a gentleman sauntering by with a female companion. 'You brazen bitch,' he whispered, still smiling at the couple. 'I shall enjoy making you take back every one of your vulgar words. One day soon, you will apologise most profusely, most abjectly, for that outrageous impertinence.' Eyes like watery sky narrowed on her, but his set smile didn't waver. To an idle observer they would have passed as stylish people engaged in polite chit-chat while shopping, rather than bitter adversaries trading vicious insults.

'And what of your vulgar words and outrageous impertinence, sir?' Elizabeth demanded in a low, vibrant tone. 'Will you ever find the good grace to apologise for your appalling insults to me over these many years?'

'Apologise to you?' he sneered. 'Apologise to a devious little slut who thought to trifle with my affections and make of me a laughing stock? Apologise to a harlot who's known the dregs of society? Perhaps that's why you visit the slums so often, is it? Have you a taste for rough trade now? Do you like knowing dockers, as you knew highwaymen: in the biblical sense? Do you? Tell me!' he rasped imperatively. 'Does the vicar watch as they tumble you in the gutter? Is that what you like? Have you raised your skirts for the clergyman, too?' Torturously aroused and enraged by what he was saying, what he was feverishly imagining, his face flushed and swelled with rampant lust. His hips squirmed against the counter and his skinny fingers thrust between his neck and his cravat, trying to ease a little air to his throat. Huge-pupilled eyes locked on to her shocked, pallid face, then slithered down her rigidly held little figure. For a moment he looked and sounded like a man in direst torment. 'By God, you'll raise your skirts for me before I'm done.' He closed his eyes, took a deep breath that pinched and whitened his nostrils. 'I'll have you if it's the last thing I do…' he exploded in a strangled whimper.

Elizabeth backed away from the naked hunger and hatred blazing at her from his bulging eyes. In her haste to get away, she collided with someone just approaching. She had a vague impression of a pretty, dark-haired young woman, elaborately garbed and rouged. A strong, sweet perfume wafted, heightening her sense of nausea. Begging her pardon for bumping into her, Elizabeth glimpsed glittering black eyes assessing her. Then the woman had swept past to clutch proprietorially at one of the Earl's arms. 'I have found just the thing, Caddy. 'Tis scarlet and there is matching lace...' Elizabeth heard her say before she quickly distanced herself from them.

'Do you want to go?' Sophie asked sympathetically as Elizabeth occupied her trembling fingers by testing various fabrics on the opposite counter.

'No. He shall never cow me,' Elizabeth averred in a choking whisper.

'Vile man!' Sophie muttered with a poisonous glare at Cadmore. 'You would think, would you not, after all this time, he would have got over you rejecting him. What a lucky escape! Mama says the Countess looks more sourly countenanced than ever. And little wonder with such a sickening spouse and no babes to love. It looks as though he has his lightskirt with him.'

'I think perhaps I would like to go after all,' Elizabeth whispered, gazing past Sophie. 'Perhaps we could try another warehouse,' she croaked on a strained smile. Her eyes immediately slid to the entrance again. A strange coldness was dousing the fiery umbrage she had felt at the Earl of Cadmore's malicious assault. She wanted to look away, turn away, but couldn't. She wanted to tell herself she didn't care, but oddly, she seemed to. The queasiness in her stomach was giving way to hurting cramps.

She stared at the couple who had recently arrived. The woman idled by the entrance to inspect a fall of beryl blue muslin that Elizabeth recalled had caught her own eye on entering.

Viscount Stratton was looking at the fabric, too, with very indulgent interest. He appeared to make some favourable comment and the woman smiled beatifically up at him. She was more than simply pretty; she was extraordinarily beautiful and extremely elegant. This was no comely courtesan: the sort of woman with whom Elizabeth imagined he dallied. This was

a stylish and refined lady who exuded an aura of gentle serenity. But then there was deep affection between them, that
was obvious. Their bodies were close; one of her hands
clasped his arm in a touch that was casual yet confidently
intimate. They made such a strikingly handsome couple that
people close by were turning to look at them. Neither seemed
caring of the interest they were generating; their attention
seemed reserved for each other. It wasn't. He was aware of
her.

Elizabeth's eyes had darted from reluctantly admiring the
woman's graceful profile and honey-gold hair, to target her
prospective husband's dark visage. He was returning her gaze.

Heat was back. It furnaced, while a detached part of her
brain regretted that her shopping trip with Sophie was turning
into such a farcical disaster. The last place she would have
expected to meet either of the men who were plaguing her
was in a fabric emporium. It seemed there was to be no re-
spite, even for a few hours! All that was lacking was Hugh
Clemence's presence here, searching for her, and her nightmare would be complete.

'Come, Sophie,' Elizabeth quavered with strengthening
persuasion. 'Let us try Baldwin's. I hear they have had a
consignment of Brussels lace…'

So, he took his mistress shopping only hours before he was
due to speak to her grandmother about their wedding plans.
The knowledge trampled her pride with far greater success
than anything the Earl of Cadmore had said or done. She
didn't care. Why should she care? And why should he not do
so? She knew he had no intention of altering his life for someone as trifling as his bride. He was wedding a dowry and
being saddled with a wife. She was well aware of that. For
her part, she was simply interested in regaining her precious
Thorneycroft jewels. She didn't want or need a husband. Or
any intimacy. Should this madness run out of control, and the
nuptials took place, she would be glad he took his pleasure
elsewhere. She wasn't bothered at being brought face to face

with the woman he…did he love her? She had the look of a woman cherished.

She refused to think of it further. Her chin tilted and she smoothed her gloves with unsteady fingers. Now he had seen her, she would let him know she didn't give a fig on whom he frittered his cash. On whom he might soon be squandering her cash! That did gall! But still she wasn't about to scurry away like a timid mouse. She would pass them, acknowledge this inopportune meeting, let him know his adultery would be of no consequence whatsoever.

Arm in arm with Evangeline and Sophie, the trio proceeded towards the door. Elizabeth knew he was watching as she drew closer; although still chatting with his companion, he had one eye on her and was well aware of her approach. Without looking directly at them, Elizabeth knew when they moved away from the turquoise fabric. With a penetrative peek from beneath a fringe of brunette lashes, she realised just why the woman favoured it: her eyes were the most wonderful shade of green-blue.

They were about to pass! Elizabeth gripped tighter to her friends for support, obliquely aware that Evangeline and Sophie were swapping idle comments on the shop's stock. Bravely, she looked up, met his eyes squarely for a moment before mirroring his courteous nod.

'Lady Elizabeth…?' The greeting was warm, polite.

'Viscount Stratton…' She matched his words, if not his tone. He was stopping, turning, expecting her to do the same. She swished about. So did Sophie, her mouth agape as she recognised the name of the handsome stranger.

'I'm sorry, my lord, we must hurry on. So many warehouses to visit and so little time. I am expected home shortly for a…tiresome engagement…' Elizabeth watched, exultant, as his eyes and mouth narrowed at the barb.

'Well, I mustn't delay you from something so important.'

'As if you could…even for a trifle…' Elizabeth lightly trilled with such an overflow of honey in her tone that his companion looked from one to the other of them, a small, enquiring smile hovering about her lips.

Close to, Elizabeth could see that she was older than she herself, yet still so breathtakingly lovely that her insides clenched. Why could she not have been milk-maid buxom, or garishly painted? Why did she have to be so…so perfect?

She stretched her lips, hoping it resembled an insouciant smile, before sweeping on. She talked with Evangeline about ribbon, gripped hard at Sophie's arm to make her look away and close her dropped jaw. Turning from one to the other of her friends, she laughed at nothing, aware of everything behind. Especially that she was observed. Then they had gained the door and turned the corner. Out of sight, her shoulders slumped, her eyes closed and just one phrase trudged through her mind: Damn you, Stratton! *Damn you!*

Chapter Nine

'Damn you, Stratton! Damn you!' Cecily Booth muttered under her breath.

The man at her side was also cursing inaudibly on catching sight of the Viscount, but for a very different reason. Far from feeling piqued at being overlooked, as Cecily was, Cadmore was uneasy at being the one to have drawn those lupine eyes.

A few days ago, the Earl would have believed Cecily unavailable to him for two reasons: she didn't come cheap and she was besotted with Ross Trelawney. Being a parsimonious poltroon, he thus looked elsewhere for female company.

It was common knowledge that Cecily had been angling for Trelawney's protection for some while. It must have seemed significant to her that she was victorious just as he received his peerage. Soon she'd felt confident enough of becoming a Lady to broadcast hints of mutual devotion and matrimony. She'd seriously misjudged in applying sly pressure. A few days ago, so rumour had it, the Viscount was ribbed about his aspirant 'fiancée' at Gentleman Jackson's, while sparring with Guy Markham. Before nightfall, his deluded young mistress was in need of a new protector.

Linus Savage made his move while Cecily was still reeling from the rejection and susceptible to flummery and negotiation. Earlier he'd been congratulating himself on a shrewd deal…now he wasn't so sure.

Now he was fretting that that vicious look in Stratton's eyes must mean he still had a fancy for the woman clutching his arm. He attempted loosening Cecily's grip and adopting an air of nonchalance.

Cecily's mouth skewed into a scarlet slash at the sight of the Viscount and his companion. To be replaced so quickly—and with such an exquisitely beautiful lady—was mortifying! Then, recalling how brusquely she'd been discarded, she reminded herself she'd hooked an Earl. What would she miss about Ross? His witty charm? His generosity? His energetic…inventive…wonderful lovemaking? Cecily's feigned unconcern faded into an involuntarily gulp of despair. To cheer herself, she surmised bitchily that the blonde was possibly his own age: a decade older than she herself. That made her feel better. Angling her head coquettishly at Cadmore, she hoped her youthful bloom and vitality were much in evidence. Her simpering smile drooped. She couldn't ignore the contrast between this puny-chested fop and the muscular physique of the handsome, rugged man not three yards away now. The elaborate, padded waistcoats the Earl favoured never quite disguised his lack of girth. She shuddered inwardly, realising that about midnight his fleshless ribs would be digging into hers.

'Stratton…' the Earl of Cadmore ejaculated by way of greeting as the couples finally drew level.

Ross jerked his head in curt response, but remained grim and silent. Cecily bobbed archly, dark curls a-sway, while peeping up at him with mingling plea and accusation. He returned her a perfunctory, preoccupied smile that whipped up her indignation.

'Stratton seems irate…face like thunder…' Cadmore muttered, glancing at the Viscount's broad back. He shrugged, eyed Cecily more purposefully. Perky with relief that Stratton had passed, uneventfully, by, a hand slid her back, skinny fingers burrowing beneath an arm to pinch a full, firm breast. Cecily instinctively recoiled in disgust.

Then she remembered: she'd hooked an earl. She paraded

the feat again through her mind, with much self-congratulation, turning towards him to shield his groping fingers from prying eyes. An onlooker would simply have seen a woman leaning close to whisper tenderly in her beau's ear. What Cadmore's new *chère amie* actually said before she tugged herself free, was, 'The scarlet velvet *I* fancy, my lord, is over this way...'

'I'm intrigued. Two attractive ladies: a beautiful blonde and a pretty brunette, and both looked daggers at you. The gentleman looked scared witless. What *is* going on, Ross?' his sister-in-law enquired with a smile. 'Not still breaking hearts and cuckolding husbands, surely?'

'You thought the blonde beautiful?' was all he said.

'Quite exceptionally lovely, despite that sad look in her blue eyes.'

'They're not blue, they're violet...'

'Ha...ha...' Rebecca chuckled significantly, making Ross grimace ruefully at a stack of satin. 'They are indeed violet. I noticed. So did you. Is there anything else you'd like to tell me about her?' she prompted softly, seriously. After a silent moment, she continued, 'And the brunette?'

He shrugged. 'As you said, she's pretty.'

'Ross!' Rebecca chided on an outraged laugh. 'You really are a callous rogue! Of the two, the brunette, of course, is your mistress.'

'Not any more,' summed up his lack of interest in pursuing the subject. He turned about restlessly, looked back towards the exit, then frowned over Rebecca's head at a drape of lustrous silk dangling off a roll on the top shelf. It undulated in a light air current, iridescent, mesmerising. The shade reminded him of hyacinths...and gems that were nestling on velvet in his safe. He wanted to go there and look at them, then take them to his betrothed. He wanted to tell her that if she'd just stopped for a moment or two, he would have introduced her to his brother's wife. He wanted to tell her that there was no need for her to have looked so hurt. And she had; until she realised he was watching her. Then she'd masked her distress with that haughty expression she'd perfected.

She believed Rebecca to be his mistress. And it upset her. But she didn't want him to know; so she'd brazened it out and confronted him. The message was clear: it didn't matter. It wouldn't even matter when they were husband and wife. That's what she wanted him to think. That's why she'd had to mention the 'tiresome engagement' later that day. But now he knew differently. Just for a second or two he'd seen her stripped of armour, wounded and vulnerable because he was with another woman. She cared. The idiotic thing was, he was glad. And he wasn't sure why. The sensible way would be to foster her apathy. He wasn't certain he was ready to… *relinquish all others…* After all, she was still the rudest, most infuriating little… He exhaled slowly, aware he couldn't even think of her in those terms any more.

But he could think of her. God knows, it seemed he could think of little else. He wanted to be with her; even if it was simply to parry insults. He wanted to tell her he'd seen silk that would suit her, that would match her eyes. He wanted to be shopping with his future wife. He wanted her…God, how he wanted her. She'd been out of sight a few minutes, and he wanted to follow her.

What he wanted, he impressed on himself while his teeth locked so hard his jaw began to ache, was a brain physician. The sensible way, the only sensible way, would have been to seduce her yesterday in the comfort of his own home. Had he indulged his lust for her, he might not now be acting like a moonstruck idiot. He might not be planning a wedding, simply settling in a new paramour. In all his life he'd never toadied to any woman, yet he was constantly modifying his behaviour and humouring this pert madam, sullied by scandal, who took delight in slighting him at every opportunity.

Women of all ages…all classes…liked him; it had always been that way. Since he'd been elevated to the peerage, his popularity had soared yet higher. He couldn't keep pace with the deluge of social invitations he received.

So, Lady Elizabeth Rowe was beautiful and desirable; so were other women desirable…and far more responsive to his blasé charm. So, why couldn't he think of anything else? Anyone else? Why had he, minutes ago, been on the point of inviting Cadmore to step outside, so he could hit him? All the man had done was look shifty and bark a greeting at him. He had no proof the weasel had approached Elizabeth today, let alone annoyed her. The fact that Cecily was accompanying him made it unlikely he had accosted her; as did the fact that they had been sited on opposite sides of the shop. Still he felt tense with the need to find out what had occurred, just in case he had looked disrespectfully at Elizabeth.

'Shall we go? Luke should be finished with his meeting now,' Ross suddenly burst out impatiently.

Rebecca slanted a look at him from beneath lengthy lashes, while still fiddling with fabrics on the counter. 'I'm not yet finished choosing, Ross. You used to like taking me shopping whilst Luke did business in Lombard Street…' She pouted.

'Don't flirt. You know you don't mean it,' he said with a laughing hint of apology for his brusqueness.

'That never used to worry you. You used to encourage me to practise on you. Why won't you flirt with me any more, Ross?'

'*What?* And risk my big brother's displeasure?'

'Luke knows it's he who benefits from your tutelage. Besides, that never stopped you before.'

'Before I was a disreputable rogue. Now,' he informed her on a wry, private smile, 'I'm an upstart Viscount.'

Rebecca nodded slowly. 'The violet-eyed blonde…?' was all she said as, arm through his, she steered him back towards the exit.

A long, dark finger unfurled from his fist lying idle on the desk top. It extended to touch a glossy, faceted jewel. Slowly it trailed alternate white and purple stones, stroking with a sensual gentleness. The amethysts were of highly prized deep, rich colour and perfectly matched in clarity and unusual octagonal cut. The diamonds were cabochon, clear of inclusions, shimmering rainbows in afternoon sunlight. A goldsmith of exceptional skill had crafted the piece. Ross supposed the rest of the parure to be of similar fine quality. If so, she had been right in her estimation: from what she'd described, and what he knew, he'd say about ten thousand pounds worth in total.

He was comfortable with treasures; as a mercenary and bounty-hunter he had had regular contact with precious arte-facts: Spanish gold, Eastern jade, African ivory, ancient Egyptian pottery... He'd been rewarded in all manner of currency—even recently crafted Sheraton and Hepplewhite furniture—and never turned any down. Now he was paid in diamonds and amethysts and he was devising ways he could give them back...without ceding what he wanted.

He leaned back in the chair, rested his head back into the leather, but the hawkish gleam between his lashes was still on the scintillating collar laid out on the desk in front of him.

Far, far back in his mind, it occurred to him that he ought to be travelling to Kent and directing his architect and his builder on renovation schedules for Stratton Hall. A few weeks ago, there was little else on his mind but building on his new and very gratifying success. He'd been proud of what he'd, alone and unaided, achieved.

His father's original ill-gotten gains had been laundered by the years and by legitimate transactions into an international business empire. As the youngest son he had been last in line as far as inheritance went. But he'd been reared knowing indulgence: by a father who believed in primogeniture yet compensated for it in other ways, by a mother who doted on her wild child, and by brothers who spoiled him through guilt at taking the lion's share of the family businesses and property. It didn't worry him. He let them all know it didn't worry him...not a bit. It was fair: Luke and Tristan worked harder and gave more time and commitment than he was prepared to sacrifice from his hedonistic life. He'd make his own way...and he had, very enjoyably, ignoring convention and morality along the way. He had his own codes: he never did more than flirt with women his brothers or friends cherished. He was loyal and protective to those he cherished, if unwilling to be restrained or tamed by their reciprocal concern and affection. Until now. Only there was no reciprocal affection. He was making marriage plans with a blonde temptress who disliked him. And he hadn't the vaguest notion why he was so adamant he would marry her. It wasn't the money. But he had to tell her it was, for both their sakes. It was all that was sensible to believe after such a short, stormy acquaintance. It was all she'd believe: that he was a hireling who was owed payment and was not shy of taking her dowry…or taking her as his mistress should she withhold consent to the nuptials. She was haughty, rude and defiant, yet something in her touched his soul…because he recognised the sham. She was bleeding still from a ten-year-old wound and vulnerable to the salt society used to season its contempt. He sensed a poignant wistfulness that made him want to fight alongside her, shield her from male lust and female spite. The instinct to care and protect had subtly, swiftly circumvented his lechery and a wry smile was all that rued its passing.

He sat forward, rested his elbows on the desk. One broad palm supported a tanned, concave cheek as he frowned thoughtfully at the sparking gem. Which brought him to just what the little fool thought she was about by consorting with harlots and pimps in some East End hovel. He wasn't about to have a wife of his risking assault or disease roaming amongst God knew what sort of squalid low life.

From what Edwina had artlessly disclosed, he guessed the situation to be thus: Elizabeth had risked further disgrace last night from selfless motives. She had come to collect her necklace with the sole intention of using it to redeem a fallen woman. She had planned to buy a friend's freedom with her inheritance. His eyes closed and something leaden settled in his stomach. If he'd given in to her pleas and allowed her the necklace, she would have taken it straight there. She would have actually journeyed, unescorted, into the heart of the stews with a couple of thousand pounds' worth of jewellery in her pocket. It didn't bear thinking about.

A slight smile softened the hard set to his sensual lips. He didn't think she'd want to hear that within a week of being ransomed, the drab would be back in Wapping searching for her fancy man and touting for business. Or that meanwhile her precious heirloom would be sold off stone by stone for the price of the freshest young doxy to be had, or a keg of geneva.

Her rescue plan had an almost charming simplicity. It also relied heavily on honest reciprocation from reprobates. It was naïve…very innocent behaviour…and something about that was discordant with what he knew, or thought he knew, along with the rest of society, about her past. And there was something else, something odd he recalled Edwina muttering when he'd brought Elizabeth home… His reflection tailed off and he glanced at the clock as it chimed half past two.

Palming the collar, he let it drape glittering over his bronzed skin for a moment. Was he going to hand it over to her now? Or was he going to prevaricate a while longer? He didn't want to renege on his promise to return it today. But when he'd said he would, he hadn't known why she wanted it.

He stood up abruptly and replaced the gem in his safe. She might have slipped under his guard when he wasn't looking, but he wasn't completely overwhelmed. Strong men made weak by beautiful women were worthy of the utmost contempt, so he'd always thought. Besides, if anyone was short-changed at present from this crazy deal, it was him. Edwina owed him; Lady Elizabeth Rowe damn well owed him. He'd kept himself leashed last night. One kiss they'd pacted and she'd withdrawn. He knew she'd been enjoying it. So had he…too damned much! It had started out as an ostentation of his seductive powers and finished with him luxuriating in the pure sweetness of it all. Just like some novice libertine. He'd keep the necklace awhile, and prove to himself he wasn't acting like a novice libertine. He was still in control.

* * *

Having dropped Evangeline at her door, Elizabeth and Sophie now sat in the small salon of Sophie's parents' cosy townhouse in Perman Street.

Placing down her teacup, Sophie pulled out of its wrapping the length of silver lace, then draped it over the chair back. She peered at it from different angles.

'It's just right,' Elizabeth reassured her. 'So delicate…like a cobweb… It will suit you wonderfully.'

Sophie giggled that she hoped that didn't mean she resembled a spider, but her eyes were speculative as she looked at her grave-faced best friend. 'What has upset you the most today, Elizabeth? Being accosted by that rat, Cadmore, or meeting the Viscount with a…um…lady friend?'

Elizabeth immediately sipped from her cup. It clattered back onto its saucer. 'Neither bothered me,' she blurted with a bright smile.

At Sophie's ironically winging eyebrows, the corners of Elizabeth's mouth drooped. 'Oh, very well; I admit that I certainly would have preferred missing both of those *gentlemen* in that warehouse today.' A shapely, slender hand worried at her brow. 'I hate Cadmore! He's a detestable lecher. And I hate the Viscount because…' She tailed into silence. 'I'm quite sure he's a detestable lecher, too. But I've, as yet, no proper proof, so I'll say I hate him because…because… Oh, I just hate him! He has insulted me and threatened me and done various other things.' A hand flap concluded the explanation as she slumped back into the sofa.

'He's extraordinarily handsome, Elizabeth,' Sophie tendered mildly. 'Not at all as I would have imagined. I don't think he looks rough at all. Quite the reverse. He seems…sophisticated and polished. And he wanted you to stop and talk to him.'

'I doubt his companion did,' Elizabeth remarked sourly. 'She was very beautiful, wasn't she?' was added on a twisted little smile.

Sophie grimaced agreement. 'Very. But then so are you, Elizabeth. I've always envied you your wonderful eyes and hair. You're younger than she is. You could easily outshine her, if you wished.'

'But I don't wish,' Elizabeth lilted. Picking up the lace, she draped it about her friend's slender shoulders, cocking her head to assess the effect. A violet glance arrowed at the stately burr-walnut case-clock in the corner. It was almost five-fifteen. She would leave at six of the clock. She calculated the Viscount and Edwina would have concluded their meeting by then. She calculated, too, her absence from home adequately conveyed her resistance to the 'tiresome engagement'.

Perhaps Stratton's lady love might object to his marriage and persuade him to retain the status quo. She didn't look the sort of woman to allow herself to be relegated. In fact, Elizabeth, thought dully, she looked the sort of woman who might be a little like herself: a little too proud. Wandering to the window, she scanned the busy street but saw nothing. She trusted he would leave her necklace with Edwina. She believed him a man of his word on that score. She just hoped Edwina's untimely revelation last night hadn't made him too suspicious about why she desperately wanted it. In any case, the truth shouldn't unduly bother him. Whether she kept or disposed of her jewellery would be of no interest once he had her dowry promised in its stead.

'I hate to see you looking so anxious, Elizabeth. Is something else troubling you?' Sophie asked quietly, on joining her at the window. She slipped a comforting hand through the crook of a soft-skinned arm.

'Actually, yes,' Elizabeth admitted. She sighed. 'I saw something awful when returning from Sunday School with Hugh…'

'You must stop going! You are being too reckless entering that slum to teach those poor little wretches.'

'No, it wasn't the children,' Elizabeth reassured, facing Sophie. 'I encountered a lady I once knew well. She had her come-out the same year I did. I classed her as a social equal and a friend. She has fallen on such terrible…harrowing times, Sophie.' Her voice broke and she sensed tears needle her eyes. 'Truthfully, it makes me feel so ashamed for even thinking I have problems. I must help her! But I'm not sure how.'

Sophie quickly steered her friend back to the sofa and sat beside her. Taking Elizabeth's hands in hers, she pleaded, 'Tell me, at once! What on earth has gone on?'

Some minutes later, Elizabeth had recounted all that had passed between Jane Selby and Leach and Hugh and herself late on Sunday afternoon. Sophie flopped back into the plump cushions with her neat little hands covering her lower face. Mingling horror and astonishment was very apparent in the brown eyes widening above her fingers.

'How…*awful*!' Sophie finally exploded. 'The poor woman. To be deceived so. And by a man she believed loved her. And the poor babe!'

'I didn't see him,' Elizabeth quietly explained. 'I've no idea how old he is: whether a babe in arms or a young child. What can be done, Sophie?'

Sophie helplessly shook her head. 'It seems this repulsive Leach wants money or he'll not let her go. I have a small amount left from my allowance,' she volunteered immediately.

'I think he will want a substantial amount. Hugh said that Nathaniel Leach springs from a family of thieves. His mother is a notorious bawd and a fence. They will doubtless let Jane and little Jack go free if the price is right. But *then* where are they to go? Jane maintains her parents have disowned her, and Edwina is loath to help, let alone take her in.'

Getting into the spirit of the drama, Sophie leapt up and raced to the door. 'I shall see what I have to pawn.' Some minutes later, she was back with a reticule stuffed with odd pieces of jewellery. They were tipped onto the sofa between them and picked through: silver combs and earrings, a pearl ring and a broken gold bangle. Sophie disentangled a small gold locket and pulled it to one side. 'Not that.' She smiled apologetically. 'It was Fiona's,' she explained, referring to her elder sister who had died of smallpox, aged fifteen.

Elizabeth laid a hand on her arm. 'It's very good of you, Sophie, to part with anything at all. But I'm not sure this vile man will be moved by anything less than a substantial bribe.' She sighed in exasperation. 'And Hugh will not be of any help at all! Not only is he intimidated by Edwina—she has forbidden me to go back there—but he believes it is too late to help Jane, in any case. He insists she will never leave her fancy man...that she is somehow in his thrall! What nonsense! What do men know of these things! They are all such conceited creatures. Yet I believed Hugh to be different.' She tutted her disgust. 'And Grandmama endorsed his male chauvinism; simply to frighten me into staying away, I'll warrant. But I'll not be so easily put off!' She paused for breath. 'You must keep it all confidential. Please don't breathe a word that I intend to somehow help Jane and her little son.'

'Of course!' Sophie stressed. 'And I shall assist in any way I can. 'Tis the time to do the deed.' She suddenly interjected, in all seriousness, 'Mars...planet of action...is currently midheaven. It's a good sign.'

Elizabeth gave a little choke of laughter. 'Well, we're certainly going to need all the good auspices we can get!'

'Well, miss, what have you to say for yourself?'

Elizabeth removed her bonnet in the hallway, then shook out her crumpled, pearly locks. Slender fingers combed casually through them. 'What have I to say for myself?' she echoed with mock pensiveness. 'Ah, I know, what you're hinting at. It concerns the Viscount's visit, does it not?'

'Indeed it does!' Edwina shrilled in high dudgeon.

'Well I shall oblige you then and say: did he bring it?'

'Did he bring what, may I ask? A big stick with which to beat his graceless future wife? Who could blame him if he did?'

'Did he bring my necklace?' Elizabeth enunciated, overlooking her grandmother's boiling physiognomy.

'Well, if he did, he took it home with him again. And serve you right if he did do that. Had you scraped the grace to drag yourself home before he left half an hour ago, perhaps he might have handed it over! If, indeed, he had it with him.'

Elizabeth's mouth pursed into a rosebud. The relief that she had avoided him by such a narrow margin was barely acknowledged. 'He said I might have it today!' she exploded as her foot stamped on marble.

Edwina ignored the tantrum. 'We are to dine with Ross and his family on Friday. The documents are signed pertaining to the dowry. The marriage is to take place in three weeks...' she listed out.

Elizabeth's violet eyes darkened as her pupils grew large with shock. 'Over my dead body,' emerged in a croak.

'That can no doubt be arranged. The Viscount looked murderous, I can tell you, when I said you were not yet home. By the time we had twice taken tea and talked of trivialities and he realised you had no intention of putting in an appearance, I thought he might take himself off again without concluding the deal. Even Pettifer said he'd never seen him look so fuming.'

'More likely he was aggrieved at having cut short his shopping trip with his mistress,' Elizabeth snapped into her grandmother's censure. But she couldn't ignore the writhing in her stomach on learning how well she had succeeded in annoying him.

Edwina looked sharply at her granddaughter. 'You saw him out today?'

'Indeed. He was shopping with his doxy in Pall Mall.'

Edwina's face softened, and for the first time since her granddaughter had walked through the door with September sun silhouetting her petite figure and haloing her glorious hair, Edwina felt kindly disposed towards her. She took one of Elizabeth's small hands in a pudgy palm. 'You don't want to get upset over that vampish brunette,' she cajoled, patting at white fingers. 'Trollops like Cecily Booth are soon forgotten by the likes of Stratton. She might be younger, but she can't hold a candle to you in face or figure. Ross will never give her a second thought once he has you as his wife.'

'Oh, indeed! You're absolutely right about *her*, Grandmama,' Elizabeth dismissed on a shrill laugh. 'The trollop I was referring to is actually a little older than me, I should say, and blonde and very beautiful. Mayhap, he'll not be quite so eager to cast her off. How many in all do you imagine there are?' Without awaiting a reply, she made for the stairs, aware of her grandmother stunned into speechlessness for a change. She had given her something to chew on, she knew. In a determined show of nonchalance, and ignoring her stomach's squeamishness, Elizabeth began swinging her bonnet on its ribbons as she lightly ascended the stairs. But the same phrases tumbled through her mind as had earlier that afternoon in the fabric emporium: Damn you, Stratton! I just don't care!

'I'm glad you chose that gown: I've always thought it suited you.'

Elizabeth managed a smile at the compliment. She fussed over pushing a pin more securely into her elaborate, lustrous coiffure. A slender finger wound a smoky-blonde tress into a tighter ringlet, then twiddled the damson-coloured velvet ribbon threaded there. Abruptly she sat back against the squabs, gripping her fidgeting fingers in her lap.

'Are you nervous?' Edwina asked as they rattled over cobbles in her luxurious barouche heading towards Grosvenor Square.

'Of course not!' After a moment a glossy-eyed glance slanted across the dusky interior of the coach. Elizabeth noticed her grandmother was smiling. A small, reciprocal smile slanted her soft mouth. 'Well, perhaps a little. It is a while since I socialised with anyone other than Sophie and her parents. Or Hugh and ladies from the Society of Friends.'

'You call that socialising?'

Elizabeth ignored the dry comment. 'I'm a little out of practice, that's all it is,' she explained away her uneasiness at dining with the Viscount's guests. She soothingly smoothed her unsteady fingers back and forth against the rich, plum velvet of her stylish gown, while restoking her agitation by wondering whether any of those who were to be present to-night were cognizant with her history.

Edwina had told her before they left Connaught Street that the Viscount's mother seldom left Cornwall where she led a quiet life. It was unlikely she would have bothered herself with *beau monde* scandals. His brother, although a wealthy aristocrat, now resided in Brighton with his family and used his Mayfair townhouse but rarely. Edwina had then complained she wasn't sure which other people were to be present, although she guessed Guy Markham might, and that failing was all Elizabeth's fault. Her last meeting with the Viscount had been so strained due to Elizabeth's non-appearance that she had forgotten all the little essentials over which she had meant to quiz him.

Elizabeth tilted her chin. She didn't care, in any case, which of his piffling friends were due to attend! If they liked him, that obviously cast their own characters under grave suspicion! She didn't care, either, whether they knew about her disgrace. She had no intention of playing the pariah for any *parvenu* cits! In fact, she had had no intention of playing along with this foolishness at all. She found herself travelling to Grosvenor Square this evening not primarily to dine or meet his friends and family, but to retrieve her necklace.

She had been quite certain that, once the Viscount's temper cooled a bit, he would make contact during the week. After all, they were now unofficially betrothed. But he had not. She had not seen or heard a word from him. Thus there had been no opportunity to revile him for keeping her necklace. And she had balked at the idea of again scandalising all concerned by visiting him to demand he return it. Which left just writing a note: which he would doubtless ignore, for he must still be very angry with her for again snubbing him. He hadn't even contacted Edwina; her grandmother had been a little chary of the absence, lest he was brooding on breaking the contract, and this dinner date. Elizabeth, too, had been moderately relieved he had not, for she needed to accost him tonight and wrest her jewellery from him.

In direct contrast to the Viscount's absence had been Hugh Clemence's many visits. The first one had her inwardly groaning, wondering how to deflect questions over her odd disappearance from home that had occasioned him being twice roused from his bed by Pettifer. Edwina had unexpectedly come to her rescue. Usually the vicar's arrival prompted her grandmother to disappear in the opposite direction. This time, she was all affability.

'Sorry about harrying you the other night, Reverend,' she had barked. 'If you must tick us off, blame m'granddaughter. She has this habit of secreting herself in odd corners of the house. And m'eyes aren't all they should be. Can you wonder at m'fears when she wasn't in her bed, but potting ferns in the conservatory at such an hour? I think this business with the slum dwellers is badly affecting her.' The dark hint and head tapping that accompanied the remark had been laden with accusation.

Hugh had looked mystified at being obliquely to blame for his own disturbance. On seeing his hurt bewilderment, Elizabeth had comfortingly mouthed, 'Eccentric…' with a couple of meaningful grimaces for good measure.

Whatever her grandmother said, she was determined to go as usual with Hugh to Sunday School. And she would make it her business to track down Jane Selby and rescue her. So she would need a valuable item to take with her…

Her musing was curtailed as she realised the carriage had stopped. Elizabeth noticed two flare-toting footmen, resplendent in their dark livery and moth-bright powdered wigs, approaching their carriage door. Her final reflection, before disembarking, was that the cheating, lying host she was about to be presented to presently held that necessary valuable item. But not for much longer. It was hers! And she was determined to have it!

Chapter Ten

'I've always been a tiny bit in love with Ross…'

The confession emerged in a conspiratorial sigh. Rebecca wrinkled her neat little nose at her friends, then glanced across the opulent drawing room at their darkly handsome host talking to her beloved Luke.

'I think we all feel that way about Ross, Becky,' Emma Du Quesne admitted, but her exquisite topaz eyes were on her tall, blond spouse, grouped with the Trelawney men, and no doubt discussing their copper-mining consortium. Sir Richard Du Quesne had propped a negligent elbow on the magnificent Adams' chimneypiece, while emphasising some point to his Cornish colleagues with the crystal goblet he held. His silver gaze slid sideways, merged with his wife's; it was a second or two before a private smile passed between them.

There was a third lady, resting comfortably between Rebecca and Emma on a plump-cushioned gilt-framed sofa. Viscountess Courtenay trailed an oval fingernail across delicately painted cherubs on her gauzy fan. 'It's as well our husbands trust us so much,' she contributed to the romantic debate. Victoria slanted a fond look at her dear David, chivalrously bringing to Demelza Trelawney a glass of ratafia while her sons socialised by the hearth.

All the people in the room were joined by family or deep friendship. All were enjoying this fine opportunity—while awaiting the arrival of Ross's other guests—to catch up with news on subjects as diverse as business and babies, as well as airing all the other myriad little domestic matters that were gladly heard by people whose opinion and advice were valued.

'They trust Ross, too. That's why they let us flirt with such a dangerously attractive bachelor,' Emma said. 'They've all been acquainted such a long time. Richard told me that Ross has ever been a successful charmer. I doubt it's exaggeration! In the short while I've known him, I've witnessed all manner of females fighting quite immodestly over him.'

'I feel privileged to have had his escort on occasions,' Rebecca added. 'It's been very agreeable. I'll miss his teasing remarks and wicked glances…I shall make Luke take over where his brother has left off!'

'That was quickly achieved, Lady Ramsden!' Emma drolly announced, noticing Baron Ramsden's dark eyes targeting his vivacious, blonde wife.

'What makes you think Ross might now deprive us of his delightful gallantry, Becky?' Victoria interjected. 'The few days I've been here in London, I've noticed no change in him.'

'Oh, it's hard to be specific,' Rebecca bubbled, very conscious of her husband's ardent gaze. 'He just seems different: a little preoccupied and impatient at times. He lacks his usual devil-may-care attitude to every single thing. I think perhaps he is at last taking his responsibilities seriously: he did tell me there is a mountain of work to be done at Stratton Hall before it is properly habitable. And then again he seemed very…interested in a fair lady we saw when out shopping. I think he is possibly in the process of…' Her voice became whisper-soft. 'Delicate negotiations with a new *chère amie*. We also came face to face with a brunette he had just put off! The blonde is so much lovelier…refined, too. I believe Ross called her Lady somebody or other. Mayhap she is a young widow. But I couldn't prise out of him much at all. And you know how he usually yields to a little coquetry.' She nodded

meaningfully at Emma and Victoria, and as one, they all
slanted a speculative look at Ross who was consulting his
gold hunter.

Irritably, the case was flicked shut and he looked at the
clock on the mantel, as though checking the time.

'Is Guy Markham late?'

Ross stared blankly at his brother for a moment.

'Is Markham late for dinner?' Luke repeated with slow
stress. 'Dammit, Ross, you're acting like a blockhead. You've
had your watch out three times in three minutes. Who are you
waiting on? Markham or this Mrs Sampson you've invited?'

'More likely to be Mrs Sampson, I'd have thought,' Dickie
Du Quesne chipped in drily before sipping from his glass.

'Mrs Sampson is a very old friend…in more ways than one:
she's over sixty years of age,' Ross informed Dickie with a
grin.

Dickie choked into his aperitif. 'Over sixty?' he gasped.
'Good God! That's a little too mature even for your all-
encompassing taste. You mentioned her granddaughter might
accompany her. Perhaps she has you on tenterhooks. Is she
squint-eyed and stalking you?'

It was Ross's turn to choke on his drink. He grimaced while
soothing his furrowed brow with hard, dark fingers.

Reading nothing positive in his friend's skewed expression,
Dickie guessed gloomily, 'Oh, perfect! She's not just out of
the schoolroom and liable to get all giggly if anyone attempts
conversation with her, is she?

'Well, whoever it is we're waiting on, I wish they'd hurry
up,' Luke growled. 'I'm ravenous!' Barely pausing, he continued, 'And Mother is signalling at you…for the second time.
By her look, I'd say maternal advice is in the offing. First, a
little brotherly advice,' Luke continued soberly, with a staying
hand on Ross's arm. 'Tell her what she wants to hear. For
some reason, she's been more anxious than usual over you,
of late. She was determined to come to London and see how
you do. And you know how much she hates to travel…'

With a sigh, Ross retrieved his goblet from the mantel and

dutifully strolled towards Demelza Trelawney's chair. As he hunkered down beside it, Lord Courtenay removed himself from where he'd been perching on the arm. With a parting smile, David strolled to squeeze onto the sofa beside his darling wife, Victoria, and her friends.

Demelza placed a delicate hand on her youngest son's lean, tanned face. 'Are you happy?'

Green-gold eyes lifted to hers, gazed deep into their gentle brown depths. He smiled. 'Of course…yes, I'm a Viscount, in favour at court. I've this fine townhouse and a magnificent estate—or at least it will be when I'm done with it. You must come and see it; next week, if you feel like a carriage ride to Kent.'

'You've told me what you've achieved, Ross, not what I asked,' his mother mildly reproved. 'Being a Viscount with a grand home is nice. Being content with that would make it wonderful. You're still not content. You've craved danger and excitement all your life and I've watched you indulge it way too much. Now I feel I should have been firmer with your father…with you all…and curbed it when you were younger. Oh, very well, tried to curb it,' she amended with a little moue as she read his ruefully amused expression. 'But it's gone on too long now; restlessness…inconstancy…seem natural to you.' She angled her head, attempting to lure her son's evasive feral eyes.

She gazed at his dear profile until it wavered out of focus and in her mind's eye stood a child; wild as the rugged Cornish coast, as the wind that cowed the grass along the cliff tops. Never still, never sated, never hurt. Sometimes he would come to her, out of childish duty, raise torn elbows and knees, while fidgeting to be free again. Momentarily, he might tolerate her fingers forking into his thick, sleek hair, her lips kissing better his wounds, before his wiry little body wriggled away. And then he would be gone, running…running…long dusky locks tangling with the briny breeze, his beautiful dark face once more animated…laughing…always laughing. And now…now Ross was hurt again and it was nothing a mother's kiss could soothe. Ross was in love.

Aware of her eyes on him, Ross glanced up, humouring her with a crooked smile.

'You helped Luke discover tranquillity and I know you'd like to find it, too,' Demelza resumed slowly, choosing her words carefully. 'But its lack never worried you, before. It only worried me.' She punitively waggled his square, shady jaw, emphasising her vexation. 'But now…you're different, my love; there's melancholy in your eyes. I think perhaps you finally know where it is, but still it's eluding you…'

Ross removed his mother's cool palm from his face. He looked at it, fleetingly pressed his lips to it, before linking their fingers and skimming her pale cheek with the back of his dark hand. He smiled at her appealing, fine-boned features. Her skin looked as soft as it felt: little marred by the years of coastal living, and her raven's-wing hair shining with silver skeins, rendered her still strikingly attractive at sixty years old. About to give spurious reassurance while inwardly cursing her maternal perceptiveness, Ross suddenly became aware of her eyes slipping away from his and a static silence crackling in the room around him. It was the serene curve to his mother's lips that snapped his head about.

'Mrs Sampson and Lady Elizabeth Rowe…' Dawkins, his butler, droned nasally.

Elizabeth sensed herself rooting to a spot barely a yard into the drawing room. Blood drained from her complexion until it prickled icily, and those old, terrifying demons that she thought conquered and long banished to her past, danced with devilish abandon in the pit of her stomach.

The scene was a decade old, yet frighteningly familiar. *Parvenu* cits? Her disparaging description returned to mock her as she gazed, panic-stricken, into a room that was all dignified elegance…as were its occupants. One skittering, scouting look had impressed on her these were charmed people; people of influence and gentility…and fabulous wealth. And they were all staring at her…and she couldn't bear it.

She was obliquely aware that only a few seconds had passed since she and Edwina were announced; the butler was still in the process of bowing sedately out of the room, pulling closed the enormous doors as he went. Only seconds had passed! But in a moment she would hear the whispers, see the sneers, and squirm beneath their scorn as she strove not to turn and flee.

As though Edwina sensed she might bolt, a preventive hand grabbed her elbow, attempting to urge her forward. Encouragement was hissed warmly against her ear. But her legs felt stiff and leaden, her chest too tight to drag in breath. Her violet eyes began flitting agitatedly over blonde…brunette… male…female…sparkling gems…sleek silk; never lingering long enough to register anything or anyone clearly, yet scouring, desperately seeking. *Where are you?* wailed plaintively in her head. More than anything in the world, she wanted to locate his strong gypsy face, his broad, brown-clad body. She needed him…now…so much…

Her bated breath whimpered out between her compressed, chalky lips as his movement amid the stillness arrested and held her eyes. He rose slowly, sinuously, from the side of a chair and was walking towards them. His eyes never once relinquished hers and she held to that comforting, honeyed gaze as a castaway might cling to a piece of driftwood.

'Mrs Sampson…Lady Elizabeth…I'm very glad you could come…'

The welcome was warm, sincere. His attention was courteously with Edwina as she addressed him, but his touch was immediately with Elizabeth. Slowly, discreetly, he drew her towards him, his firm familiar fingers on her cold, quaking arm. She felt the warmth of a thumb smooth back and forth, back and forth, and another shuddering little sigh escaped her. He shifted casually closer, and it seemed the most natural thing in the world to move to meet him, seek the lee of his large, solid body.

Within a few seconds of listening to discourse about the changeable weather, in particular the rainstorm earlier that had

knocked the petals off Edwina's favourite crimson rose, and
the ensuing sunshine that was so welcome but did nothing to
repair the damage; Elizabeth was calm enough to again be
fretting. This time her fears were that he would think her a
socially inept nincompoop to be standing so mute and trem-
bly, and so clingingly close to him. She took a very small
step back; it was the most she could manage.

Another superbly attired, handsome gentleman strolled to
join them. Ross introduced she and Edwina to his brother,
Luke. She believed she murmured an adequate response to a
convivial greeting from this stately aristocrat who looked
older than Ross by some years, but so resembled him, that
the family connection would have been obvious. Then Baron
Ramsden was gallantly leading Edwina away to meet the
other guests.

Elizabeth blinked rapidly at Ross's shoulder, unable to look
anywhere else. She was sure they were the focus of many
pairs of eyes, and that she was foolishly engendering further
interest, and thus her own uneasiness, by her obvious reluctance to quit his side. She despised herself for her timorous-
ness, but it was far too soon to relinquish the relief and security she found stationed so close to this man.

'Don't be nervous, sweetheart,' he encouraged with such
husky affection in his tone that Elizabeth's head jerked up.

There was amusement gleaming in his tawny eyes but it
wasn't scornful; it was gentle, understanding...and prompted
an immediate defensive indignation. She wouldn't be pitied!
Not by him! About to retort that she wasn't nervous and he
had no right to suppose she might be, the words withered,
unuttered, on her lips. The discreet caress on her arm was
again working its lulling magic; also she read from his wry
expression that he was anticipating the rebuttal. But primarily
she remained silent because she recollected him calling her
sweetheart and, even if it was mere meaningless cajolery, she
liked it.

His smile strengthened into a throaty chuckle that acknowledged the piquant mingling of belligerence and vulnerability

purpling her eyes. 'Good; I can tell you're now a little more relaxed, Elizabeth. You look almost the shrewish little madam I've come to know and love…'

Elizabeth stared at him, unable to draw breath, drowning in his golden gaze replete with a mockery that wasn't quite genuine. Her eyes dragged away and her tongue tip moistened her lips. 'I…I'm sorry if I seemed a dumb idiot just then when you introduced me to your brother.' Desperate to appear confident and capable, she flicked her bright, burnished head, setting her curls dancing, while rushing on, 'It's just…I rarely socialise in…I'm a little out of practice with people of…I rarely go out now.' She tailed off, feeling her complexion heat. 'I don't like to be stared at…' she defensively concluded her justification.

'There's not a soul here who means ill by it, Elizabeth. It's just that it's impossible not to stare when you look so outstandingly lovely. When you arrived, you stunned me into gawping at you, too, for a moment. And I'm acquainted with your ravishing looks.' His eyes became heavy-lidded, a veiled honey gaze flowing over her lush, petite body sheathed in taut plum velvet.

A hand instinctively fluttered to her low neckline as though she could shield from view the frantic rise and fall of her pearly, satin-skinned bosom.

He took the fingers, placed them in the crook of his arm, as he turned them into the sparkling warmth of his opulent drawing room. As far as her little reconnoitering glances could detect, nobody was staring, or even looking their way now.

'Come, let me quickly introduce you to everyone. Then I should like to speak to you privately before dinner.' His voice had lost its intimate, indulgent edge and become brisk.

Elizabeth felt chilled again, although her composure was consolidating. Of course, he would be businesslike now he had steadied her nerves…made her presentable. This was, after all, business, however attentive and chivalrous he contrived to be in front of his kith and kin.

When this invitation had been issued at the beginning of

the week she had presumptuously believed he was eager his family and friends should find favour with her. Now, she was more inclined to think the reverse was true. Doubtless, he wanted *her* approved by these imposing people before irrevocably committing himself. He intended she play the part of an agreeable, prospective spouse. Pride and indignation wedged a blockage in her throat. Well, she would have little choice but to cooperate tonight, even if she never did so again! And she expected him to reciprocate by playing the part of an honest gentleman and returning her necklace when she demanded it!

With a huge, settling breath, her sculpted chin tilted confidently just as they reached a sofa. She steeled herself; she was fine and ready; she was a Marquess's daughter. And then she looked down into the smiling, turquoise eyes of the lady her intended had taken shopping.

She had not realised just how literally he meant…*quickly* introduce. Within what she guessed to be under fifteen minutes, Elizabeth found herself being returned, by her host, to the double-doors of the drawing room she had so recently entered. Her head was reeling from the effort of remembering names, from an amazement at the sincerity and warmth of the welcome she and her grandmother had received from these people. She could discern no sly looks or whispered asides from the ladies as she passed by the sofa. None of the gentleman had ogled her, although she understood the approval in their eyes as they took a look at Ross in that subtle, meaningful way men had. And all present were so astonishingly good-looking! Even his gracious, doe-eyed mother was still attractive. She couldn't ever recall being in a room with so many beautiful people.

'Mr Guy Markham…' boomed out close behind them, startling Elizabeth out of her pleasant reflection.

Guy swept in, looking a little overheated and harrassed. Spying his friend at once, just inside the door, he blurted, 'Sorry, Stratt, to be so late. Blasted axle nigh on departed company with the carriage in Oxford Street. That footman of yours who's handy with the tools is giving my man some assistance with it…' Giving proper attention to his friend's companion, he suddenly declared, 'Well, Lady Elizabeth Rowe! And not looking a jot different from when last I saw you! How have you been?' He found one of her hands and gallantly raised small, white fingers to his lips.

'Very well, sir, thank you,' Elizabeth said amiably, with a little dip of her smoky-blonde head. Feeling now quite light-hearted, she was about to return the courtesy and ask how he did, but found that she was being backed through the closing doors by Ross, while Dawkins, his butler looked scandalised by his master's undignified behaviour: squeezing them a path past him through the aperture.

'Find yourself a drink, Guy, and then speak to my mother, would you? She was only asking after you this morning,' Ross sent casually back over his shoulder.

'Oh…right….' Guy said, bemused. He tilted his nut-brown head to watch his friend disappearing from sight.

'Dinner is ready to be served, my lord,' Dawkins informed his master in a cautionary tone once he had closed the doors with a precise flourish.

'Not quite yet, Dawkins. I'll tell you when…'

Dawkins inclined his head in acceptance of the dictate and marched, arms swinging, away along the carpeted corridor.

Aware of being studied, Elizabeth glanced up very quizzically from beneath her lush, brunette lashes. She looked down again, heart hammering in response to a wordless discipline she read in his eyes. A tentative move to re-enter the drawing room was blocked. Instead she found herself being steered determinedly along the corridor by a firm hand practically spanning the back of her tiny waist. He released her, swung open another door, and tersely gestured for her to enter.

His aloof manner made her exceedingly apprehensive, yet she knew she needed a little discreet conversation with him if she was to recover her necklace tonight. Inside the room, a roving inspection registered that it was a study with book-lined walls and an imposing desk spanning the entire area beneath a wide casement window. Beyond the glass, stars studded a black sky.

She turned quickly about, heart pumping. 'I know my reputation is tarnished already, my lord, and I know I have previously engineered just this sort of private tête-à-tête, but I really think, as you have company, it is best we are not alone like this.'

He had not moved away from the door and stood resting back against it, arms crossed over his chest, watching her. Some silent seconds later Elizabeth dropped her prim gaze from his hard face. The aubusson carpet, the walnut panelling, seemed less unyielding.

'I'm very angry with you.'

The bald admonishment, delivered dispassionately, rendered her speechless. She had believed he had tolerated her initial lack of social graces. She had demonstrated impeccable breeding ever since. To now remind her of her panic, fling it in her face in that…that careless manner… Glossy, violet eyes blazed at him as she chewed at her lower lip.

'I believe you owe me an apology, my dear…once again.'

Elizabeth opened her mouth to speak. Humiliation blocked the words in her throat. Her lips quivered then pressed closed. She had allowed him to lead her here imagining that, prior to announcing their betrothal, he wanted to impress upon her that the sordid details of their wedding contract be kept confidential. She had been certain he wouldn't want these eminent people to know he'd been outwitted by a wily old woman.

'I…I have already apologised,' she finally burst out in a tight little voice. 'I did not mean to act with such…such crass dependency, or embarrass you, if that's what you feel I have done. I think it more likely I have made a fool of myself. Nevertheless, as you wish to hear it one more time: I am sorry. I am sorry for ever coming here tonight—'

'Ah, I see…' he broke into her fierce defence. A small smile quirked his mouth. 'No. I didn't actually mean that, Elizabeth. Your insecurity and vulnerability don't bother me.

In fact, it's quite endearing. I like you close to me...needing me.'

'What, then?' she whispered, unable to hide her astonishment at that revelation.

He pushed away from the door. 'What, then?' he mimicked. 'What, then...about a *tiresome engagement* we had arranged earlier in the week that you failed to attend. Does that strike a chord? I'm quite happy for you to feel ashamed of that crass behaviour. Do you?'

Elizabeth bristled beneath his sharp, sardonic censure. 'No,' she snapped.

'Why did you deliberately stay away from home and avoid contributing to the wedding plans? Because you thought I had been shopping with my mistress earlier that afternoon?'

Elizabeth blushed to the roots of her silky, silver hair. 'I...I thought no such thing!' she burst out. Her complexion, if possible, became hotter, not only because it was an arrant lie but because the elegant lady she had just met, and learned was his sister-in-law, Rebecca, had greeted her with such sweet friendliness. And she had referred to her to Edwina as a doxy!

'Why, then?'

'I...I was upset by...by a certain...event. And I had more important things to do!' And all of that was the truth! she exhorted herself, remembering how shaken she had been by Linus Savage assaulting her in the fabric warehouse. She also recalled she and Sophie investigating ways to raise money for Jane Selby that afternoon after their shopping trip. Without doubt, her time had been far...far more vitally spent in that charitable occupation than in returning home to pick over a venal marriage contract with this hateful...hateful man!

'What certain event upset you?' he asked as he came closer.

'It's a private matter...'

'That you can share with your future husband. I've told you...I take an interest in my betrothed's problems.'

'Please don't,' Elizabeth rebuffed him frigidly. 'For I shall deal with all of them alone.'

'Even those that necessitate you slumming around Wapping docks to find this friend fallen on hard times?'

Elizabeth swallowed, froze beneath his astute scrutiny. 'Yes. Especially those...' she eventually forced out. He was barely a foot away now, and she was aware of his hot stripping gaze flowing over her body, lingering where the tonal velvet pile was rippling alluringly at breast and hips.

His fingers curled by his sides before disappearing to clasp behind his back. 'There are times, Elizabeth, when I'm not quite sure how I keep my hands off you.'

She shot a startled glance at him, then at the door as though measuring its distance.

His expression was bemused, self-mocking. 'Then again, if I yield to it, there's a possibility they might go straight for your throat. Such a waste...' As if to remove temptation, they were shoved into his trouser pockets. As if to remove her inclination to flee, he abruptly walked away. 'So; let's try again. What upset you that afternoon. Was it Cadmore?'

Another artless blush betrayed her.

Ross swore beneath his breath, at her wordless confirmation of his suspicions. 'Did he speak to you? Insult you? I saw him, too, whilst I was in that shop. He looked guilty as hell. Did you tell him we are betrothed?'

'Of course not! Why should I tell him any such thing?' Noting the intelligent, speculative glitter in his eyes, she blurted, 'I can deal with the Earl of Cadmore. I have been doing so for almost a decade.'

'Yes, I know. And I've just witnessed how that constant *doing so* has taken its toll on you. What did he say?'

Elizabeth dropped her eyes, her stomach churning again with sick shame as flashes of that venomous stare, that muttered invective, bombarded her mind. She didn't want to recall it...she wanted it forgotten.

'Tell me...' he insinuated silkily, sternly, into her turbulent thoughts.

Elizabeth jerked her head to frown at the comforting glow in the hearth. 'It was nothing...nothing much at all. I forget...' She choked an acrid laugh. 'He is never very imaginative. I'm sure you must know what men say to women in such circumstances.'

Ross walked close and a hand spanned her face, gently bringing it to look into his. 'No, I don't know. What did he say?'

Compliance came suddenly, unexpectedly. 'He said I was a brazen bitch who had known the dregs of society and that he would make me pay for my insolence and have me if it was the last thing he did. There! That is what he said...amongst other things. I told you he was not very original and you would already know the gist of it. Did you not say something similar to me yourself? Are you satisfied now?' She jerked her ashen face from his fingers and backed away.

Ross stared at her, his face seeming a tense, fleshless mask, as though his skin had tightened on his bones. Then he frowned as though in profound puzzlement. She noticed white bracket his mouth, a muscle close to it pull spasmodically. 'Thank you for telling me,' was all he said.

'Can we go back to the others now?'

'No.'

Elizabeth gestured futility with a pale, graceful hand. 'Why on earth not? What is to be gained by staying here alone? It can only lead to further bickering between us.'

Ross rested his weight back against the desk, braced his hands either side of him. Abruptly snapping his head up, he gazed at the ceiling. 'Come here,' he requested. When she remained still, he dropped his face to look at her and extended a hand. 'Come here.' His fingers beckoned.

She looked warily at those long, tanned fingers that a few days ago had so gently skimmed her skin, scorching fever in their wake.

'Come...'

She recognised the edge of command in that final, short summons. Slowly she approached him, halting just out of reach. Rocking forward, he grabbed her by the upper arms and hauled her between his spaced feet, holding her until she ceased straining. She was aware of his shady dark chin close to her forehead, aware of the spicy, sandalwood scent of him, the warmth of his hard masculine body.

'I'm sorry. I'm very, very sorry that I ever said any of that to you. I wanted to apologise before but got distracted. You do that to me. Make me forget things, make me say and do odd things. You've turned my world upside down... I don't know why I shall go into my dining room in a short while, and face people I care about, to announce my marriage, when privately I know my fiancée dislikes me. Unless, in a way that defies logic, I care more for her than anything else, and sense it's worth the risk carrying on because I'm hoping...chancing...that in time, she will like me...'

Elizabeth slowly raised cynical violet eyes. 'It's not the money,' he said in response to that look and the unspoken words souring her full, sweet lips. 'God knows, it's not the money. I don't need it...leastways, not that much.'

Elizabeth plumbed his eyes, searching for his soul... searching for deceit and sophistry. This was Ross Trelawney, a frantic part of her brain reminded her, as she sensed her scepticism melting beneath his liquid gold gaze and her body tilting towards his. Viscount Stratton was really Ross Trelawney, the bounty-hunter, hellion and seducer par excellence, she rigorously impressed upon herself. A decade ago she had witnessed snippets of his wild carousing with her own eyes, had heard gossip of much, much more. Only a few days ago, her grandmother had let slip he kept a vampish brunette mistress, and she had wondered how many others catered to his pleasure. He was a hard-hearted villain and a hardened rake, as he had described himself not a week since, while in this august house in a room very similar to this one. Yet he wanted her to believe such a man held tender feelings for her? That he didn't intend wedding a scandal-wrecked spinster simply to recoup the fortune a crafty old woman had tricked out of him? Only recently he had mocked her presumptuous expectation that he might propose marriage, then callously given her unchoosable options to repay him.

'If you like me, and repayment isn't important, give me back my necklace,' Elizabeth challenged in a breathy voice.

'So you can do what with it? Hand it over to a pimp in the naïve hope he'll hand over your friend? Life isn't that simple, Elizabeth.'

'It is! It's that simple!' she choked. 'Whatever you say, I know it's that simple. Just as I know you're lying when you say my dowry isn't important to you. It's everything to you. At one time you threatened me with abuse and my grand-mama with gaol simply to lay hands to it! But now you know for sure you can't have it without me, too. So you pretend to care. You're as calculating and crafty as Edwina, but to her I owe so much, not least my affection. To you I owe nothing. You don't like me! That's not what you feel at all!'

Ross looked at her. Then laughed, a bitter sound that grazed his throat. 'Very well; we'll do it your way. I'm motivated by lust and greed. In which case, you can have the necklace tonight after you give me a kiss. Not a very equal exchange, but as I've guests in the house and little inclination to scan-dalise my mother, I'll allow you to satisfy my lechery another night. Then we'll go in to dinner; pretend we're blissfully happy and I'll announce we're to be married in three weeks.'

'No.'

'No?' His dark brows hiked idly, as though he really couldn't care any more.

'Not three weeks… It's too soon…'

'Not for me it isn't,' he drawled drily. 'Three weeks.'

Elizabeth licked her full, soft lips, while she considered. He closed his eyes.

'Get my necklace.'

'When you've kissed me.'

She looked at his lean, dark face. His eyes were still closed, black lashes fanning his cheeks…child's lashes, she thought hysterically as she marvelled at their length and the slight curl to them. Unobserved, she studied the incongruous beauty of his rugged features: thick black brows, wide forehead above, softened by lengthy strands of glossy mahogany hair; straight, strong nose, flaring slightly, well-moulded lips that were a little narrow. She hastily suppressed the urge to touch a finger to the cleft in his chin and curiously test the abrasiveness of shady masculine skin along his honed jaw. His breathing was easy; his powerful chest, resplendent in figured cream waistcoat, was expanding towards the plum velvet curving over her bosom. He was composed; he couldn't give a damn whether she complied or not. She could walk away. She had wanted to before. She had been ready to forfeit angling for her necklace earlier just to escape to the drawing room and other company. Now, that seemed unbelievably craven and selfish. Jane Selby and her little son had been easily abandoned; yet she was their only hope. It was that simple!

'What sort of kiss?'

His lashes raised. 'What sort of kiss?'

'One for you or one for me?' she gravely enquired.

His mouth twisted wryly in comprehension. 'One for us, Elizabeth…' he said, adopting her solemn tone.

She looked again at his sensual mouth and he watched her. She fidgeted on the spot a little. He watched her. Her hands began to raise as though to touch him, then clasped in front of her uncertainly. She pressed her lips together. Her eyes met his.

'Come closer, you can't reach from there,' he pointed out.

'Oh…yes…' Elizabeth said on a faint smile.

He returned her the same sort of faint smile.

She shifted further forward between his spaced feet. Her hands brushed unintentionally against the twill-sheathed iron muscle of his inner thighs and recoiled. She tried to nonchalantly rest them on the desk, by his, but found it too far away. The movement left her tilting precariously off balance. She clutched at his sleeves, steadying herself, her face against his shoulder. Her eyes squeezed shut in mortification. 'I…I'm sorry but I'm no good at this. It's been too long since I…when I was last fond of someone…in the manner of wanting to kiss them, that is…it was…very long ago.'

'Are you talking about Havering?'

Elizabeth relaxed a little, not wanting to move. It felt so comfortable, so easy just being warm and close to him. But it wouldn't last, of course, he didn't want her comfortable and easy laying against his shoulder. But for guests in the house, he would have her pandering to his lechery. 'Yes,' she simply answered his query.

'He's married now,' he said in the same cool, neutral tone.

Elizabeth swallowed, closed her eyes against the soft wool of his coat. 'Yes, I know.' She pushed herself back, unwilling to discuss any of it further. 'You could do it,' she said. 'It will be more to your liking and quicker; your guests must be wondering where on earth their dinner is. Edwina said she was most looking forward to her dinner…but then she always does, of course. She guessed fifteen courses or thereabouts and was hoping that pheasant and salmon and syllabub would be amongst them…' She trailed into silence, a vague smile fading away to nothing, as she stared at his intricately folded cravat, stark white beneath his dusky chin. Suddenly she tipped against him, kissed him full on the lips.

It was shy, soft and soon done. Then, because she realised how boring and inexperienced it must seem, before breaking contact she touched her tongue tip to his mouth, as she re-called he had done when kissing her. She felt his lips part allowing it to flick inside and she was petrified into stillness, unsure what to do next. She knew if she raised her lashes, he would be watching her, probably in a scientific, calculating way. She had confessed to not having kissed in years; she wondered how long it had been since he had encountered such gauche clumsiness from a woman he desired. She doubted Cecily Booth, the vampish brunette, kissed him this way…

With that forlorn thought, she pulled back, face flushing. Immediately she walked away. 'My necklace, please…' She hoped the request sounded cool and compelling. Inwardly, she was writhing. If he laughed at her, scorned her pathetic effort by saying it came nowhere near to earning her back her jewellery, she knew she might fly from the room…from the house.

She heard the slide of wood on wood as a drawer smoothly opened, then his footsteps closing with her. The unexpectedness of cool fingers on her febrile skin made her flinch. He moved her hair from her nape, then the sleek coldness of gold and precious stones slid against her throat. He fastened the collar, then carefully smoothed her moonlight-fair hair into place before both dark hands slipped downwards to enclose her pearly upper arms.

Elizabeth raised unsteady fingers to glide against the gem she had last worn at her début ball. 'Thank you...' she whispered, her lids drooping in sheer gratitude that she once more had it.

He turned her slowly about. A long finger trailed the drape of a silky spiral of hair laying against a fragile jut of collarbone, before sliding to her face. Wordlessly he lowered his mouth to hers, courting her in just the same sort of sweet, seductive way he had before. It was a kiss for her and she was already drowning in it. Her hands raised, unbidden, slid about his neck, into his hair. Her lips opened beneath his, tracked his, sought his when he started to pull away. So it started again, until this time his mouth strayed to freedom across the satin of her cheek and she lay, enervated against him, eyes closed, mouth sleek and lax.

She felt a large hand stir in her hair, rousing her. 'Believe, me Elizabeth, I do like you...' he said softly as, taking her hand, he led her, dazed, from the room.

Chapter Eleven

Elizabeth might have had just the one relation present, but Edwina had been unabashedly joyous enough for a host of family members. Oddly, that had roused her spirits: she'd wanted to please her grandmama. Seeing her so very happy was reparation of sorts for the shelter, the affection she had needed so desperately from the only fond kin remaining to her. Even her anguish on her beloved papa's death had not softened her paternal grandmother's attitude towards her. The Dowager Marchioness considered her disgraced granddaughter as contemptible then as she had when she first besmirched the lofty Thorneycroft name.

Before the announcement, they had feasted on delectable fare. Or so Edwina described it in endless detail the following morning. As the assembly had settled either side of the stately dining table, there had been a scintillating air of expectancy. Elizabeth knew she'd eaten a little, but of what she could not say. Every morsel had turned to ashes in her dry mouth, directly after that brutal look. She had known then, with chilling heart, that kisses counted for nought; she remained unforgiven and still beholden for the necklace she wore.

She had slighted him again, rebuffed his apology, implied he was incapable of finer feelings. So be it, she'd read in those sardonic, dark-as-molasses eyes that had adhered pitilessly to hers. I can be motivated by lust and greed. Expect that of me and I'll willingly oblige.

Thus she had understood, as he'd intended she should, the cruel ambiguity in his speech. Yet it had been sublime... subtle...significant only to her. With an easy eloquence that had demolished for ever her estimation of him as a philistine, he'd conveyed that a bond of deep affection existed between them. Yet never did he actually say so. He'd managed to make her blush and everyone chuckle—she did too in mild shock— with a teasing remark that the fair faces of his children would be attributable to his wife. The ladies had blinked dewy eyes, the gentlemen had looked wise and empathetic. In his mother's gentle countenance she'd read a profound welcome; a tiny sanctioning dip of her head had held no condescension but a hint of female conspiracy.

He had publicly aired his aim to get children on her and gloated over his fortunate choice of marriage partner... Only she knew it was a fortune that had been her grandmother's bequest. The private message was clear: he was happy enough to take her body and her dowry. He had no complaints...yet she might...

A stab of piquant pain accompanied the realisation that, but for different circumstances, it might have been the happiest day of her life. Could she have chosen her in-laws, it might well have been people just like those who counted him as family or friend. Could she have chosen how her husband might look, how he might deport himself on just that occasion, it might have been as Ross Trelawney had that evening. The devastating irony was not lost on her as she was again put in mind of how perfect he could seem. Strong... handsome...witty...polished: no woman could possibly ask for more in a consort...and yet it was all so false.

During their bitter-sweet tête-à-tête he had declared he soon expected her to assuage his lust, then kissed her with mocking tenderness. He had professed to liking her, yet constantly tormented her by look or word. He had said money wasn't his prime concern, yet it didn't alter the fact that only days previously, he and her grandmother had pored for hours over the terms of transferring to him her dowry.

And nothing altered the fact that it was the Sabbath. For the first time in over a year, when Hugh Clemence had come to collect her to take her to Sunday School, she had sent him away, pleading a migraine. Or rather, Edwina had; even in that she was lacking valour. Had she spoken directly to him, she would have felt it incumbent on her to tell him of her engagement…and she couldn't—not yet. She had forsaken the children and Jane and her son because she was an abject coward, she inwardly railed as Hugh's gig turned the corner of the street and finally disappeared from sight.

With a hopeless sigh, she let the curtain flop back into place and wheeled into the room. She had not yet vowed to honour and obey. She was not even betrothed two full days, yet already she was dutiful! She was disgusted with herself!

'I'd hate to discover you've again concerned yourself with East End harlots against my express wishes,' had been his quiet parting shot as she and Edwina took a harmonious leave of his guests. She had dismissed the injunction with a low flippancy that it was her express wish he concerned himself with his own harlots.

She had been determined to carry out her rescue plan…especially since she now had something of equal value with which to barter that would keep safe her mother's precious necklace. Reflexively, she moved a hand and the diamond dazzled blindingly, looking enormous on her small finger.

She had been astonished when he gave it to her. Their short walk back along the corridor to the drawing room had passed in silence. But he had kept her hand in his, as though he had believed she might yet attempt to bolt and embarrass him. Moments before they rejoined the others, he had stayed her; drawn the ring from his pocket and slipped it onto her finger. The ritual seemed to crystallise the enormity of what she had pledged to do. It was serious; it was real; she *was* to marry this gentleman rogue.

And it was superb: a pastiche of the style of her Thorney-croft collection. The large central stone was a diamond rather than an amethyst but it was cut octagonally to match her jew-ellery. The surrounding smaller stones were cabochon ame-thysts, eight in number. It must have been specially made for her. She had intruded far enough into the life and mind of this itinerant Cornishman for him to have spared time to con-sider the specific design of the betrothal ring he gave her.

That evening, at the dinner table, blushing beneath his quiet articulate compliments, branded by the unaccustomed weight on a hand in her lap, she had felt suddenly close to tears at the horrible hypocrisy of it all. Tell them! had throbbed in her mind. Tell them all that my true attractiveness lies in a bank and comes as a lump sum on production of the marriage lines; thereafter as an annuity each January for as long as I sur-vive…

And the hysterical thought that at least he wouldn't give in to the temptation to throttle her, no matter how she riled him, had elucidated something else. *Such a waste*…had been his reasoning for keeping his hands from her throat earlier that evening. Suddenly she had understood what he meant. Such a waste, indeed! Quite absurd, in fact, to lose out prematurely on ten thousand a year…

Elizabeth irritably twisted the heavy gem on her finger. And now, instead of finding a certain equanimity with Hugh's poor parishioners and wretched Jane Selby, she was awaiting the arrival of her silver-tongued fiancé. He had yesterday sent a formal note to say he would call today at two of the clock and take her for a drive. How very civilised a courtship it had become. How very confident he was that she would not be at Sunday School but heedfully at home awaiting him. And so she was…

She ripped the ring from her finger. She would leave it in her room. It was a paltry show of defiance, but a show none the less! And tomorrow…tomorrow, she would go to Wap-ping instead, seek normality, and concern herself with as many harlots as she pleased!

'Are you not going to get changed?' burst in on Elizabeth's fuming thoughts. Her grandmother was gawping her distaste. 'You can't go out with the Viscount dressed like *that*!' Edwina flicked a scornful finger at her petite figure. 'That old dun serge is what you wear when you slum visit!'

'I know…'

'Well, don't just stand there like a…a bedraggled pauper,' Edwina barked. 'Ross will be here at any minute. Last time he set eyes on you you looked like an angel in that velvet gown and your amethysts. You can't venture out with him on your first public appearance together looking like…like…'

'Like a woman ready to teach Sunday School?' Elizabeth offered sourly. 'If that's how I look, then I'm glad. That's exactly what I intended to do today. It's what I always do on a Sunday. And how I wish Hugh would return on some pretext and give me another chance to do just that!'

Her grandmother's pale eyes widened and she cocked her head. Then she was wobbling to the window. 'It's Stratton's barouche…and what a corker it is, too…and it looks like rain… Good; he's got the hood up. Quick, get your black silk cloak: 'twill conceal all that tat you're decked in…hurry! Oh, and find a pretty bonnet, too…'

Elizabeth felt her heart start to hammer. He was here. He was actually here and she wasn't ready. Not that her modest garb bothered her, but she had hoped to mentally prepare herself. She uncurled her hand and looked at the jewel on her palm. Her ring finger stretched meekly towards the golden circlet, then abruptly joined the others in forming a fist. She dropped the opulent gem carelessly into a pocket of her old dress.

A moment later, Harry Pettifer announced in his grand way, 'Viscount Stratton…'

'I'll make excuses for you and occupy him while you change,' was hissed from a corner of Edwina's stretched mouth.

Elizabeth barely heard the instruction. Her eyes were drawn immediately to her fiancé's tall, powerful physique. Despite herself her heart lurched at the splendidly handsome sight of him.

He was dressed in a black tail coat and buff trousers. The tiger's eye stone blinked in a cream silk cravat. The snowy, razor-sharp collar of his shirt slashed a stark contrast against his lean, tanned jaw. Black calf-top boots resembled ebony glass. He looked cool elegance incarnate as he strolled forward to bow to and greet Edwina. His inscrutable dark visage turned then towards Elizabeth. Eyes like tawny agate slipped down her slender mouse-coloured body before returning to her exquisite porcelain features crowned by a chignon of sleek ash-blonde hair. Blood suffused her cheeks as she squirmed beneath a look that was pure quizzical amusement. Her chin edged up and petulance pursed her mouth. She didn't give a fig what he thought of her appearance!

'I'm honoured, Lady Elizabeth,' he murmured gravely. 'It seems it was a close-run thing who you graced with your presence this afternoon: me or the vicar. I'm very glad you were sensible enough to let me win.'

Elizabeth bridled beneath the latent mockery; it barely veiled the threat narrowing his eyes and slanting his mouth. 'You've not won!' she snapped in a low breath, excluding Edwina from the dialogue. 'And I've not missed my true vocation this afternoon simply to do your bidding.'

'Of course not. I'd never think such a thing…'

Elizabeth's small fingers spasmed at her sides at his smooth irony, but as he offered her a suave arm, and a head flick indicated that he was ready to leave immediately, there was very little hesitation before she complied.

'Are you ashamed of me?'

Ross stretched out his long legs in front of him and settled back more comfortably against the luxurious hide squabs, the reins loosely held in one large hand. The perfectly matched greys were impeccably behaved and the barouche glided evenly on. 'Ashamed of you?' he echoed on a frown.

'I thought we were to take a drive in Hyde Park, or perhaps

St James's. We have been out a full hour and still this is not Hyde Park or St James's. Are we going to Richmond?' A sideways glance darted to his impassive, dark profile before she resumed sweetly, 'No? Well, I imagine you are avoiding popular places lest we are spotted by the Town Tabbies. And I understand your fears, my lord. Speculation might start as to why an eligible nobleman would squire a scandal-wrecked spinster…with very poor dress sense.' She feigned concern. 'Heaven forbid, but a scurrilous rumour might circulate that said nobleman is in fact a scavenging *parvenu* out for an old lady's blunt…'

The abruptness with which he swung the barouche off the main track and onto a wide grass verge had Elizabeth tipping against him and gasping. She scrambled up, straightening her clothes and looking about nervously. She had been so lost in introspection, castigating herself for deserting Jane Selby, and blaming him for everything, that she had been oblivious to how properly rustic the scenery was becoming. The hedge-rows either side loomed lofty and dense; in the distance, up an incline, woodland was fringing the horizon. This didn't look like a pleasant little pastoral oasis in the sprawling metropolis. This was deep, desolate countryside.

Elizabeth felt her heartbeat pick up tempo. Quickly, she stabbed an assessing look at him. He swivelled on the seat and leaned back against the carriage, watching her in a way that did nothing to appease the alternating exasperation and anxiety that had engendered her foolish sarcasm in the first place. She ought to be working charitably and harmoniously with Hugh, not baiting this dangerous and unfathomable man. Was he brooding on that undercurrent of antagonism that had simmered between them at their betrothal dinner? Was he still angry with her for refusing to contribute to the wedding plans? He seemed quite mellow…but then it was hard to tell his mood. From past experience she knew he could treat her with unexpected gentleness at one moment, yet act like a ruthless ruffian the next…

At one side of his powerful shoulders, she spied a clutter

of cattle close to a gate, bovine-ringed noses thrusting through rough planks. 'Where are we?' she abruptly demanded.

'Just outside London…'

'*Outside London?*' she parroted, horrified. 'Well, turn about at once. I didn't give you permission to take me outside London.'

A white smile transformed into a choke of laughter. 'Have I your permission to take you inside London, my lady? If so, I'm more than ready to immediately recross the boundary line.'

She flushed scarlet and rammed herself backwards against the carriage, so they sat face to face. The knowledge that she was still under obligation for the return of her necklace pounded the forefront of her mind. Surely he was not so mean and vile as to have brought her into the wilds today for that? It was yet daylight! 'Take me…return me home now! This instant!'

She was aware of his green-gold eyes roving her face, her petite figure, and instinctively gathered the black silk cloak more tightly about her.

'You told me once you weren't afraid of me…'

Huge violet eyes flicked up to his. 'Neither am I… Why should I be?' she challenged hoarsely.

'I don't know, Elizabeth. Why should you be? Unfortunately, I get the distinct impression that you are…most of the time…even now when we are soon to be wed. I don't want that. I don't want a wife who's afraid of me.'

'Oh, well, in that case I'm terrified…' she muttered.

'My God, you're an infuriating little…' The reproof concluded, unfinished, in a sigh as he reached for her.

Elizabeth slapped out at his hand. 'What are you doing?' she hissed at him, flattening against the carriage again.

'What do you think I'm doing?' he asked softly. 'I'm preparing to kiss my fiancée—'

'Well, don't!' she shrilled, raising a guarding hand in readiness to defend her. Her eyes darted from him to the road as though seeking another vehicle. ''Tis time to turn about any-how. 'Twill soon be dark.'

'I'll turn about when I've achieved what I set out to do and not before.'

Elizabeth tensed, raked his face with purple eyes. 'Which is?'

'I want to talk to you. Properly talk to you. There's a great deal we need to discuss in depth and in private. This is private enough.' He gave her an encouraging smile. 'I'll start the conversation by answering your earlier question: no, I'm not in any way ashamed of you, Elizabeth. I don't give a toss about polite society or what it thinks of me or you. It can ostracise us both for all I care. I've no time or inclination to bother with Janus-faced bores. I have all the family and friends I need. As for your clothes: the first time I saw you at Edwina's you looked oddly dishevelled, intentionally so, I imagine…as now. Unfortunately, a shabby gown doesn't de-tract from your allure.' That mockery was directed more at himself. 'You look delectable, however done up. Besides, it's what's underneath that interests me. Your character and per-sonality,' he explained with studied gravity as a suspicious look was cast on him. 'But, you guessed correctly: I avoided the centre of town because I'm not quite ready for our rela-tionship to be made public.'

When she said nothing but continued staring sulkily at the hedges, he asked drily, 'Would you care to know why that is?'

'No. I can guess.'

'And?'

'You're ashamed of me.'

Ross swore beneath his breath. 'Do you ever listen to what I say?'

'Oh, yes. But I seldom believe you sincere.' She barely paused before jibing, 'I told you to return me home. Do you ever listen to what I say?'

'Oh, yes. But I seldom believe *you* sincere.'

Looking away was impossible; she tried, but her gaze was

again adhering to eyes the colour of caramel. This time as a hand came out slowly towards her she simply watched it, unblinking, as a rabbit might mesmerically eye an approaching snake. A solitary dark finger brushed downwards over the silken contours of her alabaster cheek, stroking, soothing. 'So…now it's your turn. I'd like you to talk to me. Tell me things…important things about your past. If you like, I'll tell you important things about my past, too. We'll share those secrets that husbands and wives should know about each other's history.'

Thick lashes screened violet eyes. She felt her heart thump painfully slowly, her lungs ache with little use. It was what she'd been dreading, yet expecting. Buried in her mind had been a thread of hope that he might be different. Yet she knew all along he wasn't. For all his clever phrasing…all his sly vocabulary of sharing and caring, all he wanted was crude titilation, as they all did. He wanted her to tell him things…of course he did.

'I need to know, Elizabeth,' he said gently. 'I don't want there to be any secrets between us.'

'You're so…so utterly predictable! Such a despicable lecher!' she spat. 'You're no different to Linus Savage or any of the others. Shall I tell you how many men have sidled up to beg or buy a few explicit details? Would you like to hear that? Did you think your smut original? Unique? I'm surprised at you, my lord! With all your filthy experience should you not have a little imagination when it comes to sordid… sordid….' The words suffocated, jammed in her throat by fury and fear. She blinked rapidly, endeavouring to quell the sob she could sense tightening her chest. A hand scrabbled desperately behind for the door, searching to liberate her. She was prepared to shelter in that herd of bulls if it meant escaping him. From the corner of her eye she noticed him slide on the hide seat towards her and she twisted to lash out blindly with both fists.

A vice-like grip crushed her hands in his, keeping them

utterly still. She couldn't move one bone in one finger, yet strangely they felt unhurt.

'If you're determined to continually throw punches at me, Elizabeth, you should learn to do it properly,' he said quietly. 'All this girlish hand flailing is far too provocative…and far too ineffectual.' He forced the left hand up, the other down and positioned slightly behind it. 'Keep your thumbs in to protect them; feint with your left, then bring the right through.' He jabbed the hand towards him, allowing her soft knuckles to graze his abrasive jaw. 'Keep your guard up all the time or you'll leave yourself vulnerable.'

As his tutoring tailed off and he relaxed his grip, she flung him off so savagely she tumbled back onto the squabs. Within a second she was recovered enough to launch herself forward again, angry humiliation puckering her features and curling small digits into claws. He was quite ready for her. Dark hands banded about her wrists, driving them back against the carriage. He slid them together above her head, anchored them there with five lean, insolent fingers while five more moved leisurely towards her unprotected face. The fork of his hand fitted over her pointed little chin, forced it up so she couldn't avoid his mockery, before slipping to straddle her willowy white throat. A thumb softly traced her mouth. 'Why don't you ever listen?' he chided, but a rueful smile just touched his mouth.

'I'll kill you,' she choked, twitching her face away from his indolent caress. 'I swear I'll kill you the first chance I get. You'd be a fool to marry me, even for a fortune. I'll catch you unawares and you'll never live to squander it. So you might as well strangle me first…before I shoot you. I've got a gun…'

'What sort?'

Elizabeth sniffed and blinked at him, momentarily shocked out of hysteria. 'What sort?' she echoed in a breathless gasp.

'A duelling pistol? A blunderbuss? A hunting rifle? What sort?'

'Oh, I don't know!' she cried. 'What difference does it

make? It's good enough to shoot you. Oh, I'll…I'll stab you then! I've a silver dress dagger that was once my papa's. I know it's a valuable Jackson and sharp. When I was fourteen I cut myself on it.'

'Did you? Where?' he asked softly, barely smiling.

Elizabeth screwed shut her eyes to deny his warm honey gaze. 'My knee. It fell out of my hand,' she whispered.

'You didn't listen to your father, either, did you? I'll wager he told you to keep it sheathed or leave it alone.'

'You think you know everything, don't you?' she hissed at him, mortified at his perception on something so precious and private. She began struggling to free her hands, still enclosed in his, over her head.

'No. I don't know everything. Some things I know. Some things I can guess. Some things I'd like you to tell me. I'd like you to tell me why Edwina said *now she really is ruined* the night I took you home. It seems an odd thing to say, all things considered. Why would your grandmother say that, Elizabeth?'

Elizabeth composed her face into a supercilious mask, flicked up her lids. 'I've no idea, my lord. Why do you not ask her?' she sweetly suggested. Then snapped, 'Let go of my hands.'

'I'm asking you. If I let go, are you about to scratch… gouge…slap? I'm getting tired of restraining you this way. That other way is far more pleasurable.'

'What other…?' The words tailed off as languid-lidded eyes dropped suggestively to her softly parted mouth.

She jerked her hands and this time he let them free. The momentum whizzed them dangerously close to his face. She panicked, snatched them away and controlled them, letting them fall to her lap where they clasped demurely.

He smiled at her. 'Very good,' he praised. 'You're taking good advice again. See how easy it can be?'

She turned her head, haughtily tilted her chin. 'I hate you,' she declared with great aplomb.

'No, you don't.'

'I do!'

'No, you don't. You can't. My mother says you're just right for me.'

Elizabeth stared at him. 'Your mother? You've been discussing me with your mother?'

'Shouldn't I? She's soon to be your mother, too. She thinks you're enchanting: sweet and mannerly and beautiful…just right for me.'

Elizabeth scoured his face for irony. So far as she could discern, his wry grimace seemed to mock his entitlement to her charms rather than her right to lay claim to them. The awful incongruity of his mother's opinion considering her recent bad behaviour made an uneasy flush singe her cheeks. Her tongue tip circled her mouth and she frowned and squirmed a little on the seat, disconcerted. 'Well…well you must thank her for her kind compliments. I…I very much liked her, too. I liked all your family and your friends. You're very lucky to have such agreeable kith and kin. I'll own to being surprised you could call them such,' she couldn't help qualifying her concessions with a sniff.

'I'm glad you like them. I hoped you would as they're soon to be your kith and kin. Everyone present said how engaging they found you. Where's your ring?' he asked without pausing. He raised her left hand from her lap and looked at the nude fingers.

Elizabeth had the grace to blush again after learning of such pleasing plaudits from such fine people…his people! She thought fast and said quickly, 'I put it in my pocket. 'Tis a fraction too large and I'm afraid to lose it. Wearing it to Wapping seemed a little ill advised.'

'Indeed. Going there against my wishes would have been equally ill advised. I'll have it made smaller for you.'

She snatched back her hand and inspected her manicure. His hand slid, palm up, into her line of vision. Speedily she retrieved the ring from her pocket, then placed it on his palm.

'Do you not like it?'

Elizabeth's head jerked back and she met his steadily

watching eyes. Part of her resented him for asking, even if it
was a quite pertinent enquiry. Every passing moment was
making her feel increasingly chagrined and churlish. She
could tell he genuinely wanted to know if his gift pleased her.
'Of course I like it. 'Tis a magnificent ring, but…'

'But I gave it to you. Had Havering given it to you, no
doubt it would have remained constantly on your finger.'

Elizabeth swallowed and said nothing.

'Do you pine for him still?' he asked harshly, returning the
ring to its rightful place with a slow, sensual stubbornness.

'Of course not,' she answered quietly, studying the glowing
jewels that seemed to obliterate half a slender digit.

'Of course not? Am I supposed to understand how you feel
about him now? All you show me, Elizabeth, is a prickly
surface. All I see is a little girl huddling, wounded, behind an
armoury of pride. Talk to me. Tell me how you feel…share
it with me!'

Desperation coarsened his voice and it curled her stomach,
made mute the reflexive cry that she wasn't wounded and how
dare he say she was. He sounded as though he cared. He
sounded as though he would comfort her, salve the pain…
With an instinct honed from ten years' injury, she reinforced
her armour, put up her shield. 'I like it best when you talk to
me.' An idle hand movement scattered a fragmented rainbow
from the diamond. 'How am I to know how you feel about
Cecily Booth if you never say?' she parodied. 'Why do you
not tell me about her?'

'What do you want to know?'

She stilled and stared ahead. She had anticipated her outrageous impertinence would have him blustering, bawling her
out, then, disgusted, taking her home. Young ladies—even
damaged young ladies—did not acknowledge the existence of
any gentleman's arbitrary amours. It was a taboo subject never
broached by the decorous. But then she had been branded
anything but that. Carelessly, she tossed her blonde head
about, then looked into his narrowed hawk's eyes. 'What do
you think I ought know?'

He grimaced thoughtfulness, while remaining totally dispassionate. 'Perhaps that she's nowhere near as classically beautiful as you. But she's pretty enough. She's some years younger, I should say, some decades more mature…more experienced…'

Elizabeth felt the same odd writhing pain as she had when she'd first seen him with Rebecca in the fabric emporium and imagined they were lovers. Well, she had asked about his mistress; and he was uninhibitedly telling her. And she wished he wasn't. She no longer wanted to know. 'How ideal she sounds!' she exploded breathily. 'As you insist you're not a fortune-hunter, I really think, sir, you ought make an honest woman of her, not me.' She had again wrenched the ring from her finger whilst speaking. About to throw it back at him, she noticed the latent triumph in his eyes, and it stirred her vexation to new heights. He understood very well how mention of his paramour had affected her. The need to thwart his arrogance helped her retain a tenuous grip on her self-control. Carefully, very carefully, she let the ring drop to the leather seat between them, then, head high, turned away. She even managed an insouciant smile at the thrush starting to warble atop the hawthorn hedge and tilted her head this way and that, examining rain clouds gathering in the distance, verdant, damp countryside: everything spied from her side of the carriage held a certain fascination.

'What makes you think she's ideal or that I might marry her?'

Elizabeth darted a quelling look at him, then found, again, she couldn't drag her eyes away. Silently, soulfully, she ceded…begged him to stop. She was not equal to this. She had again stupidly started something she was not fit to finish. She was no more able to win this verbal battle than she was able to beat him with her puny fists. Shamming indifference while he listed his mistress's attributes was beyond her. As he had pitilessly impressed on her while drawing comparisons, she possessed no such sophistication. 'Take me home, please. I…I feel unwell…I had a headache earlier…' she murmured, closing her eyes against the pretty bird bobbing close by. There was no mistaking she had made an utter fool of herself. What was he seeing now? A damaged little girl, or a cowed little mouse? A risible spectacle in either case, she was sure.

'Does it hurt?'

Unsure to what he referred, she hesitated in replying. Then, with aching perception, she realised ambiguity was intended. Did Cecily Booth hurt? Did her erstwhile, callow suitor's abandonment hurt? Did her ostracism hurt? Did her head hurt? Yes! she wanted to scream. Yes! Yes! Yes! She simply frowned at the first fat raindrops spoiling the dusty earth. They trailed the window like slothful tears. She nodded. He could make of that caitiff's response what he would.

The hand that slid beneath the pleat of hair at her nape felt warm and firm. Gently he urged her towards him and, a little token stiffness apart, she went to him. Her head drooped on to his shoulder and when his arm came across, pulling her properly close, she made no objection. Soothing fingers massaged at her neck and his head dipped until his mouth rested against her silky silver hair. 'There's one other thing you ought know about Miss Booth…' He tightened his hold on her, anticipating that her tension meant she might try to free herself. 'And I didn't intend telling you this, Elizabeth, because…' she heard the smile in his voice '…because, my frustrating, infuriating little love, there's a part of me that likes you jealous…likes to know you're not as indifferent to me as you'd have me believe.' As she melted against him, gentle fingers resumed the soporific stroking at her nape. 'But then caring about you, wanting to protect you from hurt, seems to have come out of nowhere and taken over my life. So, whichever fool has told you she's my mistress is a little out of touch with current affairs. I finished with her a while ago.'

'You don't have to tell me…I don't care…'

'I know I don't have to tell you,' he answered drily. 'God knows, it's not the sort of thing any man relishes discussing with his future wife.' As though to reinforce her status, he gently slid the ring back onto her finger, then curled it, as though locking it there. He brushed a thumb across the gem. 'But you did ask and I don't want something so trivial causing you additional pain.'

She grabbed at his arms, pushed back to look into his eyes. What she saw made her breath catch achingly in her throat. For a timeless moment it seemed she hovered in a dizzying limbo, bathed in a gilded, beatific warmth. She could see a tiny reflection of herself in his shining agate eyes, as though he had already absorbed her, used his body to cocoon her against harm. She read the words there, too, and held her breath waiting for them…waiting. She watched his lips, saw them part…then lower to hers. He kissed her and there was such tenderness in his attentive caress, such devotion in the hands that cradled her face, tremored against her flushing skin, that she gave herself up to it, kissing him back shyly with all the sweet gratitude she could muster, while in her mind she consoled herself with thinking the words she had expected to hear. Words no man had spoken to her for ten years: 'I love you, Elizabeth…I love you…'

Chapter Twelve

He had that look about him, Luke realised, a pang of anxiety cooling the film of perspiration on his skin.

Pulling off his visor, he sat on the bench, discarding his foil on the ground by his feet. He roughly dried his face, briskly towelled his damp, ebony hair, then settled back to properly spectate. His brother was advancing using a spare, efficiency that demonstrated he was keen to conclude the contest. With perfect balance and a powerful, easy athleticism, he was driving his adversary back towards the perimeter of the arena. A final riposte, and the tip of his épée threatened a thick, sinewy throat. Henry Bateman, no mean swordsman himself, put up his hands in submission, laughed, shrugged. They saluted and shook hands, then Ross was walking towards Luke, and Henry was folding over at the waist, exhausted.

'Good bout,' Luke mentioned conversationally. 'You slipped under his guard a couple of times. I'm glad the buttons were secure; you were attacking like a demon. Not in training for anything in particular, I hope?'

Ross jerked off his visor, shook his head, sending shaggy mahogany locks back from his face. He inhaled sharply, then blew, slowly recovering from the gruelling exertion. Stripping off his gauntlets, he wiped sweat from his eyes.

'Not in training for anything in particular, I hope…?' Luke

repeated, attempting to break through the deafness of intense preoccupation that, at times, left his brother stranded within his own consciousness.

Ross glanced at him, smiled absently, settled wordlessly onto the bench. Guy Markham strolled over, swigging thirstily from a cup. Having recently finished his own match, he was now eagerly awaiting the clash of the Titans. Dickie Du Quesne and David Hardinge were both skilful, evenly matched fencers. It would make excellent sport; as would a bout between these two brothers, should they decide to engage today.

Sensing Luke's observation, Ross slid him a look, challenge and reassurance mingling in his slitted lupine eyes.

Luke felt his uneasiness increase. 'What is it?'

'Don't worry. It's no problem.'

Ross turned his head away. Humidity had loosely corkscrewed the hair close to his forehead and nape into incongruous little chestnut ringlets. Those by his brow were clinging to skin, sweat sheened to bronze satin, those trailing his neck coiled down as far as the shoulders of his white cotton fencing jacket, now hunched up, as he rested forearms on knees. Luke considered his brother's perfectly composed profile: his mouth a sensual contour, nostrils flaring slightly as he regained his breath, long, sooty lashes slanting parallel with his cheekbone as he watched his foot positioning his épée on the floor in front of him. Almost cherubic, Luke judged with a wry, private smile... Yes, one might almost think that...if one didn't know better. And he, more than anyone else, knew better...

When their father was alive, some nineteen years ago, there had existed a thriving illicit side to Trelawney importing and exporting. The Trelawneys had, for generations, been Cornwall's premier freetrading clan. Then Jago Trelawney died, prematurely, from a wound sustained in a clash with a deadly rival, and, as head of the family, Luke decreed it was time to bury their infamy and lawlessness with his father. His brother, Tristan, had been in agreement, for already he was betrothed and leaning towards a quiet life farming at Melrose, their Cornish estate.

His mother had been relieved; their fleet of traders sailing out of Bristol, and their tin and copper mines closer to home, were all showing handsome profits; risking it all for criminal activity seemed pointless. Ross, alone, had seen a point to it, and had carried on regardless, traversing the channel in his own boat. The Trelawney family were by then rich enough to pay for whatever luxuries they needed. Ross needed what was unpurchasable: the skirmishing with rival gangs or the revenue, the thrill of the chase. He was just fourteen years old.

But he had first sailed with his father and older brothers on night runs at ten. By the time he was thirteen he had an impressive precocious musculature and height, and could fight with fists or sword as well as most men. By the time he was fifteen, he was a superior shot, too. By the time he was seventeen, their mother was in despair and Luke was worried. Neither mining, shipping, land acquisition nor any of the other commercial activities that constituted Trelawney enterprises at that time soothed Ross's restless spirit in the way that did smuggling. Yet he was far and away the most naturally intelligent of the Trelawney children, if not the most scholarly. Luke and Tristan had worked heedfully at their lessons, and conscientiously attended university lectures; Ross shrugged his way through to graduation.

He would shrewdly invest ill-gotten money in legitimate Trelawney transactions, then squander an awesome profit on gambling or carousing with women he seemed to barely want or use. Again, it was the chase he desired—surrender defeated him. And therein, Luke brooded, now lay the crux of the matter. This dangerous mood was a lot to do with transition and reform. It was everything to do with a woman he very much wanted but couldn't use...even supposing she surrendered. He was defeated until she loved him.

Lady Elizabeth Rowe was beautiful, and without a doubt there existed between them a chemistry of explosive proportions. At one point, when Ross was announcing their engagement, Luke had visions of the dining table going up in flames, so fierce were the sparks flying from one end of the mahogany to the other. Never before had he seen his younger brother so intensely aware of any woman's presence. Even later in the evening, when post-prandial chatter had them socially grouped yards apart and facing in opposite directions, still Ross was absorbed with the petite blonde who wistfully twisted a priceless gem on her betrothal finger.

Obviously, there existed between them, too, highly charged problems. Whether those related to her past misfortunes and the scandal that surrounded her banishment from London, he couldn't say. And Ross, it seemed, wouldn't say. His brother had not mentioned a solitary thing about her history to anyone present that evening. Yet he obviously realised, at the very least, that all the gentlemen would know. Sir Richard Du Quesne and Lord Courtenay had been rogues about town during that era and, if not engendering outrage themselves, were well aware of who was. Guy Markham had been with him and Ross when the news first broke in the clubs that the Marquess of Thorneycroft was taking his daughter home in disgrace. Luke got the distinct impression that Ross's silence was a test for them: they could judge her on hearsay or they could accept her as his chosen partner. And there was no doubt in Luke's mind where his youngest brother's loyalties now lay. If need be, he would turn his back on them all for her.

Quietly, Luke said, 'When I met Rebecca…for a while, the coward in me wished I hadn't. I knew, from the first sight of her wading in that pond, that I was lost. I couldn't do without her…I couldn't leave her…it came out of nowhere and shattered me. That's the thing with falling in love, there's no calling card…no time to prepare, and once you're in, you never know if you'll come out the other side whole.'

Ross arrowed him a humorous look.

'At times, I thought I was going insane,' Luke resumed nostalgically.

'I remember…'

Luke grimaced at his brother's dry tone. 'It's an odd feeling: suddenly being in bits, knowing she's the only one who can put them back together.' A circumspect look slanted sideways. 'Is that how it is with you and Elizabeth?'

Ross flicked his head. It was almost a nod. He kept staring ahead. 'Yes…she's the only one.'

Luke cleared his throat. He shifted a bit on the bench, then tendered hesitatingly, 'I'm here…you know…to talk…if you want…'

'I know…thanks,' Ross said, a twist of a smile softening his mouth at his older brother's gruff concern.

With that out of the way, Luke gladly turned his attention to the two swordsmen circling, lunging, parrying, and was about to make some comment on their friends' technique, when he glimpsed Ross's stealthy movement. He had dipped sinuously to collect the rapier at his feet. Luke's eyes darted to his brother's face; it was a mask of brutal satisfaction. Blowing out his cheeks in resignation, Luke looked up at the gaggle of dandified newcomers who were loitering about the arena to watch the sporting spectacle.

Without a word, Ross stood, sauntered towards them.

With stabbing little looks, Linus Savage, Earl of Cadmore, watched him approach. In fact, he'd been expecting his presence, and that of his Corinthian colleagues, at this venue. These renowned sportsmen performing here today were the reason for he and his friends stopping off at all at Harry Angelo's Fencing Academy. Cadmore felt unthreatened. Stratton was with respectable company; he was with his own eminent cronies.

Since that encounter in the fabric emporium, he'd not seen hide nor hair of the Viscount. Had it been any lingering lust for Cecily Booth that had prompted his hostility that day, it must surely, by now, have petered out or he would have taken her back. With smarting resentment, Cadmore knew the man could do just that, if he wanted. Cecily still pined for him, and the mewling, vicious little cat was not averse to hinting at shortcomings in his bedsport skills compared to her rugged Cornish lover's. A bauble or two soon stopped her complaints.

But Cadmore knew he was already becoming bored with the avaricious jade. If it wasn't for the fact Cecily knew a novel little trick or two designed to steady a man's roving eye, he would by now have discarded her. Perhaps the Viscount had schooled into her those special delights; perhaps he should thank him, he chortled inwardly. Outwardly, he greeted him affably, 'Stratton; how goes it with you, my dear fellow?'

Ross moved the gleaming rapier in mocking salute. 'It goes very well with me…now I've set eyes on you.'

Cadmore laughed, a trifle shrilly, unsure what to make of that. Was it a threat? A compliment? This man had never before sought his company. In fact, he got the distinct impression Trelawney had always despised him. For his own part, he was wise enough to tread softly about such an enigmatic warrior. 'We heard that there were to be some fancy bouts. Thought we'd call in *en masse* and take a gander.' A languid hand emphasised his entourage.

Ross seemed unmoved by any number of his foppish cronies and slung a powerful arm, terminating in a lethal weapon, about the man's effeminately narrow shoulders. He drew him slightly to one side. 'I was counting on it that you would hear and would come,' was drawled close to Cadmore's large ear.

The Earl attempted to wriggle his bony frame from beneath the controlling arm, disquiet curdling his stomach. He glanced about, noting that Stratton's black bear of a brother was swivelled on the bench, arms crossed over his chest, watching the pair of them through slitted eyes.

'You wanted to see me? About what?' he protested.

'About a woman.'

'Cecily?' Cadmore snorted, disbelief plain.

'No…not Cecily,' Ross said, mildly disparaging. 'I want to talk to you about Lady Elizabeth Rowe.'

Cadmore gawked at him, as though unsure he'd heard right. Then, slowly, slowly, comprehension dawned. A sly leer distorted his fleshy mouth. Of course! Why had it not occurred to him before? Ross Trelawney was notoriously popular with the ladies and notoriously fond of a challenge. That haughty whore would be a prime target for his fastidious but jaded eye. She was high born and would doubtless prove a trial, even for such a successful womaniser.

Over the years, fine sport had been got wagering who would be the first buck to bring her down to earth and strip her of disdain. In his arrogance, and with his luck running so sweet, the Viscount probably thought it would be him. He probably thought she'd fall like a ripe peach! He was newly ennobled, in favour with his Majesty, and to top it all, just to trumpet that he could, he wanted that frigid bitch pleasuring him in bed. What a fine joke! Cadmore barely suppressed a snigger. He would hazard a monkey that the erstwhile cool Cornishman was in hot pursuit of the lady.

Stratton moping about in a fabric warehouse had nothing to do with the lightskirt he'd discarded; it was everything to do with the one he'd set his sights on. Lady Elizabeth Rowe had been in that shop the afternoon this man had looked daggers at him. He must have been irked at seeing them together. It was no secret that he had been stalking her himself for years. Just as it was no secret that she had made a laughing stock of him, playing up to his court simply to disguise her interest in that snivelling puppy she'd run off with. Cadmore surfaced enough from malicious memories to spy wolfish eyes preying patiently on him, analysing his reaction. Why not encourage him? He wasn't renowned for lengthy liaisons. If Trelawney succeeded in seducing the ice maiden, he'd make sure he was handy when the thaw set in. He wasn't too proud to shun a peer's cast-offs. After all, for ten years past, he'd been chasing what a pair of gentlemen of the road had ditched.

So what was it this man wanted? Cadmore ruminated foxily. Was he going to warn him off? Demand a few salacious snippets about her? It was common knowledge that he had followed the scandal with fanatical relish. The poor fool wanted a favour or two. Perhaps, he might just oblige him.

'What is it you'd like to know about the...erm...fair *lady*?' Contempt stressed the title; a smirk was circulated for those of his chums who were cocking an ear to glean some gossip from this unlikely tête-à-tête.

'What is it you'd like to tell me?' Ross rejoined softly, staring over Cadmore's fussily crimped head at nothing.

'Well, let's see… To start,' Cadmore lectured, 'if you're interested in offering her your protection for a time, I'll warn you that she's deuced difficult to approach. That is your intention, I take it?'

'Oh, yes,' Ross said. 'That's definitely my intention.'

Cadmore nodded, licking his lips; he was enjoying himself, playing up to the attention he was generating. 'Well, you obviously know that I am…er…have been interested in doing likewise; with little success. It's not easy; she has an unconscionable high opinion of herself, has lovely Hoar Frost.'

Feral eyes, looking like green-flecked jet, sprang to his face. Dark brows lifted, demanding an explanation.

Cadmore obligingly expounded, while grinning at a couple of friends who were in on this private joke, 'Just a little pun. The sobriquet stuck at the time of her…umm…unfortunate escapade. For, lord, with that silver hair and wintry way she has, who'd ever think she'd been broken in by a couple of hot highwaymen. Mayhap, that night, they felt like riding a different sort of mare…' He guffawed and a few of his friends snorted humorously too. Most, however, looked a little uneasy on noting that the man Cadmore was hoping to impress seemed singularly unamused.

Wiping tears of mirth from his prominent eyes, Cadmore patted a fey hand on a solid shoulder. 'Let me know how pleasurable it is in that particular saddle, won't you now? If anyone can rein her in, I reckon you can. Anything else you want to know?' he asked chummily, still smearing wet from his eyes.

'Yes. How do you want to die? Your choice of weapons. Five o'clock tomorrow morning, Wimbledon Common.'

The next minute seemed to spin endlessly in time. Gentlemen, who moments ago had been dissecting superlative fencing skills as demonstrated by Sir Richard Du Quesne and Lord

Courtenay, now stared at the stupefied Earl of Cadmore and his vicious-eyed challenger. For a short while the metallic swipe of steel on steel continued, then lessened until there was no sound but echoing silence.

Ross walked away from Cadmore, drooping grey-faced in disbelief, and into the group of macaronis. He smiled slowly, thoughtfully, in a way that had some of them fidgeting, looking about nervously. He started an easy stroll about the loose circle, making it open as gentlemen shuffled back, giving him a wide berth. All were exceedingly conscious of the silver blade in his brown hand and of this man's craft with it.

'Has anyone else got any interesting anecdotes about my fiancée?' Ross asked quietly. 'Anything that I should know about Lady Elizabeth Rowe's past, or their part in it?' He halted, pivoted on a heel, eagle eyes swooping to rake an arc over slack-jawed faces. 'Come…don't be shy. There must be something: an insult…a grope…a proposition, that I'd like to hear about. No?' He read sarcastically from ruddying, perspiring complexions. Fingers were being thrust to loosen collars, frantic glances were shooting at Cadmore, lingering, fascinated, as though seeing the man for the final time. Facial expressions ranged from numb horror to mischievious relish.

Luke paced stealthily closer; Dickie and David and Guy followed. In harmony, without a passing look or word, they positioned themselves about the ring of men and waited, grim-faced. Not that any one of them believed Ross to be in any danger. Far from it. In fact, as he seemed to be the only one armed, both with weapon and lethal intent, protecting him from his inexorable quest to avenge seemed the most pressing need.

Linus Savage, darted an arid tongue about his parched mouth. 'Fiancée?' he managed to shrill with a sickly grin. 'Why did you not say, my dear fellow? Of course, I'll apologise for any misunderstanding about your interest in the lady, and for any offence unintentionally given. Naturally, I'll never again approach her. I'll not accept the gauntlet on this occasion.' He started a backwards glide towards the door, ignoring the frank looks of astonishment and disgust from his comrades as they observed him desperately trying to wriggle free of the hook. He might be, literally, fighting for his life, yet the expectation was that gentlemen should resign themselves with dignity to their fate, and preserve their own and their family's good name at any cost. Death before dishonour was a truism scrupulously adhered to.

Lord Grey, a longstanding acquaintance of the Earl's late father, inclined towards him and hissed furiously, 'Think what you are doing, man! How can you refuse him satisfaction? We all heard what you said about the lady. It was unequivocal defamation! If you fight shy now…think of the disgrace! I'll stand as your second; Beecher will, too.' He indicated a younger man with a dip of his balding head.

The Earl of Cadmore did think; he thought as hard and as fast as his scrambled brain would allow. And came up with nothing good. Death, maiming or ostracism were already his. All he had to do was choose. The situation seemed nightmarish…unreal, as did the venom that started spitting through his teeth. 'That bitch has plotted this.' He was unable to control himself, even when Ross reacted to him colluding in his own destruction by laughing. 'You're probably not even betrothed to the trollop. Has she hired you to kill me? Are you bounty-hunting for me dead or alive? Run through or ruined? Are those your orders?' He snickered in shock, for a corner of his mind retained lucidity and was screaming at him to cease, or he might be right here, a dead man. 'What's your fee? A tumble in the gutter with the whore? She likes rough trade: thieves and dockers… She'll go for you.'

In a fast fluid movement, Ross faced him, pinned him to the wall with his blade through Cadmore's coat. It effectively cut off his escape route and his raving. The Earl visibly shook and looked as though he might retch.

Slowly, deliberately, Ross took his fencing gauntlet and swiped it, with insulting lightness, about one of Cadmore's sallow, quivering cheeks. 'Just to formalise matters,' he said softly. 'Tomorrow, Wimbledon Common, five o'clock. Grey and Beecher have offered as seconds.' Ross indicated his own men with a backwards flick of his dark head. 'Ramsden and Markham stand as mine. Your choice of weapons. Now you can go.' He jerked free the blade.

Luke frowned, watching the last of the subdued gentlemen troop away. Before going, some had sidled over and mumbled their disgust at Cadmore's astonishing vitriol and base cowardice. Others had simply swayed their heads, solemnly acknowledging the gravity of what had taken place here today, while exiting at speed. Doubtless, they were keen to begin circulating this juicy gossip in clubs and salons peopled by the *beau monde*.

'He's going to choose pistols and shoot early,' Luke warned.

'I know…' Ross replied.

'You could try for rapiers,' Guy chipped in. 'You're undoubtedly the injured party in this and could exercise the option to choose.'

'He'll never go for that,' David said drily. 'Cadmore knows close combat would be a massacre.'

'And over in thirty seconds,' Dickie added. 'Whatever the outcome tomorrow, even if Cadmore fails to show or fires early, Ross has finished him here today. Everybody knows that, including him.' He looked at Ross shrewdly, and with not a little admiration in his silver eyes. 'You crafty bastard! You planned it that way. You got us here this afternoon— arranged these bouts—just to draw him in, didn't you?'

'Would I do that?' Ross drawled, as, whistling, and apparently unperturbed at the thought of stopping a cheat's bullet, he strolled off to change.

'I don't know whether I ought to tell you this, Elizabeth…' Elizabeth glanced at Rebecca with a small enquiring smile. 'I feel embarrassed at ever having thought such a thing.'

'Well, *the thing* sounds intriguing. I think you now must explain.'

Since being formally introduced a few days ago, the two

women had spent time together shopping or taking tea or a carriage ride in the park, and had settled into an easy camaraderie. Elizabeth had met the Ramsdens' two delightful little sons at their beautiful townhouse in Burlington Parade. Today they were strolling along Bond Street, chatting and window shopping, oblivious to their differing blonde looks drawing admiring male glances and envious female scrutiny.

'As we are soon to be sisters-in-law, and I already like you very much, I shall tell you.' Rebecca giggled. 'Besides, if I do not, Emma or Vicky might let it slip at some time—for I told them both,' she said with a backwards peer at their companions strolling some paces behind. 'Then I would really be in a fine pickle for not owning to once having imagined that you…'

Elizabeth felt a slight chill creep over her. Was Rebecca hinting she had heard tell of a scandalous Lady Elizabeth Rowe from years back? Was she about to embarrassingly say she couldn't conceive her to be the same person?

'When I saw you fabric shopping last week,' she broke into Elizabeth's anxieties, 'and I noticed Ross paying you such particular attention, I imagined you and he…that is, I believed you might be his…*chère amie*…' Rebecca pulled an apologetic little face, but her smile was wicked.

Elizabeth choked a laugh in her relief at that news. 'Well, Lady Ramsden, as you have been honest, I must be, too. I imagined you already filled that role when I spied you with him. I almost dropped through the floor in shock and embarrassment when you were introduced as a relative.'

Rebecca squealed with laughter. 'You believed *me* to be his mistress? How famous! He is rather gorgeous…' She grimaced. 'Oh, sorry! I meant nothing by it, of course. It's just— with Luke's blessing, naturally—I have grown accustomed to flirting innocently with Ross over the years. He has been the best ever brother-in-law; so interesting and amusing. And his nephews haunt him when he visits; Troy, that is, for Jason is but one and a half and not yet able to play soldiers and pirates or ride a pony. But he laughs happily when he spies his uncle

Ross. Ross is a natural with horses, and knows exactly which ingredients to mix as poultices for swollen fetlocks and so on. All the grooms are most impressed by his herbalism...Miles, too. Oh, he's our butler and a sweet old cove...' At Elizabeth's continuing quiet, Rebecca ceased her chatter and groaned regret. 'I imagine you must be heartily sick of females fawning over your future husband. How tactless of me to go on so. I shall caution Vicky and Emma, for they both adore him, too.'

'Say nothing to them.' The clipped words were followed by an insouciant smile. 'It doesn't matter. I'm barely aware— or caring—of his popularity. Besides, knowing he is kind to children and dumb animals is most welcome.'

Rebecca smiled at the wryness in Elizabeth's tone. She had just last night discussed with her darling Luke the tension that seemed to exist between this couple. 'Nothing worth having comes easily, sweetheart,' Luke had reminded her huskily with a meaningful look that made her blush and reminisce about their own very bitter-sweet courtship.

'Oh, Ross does have his gentle side,' Rebecca communicated archly. 'I am never more aware of that than when he looks at you, Elizabeth.'

Elizabeth retrieved her neutral smile, while pointing at an interesting window display. She urged Rebecca towards it.

The three ladies strolling a few yards behind joined them in inspecting glorious fabrics draped into enticing approximations of the newly arrived Paris fashion plates depicted. Victoria, Emma and Sophie were also enjoying a stroll along this busy street this fine September afternoon.

'Do you think our husbands will have exhausted themselves fencing and soon be home?' Victoria asked. 'Lucy will expect her papa to be energetic enough to take her on his back and gallop around the floors,' she said, referring to her three-year-old daughter's predilection for using her doting father as a pony.

'Heavens! I hope they won't be too tired out,' Emma said,

aghast, causing Rebecca and Victoria to exchange a look, then chuckle.

Emma, not long married, blushed prettily then tutted her mock disgust. 'Oh, I give up with you two vulgar hussies,' she fondly chided. 'I simply want my husband in a fit state to visit my parents. When we pluck up courage to go to Cheapside, I assure you Richard needs all his wits about him to fend off their importuning. Papa for money and Mama for invitations to Silverdale.'

Elizabeth felt at ease with the casual banter between these sweet, unassuming ladies. The thought of Lord Courtenay down on all fours with a child atop his broad, elegant back was enough to have her chuckling, too. Her amusement soon faded. There was a woman's reflected image visible in the shop window to one side of her. She seemed familiar. Yet this was the West End of London. The last time she had spied that gaunt profile, framed by dark curly hair, she had been dockside with Hugh Clemence! With careful casualness Elizabeth half-turned to slant a look.

Jane Selby was hovering close to the road, a child's hand gripped in hers. On this occasion, she was dressed quite neatly and soberly. She certainly didn't look out of place amongst the Quality promenading along Bond Street. But the furtive peeks that were sliding from beneath her bonnet brim at the shoppers were definitely suspicious. The boy by her side looked to be about five or six and he, too, was tidily turned out. But his expression was anguished: he was gazing up at his mother with such huge sorrowful eyes that Elizabeth felt her heart ache. What she saw next was still more disturbing and caused an icy shiver to hurtle through her.

Although no one stood with them, they were not there alone. And, by now, Elizabeth's clandestine observation led her to believe that they might be up to no good! Jane was nodding at a young girl, perhaps fifteen years old, who was stationed some yards away. In response, the girl tapped at her pocket, then flicked a sly finger towards a lone matron promenading.

At the signal from her accomplice, Jane pulled her hand free of her son's and whispered in his ear before pushing him away. The child swayed his head and looked at his mother with supplicant's eyes. She rejected him with a terse brush of a hand. With tears on his face, he sidled to the target, skimmed inconspicuously against the woman's ample hip and came away with a scrap of lace in his hand. It was quickly scrunched into his small fist as he took a circular path back to his mother on spindly legs that were visibly shaking. He immediately offered up to her his booty.

Aware, suddenly, that Rebecca was talking to her, asking her if she would step inside the shop with them, Elizabeth swayed her blonde head. It was the most she could manage. She felt mute with shock at what she'd witnessed. 'I've a slight headache; it's uncommonly warm,' Elizabeth blurted. 'Please, browse to your heart's content. I shall stay here, in the air, with Sophie.'

Sophie scoured her friend's face, having read an unspoken plea in her violet eyes and the breathless tenor of her voice.

'We'll be but a short while,' Victoria said as, arm in arm, the three ladies proceeded inside the shop.

Before they were properly out of sight, Elizabeth had urged Sophie into a recess between buildings and discreetly indicated Jane Selby and her son. Frantically, she whispered who they were and what she had just seen. She concluded with, 'They are teaching the little lad larceny and he looks barely six…and so distraught! How can she be so cruel and stupid! I shall tell her I know what she is about. It's a wonder no one else saw him pickpocket and raised the alarm! They might all be before a magistrate tomorrow!'

Sophie had her wide, brown eyes riveted on the mother and child. 'Good grief! Quick, approach her now, Lizzie, for I do believe she is about to send him thieving again!' she squeaked.

Elizabeth did move then, faster than Sophie could keep up with her. Weaving, almost at a run, through the strollers, and ignoring their curious looks, she was soon at Jane's side.

The woman's black eyes were wide and apprehensive as she recognised the beautiful woman who seemed to have materialised from thin air. Elizabeth grabbed the child by the shoulders as he began his stalking, and gently directed him back to his mother. 'Your son, I imagine, Jane?' she enquired by way of greeting. 'Little Jack, I believe you said was his name?' She looked down at the small boy's solemn, tear-streaked face. 'He seems distressed…'

Jane's astonishment at being thus accosted vanished; wariness instead pinched her wan features. Her eyes darted vigilantly about, then hovered on one spot and naked fear dilated her pupils.

Elizabeth turned her head to investigate and immediately saw why the wretched woman looked so terrified. The girl who had been loitering as look-out had disappeared. In her place was a man Elizabeth instantly recognised. Nathaniel Leach, dressed in dapper dark garments, had his slitted gaze on them. He touched his hat in insolent salute then, crossing his arms over his brawny chest, adopted a menacing stance and continued staring fixedly.

Elizabeth drew a deep breath; he might frighten Jane, but she wasn't so easily intimidated! she exhorted herself, and with a haughty toss of her head, ignored him. 'I saw you sending your son to pickpocket. What on earth are you about?' she demanded angrily. 'Even if that vile Leach has you in his power, how can you use your own son so? He is so young! So vulnerable!'

'Go away and leave us be!' Jane bit out, jerking her son back by the shoulders and into the shelter of her skirts. 'You're making things so much worse for us both.'

Elizabeth laid a comforting hand on her thin arm. It was immediately shaken off. 'Don't you realise the jeopardy he is in?'

'Don't *you* realise the jeopardy he is in?' Jane bitterly countered. 'You know nothing! You with your kindly, rich old granny and your doting pious vicar and your fine clothes and your fed belly! What do *you* know of any of it?' she choked out in despair.

'Jane, please listen…'

'No! *You* listen,' Jane croaked across her words. 'If he's to survive, he's to toil. And this is how we must earn. For if Leach sells him to a sweep, as he's threatened to do, he'll not last this winter out. This way, he's close to me,' she breathed fiercely. 'This way he won't burn or starve…not before I do.' Her fingers reflexively bit into her son's fleshless arms, making him whimper and look up. 'Now away with you. And your friend,' she spat, jerking her dark head at Sophie who was hovering close by, tears glossing her eyes at what she'd heard.

Elizabeth felt impotent rage thickening her throat, as it had once before when she'd learned harrowing details of this woman's predicament. 'It can't be! He wants to sell your son to a chimney sweep? No!'

'Oh, yes! Why should he keep the snivelling little runt? he says. He's old enough to make a bob, he says.' Jane swiped moisture from her eyes.

'How much do you owe him, Jane? How much can it be that keeps you tied to such a monster?'

Jane shook back her head and sniffed before grunting a mirthless laugh. 'How do I know? He's bribed the bailiffs on my account. Paid my fines and my debts after the bigamist left me. Sometimes he's kind like that…fights my battles,' she explained with a poignant seriousness. 'I lost count at four hundred. Must be more now what with the laudanum and the interest. He knows I'll pay any price for Jack's laudanum. If you want a reckoning, ask Leachie…he's the tally-man,' she concluded with an impatient snap.

As they stared at one another Jane murmured wistfully, 'I really thought you'd come back to Wapping, even though I told you not to. I thought you meant what you said, about helping, being as you'd had bad luck, too.'

Elizabeth winced; felt the pain filter from her throat to her toes. Her fecklessness whipped at her like a thousand scourges. She wanted to impress on Jane that she had not forgotten, that since their first meeting in that hovel, never an hour passed in any day when she did not recall the horror of her plight and fret over how she could help.

Such empty sincerity! The truth was that she was as much a man's puppet as Jane was. Lord Stratton's threats might be smoother, more sophisticated, but it was manipulation just the same. He had forbidden her to visit this wretched woman in the stews...so had her grandmother...but it was him she was chary of defying. He was the reason she was shopping with genteel friends; he was the reason she had simply locked all charitable thoughts to the back of her mind while she made idle excursions to furnish a trousseau.

She felt utter shame swamp her as she looked deep into Jane Selby's despairing black eyes. There but for the grace of God and a fond grandmother went she. How soon she had forgotten that maxim. Immediately she turned and walked away.

Chapter Thirteen

As Elizabeth strode purposefully closer, Nathaniel Leach peered furtively about, slack-jawed in disbelief. In truth, *she* couldn't credit either her audacity in approaching him so openly. An ocean was roaring in her ears, her ribs quivered with the pounding beneath them. But her mind's eye was focused on Jane and her son, and this man's part in their dismal lives, and she forced her wobbly legs on.

'Do you know who I am, Mr Leach?' was bitten out with cold fury as soon as he was within earshot.

Brackets deepened either side of his mean mouth and sunbursts radiated from slitted sky blue eyes as far as his hairline. 'I do h'indeed, Lady Elizabeth,' he enunciated with mocking humility. 'Marquee's daughter, 'n't yer? Jane told me a foo int'resting fings about yer. Now 'oo'd've fawt such a top-lofty gel bin in such bad trouble? 'Course…we all makes mizdakes…I understands that…an' never judges folk.'

Elizabeth glared frigidly, unabashed by his smirking innuendoes. 'Yes, I am a Marquess's daughter,' was all she icily confirmed. 'And I shall make life very difficult for you if you don't do exactly as I say.'

'An' what exackly do yer say, my lady?'

Her stomach squirmed at his sinister purr; she knew he would very much like to cow and bully her as he did Jane. Nevertheless she bit out coldly, 'I say, Mr Leach, that you immediately give Jane and her son into my care or you will be very sorry.'

Stout fingers scraped at his chubby, stubbly jaw. 'Well, now…'s'up to Jane what she do. She's as free as you'n me. Soon as she pays 'er reck'nin' she can be on 'er way an' good riddance. An' the nipper…'

'How much is her reckoning?'

He smiled…really grinned in amusement. 'A lot. A lot even by your fine standards, m'lady. 'N all noted 'n signed fer. She's a greedy little gel, is yon Jane. 'S the trouble wiv shabby genteel…they want luckshriz. They gotta pay fer 'em…everyone gotta pay. Now, shall I tell yer what I say, my lady?' he sneeringly parodied her words. His black beaver hat brushed her face as he inclined close to slyly leer at her small, curvacious body. 'I says that I was right about yer firs' time. I could tell from them knowin' eyes o' your'n you'd 'ad a little ruff 'n tumble in yer time. You should've come back to see Leachie…we'd deal right well togevver. I could intradoos yer to a foo of me Quality gents…set yer up right good. Betimes this turns proper grey…' He tweaked one of her smoky-blonde ringlets where it draped close to her bosom. 'Yer'll have a tidy nest egg…me 'n all.'

Elizabeth shot him such a poisonous look that his grin drooped and his impertinent fingers withdrew to twiddle on air. Sunlight was making a beacon of the dazzling diamond being spun agitatedly on her finger. His eyes swooped and greed tautened his face. A crafty peek slanted up at her from beneath his shaggy eyebrows. 'Might jus' do it…' was all he croaked, snapping down his chin. 'More'n a fousand pounds is doo…'

Her finger curled protectively. 'No. But I have something of equal value…a necklace…' Instinctively she had opted to lose her heirloom rather than her betrothal ring and that astonished her to such a degree she hardly noticed his uncontainable excitement. His Adam's apple bobbed as he fitfully swallowed, he shifted from foot to foot, he assessed her with his craggy face cocked this way then that, keen for her to elaborate.

Surfacing from her daze, Elizabeth blurted sharply, 'I can't meet you later today, I have an appointment. I'll meet you tomorrow; at dawn at St Mary's. Bring Jane and her son and I shall let you have the necklace.'

His mouth pursed in suspicion; he scratched at the mottled skin on his neck while considering, but she could tell avarice was winning. Enticingly she allowed the ring to escape concealment in her skirts, and flashed it back into view. 'And I require proof Jane's debts are paid, too.'

'Fair 'nuf...' was all he grunted.

Spying, through milling shoppers, Sophie hesitantly approaching them, she slipped past to prevent her coming closer, and under this evil ponce's scrutiny. 'Five o'clock in the morning. I shall be with Reverend Clemence so don't think to try and cheat me or browbeat me, for it will be the worse for you,' was launched at him, low and fluent, before she finally hurried away.

Now that they were betrothed, Edwina deemed it permissible...nay, necessary...that her granddaughter privately get to know her fiancé. As soon as an elegant hessian trod over the threshold of Number Seven Connaught Street in the evenings, Edwina made herself scarce.

Elizabeth did learn more about the Trelawneys, too. Ross had told her about his brother, Tristan and his sister, Katherine, both of whom she had yet to meet; and of his clutch of nephews and nieces. Each of his siblings had two children and she could tell he was indeed fond of all of them and proud that Katherine was soon to make him godfather to her baby son.

He told her of Melrose, the family's Cornish estate that spanned the clifftops at Pendrake. With a quiet passion that held her captive, he'd described breathtaking views with such evocative eloquence she was sure she could hear the ocean's shingle-sucking hiss, its rock-battering roar; she was blinded by the glare of sun on water, by spectral mists rolling in; she could smell and taste the tang of fish and brine.

He was content, he'd said, that their new home, Stratton Hall, had its southerly aspect facing the Kent coast. Elizabeth had been oddly pleased that he already considered it her home. She found herself telling him that she, too, was lulled by the sound and sight of the sea, and had enjoyed trips to Lyme Regis and Brighton with her papa.

When it was her turn to contribute a little family background, she told him of her mother's premature demise after a fall on ice that fractured her pelvis, and that she still missed her beloved papa dreadfully since his death, a few years ago. She also admitted to seeing little of her father's relations since his funeral. The very same day he was interred, she had travelled from Thorneycroft to London to live with Edwina. A pause had followed that statement, but she had simply resumed by stating that she missed her young half-brother, Tom, and feared that at seven years old he might eventually forget her. That had left her gruff-voiced and dewy-eyed and, to deflect his steady attention, she'd boldly asked whether he had killed many men and had a partiality for liver for breakfast.

He'd looked unruffled, as he always did, by her impertinence while telling her that in his trade sometimes killing a man was the only way to stay alive, and that, personally he preferred ox kidney for breakfast. With a defeated flounce she'd then taken herself off to bed. But since that first, icebreaking session, they had settled into an easier rapport. Even when she retreated within herself to ruminate again on his motives for wanting to marry her, and nothing much was said, silences passed comfortably. He'd never again told her that her dowry wasn't important. He'd never again sought to justify himself at all, and seemed content to remain quiet while she brooded, as though allowing her to privately make sense of it. Inexplicably, that piqued her; as did the lack of any flirtation. He flirted with his sister-in-law, with his friends' wives, but not with her!

'I hear you went missing today, whilst out shopping,' was

dropped into this particular cosy quiet, curbing her introspection.

'Oh…oh, y-yes…that's true,' Elizabeth stuttered, thinking that silences were definitely preferable at times as she recalled the reason for that absence. 'Sophie and I simply spied another acquaintance a way along the street. When we returned to the draper's, Rebecca and the other ladies had gone. Possibly they thought we had already set off home. For I felt unwell…' she disjointedly explained. 'I shall apologise to them. It was rather rude to go off and chatter for so long without saying.'

'No harm's done. You're safely home…and better now?'

Elizabeth bestowed on him a small smile, and nodded, while flicking over pages of the journal on her lap, and wondering how soon she could encourage him to leave. She wanted him gone so she could fly to Hugh, yet every evening when he left at about ten o'clock, she felt restless and wished he'd stayed a little longer. She soon missed him. He could be amusing and interesting company; just as Rebecca said he was. Just as, no doubt, his other female admirers would describe him, she thought acidly. A soundless sigh escaped. Why had she just wasted a perfectly good reason to curtail his visit by answering in the affirmative when he asked if she was well?

Ross settled his powerful shoulders back into the chair, a polished boot raising to rest atop his knee. 'Did Madame Vallois attend you this afternoon for a dress fitting?'

'Yes,' Elizabeth said with a spontaneous, sweet smile as she dwelt on the beautiful silk shift that was being prepared for her wedding day. Earlier, with Edwina and the modiste clucking and fussing over her, she had got caught up in the infectious excitement of it all. As Edwina directed first this, then that luxurious fabric be draped about her undergarmented body, she was soon as absorbed as they by embroidery and lace and net covered with seed pearls. The need to steal away and speak urgently with Hugh about their meeting with Leachie early in the morning had soon slipped her mind.

'What sort of material did you choose?' Ross enquired casually, his eyes on a newspaper spread open on a side-table. He sipped from his teacup while awaiting her answer.

'Is the announcement of our betrothal in the paper today?'

He smiled at her evasion. 'No; but be prepared for a deluge of attention tomorrow,' he warned, his smile wryly distorting. No doubt the gentlemen's clubs were already awash with varying versions of the furore at the fencing academy. Over the years he'd issued or taken up a score or more challenges. All of them had been appointments with worthier opponents than Linus Savage and he'd walked away from each. Yet the Earl was a passable shot, and he was probably not going to wait for the call. It was odd; settling down was having an unnerving effect on him. He'd been confident enough of his technique before when facing cheats.

Elizabeth was also ruminating on a dawn rendezvous: fretting that Hugh might refuse to get involved, and she was certainly chary of meeting the blackguard alone. With a guilty pang, she reassured herself that Hugh was quite easily wound about her little finger. If only this man was…

'What sort of fabric did you choose?'

Elizabeth started to her senses. 'Bridegrooms are not supposed to ask such things,' she demurred. 'You're supposed to be totally enchanted with the vision of loveliness I present as I walk down the aisle…whatever I wear.'

'And so I shall be, sweetheart,' he said huskily. 'Totally enchanted…I'll be surprised if it's not white silk.'

Elizabeth jerked the journal up from her lap to study a mediocre hat. She lightly laughed, 'Please don't probe, for I'll not tell you.'

'You don't have to, Elizabeth. Some things I know…' he said softly.

'Were the fencing bouts to your liking? Did you win?' she blurted.

'They were very much to my liking, thank you. And, yes, I won,' he said with such a hint of wry humour in his studied politeness that a violet peep slanted at him from beneath a curtain of dusky lashes.

Her shy look elicited such an affectionate smile that she began agonising again whether to confide in him. Might he be sympathetic if she told him of Jane Selby's plight? Might he perhaps offer to escort her instead of Hugh in the morning? Certainly, that beast, Leach, was more likely to keep his side of the bargain if this striking man was present... No! it was out of the question! She scathed herself for being swayed by his mellow mood. He was an enigmatic, unpredictable man. He might get angry on learning of this dangerous escapade and again forbid her consorting with East End harlots. She wasn't sure of him, didn't quite trust him; yet the idea of returning to fearing and despising him as she once had was also out of the question.

In a way she wished she could resuscitate her passionate dislike; at least it was unequivocal and relatively painless. Now she no longer knew what she felt for him, other than it was bittersweet and frustrating. Her equilibrium was ruined: her thoughts constantly dragged to him, whatever she did, wherever she was. She had reasoned that discovering his opinion of her might help. She wanted to specifically know whether he regarded her as good, bad or indifferent.

He had admitted to liking her and wanting to care for her...but that wasn't enough. There had to be more to it than that...or less. Horrified, it occurred to her that sympathy might play a dominant part. Perhaps he pitied her still paying for her youthful folly a decade on. She knew he'd been livid on learning of Cadmore's abuse. Well, she had looked after herself thus far and had no wish to receive as well as bestow charity! Especially not from an upstart! She winced at her unwarranted meanness. Besides, now she knew him, and his fine connections, it was an ill-fitting description.

She stared at the side of his gypsy-dark visage, cocked to one side, as his fingers flicked over the newsprint. She was no longer convinced he was a fortune-hunter who wanted to fritter her dowry on licentious living. He seemed to possess an innate dignity that would disdain something as vulgar as money or revenge dictating whom he married. Or would he? She willed him to look up so she could scour his beautiful green-gold eyes for clues in her hunt for the truth. Before she succeeded in luring them, his mouth tilted, almost as though he could sense her observation…her neediness. She melted contentedly beneath the honeyed caress that bathed her from between long, curved black lashes, for it couldn't disguise a smouldering neediness of his own. Whatever else he felt for her, he still wanted her. The knowledge no longer alarmed her as it once had. In fact, for the first time in ten years she was exulting in being found desirable.

Blushing, she dropped her eyes to the journal in her lap. It was astonishing they were the same couple who a short time ago had met in this room and traded vicious insults. She'd resentfully given him her necklace and cursed him as a devil. He'd made no attempt to disguise his despising either. She'd been very conscious that he'd wanted to demean her; punish her haughty insolence by dragging her to a sofa, and putting her on her back.

Now he'd only need to kiss her once and she'd willingly walk there, she mocked herself, recalling a few days ago reclining languidly on to a hide seat and allowing him unlimited liberties with her person while dusk discreetly curtained them, and birdsong serenaded them, and a patter of drizzle hit the hood of the barouche, contributing an earth-scented ambience.

She had been…a wanton at his mercy that afternoon. And he had been…the perfect restrained and respectful fiancé. It was he who had imposed boundaries on their passion, he who abruptly lifted her upright, straightened her clothes with unsteady hands while muttering it would be prudent to head home. As the memories swept through her, sensations tantalised too. Her flesh fizzled in reaction to the haunting touch of brown fingers on white skin. Her stalwart inhibitions had been no defence against such insidiously sweet sensuality.

Even though he'd not once said he loved her, she'd willingly cuddled up to him on the way back to London. Almost as far as her own doorstep, she'd clung to him, vine-like, with the witless abandonment of one intoxicated. The euphoria endured for some hours after he saw her within doors, then departed.

By the time she was soaking in her tub at bedtime, she was soberly assessing her behaviour and feeling stupid. Randolph Havering had never touched her so intimately, yet he had declared undying devotion at least a dozen times a day. An infamous womaniser showed her a little contrived gallantry and she wanted to believe he was in love with her. She'd believed herself adept at rebuffing amorous males. Pitted against his expertise, hers failed dismally.

He could have succeeded where so many others had failed, but had chosen not to. She supposed it was enough that he now knew he could...and she did too. Of course he would employ a little of his seductive charm to sweep away lingering bitterness and aggression between them. He seemed a gentlemen who would exact a certain civility from his wife and a certain physical compatibility. Thus a harmonious household would be enjoyed, as would getting those many heirs he wanted. It was all very respectable and sensible. Not virtues much previously associated with Ross Trelawney, Cornish hellion. But, now, of course, he had left notoriety behind and was fêted by the *beau monde*. Such an ironic reversal of her own situation!

'Why are you sighing so?'

Elizabeth looked up from sightless perusal of the journal, to see he had folded the paper and was watching her. 'What are you thinking about?'

'Oh, nothing!' she rebuffed with unwarranted sharpness, frantically fluttering pages as blood stained her porcelain complexion. 'What are you thinking?' she demanded quickly.

'The same as you, I imagine...judging by your blush...' he said, gently amused. 'It was madness, I know...'

'What was?' she snapped, afraid to look up and see mockery in his eyes.

'Acting the perfect gentleman.'

'And so out of character,' she sweetly scoffed.

'Indeed. But, as I've said before, you make me behave oddly, Elizabeth.'

'So sorry,' she jibed, still inexplicably smarting.

'Not nearly as much as I am, I'm sure.'

'I hope you're not out for sympathy tonight.' A page tore beneath her furious fingers and she tossed aside the journal.

'No…' He laughed. 'Actually, I'm out to rectify matters tonight.'

Violet eyes sprang to his face, and she nibbled at her soft lower lip.

'I want to marry you…'

'Indeed…I thought you were to, sir…' was quipped breathily.

'Now. I'd like to marry you now. I've got a licence.'

Elizabeth stared at him. He seemed quite serious. 'What…what do you mean? Elope? W-why?' was all she could stutter.

'I want to marry you tonight…because tomorrow…who knows what tomorrow might bring? I want you as my wife now…tonight. Shall we get married tonight?' Too late, Ross understood why she looked so stricken. She'd heard something similar before. Havering had probably used much the same pathetic phrases when coaxing her to elope with him…and look where that indecent haste had led. But he couldn't tell her he wanted her immediately protected by his name, his reputation, because tomorrow if things went awry she might be prey to some lecherous bastard again. Even the idea of it locked his jaw, made him silently vow to exact a promise from Luke tonight that he would always watch over her should the need arise. And way ahead of all the worthy practicalities, was a basic need to possess her…an atavistic urge to impregnate his chosen mate with his seed. He wanted a chance to gift her a legitimate child, because, on some subliminal level, he understood that there was nothing she needed more than a baby.

Elizabeth was in shock. Her good opinion of his recent

honourable conduct seemed to disintegrate into dust. He was slipping through her fingers...and the tragedy was she yearned to hold on to him despite suspecting what he was now offering was no better than Jane had got from her colonel; that had been no real marriage either. 'Are you now proposing the sort of union that reaps you all the benefits and none of the drawbacks?' she demanded in a voice raw with hurt and loss. 'The sort of ceremony conducted by a charlatan that might pass muster and get you your money and your wedding night...followed by an annulment at some later date when certain legalities are found to be lacking?' Her wide, violet eyes attacked his. 'Why do you not simply ask me to sleep with you...as all the other men do?' She jerked to her feet, tilted her white face, slashes of angry colour accentuating her winging cheekbones. 'It is late, my lord. I wish to retire.'

'I want to make love to you, Elizabeth...'

'Goodnight!'

'I love you, Elizabeth...' flowed out low and vibrant.

She hesitated by the door, flung herself about to glare at him, dithering over whether to jeer at the untimely, pathetic lie, or fly back and hit him for daring to stoop so low and use it. She managed neither, simply stared, glazed-eyed, at him. His face dropped and a grunted curse emerged through his fingers, followed by a despairing laugh.

He shook his head back, addressed the ceiling. 'It's the truth...but go to bed anyway. I'm sorry I made such a mess of telling you. That's how you affect me, Elizabeth. I'm barely able to pass muster as a bumbling idiot.'

She had her hand on the door knob behind, felt sure she would quit the room before he reached her, but something in his slow weary pace kept her spellbound. A dark finger traced an alabaster cheek, persevering when she flicked him off. 'Don't believe anyone who tells you I'm a practised philanderer, will you? I can be the veriest callow youth about you.' He lowered his head and she immediately swung hers about so his lips grazed her soft platinum hair.

'Please...'

She heard the catch of need mingling with his wry humour. 'One kiss…one for you…' he cajoled.

She faced him, mouth pursed tight. Invective, battering to be vented, died on her lips as she noticed a suspicious sheen burnishing the gold of his eyes. The anger on her face transformed into a look of mute disbelief. And then his mouth was slanting back and forth with silky heat over her rigid lips. They slackened. Her hands climbed his chest in weak pulls, then linked at his nape and her body pressed reflexively against his. He lifted her abruptly, as though she was featherlight and instinctively her thighs opened, her calves clasped him. And far back in her mind she thought that if only the callow youth she had entrusted herself to ten years ago had been like this one, things might have been so very different.

Freeing his mouth, his thumb slid comfortingly over her slick lips as they immediately sought his again. 'Go to bed… It'll all come right in the morning,' he said huskily, and gently placed her down behind him before he quit the room.

The last time Luke had seen that look of savage composure, had he but known what it heralded, he would have shackled him to the stairs.

But since he was a small boy, there was no helping and no hindering Ross.

He'd been standing on the clifftop when Luke eventually came upon him that morning having searched and shouted for him for some while. His brother had been needed at Melrose to help with a particularly bad foaling that was defeating the stablehands, but might just prove a mere half-hour's inconvenience for Ross, on this his nineteenth birthday.

And something in the way he'd been balancing there, so still, so close to the edge, had choked the raucous cries in Luke's throat. For with Ross it was impossible to tell if the quest for novel stimulation might at some time take him to sanity's outer edge.

It was seeing him shoeless that had made him panic. Then he'd noticed how little else he had on: dark breeches, white shirt, his glossy locks knotted by a summery breeze. Ross had flicked his brown countenance clear of snarls, laughing in that exasperating way he had when nothing could be done.

Luke remembered crying out, as in a nightmare, when all the horror is there in abundance, but no sound quits the throat. His own feet had seemed rooted to turf as he watched his brother launch to soar like a swallow before he swooped gracefully and was falling like a stone.

Madly, he had raced to the cliff edge, gaped at nothing, sped to the path and slithered, slipped, scrambled to the beach so fast. It seemed like hours, not minutes, later he was racing along it. Ross was there. Dripping wet and with his hands pillowed behind his sleek, black head he lay on smooth rock, grinning up at him. 'Told you it could be done,' he'd said.

Luke had beaten him; in relief and fury he had thrashed him, until Ross felt he'd allowed contrition enough. With one punch he'd freed himself. 'Don't tell Mother,' he'd said and walked away. Then he'd turned, pacing on backwards through salt-stained, sinking shingle. 'Try it,' he'd called. 'Nothing in the world like it. But stand where I did. There's nowhere else. When the tide's high, that's the spot.' Then he was gone; and the foal was fine, the mare, too.

And Luke did. He tried it. Loved it. There was nothing like it. The exhilaration…the thrill…the rush of breathtaking atmosphere before a quiet tranquillity, before the icy sting of brine. There was nothing like it: diving over a hundred and fifty feet into the Cornish sea.

And he had realised one day as he lay, drying off, hands pillowed behind his head in exactly the same way he'd found Ross that first time, that it had been no wild whim that took his youngest brother to the edge of the cliff the day he turned nineteen. It had been, in all probability, the end of many months of observation, of stringent calculation of water depths, of trajectories, of tides.

Ross was an adventurer by chosen trade; assessing the odds on survival and coming through was his business. And nobody did it better. And now…this misty September dawn…he was looking scientific again.

'Hair-trigger flintlocks are unpredictable bastards,' Guy Markham muttered.

Luke nodded, but his black eyes were fixed on the men pacing away from each other. He shot a look about at silent figures: the surgeon, Dickie and David by the hedge, still as statues. Lord Grey and Lord Beecher and various others…Cadmore's men. His eyes jerked back as they reached the marker and began to turn. He watched Linus Savage with a ferocious fascination as he immediately swung up his arm, and a shot rang out.

Ross staggered, somehow kept to his feet. The surgeon sprang forward. Cadmore's seconds looked at each other, shook their heads in disgust. He'd fired before the call. Luke's lips curled back from his teeth in impotent rage as he saw a crimsoning on the snowy cambric of his brother's shirt. He heard Guy's savage string of curses, glanced at Dickie and David as they separated in a seething, aimless perambulation.

With a jerk of his head, Ross dismissed the fussing surgeon. He turned his attention to Cadmore quaking on the spot. The spent weapon in his hand still smoked, flopped to point at the floor.

Slowly, carefully Ross transferred the pistol from his useless right hand to his left. He raised it all the way up until it was levelled at the Earl's head, then pulled the trigger.

'Are you warm enough? Here, take this rug.'

Elizabeth smiled at Hugh. 'I'm quite comfortable,' she said, but draped the proffered travelling rug over her jittery body. Her gloved fingers dashed away a cold nervous sweat on her top lip. She forced herself to settle back into the gig. 'What time is it, Hugh?'

'Five thirty…'

Elizabeth nodded, frowning into the chill morning mist. Her fingers crept to the heavy stones in her pocket, needlessly testing for the hundredth time that she had brought the jewel. 'I'm grateful for your escort, Hugh.'

'You know I'd do anything for you, Elizabeth,' he harshly responded. He choked a bitter laugh, 'Even what I shouldn't. Your grandmother will probably kill me for aiding and abetting...if your fiancé doesn't...' Mournful brown eyes slid sideways at her. 'Why could you not tell me yourself? Why did I have to learn from Sophie that you were soon to be wed? And to such a man as he?'

'He...the Viscount is a good man,' she championed quietly. 'And I...I would have told you, Hugh. It's just...oh, everything has been such a muddle. First I thought I would not marry him...then I would... Now I...now I think I shall...' A restless hand went to her head, worrying at her cool, creased brow. 'Please don't ask me to explain; I hardly understand it myself.'

How horribly true that statement was! What was she to make of what had occurred last evening? He'd wanted her to elope with him at eight o'clock, for no proper reason. He'd called himself a callow youth for declaring his feelings with such a lack of finesse. How then out of such ineptitude had he drawn her surrender? And her love? With an awful remoteness she had realised she loved him and that if he asked her again to go with him, she would, and devil take bogus clergy, sophistry and anything else.

She just wanted him. Even knowing other women did too, and might have been similarly won over by seeing him look so uncharacteristically vulnerable, made little difference. Was playing the dilettante just a subtle skill in his seductive repertoire? God knows it worked!

Was she just an infatuated fool? She was here, now, with Hugh, cold and nervous, because she was endeavouring to save a poor wretch broken by circumstances she had again contemplated embracing herself. Jane Selby's unwise trust and unrequited love for a trickster had brought her and her son to the brink of disaster. What reason could there be for Ross to want to marry her with such indecent haste? Surely, none other than base selfish motives? She sighed it all away. For the present she must simply endeavour to help Jane. It suddenly came to her that for a decade she had been doing that: concentrating on others' misfortunes; helping the poor and needy because she couldn't bear to closely examine her own barren life and situation.

'If I thought Stratton could make you happy, I would bless the union myself,' Hugh piously pierced her perceptiveness. 'But what I have heard of his...gross licentiousness gives me no hope to think he will make a worthy or even a discreet spouse. Of course you might overlook his misdemeanours. I hear he has a persuasive way with the fair sex...' His stricture broke off as he squinted into pastel morning light. Elizabeth heard the vehicle, too.

Within a moment, a hackney cab drew up close by. Before it was properly stopped, Nathaniel Leach jumped down, leaving the door swinging and, hands in his pockets, swaggered over to them. Elizabeth's eyes were immediately swerving past to the two pale ovals visible at the aperture. Mother and son were staring back at her.

Leach doffed his hat. 'Reverend...m'lady,' he greeted affably as though no inhuman trade were about to take place and he was simply emerging from Sunday service.

Hugh was barely able to acknowledge him, so huge was his antipathy. After a curt nod, he snapped, 'Bring Mrs Selby and her son closer.'

Nathaniel Leach beckoned to the cab's occupants, while sliding a look at Elizabeth. 'Believe yer've got a little summat fer me, my lady?'

Elizabeth withdrew the necklace from her pocket, but held it fast in a clenched fist. Leach's eyes were like limpets on the treasure. Even in the insipid dawn light it sparkled its magnificence. He raised thick fingers and beckoned impatiently as Jane helped her young son alight. A small dog-eared book was dropped on the seat of the gig. 'Tally book fer yer, as y'arst. All fair 'n square.'

Elizabeth simply nodded, reluctant to relinquish her heirloom even though mother and child were now by the villain's side. Their blank, bleak countenances loosened her grip on the necklace far sooner than any of Leach's threats might have.

Nothing escaped Leach's cunning comprehension. Jack was lifted and plonked on the seat next to Hugh. 'There y'are. Be a good boy fer the lady…' he cooed while holding out a casual hand.

With an unsteady breath rasping her throat Elizabeth placed the jewel on his flat palm. His fingers sprang like a trap as soon as gold touched skin. Within a moment it was lost to his pocket. Elizabeth shifted to make room for Jane on the seat, swallowing the bitter bile in her throat. It really was done. She'd lost her mother's necklace to this loathsome man.

'Be on yer way, then…' Leach said with a triumphant smirk.

'Jane, too…' Elizabeth swung about to gaze appealingly at Hugh. 'He said he would free them both.'

'I said nought but I'd let yer pay 'er doos. Yer've got the tally…an' the nipper. Yer can't 'ave me wife. 'S' not right nor legal ta separate a man 'an 'is wife. 'N't that so, Reverend?' he taunted, then laughed aloud at the defeat that lowered Hugh Clemence's strained features towards his clenching fingers.

Chapter Fourteen

'I have vital news, Mrs Sampson.'

Edwina leapt up from the breakfast table, linen blotting her mouth. She frowned; her butler looked agitated and breathless as though having sped to the dining room. That agitated her. Pettifer could be relied upon to cope imperturbably with any eventuality—good or bad. It was customary for Harry to damp down the fire, she supplied the bellows.

'What is it, man? For God's sake, tell me, before I expire from the suspense. Remember m'age.'

Immediately, he launched into, 'The whole town is abuzz with gossip of a duel…between Viscount Stratton and the Earl of Cadmore. Allegedly, the challenge was issued yesterday by the Viscount and the meeting took place at dawn today on Wimbledon Common. The first account has it that Cadmore fired before the call and injuries were sustained. I have returned immediately to tell you, but will try and glean more details…'

Edwina sank back down to the table, a plump hand pressed to her heaving bosom. The other reached for her knife. Feverishly she began buttering her toast. 'You have frightened me witless for that! Of course there's been a duel!' she snapped testily.

'You were aware of it?' Pettifer's usual baritone trebled in astonishment.

'Oh, I've heard nothing. But I've been hoping Stratton would call the blackguard out. Indeed, I've been relying on it that he would. I knew he'd live up to m'expectations.' She shot Pettifer a wicked smile, it transformed into a gleeful, triumphant chuckle. Happily she crunched on toast.

Pettifer stared at her, his firm jaw sagging. 'Injuries were sustained, although no specific news as to whom or the severity. Are you not overset that the Viscount might be mortally wounded by that caitiff's bullet?'

Edwina waved an airy hand. 'I have every confidence in m'new grandson. God knows he's certain to have kept appointments with cheats before. I've heard tell he's blazed successfully so many times gunsmiths outdo each other supplying him with fancy pistols, gratis. Good for business, I suppose. He'll never countenance a weasel of Cadmore's calibre drawing his cork!' She snorted sheer disbelief. 'It's as like the reverse might be true and Cadmore's soon to push up the daisies!'

Harry Pettifer sighed, shaking his stately grey head.

'Don't look so Friday-faced, man! Apart from ridding ourselves of Cadmore, there's a little added bonus to this morning's work.' An arch look slanted at him. 'I was confident enough of the Viscount seeing Cadmore off to bet on it...with your new mistress. She sniggered in my face when I wagered that before the end of the month Cadmore would be less welcome in town than a dose of the pox. Can you guess what I persuaded her to stake?'

Harry Pettifer allowed a smile to quirk his lips. 'I believe I can, madam. Although I had no intention of staying with Mrs Penney longer than the six months I signed for, in any case.'

'You probably wouldn't have summoned the stamina to do so...' Edwina sourly muttered. Then, loudly, 'Well, now you're not to go at all. I've saved you from a sordid fate. You're once more my man...'

'I've ever been that, Mrs Sampson,' Harry said quietly. 'That's my fate...'

Edwina looked at him; her chewing slowed and dawning comprehension flushed her chubby cheeks. 'Is m'granddaughter still a'bed?' she spluttered.

'I believe she must be. I've not yet seen Lady Elizabeth this morning.'

Edwina glanced sideways at him. An odd feeling stirred. She shook herself mentally. She'd not thought of *that* since her beloved husband died. Heavens! She must be as wanton as that bad Penney! Her blush grew hotter. She sought refuge in hearty conversation. 'It might benefit if this news reached Lizzie's ears. She's softening towards the Viscount. Perhaps a little shock might clearly focus her affections and Stratton's fine qualities. He's done this specifically to coincide with the announcement in the paper.' The knife's hilt thumped on *The Times* folded by her plate. 'He's made public his honourable intentions towards her and restored her position and reputation.' She grinned mischievously. 'A little side bet? I'll wager that before the day's out we're lining up visiting cards and invitations on the mantel. Come, a guinea says…mmm…six by noon!'

Fifteen minutes later, Edwina was going upstairs, mightily pleased. In a pudgy hand was the first proof that Harry's guinea might soon be hers. She started to hum while again reading that Lady Regan hoped Mrs Sampson and Lady Elizabeth Rowe might this afternoon grace her little salon at Brook Street with their most welcome presence.

'Where are you off to with that?' she suddenly barked, spying her granddaughter's maid hurrying along the landing with a tray of food. Josie screeched in surprise and jumped on the spot, slopping milk on to the carpet. Edwina stomped on up the treads to join her. 'You clumsy chit. What are you doing with it? Is Lady Elizabeth to breakfast a-bed?'

Josie goggled at her employer and simply nodded her head affirmatively.

Edwina's eyes hovered over milk, scrambled eggs, toast, butter and jam. She frowned. 'Is she ailing?'

Again Josie's head quivered confirmation, her eyes a passable imitation of the saucers she was carrying.

'Well, she can't have much to complain about if she intends tucking all that away. She's not fancied scrambled eggs for breakfast since she was a youngster.'

Josie gulped audibly, making Edwina shoot her a look. 'Here, I'll take it. I want to speak to m'granddaughter.' There ensued a see-sawing tussle for possession of the tray which occasioned milk to again puddle the floor. Retaining a contesting grip with one hand, Edwina's other delivered a stinging smack to one of Josie's, thereby further depleting the milk jug. 'What are you doing, you insubordinate hussy?' Edwina roared. 'Are you keen to be shown m'door without a character in your pocket to warm you on your way?'

Josie wobbled her head in denial, her bottom lip trembling. She burst into tears and abruptly let go of the tray.

Edwina tottered backwards; the crockery tilted, but she managed to find her balance without mishap. 'Cease that blubbing and make yourself useful,' she growled. 'Open Lady Elizabeth's door for me.'

'What is all the commotion, Grandmama?' Elizabeth emerged from her chamber and shut the door behind her. She was dressed in a powder-blue embroidered night rail, her pearl-fair hair cascading shimmery tendrils to tip about her tiny waist.

'Oh, nothing,' Edwina snarled. 'Just this saucy minx making me cross.' She turned her bulk sideways, looked expectantly at Elizabeth.

'Thank you, Grandmama.' With a vague smile Elizabeth took the tray.

'Oh…I'll come in and sit with you while you eat, dear. I've some very interesting news for you. What's ailing you, in any case?' she demanded with a scouring peer at her granddaughter's wan complexion. 'You've more mauve in the hollows beneath your eyes than in them. Did you sleep badly?'

'Yes, I slept ill,' Elizabeth immediately conceded. 'I've been feeling queasy. I shall rest a while longer, then come down in an hour or so and you can tell me your news.' She gave her grandmother a sweet smile. 'Josie,' Elizabeth called. A small head movement indicated to her maid to attend to the door.

Before disappearing inside the chamber, Josie's triangular, goggle-eyed face peeked back through the aperture. Edwina scowled and reflexively the maid slammed the door shut. Elizabeth grimaced warningly, a finger to her lips, as Josie took a shivery breath about to recommence blubbing for having been twice unintentionally insubordinate.

On the other side of the door, Edwina slid her head sideways on her chubby shoulders and pressed an ear to the panels. She shrugged, looked at the invitation in her hand and strolled off, smiling, to inspect her wardrobe for fitting attire for an afternoon salon in Brook Street.

'Are you hungry?' Elizabeth asked kindly.

The small boy simply stared solemnly at her.

She crouched close to him and took one of his tiny hands in hers. 'Come, Jack, eat a little of this and you will feel so much better.' She watched his eyes fill with tears and his lips quiver and immediately cupped his mouth with a gentle hand. 'Don't forget…this is a game…like hide and seek…and who is quietest wins. But…if you are to win…and get the cake I promised…you must be as quiet as a mouse.'

'Don't want a cake. Want my mam,' the boy choked miserably.

'I know, my love. I promise I will try and get her for you,' Elizabeth said with a fierce glower into space. Lifting him off the small pallet where he'd cat-napped on the floor by her bed, she put him on his feet.

After an awed gawp at the laden tray balancing on the dressing table, Jack's hunger overcame all else and his fingers stole towards the toast. Soon the eggs tempted him too and he shovelled them up with a spoon.

Josie was clutching double-handed at the bed post, transfixed, as though in the presence of a spectre.

'We must bathe him, Josie. He looks a little…'

'Scummy…' Josie supplied, uninhibited by the delicacy that limited her mistress to wrinkling her nose, and with unaltered pop-eyed entrancement.

'Fetch hot water and fill the bath. My grandmother will be away in her chamber at this hour. She will not spy you.'

Keen to avoid the old harridan, Josie fled to do her mistress's bidding. Within five minutes she was back with the first pitcher of water. Within ten minutes, Jack had cleared the tray and the tub was half-full and steaming.

Coaxing him from his clothing, Elizabeth realised, was to be no easy task. He was eyeing the water, and the soap in Josie's hand, as though it might be poisonous. Elizabeth groaned inwardly. If only she had been able to persuade Hugh to give the boy shelter until they could fathom what next to do! But although the vicar claimed he would do anything for her, it didn't extend to donning the trousers in his own house. His elderly mother had no qualms in ejecting the lad before he'd set both feet in the hallway of the vicarage. Strict directions were given to the closest foundling hospital, as though her son might have forgotten the location since Tuesday when last he read scripture there! Sheepishly Hugh had offered to drive them either to that bleak institution or Connaught Street. Elizabeth had no intention of little Jack exchanging one miserable existence for another, so had brought him home.

Prising Jack from his mother to take him anywhere had been a heartbreaking feat. Nothing would sway Leachie into letting Jane go. Not her son's howling, nor Hugh's appeals to the man's conscience, nor Elizabeth's irate insistence that he honour his word to do so. Quietly resigned to sacrificing her own health and happiness for her son, Jane had begged them to go and keep Jack safe from sweeps and pickpockets. The lad's fate if left behind was inducement enough for Elizabeth to concede defeat. Besides, demanding back her necklace from the duplicitous devil would have been quite futile. He would have laughed in her face. So, home she brought Jack, with him sobbing all the way. Hugh passed the time muttering the marriage was probably a sham and Leach was simply keeping Jane to put her back to work.

Her grandmother was still abed and, thankfully, the only two servants in the vicinity of the side doorway were Josie and Peter, the youngest groom. They were sweethearts and had been bestowing a hearty good morning on each other away from prying eyes, as Elizabeth and Jack slipped in at seven o'clock. They had been equally disconcerted at the untimely encounter and were easily sworn to silence. In all, things could have been worse. With that encouraging thought, Elizabeth confidently advanced on Jack. He backed away to the window. 'Your mama will want you to be a nice clean boy when you again see her. I shall tell her you've been very good.'

It seemed to strike a chord. With his sweet solemn face lifted to hers, his small fingers picked at his buttons to undo them and the toe of one boot fastened over the heel of the other to remove it. Gratefully, Elizabeth sank to her feather soft mattress and, as slowly, shyly, he revealed a skeletal, milky body filmed with grime, she felt enraged that it might so easily have been crusted with burns; or blackened with soot...or bruises from Leachie's fist should his stepson's pickpocketing fail to satisfy his avarice.

She knew she couldn't keep the boy secreted indefinitely and there was only one person left to turn to for aid: Ross. He had asked her to share her problems with him before and she had rudely rebuffed him. Now she wished she had confided in him yesterday. He had the strength and experience to know what must be done. He would doubtless be cross she had disobeyed him...but...she needed him now. She must humble herself and beg his help in finding a solution to this regrettable fiasco.

'It is a miracle he is alive.'

'He has sharp reflexes. How do you think he has survived so long in such a perilous trade?' Edwina remarked, while tipping her head this way and that, assessing her butler's contortions.

'Rumour has it that Cadmore was so early with his fire he could have shot him in the back!'

'What are you doing, Pettifer?' Elizabeth asked from the parlour doorway, while frowning at the spectacle of their sedate butler standing sideways with his lofty frame bowed and one of his arms up as though he were taking aim at an imaginary adversary.

Pettifer straightened his shoulders and his black uniform. 'Er…I am…er…demonstrating a particular method of protecting one's self whilst engaged in a duel, Lady Elizabeth. It is, by all accounts, no mean feat to master the art whereby a ball needs to pan all the way up the arm before touching a vulnerable part.'

Elizabeth chuckled. 'Are you to duel then, Pettifer? With whom, may I ask? Have you and Grandmama been at odds again?'

'Why, no, Lady Elizabeth. Your grandmother and I are…ever harmonious…' That elicited a blush from Edwina…and a smile from Harry when he saw it. 'Besides, my technique may not match Mrs Sampson's. She may have received tuition from her friend.'

'Good. The Bow Street Runners might arrest you both. Duelling is stupid and criminal, too!'

'Also heroic,' Edwina interjected, patting the sofa cushion invitingly. 'Especially when life is risked to avenge wrongs done a lady.'

'I'm sure the lady would rather not have such barbarism on her conscience…' Elizabeth's voice faded, her skin crawled fearfully.

Harry abruptly busied himself clearing away the coffee pot and the depleted dish of sweetmeats. Quietly he quit the room. His retreat seemed diplomatic. It also seemed to confirm Elizabeth's dreaded suspicions. 'Who were you talking about, Grandmama? Which friend might have taught you a duelling technique?' Before Edwina could reply, she resumed in a panic, 'What was it you wanted to tell me, earlier?'

'Well, m'dear, am I right in thinking you've grown a little fonder of the Viscount recently?'

Pansy-blue eyes grew dark and large in a snow-white face. She simply nodded jerkily and small teeth sank into her lower lip.

'Your good opinion of him is overdue but well deserved, Lizzie. Ross has put life and limb in jeopardy returning you status and respectability. This morning the announcement of your betrothal is in the paper; it coincides with him meeting Cadmore on Wimbledon Common...'

Elizabeth heard no more. Her heart had vaulted to her throat where it pulsated crazily. An anvil was pounding in her fragile head. She grasped at the nearest chair and lowered herself stiffly into it. She could see her grandmother's mouth working, realised she was explaining about the cards she was fanning out on the sofa-table. There looked to be at least eight. Edwina was tapping a fingernail on one of them.

'So of them all, I think we ought go to Lady Regan's first, then on to the Braithwaites' later. Unless you've a preference for one or two of the others.'

'Is he dead?' exploded in a whisper.

'Ross? Dead? Of course he's not dead!' Edwina snorted. 'He wouldn't be wounded but for that lily-liver getting a shot off early, but...'

Elizabeth sprang to her feet. Her complexion was now ashen, her eyes bright with tears dammed by shock. 'Badly wounded? Are surgeons attending him?'

'It's a flesh wound, I've heard. As Pettifer was demonstrating—quite admirably, I thought—there is a technique whereby one can use an arm as a shield to cover oneself. Obviously Ross has long ago mastered it...'

'What of Cadmore? Is he dead?' Elizabeth breathed.

'He deserves to be. Ross shot off his hat, by all accounts, when all present believed he would put a bullet between his eyes.

'Thank God, he missed…'

'He didn't miss!' Edwina scoffed. 'Ross spared him. He's given the skunk a stripe straight across the pate, so rumour has it. Cadmore's branded as the poltroon he is. Not that he's likely to again show his face in public. Ross is a marksman…even left-handed,' Edwina said on a proud, emphatic nod.

'Where is he? I must see him…' Elizabeth gasped, twisting about agitatedly on the spot.

'I believe he is with his brother. Luke will ensure he gets the best physician. You would not want to see him all bloodied. I understand the surgeon has extracted the bullet.'

With nausea bubbling in her throat, Elizabeth stuffed a fist to her mouth and turned and fled.

'Open this door at once, Lizzie. Do you intend to stay in there for ever?'

'I'm staying home this evening, Grandmama. I'm tired.'

'Tired? You've slept the clock round these past few days. How can you still be tired! You must venture abroad this evening,' Edwina wheedled. 'Look…it is the most prestigious invitation yet,' she enthused. 'From the King's favourite: Lady Conyngham. Now what do you say to that?' The thin card was slipped under the door.

Elizabeth retrieved it, saw it boasted an Italian diva performing at a notable Mayfair address. Listlessly she dropped it onto a sidetable to join a pile of others with which Edwina had recently tried to lure her out.

'Is the Viscount yet back in town?' Elizabeth asked huskily. There was silence for a long moment from the other side of the door.

'I don't think so; but men always take themselves off for a while after such scandals, Lizzie. Gentleman that he is, Ross is probably allowing Cadmore time to scuttle back to his wife in the country before he returns to town to be fawned over. As his fiancée, *grandes dames* are falling over themselves to secure your presence at their little functions. Bets are being laid as to who will first manage to tempt you out. We could lay a discreet wager and collect a tidy sum...'

'Has he a fever, Grandmama? Has the wound become infected, do you know?'

Edwina let out a mighty sigh. 'No, I do not know! But he has fought battles with soldiers, with smugglers, with the revenue, with drunken cronies and come through them all. He's as strong as an ox and has taken more stitches over the years than you'll count in your bridal gown! Besides, not so long ago, you would have filled him with lead yourself, given the chance! Oh, I shall go with Evangeline then,' Edwina mumbled and was heard rustling away.

Elizabeth sighed; her grandmother regretted resorting in pique to that last accusation. She was equally ashamed, for it was quite valid. She leaned her head against the door panels, again tortured by the vision of him raddled with ague and poisoning of the blood. She might never again look upon his gypsy face, never again hear his voice, feel his strong, dark fingers fasten gently on her. She might never have the opportunity to apologise for her rudeness...and say she loved him...

Edwina stomped, muttering, down the stairs. In truth, she was a mite worried herself now. Little was known on the grapevine of Ross's recovery or his whereabouts. She frowned, wondering whether to call at Grosvenor Square on her way out to Lady Conyngham's and see if he was yet at home. She was spared the need. In the hallway, Harry was in the process of taking her prospective grandson-in-law's coat.

'Where have you been?' she barked at Ross, sheer relief making her irritable. 'It's as well you're here! M'granddaughter's acting very strange. Even before she knew of the duel she was pasty-faced and ailing. She's barely quit her room since discovering you were hurt...' Enlightenment abruptly dropped her chubby jaw, and she gawped at the handsome, virile man who had his fierce agate gaze angling up the stairs.

Edwina's gimlet eyes attached to his dark profile while she reflected on the time her Lizzie had disappeared from home. She'd been brought back close to midnight by this charming romeo. 'Morning sickness…damn!' she groaned to herself. 'Why did it not occur before? Blast that Wapping drab! It's her fault! No wonder Lizzie's fretting so. Not yet wed and really ruined…'

'What?' Ross frowned, obliquely aware of Edwina glaring and mumbling.

'You'd best get her respectable as soon as maybe, or I'll fill you full of lead m'self. See if I don't!' She flapped a hand. 'Oh, go on up. Third door on the left. No point in standing on ceremony now. I'm off out to hear Signora Favetti…' trailed back at Ross who was taking the stairs two at a time.

If Josie's short double tap at the door seemed a little heftier than usual, it didn't disturb Elizabeth enough to stir her from her comfy spot on her bed. A call to enter vied with a yawn as a slender finger touched a lock of hair away from Jack's brow. She smiled tenderly as he snored; in the short while he had been with her he looked healthier, with colour in his cheeks. She was sure he had even put on a little weight. He rather resembled her little half-brother, Tom, she judged, assessing his small regular features and mop of flaxen hair. And of a similar age, too…

'Is that the problem? I'm too old for you?'

Elizabeth's finger froze by Jack's head. Abruptly she squirmed on to her stomach on the counterpane. Pushing back on her elbows, her satin-sheathed derrière poked provocatively into the air, before she made it onto her hands and knees, where her eyes were immediately level with muscular buff-coloured thighs. She swallowed, her violet gaze sliding upwards over blatantly hardening masculinity before skittering hurriedly on to encounter an elegant chestnut coat. She stared up at him, unblinking, as though he was a ghost, and a small hand actually fluttered out to test his arm. Her weak prod blunted on healthy muscle. The light, hungry touch transformed into a furious slap. Platinum tresses danced about her slender shoulders as she shook back her head to get a good look at him. 'You…you absolute devil! Why did you do that?' she squeaked. Instinctively she'd lowered her voice to avoid waking Jack, yet her tone quavered with despair.

'Why did I do what?' he asked huskily, his eyes hot as molasses and coating her curvacious body. Her breathing was coming in sharp bursts and her nipples were clearly visible beneath the sleek negligée. With a groan he reached for her, but she reared back onto her heels away from him, then scrambled to the edge of the bed.

'What did I do? Startle you? I'm sorry…'

Elizabeth drew herself up to her full five feet three. He seemed larger and darker than usual; apart from that he was perfectly normal. The agonies she'd endured imagining putrefied flesh and amputated limbs seemed now so wildly unnecessary. She rushed to the table, strewn with invitations and grabbed a handful. 'This!' she hissed. 'This is what you did!' She advanced back towards him, bristling like an angry kitten, then lobbed them up at him.

Ross turned his face and the cards fluttered about his long dark hair before scattering on the floor.

'You risked your life to get me this?' she choked. 'You thought I'd be impressed by some…some grand gesture allowing me to ride back into the *beau monde* on your undertaker's coat tails? I don't want society invitations!'

'What do you want?' he asked immediately, softly.

She could feel the pull of his eyes on hers, insisting she look at him. The small space between them was cramming with heat, with tension, with unspoken words.

'Come, tell me,' he said. 'You can do it…you're a very brave woman. Tell me what you do want, Elizabeth…' His voice was low, hypnotic and drew a single, croaky syllable from her.

'I'm all yours, sweetheart,' he said with hoarse contentment. 'And I did it…because it needed to be done, that's all.'

'I thought you might be dying of fever or poisoning,' she gasped.

'I'm fine. I've been at Stratton Hall for a couple of days. I usually go to the coast when I'm wounded: sea water's healing.'

She backed away, tears sliding her face, sticking silky curls to her cheeks, scraps of shock and anger still writhing in her.

He cornered her and exasperatedly she flung up her fists. They froze in mid-air. 'Where are you hurt?'

He smiled down at the top of her smoky head. 'Everywhere...' he purred as he lifted her up so her face was level with his. 'Where are you hurt?'

'Everywhere,' she echoed.

'Good...it'll all need kissing better...'

With a defeated sob she wound her arms tightly about his neck and ran her lips fleetingly over his face, covering his skin from bronzed brow to abrasive jaw. It was tender, at odds with the punitive fingers that twisted in glossy mahogany hair.

'Have you something else to tell me? Something I'd love to know?'

Elizabeth opened her eyes and, past his head, Jack stirred in his sleep. 'Promise you won't be angry...he's a good little boy.'

'I didn't mean that, actually, sweetheart,' he said wryly. 'But now you've mentioned him...is he your half-brother?'

Elizabeth looked at his frown. Her tongue tip nervously moistened her lips. She struggled to free herself, to act decorously when she explained. As she pushed against his right arm he winced. Immediately she was still and hugging him. 'Sorry...oh, I'm so sorry for everything, Ross. Promise you won't be angry with me...' There was raw plea in her voice for she so wanted to build on this new harmony and affection, not destroy it with her revelation.

Ross sat abruptly in the armchair. Gently, deftly he manoeuvred her to face him so her knees straddled his thighs. As she attempted to sit more demurely on his lap, he stopped her, took her mouth in a slow loving kiss that drained her of energy or will to move at all. She flopped against him, breast against breast, her pert behind tilting ceilingward.

Ross abruptly curtailed the kiss, as though his mind had been working throughout. 'Who is he?' he asked mildly, but she recognised the suspicion and intelligence in the question.

Her arms tightened about his neck, as though to restrict his temper. 'His name is Jack; he's the son of an old friend of mine…the one who presently…who is unfortunately…'

Loosening her grip, he firmly held her back from him by her wrists, so he could see her face. His dark countenance was a study of ironic disbelief. 'You've abducted a harlot's child?'

'No! She begged me to take him. Jane was to come, too, but that monster wouldn't let her go. Edwina doesn't know of any of it, or that Jack's here.'

He swore beneath his breath. 'Life isn't that simple, Elizabeth, is it?' The sheer fear of what she might next admit to having done coarsened his voice to a gravelly explosion. 'Have you been back to the docks to barter with a pimp? Alone?'

'No…with Hugh…Reverend Clemence. He's a good friend of mine and very obliging to me… Don't be angry!' She banned his annoyance in a whisper, blazing appeal in her jewel-bright eyes.

For a moment his expression didn't alter, he simply held her gaze with its odd mix of meekness and defiance. He studied the perfect contours of her fine-skinned face, the lucidity of her grave amethyst eyes. Despite his best attempts at sang-froid, his blood was boiling, dragging his appreciation lower, to the soft, rounded body tempting his. His half-smile was self-mocking, already defeated as he said thickly, 'An upstart Viscount wouldn't be lenient…would he?' He felt his loins answer before she did.

'I…I don't know, sir,' she answered coyly, hiding her blush against his shoulder. Her breasts throbbed, felt heavy and full; the apex of her parted thighs grazing his body seemed hot and dewy and these new sensations were exciting…and terrifying her. 'My Viscount is a brave and honourable gentleman who would never abuse his position of power, even if sorely tempted.'

'He is sorely tempted, sweetheart…'

'I know…' Excitement won. She instinctively pressed her hips forward and her lips to his, just as a knock came at the door.

Josie was in the room before Elizabeth had time or mind to scramble from straddling her fiancé's lap. The maid stopped short, brought her dropped jaw together with an audible clack of teeth and garbled, 'Pettifer says as there's visitors to see you, Miss Elizabeth…' Her goggling eyes blinked once, then she was gone in two precise backwards steps. With contained hysteria Elizabeth realised that Josie no longer had the capacity to be scandalised.

Chapter Fifteen

'You!'

Elizabeth advanced into the room, her expression tight with wrathful disbelief. She glared accusingly at Hugh, then turned her back on him, causing him to redden and abandon explanation.

Josie had fled before Elizabeth could discover the identity of the visitors. She had told Ross she suspected it might be Hugh and Sophie come to see how Jack fared. They were both aware of his presence at Connaught Street and timed their visits to coincide with Edwina's social sorties. She was half-right! It was Hugh...and with him was Nathaniel Leach! She understood how he had got past Pettifer's rigorous scrutiny. Soberly turned out in smart, dark clothes, clean-shaven and with slicked-down hair, she barely recognised the villain herself. He could have passed muster as the vicar's apprentice, he looked so meek and mild!

Ross had quit her chamber first, giving her time to hurriedly pull on a gown. She guessed he was being diplomatically discreet in allowing her time alone with her friends in the drawing room while he kicked his heels in the parlour. She was sure he wouldn't go without saying goodbye. She found herself hoping fervently that he had not.

'Why on earth have you brought him here?' she heatedly demanded of Hugh.

'If I've mistaken your commitment to Mrs Selby's welfare, I apologise,' Hugh said with pained primness. 'Mr Leach came to the vicarage in a panic, saying he had urgent news concerning Mrs Selby's health but would only recount details to you personally. I thought you would be overset if I did *not* immediately act on it. I ensured your grandmother was out before calling.'

Elizabeth hoped to God Edwina didn't return early. She would have a purple fit on finding this rat infesting her drawing room. And how credulous Hugh was! Or perhaps a few unhappy dealings with this trickster had made her a cynic! A glacial glare accompanied her snapped, 'I've nothing more to give you, if that's your intention in coming here, Mr Leach.'

He gestured unctuous apology with the hat in his hand. 'Fergive me, m'lady, fer the introoshun. Beein' as yer've suffered some too, an' come from sim'lar stock as Jane, I 'opes yer'll be kindly disposed ta listen. She's frettin' so over the little lad, she's dosed 'erself nigh to deaf wiv laudanum. I'm at me wits' end. She's fadin' afore me eyes,' he intoned with theatrical gravity. 'She'll only rally, I reckons, if 'er 'n' the nipper can be togevver.'

'Have you brought her with you, then, so mother and son can be reunited?' His Haymarket histrionics seemed to vindicate her scepticism; she was sure all that ailed Jane was this vile man's rapacious greed.

'No, 'cos I'm sure yer'd agree that a man deserves compensatin' fer losin' 'is wife,' he crooned.

'She's no more properly married to you than I am!' Elizabeth furiously remonstrated.

'That's a relief...' was drawled from the doorway.

Ross walked into the room, a half-filled brandy balloon cradled in his hand. He set it down on a side-table before assessing the men with calm, feral eyes.

Both Hugh and Nathaniel Leach were statue-still, gawping warily at this imposing gentleman who had quietly, confidently joined them. Hugh shot Elizabeth a stern look: the roguish Viscount seemed quite at home, while Edwina was away. Nathaniel Leach was also eyeing her, but with approval. She knew exactly what he was thinking, too: she'd found herself a Quality gent without any help from him.

'Are you not going to introduce us, my dear?' Ross gently prompted as her guests began shifting uneasily beneath his appraisal.

'This is Viscount Stratton,' Elizabeth announced, feeling very pleased as Leach's hooded lids unshuttered. Obviously Ross Trelawney's reputation preceded him even to the further reaches of the East End. 'Reverend Clemence is a good friend of mine and is vicar at St George-in-the-East. Mr Leach is no friend of mine and is responsible for cruelly separating Mrs Selby from her son.'

''S'why I'm 'ere, m'lady,' Leachie whined. A vigilant eye stayed on the Viscount. He was unsettled by Trelawney's unnatural stillness, his profound, impassive attention. 'You've got me all wrong: I ain't an 'ard-'earted cove.'

'You'll be keen to immediately return the lad to his mother then.'

'No!' Elizabeth cried, rushing to her fiancé, her stricken face turned up appealingly to his. 'If Jack goes back to Wapping, he'll be forced to pickpocket again, or be sold to a sweep…'

Leach looked equally disconcerted at the idea of being foisted with the brat he'd just offloaded at a tidy profit. Jane was still of some commercial use, but nothing like as valuable as that rock-like diamond he'd seen flashing on this classy strumpet's finger. He'd duped the vicar into bringing him here with the intention of relieving her of it. But now he was nervously cogitating that this infamous rakehell might have given it to her…and that necklace…and he was cursing himself for a dolt coming here at all. He'd thought the mooning-eyed vicar was her beau. He'd plucked out of Jane that m'lady had been ravished and was no longer marriageable merchandise in high society, although many a nob wanted her for a liaison. Had he known she'd secured Ross Trelawney's protection…

He chewed the inside of his cheek, surreptitiously sidling towards the door. Home ground called.

'How much?' Ross asked quietly, lifting the brandy balloon to his lips.

'I've paid him already!' Elizabeth thoughtlessly cried.

After a long swig, Ross replaced his drink. 'The necklace?'

She nodded, colouring miserably. She'd never felt more of an incompetent idiot. Leach had intended this all along: he had no real wish to keep Jane or her son, but desired extracting as much as possible for their release. Having easily parted her from one gem, he'd felt encouraged to return for more.

'I want the necklace back,' Ross stated.

Leachie licked his lips nervously. 'Well now…m'lady give it to me in exchange fer the nipper an' 'er friend's tally…'

'It isn't my fiancée's property. It's mine. I'm willing to negotiate a price for its return. I take it you've still got it?' he enquired silkily. A smile touched his lips at Leach's startled expression on learning Elizabeth was properly under his protection.

Leachie nodded slowly. His interest was quickening, so was his caution. *Fiancée?* 'Struth! Yet he'd rather not have the bother of prising stones from gold to sell for a fraction of their worth. It was too much of an exquisite, noteworthy piece to fence whole.

Exactly reading his thoughts, Ross interrogated, 'Is it undamaged?'

'It is, m'lord.'

'Good. I'll do business with you tonight. Do you know Cinnamon Wharf?'

'I should think I do,' Leach smirked. 'It's my manor…'

'Good,' Ross repeated in a satisfied drawl. 'I'll meet you there at ten o'clock. I'll show you out.'

Elizabeth recognised the deceitful smoothness in her fiancé's voice and smile from her own early dealings with him. A chill assailed her. There was to be dangerous trouble and Ross was already injured…

Leach kept a respectful distance behind the tall, athletic

figure striding easily along the hall. By the door, Ross curbed the instinct to accelerate the slimy toad down the steps with the toe of a boot. Instead he said, 'Ten o'clock, then. Don't be late or make me come looking for you...'

'I'll be there,' Leach vowed. 'Might I be so bold as to ask...what sorta price, yer lordship?'

'No,' Ross said and shut the door.

'Do I need to show you out, Reverend, or do you know the way?' Ross asked quietly, on re-entering the drawing room.

The fading heat in Hugh's cheeks re-ignited and, mumbling farewell to Elizabeth, he curtly nodded at the Viscount before hastily removing himself.

Elizabeth started after him, hissing, 'Did you have to be quite so rude?'

'Yes, I did. What's the man thinking of, bringing a thieving pimp into the house? If I hadn't been here, Leach might have felt inclined to help himself to a few valuables before he left. A few virtues, too. The vicar would have gone down with one punch.' He blocked her way, preventing her pacifying Hugh.

Elizabeth stiffened in shock. It had not occurred to her that Leach might cause such havoc. There *were* several attractive female servants in residence, and personally she was very vulnerable to his savage spite...

Ross swore beneath his breath and enfolded her close, rocking her soothingly in his arms. 'I'm sorry...I shouldn't have said that.'

'No, you're right! He is a fiend! I don't want you to meet him later. He's going to try and trick you. He might bring accomplices and beat you and rob you and you're already hurt...'

'Hush...it's a simple enough exchange.'

'What of Jane?'

'I'll do what I can. The boy needs his mother. I've no intention of starting married life with a ready-made family. I'd rather make my own...' He kissed her blushing cheek and with a rueful sigh put her away from him. 'I had every hope of a quiet, romantic evening...' was his wry farewell.

Cecily Booth emerged from the shadows and watched the curricle pull away at speed. Her rouged lips pursed as she stared malevolently across Connaught Street at the neat façade of Number Seven. Her recent aspiration to win Ross back and become a Viscountess, or failing that, retain her status as paramour to an Earl, lay in tatters.

She'd tracked Ross here before and believed he was simply visiting the old woman he classed as a good friend. Now, she knew differently. Along with the rest of the literate populace, she'd read of his betrothal to the late Marquess of Thorneycroft's daughter: that virago's granddaughter! To add insult to injury that day, she'd also learned Linus Savage had been socially crippled after a duel with Ross over the same woman.

Cadmore was repulsive but powerful; he'd provided an adequate meal ticket and, as his mistress, she'd gained entry to the fringes of the *ton*. Now, without even a farewell, he'd fled, with his tail between his legs, back to his wife in the sticks. There had not even been a chance, before he'd absconded, to importune for help with unpaid bills and the rent due on her villa in Chelsea. The idea of resorting to fully satisfying the stump-toothed oaf of a landlord she'd recently mollified made her stomach heave.

She'd lost everything! And it was all due to a trollop who was no better than she ought to be. She'd been eavesdropping when Mrs Penney thus maligned Mrs Sampson's high-born granddaughter to that woman's face. A few evenings ago, at Maria Farrow's musicale, the two widows had constantly spat venom at one another behind a potted palm, believing themselves unobserved. Edwina Sampson had bested every insult. Gloatingly, she'd described in fine detail the magnificent betrothal ring her besotted grandson-in-law had lavished on his beloved until, boiling-faced, her enemy bounded away in defeat.

On overhearing it, Cecily had been cut to the quick, too,

yet still she had harboured hopes of being reinstated as his mistress. She was very adept at pleasuring jaded men. Lady Elizabeth, on the other hand, was rumoured to be a virtual recluse, more used to pandering to scum in the slums. But earlier today even the consoling hope of enticing him into a discreet liaison after his nuptials foundered. Stratton had noticed her loitering about his house this afternoon, as he had on many other occasions. Before he would acknowledge her with a bored tolerance. Today there was nought but disgust and irritation in his hard face. She finally saw she was nothing to him. Yet just relinquishing him to the woman who had wrecked her life was impossible. She wanted something in return: revenge, and, ambitiously, a valuable diamond and amethyst ring. That would certainly cosy her way north to Yorkshire and her doting old godfather.

Ross had only been gone a few minutes when Elizabeth had dashed off a letter to Luke concerning her fears that his brother would be ambushed at Cinnamon Wharf by an East End rabble. She was sure that Luke could dissuade Ross from such a hazardous rendezvous when he was wounded. Harry Pettifer had been despatched post haste to deliver the missive to Luke's mansion on Burlington Parade and she was now impatiently awaiting his return.

When the rap came at the door and no footman responded, she dithered over the wisdom of doing so herself. It was dusk; it was possible Leach might have returned for some reason. Opening the door just a crack, she found herself peering at a dark-haired woman who looked familiar.

'May I speak to Lady Elizabeth Rowe?'

'You are doing so.'

Cecily Booth lowered her eyes, shielding her annoyance at her rival's loveliness. Even with so little of her perfect features and lustrous pale hair visible through the aperture, she recalled having spied this beauty with Cadmore in the fabric warehouse. The Viscount had been there too that day. She'd unearthed the identity of the blonde woman he'd been escorting and recalled a smug relief on discovering it was his brother's wife. Now that small comfort was ripped away. Even then Ross had been more interested in this blonde...so had Cadmore. The bitch had her pick of the two men lost to her. 'May I come in and speak to you, my lady?' she asked meekly.

'May I know who you are?' Elizabeth responded coolly. Something in this young woman's flamboyantly stylish garb seemed at odds with her diffidence.

'My name is Cecily Booth...'

Behind the door, Elizabeth flinched as though she'd taken a blow to the stomach. Her tongue darted to moisten her arid mouth; still her voice sounded hoarse. 'Why do you want to talk to me?'

Cecily modestly hung her head. 'I find myself in a...very delicate situation, my lady, as a result of a...friendship with your fiancé.'

Some silent minutes later, Elizabeth was conscious enough of seeming an imbecile to abruptly jerk wide the door and invite her in. An unsteady hand gestured at a hall chair for she'd scraped together sufficient composure to deny her any better hospitality. Cecily seated herself, then threw back her fancy bonnet so her long dark ringlets bounced about her shoulders.

'Thank you for allowing me a little of your time, my lady. I shall be brief and to the point. I read of your betrothal to my erstwhile fiancé. I congratulate you and wish you better luck than I enjoyed with the Viscount. I managed just a few secret weeks as his intended before he demanded I return my betrothal ring, then ruthlessly cut me out of his life. I was devastated...knowing as I do that we will ever be linked by blood.'

Elizabeth felt her world begin splintering apart, yet with admirable, cool civility, she asked, 'What is this leading up to, Miss Booth?'

A sad smile played on Cecily's mouth. 'Unfortunately for us all, it is leading up to the Viscount's first born...in about six months' time. Yet I am nothing to him now, just a discarded plaything, although once he professed to adore me. He refuses me even the token of the love we once had. At the very least, returning my betrothal ring would provide some security for his unborn child until such time as I find employment. I have been left destitute.'

'Betrothal ring?' Elizabeth echoed faintly.

'It was unique; fashioned to reflect the eight wonderful months we'd shared, so he said. A central octagonal diamond surrounded by amethysts.' She choked a mournful little laugh, pressed fingertips to her eyelids. 'I'll own to being a fool. I had heard of his reputation as a pitiless philanderer…but when in love…we women do foolish things, isn't that so?'

Elizabeth was again rendered speechless. The most she could do was touch her ring finger again and again to satisfy herself that this woman hadn't somehow craftily glimpsed the gem. But she knew quite well it lay in a drawer in her chamber. Jack's presence had restricted her to the house for days. How could she describe it so accurately? Had Ross told her about it? Why would he? He'd said he'd finished with her a while ago. Who was lying? He? She? Both of them? Suspicions whirled faster, making a vortex of pain scour the inside of her head.

Cecily Booth *had* had a relationship with Ross; her own grandmother had let slip she was his vampish brunette mistress. She might well be carrying his child. He might well have promised to marry her before Edwina schemed to trap him…for her. The ring might have been made for someone with a slightly larger finger. Was it just a horrible coincidence that it bore a resemblance to her Thorneycroft parure? It was no strict match…

Elizabeth stood silent and still, feeling as though her clothes and the skin from her body were slowly being stripped from her, leaving her raw and bloodied. 'I'm sorry, I cannot help you with any of this,' she announced stiltedly. 'Speak to the Viscount direct about his responsibilities. Good evening.' Rigid-backed, she swept to re-open the door on legs that shook so that, on gaining it, she put a hand to the wall to steady her.

Cecily Booth slid a crafty glance at her successor's chalky complexion, her large shimmery eyes…amethyst eyes. Despite the blonde's dignity she was devastated. A wedge was driven between the Viscount and his love and she revelled in the knowledge. At the very least he would have some serious explaining to do. She hadn't realised revenge could be so sweet. Appropriating the ring had always been an unlikely bonus. Joining Elizabeth at the door, she dredged up a wan smile. 'It seems so unfair, does it not,' she breathed with sisterly concern, 'that men are able to treat us so appallingly and never be marked with scandal they supply. I have heard you experienced similar misfortune when younger, and that you show sympathy to poor wretches ruined by men's lust. My only reason in coming here at all was to beg you understand why I must keep in discreet contact with your future husband.'

Unable to respond to that, Elizabeth closed the door, leaned back against it for a moment before folding over at the waist, her wet face cupped in quaking hands.

'Are you going to call or ogle that redhead all night?'

Guy Markham looked away from the titian-haired temptress who was fluttering her fan and her eyelashes at him and paid attention to the cards in his hand. 'Hearts…' he announced to Baron Ramsden with a meaningful grin.

'If you say so…' Luke responded drily, with an oblique glance at the demi-rep. He examined his hand, shifted cards about into suits.

'I thought Ross was back in town,' Guy idly remarked, laying a Jack of diamonds.

'He is…' Luke confirmed, beating it with the Queen.

'Where is he, then?'

'Where d'you think?'

Guy peered at Luke over a semi-circle of trumps. 'It's a love match, isn't it?'

Luke smiled and his dark eyes strayed sideways to where his own love stood chatting with Emma Du Quesne and Victoria Hardinge. He watched her graceful fluttering mannerisms, the way she laughed with just a hint of mischievousness, and savoured anew her ability to enchant him.

Dickie Du Quesne and David Hardinge had returned to distribute drinks to the ladies. Rebecca turned with her glass at her lips. Meeting Luke's eyes, she slipped away from the group and came over. A slender finger shaved her husband's lean jaw on its way to lay a card for him. Guy immediately trumped it and chuckled.

'Come, hurry up with this,' Rebecca coaxed. 'Signora Favetti is to perform in a few minutes. And I have spoken to Mrs Sampson,' she added conversationally. 'She says that poor Elizabeth is still indisposed and not due to attend. But she is certain tomorrow she will be so much better! I expect it is no more than a malaise brought on by the worry over the duel. Ross is a rogue to terrify her so! I must have been asked a score or more times if Viscount Stratton will attend tonight. How famous! Ross is all the rage. Do you think he will put in an appearance?'

'No,' her husband succinctly supplied, with a smile for his talkative wife. He turned his face so his lips discreetly brushed the delicate wrist bone close to his shoulder.

'Baron Ramsden...an urgent message for you, my lord.' One of Lady Conyngham's bewigged footmen was proffering a silver salver.

Luke frowned and took the note, breaking the seal. His thoughts were immediately with his mother at Burlington Parade. She had not accompanied them to this recital, preferring to spend all her time with the grandsons she infrequently saw. The message *was* from Demelza, simply to enclose another note that had been delivered that evening.

Luke's lips thinned to a tight white line as he read Elizabeth's hastily penned anxieties over Ross's safety at ten o'clock that night. He handed the note to his wife, simultaneously checking his watch.

'Oh, no! You must go to him, Luke! Stop him! Do something…!'

Sensing vital goings on, Sir Richard Du Quesne and Lord Courtenay joined them. Rebecca's stricken countenance and Luke's cards suddenly skimming the baize prompted the two friends to exchange a look then, abandoning proprieties, read the Baron's letter. It was handed on to Guy.

Rebecca rushed to quickly impart news of a threatening catastrophe to her friends.

Emma was soon at Richard's side. 'You must go and help,' she told her husband, her elfin face turned up appeallingly to his. She was terrified for Ross. It was too cruel he might be in mortal danger and never know wedded bliss with the woman he loved. She recalled all the drama and laughter they had shared. He had courageously saved her from the clutches of a sadistic suitor, he had protected her, charmed her… helped becalm the stormy passion between she and her darling Dickie in the advent to their marriage. He had ever been the man she secretly would like to have married…could she not have had the man she loved.

Richard's thoughts were treading a similar path to Emma's as he dwelt on the gratitude, the unpayable dues he owed Ross Trelawney, friend, comrade-at-arms, business associate. His lips lingered at his wife's fingertips, then, wordlessly, he was striding behind Luke who was already threading through the throng towards the exit.

'Be careful…' was the sum of Victoria's encouragement to David. He smoothed her raven's-wing hair, smiled as she turned her face into his palm. Then he, too, was gone.

Guy was examining the cards strewn on the table with great interest. Gathering them all up, he laughed. 'I would've won.' The few guineas were scraped together and he pocketed them. An easy smile was flashed at the three anxious ladies watching him. 'No rush,' he said airily, reading their collective thoughts. 'Unless there's a dozen of these dockers, injured or not, Ross'll see them off.' He pushed out of his chair and sauntered away, detouring past the redhead. She smiled, triumphant, as he dipped his head to murmur something to her on his way to the door.

At the first faint sound he crouched instinctively, hands going to cold metal in his pockets. He listened to the low guttural hum become distinct voices, heard the shuffle and pat of footsteps. He individualised them. At least six men, with all the stealth and finesse of a herd of elephants. He grimaced a smile. Sometimes enthusiastic amateurs were the worst to deal with. He had no desire for any carnage. His desire lately seemed to run solely in one direction, he mocked himself as he came fluidly upright then came out behind them. He watched their scruffy backs for a moment: it could be so easy. Like taking candy from a baby. If the runt had brought the candy with him of course. He saw the small woman being pushed in front of a thug toting a torch. A line of yellow undulated on the oily swell parallel to the jetty.

'Leach?'

They sprang about in unison, clumsily…except one. One knew what he was about and was balancing on the balls of his feet, hand at his pocket, already shifting sideways out of weak light into shadow.

Nathaniel Leach stepped forward, holding high a flare. He bowed mockingly but his eyes were up and vigilant, peering past Ross's solid silhouette into a nebulous murk.

'I came alone,' Ross volunteered drily. 'Is that the boy's mother?'

Leach beckoned and a henchman urged Jane forward for inspection. Oddly, the fact that Trelawney was unaccompanied yet undaunted by his burly accomplices unnerved him. Even with the Viscount's reputation as a fearless fighter, one against six was poor odds. Leach could feel the flare's cone sliding as his palm leaked sweat.

'The money?'

'The necklace?' Ross mimicked sardonically.

The glittering collar emerged, sinuously, from a pocket to

swing tauntingly between thumb and forefinger. 'Come and get it, m'lord.'

Ross's long fingers curled about the gun in his right pocket. It was a four-barrelled duck's foot, and he knew, at this distance, he could incapacitate at least three of them with no problem…four if they moved closer together. There again, if they liked the idea of returning him the gem, releasing the boy's mother, and getting nothing in return, they could all walk home. The hackles on the back of his neck stirred, causing him to smile wryly. Obviously it wasn't going to be that easy. He crouched, bringing the duck's foot out of one pocket and a dagger-fitted flintlock out of the other.

'Don't shoot…I'm on your side…' Dickie drawled, emerging from between tarpaulin-shrouded pallets on his left.

Ross was already lowering the weapons and pushing out a string of expletives through scraping teeth. He could identify this man quite easily in darkness. They'd fought side by side too often for him not to react to his stature and pale hair. 'You infernal idiot! I could've given you a belly full of lead!'

'Why…reflexes shot to pieces?'

Ross curled a sarcastic lip at him. There was a troubling truth in that. Other familiar figures were now visible approaching along the wharf.

Close to, Dickie could read the naked disbelief in Ross's eyes. 'Don't blame me,' he said. 'I thought it was just Luke and me didn't like sopranos…'

Ross's dark head tilted back. 'This is embarrassing…' he told the stars.

Luke strode up with belligerent speed. *'Embarrassing?'* he snarled. 'You damned lunatic. You'll only take one direct blow on that arm and the stitches will burst open. That would be bloody embarrassing! The way I feel, I might land you one myself.'

'You could try…' Ross bit out but with conciliation in the challenge. He could feel his brother's anxiety radiating from him with blistering intensity; as it always had his life through when he did something Luke deemed needlessly reckless.

Now he understood: commitment made you cautious. But it was a strength, not a weakness. From the age of twenty when their father died, Luke had been dogged with responsibility. Luke lived to live and provide. Ross had lived to die and provide himself with all manner of self-indulgence until that day...until now.

Coming here alone with a fresh wound hampering him, knowing Leach intended cheating him, had been idiotically reckless. For quite some time now he'd been thinking with his heart, not his head, and it was a foreign and disorientating phenomenon. He didn't want to go back and tell Elizabeth he'd killed or maimed men tonight. He just wanted to go back to her...whole...strong enough to be a good husband and father...in his brother's image. But for his own sake he couldn't return without taking those things she wanted: her necklace and her friend.

'The notorious Ross Trelawney needs a few nob friends to help him,' Leachie sneered, but he was frustratingly aware that his cronies were not looking quite so confidently aggressive now the odds had evened. 'Togged out in fine duds, too,' he mocked the gentlemen's sartorial splendour.

'That's a point,' Guy moaned, sotto voce. 'These threads are new...first time aired.'

'I reckon yer've a yella streak, Trelawney. Yer lucky I'm jus' int'rested in the colour of yer money,' Leach blustered, keen to get the cash in his hand, before incidentals like brawling or chicanery, robbed him of it.

'I don't buy back my own property.'

'Yer said yer would,' Leach bellowed in rage.

'I said I'd negotiate. I'll do so now. I get the necklace in one piece, you get to go home in one piece.' Ross turned to fully face him, conscious of men fanning out behind him.

Leach's lips strained back over stained teeth. He could hear the disgruntled muttering of his pack. He'd promised them a tidy bit of blunt from this night's work. In sheer exasperation he flung his shaggy head about. His savage gaze alighted on Jane, visibly quaking against a backdrop of rocking water. In fury and frustration he strode towards her and slammed the heel of a hand against her breastbone. 'You an' yer fancy friends!' he snarled.

With little respect for his excellent tailoring, Guy hit the Thames within a second of Jane disappearing, with a shriek, beneath the oil-filmed water.

Ross advanced as Leach backed away; they paced in unison until Leach abruptly turned tail and fled. Ross sprinted after him along the jetty, idly tripping and kicking a henchman off-balance and into the river as he tried to block his path.

David Hardinge grinned at Dickie, with one eye on the remaining rabble. They were shifting, goading each other with jeering comments on the fighting ability of the dandies. 'I think they *mean* Corinthians.' David allowed them the benefit of the doubt. 'Shall we oblige them? It's been a long time…'

With Luke sighing resignedly behind them, Dickie and David took off their elegant jackets, discovered the best place on the pallets to lay them, then strolled forward.

'Come away…you'll go blind…' David mocked as Guy gravitated towards a trio of ample-bosomed strumpets lounging against brickwork. The women immediately scuffled competitively as Guy's eyes swept over them. The stoutest flung off her colleagues and began to hip-sway forward, undeterred by the fact that her prospective punter was sopping wet.

Along with a good deal of the other residents of this Wapping tenement, the women had emerged from the building to see what the commotion was all about. The heap of groaning bodies slowly disentangling on the jetty drew few curious glances. Five society gentlemen of obvious wealth and prominence strolling off Cinnamon Wharf, and up the alley, all bloodied and dishevelled, was a far more unusual and intriguing sight.

Dickie shrugged into his tidy coat that a moment ago had hung over his shoulder on a crooked finger. 'Who trod in that heap of dung?' he ribbed his closest friend. 'We all avoided it. I'll buy you a lorgnette…'

At the reminder, David lifted his boot and grimaced distaste at the mucky sole as he hopped along. The foot found the ground again with a scrape of leather against cobble.

Ross flexed his aching shoulder. His other arm drew the shivering, dripping woman close to his side to warm and calm her as they made for his carriage. In his pocket the weight of gold and precious stones was comforting. He felt content. His mind turned again to that blissful interlude earlier that evening in Elizabeth's bedroom. He felt himself growing so warm that he carefully shifted away a little from Jane in case she started steaming, before again allowing himself to picture Elizabeth on his lap. A few more minutes and she would have said she loved him, he knew it. And he would have shown her just how much he loved and wanted her…in a time-honoured way that would have been the first of her many trips to heaven. He thought of her white silk wedding gown and smiled ruefully.

Chapter Sixteen

Ten minutes ago, the chaos of getting Jane out of her wet things, and into a hot tub had taken every scrap of Elizabeth's time and attention. It was paramount that mother and son were settled out of sight before Edwina walked back through the door.

Josie had excelled herself; dealing with drabs fished from the Thames might have been a mundane duty for a lady's maid at Number Seven Connaught Street. Good naturedly the young maid had responded to Jane's plea to know how Jack fared with, 'Little lad's never stopped eating, m'm. You'll hardly recognise him, he's plumping out so.'

But now the hallway was quiet again; the brackish water that had seeped from Jane's hem to pool on the marble was a sole reminder of the pandemonium. It pulled between them now, widening an unbridgeable gulf.

'What's the matter?' Ross repeated, cracking the tense quiet. 'You've barely spoken to me or looked my way since I walked through the door. Has the vicar been back to warn you I'm a godless villain?'

'I don't need Hugh to tell me that!' was snapped out before she could even think, let alone act, judiciously.

Ross smiled. It didn't reach his eyes.

She took a steadying breath, determined to act with dignity and prudence. 'Are you injured?' was the first example of it.

Her eyes scanned his face and body. Apart from a mark close to an eye and his fine clothes appearing torn and muddy, he seemed undamaged. 'I hoped Luke would intercept you. I feared you might be ambushed by a mob.'

'I was. It's cheering to know my safety worries you.' His ironic tone heightened her colour, otherwise she seemed unmoved. 'Had it not been for Luke and the others arriving at the eleventh hour, the outcome might have been very different. As it was, little blood was shed on either side. I owe my brother and my friends a great debt of thanks. And you, too, for sending them after me.'

'And I owe you a great debt of thanks,' she returned with acid equity. 'You've reunited Jane and her son and reclaimed my necklace. But then you had a vested interest. The necklace is part of my dowry, and thus well worth retrieving, and I know you were keen to eject cuckoos from the nest.'

'Are you annoyed because I made some comment about wanting to make my own family? I hadn't intended to sound callous about the boy.'

His patient self-possession simply exacerbated her indignation. As did the unshakeable vision of a host of voluptuous women parading gypsy-visaged children for their father's approval. Her tenuous hold on her composure slipped away. 'I'm annoyed that you hadn't thought to mention you'd already started making your family. Perhaps you deem your first born none of your future wife's concern.'

Eyes like twin gold coins gleamed at her until her savaging gaze turned on the wall. 'Already started? First born?' he selected with silky softness.

'Your paramour came here, inveigling for funds to support the bastard she is expecting. She claims you were once secretly engaged and that you cruelly abandoned her. Was that when Edwina bought you for me?'

The silence was catastrophic. Finally he quietly summarised, 'Cecily Booth came here tonight and said we were engaged and she's expecting my child?'

'Yes.'

'I apologise for her outrageous lies and impertinence. She won't ever again accost you or bother you in any way.'

'I'm sure,' emerged sweetly through clenched teeth. 'I think she's more interested in again accosting and bothering you. I agreed that would be best.'

'Elizabeth…look at me…'

Elizabeth responded to the hoarse plea in his voice.

'Are you going to let something so patently false and malicious poison what you feel for me? Look at me!' he blasted when she swung her face away. 'I'm the same man who held you in your bedroom not two hours ago, who kissed you. What did you tell me then? Say it now! Tell me what you want.'

When she remained silent, staring at the wall, he resumed harshly, 'If she's pregnant—and I doubt she is—Cadmore's the culprit. I know enough about the workings of the female body to be sure she's nurturing no child of mine. She was regularly indisposed the short time she was under my protection.'

Elizabeth flushed; embarrassment fanned her feverish need to hurt him…topple his composure.

Gently he reasoned, 'She'll win if you reject me, Elizabeth. Is that what you want? To let some scheming harlot get the better of you by wrecking your happiness and mine? Come, I'm exhausted and you're overset. It's been a chaotic day for us both. Let's not give credence to this paltry fiction by discussing it further.' He withdrew her necklace from his pocket and held it out as a peace offering. 'Do you not want this?' he asked on a boyish smile that flipped her heart.

Elizabeth stared at gleaming octagonal amethysts. Similar stones to those in her betrothal ring. Was it hers? Was the ring a complement to this necklace or to eight months' fornication? 'No.' She rejected the olive branch. 'You've earned it. Keep it as payment for tonight's work. I intended the necklace should buy Jane's freedom.'

A dark thumb began sweeping the glossy jewels; his eyes

tracked the movement, as though he was lost in thought. 'You'll want it back,' he eventually said.

'You told me that once before,' she mocked.

'I was right once before. Take it now, or you'll come and find me again and plead for it. Think what you're doing. Think carefully, Elizabeth, for I'm done with being honourable and lenient.' He looked up and their eyes tangled, strained, while he waited, allowing her time. A hand hovered over his pocket, then, fascinated, she watched the jewel slink shimmering out of sight.

'My lord?'

Ross pivoted on a heel, close to the door, his face a tense, expressionless mask.

'You've forgotten something, Viscount Stratton. Here.' The ring was whipped from her pocket and thrown straight at him. He put up a hand instinctively, deflecting the missile with a palm. That same hand arrested the ring a foot from the flags.

'Give that back to your whore. She's sorely missing it and the eight wonderful months it represents,' Elizabeth stormed raucously.

A mirthless laugh cluttered his throat as he looked at the priceless ring. Within a moment she was alone.

'You say the Viscount was in on this! I'll skin him alive!'

Elizabeth put soothing fingers to her aching head. 'Please try to understand, Grandmama, they have nowhere else to go. How in the name of Christian decency can they be turned onto the street? I have told you Jack will be forced to pick-pocket or climb chimneys if Leach has his way. And Jane—'

'Oh, I know…*and Jane*…' Edwina mimicked ferociously. Jane coloured miserably and pulled Jack back into her skirts to shield him from the woman's withering glare.

'I have been truthful in apprising you of their presence, Grandmama,' Elizabeth said with just a little blush that her honesty was somewhat tardy. Jane had been in residence thirty-six hours before Elizabeth realised it was pointless concealing them longer. For her own conscience's sake—and, less worthily, because of mundane practicalities such as providing them with basic necessities—she had had to own up, beg forgiveness and appeal to her grandmother's humanity.

'Well, as Stratton involved himself in hoodwinking me, you can get him to find a respectable lodging for the pair of 'em. They'll not stay longer beneath *my* roof!'

'I can't do that, Grandmama…'

'Why not? He's your fiancé. You're all but wed,' she hinted darkly with a peer at her granddaughter's waistline. 'Twist him a little more about that betrothal finger of yours. Where is your ring? Give it to me for safekeeping.' Jane and her son received another dubious look. 'Pickpockets, you say…' she muttered, a hand diving into the silver dish at her side. A piece of marchpane was picked then, with an irritated tut, discarded. Jack, having seen the sweet, crept closer and peeped into the dish. Edwina glowered as he raised his large child's eyes to hers.

'I suppose you want it,' she accused him.

He simply blinked.

'Oh, take it then!' She grumpily pressed the dish on him then flapped a hand to wave him away from her. He whispered solemn thanks and was soon back with his mother. 'Take yourselves off to the parlour,' she ordered Jane. 'I want to speak in private with m'granddaughter. Leave the dish!' she bawled as Jane opened the door.

'Why is it you can't do that?' Edwina demanded, one gimlet eye on the silver dish as it was safely replaced.

Elizabeth winced. This was another piece of news she hadn't relished breaking to her grandmother. Not least because tears needled her eyes simply at the thought of it. She didn't want to discuss it and be torn to shreds.

'Where was Ross yesterday? Usually he visits every day.'

'We have quarrelled, Grandmama,' Elizabeth said huskily.

'People in love always quarrel.' Edwina flicked a dismissive hand.

Elizabeth swallowed painfully. The lump stayed in her

throat. 'It was a bad quarrel. We are no longer betrothed. I returned his ring.'

'You have broken the engagement?' Edwina looked too shocked to be angry. 'In God's name, why? I know you love him. And little surprise in that! He is the most eligible man around. You are sought after by all the top hostesses...as his intended. He has helped you rescue these...these waifs. *Now* you refuse him?' Edwina was utterly bewildered, but Elizabeth sensed anger, too, simmering close to the surface. 'Has he lectured you on the wisdom of involving yourself with riff-raff? You can be stubborn and haughty once you get ideas in your head, Elizabeth.' A plump finger was wagged cautioningly.

'The cause was *his* failings, not mine,' Elizabeth blurted out indignantly.

'His women?'

Elizabeth pressed tight her quivering lips, but her heightening colour betrayed her.

'I suppose that silly strumpet's been following him about again and making a nuisance of herself and you've come to hear of it.'

A sharp, violet look demanded further explanation.

'That blasted brunette is a figure of fun for mooning about after Ross. Even when Cadmore took her on, she still set out to entice Stratton back...and made it very plain. Damned if she wasn't eavesdropping on m'conversations last time I was at Maria's. Everywhere I turned, there she was, watching me. Probably hoping to hear where Ross was to be found. Cecily Booth is a jealous minx up to no good, you mark m'words!'

Elizabeth did. Her heartbeat was painfully slow as she ventured, 'What did she overhear? Were you boasting of my engagement to the Viscount?' An icy suspicion shivered her. 'Were you boasting of my ring?'

Edwina frowned reflectively, then chuckled. 'Yes. That's it. Alice Penney was boiling mad when I regaled her with it all at Maria's.'

'Was he engaged to her, Grandmama?'

'*Engaged to her?* Hah!' Edwina shrieked a laugh. 'She'd like to think so, I'm sure! She let it be known she figured on becoming a Viscountess. As soon as Stratton got wind of it, his lawyers were figuring her a pension fund. Impudent hussy! A month or two warming an aristocrat's sheets and she gets fancy *ideas*?'

'Were they together eight months?'

'Eight weeks more like. Can't say I ever recall Ross spending eight months with the same filly…' Edwina coughed and shifted on her chair. 'Well now, that's enough of that indelicate talk. What I'm saying is…'

Elizabeth closed her eyes in consternation. She knew what her grandmother was saying better than she did herself. She'd been an utter, utter fool. She'd been swayed by malicious lies because she was too sensitive and too woefully haughty. Finally she accepted he had never wanted her for her dowry, but it was too late. He had warned her where acrimony would lead; he had tried to deflect and soothe her jealous hurt before she let a spurned woman wreck their future together. A smuggler's son had the graciousness to apologise for his lapse in conduct, to offer her the opportunity to do likewise when she yielded to temper. Still she resisted behaving properly; a Marquess's daughter was loath to stop being a rude, supercilious little bitch.

Pettifer announced, 'Mrs Trelawney and the Ladies Ramsden, Du Quesne and Courtenay are arrived, madam, with their children. Shall I show them in?'

Edwina frowned at Elizabeth's wraith-like complexion and wide shame-filled eyes. 'Well, Ross has kept news of the rift to himself, that's obvious, if his kith and kin are paying us a call. Thank Heavens! Perhaps you might yet persuade him you're just an impetuous madam…as if he don't already know!'

Ross was in Kent, overseeing repairs to Stratton Hall, Elizabeth had learned from his mother. She implied she knew of his whereabouts, of course, to avoid awkward questions. The ladies had kindly come to see how she fared and whether her indisposition was finally gone. She had felt the fraud she undoubtedly was, and a little tongue-tied with them. Demelza Trelawney had taken particular care to sit close, take one of her hands, and tell her again how glad she was to welcome her into their family. She chatted about the quiet ceremony planned at a local church and how it was drawing close. She said she was sad Katherine and Tristan would miss the wedding and how they had both written to say they were eager to meet their new sister-in-law. Every time Elizabeth met Ross's gentle mother she liked her better and she knew the woman's regard for her was genuine. After recent events and the appalling way she had treated her youngest son, she felt an unworthy recipient of such esteem and affection.

Rebecca's children, Troy and Jason, and Victoria's daughter, Lucy, had played on the floor with a rag doll and tin soldiers while tea and cakes were distributed. Victoria had a second daughter, Faye, but as she was still a babe-in-arms, just months old, she had been left with her nurse for the afternoon. When the children had got bored with that game, Edwina had huffed down there with them and showed them how to flip a coin with another coin into a cup. Gruffly she had bid Elizabeth fetch Jack, so he could play. Jane came, too, and was introduced as an old friend who was staying awhile. Elizabeth had studiously ignored Edwina's dry cough at that comment. All the ladies had greeted Jane kindly, and if they thought her overly diffident or recognised the gown she was wearing to be one of Elizabeth's, they kept it to themselves. If they guessed at her identity from what their husbands had told them of the fracas on Cinnamon Wharf, that kindly went unremarked as well.

But now the drawing room was quiet again. Jane and Jack had repaired to the parlour, obviously deeming it best to avoid Edwina as much as possible.

'Fine people,' Edwina enthused, observing their departure through the window. 'Joining that circle is a privilege not to be lightly dismissed.' She seated herself again in her comfy fireside chair and looked at Elizabeth. 'So where were we? Ah, yes. You've made a bad mistake, m'girl, haven't you? You've overreacted to tittle tattle and you're too proud to admit it.'

'No, I'm not. I readily admit it,' Elizabeth croaked, blinking rapidly.

'Well, that's a step in the right direction. To help you take another…I'll allow your friend and the boy house room for a few days.' At Elizabeth's immediate thankful expression, she added, 'On the condition that you eat humble pie with your fiancé. Yes, he is still your fiancé, I'd stake m'life on it.'

Elizabeth dropped her face into her hands. 'I can't…'

'You can and you must. Are you still feeling queasy in the mornings?'

Elizabeth nodded. God knows her stomach churned and curdled the day through. As a possibility penetrated, she quickly looked up, scouring her grandmother's face with apprehensive eyes. But Edwina seemed unconcerned about following up her leading question.

'No brass-faced baggage is about to ruin m'granddaughter's happiness and good name. A few days ago you had both those things. You'll have 'em again or I'll eat m'wedding hat!' She gave Elizabeth an indulgent smile. 'Go and get yourself ready; Josie can travel with you.'

She heard the ocean before she saw it. The sound of surf rushing on shore kept her still for a moment, straining to listen. A violet gaze swept the meadowed horizons; no blue but the sky was discernible.

Aware that the coachman was hovering for a gratuity, she opened her reticule and counted out some coins. Soon the hired rig was turning on the circular forecourt, then cracking back along the gritty drive that meandered a good half-mile, Elizabeth had judged, to the main road.

Josie was dubiously eyeing a crenellated and slate-slipping roofline that crowned the brick-and-timber façade of Stratton

Hall. Her wide-eyed stare turned on her mistress. She grimaced. Elizabeth forced her faltering smile to strengthen, as she nervously assessed the decaying Gothic mansion of which she might or might not yet be mistress. Josie began creeping towards the curve of stone steps that lead up to weatherbeaten double doors stranded between crumbling portals.

'Wait here a moment longer,' Elizabeth checked her maid. 'I don't want to go in just yet. I must find the sea.'

Leaving Josie encircled by travelling bags, Elizabeth calmly got her bearings, then set out across rough, unkempt grass towards the southerly horizon. She passed through the detritus of what once must have been a fine orchard. Rotting fruit was scattered stickily beneath branches that contorted low to the ground. The lush scent of cider cloyed in her nostrils. Insects fidgeted close to her hem, then flew up to worry her for disturbing them. She flicked her shining head and walked on. She noticed shards of broken timber entwined with bellbind. What remained of the rickety fence swayed in a tepid breeze. She plucked a grass stem from a matted clump, drew the feathery frond through her hand, then abruptly shed its seeds onto the ground. She did so again and again with fierce concentration while weaving a path through thigh-high reeds, her skirts gathering dew from the roots of a confusion of uncultivated wild flora.

As the natural melody penetrated her thoughts again she looked up. Slowly she took the last few steps and stopped and stared. Below, sun-sparkling water was rimmed by the silver sand of a small, pretty bay. Captivated, she watched as an arc of foam plunged to race and recede…race and recede.

Finally she became aware of him, slightly behind and to her right. Instinctively she turned away, smeared wet from her eyes and let the fresh sea draughts dry her skin. 'It's closer than I thought. So close…'

'Move back from the edge. The chalk's crumbling. It's possible the house might cover the beach at some time.'

'That should please you,' she said with a wryness in her voice. She took two careful paces back and turned to look at him. Her stomach tipped over. This wilderness of rough beauty and decadence was his natural habitat. With gnarled applewood at his back, he merged with the landscape, dark clothes, dark hair wind-tangled, golden hawk's eyes narrowed…preying on her. She saw a Cornish brigand for the first time.

'You'll have to excuse the mess in the house. There are few servants at present. Just a few old retainers. If I'd realised you were coming today I'd have got them to tidy up. You're here sooner than I thought.'

She was aware of the hard satisfaction in his tone, the idle triumph. But then what had she expected? *Think what you're doing*, he'd said. *Think carefully, Elizabeth, for I'm done with being honourable and lenient.* But she'd come anyway. She saw now, in his glittering beast's eyes, in the ruthless amusement curving his mouth, that he'd meant what he'd said. Apprehension needled her skin, but proudly she tossed up her head, letting a soft salty zephyr beneath her bonnet to soothe her warm face. 'Are there steps?'

'Yes. But you're not going down there now.'

She heard the implacable note in his denial. He was waiting for her to challenge his ruling. He wanted her to. 'No,' she murmured. 'Not now,' and walked past him and back towards the sombre house.

The red salon was, he'd said, the only reception room in a reasonable enough state to receive guests. Is that what I am? she had wanted to ask him. A guest? But she had not found the temerity to do so.

It was a dusty room, but well appointed with a view through large leaded casements over an expanse of unmowed parkland. It held some quite exquisitely dainty furniture that seemed at odds with the rough, masculine tenor of the property. They were, she realised, the last chatelaine's taste.

Josie had been led away to the kitchens by Maude, a maid-servant, the pair boldly taking each other's measure as they walked side by side. Maude had returned, as directed by her master, within a very short time with a tray of tea and cakes for Elizabeth. She had barely managed one sip and swallow before agitatedly rising from her chair and pacing the room.

'I think a pianoforte might suit that corner…' The observation held a brittle gaiety and was met by the sound of glass hitting wood as his brandy balloon found the table. She took a few more forlorn steps about the faded salon, still inwardly praying her tentative rapprochment might elicit some favourable response.

The silence stretched. Her small teeth worried her bottom lip, her pellucid eyes pleaded for a small indication that he was not as unyielding as he seemed; that he might yet forgive her. Her wistful, shy appeal elicited just a small movement at one side of his mouth. He swiped his drink from the table again and downed a quantity while a booted foot rose to balance on the edge of a footstool in front of his worn hide chair. Eyes the colour of the cognac imbibed watched her over the rim of his glass.

With sinking heart, and fingers twining in front of her, Elizabeth continued perambulating. He had no intention of making this easy for her. But why should she expect him to? In London she had taken for granted and abused his respect, his consideration, his humour and patience, secure in some innate female sense that he would tolerate her petulance. Now she was isolated in Kent in a house that seemed as cold and forbidding as its new master. For the first time a fearful uneasiness stole over her. Perhaps Edwina was wrong about her roguish gentleman; perhaps he no longer deemed himself her fiancé at all…

She touched a chipped Meissen bowl on a sideboard; her nervous fingers flicked pages of a leather-bound volume on copper mining in granite. She was tempted to provoke him into conversation on that subject. Little matter that she would understand none of what was said. She moved on. The throbbing atmosphere seemed to dog her footsteps. Her damp palms were dried on her delicate rose-pink skirt. Forcing a little smile, she examined a small clock on the mantel. 'I…I see…understand why you must have been very angry with Edwina…for tricking you out of your money. The renovation costs here must total quite a sum.' In case that sounded like a criticism of his home she quickly added, 'But I…I think it has great potential…'

'It's a derelict dump.'

'You don't like it?'

'I like where it is. His Majesty let me choose between this or an estate in Warwickshire. The house and grounds there were in far better condition, having only recently been returned to the crown. This has been empty for about nine years.'

'You wanted it for the sea?'

'Yes.'

''Twill someday be fine again. I like it…'

He drank from his glass.

Desperate not to let the conversation stop and thus endure that stifling silence, she bubbled, 'I meant to tell you…your mama and your friends' wives called on us. That's how I discovered you were here. I pretended I knew. I thought it might seem odd that you had not told your fiancée of your whereabouts.'

'When last we spoke I got the distinct impression you wouldn't ever again give a damn where I was.'

Elizabeth winced and flushed but felt heartened that he hadn't denied she was his fiancée. 'And Edwina now knows Mrs Selby and Jack are in her house. She said she will flay you for helping me rescue them. But they can stay awhile, so long as I…that is, at least until I return home,' she hastily amended.

'A roof over their heads so long as you keep me company?' he astutely guessed. 'Is there no limit to your philanthropy, my dear?'

Elizabeth swung about to look at him, her chin came up. 'I would have come whether Edwina allowed them shelter or not. It was my decision to come.'

'Was it?'

'Yes!'

'To what end? Tell me what's brought a Marquess's daughter into a Cornish brigand's lair.'

'I…I want to apologise to you. I know now you were right in what you said about…about that woman's malice…and where it would lead…'

'And you've come for this,' he stated, ignoring the reference to Cecily Booth.

She watched as he drew her necklace from the table close to his glass and let it swing between thumb and forefinger.

'I said you'd want it back.'

'I know,' she hoarsely whispered.

'Do you remember what else I said?'

Their eyes locked. After a moment whitish tresses swayed about her alabaster neck as an almost imperceptible nod answered him.

'Good. Come and get it then.'

Elizabeth hesitantly approached. As she came close an idle shove with a foot sent the stool a fraction away from him. 'Sit down,' he directed.

She sank to the tapestry-covered seat before his chair, her fair head low against the broad, dark expanse of his torso.

After a moment he leisurely leaned forward so his elbows rested on his knees and their heads were close. 'Now what I want you to do…' she visibly flinched as the ellipse was deliberately protracted '…is give me one good reason why I shouldn't act the rampaging heathen you've always thought me.' The necklace was draped across the milky fragility of her wrists held neatly on her lap.

'You said you loved me,' she answered him as the glittering manacle blurred into purple fire.

'You said you wanted me.'

'I do,' she affirmed in a weak croak.

'Prove it.'

The small clock chimed, making her start and wonder how much time had passed since his challenge. How long had she sat before him, wanting just a small sign that this callousness wasn't meant; that he would soften, as he always had, beneath her demanding pride and innocence. A hand slid from beneath the precious weight. She placed the necklace on the stool close to her dusky-rose skirt, then stood, smoothed out the silk and took the one pace to his chair. Crumpling her skirts again with trembling fists, she climbed onto his lap with her knees spread, straddling him as he had positioned her before, in her bedroom. She tilted forward, blindly searching for his mouth with hers. Her lips found the lean plane of his cheek, tasted the salt of the sea air, slid down to sweep sweetly over his mouth.

He returned the shy salute with just enough restraint to prevent bruising her lips, with a savage skill that craftily eroticised the pain. She kissed him back. In her own way she persevered with trying to please him while the tears filling her eyes spilled and slipped between them.

She felt cool air then the harsh heat of his mouth on her shoulders as he bared them. As her demure bodice was pulled lower she curved into him, trying to shield her nudity with his body. His hands girdled her dainty rib cage, thrust all the way up until her small firm breasts were raised then covered by his palms, offered up to his tormenting, treacherous mouth.

Her fingers slid into his hair, twisted at the outrageous pleasure that put a moan in her throat and a coil of fire in her belly. Still she made no move to deny him, even when her skirts were ruched up by an insolent hand flowing from knee to buttock. Hard fingers pressed over her thigh; one insinuated beneath the rumpled hem of her drawers, turned so the back of it tormented the satiny skin near the moist core of her.

'Do you want to go home? You've only to say.'

'No,' she gasped.

He wound a hand into her thick soft hair, tilted her head back to look at her tear-smeared face with smoky-amber eyes.

'No?' he echoed tauntingly. 'You want to stay? Is this how you prove you want me? By crying when I touch you?'

'You said you loved me,' she choked fiercely, her vivid eyes accusing, pleading, before snapping closed to stem a fresh surge of brine. 'Is this how you prove it? By being so cold...so insulting?' Then she was tipping forward again, trapping him against the chair, already fearful he might reject her because of what she'd said.

'You didn't like me honourable and lenient, either, Elizabeth. I thought I'd try this instead...'

She heard the hoarseness in his sarcasm, recognised the first hint of her victory and her arms tightened about his neck in thankfulness. 'I'm sorry...I will be different in future, I promise. I liked you as you were...'

She heard the low laugh...followed by low cursing as he fought her gentling him, fought his own male need. His hands fastened over hers at the back of his head as though he would push her back, make available her body. She let her head droop against his shoulder, pressed her bare breasts against the soft wool of his coat.

'Randolph thought they would kill him.' She halted, heart thumping, wondering why she had said it, for she had not been conscious of thinking of anything past. She frowned her confusion at his shoulder, barely aware of a new delicacy in his touch. His hands released hers, moved to splay over her back, warming her goosepimpled flesh. She felt comforted, comfortable. 'I thought they would, too. I shouted at him to flee...but I never seriously thought he'd go completely away. I thought he'd return for me later. The highwaymen had no bullets left and had intended tying him to the tree to steal his carriage...not to execute him. They wanted the gig and money to escape for the dragoons were closing on them. Randolph didn't even have a loaded gun for them to steal. My father was most furious at that.' She gave a watery sniff, knuckling wet from her eyes to keep it from soaking his neck. 'He said a military man should know better than to travel at night without a loaded weapon...' She paused. 'Do you think that?'

'Yes.'

She nodded. 'He was so young...barely twenty. He said he was a bad soldier. His father bought him a commission. It was his sole help. Randolph was for ever cursing primogeniture. He hated the army; he'd rather have studied medicine.

'The Boar's Head was close by and they talked of breaking into a barn. They took me with them for one of them, the leader, thought I might be worth a ransom or useful as a hostage. Also, the dragoons were looking for two men, not three people travelling together. He told his accomplice to find some food while he guarded me. I knew straight away what he intended for he'd been looking slyly at me.' She paused, resumed in a faraway voice, 'By the time his partner returned he had stripped me of my gown and punched me twice…no three times, I think, for I never stopped fighting him. And then…'

She felt long, tender fingers slide up beneath her hair, cradle her scalp. 'His wife was back and hitting him with a shovel. She hit him so hard her hat was knocked off. She had very long hair all wound into a bun and hidden in its crown. I thought at first she had killed him. He was unconscious for some time. She helped me…with her calloused gentle hands…she helped me dress…gave me some food, cursing him for a stupid lecher all the while.

'Then the dragoons were in the courtyard. I could have screamed I suppose; she looked at me, thought I would. Still she left me unharmed…unbound. The dragoons were looking for two men, I reminded her. I took off my dress again…gave her it and my best wishes. They got away, I think. I hope she escaped the gallows or Newgate. When prison visiting or at Bridewell I used to look for her. I shan't ever forget her face.'

After a silent moment, soothed by the fingers moving against her body, she resumed, 'My papa had already started after me…as soon as he discovered I'd eloped. He found me a day or two later. It seemed like a week I was there, hungry…hiding in just my underclothes. I hid in case the dragoons came back to arrest me for aiding and abetting…or to misuse me. I told Papa honestly all that had happened. He never blamed me, but he was so sad, so angry at circumstances, at Randolph, at himself. He blamed himself for not caring well enough for me when no one ever had a better papa. My grandmother, the Dowager Marchioness, said it mattered little what they had or hadn't done to me, I was ruined the moment I set out with Randolph, then returned unwed. She wished I hadn't returned…that they'd killed me, I'm sure, although she never actually said so. I hated her thereafter; just as she hated me for tarnishing the Thorneycroft name. Perhaps I'm too like her: too arrogant and proud.'

Slender white fingers smeared wet from her cheeks. 'Papa was a very private man…although well-liked and sociable,' she explained with a touching earnestness. 'But the scandal…the contempt and abuse from people who once he'd thought were friends, was too much too bear. Even the birth of his son, the heir he had wanted so much to prevent his cousin Cyril having the estate, couldn't cheer him. He didn't see Tom grow. Tom was but three when Papa died. My stepmother hated me too. She blamed me for putting her husband in an early grave, my grandmother blamed me for the loss of her son. They hated me so much.' She gasped in a shuddering breath. 'I deserve it, I know…they were right…'

'It's not your fault he died…'

'I know…' she whimpered.

'It's not your fault, Elizabeth…none of it's your fault. You're brave and selfless and wonderful,' was whispered against her hair, while his hands slid across her back. She felt the wool of his sleeves against her nude skin as he pressed her against him. 'Edwina told me his heart was weak. Your father might have died at any time.'

'But I broke his heart…I know I did…' she shrilled in anguish.

'It's not your fault, Elizabeth…'

The sob, gathering momentum, jolted her violently against him. She buried her face into his neck, keening as though her own heart might shatter into a million pieces.

Chapter Seventeen

Elizabeth woke suddenly, yet remained quiet and still. Her eyes raised, focussing on a faint scar that ran parallel and slightly beneath his jaw. His steady breathing was raising and lowering the burden of her body in a soporific rocking rhythm that weighted her eyelids again.

He was unaware she was awake. His eyes were lost between long close lashes as he stared ahead, deep in his own thoughts. A cigar was smouldering, forgotten, between his fingers resting on the chair arm. Curiously, it was then recollected. She watched his mouth, lips that could savage or soothe, curse or comfort, as the ash glowed a dull red. His head angled lazily, a strand of his dark hair stroking her forehead as smoke was directed away from her and at the ceiling. The pressure of a hand was on her back but not tactile skin. He had dressed her; put up her bodice and smoothed down her skirts while she slept.

She felt too luxuriously content to move; in this shadowy, shabby room she'd found peace and home. This was her home...not Thorneycroft, not Connaught Street: both had housed her in her tender years. This sea-worn mansion was her's. So was this man: this Cornish rogue who had warred and seduced his way to nobility; who'd shed infamy and fecklessness, for her; who'd cradled her carefully in his arms while she wept and slept. He'd believed in her, waited for her, finally taught her to trust enough to let him, with a few simple words, conquer her haunting demons and take her heart and soul. 'Say you love me.'

He didn't smile, didn't look at her. But with a soft vibrancy, an immediacy that denied a need for thought, he told her what she wanted to hear.

'I love you,' she echoed softly.

That did make him smile. 'I know,' he said and brought his tobacco-scented fingers to stroke her face.

Elizabeth turned into the caress, then snuggled closer and kissed his cheek. 'You wanted to elope with me because you knew Cadmore would cheat. You thought he might kill you and I'd again be at his mercy. You wanted to protect me…as your widow…your beneficiary…'

'Something like that…' he said wryly.

'Why didn't you *tell* me?'

'Because you would have stopped me meeting him.'

She gently tested his right arm to see if it still pained him. 'You won't seek out Randolph…not now…will you?'

'No. In a perverse way, although I despise him, I admire him, too. He saw you, wanted you, had the fortitude to persevere knowing there was a good chance he'd be rejected. I withdrew at the first fence…'

'You? You didn't even know I existed ten years ago.'

'Of course I knew…'

At his stinging self-mockery, she sat back on her heels on his lap to study his dark, satiric expression. Dusk was enclosing them as shadows elongated in the quiet, fire-daubed room.

'I always knew where you were to be found. Sometimes I'd allow myself to go there…sometimes I wouldn't. I'd never have let myself endure the humiliation of being summarily rejected. No courage, you see…'

Elizabeth put a soft hand to his hard cheek, devilishly lit by the glowing coals in the grate. 'That's rubbish. You're the bravest man I know.'

'No, I'm not. I'm the most self-indulgent man you know.'

'Not any more. You'd deny yourself anything…do any-thing…for me.'

He smiled at the truth of it. 'Do you know what really rankles, Elizabeth?' Silky blonde tangles were smoothed from her face as he cupped it double-handed, brought her close. 'I know now you wouldn't have rejected me.'

'You fascinated me then, too. I wanted you then, too,' she shyly admitted.

'So…what would your papa have said,' he breathed against her warm parted lips, 'when you told him you'd settled on a Cornish smuggler's son?'

'Oh, that's easy…he knew people…he'd just have said… well done…'

He discarded the stick with which he'd patterned the sand in front of him, and looked at her again. He squinted through twilight; just a blush on the horizon, dappling glitter on the grey sea showed there had been a sun.

Ross leaned back on an elbow on the smooth flat rock at the base of the cliff. Overhung by craggy strata and straggling brush, it formed a natural windbreak; a shelter from the ele-ments and prying eyes. He watched as Elizabeth sifted through pebbles for shells by the water's edge. There was something almost primitive in the way she was foraging, fas-cinated, her glorious hair already thick with salt and gleaming like mother of pearl. She resembled a mermaid, he decided with a smile, the way she was resting on an elbow, with her legs sideways and hidden in a cone of skirt. Beneath that cascade of ivory locks she might have been naked to the waist. She stood abruptly, skirts raised to carry her beach booty, displaying shapely calves and ankles, tiny feet, putting paid to his mermaid fantasy. She was about to wander further away so, as she glanced at him, he beckoned.

She obeyed with an eagerness that was sweeter for being transient. A few more hours would help restore her proud independence and he could be patient a little longer. At some time he'd share a confidence of his own: tell her that he had been on the point of returning to London to see her and try to win her over, when she'd showed up today. Eventually she would ask where were the builders he was supposedly setting to work.

Elizabeth dropped to her knees before him, scattering an assortment of sea shore on the smooth rock.

'Is that for me?'

'Yes.'

'Thank you,' he said with a gracious dip of his head and a hot golden look arrowing at her.

She laughed. 'You look a little disappointed, sir. Were you hoping for a crab? A fish? A turtle?'

'None of those. Something a little sweeter,' he said huskily.

Elizabeth felt her heartbeat hammering with a wild excitement, a calm acceptance. It was time. Despite the sea-breeze her skin felt febrile, raw with wanting him to reach out and touch. 'Such as?' She shook back her hair from her exquisite face so the heavy tresses separated into rope-like silver skeins.

His low-lidded eyes swerved past hers to stare out to sea.

Elizabeth raised a soft hand to slide along his abrasive jaw, brought his eyes back to hers, exulting in her power in this mating game. 'Such as?' she repeated. She could see his turmoil, his pain and regret for having succcumbed to a vengeful lust earlier, vying with his need for her now. Her fingers went to her bodice, working until it gaped. She was aware of his stillness, his eyes tracking the movement. He dipped his head, watched the heel of his boot score a furrow in sand. She brought his chin up, tilted forward to boldly kiss him. 'I love and trust you. I want you. Let me prove it.'

'You don't have to. I believe you,' he said hoarsely. 'I was acting stupidly when I said that, like an uncouth lout. Or an upstart Viscount, perhaps…'

She moved closer on her knees, slid her arms about his neck, pressing herself against him. He felt hard and hot. So hot that she sensed his torso toasting hers. 'I thought you wanted me, too, Ross…'

The rumbling laugh shook him backwards. He took her

with him so that she was lying atop his tense, pulsing body, then studied her beautiful face, her serene, inviting smile. 'What about your white silk wedding gown?'

The question was unnecessary; she knew from his blackened pupils, his subtle manoeuvring to ease his tortured pelvis, that she'd won. He couldn't go back. 'I won't tell if you don't.'

'I think Edwina already believes you to be *enceinte*.'

Elizabeth giggled. 'I know and I swear she's secretly pleased.'

'And you? How pleased would you be?'

Elizabeth looked deep into his velvet eyes as though the reality had never occurred to her. 'A baby?' Wonderment made her yearning sound ragged.

He turned her gently on to her back, shifting them from hard rock to soft sand. His hands pillowed her scalp, lost in hair that veined platinum on gold. 'You know I'd do anything for you, Elizabeth…' He was still smiling as his mouth merged with hers.

Epilogue

'**D**amme... She got her way after all,' Edwina said, but with a grin for her grandson-in-law. 'Lizzie was forever trying to spend her dowry on waifs and strays.' She looked up at the sturdy building and read the caption beneath the roofline: *The Lady Elizabeth Rowe Charitable Foundation.* Cast in bronze, it was an enduring tribute to her granddaughter's benevolence.

Ross disentangled his hair from his son's strong grip, slipped a long forefinger into his plump, curled fist. He smiled as it was immediately used to soothe toothless gums. He looked at his wife, wanting to cut a swathe through the town dignitaries encircling her, and carry her off home. The need made him feel guilty and selfish. For weeks she had looked forward to this day, but he wanted to curtail it to make love to her...properly make love to her.

'Here...I've something for you.' Edwina regained his attention. She handed him a document she had pulled from her reticule. 'Thought you might like it...now m'ship's come in.'

Ross shifted his wriggling infant son in his arms. Unfolding the parchment, he quickly scanned it. He frowned. 'This *is* a ship, Edwina.'

'Yes...I know. Thought you might like it. It's a good one...as fine a trader as you'll buy anywhere.' She assessed him shrewdly. 'Why did you never badger me for repayment? You've spent the dowry on this building and pledged the annuity to a charitable trust. You're seriously out of pocket now you've renovated Stratton Hall from your own funds, too...'

Ross's golden eyes raised. He smiled at the Heavens, shrugged. 'It's just money. You gave me far more than I gave you...'

'You're a fine man, Mr Trelawney,' Edwina said with a choking huskiness in her voice. 'And don't even try and give me that paper back,' she threatened as, suspiciously dewy-eyed, she waddled off to mingle with the pillars of society from neighbouring parishes and more local and lowly towns-folk.

Ross threaded his way through the crowds towards his wife. He passed by Guy Markham, chatting to Elizabeth's best friend. 'So what birth sign were you born under?' he heard Sophie earnestly ask Guy.

'Virgo...' Guy promptly answered with a grin. 'I think...'

'Think again...' Ross muttered drily as he strode on.

Aware of a spicy sandalwood scent, Viscountess Stratton turned towards her husband and gave him a blissful smile. Amid the press of chattering, laughing people, their eyes locked exclusively as they stood face to face, each cradling a baby in their arms. 'I'm so happy, Ross...'

'Good. You look it...and quite beautiful...blooming...' A discreet hand moved to touch her, a thumb caressing her arm in an old familiar way.

Elizabeth sensed the tremor in his fingers, the hunger he was still repressing. She lowered her eyes. Her confinement had only recently come to an end and she was feeling stronger every day. Five months only to recover from the birth of twins was exceedingly good going, Edwina had assured her. 'I feel blooming. Very well, indeed,' Elizabeth impressed on her patient, wonderful husband as her eyes merged meaningfully with his. 'Here, take your daughter.' She swapped the chestnut-haired blue-eyed angel dozing in her arms for her bobbing blond-haired son. His alert little eyes were already showing signs of turning the colour of autumn leaves. 'I must just speak to Hugh and Jane...then I should like to return to Grosvenor Square for some papers for my speech later at the Guild Hall. Will you take me there?' she asked with a provocative amethyst glance slipping at him from beneath her lush lashes.

'Of course,' Ross said, softly laughing. 'You know I'll do anything for you, my love.'

Hugh was being led away from Jane Selby by a colleague just as Elizabeth was approaching. Hugh greeted her in passing and smiled at her lively son.

'You're settled here, Jane?' Elizabeth asked, indicating the building in which her friend was now installed as matron. Edwina's initial reluctant few days' hospitality for the Selbys had extended to almost fifteen months harmonious cohabitation. After Elizabeth's marriage, Edwina had been gruffly appreciative of her live-in female companion and her engaging little son. But now circumstances had changed for all of them. Edwina wanted back her privacy. Jane was more than ready for financial independence and self-fulfilment. These were to be gained from managing an institute that provided shelter and an education for orphaned and abandoned children, and refuge to destitute women of the locality. Who better to give support and sympathy? she had said on applying for the position.

'Oh, yes, I'm settled. And Jack, too.' A proud maternal look arrowed to a lively blond boy chasing a few young friends on the fringes of the crowd. 'I can't ever thank you enough, Elizabeth, for what you've done for us.' Jane's voice vibrated with emotion and gratitude. Before Viscountess Stratton could demur or look concerned at her friend's tear-choked tone, Jane quickly changed the subject. She raised a hand to touch the petal-soft cheek of the boisterous infant in her friend's arms. 'You've fine babies; honeymoon twins... How wonderful...'

'Yes,' Elizabeth said with a small private smile as the tang of brine and the sound of rushing surf assailed her senses. 'Wonderful...' And then with a parting wave she was returning to her husband.

'Now go to your grandpapa, my love...' Elizabeth handed

over her precious burden to a stately, steel-haired gentleman who immediately put the child to his shoulder as though practice had perfected the move. Her husband carefully placed their still-sleeping daughter in Edwina's fond embrace.

Settling sedately into their elegant carriage, Elizabeth waited for it to move away along the street before she slid the seat and, giggling, fell into Ross's welcoming arms. She hugged him close. Then with a mother's instinct disengaged herself, angled her head to see through the window, and watched serenely as Harry and Edwina Pettifer hugged their great-grandchildren.

'I'm so lucky,' she whispered to Ross. 'How did you do that? I would have been thrilled with one baby...but two...' The frank adoration and awe in her glowing violet eyes made him smile crookedly before bending his dark head to hers. He touched their lips together lightly, then with a hunger that made her weld against him and encircle his strong neck with silken arms. With a wry modesty he murmured against her slick, soft lips, 'I thought you'd like it that way, sweetheart: one for you and one for me...'

* * * * *